DARK FORTUNES

DARK FORTUNES

FROM THE BOOK

D ale looked at Bruner and begged, "Please don't say anything further. Send us to a prison camp. We have rights under the Geneva Convention. It would be in everyone's best interest."

The general shook his head. "The Geneva Convention has no meaning in this room — besides, it's too late for that, because both of you already know too much. I'm convinced that after you listen to my proposal, you'll participate. This has nothing to do with the war and everything to do with mutual survival."

Dale was noticeably rattled. "So we won't leave this room alive unless we participate?"

Bruner nodded. "It's guaranteed. Now listen very closely."

DARK FORTUNES

Manufactured in the United States of America

ISBN: 978-1-886591-36-3
Library of Congress Control Number: 2024923103

BLUE CREEK PRESS
Heron, Montana
www.bluecreekpress.com

DARK FORTUNES

 KEITH BECK

ABOUT THE AUTHOR

Keith Beck is a Midwestern boy who honorably served in the U.S. Army Artillery from 1969-71. During college he concentrated on Science and Engineering but enjoyed creative writing. He also studied English Literature with his soon-to-be wife, Cindy.

After marriage, they moved to Philadelphia as owners of an elevator company. During this period, Keith invented and developed numerous U.S. Patents, which led to a lifelong career of engineering, product development and manufacturing.

As President of a mid-sized corporation, he honed his writing skills by providing technical articles for trade magazines as well as comprehensive product catalogs. He provided insight and guidance to various government agencies for disabled access and was appointed as an advisor to the U.S. Access Board.

In 1998, he and his wife's company was honored as SBA business of the year. Keith also served as a Board Member for the Montana Manufactures Association, an extension of Montana State University in Bozeman.

Upon early retirement, Keith purchased a Montana cattle ranch. He also spent six summers on his fishing boat exploring Alaska's inland waterway from Ketchikan to Homer. He also spent time in the Kodiak Island chain. During this chapter of this life, he wrote *Dark Fortunes*.

THE TALE
OF THE TALE

In 1999, Keith Beck was contacted by a 95-year-old German physicist from Berlin who claimed to be his grandfather's sister's son, making him Keith's first cousin, once removed. He spoke of events that only could be known by family members. His authenticity was verified by Keith's mother, who spoke fluent German and had numerous conversations with him.

Afterward, a new understanding of the family history was uncovered. The original family were Norsemen who sought asylum in Germania via the Catholic Church in the late 1300s. They purchased land from German officials and built a Catholic church in exchange for anonymity and new identities. The church stands today.

The family clan prospered for over 550 years, but during World War II, all male descendants of breeding age were either killed or simply vanished. The old physicist hoped to uncover the status of his mother's brother (Josef Johann, who came to America in the early 1900s). Josef was Keith's grandfather.

The old physicist asked about Josef's descendants to ascertain if the blood line from the original family survived in America. He also asked if anyone claiming to be distant relatives from Germany ever contacted Josef's descendants. Oddly enough, just a year earlier, a person from the West Coast had contacted Keith, claiming to be a distant cousin.

Unconvinced of his claims, Keith arranged a meeting over a few drinks and a barbeque. The man disclosed facts about Josef's youth that only family members knew. None of Josef's offspring knew or had heard of this man, but his facial features were strikingly similar to Josef.

Due to business commitments, Keith lost contact with the cousin. Ironically, according to the old physicist, a family member with the same name as the cousin had gone missing during the war.

The encounter with the old German physicist seemed like something out of a movie. The circumstances surrounding his family's history — dating back to 1400 — plus the disappearance of former Nazi soldiers and missing German gold gave Keith the idea for his book *Dark Fortunes*.

A special thanks goes out to my family and friends, and in particular to Cindy, my wife and partner of over 52 years. Her support has kept me focused while navigating the minefields of life. Our journey together has been an 'absolute trip.'

The rock star Joe Walsh said it best, "Life's been good to me so far."

CHAPTER ONE

June 8, 2008 — Angoon, Alaska

The old trapper's thin and wrinkled hands trembled with excitement as he twisted the cork from a newly-opened bottle of Wild Turkey. It had been nearly five months since he had store-bought whiskey. After carefully pouring two portions, he swirled his glass to watch the lines of alcohol merge into the beautiful amber-colored bourbon. He handed the second glass to the blocky, middle-aged man sitting across from his kitchen table and smiled.

The old man softly spoke. "Jim thanks for the whiskey — the only time I get to taste good stuff is when ya bring me some. Village laws don't give a hoot about geezers like me."

Jim Bennett raised his glass, offering a toast to Ernie McKinnon's recent birthday. "To my trapper friend — like fine bourbon, aged to perfection. How many years does this make Ernie?"

"Turned eighty-three on the 5th, which was last Thursday. I always celebrate for two days. One for my birthday, then again for D-Day, which is June 6th." He raised his glass and said, "Here's for D-Day."

Jim added, "Then we're toasting two great events in history, your birthday and D-Day."

Both men smiled and sipped their drinks. Ernie swirled his glass and smelled the bourbon and said, "Sure wish this wasn't a dry village. Tlingit law shouldn't apply to me." He pointed toward the pantry. "I'm tired of making hooch in that old still — I just can't match Kentucky bourbon — got something to do with their water and those charred oak barrels."

Jim glanced across the cluttered room at a small copper still sitting on the floor and said, "Nobody gives a rip about your still or what non-natives do behind closed doors as long as it doesn't interfere with their way of life. The village is simply policing

1

their own. They nearly lost their culture because of booze and pills, so I'm glad they've finally decided to do something about it — besides, I'll see that you've got enough whiskey to keep you stocked for the winter."

"I ain't so sure about your behind-closed-doors stuff. The Village hired a town cop named Crane, and he confronted me about buying corn meal and barley from Engel's store — asked if I was moonshining. He also grilled me about a rifle stolen from the fuel depot on Killisnoo Road. Then he demanded that I give him the pistol I was wearing on my hip — said I'm too old to safely handle guns. I told him a bear's been hangin' 'round town, and he could kiss my old wrinkled ass. Pete Engle got involved and demanded that the asshole leave me alone or he'd call Clan elders. Crane backed down and left. Pete told me Crane got fired from his job in Sacramento and that's how he ended up in Angoon."

Ernie shook his head and added, "You'd think bein' married to a Tlingit for over fifty years would give me some kinda standing with the Clan."

Jim sipped his whiskey and wondered why a newbie cop in Angoon would hassle a harmless old man. "The new cop's probably desperate for employment," he offered. "Otherwise he wouldn't have ended up here. I doubt that the Clan set him loose on you for making hooch and his actions are probably self-driven. Look, he can't take away your pistol, and the Clan won't back him up when it comes to you making your own whiskey. Just ignore him."

Jim stood and said, "I need to take a leak."

He set his glass down, stood up and walked onto the wooden porch. It was 10:30, dusk and too chilly to be wearing a short sleeved shirt. Goose bumps covered his muscular arms as he urinated from the porch onto the mossy gravel below. The sound of an approaching float plane roared through the bay, making Jim wonder why it was arriving so late. After relieving himself, he removed an electronic device the size of a cigarette pack with a telescoping antenna from his top pocket and turned it on. He studied the device's screen; slowly pointing it in different directions as if searching for something invisible. Satisfied with the results of whatever information was on its screen, he shut the unit off and returned it to his shirt pocket. Bennett then grabbed several split logs from what remained of a firewood stack he'd piled for Ernie last fall and brought them into the old man's cabin. His chiseled biceps were well defined as he tossed several logs into the wood stove. Red sparks exploded within the firebox, reminiscent of tracer rounds from his army days. While returning to his chair, he noticed a holstered German Luger hanging on an adjacent support post.

Jim said, "Don't worry about the new cop — I'll talk with Clan elders about your concerns. I'll email TacSec and run a background check on him. That way we know who we're dealing with."

Jim could hear the bush flight taking off again and asked, "Who the hell flew in this late?"

"Probably that rich fella Santos — the guy who built the house in Hood Bay. I heard he's got a big group comin' in this summer, so he's gettin' things ready."

Jim swatted a mosquito as it bit his temple slightly above an old, deep scar that ran across his cheek bone to his mid ear. The ear was obviously sewn back together at some point in time. His flattop haircut with neatly-cropped sides seemed to attract mosquitoes. He often wondered if the heat from his head was what attracted them. After scratching the newly formed welt, his fingers ran across the deep scar. "I'm thinking of letting my hair grow out this summer — maybe then these damn bugs will leave me alone."

"Shit, you're lucky he didn't bite your pecker off when you was using my porch as your personal outhouse."

Bennett smiled and continued to rub the rising welt, then asked, "Why would Santos stop here instead of landing at his place in Hood Bay?"

"Ice destroyed his dock this past winter, so his catamaran's been parked at the marina. Locals been poundin' replacement pilings and buildin' a new pier. I was told it's gonna take another two days to finish the job. They got a barge with a pile driver doing most of the work. Meanwhile, his caretakers use a small skiff for stocking the place and gettin' ready for his guests. He won't let hired help use his million dollar catamaran. If that's him who flew in, he'll sleep on his boat somewhere in the channel — probably go to his place in the morning."

"Sounds as if you don't care for the man. Have you ever spoken with him?"

"Tried last year but his bodyguard shuffled me aside. He seemed annoyed that I tried to introduce myself. The way I see it, anyone who won't say 'howdy' is an ass."

Jim nodded. "I agree. I've never met the man and don't care to — just saw his place while fishing for salmon in Hood Bay. I heard a rumor that he made a pile of money in the Brazilian oil fields. That's probably why he's got a bodyguard."

"He sure didn't make a fortune being nice to people. I bet he needs guards to protect him from all the people he's screwed over."

Jim questioned whether Ernie's attitude was justified but played along. "Astute observation." Jim again scratched at his bite. "What about his family?"

"Don't think he's got any — at least I never heard that he's got a wife or kids."

Jim reached down and pulled a small backpack onto his lap from the cabin floor. After producing another bottle of whiskey, he pulled out a neatly-folded flannel shirt and handed both to the old man.

"Here's a little something to take the sting out of cold Alaska nights. If the shirt doesn't fit or you don't like the color, I've got the receipt and can exchange it for another. The whiskey should hold you over until my kids arrive. I also bought you a DVD player, but I left it at the house. I purchased every old western I could lay my hands on — new stuff too — certainly enough to keep you occupied for a while. I'll see that you get it tomorrow."

Ernie looked astonished and then smiled. "You're an OK fella Jim — a real good friend. I know you're a man of means, but you're down-to-earth — not like the asshole in Hood Bay." Ernie hesitated, then asked, "Can ya answer me a personal question about yourself?"

Jim sidestepped the question by offering, "I'm not a man of means — just comfortable. My home in Denver and this place are paid for and I've got a few nickels put away to get me through retirement — that's all."

Ernie pressed for an answer. "I'd really like to know what possessed ya to build a place in Angoon? I know you're involved with computers and stuff, but there's gotta be more. Why would a high flier like you come here?"

"Trust me, you don't want to know my life story — too much baggage."

"Honest. I'd love to know, cuz you're the only real friend I've got — everyone else is either senile or dead."

Bennett considered ducking the question but figured that Ernie was harmless. Once again, Jim removed the electronic device from his shirt pocket. After pulling out its antenna and studying the screen, he responded to Ernie's request. "OK, I'll give you an official but abbreviated version if you promise to keep this conversation private."

Ernie wondered about Jim's need for privacy, but nodded. "Absolutely — I keep secrets better than most. What's that gizmo you have in your shirt pocket?"

Jim answered, "Um, it's a monitor for texts — that's all."

"So, are you gonna give me the Jim Bennett story?"

Jim hesitated about divulging his true past as a CIA/SOG agent to anyone, so he offered a response that would provide a somewhat accurate account of his life while protecting his need for secrecy. He began. "What it boils down to is I needed a place to clear my head. As a kid, I grew up on a cattle ranch in northwest Wyoming — near Cody. My parents and wife's parents came from a long line of cattle ranchers. My father graduated from Yale and later became a five term Senator in Washington — you may have heard of the late Senator William Bennett."

"Yep. Didn't he die in a plane wreck several years ago?"

"That's him. Anyway, because he was gone so much, I felt obligated to help run the ranch. After graduating from high school I wanted to join the army — needed to get away from Cody — but my dad insisted that I go to college. I was set on joining the army, so we reached a compromise: he pulled strings to get me into West Point. After West Point, I transferred to Fort Bragg and became an Airborne Ranger."

Jim considered stopping, but decided there wasn't any harm in continuing. After a brief pause, he said, "Because I excelled in Ranger School, I was asked to join Delta Force. Have you ever heard of Delta?"

"No. What is it?"

"Delta's an elite and covert military organization closely tied with the CIA. They have tremendous flexibility and autonomy — dressing in civilian clothes, long hair, sporting beards, looking like ordinary people; but doing whatever is necessary to gather information from foreign governments and terror groups. Much of my work was focused in hot spots like Central America — El Salvador, Nicaragua, Panama, Granada, Cuba, then finally in Afghanistan, Pakistan, and Somalia."

"Sounds like Oliver North kinda stuff?"

"Indeed it was. In fact, I worked directly with Ollie for almost two years. He's an honorable soldier and patriot. Anyway, after being promoted to Major, I was transferred to an actual military unit and commanded a squadron of three sections — 75 men. Two of my sections were assault teams — highly skilled commandos — while the third was a reconnaissance unit. I ran this operation from a twelve man Recon troop we called the "Funny Platoon." I gathered intelligence in concert with embedded CIA agents, then my assault teams acted on that information. We basically killed enemy leaders, backed key political supporters, and provided training to pro-American rebels. I had immediate communication links with the Pentagon and certain CIA officials."

"For Christ sake Jim, that's dangerous stuff!"

"It certainly was — these were secret wars with a secret army orchestrated by the CIA, and backed by the President. If we weren't able to topple key leadership within hostile regimes, we'd simply kill them — making it look accidental, or a result of health issues. That was the best way of handling bad actors."

"The CIA provided us with private contractor mercenaries, which made our involvement invisible. The mercenaries were paid by the rebels, who we financed."

"You were involved in Granada?

"Somewhat — my commandos were involved during the invasion. We weren't allowed to infiltrate their leadership and kick out the Cubans. Instead the Pentagon decided to invade, which nearly cost the mission. They lacked 'real-time' intel and used antiquated communication systems. My unit could have handled it without the invasion, but the Pentagon thought otherwise. Those failures reshaped their thinking, however. If you're going to invade, you must embed personnel who can provide accurate intelligence, advanced communications and superior weaponry. Our unit would have satisfied those needs. Rather than sending troops, send missiles and drones. When everything's in place we can topple any third world regime.

Ernie asked, "How about the Sandinistas?"

"We crushed the Salvadoran Revolutionaries by creating an insurgency from within. We infiltrated the Sandinista leadership, which gave us vital information. While that was happening, we trained the Contras and provided them with advanced weapons and intel. The Sandinistas never knew what was happening until it was too late. The entire operation required 75 Delta operatives and four CIA agents."

"The CIA also provided us with mercenaries; former US soldiers who led assaults with the Contras against the Sandinistas. It looked as if our military wasn't involved in the conflict, even though we were up to our eyeballs in the entire affair."

The old trapper frowned. "Seventy-five men defeated the Sandinistas?"

Jim nodded. "Yes, sir — the Contras did America's dirty work while Delta provided them with training, surveillance, weapons and computers. As for Granada, we could have eliminated the Cubans with the same outcome. No invasion needed."

"How do you fight with computers?"

"Computers enable us to combine three key elements — satellites being our eyes, communication links our ears, and advanced weaponry our muscles. The same techniques were used against Noriega in Panama and Saddam in Desert Storm."

"That's a whole lot different from World War II. I like your term 'secret wars.' You guys did this without getting caught — no fanfare — no hoopla."

"It's the modern way of fighting — it avoids world wars. We're doing the same thing against Al Qaeda, Hamas and Hezbollah in the Middle East and Southeast Asia. You name it, we're there. Many hostile regimes are actually shills for the CIA who supply us with an endless stream of Intel on the Russians and Chinese. You might hear about it years later, but usually it remains hidden. By avoiding capture, our government can deny involvement — it's called 'plausible deniability.' But if we're caught, we're treated as civilian mercenaries with no connection to the Pentagon.

Ernie shook his head. "My Lord! I knew our government was tricky, but not like this. You're saying the CIA has its own army that works behind the scenes?"

Jim nodded. "In a simplistic way, yes. Here's another example — my crew assassinated Pablo Escobar. One of my commandos put an M4 round through Escobar's head from a distant rooftop while he was trying to escape,. There was so much bad press in America about Delta sponsored 'Death Squads' that we had to deny killing him. We provided the Los Pepes para-military of Columbia with a list of known cartel members, which made their job easier. They took credit for Escobar's death and methodically eliminated the cartel by deploying death squads who we in fact trained."

Ernie sipped his drink. "I knew we had spies and stuff, but this sounds like a damn movie. Is that how ya got the scar on your face?"

The former colonel looked at his drink when Ernie mentioned "spies and stuff," then ran his right hand over the scar. "Yep. Got this souvenir while ousting Noriega in Panama City."

Ernie took a good look at Jim's scar. "What happened?"

"Three of my men and I were undercover as Miami drug runners with the Columbians. Escobar and Noriega were funneling Columbian cocaine through the Canal Zone so we embedded ourselves by purchasing four thousand kilos of coke. During the transaction we learned that one of our CIA agents had recently been uncovered and captured. He was about to be executed. I immediately contacted Washington and explained the situation. Old man Bush had been preparing to invade Panama, but that was the last straw. My mission was to extract our agent minutes before the invasion. During the rescue, a prison guard shot me in the side of the face and shoulder with an AK-47. Fortunately he ran out of ammo. The guard wasn't so lucky. I killed him along with six others."

"Did ya save the agent?"

Jim nodded. "Indeed we did. In fact, he and I have become close friends."

"How'd ya manage to raise a family during all of this?"

Jim sighed. "Ah, there's the rub — I didn't. My absence exacted a huge toll on my family, and to this day, I feel terrible. I was seldom home and couldn't communicate truthfully with my wife. She never knew where I was or what I was doing. Had I been captured, our government would have disavowed my connection with Delta and I'd have been tried as a drug trafficker or mercenary in a foreign country. It was a bad situation."

Ernie asked, "Did your wife make ya leave the army?"

"No. Just before Clinton took office I was promoted to full colonel but the political landscape had changed. It all comes down to politics. We knew that Bin Laden was behind countless terrorist attacks so my unit infiltrated Sudan's government and bribed their Foreign Minister into giving us his exact location. Everything was in place and we were ready to kill him with a cruise missile but Clinton ordered me to stand down. Days later I confronted Clinton during a debriefing with the Joint Chiefs of Staff at the oval office. I openly challenged his decision. He wagged his finger at me and said 'shut your mouth.' "

"I lost it, and said, 'Mr. President, you only have balls for fucking interns — you'll soon regret not taking out Bin Laden.' Clinton said I was insubordinate and ordered me out of the room. Within hours I was forced into retirement. At that point, I knew the only constructive way to serve this country was to improve military weapons with computer technology. Hence my company, TacSec, short for Tactical Security."

"So ya got booted from the army and went into business. They're different worlds."

"Not at all. I assembled a team of computer programmers and we developed various software systems for existing weapons. I captured a niche market."

Ernie asked, "So what do you make at TacSec?"

"Two things. One facet supplies the Pentagon with encrypted communication capabilities from anywhere on the globe, while the other provides digital software for new weapon systems. The Pentagon is my biggest client."

Ernie looked confused. "But how'd you end up here?"

Jim smiled. "Luck I guess — an investment group took my company public after 911, so I cashed out. By then my marriage had collapsed, I hardly knew my children, I'd killed scores of people in the cause of national security, and I was psychologically drained. I needed a place to rediscover myself, get a handle on what was left of my life and try to rekindle a relationship with my children. I love the outdoors and always wanted to visit Alaska. I stumbled into Angoon by talking with a general who'd fished these waters. I fell in love with Angoon because of its remoteness and the Natives. Unlike touristy Alaska, Angoon is like it was during the whaling days. By coming here, I have time to reflect and relax. Now I'm closer to my kids than I've ever been. Things are working out for me and I'm glad to be here."

"Holy crap Jim, that's some story. I had no idea you were a colonel and all this other stuff."

Even though he was far removed from his past, Jim knew he'd disclosed too much. On the other hand, he was relieved that Ernie didn't seem alarmed. He looked into the old trapper's eyes. "Look, don't share this conversation with anyone else — I must remain incognito."

"I won't say a word. You're an amazing man and deserve respect for being a patriot."

Jim shook his head. "I'm not a patriot. Real patriots are the brave men and women who've died for this country. They've given everything a person can possibly give. I've done nothing that most people wouldn't have done under similar circumstances. If anything, I'm an opportunist."

Ernie shook his head and wondered why Jim would downplay his accomplishments. He took another sip of courage and contradicted his friend. "Baloney, I read a book this winter about Old Blood-and-Guts — Patton. He once said, 'The object of war isn't to die for your country but to make the other bastard die for his.' You did exactly that, so don't downplay your past. I'm honored to be the friend of a modern day patriot."

Ernie then stretched his hand out and shook Jim's.

"Well thank you," Jim said. "I'm honored to be yours as well. I've come to realize that family, friends and relationships are the most important things in life."

Careful not to spill any, Ernie poured another two portions. "I'm taken back about what's going on in the world. A person doesn't see that living in Angoon."

Ernie unfolded the new shirt and held it up, then smiled. "How long do ya plan on stayin this season?"

"Most of the summer. I may go back to Denver for a few days, but I want to stay here until late September. Unfortunately, the director of TacSec expects me back as a consultant for a magnetic pulse missile jamming system in October. It seems the Pentagon's having problems with excessive response times for intercepting surface to air missiles. I'm convinced it's a software issue. I'd planned on going to Mexico for a few months next winter, but I'll probably end up spoon-feeding a bunch of government geeks unless I can talk my way out of it. Otherwise, I look forward to seeing my kids and a few old friends this summer."

"We'll fish, visit the hot springs, hike, maybe even explore that old abandoned village — Neltushkin. I'll try making a treasure hunt out of it — perhaps bring my metal detectors and kick around the old cabins. My kids really enjoy that sort of thing."

When Jim mentioned a treasure hunt, an off-the-wall idea struck Ernie. He looked at the Luger hanging on the post and considered divulging his memories, then dismissed it.

He sipped his drink. "It'll be good to see both of 'em. Young Audra's a kick in the shorts — never stops asking questions — and your son's a chip off the old block. He looks and acts just like his old man. The kid's got a lot more muscle than you though — kinda like one of them body builders."

"Audra's not so young — she turned 26 in January, and Danny's 28. Audra received a Master's in marketing and starts working for Boeing in a month or so. Danny may look like me but that's where the similarity ends. He lacks discipline, which is my fault. It took him five years to finish college and he's done nothing with his degree since graduation. Spends his time roofing, landscaping, concrete and carpentry work. That's probably why he's so muscular. Here's a kid with an electrical engineering degree who's working like a dog in the trades."

Ernie wanted to tell Jim that he was too demanding of Danny, but gave a watered-down response. "Give it time. Today's kids think if they get settled in, their life's over — they'll become their parents."

Jim knew that Ernie never had children, yet his remarks seemed incredibly wise. "That's a fresh approach of looking at it. You think he's afraid of becoming me?"

Ernie nodded. "That's how I see it — besides, he probably enjoys doin' what he's doin."

Jim never considered that Danny didn't want to become Jim Bennett's clone and that he might enjoy manual labor. Almost convinced, he murmured, "Maybe so."

Jim sipped his whiskey and looked toward the holstered Luger hanging on the post. "Today's the first time I've noticed the pistol hanging there. How'd you manage to get hold of that relic?"

Ernie rose from his chair and retrieved an old rusted cookie tin from a shelf above the dirty porcelain sink. He pulled the Luger from the post and sat back down. He unholstered the gun and handed it to Jim. "I'm glad you noticed it — careful, it's loaded. I was meanin' to tell a story when ya mentioned treasure huntin' with your kids." Ernie opened the tin, pulled out two strange looking medals then slid them across the vinyl coated red and white checkered tablecloth.

Jim inspected the Luger. He cleared the chamber, then looked down the barrel toward the overhead light. Other than one minor rust pit, it was in remarkably good condition. His attention shifted to the medals, which appeared to be Nazi. Ernie smiled as he retrieved a fierce looking dagger in a sheath and handed it to Jim. The knife was eight inches long, with a black ebony handle. The bottom of the handle had a polished nickel cross guard and directly below the upper cross guard was a circular nickel button with the letters "SS" cast into the metal. The ebony handle center contained a silver inlaid Imperial Eagle on top of a German Swastika. Its blade was engraved in gothic German text: *Meine Ehre Heißt Treue.*

Jim was stunned. He turned the knife in the light. "I'll be damned — this is an authentic SS dagger. The inscription says, 'My Honor Is Loyalty.'"

Ernie bubbled with excitement. "I found the Luger, knife and these medals in 1945."

Jim carefully examined the Nazi medals, which appeared to be naval. One medal was oblong and made of pewter. The outside of the oval was outlined with an outer wreath while the inner oval contained a finely detailed U-boat with the number U-740 emblazoned on its conning tower. Above the oval stood an outstretched Imperial Eagle and Swastika. The second medal was perfectly round and obviously silver. Its inner circle contained a detailed engraving of a Viking ship. The ship's bow culminated with a fierce dragon head. SS lightning bolts adorned the main sail while a Swastika flag topped off the main mast.

Jim shook his head. "Unbelievable, Ernie. Where did you get these?"

"Found them south of here."

Jim thought while he turned the U-boat medal between his thick fingers. He picked up the Luger and asked, "Who knows about this?"

"You're the only person I've shown these to, other than my late wife Jenny — gospel truth. Get this Jim, there's a writer fella stayin' at the Killisnoo Lodge — he's writin' about Tlingits — he interviewed me last month, and noticed the Luger hanging there. He completely changed his tune and kept askin' about it — asked if I knew any Nazi's during or after the war. He offered to buy the gun for $2,000, but I told him it wasn't for sale. His constant questioning bothered me, so I asked him to leave — said I was feelin' tired."

"Do you really think this guy's an author?"

"Can't say for sure but he strikes me as odd."

"We'll revisit this fellow later. Where exactly did you find these?"

"I found them on the south end of Admiralty Island."

Jim shook his head. "Not in 1945 — Germany never fought here."

Ernie broke into a huge grin, leaned back into his chair and sipped his drink. "I was a civilian cook on the Alaska Highway during the war. Froze two toes off near Watson Lake and was sent to Juneau for treatment — that's where I met Jenny. She was a kitchen helper from Hoonah, and I became a volunteer civilian cook at the same mess hall. After Germany surrendered, we married and moved here. Tlingits are a matriarchal society and Jenny's grandma was the oldest leader in Angoon. She was head of the Dog Salmon Clan, so she was able to give us this land. We built our cabin here, then worked for the fish processing plant by Killisnoo. Like most Tlingits, we were subsistence harvesters — fishing and hunting when we weren't working at the plant. I was setting beaver traps in Whitewater Bay during early fall of '45 when I noticed three eagles feeding on shore. It was low tide, so I beached my skiff and walked across the mud flats to where the eagles were. I found the bottom half of a decomposed human above the high tide line. It was wearing torn trousers and leather boots with the Luger, holster and belt still fastened to the loops of the trousers. I assumed it was a man. There was hardly any flesh left on the guy — it looked like a bear killed 'im. At first I thought he washed ashore durin' a winter storm, but realized the tide couldn't have washed him into that bay."

Jim tipped his head to one side. "Are you bullshittin' me?"

Ernie looked Jim in the eyes. "Gospel truth Jim. Afterwards, I spent every spare minute searchin' the bay for more evidence of the dead guy. On my second trip I found a metal pipe with handles welded on each end. The dagger and medals were inside the pipe. It wasn't even 50 feet from where I found the body. After many other searches I gave up. I figure the guy musta beached in a boat, then got killed by a bear."

Again Jim examined the Luger, dagger and medals. If Ernie was fibbing, he was awfully convincing. Jim countered, "I doubt a bear killed him. He'd have used the Luger. It wouldn't have been holstered. How long do you think the body was there?"

"Less than a year. The bay's cold water and damp weather acts like an icebox."

Jim's experience as an interrogator told him that Ernie was telling the truth. "Very puzzling," he continued, "because the time frame is wrong. Germany surrendered in May of '45, and they never fought here. There's no logical explanation for a Nazi to be in Alaska unless he was a spy. This could be evidence of a covert operation."

Ernie nodded. "I never thought of that. I kept going back lookin' for more stuff but came up empty."

Jim considered the use of a pipe as a container then asked, "Describe the container these artifacts were in. Where is it now?"

"I'm sure it was special-made cuz it was machined — it was eight inches 'round and over a foot long. Each end of the pipe had finely-threaded end caps with welded handles for carrying. It was made from lightweight aluminum or pot metal. Ervin Weller traded me two six packs of beer for it in the '50s — said he wanted it for a crab pot float."

Jim asked, "I've never heard of him — who is he?"

"He lived with Martha Franks for over thirty years. Ervin's taking the 'big nap' at Cemetery Park — he died of a heart attack in the '70s. He and Martha had two kids — Mel and Eva Franks. I bet it's still tied to one of Ervin's old crab pots."

Jim smiled. "I know Mel Franks fairly well — in fact I brought him some goodies from Denver. I'll ask him about any old crab pots he might have. Why'd you show me these things Ernie?"

"You said your kids like treasure huntin' so there it is. Bring your maps tomorrow and I'll show you where I found the body. When you're done snoopin' round, I'll tell you a few other juicy tidbits, like the one I heard from Jenny's cousin. It's about Nazis in Alaska during the war."

Jim grinned. "Outstanding. I'll take you up on it. My kids are going to love this. Just a few more questions. Was there wreckage from a boat or anything unusual during the time preceding your discovery?"

"Nope. Never heard or found nothin' else. If I hadn't seen the eagles feeding, I'd never have found what I did."

"What did you end up doing with the body?"

"I dragged it into the water and the tide took it away."

Jim returned to Ernie's comment about the author. "Tell me about this writer — what's his name?"

"Rigby. Don't know his first name."

"Did he ask you how you came upon the Luger?"

"Yep. I told him I bought it from a pawn shop in Juneau."

"Do you think he believed that?"

"I think so, but he wanted to know the name of the pawn shop and when I bought it. Then he wanted to inspect the Luger. That's when I asked him to leave."

Jim shrugged his shoulders. "Who knows, maybe he's a collector. Look, when I get home, I'll research the internet for missing boats and planes from 1944 and '45. I may be pissing in the wind, but it's worth a try."

Ernie had often wondered about his random discovery. "Let me know what ya find," he said.

"I'm jacked about this Ernie. Tomorrow morning I need to launch my boat and check it out for the season. My tackle's a complete disaster and needs sorting out too. I should be off the water by noon so give me your shopping list and I'll grab your groceries from Engle's before picking you up. I'll be over by early afternoon to pick you up. We'll eat at my place — I'll heat up some elk stew. After dinner we'll talk about the upcoming treasure hunt."

Ernie smiled and nodded. "Can't turn down home cookin'. I'll be here all day — just like every day."

Jim left the weathered cabin and headed to his refurbished Humvee, brushing away a swarm of black flies. He knew tomorrow would be nice because black fly hatches forecast calm, warm weather. He watched the Santos catamaran heading towards Chatham Strait. Ernie was right — Santos would probably spend the night in the channel. His attention shifted to Ernie's story as he turned the Hummer onto Killisnoo Road. He wondered how the hell Nazi artifacts ended up on Admiralty Island. His kids would love the mystery and upcoming treasure hunt.

Back inside the weathered cabin, the old man considered how nice it was to have his friend back for the summer. Since Jenny's death, not many people visited or seemed to care much about him in this remote village, but Jim was different. He always checked on him and helped out. It made him feel good that someone still cared. Perhaps the story of Whitewater Bay would make up for some of Jim's generosity. Ernie poured one last short drink and looked at his new flannel shirt. After unfolding the gift, he hung it on his bedpost. He'd wear it tomorrow to please Jim.

The old man picked up the dagger and medals and placed them back into the rusted cookie tin. While replacing the items, he lingered over a folded paper and other documents in the tin. He spoke out loud. "Wait till Jim see's these — he'll crap." He closed the tin and placed it on the shelf above the sink. After hanging up the Luger, he finished his whiskey and crawled into bed.

Thoughts of Whitewater Bay, the corpse, and his attempts to solve the puzzle haunted Ernie while drifting toward sleep. Computers were foreign to him but perhaps Jim could use his skills to unravel the mystery. Jim was a smart man — if anyone could figure this out, he could. Ernie simply wanted to know before his own "big dirt nap" at Cemetery Park.

Jim arrived home and entered the expansive log house facing Chatham Strait. The panoramic view through the high vaulted ceilings and glass front was breathtaking. A crescent moon reflected off of Chatham, providing a surrealistic setting.

Dark Fortunes

He'd built the retreat five years earlier, anticipating an early retirement. His children enjoyed Alaska and made a point of coming up twice each summer. Jim made it easy for them by providing first-class airfare and traveling cash. After turning on the propane fireplace, he put on an Alan Parsons CD, walked into the study and turned on his PC. Unlike the rest of Angoon, his computer was linked to a stand-alone satellite system which TacSec technicians had installed. This provided him with immediate and secure internet and Pentagon access.

Jim logged on and emailed Lori Phelps , his Security Chief at TacSec. He asked her for a background check on Richard Crane of Sacramento.

Jim knew Lori had a crush on him even before his divorce became final, but he refused to fraternize with employees. Former military policy was difficult for him to overcome. They'd gone to company functions together but nothing more. After selling TacSec, he considered asking her out, but the Board of Directors exercised a consulting clause in Jim's buy/sell agreement. He'd wait another six months before approaching her. By then he'd be clear of all ties to his former company and free to do as he pleased.

Jim searched the internet for the type of Nazi artifacts which Ernie had shown him. Several sites indicated that they were authentic. Jim learned that U-boat pins were given to kommandants and crewmembers of each commissioned sub. The U-740 was captained by Oblt. Günter Bruehl. It was destroyed in the English Channel on D-Day, June 6th, 1944, with 51 men on board. It was impossible for anyone who died in the English Channel to wash ashore in Alaska. The second medal with the Viking ship was given to every member of the Kreigsmarine — the German Navy. The SS dagger found on the body was issued to the Allgemeine branch of the Third Reich. This was the political and administrative branch of Hitler's regime. A U-boat commander wouldn't have access to a high-ranking officer's SS dagger. It was reserved for non-combat generals or political big shots. The dagger and navy pins didn't belong together.

After hours of accessing secure sites of the Coast Guard, FAA and US Navy, he stumbled onto something — three situations that occurred in late August of 1944. The first event was an unusually large fuel oil slick in Cross Sound near Elfin, Alaska, on August 27. Elfin is northwest of Angoon by fifty air miles. The second event was a lost bush flight originating from Pelican, Alaska, and going to Bellingham, Washington, which disappeared on the same day. The plane was never found and presumed crashed due to bad weather; another case of small planes being swallowed by Alaska's endless wilderness. The slick was reported several hours prior to the bush flight's departure from Pelican and was obviously unrelated. The third incident was a stolen fishing boat from the Sitka harbor on

August 24 Like the missing airplane, it was never found. The proximity of the three events was within a 60-air-mile radius of where Ernie had found the body.

Jim focused on the missing float plane. Navy records from Juneau indicated that the North Star Cannery reported their float plane with a two-man crew missing on the afternoon of August 27. The Navy searched for five days without finding anything. Several independent pilots searched coastal Alaska for another week. The logical flight course would have taken the plane directly over Peril Straight, which intersects Chatham. This intersection is very close to Whitewater Bay, where Ernie had found the artifacts, but the Navy believed the plane crashed somewhere in the inland waterway near Ketchikan and sank without a trace.

Jim shifted his attention to the oil slick in Cross Sound. The slick was located in an area near Pelican — where the missing plane originated from. The slick remained visible for several days, but a storm and strong tides made it impossible to pinpoint its origin. The Navy assumed that an unregistered fishing boat or the stolen boat from Sitka ended up sinking in Cross Sound. However, wreckage debris was never found. Jim wondered if there was a connection between the missing plane, the oil slick and Pelican Cove. To find out, he'd need help from a friend at the FBI.

Jim then considered the stolen boat from Sitka. This was problematic because it would be virtually impossible to hide something that large without getting caught. If someone tried removing a vessel from the area, the Navy would certainly have run across it. The report suggested it probably sank somewhere near Sitka, or was stripped of its contents and scuttled.

Jim refocused on the town of Pelican and the North Star Cannery. The history of Pelican was brief but directly connected to the cannery and a cold storage facility there. Without the cannery, the town wouldn't exist. The entire complex was sold to the Northern Cross Company of Seattle in 1955 for 1.7 million dollars, which was a huge amount of money in that day. There was no other information on the area other than modern demographics.

Jim got up and changed the music to laid-back Moody Blues CDs. He mixed a drink and sat in front of the vaulted windows. It was 4:00 a.m. and getting light. He'd been on the computer for nearly four hours. After finishing his drink, he decided to call his friend and Colorado neighbor, Doug Borland, section chief of the FBI field office in Denver. Jim knew Doug was an early morning person and probably on his way to work, so he called his private cell phone. Both men had encryption modules on their phones paired to each other, making it impossible for anyone to intercept or monitor their conversation.

Doug answered, "Hey, how they hangin', Jim? It's 6 a.m. — what's up?"

Jim apologized. "Doug, sorry to bother you this early but I need a favor."

15

Doug was sitting at a red light in his silver Mercedes. He smiled. "I'm flipping you shit buddy. I'm in my car heading to work. Let me guess; you're bored with semi-retirement and want a job at the Bureau."

"That's very funny Doug. I really need a favor."

"What do you need?"

"I'd like you to find everything you can about the North Star Cannery of Pelican, Alaska. It was founded in the late '30s or early '40s, then sold to the Northern Cross Company in 1955. The cannery reported a missing plane on August 27, 1944. Get me everything you can on the owners, their family and the missing plane. In particular, I want to know who the crew members were. There was another incident that occurred in Sitka on August 24 of '44. A fishing boat was stolen from the harbor, and was never recovered. Perhaps there's a police report associated with the investigation. I'll owe you and Sharon a salmon barbecue when I return."

"Shit Jim, these people died decades ago. What the hell do you want with crap like this?"

Jim could only offer a terse theory. "I'm doing historical research with a friend. I've come to believe the cannery was a German front or the missing plane's crew were Nazi spies. It's also possible that the stolen boat was used by the Nazis or a sympathizer. Find out what you can about the owner and his background."

Doug turned the Mercedes into a parking lot. "Who really gives a shit? The Krauts lost. You actually need this crap?"

"I wouldn't be asking if I didn't."

Doug shook his head and sighed, as if Jim was being a pain in the butt. "OK, I'm on it. I doubt we'll uncover anything, but I'll put one of my greenhorns to work on it. It'll cost more than a damn barbecue though. I'm thinking a candlelight dinner at Chez Paul. You'll need to bring Lori Phelps and make it a foursome. Sharon thinks you guys would make a great couple. She sees Lori at the gym several times a week. And get this, Lori told Sharon that she likes you — a lot."

Jim was pleased to hear that Lori had feelings for him but downplayed Doug's statement. "If it makes you happy, we'll all do dinner when my employment contract is up. You know how I feel about fraternizing with employees. Could you research this right away and email me the results?"

Doug took a deep breath. "You've got it. Look, I'd like to talk more, but I've got an interview with one of my agents in twenty minutes and I haven't had any coffee yet. Email me particulars on what you want and I'll forward my report. Is your computer formatted with our encryption program?"

"Only if you're using the SE-200 system."

Doug answered, "That's what we have — with version 3 upgrade."

"That's what I'm using. Hey thanks Doug. I'm sending you an email as we speak."

"Good, because I'm pulling into a Java Hut. I'll get back with you. Ciao."

The sun was up and striking the crystal waters of Chatham. Jim knew he needed sleep if he was to get anything accomplished today, so he quickly chewed a third of a sleeping pill and washed it down with a shot of Crown Royal. After setting his alarm, he laid down and considered the Nazi relics Ernie had found. His thoughts floated back into the jungles and small villages of Central America; wondering what secret wars were presently being waged. Perhaps his unit was working in Venezuela to bolster Hugo Chavez, actually a CIA shill. Twenty minutes later, as the pill kicked in, his mind slowed down. He closed his eyes and slept.

CHAPTER TWO

June 9, Late Morning — Patrick's Point, California

A black stretch limo with darkly-tinted windows pulled onto the west road of the cemetery overlooking the seaside cliff of Patrick's Point. A freshly dug hole awaited an upcoming funeral service. A finely polished chrome casket rack spanned the grave and excess dirt was neatly covered with green Astroturf. Large pots of cut flowers surrounded four rows of wooden chairs on top of a red carpet.

It was an unusually warm California spring morning next to the Pacific Ocean. The gravesite was void of people other than two groundkeepers dressed in gray jumpsuits ready to fill the grave. A distant yellow backhoe stood ready. The limo drove beyond the gravesite, then turned around in order for its occupants to have an unobstructed view of the upcoming ceremony. Within moments, a white, late-model television news van parked across the road from the limo. It had two small satellite dishes on its roof and a KVIQ — TV-6 logo painted on its side. Both vehicles were perfectly positioned to view the coming service.

An elderly, white-haired gentleman in the limousine's rear seat tipped his head forward and rubbed his burning eyes with his left hand. A peculiar sound came from his robotic right arm as it extended downward. His artificial right hand pressed the button controlling the plexiglass partition separating him from the limo driver. He spoke softly to his chauffeur. "William, please contact the surveillance team and connect them to my rear intercom."

The driver obediently responded, "Yes, sir." He picked up a telephone and pressed a button on the dashboard. "This is Blue Marlin to Central — do you copy?"

A short, solidly-built, red-haired man inside the news van answered. "Roger Blue Marlin, we copy."

William turned toward his employer. "We're connected to the van, sir and I've shut off the front intercom — you may proceed. Shall I close the partition?"

"Yes please."

After the partition closed, the white haired gentleman began, "Rusty, do you copy?"

"Loud and clear, Mr. Reid."

The old man continued. "As ordered earlier, photograph everyone we can't identify as immediate family or friends and run every license plate through our DMV software. I want a shadow team member to follow anyone we tag as suspicious. During the service, contact Catherine and give her my message. Intercept and apprehend anyone who attempts to follow me — understood?"

"Yes, sir. Understood. Is your driver armed?"

The old man looked toward the van. "He's armed and so am I, but no shooting unless it's absolutely essential. They'll be looking for me and my cousin, not the Weddell family; however, protect Catherine and her family at all costs. They'll want them to locate me."

The red-haired man answered, "Affirmative, sir."

"We'll talk as people start arriving — assemble your crew and pay attention."

"Yes, sir." Rusty Miller, a stocky man in his early fifties, sat back in his leather seat and talked with two other men and a woman inside of the van. "Time to position ourselves — team leaders, contact your people. The blocker team must get behind the limo immediately after the service. Our shadow members must follow every vehicle and individual I determine as suspicious. Position two body guards behind Catherine's family. Stay with each target and maintain surveillance until I say OK or back-up arrives. I expect constant radio and cell phone contact. Finally, no shooting unless family members are in imminent danger — that includes the 'Old Man.' We've rehearsed this, so I demand perfect execution. Questions anyone?"

An albino man in his late forties with white shoulder-length hair said, "You mentioned an incentive bonus earlier. What did you mean by that?"

Rusty apologized. "Sorry, I didn't elaborate earlier Whitey, but I got wrapped up in the big picture. Beyond our normal fee, the Old Man's offering the team an additional half million if we determine who's responsible for Weddell's death. That means capturing and interrogating all verified operatives in order to find out who's behind this. Reid expects no loose ends to haunt him, so get the word out to your men — capture every target and keep them alive for interrogation."

Rusty's three subordinates looked at each other and smiled. The men exited the van with their red-headed boss, leaving the woman to operate the expansive control panel. Within the van, four closed-circuit television screens adorned the wall and two computer monitors were surrounded by an array of buttons and dials. A young, strikingly beautiful woman — Helen Moorcroft — sat at the console and talked through her headset to the surveillance team. Her short-cut black hair, tightly-tailored blue jeans and calf-high, black leather boots projected a Euro/punk-rock persona. A tight, black tank top exposed well-crafted tattoos above each elbow and her well-developed breasts. A silver chain necklace with attached miniature handcuffs rounded out her desired look. Smooth, lightly-tanned skin and crimson lipstick added to an eerie, intimidating aura. Every man on the crew considered her as attractive and "kinky hot," yet no single team member had the courage to ask her out. An English accent added to her dark-side allure. As a former British Intelligence surveillance officer, Helen's knowledge of computers and electronics made her an indispensable team leader.

Inside the limo, the old man opened the rear compartment partition and sat back with a *Eureka Times*. At the top of the obituary page was a two column obit for Henry Weddell, his friend and business partner for over sixty years. The old man had read the article at his home in Port Angeles, but he couldn't believe Henry was dead. Oddly, there wasn't an accompanying photograph in the obituary. The obit portrayed Weddell as a successful entrepreneur and generous benefactor. His accomplishments included the formation of Caribou Mines, Ltd., in southern British Columbia, where he'd made millions in the late '40s developing two lucrative gold mines. This led to creation of the infamous Caribou mining district. Further ventures included the purchase of Pacific Cargo International (PCI), a large shipping and air cargo company based out of Seattle. Later, PCI became the parent company of Coastal Airlines, Alaska Freight & Marine, Island Transport of Hawaii, and Holiday Cruise Lines. Simply put, Henry Weddell was a multi-billionaire.

His business savvy was eclipsed by his generosity and philanthropic activities. Henry created countless scholarships at prominent universities, funded medical research facilities and created the robotic prosthetics department at Harborview Medical Center in Seattle. Every year, the Weddell family trust donated millions to various charities and organizations including the Jewish Documentation Center, the Sam Wiesenthal Center, the American Cancer Society and many more.

Though he was a corporate titan and philanthropist, Weddell led a secluded, low-profile existence. Individual family members weren't mentioned in the obituary. Only close friends were included into his inner circle. Donations were always made without his presence and his business transactions were typically performed via proxy and attorneys. Most of the world's business leaders wouldn't recognize him even if they sat at the same table. That's how Henry Weddell wanted it and that's exactly how things went in Henry's world.

The old man's reading was interrupted by the chauffeur. "Mr. Reid, would you care for a sandwich and something to drink? The hearse won't arrive for at least another half hour and you haven't eaten in days."

"No thank you William, although I truly appreciate your concern. Perhaps I'll lay back and rest my eyes. They're burning from lack of sleep. Please inform me when people arrive."

The chauffeur responded, "Yes, sir."

Reid picked up a small embroidered pillow his late wife Delores had made and placed it against the limo's door jamb. He nestled his head into the pillow and reminisced. Initially, he had despised Henry. They were bitter enemies, but later they became the best of friends. He would miss the friend he affectionately called "The Wizard," just as he missed Delores. He asked himself, "How did our lives get so out of control and boil down to this?"

The old man's eyes became heavy and closed as he entered the dream ether — the land of "Oz" where past dreams and nightmares often merge.

March 10, 1944 — Over Hamburg

The skies over North Germany were cold and crisp. Captain Dale Olsen shifted his body in the seat and readjusted his oxygen mask. His tall, lanky frame made it difficult for him to get comfortable within the close quarters of a B-17G cockpit. Only 21, this was his seventh mission with the 457th Bomber Group. He was cited for bravery on his fourth mission after piloting his badly-crippled ship home from Leipzig. They'd been assigned "Tail End Charlie" position on that flight, becoming the formation's sacrificial lamb.

The first leg of today's mission was expected to be "gravy," but the bombing run would be risky, especially after the formation separated to move toward their two targets. One-hundred-sixty-two bombers left England that morning, hoping to destroy the Bruner-Visse shipyard and a railway complex southeast of Hamburg. A brilliant orange sunrise grew directly in front of the fleet and a blanket of clouds presented a colorful array as the bomber group approached the target area. Captain Olsen enjoyed the early morning skies despite their dangers.

The cloud cover was 3,000 feet lower and thicker than expected. The pre-flight briefing was wrong, so Colonel Lupner got on the radio and ordered the formation to drop to 19,000 feet. He expected them to be completely leveled out and at the prescribed speed before splitting into two separate squadrons. One-hundred fortresses would follow the colonel toward the railway hub while the remaining aircraft would follow Captain Olsen to the shipyard. The formation was 20 minutes away from the split point when they began their gradual descent.

Dale Olsen was thrilled to be in charge of his own bombing run. On their left, countless P-47 vapor trails lined the skies 500 feet above the formation. Their much-needed air support had arrived.

Captain Olsen communicated the elevation changes to his navigator and bombardier. He expected them to obtain a visual fix on landmarks as soon as they reached

19,000 feet. Fifteen minutes later, the formation reached the new altitude to find a broken but acceptable view of the German countryside. Olsen re-trimmed his aircraft, leveled out, then adjusted the autopilot settings. Colonel Lupner gave the order to split the squadrons into their respective flight paths.

Captain Olsen spoke to his squadron. "Tighten up men, We're entering the final leg before our turn. Trim your birds and follow my lead."

He switched to the on-board intercom. "Mr. Kowalski, what's our ETA for target acquisition?"

"We're three minutes from the way marker, sir".

He shifted his conversation to the bombardier. "Mr. Fowler, have you recalculated the new glide path yet?"

"Yes, sir — no problems here."

The captain asked, "Mr. Fowler, what do you need from me?"

"Hit the final marker as planned; then change course to twenty one degrees north. That'll place us directly into our bombing lane. After turning, give me exactly 245 mph with bomb bay doors open and perfectly level flight at 19,000 feet Then re-trim the bird for auto-pilot. I'll engage my clutch and let the bombsight take over from there."

Captain Olsen responded, "You've already got it. We're in perfect trim, level and exactly at 19,000 feet. Mr. Kowalski, we should be approaching our final marker. What say you?"

"One minute, ten seconds, sir."

Olsen radioed his squadron. "One minute to our turning marker. Keep it tight gentlemen. Maintain 245 mph with bay doors opened."

Ground fire desperately reached for the formation but was at least 1,000 feet below the fortresses. At 19,000 feet it's difficult to hit something moving at such high speed, but sooner or later, ground fire would find its range and begin pummeling the squadron with 80-mm shells.

Dale Olsen knew once that happened, his squadron was within easy reach of ground fire. At this altitude, the B-17s had marginal floor space if they needed to recover from a hit.

Olsen took a deep breath as the formation executed a flawless turn toward the Hamburg shipyard. He spoke into the intercom. "Mr. Fowler, do you have target acquisition?"

Fowler peered through his newly-installed Norden bomb sight. He cupped his left hand over the eye piece, blocking out surrounding light, giving him a perfect view of the upcoming shipyard. He adjusted the lens dial while placing the crosshairs onto the bombing lane. "Yes, sir, I see it. Gyros on — engaging clutch in five, four, three, two, one — targets locked. I'm in control, sir."

Captain Olsen radioed the squadron. "Mr. Fowler's in control — bombing orders will come from him. Keep it tight gentlemen. We're so far up Hitler's ass, we'll see his breakfast."

Black, greasy-looking flak surrounded the formation as they closed on the shipyard. The formation had entered the hostile zone known as "Flak Alley." Final moments of bombing missions were always tense and intercom chatter ceased as every crew member concentrated on his duties.

The eerie silence was broken as Fowler warned the formation, "Easy does it — big flack zone ahead. Hang on, it's gonna be rough. Get ready to give these goose-stepping assholes a taste of hot Pittsburgh steel."

Olsen addressed his ship. "OK, men, bases are loaded and we're at bat. Gunners on your toes for bandits."

The B-17s seemed to crawl toward the drop zone. Ten seconds before reaching the drop zone, the radio blasted, "Red Hawk 3 is hit — two engines gone — they're on fire and falling out."

Olsen looked over his left shoulder and saw the plane roll onto its side below the lower formation with smoke trailing. A red and yellow fireball was followed by a tumbling right wing. The single-winged aircraft spun in a crazy corkscrew spiral towards earth. As he lost sight of it he said, "Remain focused everyone — on your toes."

Fowler engaged the trigger and yelled, "BOMBS AWAY! BOMBS AWAY!"

Flight engineer Decker slid down from the upper turret to watch as the bombs slid effortlessly from their racks.

Olsen loudly confirmed the bombardier's order to the squadron by repeating, "BOMBS AWAY, GENTLEMEN."

Each Flying Fortress immediately ascended due to the 5,000 pound weight reduction. Moments after the last bomb cleared the bay doors of Olsen's ship, a vicious explosion rocked the B-17 directly under its nose. The relentless ground fire had struck home.

Switching back to manual control, Olsen calmly said, "Mr. Kowalski, damage report — what just happened?" There was no answer. "Kowalski — Fowler report." There was no response, but the flak stopped. The B-17 lost altitude and Olsen felt ice-cold air rushing into the plane.

Co-pilot Lieutenant Adams grimaced, holding his left knee. "I'm hit in the leg. Hold us steady while I tie off my wound."

Olsen banked the aircraft to the right and nudged the nose down to avoid being struck from behind by the trailing B-17s. Realizing that they'd been hit from below, he spoke over the intercom. "Decker, we've been hit under our nose — give me a visual."

Decker had been knocked against the fuselage during the explosion and paused to gather his composure. After his foggy state lifted, he peered into what remained of the B-17's nose. "You won't be reaching anyone up front, captain. The chin turret's gone. There's nothing but empty sky where our nose was. Fowler and Hanson are missing — Kowalski's dead. It's an ugly scene — we'll have a tough ride home."

Decker climbed back into the upper turret. P-47s were engaged in dogfights on both sides of the aircraft. Olsen maintained control of the plane as his squadron perform a 90-degree turn toward home. He began his own lumbering turn. Flight engineer Decker in the upper turret yelled, "Two bandits at six o'clock — one bandit at four — Christ, one more directly above at twelve o'clock." 50-caliber machine guns barked from the ailing ship and the interior of the B-17 smelled of spent gunpowder.

Olsen reached to disengage the autopilot master bar as two Messerschmitt 109s unloaded on the crippled aircraft, tearing across both wings, taking out the number three engine, badly damaging number two and tearing through the cockpit. Burning pain tore through his right arm, upper left back and scalp above his left ear. Co-pilot Adams was slumped over the wheel, his right forehead missing. Adams' body weight against the yoke was forcing the B-17 into a rapid descent.

Captain Olsen became overwhelmed and dazed as his world transformed into slow motion snapshots - suspended animation. Sparks flew and smoke billowed from the radio room as the captain's consciousness separated from his body. Sounds became distorted and hollow while he rose above his own body. He saw his right forearm dangling from the elbow socket while floating above the eerie scene.

Decker yelled into the intercom, "The cockpit's been hit. I'm taking a look. Side gunner, man my turret."

Crews of the squadron's last few planes watched Olsen's fortress slowly list onto its right side. One of the formation tail gunners addressed his pilot. "I've got a visual on the captain's plane — they're going down, sir. Their nose is gone, number two engine's burning and number three's out. The cockpit looks torn apart. I've not seen anyone bailing out."

The pilot answered, "Keep an eye out for silk. If anyone bails, give me a count."

The formation's radio chatter became silent as Olsen's badly-damaged fortress slid toward the German countryside. Their esteemed leader was earthbound.

Andy Decker tore off his oxygen mask and scrambled from the upper turret to the freezing cold cockpit. With the chin turret gone, open bomb bay doors and fist sized holes in the cockpit and windshield; the B-17 became an enormous wind tunnel. Decker yanked the dead co-pilot back into his seat and pulled back on the yoke. Frozen blood and tiny specks of brain covered the controls. Just as the B-17 leveled out, another ME-109 approached from the left side of the Fortress. Decker desperately scanned the instrument panel while the waist and turret gunners fired at the approaching aircraft. The bandit was destroyed, but only after it shot across the fuselage, wounding the waist gunner. The gunner fell to the floor, holding his leg in agony while thick smoke raced through the rear of the aircraft.

Decker yelled at Captain Olsen to hold the wheel with his left hand. Somehow, Decker's shout enabled the pilot to regain his senses. He found himself back in his body and behind the controls. Adrenaline rushed through the captain's veins, and he instinctively pulled hard on the yoke with his good hand and held the plane steady. Decker unstrapped Adams from the copilot's seat and pushed him into the cavity where the chin turret had been. He slid into the co-pilots seat and steadied the shaking control wheel.

The B-17 was sluggish and losing altitude. The captain looked at the burning number two engine and dead number three engine. He instructed Decker to cut the down engine's throttles and propeller pitch. Andy reached over to the control panel with his left hand and cut power to both engines. Down to two engines, the plane helplessly slid to the right from lack of power.

Captain Olsen pulled off his mask with his left arm and scanned the instrument panel. Number one engine's oil pressure had suddenly dropped into the danger zone. He glanced at the engine and saw a thick trail of oily black smoke. The altimeter showed 9,000 ft. Olsen shook his head.

"Fuck it Andy, we're done here — this plane's had it. Hit the bail-out alarm, I'll hold her steady while you and the crew punch out. I'll follow."

Andy hit the red alarm button three times, yelled into the intercom to bail out and trimmed the plane one final time. Intercom chatter reached a frenzy as the surviving crewmen bailed out. Decker ran behind the pilot, located their chutes and unstrapped Captain Olsen from his seat.

"You're coming with me," he yelled

The captain countered, "Damn it, Andy! There's not enough time. I'll get out on my own."

"You'll never get your chute on with that arm. You're wearing a body harness so it'll only take me seconds to attach your chute. Come on, let's go."

The captain argued. "I gave you an order, mister — hit the silk."

"Shut the fuck up or we'll both be killed! Now let's go!"

Stumbling in the cramped cockpit, Andy grabbed the sandy-haired pilot by his flight jacket. As they reached the bomb bay doors, bullets rattled across the wings and through the cockpit as another ME-109 strafed the dying ship. Andy quickly attached his chute, then struggled with Olsen's. Managing to secure the captain's chute to his body harness, Andy positioned Olsen next to the bomb bay doors. He cut a piece of cargo strap with a switchblade knife he carried in his jacket pocket. His hands became covered in Olsen's blood as he tied a tourniquet around the remains of Dale's arm. He was surprised at how sticky blood became while drying.

The B-17's metal skin looked like a cheese grater as sunlight penetrated the countless bullet and shrapnel holes. Number one engine sputtered and coughed, and the plane listed heavily to its right side and the nose dropped. Andy shoved the captain out the bomb bay doors and yelled, "See you on the ground, pal."

Decker quickly followed. Seconds later the ship rolled over, broke apart and tumbled toward the ground. Debris from the plane littered the sky like confetti falling from tall buildings during a parade.

The rushing ice-cold air took Captain Olsen's breath away. He fumbled with the rip cord handle several times before the chute finally deployed. The jolt of the opening chute was excruciating and it felt as if his lower right arm had torn completely off. He became light-headed, dizzy, and then passed out.

The parachute silently floated like a feather in the wind as the pilot swung back and forth toward the forest below. His immobile hulk crashed through a tall pine tree and the chute and cords became entangled. Snow rained down to the pilot's motionless body from the upper branches. He came to rest four feet above the ground, swinging from his harness. Blood trickled from his right arm and made circular designs onto the crusty snow below.

Within seconds, a Nazi half-track clattered toward the tree. When it arrived, three soldiers jumped out; yelling, running and stumbling through the snow toward the tree. They pointed their machine guns at the motionless pilot. They were about to shoot, but their sergeant ordered them to halt.

"Cut him down. He looks to be an officer. If he lives, he may be of value."

Rude Awakening

The chauffeur spoke to the old man. "You need to wake up, sir. People are arriving. Mr. Reid, please wake up. The hearse is approaching."

Sweating and groggy, the white-haired man managed, "What?"

"Mr. Reid, you must wake up."

The old man looked confused and disoriented as he sat up. His throat was dry. "I'm sorry, William. I was having a nightmare. Was I snoring?"

The chauffeur acknowledged, "Yes, sir. Would you care for something to drink?"

"Yes please, a ginger ale would be marvelous."

He looked around as the hearse pulled up to the grave site. He saw Rusty operating a television camera supported on his right shoulder. Another security agent played the part of a television reporter, with a microphone in his left hand, facing the camera. The limo's radio beeped as William handed the old man a ginger ale.

Mr. Reid turned on the rear intercom and closed the partition and spoke. "Blue Marlin to Command."

Helen responded, "This is Command. Everything's up and running, sir. I can connect your audio with the entire team whenever you'd like and your television monitor is live-stream. I can transmit any individual camera or send you a four sectioned split screen."

"Excellent job, Helen, split screen is best. Connect my intercom to the crew please."

She pressed a button at her console. "You're connected, sir."

"Rusty, do you copy?"

The red-haired man had an earpiece and spoke softly into a button on his left shirt cuff, "Yes, sir, I copy. Over."

"Good. I'm watching our live cams. This is shaping up to be a modest ceremony — maybe three dozen people. It should make our job easy. They'll stick out like sore thumbs. I see that Catherine and her family came in Henry's limo. Watch them closely. Blue Marlin out."

Chatter filled the radio channel as team members began scrutinizing each arriving vehicle. People filtered toward the grave as eight pallbearers carried the cherry-wood casket to the chrome rack that straddled the open hole. The security team mingled among the crowd as if they were part of the procession. Small tie clasps with concealed cameras sent a constant stream of video to Helen within the van. Rusty's news camera received the same barrage of live video. Within five minutes, all but three individuals were identified and cleared. Those three were immediately surrounded by the shadow team.

Rusty keyed in on the three targets, taking high resolution photographs. The van immediately forwarded them by satellite to a Seattle office for facial recognition. DMV software processed each and every license plate as bodyguards maneuvered themselves between family members and the targets. A sharply dressed, heavy-set Black man walked to the casket, placed a single white rose on its lid, then turned and faced the small gathering crowd.

A tall, blonde woman in her late thirties accompanied by an older woman walked to the front row and sat down. They were wearing black dresses and sunglasses and appeared to be related. The younger woman turned and motioned to a man standing behind the rear set of chairs. He grabbed a grade-school-age boy's hand and hurried to join her in the front row. He sat next to her, placed a hand on her shoulder and offered his handkerchief. The restless young boy stood up, adjusted his belt and looked around. He noticed that the cemetery workers in gray jumpsuits were taking photos of him. One of the men had a camera with a telephoto lens, while the other was using his cell phone. The boy immediately sat down and whispered into his father's ear. They weren't the only people who noticed the two men.

Rusty whispered into his left shirt cuff, "We've got two hot targets in gray jumpsuits fifty meters south of my position. They're taking photos of Catherine's family."

Mr. Reid looked at his monitor and barked, "Of course. We should have picked up on them when we arrived. I thought they were legitimate,"

Rusty backed away from the grave, blocking the two men's view of him. Once hidden, he spoke. "Whitey, have your men flank them. Don't let them escape. Apprehend them when the service's over, but avoid making a scene."

The albino immediately nodded at another guard, and they walked far to the sides of the groundskeepers, leaving the seaside cliff as their only escape route.

Rusty spoke. "They may be connected to one or all of our targets. If they draw weapons on the family, shoot to kill. Helen, do you have anything on the other three targets?"

She responded, "Not yet. Wait — just got a hit on the guy in the tweed suit. He's a local physician named Paul Linton. He treated Mr. Weddell before his death. Hold on — got info on the other two. They're both lawyers for Weddell. One's chief council for PCI. by the name of Craig Johnson. The other guy's Howard Bradley — he runs the Weddell family trust."

Reid interjected, "Henry spoke highly of the last two men. I've never met them but if their faces match the biometric program, they're clean."

Helen said, "They match, sir, but Doctor Linton and the jumpsuits are solid targets."

When the ceremony began, one of the groundkeepers walked north and paralleled the bluff. Whitey casually meandered along the cliff side, maintaining a flanking position. He knelt by the nearest headstone as if praying, then talked into his cuff. "Jumpsuit One has a slight limp. He's changing direction, heading east toward the limo. Bill, intercept him if he gets too close to Blue Marlin."

The limping man stopped thirty feet from the rear of the limo, bent over, pretending to pick up something from the road while using his phone to photograph the limo's license plate. Rusty watched as the man stood up, turned and made a call. Within seconds the doctor reached into his pocket and looked at his phone, then glanced toward the limo. The limping man reversed course and slowly made his way back to the trees where his partner stood.

Again Rusty whispered into his left cuff. "Jumpsuits and Linton are together — they just communicated via phone. After the ceremony, my team will apprehend the Doc. Whitey, you and your team grab the jumpsuits."

Whitey whispered into his shirt cuff. "Roger that."

The well-dressed Black man placed a hand on top of the casket as he finished the eulogy. "So let us celebrate the life of our brother Henry rather than dwell upon his passing. The measure of a man can be seen in the lives of the people that he's touched and I'm convinced that Henry Weddell has managed to touch everyone here today — with his kindness, his generosity and brilliant intellect. He once confided in me that he wasn't a religious man and that his sense of God could not be found in church but in the everyday moments of life which most of us take for granted — like a plant turning toward the sun, the song of a meadowlark or the laughter of children playing. Henry celebrated God in the simplest of things. He took pleasure in watching people smile and did his best to make us smile. May his legacy live on in our smiles as we remember this extraordinary individual. God bless you, Henry Weddell."

The man turned to the casket cradle and began cranking a long chrome handle. Henry Weddell was lowered into the grave to rest beside his wife for eternity.

People stood and formed small groups away from the grave. Rusty held out his right hand to Catherine while placing his left hand onto her shoulder. As they shook hands she felt a small folded paper being passed to her. He whispered something into her ear, then retreated.

Upon reading the note, she looked at the black limo, then back at her father's grave. A short man wearing a kippah was kneeling and chanting something in Hebrew while tossing flowers on top of the lowered casket. She quickly gathered her small family and walked toward the limo. Doctor Linton tried to intercept the family group as they approached the limo, but instead found himself surrounded by Rusty and the TV-6 news team.

Three Targets

The doctor was upset after being surrounded with newsmen from the Channel 6 team. He had hoped to intercept the Weddell family before they reached the stretch limo on the opposite side of the roadway.

The red-haired "newsman" stood in front of the doctor and asked, "Sir, could we have a moment of your time for a quick interview? This will only take a minute."

The doctor shook his head. "No, I'm pressed for time and need to speak with Mr. Weddell's daughter before going back to work."

The newsman pressed on. "Lucky you. Catherine plans on returning to our news van as soon as her family leaves for Mr. Weddell's estate. She'll be here in less time than it takes for the interview. How about it, sir?"

Linton looked around and saw people were entering their cars and leaving. Unable to see his partners anymore, he declined. "I don't wish to be rude but I really must be going. I've got a two o'clock appointment which can't be rescheduled."

Rusty nodded to two of his men who stood near the van, then opened his baggy suit coat showing off a gold chain with an FBI badge hanging from its end. A holstered pistol hung under his left armpit. "There's no time like the present, doc. Don't say a word and get into of the van. If you don't comply, the agents standing behind you will cuff and arrest you."

Linton turned and saw two men standing directly behind him. He frantically looked for his accomplices, then turned toward his car. Rusty stuck out a leg and tripped the doctor, who fell hard onto the pavement. The three men picked up the doctor and brushed him off.

"I'm sorry, Doctor. How clumsy of me. Let's get you cleaned up inside the van,"

Before anyone had noticed, the doctor was shuffled into the van. Within seconds, duct tape covered his mouth and plastic zip ties had him hog-tied.

Helen was sitting at her consul holding a report. She spun around and commented, "Bravo! Jolly good show, guys. My first customer of the day." She looked at the terrified doctor. "Let me see. Says here you're Dr. Paul Linton, orthopedic surgeon, UCLA medical school graduate. This will be an interesting afternoon after all."

"Focus on your work, Helen," Rusty said. He spoke into his radio. "Whitey, what's the status on the jumpsuits?"

Whitey responded, "They're standing on the bluff, looking over the edge. There's no safe way down They saw you grab the doctor and are looking for options."

Rusty considered the situation. "Fuck 'em! Take them now — alive."

Whitey and four armed men spread apart and hurried toward the bluff, and both targets began negotiating the steep cliff toward the Pacific below. There was no pathway to the ocean there, only loose rocks and brush. Whitey sprinted several hundred yards along the cliff to the north. He located a steep trail heading to the secluded, rocky beach below and moved quickly and carefully down the path. As the other pursuers reached the bluff, the limping man lost his footing and bounced down the embankment to the rocky beach below. The final stretch to the shore was a 15-foot freefall,. After bouncing like a rag doll, the man landed head first on top of the rocks. He lay motionless, unconscious or dead. His accomplice watched in disbelief; still hanging onto brush and continuing down the steep incline. One missed step or bad hand hold would result in his partner's fate.

One of the security men looked at the motionless man below and commented, "Oh wow! That must've hurt. Think he's dead?"

Another said, "Yep. C'mon! The other guy's getting away." The men began a tenuous trek down the steep cliff, careful not to share the first man's fate.

Moments later, the second groundskeeper managed to reach the beach below. He glanced toward his motionless partner and realized he was probably dead. Huge rock outcroppings and vicious breakers prevented him from escaping in that direction so he scramble north along the wet, rocky beach. Nearly out of breath, he turned to see if anyone was following him. Three men in suits approached the base of the cliff from above. Panicked by their persistence, he turned around and found Whitey standing less than fifteen feet away.

The albino's pistol was aimed at his chest. Whitey said, "Stay where you are! Put your hands on top of your head and drop to your knees."

In desperation, the fugitive lowered his head and charged the albino like a linebacker rushing a quarterback. The albino stepped to his left and struck the passing man in the back of the head with his pistol. The "groundskeeper" fell face first onto the gravelly beach and the albino pounced on top of him and put a knee onto the neck of his captive. He shoved the pistol barrel against the man's head and ordered, "Alright, asshole. Move again and I'll kill you."

The captive whined, "Don't shoot. Don't shoot. I didn't do anything."

The other shadow team members arrived, cuffed the captive's hands behind his back, then rolled him over. One laughed and said, "Fuckin' a — great job, Whitey. I thought we'd have to run this jerk down or shoot him in the legs."

Whitey proudly responded, "Just trying to keep ahead of you young pups."

They pulled the terrified man to his feet. A red, embroidered name tag on the jumpsuit identified him as John. They frisked him and found a cell phone, wallet and a small semi-automatic pistol.

"Grave diggers with guns," Whitey commented. "What's this world coming to? OK asshole, where's the camera?"

"What camera? There's no camera. You know the drill — read me my rights. I wanna lawyer-up."

Whitey kicked the man in the groin, buckling him to his knees. "We're not the heat, asshole; we're your worst nightmare. I'm not playing games, now where's the camera?"

The captive moaned in pain and fell to his side. He hunched into a fetal position, trying to collect himself. He finally managed a faint response. "My cousin's got it — the guy who fell."

Whitey looked at his men. "Sam, you and I need to get this guy upstairs. There's a fairly decent pathway about one hundred yards ahead. Bill, get over to the other guy and see if he's still alive. If not, strip him clean of all I.D. and phones — and find that goddamn camera. I'll call you when we reach the top. Don't leave until I give you an all-clear."

Bill obliged. "Got it."

Whitey turned to his captive. "On your feet — what's your name?"

"Gary — Gary Wiser."

Whitey opened the man's wallet, looked at his license, then grabbed his ear and pulled. "Says here your name's John Hart. Better start explaining."

In pain, the man spoke. "It's Wiser — that's a fake I.D."

The albino let go of the ear, and spoke into his sleeve. "Whitey to Command, over." There was no answer. He repeated the message without a response. He turned to his partner. "We're out of range down here. Let's get our new friend up to the van." He looked at the captive. "Start moving asshole."

After the kick to his groin, the man struggled to walk. He finally managed to move when Whitey kicked him in the buttocks. "I told you to get moving — we don't have all day." After five grueling minutes of climbing, the trio reached the summit. They were out of breath when the albino finally made contact with the van.

Rusty responded, "Go ahead, Whitey."

"We've got both of them. One fell off of the cliff while trying to escape. He's probably compromised or at least seriously injured. Bill's checking on him now. I'm coming in with the live one."

Rusty wasted no time. "No, wait there. You were out of radio contact and you're the only link to Bill. If the other target's salvageable, keep him alive, otherwise make sure he's expired goods. No bullet holes. I want a photo of his face for the biometric program. Get that damn camera."

"Yes, sir. Hold while I contact Bill."

Whitey stood at the bluff's edge and watched Bill rifle through the man's clothing. "Bill, this is Whitey. What's up with our mark? Is he conscious?"

"Negative — he's done. I've got his camera, phone and ID. My job's complete. The tide's coming in and my new wing tips are getting soaked."

"Wait," Whitey ordered. "Get a photo of his face. He could be in our database."

"Already did that. Am I going to have trouble finding the path you talked about?"

"No. High tail it back here. You won't have problems finding the path — it's about a hundred yards beyond the spot where we cuffed our friend. There's an enormous chunk of driftwood by the trailhead."

"Good, I'll meet you at the van in ten minutes."

Whitey spoke to his radio. "Rusty, I gather you heard me talking with Bill. The other guy's compromised and we've got everything you asked for."

Rusty responded, "Excellent! Come on in."

As the three targets were being apprehended, Catherine and her family entered the long black limousine, unaware of what was transpiring around them. She immediately threw her arms around the old man and sobbed. "Uncle Frank! You've made it. I'm so glad you're here. Where are Anna and Peter?"

The old man spoke softly. "I'm thrilled to see everyone as well. I wish this reunion was under happier circumstances. My children wanted to attend but I advised them to remain at home. After we talk, you'll understand why they're not here. It's extremely important that we discuss things about your father and I. This happens to be a very sensitive subject and quite personal, so I strongly suggest that we have this conversation in private — just you and I."

Catherine frowned. "Nonsense. This is my family. They can hear anything you have to say unless it might upset my grandson."

The old man shook his head. "Would you mind if young Henry joins William in the front seat, or returns to Henry's limo? Trust me, this requires complete privacy."

Catherine looked confused. "Why? What's going on?"

Before the old man could answer, Rusty radioed the limo. "Blue Marlin, do you copy?"

The old man patted Catherine on her knee with his left hand and looked her in the eyes. "I'll tell you everything, but I must take this call."

He turned his attention to the intercom. "Yes, Rusty. I'm with Henry's family, so please speak in general terms. How are things on your end?"

"Things have developed quite well, sir. All targets are under our control — unfortunately one of them had an accident and I regret that he won't be of any value. We've pulled the vinyl logos from the news van. When Whitey returns with his team, we'll be ready to leave."

"Wonderful. Get our targets to the warehouse and prep them for interrogation. Have the other two guard vehicles stay behind my vehicle and Henry's. Catherine and I are going to talk briefly. I'll leave for the warehouse as soon as we're done here. I'm going to turn off the radio while I speak with Catherine."

"Affirmative, sir. I'll contact your driver if I need to speak with you."

"Fantastic job, Rusty. We'll talk soon."

Catherine was staring at her uncle. "What is this? Why all the intrigue?"

The old man looked at her and winked, then patted the young boy on the shoulder. "So young Henry. How about a personal ride in your great-grandfather's car? Rumor has it that there's a bag of goodies inside the center console and I'm sure you know about the small television that unfolds from the ceiling. I believe there are several episodes of *The Simpsons* on DVD, which I understand appeals to you. They should be in the carousel next to the bar."

Excited, the boy turned and looked at the other limousine. He asked his parents, "Can I go? Can I please?"

Patty answered, "Absolutely — but only one can of soda."

Patty's husband Travis assessed the situation and commented, "I think it would be in everyone's best interest if I joined Henry. This sounds far too personal for someone who's not flesh and blood."

Frank thanked him for his discretion. Travis opened his door and walked to the other vehicle with his son. Opening the door of the other limousine, he saw an albino escorting what appeared to be a handcuffed cemetery worker into the news van. He shook his head.

Both limousines sat idling, and the partition in Frank Reid's closed. Catherine and Patty listened as Frank began. "You're aware that your father and I weren't actually brothers — Henry said he had that conversation with you years earlier."

Catherine nodded. "Yes he did, but what does that have to do with anything?"

"Unfortunately I can't elaborate right now because of time constraints, but what's important for you to understand is that my actions are at the request of your father. Henry was murdered by people from our past. The gentleman I was talking with on the radio is part of our security team and he's managed to apprehend three of the individuals involved in your fathers' death. One of them is the doctor who treated Henry."

Catherine was noticeably shaken. "Nonsense! Father wasn't murdered; he died of heart failure after breaking his arm and hip. He was 97 years old and the sweetest person on earth. Why would you say such a terrible thing?"

"I'm not saying these things to upset you. I'm here to ensure your safety. Henry and I spoke two days after he fell. He informed me that a group of people from our past have become a threat and if anything happened to him that I was to protect both of our families. The next day, Henry died."

Catherine winced. "You actually believe that father was murdered?"

"Yes, I do, and unless I can gather information from our captives, the gravity of the situation is unclear. Until I determine the depth of their organization, all of our lives are in jeopardy. That's why my children remained at home. I believe these people are only after your father and I but they'll use our families as bargaining chips."

Catherine said, "You're saying that people from Father's past are behind his death and that our lives are in danger?"

The old man squeezed his lips together and nodded. "That's correct."

She was rattled. "Then why haven't you gone to the police?"

The old man shook his head. "That's not an option. The authorities must be left out of this. Once you know the truth about our past, you'll understand why. Trust me — no police, FBI, or anyone other than my security personnel."

Catharine's daughter Patty interjected, "You're scaring us to death Uncle Frank. If we need to know something, then get on with it so we can prepare ourselves."

"I'll tell both of you about our past when I'm done at the warehouse. Meanwhile, I'm asking that you work with me. Your cooperation is essential. Remain at Henry's estate, contact no one, and allow my people to establish a protective perimeter until my return."

Knowing her father and Frank were as close as brothers, Catherine grudgingly cooperated. "I trust you Uncle Frank. What do you want us to do right now?"

"Return to the estate in Henry's limo and wait for my return. I'll need to spend the night there with our security team. We'll talk either tonight or first thing in the morning."

Patty asked, "What do I tell my husband?"

Catherine said, "Tell Travis nothing. We'll decide what to share with him once we know about Father's past."

The old man kissed Catherine on the cheek. "Excellent idea. I'll see both of you later."

The women left Mr. Reid's vehicle and returned to Henry's limo. Each limousine was followed by a two-vehicle escort filled with armed guards as they left for their respective destinations. By early evening, Frank Reid expected to have some answers.

Mid Morning — Angoon, Alaska

The alarm went off at eight-thirty. The former colonel stumbled to his feet, rubbed his face, then looked out the large windows. A lone humpback whale passing to the north blew a spout of mist directly in front of the house. Jim considered it a lucky omen to see whales. He went into the kitchen and made a small pot of coffee. After pouring a healthy shot of Irish Cream into his mug, he walked to the study and booted up his computer. Checking his email, he was surprised to see that Lori had already responded to his request. She also asked that he call her at 4:00 p.m. The Crane background report was attached to the email. Jim sent it to his printer and shut down the computer.

Typically, bad or questionable individuals are easier to locate than people with clean slates. Such was the case of former police Sergeant Richard Crane. He'd killed a 14-year-old boy in 2005. The boy was an MS13 gangbanger dealing cocaine outside of a convenience store. Crane and a subordinate officer named Mendoza were staking out the store without permission. After witnessing several drug transactions, Crane left his vehicle, yelled, "Police!," drew a 9-mm pistol and fired on Ruiz when he ran. Young Jose Ruiz was hit in the back and died two days later.

An internal investigation concluded that Crane was acting without authority and that he was involved in a turf war between the Hell's Angels and the South American MS13 cartel. Hearsay evidence suggested that he had ties with several motorcycle gang members and accepted bribes to protect their turf. At the very least, he was a trigger-happy cop with a history of police brutality and prisoner abuse. After being fired, he was arrested three times; twice for beating his wife — now divorced — and once for hitting his neighbor in the legs with a baseball bat. Prior to becoming a policeman, he spent a short stint as a Marine Corps MP, but received a general discharge for assaulting an inmate. His psychological evaluation indicated a troubled individual who was dismissed for cause. Jim printed the four-page report and put it in his filing cabinet.

The outside air was warm and damp as he attached the *Sojourn* and its boat trailer to his restored, military surplus Humvee. The black flies of the previous night proved to be accurate weather forecasters. After securing the trailer's safety chain, he noticed movement to his right. An unusually large brown bear with a white patch above his right eye walked up the gravel driveway toward his house. He immediately opened the Hummers door and blew the horn. The bear was unphased and continued forward. Jim grabbed a .44 caliber Desert Eagle pistol from under the front seat and stood behind the door. When the bear had come within fifteen yards, he fired a round to the side of the bruin. The bullet spit gravel skyward, causing the bear to bolt into the timber. This was the bear that tried breaking into his house the previous fall. If it returned, he'd ask the Clan to have it trapped or destroyed. He returned to the house, poured another cup of coffee, flipped a hidden switch above the coat rack, secured the front door and headed to the launch.

There were less than ten miles of road in and around Angoon, so it took only five minutes to reach the marina. It was 9:30 a.m., and the docks were void of activity. Anyone else going fishing had left hours ago. Though the sun was up, it had yet to crest over the looming, snow-covered peaks to the east, making for a spectacular view. He launched the *Sojourn* and tied it to the pier, then drove the Hummer and trailer up the hill to a small parking area. He walked back to his boat, brushing away black flies as an old police car drove past him and stopped on the ramp below. A young Tlingit boy rode up on a beat-up bicycle with ape-hanger handlebars and a banana seat, and stopped next to the police car. He sat on his bike and watched a large, barrel-chested, dark-haired policeman get out of the cruiser. He stood between Jim and the dock. The officers' temples were slightly gray, and he reminded Jim of someone, but he couldn't remember who. A 9-mm Glock hung from his right hip and a black wooden nightstick balanced out his left side. He wore wrap-around silver reflective sunglasses, which prevented people from making eye contact. The man obviously tried to look intimidating. Jim already knew he didn't care for Officer Crane, and this confirmed it.

The policeman wore a baseball cap which had an embroidered gold star on its front along with ANGOON POLICE.

He spoke. "You the fella that has a place in front of Chatham?"

Jim was solidly built and muscular, but Crane stood two inches taller and was at least fifty pounds heavier. Jim answered, "Yes, sir. How can I help you?"

Crane had a toothpick into the right corner of his mouth. "Just making sure you're not a thief trying to steal his boat."

Jim knew this was a ridiculous statement and challenged Crane. "I appreciate your concern, officer, but there's no place for a person to hide a stolen boat around here. We're on an island in the middle of nowhere and Native culture forbids stealing. They don't tolerate thieves. I'm certain you already know that and I bet you know who I am. You watched me arrive on yesterday's ferry. I saw you glassing people from your cruiser."

Crane acted annoyed, turning the toothpick in his mouth. "I watched you leaving the ferry with that tricked-out Humvee. Looked like it was stuffed with boxes. What's the likelihood of contraband being in some of those boxes?"

Jim wondered why Crane was so confrontational. "So this isn't about a possible boat theft. Shame on you, Mr. Crane. That's a rude way to introduce yourself. You have a peculiar method of dealing with people. After all, you're a public servant. Let me demonstrate how this is done."

Jim outstretched his right hand and said, "Hello, my name's James Bennett and I'm very pleased to meet you Officer Crane. Now isn't that much better?"

Crane pulled the toothpick from his mouth and tossed it at Jim's feet. "So besides knowing my name, you're a mouthy prick. Makes me wonder about you."

Bennett wanted to punch the man but refrained. "I'm trying my best to be civil, but this isn't working, so cut to the chase. What do you want?"

Crane barked, "Get something straight asshole, I'm the law in Angoon and I take my job seriously. That means you and Ernie McKinnon are on my radar. I've been watching him and think he's involved with a rifle theft from the fuel depot and I'm convinced he's a moonshiner because locals say he's got a still. Besides that, he avoids answering questions about his past, which tells me he's got something to hide. You're real chummy with him, so maybe you've got something to hide too. Listen up mister, I won't tolerate either of you breaking the law around here and making me look foolish."

Jim wasted little time getting into Crane's face. "You don't need help looking foolish — just look in a mirror. If you suspect us of breaking the law, then arrest us or get a search warrant from Juneau. As for the rifle theft, try talking with some of the seasonal help from the fishing lodge on Killisnoo. Most of them are college kids from the Lower 48 working for minimum wage and tips. Furthermore; Ernie would never steal from anyone and he certainly has no need for additional guns. He doesn't have to answer to you about anything. He's lived here for over 60 years, so leave the old timer alone."

The officer shook his head. "You don't tell me anything and I'll see about that warrant. Meanwhile, I'll jump your sorry ass if you so much as fart. You're nothing more than an arrogant corporate piss-ant, and I don't like you."

Jim lifted his leg as if farting. "Oh my, does that mean we'll never exchange Christmas cards? You're a predatory bully who takes bribes, shoots teenage kids, beats up women, and pushes people around. Listen up, Crane. You don't scare me, and if you think you're man enough to have it out with me, let's roll. Otherwise get out of my face and leave me and my friends alone."

Jim waited several seconds, then walked past Crane toward his boat.

Crane placed his hand onto his pistol and yelled, "Hey, get back here! I'm not done."

Jim continued walking to his boat. He yelled over his shoulder, "Arrest me or fuck off." After reaching the boat, he turned around and flipped Crane the middle finger.

The Native boy tore off on his bike toward town; in a hurry to tell *someone* what he'd seen. Crane stood dumbfounded. Jim untied his boat, started the engines and headed down Kootznahoo Inlet. Before reaching the outlet to Chatham, he turned left toward Mel Frank's dock. It was nearly 10 a.m. when he tied up. He hurried up the steps to Mel's house and loudly knocked on the door. A stained window curtain moved slightly to one side, announcing someone's presence.

A short man in his mid sixties answered the door. "I'll be damn. It's good to see ya, Jim."

The two men shook hands and Jim said, "Sorry to bother you Mel, but I just had a run-in with the new town cop down by the marina. He tried picking a fight with me. He also accused Ernie of being a thief and moonshiner. He'd better chill out before someone gets hurt. Crane's combative behavior's bad for Angoon, and Ernie told me he's been harassing him, so I pulled a background check on him. I'll provide you with a copy. He's got a checkered past."

Mel shook his head. "Come in for coffee, and we'll talk."

"I'd like to, Mel, but I've got a pile of things going on today. I need to check out my boat, organize tackle and go shopping for Ernie."

"I'm sorry he gave ya a hard time, Jim, but he's been nice from what I've seen and heard."

"Then he's blowing smoke up your butt. Talk with little Otto Kankesh — he witnessed what happened at the marina. Even Pete Engles stopped him from harassing Ernie and considered banning him from his store. Crane's a complete jerk."

Mel nodded. "Guess I'm gonna need that report. I'll talk to Otto and his folks — maybe swing by Pete's store and talk with him too. Ya know it's tough to get anyone decent for this sorta job. He'll end up just like the others, either fired or quit. Between you and me, we don't need a cop in Angoon, but some Clan members felt it would reduce domestic abuse. We got a few bad apples that get blitzed every night and wanna fight. When the Clan got an offer it couldn't refuse, they hired Crane."

Jim frowned in confusion. "What do you mean 'offer?' What kind of offer?"

"Santos asked through his lawyer for local law enforcement in exchange for hiring locals to rebuild his dock. He'd also donate $30,000 each year toward a cop's salary — we're gettin' Crane for free. He's even buying us a police boat if we patrol Hood Bay, so the Clan jumped at the offer. The boat should be here any day."

Jim shook his head. "The village has no authority on the water or on privately deeded land; you know that. Only state troopers can perform those functions. Clan law doesn't apply to non-Clan property or boats on the water, so what's the point?"

"We told his lawyer that, but he wants it patrolled anyway. He bought us a new boat and he's paying Crane."

Again Jim frowned and asked, "How'd you end up choosing Crane?"

"Santos' attorney hired him."

Jim cocked his head to one side. "This situation is bizarre. After reading Crane's history, you'll be as skeptical as me. I'm convinced that things are different than they appear. Do you have telephone numbers for both Crane and Santos?"

Mel nodded. "Inside the house — they're written on top of my phone book."

Jim's mind raced. "Do you happen to have a photograph of Santos or know where I can get one?"

"So happens that Hank Stytes took pictures of Charlie Deshitan shaking hands with Santos and his attorney while they were giving the Clans a check for Crane's salary. The pictures were used in our school newsletter."

The former colonel smiled. "Outstanding. Can I have a copy?"

Mel nodded. "You bet. As for Crane, after speaking with Pete and Otto, I'll have a pow-wow with the elders 'bout what happened. Hey, I'm sorry 'bout this. Please don't think he represents the feelings of the village cuz we respect ya and we're glad you're here."

"I appreciate that Mel. It's great to be back. On a more personal note, I have the cigars you asked for and a few other things from Denver. I'll bring them down after I get caught up — maybe by mid-afternoon. I'll pick up the photos and telephone numbers then. We'll talk about the smoked salmon idea from last fall and the new health clinic. I wrote up a business plan for the salmon idea and made good progress with a major grocery chain."

Mel smiled. "That's great news. I'll be home all afternoon."

Sensing the timing was right, Jim seized the opportunity. "By the way, do you have a crab pot that I can either purchase or rent? My kids are coming up in two days and I'd like to make them some crab cakes"

Mel nodded and pointed toward his pier. "There's several next to the old skiff behind my tool shed. You can have 'em. I'm too old to wrestle with 'em anymore."

"Fantastic. I only need one, and I'll return it when I'm done."

"Keep it Jim. Bring me a couple crabs every now and then, and we're square."

They shook hands again, and Jim headed toward the pier. He found the crab pots behind the skiff and found the metal tube Ernie had traded to Mel for beer. His heart pounded with excitement as he lifted the heavy cage. The corroded metal cylinder was attached to it by a length of rotted rope. Another element of Ernie's story was verified.

Perhaps a Nazi *did* make it to Admiralty Island, Jim thought. He swung the pot onto his boat's deck and backed into the bay. It was time to check out his craft for the upcoming season.

After leaving Kootsnahoo Bay, he entered the two-hundred-mile-long Strait. Jim noticed a small white ship against the opposite shore near the entrance of Peril Strait. Peril is a small narrow that offers a shortcut to Sitka. However, strong tidal rips throughout the passage had proved deadly at times. Another smaller vessel, which appeared to be the Santos catamaran, was within several hundred yards of the ship. Jim looked through his binoculars and verified the identity of the drifting catamaran. He wondered why Santos was near this dangerous passage.

Jim was unable to identify the larger ship's markings, so he continued his journey by engaging his GPS autopilot and running the large aluminum cabin cruiser south. Twenty minutes later, he shut down the engines and allowed the boat to drift south while he arranged his fishing tackle. He drank a cold beer and set a short, thick halibut pole baited with herring bouncing the bottom.

Placing fresh line onto reels, sorting through tangled lures and organizing his boat for the season was tedious, and keeping it organized was a challenge. But in spite of the work aspect of maintaining an Alaskan summer home and boat, Jim felt that the experience was a privilege. He expected visiting family and friends to simply catch fish, drink beer, eat meals and enjoy the ride without having to deal with mundane chores. He considered it therapeutic, which was a far cry from the corporate world and his past military exploits. He missed neither.

By 11:30, the boat had reached the mouth of Whitewater Bay. He'd caught several large cod and placed them into the boats live well. Jim glassed the mountains with his binoculars. The steep mountainsides, with countless rushing streams and old growth timber, were stunning. He noted that the inner bay had been logged off many years ago and the distant lower reaches of the mountains were second-growth timber with moderate-sized trees, which detracted from the overall setting.

Overall, the bay looked inviting and serene, so he reeled in the halibut pole and set up a downrigger for King salmon. The boat slowly trolled the shoreline as he fileted the cod on the rear deck. He kept the skin, heads, tails and entrails for the crab pot. After fifteen minutes of trolling, a vicious strike disengaged the line from the downrigger and the battle was on. Jim placed the engines into neutral as the fish peeled out line. It fought hard for over ten minutes, then finally broke the surface. After another five minutes, the salmon tired, and he netted the King, which weighed 25 pounds. He put the boat in gear and slowly motored toward the headwaters of the bay, carefully studying his depth finder. It was almost high tide on a waxing moon, yet the depth was only thirty feet. This was the inlet Ernie had described, and Jim understood navigating the inner reaches of Whitewater could be a dangerous proposition.

Jim fileted the salmon and placed its remains along with the cod's into the crab pot. He retrieved a fifty-foot length of rope from the anchor compartment, and the pot was tied off to an orange marker buoy and thrown overboard. He thought fresh Dungeness crab would be on the menu when his children arrived.

The inlet's steep, rocky north shore gave way to a second channel which led into a small lake. Though most of the lake's shoreline was obscured, Jim knew from his topo maps that the entire area was gently sloped and timbered. When the tide was out, flats stretched east on both sides of the lake. The north slope is where Ernie found the body in 1945. Jim was tempted to enter the inlet but better judgment prevailed. The narrow inlet reminded him of a mangrove swamp where he had ambushed and killed a platoon of Sandinistas.

Uneasy about the opening, Jim decided to head home. After backing out of the channel's mouth, he accelerated the 34-foot boat until it reached its "step" speed and skipped over the water at 22 knots. Within minutes, the boat cleared the corner of the long bay and turned north toward Angoon. Dolphins swam next to the boat for a bit, but soon tired and disappeared. Even at high tide, rocks were noticeable at Russian Reef, two miles outside the mouth of the bay. Jim heard rumors that several whaling ships had run aground and sunk there during storms. He thought how strange it was to be in 250 feet of water, and suddenly encounter rocks. The geology of Alaska fascinated him.

Forty minutes of wide-open running placed the boat near the southern tip of Killisnoo Island, which had been a whaling factory during the 1800s. A distant storm raged thirty miles to the north toward Juneau, but experience told him that it wouldn't make its way south. Unlike the rest of Southern Alaska, Angoon seldom received a lot of precipitation. The surrounding mountains protected the village and provided a unique "rain shadow." Jim enjoyed not getting drenched when he was out on the water and chose Angoon for its mild weather and down-to-earth people.

He entered Angoon's Kootznahoo Inlet as the tide was going out. A torrent of swirling eddies greeted him as he sped through the narrows toward the widening bay and marina. Jim understood that deliberate speed was the only way to safely navigate the narrow inlet during an outgoing tide. Tlingits told stories of strong tide rips during which opposing winds stacked up walls of water, causing boats to capsize. People who go down in those situations were usually never found and locals seldom bothered searching for bodies.

The marina was quiet, just like early morning. Two people in a small aluminum boat trolled for King salmon across the bay, but Jim knew it was too early in the season for them to be successful. It would be at least another week before the Kings began moving into the Angoon river system prior to spawning. He crept into his slip, tied off the boat and flipped a small concealed switch located under a cup holder. Because of his covert past, the boat was equipped with several secretly-positioned infrared motion sensors and cameras, making it easy for him to keep tabs on his belongings with high tech equipment. Jim didn't worry about theft but liked to know who was sniffing his turf.

He headed to his cabin in the Humvee with the empty boat trailer. While disconnecting the trailer, he noticed a fresh pile of bear scat near his back-up generator. The bruin had returned. *Better start wearing a pistol,* he thought.

He stepped onto the porch and focused his attention on a hanging planter containing plastic flowers. The largest daisy contained a tiny hole in its center with an LED flasher which was activated by any of eight fiber-optic cameras surrounding his home. The flasher was detectable only with specially tinted sunglasses. Jim put on his shades and looked at the daisy. It was flashing. He returned to the Humvee and grabbed his Desert Eagle. After walking the perimeter of the house, Jim entered the seaside door. Another LED flasher on the stereo was unlit, indicating that the home's interior hadn't been breached. Jim flipped the coat rack switch off — which controlled the system — and walked into the kitchen. He pulled out a built-in wooden cutting board from the counter top and turned it over. The underside of the board contained a recessed computer monitor and keyboard. Its base contained a USB connection for a computer. He reached behind the refrigerator and pulled two thin retractable cords from near the condenser coils. After making the necessary connections, the monitor lit up. This was Jim's secret computer system — separate from his PC in the study. It was well-hidden and a "stand alone" unit.

The computer required entry of a seven-digit security code within 30 seconds of activation or it would automatically hibernate for 12 hours. He entered the code and the operating system kicked in. He opened the camera system and viewed the videos from eight exterior cameras, which produced a four-minute video of the brown bear walking across the porch and sniffing around. More concerning was a two-minute video of Officer Crane walking to the front door, then walking the cabin's perimeter. He was wearing latex gloves and tried to open all three entrances. Jim pressed the print button, shut off the computer, retracted the cords and returned the cutting board to its rightful spot.

Blood was pounding in his temples as he paced the living room. His immediate reaction was to confront Crane, but after taking several deep breaths he cooled down, and a peculiar calm overtook his anger. He sat down to consider his options.

Jim soon understood that he controlled the situation — Crane was his for the taking. The dirty cop was nothing more than a sloppy fool who didn't have a clue who he was dealing with. What really troubled Jim was Vicente Santos' connection to Crane. He thought, *Why would Santos hire someone with such a sordid past and why would he want the bay patrolled? Perhaps Santos didn't know about Crane's past and simply allowed his attorney to select the patrol officer.*

Jim gathered Crane's rap sheet, surveillance photos and the items he promised Mel Franks. He opened an end-table drawer and retrieved a .357 magnum derringer. The tiny stainless steel gun had a 2" barrel and neatly fit into a sewn-in pouch in his upper right boot. He liked the pistol because it fit into a person's palm without detection. Special Ops called these "pocket rockets," because they were easily concealed, yet brutally lethal at close range. Because of Crane and the bear issue, he'd pack it with him until he had answers. After locking the house, Jim reset the security system and left for town.

Mid Afternoon —Angoon

The Humvee pulled into a parking lot adjacent to a small store with rusty metal siding. A bleached-out, orange "For Sale" sign that had been there for 3 years adorned the front window. The only other vehicle in the lot was a white minivan that belonged to the owners, Pete and Candice Engels. Jim entered the small store and greeted Pete, who was busy stocking shelves. Candice was nowhere to be seen.

Jim called out, "Hey Pete. Haven't seen you since September. What's new?"

Pete was a bitter old man in his late sixties. He replied, "Same shit, different day."

Jim hated that cliché, but played along. Pete was an ornery old cuss who disliked his store, his wife, Angoon and basically everything about life. He inherited the store from his dad, who was a raging drunk. Rumors had it that Pete was abused as a child and that he treated his children the same way. Because of that, Pete's kids moved away as soon as they finished school. He was a angry, aging man, trapped and rotting in his own rage.

Jim asked, "How's Candice?"

"Who gives a shit? I sure don't."

"Sorry for asking. Here's a list of things for Ernie. Can you help me out?"

Pete grabbed the list and began pushing a small cart through the store's narrow aisles, filling the order.

"What's that old coot up to?" Pete asked. "Haven't seen him in over a week."

"He's OK," Jim replied, "just getting old. Arthritis makes it tough for him to walk this far . Without transportation, the uphill climb is overwhelming."

Pete eagerly offered, "We deliver for an extra charge."

"I know, but he doesn't have a phone and can't call to tell you what he needs. I plan on helping out while I'm here but when I'm gone, maybe I could pay you to pick him up every week so he can shop. Besides, he could use the company."

"I ain't a damn nursemaid — find someone else. I'm too busy."

"Here's the deal Pete, I'll pay you twenty dollars a week to check on Ernie while I'm gone — payment in advance."

Pete countered, "Forty bucks and you've got a deal."

"You drive a hard bargain Pete. I'll pay 40 if you agree to pick him up — then have him call me on this cell phone."

Jim handed Pete a disposable prepaid phone he'd brought for that purpose. He knew he could get Pete to agree — for a price. "My number's in the memory as 'Bennett.' Do you know how these work?"

Pete looked annoyed. "I'm gettin' old, but I ain't stupid."

Jim asked, "Do we have a deal?"

"It's a deal. I'll start when you head back to Denver. He's lucky to have someone like you for a friend."

Pete grinned, showing off his darkly stained teeth. Dental hygiene was a low priority in his world. "Ever feel like adopting me?"

Jim laughed. "Maybe when you're eighty three and not so damn ornery."

Pete finished filling the list and began ringing it up at the register. "Seen the new village cop yet?" he asked

"Yes, indeed I have. We met this morning and he seems like a fine gentleman."

Pete reared his head back and gave Jim a dirty look. "What planet are you from? He's an asshole. I told him to get outta my store the other day. He's always asking questions about everyone — keeps notes too. Him and that writer fella are both jerks — they must be in cahoots. Mel Franks was by earlier asking 'bout Crane, so I gave him an earful."

Jim knew that Pete had a keen sense of observation, then asked, "I'm yanking your chain Pete. He's a jerk, alright and probably won't last a month. What's this about the writer and him being friends?"

"They're pals alright. I've seen Rigby walkin' into Crane's motorhome many times. Every now and then Crane drives him to the dock by the old fish plant because Rigby stays on Killisnoo Island. Either they're queer as a steer or comparing notes. Both of 'em are always asking questions and hanging out together."

Jim considered Pete's remarks and asked, "That's odd. I've been wondering why either of these guys would be hanging out in Angoon? Do you know Rigby's full name?

"David Rigby. He's an author writing about Tlingit culture, but he's hung up on Angoon during the war. If ya ask me, he doesn't give a shit about the Tlingits. As for Crane, he wants to know everything about everyone. I bet he knows how many times I wiz and when."

"Do you have a photograph of Rigby or a copy of his book?"

Pete took a color brochure for Killisnoo Fishing Charters from a stand-up holder near his cash register. He handed it to Jim.

He pointed to a short bald man in his sixties. "Here's a picture of him holding a nice halibut he caught last fall. The lodge made a new color brochure this winter and that's the weasel right there."

Jim asked, "Can I keep this?"

"Sure, there's plenty more where that came from."

Jim asked, "Do you happen to have Rigby's cell phone number?"

Pete scrolled through a Rolodex behind the cash register. "Just so happens I do."

He took a pen from his shirt pocket, wrote the number on the brochure and handed it back to Jim.

Jim continued, "Have you ever seen Crane or Rigby with Santos?"

"Nope. I doubt that rich fella would associate with either one of those losers."

"Ernie told me Crane wanted to take away his pistol and you stopped him."

Pete nodded. "Yep. Crane was giving the old coot a hard time so I called him on it."

Jim nodded. "Good for you. How'd you find out he was fired from his last job?"

"He sorta said so. I told him if he kept pestering people in my store, I'd ban him from my place and get the Clan to fire him. He laughed and said it wouldn't be the first time he was run out of Dodge — also said the beaners in Sacramento could kiss his lily-white ass."

Pete punched numbers into his register as he placed the groceries into a cardboard box. "That's gonna be $87.30 for the grub. Should I put this on Ernie's tab?"

"No, sir." Jim handed Engels a crisp hundred dollar bill. "Apply the balance to Ernie's account."

"Say hello to the old coot for me. I'll start our arrangement when ya leave this fall."

Jim nodded. "Catch you later Pete."

Jim grabbed the box of food and packed it to the Humvee. Starting the truck he thought, *A person doesn't get much for ninety bucks in Angoon.* Driving to Ernie's cabin, he passed Officer Crane driving in the opposite direction. Crane looked away as the two vehicles passed, refusing to make eye contact .

After unloading the groceries, he and Ernie made ready to leave for Mel's. Jim grabbed a farmer's match from the center console of the Humvee and returned to Ernie's porch. He opened the screen door slightly, then stuck it between the door and its jamb. Upon returning to the vehicle, Ernie asked why he did that. Jim said he was keeping track of the riffraff. Confused by Jim's response, Ernie shrugged his shoulders.

Minutes later, Jim's truck pulled up next to Mel's cabin. The Tlingit elder was on the porch reading a newspaper. Ernie hadn't seen Mel in over eight months. He realized he needed to get out more often. As Mel greeted them, the old trapper struggled to step down from the tall vehicle

Mel shook hands and patted Ernie on the shoulder saying, "Good seein' ya, partner. It's been ages. Please come in"

In the living room, Jim and Ernie sat on a tattered orange couch and Mel in a recliner directly across from them. House cleaning wasn't Mel's strongest skill. The house was messy and cluttered. Ernie thought to himself that the place really went to hell after Mel's wife passed away last spring. As Ernie settled into the couch, a fat Cheshire rubbed up against his leg. He kicked at the cat, which darted into the kitchen, then jumped onto the kitchen counter top near a stack of dirty dishes.

Jim handed a large envelope to Mel. Slyly viewing the screen of the electronic device from his shirt pocket, he managed to swing the unit in all directions without causing suspicion. He folded it and returned it to his pocket.

Mel placed the envelope onto his lap. "What's it say? Gimme the short version."

Jim began, "Crane's a bully with a long history of abusing people — family, neighbors, strangers, prisoners — you name it. He has no friends, only acquaintances.

He gunned down a 14-year-old kid in Sacramento and lost his job. He's been arrested twice for felony assault, but each time, the victims dropped the charges. The Sacramento P.D. investigated him for taking bribes from a biker gang, but couldn't prove it. Frankly you've got a dirty cop working for you. Police profilers and psychologists classify him as a sociopath. He worked his way into a position of authority. Sociopaths are typically intelligent and can't resist the rush of tormenting people. Judging from my altercation with him, it's only a matter of time before someone gets hurt."

Mel rubbed his cheek. "Oh my. This ain't good at all. The report spells this out?"

"Yes, but I suggest you have the Clan's attorney in Juneau look at it. He'll verify what I'm saying and may have ideas on how to replace him. If the Clan is serious about having law enforcement, I can provide you with a list of qualified people and offer complete background checks on any candidate you choose." Jim then handed Mel his surveillance photos of Crane wearing latex gloves trying to enter his home.

Mel studied the photos of Crane and shook his head. "I'm gonna hold a private Clan meeting about this. We can't have this kinda lunatic running round Angoon. I'll let them know about your offer."

Jim nodded. "Good idea — sooner the better. Did Crane contact you to discuss what happened at the marina or apologize?"

"Nope and none of the Clans know. I talked with young Otto and Pete Engels. You're right about Crane — he's a problem."

Jim thought for a moment, then said, "It's troubling that Crane hasn't approached you about the incident. Maybe he figures Santos and his attorney can protect him."

Mel shrugged his shoulders. "I couldn't say."

"What do you know about David Rigby? I've heard he's pals with Crane and asks a lot of strange questions."

"He was here last fall for a while, then returned two weeks ago. He's staying in one of the old cabins at the fishing lodge on Killisnoo. Folks say he's a writer. At first, the Clan liked the idea of someone telling the Tlingit story, but he's sorta wearing thin on folks. I never knew he was chummy with Crane though."

Jim asked, "Do you know of any of the books he's written?"

"I'm sure he told other Clan members but I don't remember the name. Says he wrote a book about Hawaii."

Mel handed two photos of Santos and a folded paper to Jim. He added, "I promised these earlier — the phone numbers for Santos and Crane."

"Excellent. Would you also happen to have a photo of Rigby? I've got a picture of him in a brochure, but I'd love to have an actual photograph."

"You bet. Hilda, of the Raven Clan, had her picture taken with him while she was being interviewed last fall. It made the November school newsletter."

Mel groaned as he struggled out of his recliner. After rifling through a desk drawer, he handed Jim a five-by-seven colored glossy and sat back down. "There ya go — it's all I got on 'im."

Jim examined the photo of two smiling people sitting next to each other at a long table. Rigby, a mostly bald man in his sixties, had a small tape recorder and notepad. Hilda was dressed in her Clans ceremonial regalia. Jim smiled, knowing he could now check out Rigby.

"Thanks Mel. I'll return the photo after I scan it. For the record, if Crane tries breaking into my place again or confronts me like before, I'll take him down."

Mel agreed. "Do what ya need ta do ta protect yourself. I'll back ya up when it comes to other Clan members."

"I appreciate that." Jim retrieved a small cooler from the Humvee and gave Mel three large packages of frozen elk steaks. He also handed him two bottles of sixteen-year-old single-malt scotch and a wooden box of Cuban cigars. Mel was shocked by the quality of Jim's gifts.

"Oh mercy, this is too much. I can't accept these. All I asked for last fall was a couple of Fuente cigars. How much do I owe ya?"

"Nothing my friend. Enjoy. On another subject, I noticed the new single-wide trailer near the school. Is that going to be the village health clinic?"

"Yep. It was delivered and set up two weeks ago by the Feds. The health grant ya wrote for us last fall came through like butter. It's being stocked with supplies and we hired a nurse from Kake to run the whole shebang. She's a Dog Salmon clan member. We can't thank ya enough for everything you've done."

Jim smiled. He knew that receiving federal funds for the project was the only way the Clans could afford a primary care facility.

"My pleasure Mel — it was easy. Has the village done anything further about converting the old fish processing plant into a smoked salmon facility?"

"We looked into it but we ain't got the money to pull it off. We figured it would cost at least $150,000 to get it goin' again, which we don't have."

Jim thought about the situation and added, "Just so you know, on a business trip to California, I met with an organic food store chain. After the marketing director and purchasing agent sampled your smoked salmon, they committed to handling your products. They require USDA approval and want a snappy label. The marketing director said he'd create a totem pole label with a small spiel about the Tlingits. They're convinced they can sell as much as the village can produce. USDA approval is nothing more than paperwork and a list of the ingredients. I can have a friend help you with that."

"Thank ya Jim. We're so lucky to have ya here. I'll let the Clan know what ya told me. Maybe we can find a way to raise the money."

Jim stood and looked at Ernie. "Let's make some dinner, old timer. Oh, I nearly forgot. Mel, there's an old brown bear with a white patch above his eye that's been hanging around my place. He's awfully bold and I can't seem to get rid of him."

"It's probably the same one seen hanging around town. Hank Stytes promised he'd trap the bugger and move him south of here."

Jim smiled. "Wonderful, because I don't want to deal with him alone."

The three men walked outside to the Humvee. Mel leaned on the window jamb after Ernie got in and commented, "How 'bout I stop by and visit every now and then? I've been kinda lonely since Angie died. I suppose you've been the same since Jenny passed. We could play cribbage and shoot the breeze."

Ernie developed a huge smile. "I'd enjoy that Mel — really I would."

Mel patted Ernie on the shoulder and said goodbye. He waved as the Humvee backed out of his driveway. Jim turned the vehicle around and drove toward home. Leaving the pavement, he turned onto his one-third-mile-long gravel driveway. As he approached the parking area, a grouse ran into a thicket of devil's club. Ernie chuckled, calling it an "Admiralty Chicken."

Jim helped Ernie out of the vehicle, then put on his infrared sunglasses. The LED light on the planter was blank, indicating nothing had triggered the cameras. They entered the dwelling and Jim disarmed his security system. Ernie sat facing Chatham while Jim produced two cold beers from the bar's refrigerator. He placed the beers on the glass coffee table and sat next to his aging friend. They drank their beers, and Jim explained the marina incident in detail. Afterwards, he cooked an early dinner.

Mid Afternoon— A Eureka, California, Warehouse

Mr. Reid's limo paralleled Humboldt Bay, then turned onto Cod Street. Directly in front of the limo, an enormous gray metal building spanned two floating cement docks. The 100-foot-wide building had large overhead doors on each end. This is where Henry and Frank housed their mutually-owned 184-foot yacht. Two massive horseshoe cranes suspended the yacht above waterline. An overhead door on the street end gave vehicle and machinery access to the beautiful ship while another dockside passenger door provided access to the street.

Frank called Rusty on his cell phone and the warehouse side door quickly opened. The old man exited the limo, leaving William and the two blocker vehicles behind. Inside the building, the massive white yacht spanned the two docks. One side of the warehouse was partitioned off with walls that ran the length of the building. Small, segregated storage rooms were built into the long wall. The captives were held in two adjoining rooms. Helen and four men stood in a small circle talking near the suspended yacht.

Miller spoke to the group. "Mr. Reid and I will take over from here. Helen, I need you inside of the van manning the control panel. Process the three cell phones through the Seattle office. If any of the three phones ring, contact me immediately but don't answer them. I need everyone else to guard the outside perimeter but remain out of sight. I want everyone's radio turned on and connected to me in case there's trouble. I'll let you know when we're done."

The group split up and Miller and the old man spoke in private. Rusty explained his plan for questioning. He'd initially frighten and torture if needed, then follow up with drugs to compare results. Frank agreed, then shifted the conversation.

He asked if Rusty would work directly for him. Frank assured him that he'd retain the services of Dark Star for ongoing security issues. However he wanted Miller's expertise and confidentiality for the ongoing investigation.

Rusty wondered why Reid wanted him as his personal employee, but then it struck him: Reid wanted Dark Star out of the loop because he had something to hide; something that couldn't be shared unless you were within his inner circle.

"First off," he responded, "what kind of money are you talking about. Second, I require long-term employment. Dark Star will never hire me back if I resign."

"I'll double what Dark Star pays you, and throw in a million dollar bonus if you're able to eliminate everyone involved in Henry's death."

Rusty raised his eyebrows. "I guess the bonus makes long term employment a moot issue. My rate at Dark Star is 200 bucks an hour. You're prepared to double that?"

"I certainly will. How much notice will they need?"

"Like all Dark Star paramilitaries, I can leave at my leisure; but they'll never consider having me back once I quit."

"How do I continue to utilize their resources? Things like databases, computer links, hired guns?"

"Don't worry. When I quit, they'll immediately assign a new agent to take my place. You'll deal directly with my replacement and be able to interface with their assets through him — just like now."

Frank Reid smiled. "Excellent. Do we have a deal?"

There was a pause while Rusty thought to himself, *You bet your ass we do — now I can retire. I'll get that million dollar bonus and then some.* Rusty finally responded. "It's a deal, providing you tell me the reason why these guys are after you."

Reid briefly alluded to Henry's past and a possible ODESSA link to his murder. He told Rusty ODESSA was a Nazi organization after Henry's fortune but didn't elaborate further. He assured Rusty that he'd disclose more on a "need-to-know" basis. Following Frank's comments, the duo walked into the first makeshift interrogation room.

Interrogation One — Mr. Wiser

Inside the small, brightly-lit, drywalled room was Gary Wiser, somebody's hired gun. He was naked and secured to a gurney with his mouth duct taped shut. He had a short dark beard, long greasy black hair and his body was covered in tattoos. Both arms and legs and his head were tightly strapped to the gurney, making it impossible for him to move.

Miller walked over and ripped the tape from Wiser's mouth. "We're going to talk and I expect truthful answers — the more you talk, the longer you live. If you cooperate, I may spare your life. The concept is simple: don't cooperate or lie to us and you'll be killed. Not quick, but a slow painful death. I'll inject you with a poison that has no antidote. You'll remain in agony for hours — virtually paralyzed — then die. Do I make myself clear?"

The captive barked out, "Go fuck yourself — you'll kill me anyway."

Rusty knocked the wind out of him by punching him in the stomach. He elevated the foot end of the gurney while Wiser struggled to breath. The captive's feet were now elevated above his head. Rusty placed a wet towel over Wiser's face and said, "Alright tough guy — let me know when you're ready to talk."

Miller picked up a plastic bucket half-full of water and slowly poured it over Wiser's face, into his nostrils and mouth. Wiser gasped for air and attempted to turn his head away from the constant rush of cold water. It was hopeless. The straps kept his face directed into the oncoming stream. He choked and gagged while trying to hold his breath but Rusty continued pouring water onto the prisoner's face. Wiser couldn't take anymore. He managed a gurgled scream. He was certain he'd drown.

Rusty quit pouring and spoke. "Like I said before, do I make myself clear?"

Coughing and choking, Wiser managed, "Yeah — alright — no more."

Reid looked at Rusty. "Very effective — where did you learn that?"

"In the Army, they perform this on every Special Ops soldier. It's called waterboarding — there's a lot of controversy over its use, but it never fails. No matter what people think, it's a great tool for hard asses like this."

He pulled the towel off of Wiser's face. "Who do you work for?"

Eager not to have another round of what had just happened, he answered, "I was hired by my cousin Greg — the guy who fell."

Rusty took a pair of vice grips and clamped Wiser's big toenail. "Wrong answer asshole — if I pull it's gone. Who do you work for?"

"Some guy my cousin Greg met. I've never seen him — only heard Greg talking with him on the phone. His first name's Al, but I don't know his last name. Greg said he's sixty-some years old, bald and has a European accent."

Rusty continued, "How did your cousin get involved with Al?"

"Through a dirty cop he knew in Sacramento."

"What's his name?"

"I don't know — Greg never told me — just said it was a dirty cop."

Reid interjected, "Have you ever heard him mention the name Karl Obert?"

"No."

Reid continued, "How about ODESSA?"

"No."

Miller and Reid looked at each other and smiled. Rusty continued, "Where does Al live and how did he and Greg meet?"

"I don't know, but Greg said he comes from Europe. He and the dirty cop approached Greg several months ago and told him to apply for a job working with the gardening company that Weddell used. Al wanted pictures of Weddell and a layout of his place. Weddell fired the lawn company after discovering Greg was a felon. Turns out he does background checks on everyone who comes onto his estate on a regular basis."

Rusty continued his questioning so fast that Wiser didn't have time to think. "What did Al want with Mr. Weddell?"

Wiser hesitated as if he was thinking for a creative answer. "Information about his habits and business ventures I'd guess."

"Bullshit. This is going nowhere." Rusty reached over, grabbed the vice grips and pulled off his large toenail. "I bet that hurts."

The old man turned away as the prisoner screamed in pain and blood spurted into the air. Wiser desperately struggled to move but couldn't.

Rusty yelled, "Get busy asshole — tell me the truth or another one bites the dust. Tell me everything you know."

Wiser screamed in pain. "Fuck." He closed his eyes and grimaced while thrashing around to free himself. "Jesus Christ, you mother fucker — look, I'm trying."

Rusty showed him the vice grips with the attached toenail. "Get busy or the other one's gone."

"OK, OK! No more." Wiser took a deep breath and began, "Al thinks Weddell stole his family's fortune during WWII. His dad and Weddell were partners — he said Weddell killed his dad for millions in gold. He thinks Weddell still has tons of gold hidden somewhere. Al wanted us to kidnap Weddell's family and use them for ransom but we couldn't locate them. Weddell's family and friends were too well hidden. When the old geezer fell and got busted up, Greg paid his doctor twenty grand to administer a truth serum called scopo-something — just before his surgery. The doctor had a gambling problem and jumped at the dough. Greg and I dressed up like hospital staff and got into the old man's room after Linton administered the drug. He left us alone with Weddell — the old man was in and out of it but we got good info."

Rusty said, "Keep talking."

"Turns out Weddell didn't kill this Al guy's dad. Al's dad was Karl Obert. He and Weddell were German deserters. Weddell said Obert went crazy and tried swimming across some fjord. He figured the guy died while striking out on his own. It happened in 1944 at a place called Pelican — I think it's in Alaska. Weddell spent days searching for Obert but never found shit. Two cousins named Olsen, two brothers named Bruehl, and a guy named Decker were all involved. Weddell mumbled that everyone was probably dead except the Olsens. Before we could find out where his family was, a nurse entered the room and wanted to know what we were doing — she demanded to see our IDs. We escaped through a stairwell to an outside parking lot. Greg stumbled down the steps and rolled his ankle — maybe broke it. We barely got away."

Mr. Reid barked, "I asked if you ever heard the name Karl Obert and you said 'no.'"

Fearing additional torture, Wiser explained, "You asked me if Greg ever mentioned that name — not if Weddell did. I'm sorry — I won't hide anything else."

Rusty immediately knew why Frank didn't want Dark Star personnel involved with the details of this operation. Somehow, the old man was connected to a fortune in stolen gold. He wondered how to proceed and asked, "Then what happened?"

The captive answered, "Al called that night and Greg told him about the questioning. Al said he needed more information to locate Weddell's family. He told Greg to offer the doctor another twenty grand to make a house call and check on Weddell. The three of us drove to the old man's estate but since Weddell knew Greg's face as the fired gardener, Greg stayed in the car while I played the part of the doctor's assistant. Greg directed the questions to me from the car by cell phone. As soon as I entered the old man's room, he remembered me from the hospital. I held him down and covered his mouth while the doctor sedated him. After he settled down, Linton administered the truth serum — shortly after that, Weddell had a heart attack. We tried to revive him but couldn't. It was an accident — we only wanted information."

Rusty's questions continued at lightning speed. "How much is Al paying you?"

"Hundred fifty grand plus expenses."

"Has he paid you anything so far?"

Wiser answered, "Fifty grand."

The two interrogators walked into the corner and whispered to each other, then returned. Rusty continued, "When was the last time Greg spoke with Al and what's the timing for the next contact?"

"Greg talked with him last night and early this morning. He's supposed to call Greg at 6:00 p.m.."

Rusty Miller looked at his watch. It was 5:35. He spoke into his radio. "Helen, do you copy?"

She answered, "Go ahead — read you loud and clear."

"I need all three phones in here immediately. Hurry up — it's critical."

Within moments, someone knocked on the door. Rusty opened it and the stunning, raven-haired woman in a custom-tailored black leather jacket entered. She winced at the gruesome sight of Wiser secured to the gurney with blood streaming from his right foot toward his head.

Shaking her head, she said, "You gag me, Rusty. Your methods are gross. Next time, get one of the guys to do this sort of rubbish."

"Sorry. I'm in a hurry. Your tough-chick presentation must be all show and no go."

"I can handle myself, dude, but what you're doing in here's sicko." She handed the phones to Rusty. She noticed Wiser's tattoos. "Ooh, check out these tats — this guy's a hard-core biker and a skinhead."

Rusty frowned. "How could you possibly know that?"

"Look at his shoulders: a wing and skull inked onto each one. Now read what it says; " 'Hell's Angels' on top and 'Sacramento' on the bottom — it's a classic Hell's Angels tat. The 'Terminator'-looking skull with outstretched wings in the middle of his chest? See the words 'Hell Bent' at the top and 'Ride Hard' on the bottom? He's with the Hell Bent Chapter of the Hell's Angels out of Northern Sacramento. The red diamond with '1%er' inked inside of it? That's a typical hard-core biker statement — it means you're in the top one percent of all bikers." She pointed to his left arm. "The Nazi Swastika and the number 666 buried into the matrix of this spider web? It's how skinheads identify themselves in prison. The spider web denotes being in prison and the 666 inside of the Swastika tells other inmates that you're an Arian Nation member. The numbers '8 – 8' are codes for 'H – H' which stands for 'Heil Hitler' — he's a bloody skinhead, alright."

Rusty looked at the tattoos and smiled. "Well, well, it seems Mr. Wiser's a hard-ass — an ex-con, a Hell's Angel and a skinhead too. Where did you do time and for what?"

"I spent four years of an eight-year stretch in Folsom for weapons and drugs."

Sarcastically, Rusty added, "I bet you were innocent too. Was your cousin a biker and skinhead?"

"Yeah, we're both Angels — I ride with the 'Hell Bents' from Sacramento and he's with the Angels from Frisco.

Rusty continued, "Charming. What was Greg in for and where?"

"Folsom — weapons, drugs, receiving stolen property and witness tampering. He spent six years of a ten-year stretch."

Rusty turned to Helen. "Listen up; Prince Charming here's expecting a call. When it happens, find the number and triangulate its source. Get the Seattle office involved as well. I'll keep the caller on the line as long as possible. This could be a big break. Don't get soft on me. Turn around and don't watch this."

She turned toward the corner while Rusy grabbed the vice grips. After clamping Wisers other big toenail, he spoke. "Has Al ever heard your voice?"

Terrified, Wiser offered. "No — honest — never."

"Did he supply you with the fake I.D. and cell phones?"

"No, Greg got them from his cop friend. The phones are ours."

Rusty continued. "Is there any way he'd know it wasn't you if I talked with him — any codes or secret passwords — anything I need to know?"

"Greg called it Corona."

Frank interrupted. "A Corona's a gold coin — it fits."

The phone rang. It was 6:02. Miller stuffed a rag into his captives' mouth. He showed the phone screen to Helen. There was no number, merely the word "Private."

"Keep him on the line," she said "I'll trace Wiser's number to find the connection and location — I need at least 4 minutes." She darted toward the van.

Rusty placed the phone near Frank's head so they could both hear, then pressed the talk button. "Yeah, I'm listening." There was dead silence on the other end. "We've got problems — talk to me or I'm hanging up."

The voice on the phone asked, "Who is this?"

"Gary Wiser, Greg's cousin and partner — and you're Al. Now cut the bullshit — we've got problems."

The voice on the other end asked, "Where's Greg?"

"He's dead. A couple of Weddell's goons tried grabbing us at the funeral. Greg fell off the cliff by the cemetery. I managed to get to Greg before Weddell's men got to him — I stripped him clean, and escaped up the beach. There are people after me and I don't like it. I wanna know how they knew about us?"

Unconvinced, the man asked, "What's the name of our project?"

"Corona — listen to me fuckhead, I'm tired of your Perry Mason bullshit. I was nearly greased doing your dirty work and people are after me. The price has just gone up because I've got what you need — I know where the Olsens live and how to get to Weddell's family. I also know about the gold and your father — I want a quarter million cash by tomorrow."

A long pause was followed by, "I can't raise that much money in a day. Besides, I need approval."

"Then you're a fucked monkey aren't you? Greg said you were the 'Head Honcho' but you're nothing more than somebody's bitch. Tell your boss that he needs to meet me tomorrow with the cash or I'll get a few of my boys to find the gold. Old man Weddell told me a lot more than I told Greg. He didn't instantly drop dead during our last talk so I expect your boss to deliver the cash by tomorrow."

Another pause followed. Finally the man said, "That's impossible — my people will never expose themselves under any circumstances. I can arrange a drop point once we have the information."

"Fuck you! I'm not stupid. This is how it's gonna be — you meet me face to face tomorrow at a place of my choosing. Give me the cash and I'll tell you everything. I'm the only person who knows how to get at the people you want — ya got that?"

"So Mr. Wiser, you have everything I need to make this work?"

"Damn straight I do — I know Olsen's new name and where he lives. I also know where Weddell's family's located."

Another long pause followed Rusty's comments. The man finally spoke. "You couldn't have gathered that much information so quickly. Greg knew none of these things when I spoke with him this morning."

"That's why he's dead — he was a dumbass. Last night while Greg was drinking beer and watching TV, I tracked down the pilots of two private jets located in Redding, which happen to belong to the people you want."

This time the man responded immediately. "You impress me Mr. Wiser. I'll call at noon tomorrow to arrange a meeting — just the two of us. I need to fly into Sacramento and rent a car so it'll be evening before I'm there. What became of Doctor Linton?"

"He bailed on us. The candy-ass called Greg and said he was finished — couldn't take the drama. You bet your ass he's finished, because it's his fault Greg's dead. We needed a third set of eyes and a diversion, so we wouldn't stand out — I'll kill him tonight."

"Excellent. We'll talk at noon tomorrow, Mr. Wiser."

The phone went dead. Rusty was a bundle of nerves. He looked at Mr. Reid. "What do you think, was I convincing? Did he swallow the bait?"

"You convinced me but I don't know about this Al fellow. I was thinking, he won't be going through Sacramento because Redding's closer. He lied to us."

Rusty nodded. "I thought the same thing. I hope Helen was able to triangulate his location."

There was a knock on the door. Rusty peeked out and saw Helen sporting a huge grin. "You'll never guess where the call originated? C'mon guess."

Rusty didn't like the way she was showing off. "Christ, I don't know — Timbuktu?"

"Close, but no cigar. I narrowed it down to translators between Juneau, Gustavus and Hoonah, Alaska — he's on the ocean. I also have his number — it's got a Seattle area code. I should have the owner's name within minutes."

Reid hugged her with his left arm. "You always amaze me young lady. You possess a masterful understanding of modern technology yet you have this primal fetish for the macabre — like understanding bizarre tattoos and dressing like a black widow spider."

Helen loved the flattery. "Watch out Mr. Reid, or I'll think you're hitting on me. Be careful — black widows are man-eaters. Maybe someday I'll show you a few of my tats — just the ones on my arms of course. They're far more interesting than what Prince Charming has."

Mr. Reid flushed and looked embarrassed. "Don't be silly, I'm old enough to be your great-grandfather and at times I swear I am."

Rusty Miller smiled while ushering her to the door. "Good job, Ms. Spider — take the other two phones while I finish up with Prince Charming. If they ring, don't answer — just contact me immediately. I'm keeping this one in case he calls again. I recall seeing two motorcycles parked on the street before we entered the cemetery — they must belong to this guy and his dead cousin."

He turned to Wiser, removed his gag and asked, "Were those your motorcycles with the tall handle bars?"

The captive nodded. "Yeah."

"Are your club jackets with the motorcycles?"

Eager to avoid more punishment, he answered, "Yeah — they're in our saddlebags"

Rusty looked at Helen. "I'ave two of our men retrieve the motorcycles and bring them here."

Helen giggled, and placed her hands into her jacket pockets.

"They're called 'ape hangers,' not 'tall handlebars'. They're 'bikes,' not 'motorcycles'; and they're 'colors,' not 'jackets'. If you're going to play the part of a hard-ass biker, you'd better start acting like one. Sometimes you're such a dipshit."

She shook her head and returned to the van.

Rusty smiled and looked at Frank. "Whoa! I guess I'm out of my league when it comes to motorcycle gangs. I'd better take classes from Helen. But I do know this: Al's in Alaska, possibly lives in Seattle and almost all flights from Juneau go through SeaTac airport. Let's put some resources at the arrival gate for every in-coming Juneau flight. There can't be very many — maybe three or four a day. We'll try to intercept him before he gets here."

Frank Reid asked, "What if he uses a charter service or has his own set of wings?"

"Then we nail him at the rendezvous. Either way, we'll catch him."

The old man wondered, "What'll happen with our two guests?"

"We'll decide after interrogating Doc Linton. Do you have a preference?"

"Not in here. Let's talk outside," whispered the old man.

After discussing the potential pitfalls with meeting Al and their assessment of Wiser, the two men returned to the room. Rusty opened a small gym bag and pulled out a needle, syringe and small vial. Wiser was terrified and desperately tried to free himself while being administered the drug.

Rusty said, "Chill out Prince Charming, it isn't poison. We'll see how truthful you've been. If you've lied, poison will be the next injection."

As soon as the serum entered his vein, Wiser's eyes fluttered. His tense muscles relaxed and a sense of calm overtook the prisoner. Frank asked if it was the same truth serum used on Henry, and Rusty explained that it wasn't. "It's a drug known as SP-17, developed by the KGB, and much faster and more reliable than scopolamine."

The two men grilled their captive for another thirty minutes. There were no discrepancies from their initial interrogations and his story matched everything previously disclosed. Both men were convinced that Mr. Wiser was a nasty indi-vidual capable of just about anything, and Frank commented that whoever hired these men was probably as bad, if not worse.

Interrogation Two — Dr. Linton

Several doors down from the first interrogation room was another one set up exactly as the other — the only difference being its occupant. Dr. Linton was anx-ious. "I'll tell you everything I know. This whole thing's a terrible mistake. Please don't prosecute me. I've got a family and . . ."

Frank interrupted. "You should've thought about that before you killed my friend. We're going to dispense with the formalities and get right to it. Tell us everything from the beginning. If you lie, you're dead."

"You're the FBI — you can't kill suspects."

"Hel-looo," Rusty responded. "We're not the FBI, dummy. We're death knock-ing on your front door. I suggest you get busy talking or else."

Terrified, the doctor stuttered, "I'll cooperate! Please don't hurt me."

"Then get on with it," continued Rusty.

"I'm an orthopedic surgeon — Mr. Weddell's treating physician when he entered the hospital. He'd fallen down several steps and broke an elbow and a hip. The elbow required a small screw to repair and the hip was unremarkable. A man named Greg Wiser approached me about letting him talk with Henry before his surgery; said he had people who wanted to know about Mr. Weddell's past. He offered me twenty thousand if I'd administer a truth serum. It's customary to provide Demerol prior to surgery, so I added a few cc's of scopolamine."

"Why did you accommodate his request?" Frank asked.

"I needed the money. I owe a bookie thirty thousand."

Rusty asked, "Then what happened?"

"After giving him the injections, I left the room so they could question Mr. Weddell. I know it was wrong but considered it safe. Besides, I figured no one would ever find out. After the surgery, Greg approached me again, offering another twenty thousand if I'd give Mr. Weddell another injection at his home. I'd scheduled a house call anyway, so greed overcame my rational side. This was a chance for me to satisfy my bookie."

Rusty pressed on. "Keep talking."

"When we entered the room at his estate, Henry recognized Greg's accomplice and panicked. I gave him a small dose of Demerol and he settled down. After injecting the serum, he began having arrhythmia, then fibrillations. Within minutes he'd expired. We told the butler that Henry was sleeping and shouldn't be disturbed and left. That's it — that's everything."

Frank asked, "How were you able to identify Henry's daughter?"

"It was an educated guess — nothing more."

Frank continued. "Why did you want to speak with her?"

"I wanted to offer my condolences for Mr. Weddell's death. I feel guilty."

"Were you going to tell her the truth about what had happened?"

"I considered it, but was afraid of what the Wisers would do to me. I just wanted to offer my condolences."

Miller opened his gym bag and produced the syringe and the bottle of SP-17. Linton looked up and asked what he was doing.

Frank asked, "Who else was involved in this?"

"Nobody — honest."

Rusty asked, "Who do Greg and Gary work for?'

"I have no idea."

Rusty administered the dose of SP-17, and the drug's effect was immediate. He relaxed and began to sing, "I'm a little teapot short and stout, this is my handle, here is my spout."

Rusty and Frank looked on as Linton delivered an extended chorus of children's songs. It took several minutes before he was cognizant enough to be further interrogated. They spent another twenty minutes questioning him. He'd told the truth during the initial interrogation.

Rusty asked Frank, "What do you want me to do with these guys?"

"I suppose it's up to me, isn't it?"

"Yes, sir. I'm not the one who wanted them — it's your call."

Frank pondered the situation. The doctor's conduct had killed Henry. He'd been exploited by the two convicts and their boss for forty thousand dollars.

"They recklessly killed my best friend. I'd just as soon see them dead but then I'd be as bad as they are — what are my options?"

"Their value to us is gone," Rusty began. "We've extracted what we need. At this point, they're a liability. They know too much about us and 'Corona.' I can either kill them and make it look like an accident or administer a drug that will cause amnesia for months, if not permanently. It's a combination of psychotropics, PCP and barbiturates. They'll probably survive, but they won't function in a meaningful way for a long time — if ever. When a person's given this, they're never the same. It mimics psychosis. Imagine being on a constant acid trip. Afterward, we can dump them onto the streets of San Francisco. They'd fit right in with the bums and street people."

Frank seemed intrigued and asked, "You can actually do that?"

"Absolutely."

The old man nodded. "So be it. At least we won't kill them. Tell me something, if the doctor receives a lower dose, will he eventually function in a normal capacity?"

"Possibly. Are you willing to risk his knowing about us?"

Frank pondered the situation for a while, then offered, "Yes. He actually knows very little and I'd hate to see his life destroyed because of a gambling problem."

Rusty shrugged his shoulders. "Alright, I'll cut his dose in half."

After injecting the two detainees, Miller grabbed his gym bag and returned to the van with Mr. Reid. On the way, he instructed two of the outside men to clear the warehouse of all incriminating evidence, then dump Dr. Linton and Gary Wiser in downtown San Francisco.

Inside of the van, Helen was looking at one of the monitors and listening to her headset. She turned to Rusty saying, "The cell phone used to contact Wiser is a disposable purchased from a Radio Shack in Bellingham. It was paid for in cash by Vincent Merlison of Spokane. I checked out the name and address — it's bogus. The call log for Greg Wiser's phone has outgoing contact with the Merlison phone — all within the past two weeks."

Rusty looked at Mr. Reid. "Unless Al calls tomorrow, we could be forced to call him. We'd need to set up shop in Juneau, then make the call — hopefully he'll answer or use his phone so we can pinpoint his exact location."

The old man spoke. "We'll do whatever it takes. I must be getting to Henry's, and I'm sure both of you are hungry and tired. You should come to the estate with the van as soon as you're wrapped up here and we'll develop a plan for tomorrow."

Rusty nodded. "We're done here. We'll follow you to Mr. Weddell's."

"Very well. Rusty, you ride with me and I'll give you some details about my past. Helen can drive the van while we talk."

Rusty nodded. "That's fine. Let's do it."

The limo, van, and blocker vehicles left the warehouse and drove down Cod Street toward the bay. Thirty minutes later, William turned right off of Stagecoach Road into Henry's private drive, approached the stone gatehouse and rolled down the window.

The guard smiled and saluted the chauffeur.

The guard said, "William, so very good to see you again. I see that Mr. Reid has two additional vehicles with him. Is Mr. Reid in the back seat?"

William answered, "Hello John, good to see you, old chap. Yes, Mr. Reid is indeed in the back seat. Would you care to speak with him?"

The gatekeeper nodded. "If you wouldn't mind. Simply following orders."

The back window lowered and the old man spoke. "Hello John. Wonderful to see you again."

"I'm pleased to see you as well, sir. Are the other two vehicles with you?"

"Oh yes. They're with me and I appreciate your diligence. Please don't allow anyone else onto the grounds without Catherine's authorization."

"Yes, sir, I've already been informed by her about the latest security measures. She also informed me about your arrival. I'll open the gate." John pressed a button, and the large steel gates supported by two massive stone columns swung open. Each column top was accented by bronze eagles with outstretched wings.

A beautifully-manicured lawn stretched far to the west and cliffs overlooking the Pacific. At the crest of the rise loomed a sprawling, two-story, red brick mansion. To the left of the mansion stood a much smaller servants' dwelling. A sleek blue and white Bell 430 helicopter was parked on a helipad located several hundred yards to the right of the main house. This had been Henry's primary residence. It sat on 640 verdant acres southwest of Trinidad, California. With a mile of private oceanfront and an enormous State Wildlife Sanctuary to the south, Henry had been afforded the privacy he expected.

At 7:30, Catherine and Patty met the group as they arrived at the cobblestone vehicle entrance. An enormous protective roof supported by brick columns covered the unloading area. After introductions, the group entered the 20,000-square-foot mansion, where they feasted on a gourmet meal of roasted game hens and stuffing.

After dinner, Frank held a private meeting with Catherine and Patty in Henry's library. He informed them about the three accomplices and what had led to Henry's death. Both women were livid that Henry died as a result of forced questioning and there was little consolation in the men's confession. Frank also disclosed that he had intercepted a phone call meant for one of the captured men and that others were involved. Frank assured them that the people involved in the day's activities were adequately dealt with, which both women assumed meant "killed."

Catherine broached the subject. "I want to know about fathers past and why these people did what they did?"

"Can it wait until tomorrow morning?" Frank asked. "Forgive me Catherine, but the questioning today took much longer than expected and I'm physically drained. Since your father's death, I've had less than four hours of sleep. Can we meet here at 8:00 a.m. sharp?"

Catherine looked at the haggard old man and nodded. "Alright — 8:00 a.m. sharp."

Bennett's House — Angoon — Early Evening

The grandfather clock chimed 6:00 p.m. as Jim and Ernie enjoyed a modest meal of elk stew and biscuits. It was easy for Jim to prepare because he'd pre-canned several batches before coming to Angoon. Every fall, his neighbor Doug traded Jim half an elk for two 70-pound boxes of Alaskan fish filets.

After dinner, Ernie sat on the couch, and Jim finished cleaning the kitchen. The phone rang as Jim walked to his well-stocked bar. It was Lori Phelps. Jim was pleased to hear her voice.

"You never called me at four o'clock Mr. Bennett."

"Oh hell! I'm so sorry, I got wrapped up and forgot. And what's this 'Mr. Bennett' crap? You know I hate that."

Lori apologized. "I'm being facetious. Sit down because I've got very bad news."

She paused for a moment, allowing Jim time to wonder. "You've been terminated by TacSec. Your employment obligations are fulfilled. The board of directors informed me they won't require your services anymore. They sent you a certified letter this afternoon."

There was absolute silence. At first Lori thought she'd lost the connection. "Hello? Hello? Jim, are you there?"

"I'm here. I mean, heck, this is outstanding. For a minute there, I thought something bad had happened. What about the Magnetic Pulse program and the big stink they made in March when I asked to be excused from my contract?"

"I convinced them you weren't needed and that Hadley could handle the project. It saves the company several hundred thousand and eliminates further stock options. You're off the hook, Jim."

"Outstanding. You're stellar. I can't thank you enough. I owe you big time."

Lori continued, "Did you get my email this morning?"

"Indeed I did, and it's exactly what I needed. Thank you."

"Well, I personally wanted to tell you about the boards' decision."

After a brief hesitation, she added, "It's been a pleasure working with you and I thank you for the employment opportunity. Perhaps we can keep in contact."

"Whoa, whoa, whoa. Hold your horses, lady. I'm officially unemployed, and there's something I've wanted to say for quite some time. First off, as a fellow worker, you're bright and talented. You've earned your position at TacSec and I had nothing to do with your success. That being said, as a woman, you're an absolute knockout."

"I've been dying to know you on a personal level for years, but my business beliefs prevented me from doing that. Now that I'm actually retired, I'm free to do as I please and it would please me very much to know you beyond the employment scene. How about coming up and visiting Angoon; maybe do some fishing, hiking and sightseeing. If you can't swing a trip, perhaps I'll fly back to Denver so we can have dinner. Whatever works for you — unless you're in a relationship or something?"

Lori didn't hesitate this time. "No relationship here other than my career — you know that. And I'd love to meet you in Alaska. I have to burn another two weeks of vacation before September, otherwise they pay me out and I lose it, so coming to see you would be marvelous. What time frame works best for you?"

Jim offered, "How about tomorrow?"

"You can't be serious Jim? TacSec doesn't operate that way."

Jim kept the momentum going. "I'm dead serious. Sooner the better works for me. I don't know if this matters, but my children are coming up tomorrow. They'll be here for ten days, but you'd still have your own private accommodations."

"Having your kids there doesn't bother me at all. I've met them several times and think they're wonderful. I doubt if I can get off with such short notice, but let me talk with Frasier in the morning. More than likely he'll say 'no,' then try to reach a compromise."

"Fantastic. Listen. I watched a whale in the waters by my front window this morning and knew it was a good omen. Natives say that seeing a whale brings luck, and I'm feeling very lucky right now."

Jim knew he was acting like a teenager but didn't care. Like his "ex" said — fifty-one, going on fifteen.

Lori said, "I'm thrilled. I never expected an invitation. I can't wait to see you."

Jim added, "The feeling's mutual."

There was awkward silence as they both wondered what to say next. Jim finally broke the ice. "I hate changing the subject, but there are a few things going on up here that could use your expertise with background checks. Do you have time to run a few marks?"

Lori answered, "Sure, what do you have?"

"First, there's a fellow named David Rigby who claims to be a published author — wrote a book on Hawaiian culture. He has a European accent — maybe Dutch, but I haven't the foggiest on where he's from. Then there's Vicente Santos, a wealthy oil producer from Brazil. Pull out all the stops on these guys. Contact Diller at the CIA and have him run complete biometrics — facial recognition, prints, the works. Make sure he uses the INTERPOL database as well. Also run their names by Doug at the FBI. I'll email you their photos. I need this encrypted and sent to my 'high security' email account."

"What the hell's going on up there? You're retired, remember?"

"It's probably nothing at all, but I'd sure like to know who these people are. They're connected with Crane and you saw what a shady character he is."

Stirring up a hornets nest as usual," Lori joked. "I'll call Diller first thing in the morning."

Jim continued. "Please get me what you can ASAP."

"I'll do my best. Hopefully Frasier will cut me loose for a few weeks so I can visit metropolitan Angoon."

Jim grinned. "Terrific! Tell Frasier I owe him a smoked salmon for giving you time off on such short notice."

"What are you thinking Jim? I'm not telling him anything. I can hear it now: 'Sure, get Bennett off the hook, then spend two weeks with him.' Not the best career move."

Jim laughed. "You're right — he'd give you a pile of crap. I'll call tomorrow at 1800 hours to see what's shaking. I promise I won't forget this time."

"You mean '6:00 p.m.', not '1800 hours.' For Christ's sake Jim, you're no longer in the Army either. I'll expect a call tomorrow. Bye."

Jim hung up the phone and looked at Ernie. "She really likes me."

"Gotta new honey?"

"I think so. She's a terrific gal. Maybe you'll have the pleasure of meeting her. If she can get time off, she'll be here within a few days. You'll like her. I know I do."

Ernie offered, "I'd love meeting her. I'd even take a bath, comb my hair and wear my best cologne. I wanna make a good impression."

The old man changed gears. "Pull out your map of Admiralty — I'll show ya where I found the body."

Jim went into his computer room, sent the photos from his scanner to Lori, and returned to the living room with a neatly folded USGS map and laptop computer. After laying the map on the coffee table, he turned on his laptop. Ernie leaned over and studied the map. He pointed to the exact spot that Bennett had visited earlier in the day. Before Ernie could take another sip of whiskey, Jim produced a satellite view of Whitewater.

Ernie shook his head. "This is crazy."

Jim pointed to the screen and used his cursor to circle the area he thought Ernie had described. After reducing the magnification to get a wider view of the lake he said, "Take a look at this. Is this the area you were talking about?"

Ernie McKinnon placed his hand onto his chin and examined the images on Jim's computer screen. The south end of Admiralty Island and Whitewater Bay were clearly visible. He'd never seen anything like this before. He said, "This is incredible. How in the hell do they do this, from airplanes?"

Jim smiled. "This is fairly old technology, my friend — nothing more than photos from satellites in space." He zoomed in on the shallow inlet where the crab pot was placed. Pointing with a drink straw, he asked, "Is this the area where you found the artifacts?"

Ernie pointed at the end of a small lake further into the inlet. Bennett panned right and zoomed in tighter. Individual fallen trees were clearly visible lying over the tidal shoreline.

Ernie said, "There — that's it." He pointed to a small stream that entered the lake from the steep hillside above the tidal flats.

"You're certain about this location?"

"Like it was yesterday." He pointed. "This is where I found the body, and right here is where I found the tube."

Jim studied the monitor. "I was near there today but I'm reluctant to take my boat inside the inlet. I'm afraid I'd bottom out and destroy the hull."

"You can do it. Ain't no doubt ya can get inside the inlet with your boat — just wait till halfway through the incoming tide and leave at halfway before low tide. When inside, anchor near the end of the lake and transfer to something smaller — like a skiff or raft. I went in there all the time with my motor boat. I could go all the way to the far end of the lake without any trouble." He pointed at the small river at the end of the lake. "East of here is really good trappin' and this stream is where salmon spawn."

Jim studied the area, then panned back for a broader view, which included the mountainside. He asked, "How much of this area did you physically search?"

Ernie defined the search area, and Jim realized he hadn't covered much territory at all. Much of the shoreline on both sides of the inlet had been searched but the steeper area to the northwest was ignored. The steep terrain was thick timber interspersed with moss-overed boulders, while everything to the east was logged off and open. Jim panned back even further, exposing craggy cliffs, huge snowfields and the bay.

He asked, "When was this area logged?"

"In the late '50s, then again in the early '70s. I searched the area after each logging operation but came up empty."

Jim studied the unfolded contour map and commented, "The bay before the inlet is fairly deep. A good-sized boat or plane could have sunk anywhere along the north shoreline of Whitewater without leaving a trace. Only sonar, magnetometers and underwater cameras could detect a submerged wreck. Outgoing tides would probably pull anything on the bottom into even deeper water. You never found any form of wreckage or oil slick?"

"Nothin' — not a damn thing."

Jim added, "My kids and I'll take a rubber raft and search the area with my metal detectors. Would you care to join us?"

"No thanks, that's for young folk, not old farts like me. When you're done searchin', let me know what ya find."

Ernie yawned and stretched. "Between the food and drinks, I'm ready to hit the hay. Your place is mighty damn comfortable — almost too comfortable. I'd best be getting' back home. Besides, your kids are coming tomorrow."

"If you're tired, you're welcome to sleep in one of the spare bedrooms. Otherwise I can take you home whenever you'd like. I hired a float plane for the kids and they won't be here until three in the afternoon, so spending the night doesn't affect me or my kid's."

"I'd rather get back home soon. It's been a long day and I'm pooped."

Before the two could finish their drinks, the telephone rang. Jim looked at the caller ID and saw it was Doug. Jim answered, "Hey neighbor, I bet you found out Hitler's hiding in Angoon."

"I found a few things Jim, but whether it's of any value is for you to decide. Got something to take notes with?"

Jim motioned for Ernie to sit back down and refreshed their drinks. "Give me another second while I put you on speaker and grab a pen."

Moments later he said, "I'm ready, let's do it."

Doug began. "I'm only going to discuss the major events. Specifics are contained within the body of the report which I will forward via email. Here it is:

Pelican cannery was built and operated by Carl and Rita Olsen of Seattle. They married in 1926, moved to Juneau in 1928. In 1938, they borrowed money and built the cannery at Pelican. Carl worked closely with the government during the war; supplying canned salmon for our GIs. The Olsens had a son named Gus who owned a commercial fishing boat out of Pelican and supplied fish for his parents' cannery. The Olsens sold the facility in 1955, and retired to Hawaii. Carl was an orphan. He had a brother named Richard who lived in Seattle. Richard and his wife were killed in a car crash in 1930 and left behind a son named Dale, who was immediately adopted by Carl and Rita. Dale was a highly-decorated B-17 pilot during the Second World War. He was killed in March of 1944 during a mission over Hamburg. Dale was also a bush pilot prior to the war and owned the float plane Carl reported missing in August of 1944.

Doug continued, "According to Navy reports, Carl was bringing in machine parts from Seattle in order to develop another canning line and hired a fellow named Drew Pryne to fly for the cannery. Pryne had a friend named Koenig who acted as co-pilot and general grunt. Both men were from Anchorage. We found nothing on either one of them which is not surprising because Alaska wasn't a state yet. The bureau has no information or documentation on individuals from Alaska during that era unless they were criminals. Are you keeping up with me?"

Jim answered, "Sure. Don't stop now."

"Late afternoon of August 27th, Carl Olsen reported the plane missing. It failed to show up in Prince Rupert and was never picked up by Juneau's, Sitka's or Ketchikan's radar. The weather was socked in when the plane took off and turned to shit hours later. Naval and private air searches scoured the flight path for 10 days, but came up empty. Here's an interesting fact about the area where it disappeared: It's called the 'Vector 319 Flight Path' — the Alaskan version of the Bermuda triangle. Planes, boats and people seem to get swallowed up without a trace along this route. The Navy's final report was that foul weather caused the plane to crash and believed it went down in the inland waterway and sank. As for the Olsens, they appeared to be hard-working, well-respected individuals. They received the Congressional Gold Medal in 1946 for their efforts and sacrifices during the war because their cannery produced more salmon for our troops than any other single facility. Carl died of a heart attack at age 76, and Rita died of diabetes at 79. Both are buried in Hawaii."

"In 1999, their son Gus and his wife Lena drowned in a boating accident in Puget Sound. Lena was from Hoonah, which is near Pelican. Their boat was found overturned and wrecked against the coastline, but the Coast Guard never recovered their bodies. They had a son named Eric and daughter named Donna. Eric was killed in Vietnam during the Tet Offensive of '68. Their daughter Donna left home and spent time in Haight-Ashbury during the late sixties, then found Jesus and returned home. After her parents died, she grabbed the inheritance and disappeared — we can't find anything recent on her. As I see it, the Olsens led Mom-and-Pop, 'apple pie' lives —straight out of a Norman Rockwell painting. They were heroes, certainly not spies."

Ernie fidgeted while listening to the conversation. He nervously paced in front of the windows while swirling his drink.

Jim asked, "What about the oil slick in Cross Sound on the 27th?"

"I was getting to that. The oil slick was discovered on the 27th at 6:45 AM. It was reported by fishermen from Pelican prior to the missing flight. There's no connection between the flight and the oil slick because the flight left several hours after the slick was reported. The official Navy report suggests that an unregistered fishing boat sank in Cross Sound."

Jim asked, "That's it? Nothing else?"

"Hold the phone Jim, this is where things get interesting, There's an unofficial version from a Hoonah native who claimed to have seen an iron whale with men walking on its back in the middle of the night — of course it was quite light. He said it was dark black, sat low in the water and disappeared under the waves after spending thirty minutes on the surface. A fishing boat looked to be tied to the tail of the whale while it was on the surface. The man insists it happened at Soapstone Point but couldn't remember the exact night."

"The Navy immediately considered it to be a submarine sighting, but after extensive questioning, the native admitted he was totally drunk at the time. They ultimately dismissed his story because of his propensity for alcohol and the fact that there wasn't any debris. I find the story interesting because Soapstone Point is located in Cross Sound at the mouth of Lisianski Inlet — the inlet that leads to Pelican — and there's only fifteen miles between the oil slick and Pelican. A native lying about an iron whale is unlikely — a sub seems plausible because it would look like an iron whale to natives. Besides, Japanese subs were reported in the Aleutians."

Jim sank back into the couch, looked upward and closed his eyes. "Timing between the two events suggests a connection with the Olsens yet they were solid figures. Maybe the crew of the missing plane was somehow connected to the oil slick."

Doug said, "That's a stretch — there's no evidence to suggest anything like that."

Jim asked, "Then what about the stolen boat from Sitka?"

"Now, that's a good one. Mark Nussbaum of Sitka reported his boat stolen on August 18th of '44. He suggested that a disgruntled deck hand who had quit two weeks earlier probably stole the boat. However, a year later, he and a friend shot off their mouths in a bar about how they scuttled the boat for the insurance. When questioned about their comments, they denied ever saying it and were never charged with a crime. In an unrelated event, Nussbaum was convicted in 1946 for second degree murder. He pushed a hooker off of a second floor balcony while drunk at a local brothel. He died in prison from food poisoning in 1949."

Jim asked, "Is there anything else?"

"I never thought you'd ask. I saved the juiciest tidbit for last. The Sitka police reported that a body was recovered from a fisherman's net on September 4th at a place called Rodman Bay. It was a fully intact Caucasian male, with no shirt or jacket and a tattoo on its right arm — of a skull and crossbones. Get this: Below the tattoo was an SS lightning bolt. The body contained three bullet holes — one in his head, and two in his chest. Healed wounds on the corpse's left leg and torso suggested past trauma consistent with shrapnel. Are you familiar with the area where the body was recovered?"

Jim shrugged and watched Ernie pace. "No. Where's Rodman Bay?"

Doug answered, "In Peril Straight — it connects Chatham Straight to Sitka Sound. Nussbaum was known to fish this area."

Jim asked, "Was the body identified?"

"Negative. The corpse had no ID; just the tattoo, which suggested he was either a Nazi or liked the SS emblem so much that he had it tattooed to his left arm. Neither description of the men from the missing plane matched the body."

Jim asked, "Was anyone from Sitka reported missing prior to the body being found?"

"Only the deck hand who quit Nussbaum, and he was wanted for questioning regarding the stolen boat, but couldn't be located. Sitka police concluded that the body was that of Nussbaum's former employee even though Nussbaum claimed it wasn't. They considered Nussbaum as John Doe's killer but they couldn't prove anything and he denied any involvement."

"Did the Police archive a photo of the victim?"

"Absolutely." Doug said. "I've got black-and-whites of the vic's face and his tattoo. They're in the report."

Jim swirled the info around in his head. Any connections seemed vague. "So I'm at a dead end unless I can connect the events with Nussbaum to what I've found here."

"Maybe, maybe not. What do you have that's so compelling?"

"A handful of Nazi relics that were discovered near Angoon in 1945."

Doug thought for a moment, then offered, "I'm certain there were plenty of GIs at the numerous military sites throughout Alaska who had access to Nazi souvenirs. I'd say there's a strong likelihood that Nussbaum was connected to the body in Rodman Bay and that the oil slick at Pelican could be where he scuttled his boat. His involvement with Nazi memorabilia is also possible. I'll email the report when we're done talking."

"On another issue, Lori Phelps called me about an hour ago and explained the need for detailed profiles on two shady characters. What the hell's up with that?"

Jim sighed. "I'm trying to determine if Santos or Rigby are pulling a fast one on the local Clans. Merely verifying their identities and credibility — that's all. Look, send the report to my 'high security' email address with top secret encryption."

Doug sounded frustrated. "I'll do it this time but I can't continue using Bureau resources for your pet projects. If you convince me that there's a Homeland Security connection, then the sky's the limit — otherwise I can't jeopardize my job. You wouldn't want me to get into trouble, would you?"

"No I wouldn't. I promise Doug — no more favors."

"I'll send you what I have on the Olsens to your top secret computer link. Lori can forward you the backgrounds of the two marks."

"Thanks a million Doug. I'll make it up to you."

"I'm holding you to that Jim — remember your dinner promise at Chez Paul. Ciao."

As soon as Jim hung up the phone, Ernie stood. "Thanks for supper, drinks and your hospitality, but I should be gettin' home."

"OK but let me get the DVD player and CDs I promised you last night." Jim walked into his study and returned with a small cardboard box. He armed the security system and said, "If you can get the door, I'll load these into the Humvee."

Ernie opened the front door and held it for Jim. It was twilight. As Jim started his truck, a set of headlights approached the house.

Ernie asked, "Who the hell's comin down your driveway at this hour?"

Pete Engels pulled alongside the Humvee in his minivan. Sitting next to him was Hank Stytes, the area wildlife biologist and a respected Clan member. Pete rolled down his window. "We been lookin' for Ernie — figured he'd be here. That damn bear was seen breakin' into your place 'bout two hours ago. Hank set a barrel trap with fish scraps in your front yard."

"How much damage did he do?" asked Ernie.

"None. Crane followed the bear down the shoreline and watched as he tried to claw your door open. He yelled and fired a round into the air — the bear took off runnin' toward the marina. Crane peeked inside your place and said everything was fine."

Jim frowned. "Were there any other witnesses?"

Pete answered, "As far as I know, only Crane was there. After it happened, he called the Clan and explained the situation. I was with Hank when the Clan called him. We set the trap, then came lookin' for Ernie."

Jim shook each man's hands. "Thank you both. We were about to leave for Ernie's when you drove up. We'll check things out for ourselves. Hopefully Hank can catch the bastard before he hurts someone."

Hank nodded. "It's gonna be tough. I trapped and relocated him when he was a youngster. He's smartened up since then. Say, Jim, maybe you could bring me some fish scraps the next time you go fishin'?"

"No problem Hank. Should I leave them with Pete?"

Hank nodded. "That works for me."

Jim asked, "Hey, do either of you have Crane's cell number?"

Pete answered, "No, but I bet Mel has it at his place."

"Wonderful. Hey, thanks for everything, you guys."

Pete and Hank said goodbye, drove to Killisnoo Road and turned left toward their homes. Jim went back into the house and returned with a small device that looked like a cell phone. The duo took off in the Hummer and hung a left toward Angoon and Ernie's cabin. They hadn't driven more than two hundred yards when the bear with a white patch on his forehead came out of the timber from their left side and walked onto the road.

Jim pulled over and said, "See that white patch above his eye? Is this the same bear that you've seen in town?"

Ernie nodded. "Same patch — that's him alright."

"I don't believe this bear tried to get into your cabin tonight. We're over two miles from Angoon and he just came out of the timber heading toward town. Bears don't walk in circles for hours on end. I think Crane opened your door after we left. When he realized I marked your door with a match, he fabricated the bear story. And, there are no witnesses to verify his version. We need to carefully inspect the inside of your cabin to see if anything's missing or out of place."

The old trapper nodded. "I agree. I ain't ever had a bear break into my home as long as I've lived here. They'll snoop around and go after your garbage, but they're afraid of the people inside. It'd be different if the place was unoccupied for a long time."

They arrived at the cabin and passed the large, portable barrel trap. Jim aimed his headlights at the front door. He left the Humvee idling as they walked to the porch. Jim pointed to the farmer's match lying on the rough-sawn porch boards. "I bet he heard it hit the porch opening your screen door and didn't know where I'd placed it."

Ernie studied his door. "There ain't claw marks or tears on the screen. If a bear wanted in, he'd have torn the door off the hinges."

Jim inspected the door and agreed that a bear hadn't tried to break in. He pushed the inner door open and allowed light from the Humvee to flood the cabin's interior.

After turning on the lights he whispered very faintly into Ernie's ear, "Don't say anything. The place could be bugged. Take a look around and tell me if anything's out of place. I'll check for transmission signals."

Ernie frowned. "What're ya talkin about?"

Jim showed him the cell-phone-looking device he'd gotten from his house. He opened it and whispered, "This thing tells me if signals are being sent from the immediate area. Go ahead and survey the inside while I scan the outside."

Ernie whispered, "Last night ya said ya was checking for messages with that thing."

Jim shrugged. "I couldn't tell you about myself without knowing the place was secure."

The old man stood in the doorway and looked at the Luger hanging on the vertical post near the kitchen area. Something wasn't right, but he didn't know what. His attention shifted to the old cookie tin he'd hidden under his pillow. Ernie threw back the pillow and was relieved to see the old tin as he'd left it. He opened the lid and methodically inspected the inside to find everything in order. After looking around the cabin, he noticed that several dresser drawers were partially opened and his whiskey still had been moved aside in order for someone to rifle through his pantry cabinet.

Jim entered the cabin as Ernie tucked the cookie tin under his arm. The old man flicked his head toward the door and they walked outside.

Once outside, Ernie whispered, "That fat bastard rifled through my belongings."

"That figures. I'm sorry but the batteries in my scanner need replacement so I can't tell if the place is bugged. Did he take anything?"

"Near as I can see, just my dignity — I feel violated. In all my years, I ain't never seen anything like this. My doors don't even have locks — never needed 'em. Nobody has the right to do this sorta thing."

"You're right; he has no authority to enter your dwelling without a warrant. I'll take care of Crane when I figure out what he's up to. Do you have any idea what he's after or why he's dialed in on you?"

Ernie was anxious. "Beats me."

"You ought to stay at my place for a while — I'd feel much better. My house has four bedrooms and there's a hide-a-bed in my study as well as the loft — there's plenty of room. In the meantime, I'll set up a hidden surveillance system so we can monitor what's happening here. Crane's a dangerous man and your welfare may be at risk."

Ernie nodded and re-entered his cabin. He took another look around, then walked to the post where the Luger was hanging. He then realized the pistol and holster were hanging backwards. The handle was facing the front door instead of the pantry. Not knowing whether the cabin was bugged, McKinnon looked at Bennett and winked. "Jim, would ya mind if I stayed at your place till the bear's caught? I don't feel safe with him being so close and all."

Jim understood Ernie's ruse. "I'd enjoy the company old timer. Get what you need for the night, and we'll come back tomorrow."

Ernie grabbed the cookie tin and pistol, then gathered a change of clothes and his toothbrush. "Thanks for the hospitality Jim. I'll stay for a night or two if that's alright with ya. I bet Hank catches the critter before ya know it."

Jim played along. "Wonderful idea. Let's get out of here before the bear comes back."

Upon entering the truck Ernie asked, "Ya got what's needed to catch that son-of-a-bitch?"

"Yep, if he returns, we'll nail him for criminal trespass."

Driving home, both men were silent. Jim considered how chaotic things had gotten and felt something ominous looming on the horizon. Without having real-time information, a dense fog of confusion obscured his understanding of the situation. Experience told him that Crane and Rigby were acting in concert for some unknown agenda but wondered if Santos was involved as well. How did old man McKinnon and Angoon fit into this expanding puzzle? Jim also wondered why Ernie chose to lug his Luger and cookie tin along instead of a box of clothes.

Upon arriving at home, Jim disarmed his surveillance system and entered his summer house. He looked forward to his children's arrival tomorrow, and a possible relationship with Lori Phelps. Everything was happening at break-neck speed. He shook his head and thought to himself, *I'm here to simplify my life, not complicate it. I need to relax or I'll never sleep.*

Jim set up a bed for Ernie, then sat at his computer. He checked his emails on the hidden computer and found the Pelican/Olsen report. What Jim really wanted was information on Rigby and Santos. Jim knew that biometric reports typically took 48 hours and it would be that long before he had answers. Tomorrow morning, he'd lean on his friend Walt Diller at the CIA and see if he could expedite things. He and Walt infiltrated Noriega in Panama, and later they developed the Escobar project together. The colonel had saved Walt's life by extracting him from Panama during the 1989 invasion. After Jim left the Army, they kept in touch.

He shut off his computer, returned it to its hidden location, then sat on the couch in front of Chatham and stared into the inky darkness. Twenty minutes later, he stood, walked to his bedroom and fell fast asleep.

CHAPTER THREE

June 10 — Trinidad, California

Since 10:00 p.m., Frank Reid had tossed and turned in his bed, unable to relax or sleep. Thoughts of past exploits haunted him while he drifted aimlessly on the edge of dreamland. Bothered by his sweat-soaked pillow, he rolled it over to expose a fresh, dry underside. Seconds turned into minutes and minutes turned into hours. He looked toward the alarm clock, which showed 12:30 a.m. After another round of tossing around, exhaustion finally overtook the old man, and he fell asleep.

March 20, 1944 — Hamburg

Captain Olsen awoke in a small room to the sound of voices outside. At first he was confused and disoriented, then realized the voices were speaking German and that he wasn't in his army barracks. The captain reached over to scratch his right arm. To his surprise, the arm was missing, obviously amputated. It seemed surreal because it ached and itched profusely, yet it was gone. He carefully touched a long, tender scab above his left ear, then remembered being hit while flying his B-17. His attention shifted to the surroundings and he wondered what kind of facility this was. The room was approximately 16 by 16 feet, with two heavy wooden doors and a large window made of beveled cut glass.

One of the doors was fully open, leading to a spacious, white-painted bathroom. A light fixture on the ceiling over his bed was made of cut crystal and unusually bright. The walls were beautifully covered with small-flower-patterned wallpaper and several original oil paintings. White marble floors added to the room's immaculate look, and the captain quickly understood that this wasn't a prison hospital, but something quite different. Perhaps he was in a church and was being cared for by the underground. He attempted to sit up but severe pain in his upper left back stopped him. As his lanky torso sank back into the feather bed, he realized he was sweating, very hot and probably running a fever. He wondered how he got here, where he was and the fate of his crew.

The outer wooden door opened as a short, bald, elderly man in a white smock walked into the room. Carrying a black leather bag with a stethoscope wrapped around his neck, he glanced at Olsen and saw that he was awake. He mumbled something in German, took a thermometer from his upper pocket and placed it under Olsen's tongue. After pulling up a chair from the corner he examined Olsen's wounds. The stump above the amputated elbow was unremarkable but the wound at the top of his left back and collar bone looked terrible. Green and yellow puss wept from several inflamed and swollen holes. His shoulder was infected. It would need surgery to repair the clavicle and debride the wound. The thermometer verified a worsening fever. The man yelled something in German towards the door, pushed his chair back into the corner and stood.

Olsen asked the doctor, "Do you speak English? Can you understand me?"

"Nein, wie geht es Ihnen."

"I don't understand what you're saying."

An orderly entered the room with a stainless steel cart filled containing dressing materials, antiseptics, and a tray of instruments. He wheeled it next to the bed as the doctor said something in German.

The captain asked, "Can any of you speak English?

The doctor smiled and said, "Nein, wie geht's."

"What are you saying. I can't understand you."

The doctor walked to the door and looked back at him, as if saying goodbye. The orderly put fresh bandages on Olsen after cleaning the wound and said something in German which Olsen couldn't understand. Afterwards, the young orderly left the room, locking the door behind him.

Olsen laid half asleep in a bed of sweat. Eventually, he heard the door opening. A tall, thin, sandy-haired man with a thick mustache entered the room. He was in his mid thirties and wore a black SS uniform. The uniform had three clustered oak leaves with two diamond pips on each collar and gold braided shoulder boards. His red swastika arm band looked intimidating. Olsen recognized his rank as a two-star general. The uniform was accented with polished silver buttons and pins. His black hat with its imperial eagle above a silver skull, and his shiny black boots gave Olsen the impression that the general was an SS "bad-ass." The officer unbuttoned his coat, slid a chair from across the room and sat next to the bed. The coat buttons were circular death skulls that looked evil and menacing. Another ornamental skull covered the knot of his neck tie, and a black-handled dagger hung from his belt. The belt buckle contained an embossed eagle with a swastika. Having this Nazi sitting next to him was Dale's ultimate nightmare.

In a deliberate but soft spoken voice the, Nazi began, "Good afternoon Mr. Olsen. My name is Generalleutnant Bruner —the SS Group Fuhrer for Hamburg. I'm the man who controls much of the activities in North Germany. My specialty is security and intelligence within the manufacturing sector."

"You have a severe infection and your collar bone requires a plate with screws. The doctor tells me you'll soon die unless he performs more surgery and gives you penicillin. He tells me there are metal fragments in your back and shoulder, but the good doctor doesn't want to waste time or medicine on you. You've been unconscious for ten days and have lost a considerable amount of blood. If I order him to save your life, I expect to have candid conversations with you when you recover. Do you agree?"

"Dale Olsen, Captain, United States Army Air Force, serial number: RA-16473595."

"Don't display your ignorance Captain — I already possess more military information than I have time to digest. I already know who you are and where you're from and you possess no military secrets of interest to me. If we save your life, I expect to openly discuss things unrelated to the war. So the question becomes, do you choose to live?"

"The Geneva Convention requires that you provide me with medical treatment."

"Not if it means taking extraordinary measures to keep you alive. We've already done more than you're entitled to and by treating you again, I'm jeopardizing our own soldiers who deserve treatment for equally severe wounds."

Dale's back was hot and throbbed, and his missing arm continued to itch. He had a splitting headache and knew the general was right; he'd die if left untreated. Realizing his predicament, he spoke, "Are you a former American. You speak nearly perfect English?"

"No, I'm German. My mother is German but she was raised in London. I have studied English since a young age and had a personal tutor to improve my language skills. Later, my parents sent me to Princeton University to learn engineering for our family business —I returned to Germany in 1935. My great-grandfather and his cousin founded the Bruner-Visse Shipyard in 1877 — the one you tried destroying. My family are the owners. They built the Bismarck and countless other ships, including U-boats. You're a guest in my parents' home."

The general grew a dark smile. "Enough idle conversation. Do you agree to my terms or do you choose to die?"

The pilot closed his eyes and nodded slightly, "Under the circumstances, I really have no choice. But, can I ask something?"

The general nodded, "Yes."

"What day is it and what happened to my crew?"

"Today is March 24. Your flight engineer, Andrew Decker is well and sends his regards. He wishes for your speedy recovery. Three other crew members — Lambert, Miller and Ferrise —survived and are in prison camp. Edwards had a wounded leg, became tangled in his parachute after landing in the Elbe River and drowned. The balance of your crew died in your plane. The three prisoners in the camp believe that you and Decker went down with your bomber."

"That means I've lost five of my crew. Those poor men and their families."

The general looked down, "I'm sorry for your loss. This war's a brutal and tragic affair."

A knock on the door interrupted the conversation. The general pushed the chair back, stood up, looked directly at Olsen and winked, "We shall talk when you're better."

He opened the door and spoke loudly in German to the bald doctor, who was clearly afraid of him. From the tone of Bruner's voice, Olsen knew he was in complete control. The general left the room; his black shiny boots methodically clacking down the white marble hallway. Olsen wondered about this paradox of a man. He was cordial and refined, yet an assertive top ranking Nazi.

The doctor entered the room noticeably shaken. The orderly brought in a wheeled gurney and placed it beside the bed and locked its wheels. He quickly maneuvered Olsen onto the gurney and pain shot through his shoulder and back. The captain moaned and grimaced as the doctor opened his bag and pulled out a syringe and small vial. He said something in German when the stinging needle entered Olsen's thigh. As they wheeled Captain Olsen out the door, a heavy rush overtook his head. His invisible arm continued to itch as his eyes fluttered, then closed.

Reunion

Andrew Decker entered the heavily-guarded, two-story, red brick mansion. His auburn hair and short muscular frame was in sharp contrast to the tall, thin, sandy haired general who walked in front of him. This was his third meeting with General Bruner, but the first time at this location. He immediately understood that this home belonged to very powerful people.

The floors were white polished marble with black Roman borders and corners. The main entrance ceiling was over twenty foot tall, with a beautiful crystal chandelier as its centerpiece. An enormous spiral staircase stood to the right of the entry, providing access to the mansion's upper level. Directly below the chandelier, inlaid in the white marble floor, was a marble, multi-colored Viking ship with the name "Bruner" on the front sail. A blonde-haired, bearded Viking stood at the front of the ship next to the ship's dragon figurehead. He wore a metal helmet with horns and pointed with his outstretched left arm as if directing the vessel.

The mansion's interior walls were adorned with light-colored, floral wallpaper surrounding impressive oil paintings. Andrew noticed an original Rembrandt on his way into another breathtaking room, a library or study with Persian rugs lying over beautifully-finished hardwood floors. Near an arched set of windows sat a cherry wood desk and red leather couch with matching chairs on each side.

The general sat at the desk and pointed to the couch. "Please make yourself comfortable." After producing a notebook and pen, he began. "So tell me Andy, how are things at the compound? Has anyone asked you about our sessions or my line of questioning?"

"Things are fine sir, and nobody talks to me — ever. I'm kept to myself in a guarded room."

"Excellent. My subordinates follow orders. Your captain had another surgery last week and I'm told he'll survive. He's upstairs resting, and you can see him shortly. But first we must talk." The general poured Decker a cup of hot coffee from a solid silver pot, then offered him cream and sugar.

Decker thanked him and said, "I'm glad he's better and thank you for saving his life. Go ahead with your questions."

The general looked at his notebook. "How far north of Seattle is the lake you lived on?"

"Eighty-five miles from Seattle and twelve miles east of Bellingham."

"Tell me about this place, I'd like a short description. For instance, how many people are there, what they do for work — that sort of thing."

"The north end of Lake Whatcom has two small towns — maybe two hundred people combined. The south end, where my grandfather's property is located, has no population."

"How is that possible?"

Decker elaborated. "There's no work outside of farming, logging or at the docks in Bellingham. When the Blue Canyon coal mine at the lake went out of business, the area became deserted. My grandparents gave me several hundred acres at the south end of the lake when I turned eighteen. They farmed it for years but never lived there. The actual homestead is four miles to the east. They built a pier and large barn to serve as a staging point for the mine across the lake and the mine paid my grandfather to use his property. After the mine closed, my family let the land go fallow."

The general continued taking notes while asking, "So, no one resides on that end of the lake?"

"Not for some time. The mine made a mess out of the lake, so when it closed its doors in 1920, everyone moved away. The tailings killed most of the lake's fish, except on the north end where the small towns are. Blue Canyon got its name from the coal mine's endless smoke and tailing piles."

"How many people live in and around Bellingham?"

Andy had to think. "I'd bet less than thirty thousand for the city and surrounding area."

Continuing to take notes, the general asked, "How long is Lake Whatcom?"

"Maybe twelve miles."

The general asked, "What type of road system exists for accessing your property?"

"There's a small dirt road which runs the length of the lake on its south shore. It forks near my property, heading either east or south. The south fork dead-ends while the east fork heads to my family's farm on Route 9, which is called Valley Road. It runs north into Canada and south to Seattle."

The general rubbed his cheek and asked, "How much traffic is on the lake road?"

"None — there's no reason for people to be driving on a mud road when there are paved roads directly east and west of the lake."

The general sipped his coffee. "Where's the nearest police station or military post?"

"Bellingham has a small police force, but it's for the city — not the county. There's a sheriff and two deputies for Whatcom County located at the courthouse in Bellingham but they never stray from Bellingham — only if there's an accident, bar fight or theft — that sort of thing. There's a new naval base in Everett which is maybe 50 miles south of Bellingham."

The general smiled. "Thank you, you've been very helpful. If things work out, we'll discuss a mutual and beneficial endeavor. As usual, this conversation must remain private. I'll keep you from prison camp providing we maintain secrecy and things continue to develop. When I return, you may visit with your friend."

Bruner stood, left the room and walked up the large sweeping spiral staircase.

In a bedroom above, Dale Olsen looked at the annoying crystal light fixture in his room — its brightness kept him awake. He wished he could roll onto his side and get some sleep, but the pain of being on either side was almost unbearable. It was one week since his surgery and he'd lost weight and looked even more gaunt. The infection was under control, but he was severely depressed and having difficulty accepting the loss of his arm. He was allowed to walk around the room for short stretches and to the attached bathroom, but he was kept from leaving the room. When he looked out the window, he found he was on the second floor of a large mansion. It would be easy to escape through the window, but the reality of his condition tempered his ambition. The landscape below was a beautiful expanse of spring-green grass containing long rows of mature walnut trees. The trees were filled with black and yellow finches jumping from branch to branch, never staying in one spot for more than a few seconds. Despite his concerns about the future, the estate's park-like setting was soothing.

The general had stopped by twice since Dale's surgery, but not to talk. He merely monitored Olsen's condition, so the captain's only real contact was with the orderly and the old doctor who checked on him every few hours. Neither of them spoke English, and Dale found himself learning bits and pieces of German from his captors.

Dale's thoughts often wandered back to Alaska and the float plane he purchased when he was eighteen. He was an only child, and his parents were killed in a car accident when he was eight. He inherited their Seattle home, a modest bank account and an insurance policy worth $15,000. Uncle Carl immediately brought him to Alaska to live with his family in Juneau, and taught him to fly when he was fourteen.

The airplane was a Stinson with tremendous horsepower and range —an ideal bush plane. Its previous owner was a corporate big-shot from Lima, Peru, who died of a heart attack. Dale brought the plane to Seattle, had custom-built floats mounted onto the chassis and flew it to Juneau. That was the end of his inheritance but the start of a business and his flying career. He flew up and down the Alaska coast delivering mail, supplies, parts, passengers or whatever was necessary to make a living. Then came Pearl Harbor and the halt of his promising venture. As an experienced pilot he had no problem being accepted into the Army Air Force in 1942. Because of his skill level, he was top of his class. Dale made rank quickly and other pilots in his class nicknamed him "The Sharp One."

Dale loved flying, but now knew those days were gone — he'd never heard of a one-armed pilot.

As he daydreamed, the rhythmic clack of footsteps announced the approach of General Bruner. The timing between footsteps was unmistakably long, indicating a longer-than-usual stride. Today, with a Luger attached to his belt, he looked more menacing than usual.

The general asked, "How is Captain Olsen this evening? Or should I call you Dale?"

"You can call me Dale. I'm feeling better, thank you. What's your first name?"

"Rudolph"

"That's right, I remember you telling me your first name when we first met, but I wasn't very coherent. Can I call you Rudolph?"

"Perhaps in time. I have a surprise for you but first we need to confirm something." Dale answered, "Fine."

"I trust you remember the conversation we had prior to your surgery?"

Dale nodded. "For the most part, yes."

"Do you recall our agreement regarding having future discussions?"

Again he nodded,. "Yes."

"Will you honor that agreement now that you're better?"

Dale pointed upward. "Only if you agree to put a smaller bulb in that damn light fixture."

Bruner looked at the ceiling and frowned. "That can be arranged — your surprise is downstairs and will be here after I leave. I felt it important to remind you of our agreement. Don't disappoint me. You will suffer severe consequences if you resist. We'll talk tomorrow."

As Bruner was leaving, Olsen murmured, "Heil, Hitler."

Dale meant it as a joke, but the general spun around and barked, "Fuck you and fuck Hitler. You're alive because of my family's gracious hospitality. We're risking our lives by having you here. Don't ever insult me again or I'll teach you the meaning of etiquette."

Olsen realized he was out of line. "Sorry — really I am."

The general slammed the door and stormed down the marble hall, his shiny black boots loudly clacking into the distance. Minutes later there was a slight knock on the door. It slowly opened and a head peeked in —there was Andy Decker, the man who'd saved Dale's life. Both of his eyes had been blackened some time ago, and he was in civvies and handcuffs.

Dale almost yelled, "Holy crap Andy, it's you. You're not in prison. I thought the general was lying. You saved my life, amigo."

"Think nothing of it, pal — you'd do the same for me. How you feeling, you damn goldbricker?"

"Considering the alternative, swell I guess."

"That fat-cat Nazi was about to blow a head gasket when he came downstairs. What did you do to piss him off?"

"Not much —just said 'Heil, Hitler.' It was a joke. Pull up a chair and tell me what the hell's going on."

"For Christ's sake, Dale, you can't pull that sort of crap — don't antagonize him. He saved your life and kept me from prison camp. Bruner's a real shit kicker and the last guy you'd ever want to piss off. Understand?"

81

"Roger that, amigo. I apologized, but he still left in a huff. Now tell me, how'd you end up here?"

"First off, I landed in the middle of a farm field with Krauts everywhere — there was no escaping. I was captured and they beat the holy crap out of me. That's how I got the black eyes. Then they took me to a building in some small town outside of Hamburg and several SS guys worked me over a second time. Afterwards, they asked questions — not military questions but things like, 'Where are you from?'; 'Are you married?'; 'What did you do before the war?'; 'What are my plans after the war?' Real folksy stuff."

"At first I resisted, but then I thought, "What the hell, these questions aren't worth dying over." Within hours, I was taken to Bruner. He was interested in the fact that I grew up on a small rural farm in northern Washington on Lake Whatcom. He asked about the private lives of our crew including yours. He knew the 457th is from Washington State and most of us are from the Pacific Northwest."

"I'm kept in a building not far from here —it's some kind of intelligence gathering facility. I've heard horrible screams and gunshots coming from the basement — probably poor saps that managed to piss off Bruner or one of his monkeys. A lot of Russian dog faces are being processed through that place, but they keep me in an upstairs room. I must admit, they treat me like a fat cat."

"What did you tell him about me?"

"Not much — your parents were killed as a child, you were raised by your uncle in Alaska and you flew your own float plane before the war."

Dale squinted. "What does he want from us, Andy?"

"I'm not sure, but it doesn't seem to be anything military. There's a connection between Washington, Alaska, and the two of us. I get the feeling he's testing the waters for some plan or idea — keeps notes on the most obscure details. Maybe he's writing a book about prisoners from our corner of the world. Just jokin', pal. I can tell you this much, if we're combative or resist him, we'll probably be killed. Meanwhile, I'll accept his hospitality, act dumb and play along."

Dale shook his head. "If this turns out to be a military operation, we'll have to clam up, amigo. I'll face a firing squad before turning on America. I hope you feel the same."

"I do, but we ought to play this out and see what happens. Bruner's extremely intelligent —probably smarter than both of us combined — and he's up to something big. Otherwise he'd have snuffed us like spent cigars. Let him make the moves and see where it leads."

"I'll play along for a while but I'm not compromising my country for a Nazi. Speaking of smokes. You got any?"

"No. I've had a total of three fags in two weeks. Seems like a good time to quit."

Dale nodded. "Maybe so. Enough of this crap. How're you doing, amigo?"

They'd talked for another 15 minutes before the orderly entered the room. He pointed to Andy and then the door. "Auf Wiedersehen —schnell." Both men knew exactly what he meant — the party was over. As Andy left, Dale once again thanked him for saving his life.

Lying there alone, Captain Olsen wondered about their predicament and potential mine fields that lay ahead.

Questioning

The next morning was dark and overcast. Dale sat overlooking the rows of walnut trees. There was a stark similarity between Hamburg's weather and the Pacific Northwest —plenty of clouds and precipitation. Earlier, a soft leather chair was delivered and the light was changed in Dale's room. At least, now he could sit up and feed himself by means of a crude aluminum tray that spanned the chair's arms. It would also be easier for him to sleep in the oversized chair. Dale's left shoulder ached, had very little motion. It seemed locked in position, as if it were frozen solid.

He was staring out the window when he heard the infamous clacking boots approaching the door. The general entered with a fierce-looking German Shepherd at his side. He pulled up a chair, sat down and pointed at the floor to his right. The dog immediately lay down where he'd pointed.

"This is my dog Fritz. He won't bite unless I tell him to."

Dale knew it was showtime. "He's well disciplined," he offered "You've come to talk?"

"Yes. You should know that I expect the absolute truth —I already have the answers to many of my questions, so I'll know if you're lying. This has nothing to do with the war, and you need to cooperate by answering every question. Do you understand?"

"I do, and I'll try to be accommodating."

The general began, "Exactly where in Alaska did you grow up and with whom?"

Dale knew that Bruner already had the answer. "Juneau —with my Uncle Carl, his wife Rita and my cousin Gus."

"Where are your parents?"

Dale was convinced that Bruner knew this too. "They died when I was very young."

"That's sad. I'm sorry. Your aunt and uncle took you in and cared for you?"

Olsen nodded. "Yes."

"Are you married or do you have a serious lady friend?"

The captain wondered what relevance this had, but answered, "No, never had the time — too busy flying, then the war."

"What's Carl's last name?"

"Same as mine — Olsen."

The general continued, "Any other family?"

Dale wondered about Bruner's strange, folksy style of questioning, but continued to answer in kind. "Just a grandmother in Seattle — on my mothers' side. She had a stroke right after the war began and is no longer cognizant. She doesn't even recognize people — can't walk or talk either. Because my dad and uncle were orphans, I never knew anyone from that side of the family other than my uncle Carl and my mother was an only child."

Bruner asked, "What are the ages of your uncle, aunt and cousin?"

"Carl must be 50, Rita maybe 45, and Gus will be eighteen next month."

"What do they do in Juneau?"

"Nothing, anymore," he answered, because they don't live there. Before the war they moved to a place called Pelican, which is west of Juneau. My uncle sold his plane, got a bank loan and built the North Cross Salmon Cannery in Pelican. My cousin has a small commercial fishing boat and sells what he catches to the cannery."

The general continued, "What did you do for employment before the war?"

"I flew my own float plane along the coastal waterway from Seattle to Haines — chartered passengers, mail, whatever people needed in remote areas."

Bruner studied his notebook, then asked, "What type of aircraft do you own, what was its condition before you left and where is it now?"

Dale thought to himself, *Now we're getting somewhere —I wondered when you'd get down to some serious questions.* He hesitated, then answered, "I bought a Stinson Faucett F-19 in 1940 —it was manufactured in 1936. It was in perfect condition when I enlisted, and my uncle keeps it for me at Pelican. He uses it on occasion for his cannery, and I'm sure he takes excellent care of it."

Bruner considered the answer while taking notes. He leaned back and stated, "I've heard of Stinson Aircraft out of Detroit, but not a Faucett F-19. Please explain."

Dale thought, *Why is he hung up on my plane? What's he after?*

He answered, "It's an advanced conversion model of the Stinson-6MB, made in Peru — a powerful plane, with over 700 horsepower."

Bruner raised his eyes then continued, "Do you trust Carl with your plane? That's an expensive toy."

"Of course I trust him. He's a father to me — and it's not a toy."

Bruner's voice elevated. "Don't be testy. What's the capacity and range of your plane?"

Olsen immediately felt a curve ball swish by his plate — should he answer or decline? Finally he offered, "It can easily handle 3500 pounds with a range of 600 miles. Why are you dwelling on my plane?"

The general continued without hesitation. "How do you refuel when you fly to Seattle?"

Dale had enough. "Hey look, this sounds like a military operation. Tell me what this line of questioning is about or I'm clamming up."

The general bristled at the response. "We have an agreement. I ask questions and you answer them. This has nothing to do with the military and if I get satisfactory answers I may disclose my agenda. That would be the next step, but if you refuse to answer me, you'll learn what I mean by undesirable consequences. I've warned you before, and your army already thinks you're dead, so honor your agreement by answering my questions."

Dale's entire body flushed and his face turned red. He was angry and felt cornered. His mind raced. He remembered what Andy said about pissing this guy off. *What's he after?* Then it struck him. The general needed him — something to do with his plane. *That's why he saved my life —he needs my plane and Andy too — maybe he wants to defect — no, he wouldn't need me for that.*

He looked directly at Bruner. "You won't kill me, you need me — you need my plane and Andy too."

Bruner calmly responded, "Very well,. I've tried to reason with you, but frankly I'm weary of this ridiculous banter. Furthermore, yesterday's insolence continues to irk me."

The general stood and turned toward the door. "You and Decker will be dressed in Russian uniforms and killed while trying to escape. My men will be here shortly. Good day, sir."

Cornered again. *Killed while escaping — Andy too.* The general had all the cards. Dale hated being cornered and now completely despised Bruner. He turned toward the window. It was raining and he could see wind blowing through the walnut trees. He knew his situation was desperate and that Bruner wasn't bluffing.

He spoke. "OK. Wait a minute."

Bruner turned around and stood at the door.

"I can get my plane from Pelican to Seattle fully loaded with only one stop but it's risky unless the weather's absolutely perfect. Otherwise, I refuel at the docks in Prince Rupert and again at Powell River — the only safe way to make it with one stop is if it's a partial load."

"Good. You've decided to live. I won't tolerate further displays of defiance or poor manners. Otherwise we're done. My patience has worn thin with you, Captain Olsen. Do you understand me?"

Feeling beaten, the pilot nodded. "Yes, sir."

The general returned to his chair and sat. "What's the possibility of being stopped and questioned in-route?"

Dale hated himself for capitulating. He closed his eyes and answered, "I can't say for sure. This is war time, but with a registered flight plan and proper documents it shouldn't be a problem. Rupert is a sleepy Canadian fishing town and Powell's a logging camp with a paper mill. They're both quiet, out of the way and of no military significance. A registered float plane draws little attention along that stretch of coastline. I doubt if anyone would monitor an unsuspicious flight."

The general thought for a moment, then continued. "Describe Pelican and its surroundings."

"It's very small and peaceful — maybe fifty miles west of Juneau in the Lisianski Strait. The strait looks like a fjord — long and narrow and surrounded by steep mountains. It's on the north end of Chichagof Island and very well sheltered. The strait is deep and connects to the open ocean. The harbor at Pelican is shallow but deep enough for small ships, even at low tide. It's got a small store, a beer hall and a one-room school. A portable sawmill was brought in, enabling my uncle and others to build their facilities. The entire camp is elevated on pilings and has a boardwalk because of the steep shoreline. An investment group from Seattle built a cold storage plant and buys as much processed salmon from my uncle as possible. Between the cannery and processing filets for cold storage, my uncle's swamped."

Bruner frowned. "It's much larger than I imagined. How many people reside there?"

"It sounds larger than it actually is. My uncle's operation is big, but it's mostly machines and equipment. Not many people actually live there, and those who do work at the cannery. There's two bunkhouses and a mess hall for the workers. I'd guess there are 60 or 70 people living at Pelican."

The general continued. "Is there any police force or governing authority?"

"No."

Bruner said, "I assume your uncle's the person in charge — everyone answers to him?"

"You could say that. Other than Art Steller, the store and beer hall owner, there's nobody to even consider in charge. This is a small community — nothing more than a fish processing plant. My uncle's respected and the people of Pelican look up to him."

"How does he communicate with the outside world, by telephone or radio?"

Dale answered, "There's no electricity or telephone lines in Pelican. He has several generators and a radio — it's the only method of operating in such a remote environment. There's an antenna on the ridge above the cannery. It reaches as far as Juneau to the east, Sitka to the south, and sometimes, Yakutat to the north."

The general thought for a moment, then asked, "Would you characterize your uncle as stubborn or flexible?"

Dale frowned. "He's both. When his mind's made up, it's difficult to make him see another point of view, but for the most part he's fair and reasonable."

Bruner said, "Describe your relationship with Carl and Rita."

"They treat me like their son and I consider them my parents. They're wonderful to me."

After a long pause, the general continued. "Tell me about your cousin's fishing boat."

"I've never seen it —just heard about it. It's not new; probably fifteen years old —48 feet long —it's a gill net operation."

"How many pounds of fish will it carry?"

The captain shook his head. "I don't know, I'm not a fisherman or a sailor."

"Would a boat like his make it to Seattle without drawing attention or being stopped?"

Dale shook his head. "Probably not. Navy patrol boats would want to know why a fishing boat is leaving Alaskan waters for Seattle because this type of boat never strays far from the fishing grounds. Commercial boats coming from Seattle to Alaska would be less conspicuous."

Bruner nodded. "That makes perfect sense. What'll your uncle do with your plane if he thinks you're dead? Will he sell it?"

"Not likely — he loves flying and would use it for his cannery. I told him he could have it if anything ever happened to me."

The general nodded. "That's all for now. You've managed to avoid a firing squad. This conversation is confidential and never occurred. Many lives depend on it, including yours. If anything happens to me, don't speak about this. Do I have your word?"

"Yes." Dale paused. "When will you tell me about your agenda?"

"Shortly — but only if things work out. Be careful what you ask for, because you can't know without participating. Decker, you and I may meet to discuss things further, but in the meantime, I impress upon you to remain silent. You may call me Rudolph when we're alone. Then and only then."

He rose, turned toward the door and snapped his fingers. Fritz immediately jumped to his side. The door closed behind him, followed by the usual clatter of boot heels on marble floors.

Dale sat there dumbstruck and confused. He and Andy were nearly killed by a firing squad. He sat back in the soft leather chair and stared out the window at the rain. There were sounds of distant explosions, probably another Allied bombing run.

Trinidad — Rude Awakening — 2:30 a.m.

Mr. Reid yelled, "Dale Olsen, Captain, United States Army Air Force, serial number: RA-16473595," waking himself up. For a moment, he wondered where he was, then realized he was in bed at Henry's estate. He stumbled into the bathroom for a drink of water, looked at himself in the mirror and shook his head.

He couldn't help but stare at the stub of his right arm and the old scars above his left pectoral muscle and shoulder. Frank thought to himself, *Rudy, Rudy, Rudy — you'll always be my Wizard of Oz. What a tangled web we've woven through the years. If you can hear me, amigo, I need you to perform a few more tricks from behind that curtain.*

The old man drank his water, returned to bed and fell back to sleep within moments.

Planning — April 10, 1944

Two SS officers sat across from each other at a twelve-foot-long, solid walnut table. Both men remained silent with their hands neatly folded. One was short, stocky and in his early forties. He was Günter Bruehl, a major in the Kriegsmarine and a highly decorated U-boat commander. The other was of medium build and probably thirty. He was Karl Obert, a full colonel in the SS. Obert carried a Luger and had a silver-skulled SS ring on his left hand which he nervously spun on its finger. Himmler gave these coveted rings only to the most deserving officers.

General Bruner entered the room and the two men stood to attention. He walked to the window, looked outside and closed the drapes. He turned, sat at the head of the table and instructed the other two officers to sit.

He whispered "Has this room been cleared of listening devices?"

"Yes," the colonel replied.

The general looked at Colonel Obert. "How are your wounds healing?"

"My leg and side are mending quite well, sir. Thank you for asking."

"Good, then let's talk," the general said. "Tell me Günter, is the crew of U-666 hidden?"

"Yes."

"Does anyone suspect that the U-boat didn't sink in February?"

Günter answered, "No, it was very convincing — the kommandant blew several Russian casualties from the torpedo tubes. The bodies were in German uniforms and had false German identification tags. Our Kreigsmarine thinks the boat was lost with its crew."

The general asked, "Where's the U-boat now?"

"In a secluded pen at Lorient. We altered the boat's number and it's being guarded by Admiral Doenitz and his men. It's in perfect working condition."

Bruner continued, "Where's the crew being kept?"

"In a chateau near Strasbourg. I can have them here within two days."

Bruner shook his head. "Leave them there for now. I want you to visit my brother at our factory tomorrow. He will show you the model XXI U-boat."

He turned toward Colonel Obert. "Is ODESSA aware of our stolen U-boat and its location at Lorient?"

The colonel answered, "They know we have the boat, but not its location. Admiral Doenitz will remain silent. He believes he's working with Hitler and the SS. ODESSA demands another U-boat and all the gold we secure. If we give it to them now, they won't need us later. They'll take their share of the gold bullion plus our portion and disappear. They believe we're part of them and that they're playing us for fools."

Bruner smiled. "Excellent. I agree with keeping them at bay. Tell them you're working on the other U-boat and the gold. Speaking of gold, have you spoken to my cousin Alfonse Keller?"

"Yes — your cousin has been cooperative, but insists that you contact him personally so we can arrange to have his share hidden. He speaks of throwing in with ODESSA after he reaches Argentina."

Bruner shrugged. "I'll speak with him tomorrow. How much gold is available and when can we take possession?"

"It's hidden in a bunker near Bremen. We have 1,000,000 Coronas; 1,000,000 Swiss Francs; many gold bars and at least $250,000 in U.S. currency. The gold weighs 60,000 kilos."

Bruner nodded. "Excellent. As I said last week, this must be pre-war gold — nothing from concentration camps or invaded countries — nothing traced to the Reich."

Obert added, "We have seven thousand kilos of Deutsche Reichsbank bars with low serial numbers. These were from our own treasury before 1938. Is that acceptable?"

"Providing it's not from concentration camps, I'm OK with that — it can be melted down later. I want no gold stolen from the Jews or countries that were invaded. We'll keep twenty thousand kilos for ourselves. The rest needs to be evenly distributed to the three families. My cousin Alfonse can take his cut from the family distribution. Both of you need to speak with your parents and arrange transfer of their portions. I'm convinced our families will need time to secure it somewhere safe. Colonel, can you provide an undetected transfer of our portion to the Am Alten dock in Bremerhaven when I give the word?"

Obert nodded. "Yes, but it may take several trips unless I arrange for a small convoy. I can have it moved within forty eight hours."

Bruner leaned forward and spoke softly. "The war is surely lost and Operation Valkyrie is underway — Hitler will soon be assassinated. The Allies will invade this spring, so we're almost out of time. If Hitler's assassination fails, we must act with great speed. That chicken farmer Himmler will go on a rampage and purge the SS of anyone he's unsure of, which includes us."

"ODESSA can have the U-boat in Lorient, but not our crew. Günter, you will obtain another U-boat, so they believe we're part of them. Convince them that the crew is untrustworthy and that we'll assemble another one. I'm supplying us with a revolutionary new type of U-boat from my fathers' shipyard — a prototype of the XXI series. It's an Elektroboote and will serve as our escape vessel. It'll be ready by June and my fathers' engineers will brief you on its operation after you've met with my brother. Günter; you're going to take it for sea-trials and fake its loss."

"Gather depth charts for the Aleutians and Lisianski Strait. The Japanese will provide you with what you need. After we arrive in Alaska, the kommandant can take the boat to Columbia, having whatever gold we can't handle. The crew must avoid Argentina, Brazil and above all, ODESSA."

Obert played with his SS ring, turning it on his finger while asking, "What about the American prisoners. Can they be trusted? Much depends upon their cooperation."

"I believe so. I've not divulged our plan, but they'd be fools to pass up their freedom and a share of the gold. I believe they're a perfect fit because both have much to gain. If they refuse to cooperate, I'll kill them. I can find others to join us. I'm personally interviewing every new prisoner taken from the 457th."

Bruehl added, "What about travel documents, new identities, clothing — things we need to disappear?"

Bruner nodded. "Everything's under control. I've arranged to stage our deaths, so select new names for identification papers. Karl, special containers for the gold have been fabricated at my father's factory and will need to be loaded immediately. Pick them up next week and take care of the situation. Günter, if you expect to blend into America, you must improve your English.

"Finally, this operation must be kept totally secret. Tell no one about our plans for entering America — this includes family members. No one can know, because if Hitler, Goering, Himmler or ODESSA finds out, they'll kill our families and come looking for us after the war. If this is to succeed, they must think that we're dead."

Bruner looked at the two others. "Anything else?"

Günter looked at Bruner and cleared his throat. "I can arrange another U-boat for ODESSA — perhaps U-740. My brother Hans is the kommandant. We'll pretend it was lost in the English Channel. As for the new Elektroboote, is your brother expecting me? Twenty thousand kilos of additional weight will be difficult for any U-boat — I need to make adjustments."

"He'll see you tomorrow. You and he figure out the details for the added weight."

Obert looked at Bruehl, then at the general. "I believe our weakness are the American prisoners. If this is going to work, they must perform flawlessly, and assimilate with us when it's over. Frankly I think we should kill them afterwards. That eliminates one concern and leaves more gold for us. Then our only loose end is their initial performance."

Bruner shook his head. "For the Americans to perform, they must feel comfortable with us. They need to trust us and actually believe in the end result. They're not foolish, especially Olsen — he'll know if we're insincere. Accept that they'll be our partners and treat them as such. Besides, there's enough gold for everyone here. It's my job to convince them to join us. Killing them when this is over isn't an option. We desperately require their services if we're to fit into American society."

Karl Obert shrugged off the general's comments. "I'd prefer to kill them when we're finished with their services. Perhaps you'll change your mind when we reach America. When should we meet again?"

Bruner frowned. "I understand your preference, Colonel. It's not mine. I'll contact both of you when the time is right."

There was silence in the room. All three knew the huge risks they were undertaking. Anything short of complete success meant certain death. Bruner stood, adjusted his uniform and left the room. The others followed.

April, 1944 —Hamburg —Torture Room

In mid-April of 1944, Andy entered the basement room in leg irons and handcuffs. He figured this is where the screaming came from. There were blood stains on the cut stone floor and rock walls. It was apparent that the room was used for interrogations and executions. Some sort of electrical device with batteries, wire leads and electrodes sat on a wheeled cart. Another cart had a variety of tools such as forceps, drills, hammers, pliers, hypodermic needles, and more. A low, reclining wooden table with arm, leg and head restraints and a floor drain under the table's head harness looked evil and archaic. Andy wondered if he'd be subjected to the horrid contraption. Bullet pock marks riddled the rock walls. The ceiling had a chain-operated block-and-tackle hanging from it.

Andy wondered what he had done to deserve this fate. Two guards sat him in a wooden chair with his arms cuffed behind him. They secured straps around his waist and feet, tightened him to the chair and left the room. Andy tried standing but immediately fell to the stone floor.

Ten minutes later the door opened and Dale entered. He was wearing a single handcuff attached by a chain to leg irons. The two guards strapped him into another chair. One of the guards kicked Andy in the face several times, then stood his chair up. The guard yelled something in German while striking him in the groin with the butt of his machine gun. Andy's head drooped and blood ran from his nose onto his pant legs. Both guards retreated to the far wall and stood with their guns pointed at the pair.

Dale looked at his friend. "Andy — Andy — hey, wake up. C'mon, amigo. Wake up."

Andy lifted his head and turned toward Dale and moaned. "This is it, pal, We're not here for cake and ice cream."

Dale asked, "Andy, are you OK?"

"Fuck, I'm absolutely splendid. What the hell do you think? Did you piss off Bruner again?"

"I don't think so, Is this the building where you're kept?"

Andy struggled to sit up straight but couldn't. With his head tilted down he answered, "Yeah, I'm kept upstairs. I'm scared shitless, Dale. Take a good look at this room. This ain't no Sunday school class."

"I'm scared too." Dale looked at the guards and asked if they spoke English. They didn't respond. He then said, "Verzeihung . . . sprechen sie Englisch?"

The senior guard who had beaten Andy appeared amused. "Nein — Nein Englisch." Dale nodded. "Danke."

Dale turned to his friend. "Hey, it's OK to talk — they don't understand us. Bruner asked me a bunch of questions about my F-19 and Alaska. He wants to develop a plan involving us. Has he told you anything I should know about?"

Andy was still bleeding from his nose, but he managed, "He alluded to a non-military project that possibly involved us. If things developed and we declined, we'd be killed."

Dale shook his head. "Ah. That's just swell. I was told the exact same thing. The other day I refused to answer a question and he threatened to execute both of us. I thought he was bluffing, but I guess he's not fooling around."

Andy was angry. "I told you he was a powerful 'shit kicker' who shouldn't be toyed with. The staff in this place is terrified of him. His back must be against the wall and he needs more information. Take a good look at this room. He'll get whatever the hell he wants from us."

Andy stopped talking when he heard Bruner talking outside the room. The general entered and spoke with the guards. They saluted with a traditional "Heil

Hitler," then left the room. Bruner slowly walked the entire perimeter of the room, looking at the walls, ceiling, light fixture, floor and shocking machine. He pulled up a chair and sat directly across from the prisoners.

Leaning forward with his forearms on his legs he whispered, "I can't be too careful about eavesdroppers. Mr. Decker, you've been a naughty boy. Shame on you. Try that again and I'll personally kill you. Now, we need to talk, but very quietly —understand?"

They nodded without saying a word. Both men were terrified.

"I'm going to tell you about myself — as a person, and as an SS General. I'll do the same for regarding my associates, and then outline a project I've been planning for several months. After hearing the plan you must tell me if you'll participate. Look at this room. I'm sure you know your fate if you don't agree or if I feel you're insincere. By knowing my plan, you present a tremendous risk to my family, associates and myself."

Dale looked at Bruner and begged, "Please don't say anything further. Send us to a prison camp. We have rights under the Geneva Convention. It would be in everyone's best interest."

The general shook his head. "The Geneva Convention has no meaning in this room — besides, it's too late for that, because both of you already know too much. I'm convinced that after you listen to my proposal, you'll participate. This has nothing to do with the war and everything to do with mutual survival."

Dale was noticeably rattled. "So we won't leave this room alive unless we participate?"

Bruner nodded. "It's guaranteed. Now listen very closely."

"I entered the SS at the request of my father because he was concerned that the Nazis would take over his factory. Hitler had gained power and managed to convince Germany that he would restore our country to its pre-World War I stature by nationalizing everything from banking and commerce to manufacturing. Many families involved in manufacturing were unconvinced by his bold promises. The industrial might of Germany banded together and insisted on policing themselves in return for cooperation with Hitler's regime. That meant infusing SS branches into Germany's old wealth and aristocracy and Hitler's other organizations while retaining family power and wealth. It was the only way to protect our families' factories, investments and heritage."

"Prior to the war, Hitler, Goering and Himmler found it impossible to exercise any control over our group without integrating us into the new power structure. Without us, Hitler was lost. He needed us, and he knew it. We became firmly entrenched into the Reich and performed with great vigor. We had the knowledge and capability to create his war machine and we believed in a unified Germany, Prussia and Bavaria —nothing more than our original Fatherland. Conversely, Russia had tried taking over Germany politically and converting us into a Communist controlled state. Our only option was Hitler, but he lied to my family, Germany and the world. His ambitions are insane and he became a monster."

The general stood and quietly walked to the door. He pressed his ear against the door and listened, then returned to his chair.

He leaned forward and quietly spoke. "My family, their associates and I realize that Hitler's evil and we understand the war is lost. The Allies will soon invade, Europe will stand in ruins and Germany will eventually be occupied. High-ranking SS such as myself will be tried as criminals even though I've never participated in war planning, death camps, or atrocities associated with Hitler. My allegiance to Hitler is a ruse — put in motion to fool his dogs of war. Many inside the Reich fear me and because of this, I operate without suspicion — in the shadows, protecting my family and their interests.

The same is true for my two associates ,whom I've known most of my life. They represent other elite families. They're both distinguished officers —one was a Luftwaffe pilot and worked with Goering, but he was severely injured in North Africa and now works under Himmler. His family manufactures aircraft near Leipzig. My other associate is involved with the Kreigsmarine and Admiral Doenitz — his family owns the Howaldtswerke Shipyard in Kiel. The three of us are loyal to our families' coalition — not Hitler. We've been working behind the scenes together since 1939."

"I'm the senior ranking member of our coalition. The three of us refuse to spend our lives in prison for being loyal sons and patriots, so we'll leave Germany before the collapse. Our families will be taken care of while my associates and I simply disappear — our deaths staged. Others within the Reich believe in leaving as well, but they're misguided. They are politically motivated, ambitious men with dangerous ideas. They're thugs and criminals, including Himmler and Goering. They refer to themselves as "ODESSA," an acronym for "Organization of Former Members of the SS." These are upper echelon SS officers who understand that the war is lost and plan to start a Fourth Reich in South America."

"They believe that we're part of them but while they're busy planning an exodus, my associates and I will have already disappeared without a trace. This plan makes sense for us and our families. As for dear Adolph — fuck him, fuck the Fourth Reich and fuck ODESSA."

"That being said, I have at my disposal over 20,000 kilos of pre-war gold and substantial sums of authentic U.S. currency. The gold is composed of gold bars, Austrian and Swiss coins from 1935 or earlier — nothing to do with the war or concentration camps. It's a fraction of what Hitler has stolen from the German people and our families. I've arranged undetected passage by U-boat to wherever I choose, and I have chosen Alaska, due to its remote nature. It's the perfect place to gain access into the United States. I enjoyed America when I was a student and I look forward to returning there."

"This is where the two of you come in. Dale, you've a method of getting the gold and ourselves from Alaska to Washington — your float plane. Andy, you've the means of receiving the gold without detection — your remote barn on Lake Whatcom. Both of you have given much for America —especially you Dale. Both of you deserve new lives without financial worries. That's what we offer, new lives without worry — complete financial independence — a full and equal partnership."

"Once at Whatcom, we will require your assistance for assimilation — things like maps, clothing, transportation, and knowledge of our surroundings and, finally, customs. We'll furnish new identities for both of you and show you how to convert gold into cash without raising suspicion. You must stay away from your families for many years after the war. Later you can re-establish contact if you desire. By then my colleagues and I will have vanished."

"It's important to understand that we pose no threat to America, yourselves or your families. We have options other than America, but this is our first choice. If you agree to join us, you'll be relocated until we're ready to depart. I would deeply regret refusal, but if you do refuse, the guards outside will perform my dirty work. Please don't disappoint me, because I've come to like the two of you. I require an answer."

Dale turned toward Andy, then back to Bruner and whispered, "I'll be a son of a bitch. I was right about what you've been up to — but I'd never have guessed about the gold. Can I ask a few questions please?"

The general nodded and whispered, "Of course —I fully expected questions."

"What's to keep the three of you from killing us when the gold's in Washington?"

Bruner smiled. "You'll be given side arms as soon as we depart for Alaska and treated as equal partners, not prisoners. Everyone will be on equal footing. When we arrive in Alaska, you can immediately take your share of gold and hide it while my partners and I remain on board the vessel. We have no motive to kill you unless you tried turning us into the authorities which would result in bloodshed. We need the two of you for transport and assimilation into American society."

Dale shook his head. "That still doesn't stop you from killing us when our usefulness is gone — gold or not."

The general shook his head. "You're missing the point — both of you have a motive to kill us — our gold and the notoriety of capturing Nazis. Because we're foreigners in a new land, we need you more than you can imagine. None of us know local customs, attire, road systems, have maps or transportation. Without you, things become nearly impossible. There's no positive reason to eliminate you.

We are like infants who're completely dependent upon their parents. On the other hand, you have numerous reasons to kill us."

Andy asked, "OK, then how can we believe this isn't an elaborate plot to help Hitler or this ODESSA group?"

"Hitler's a walking corpse. Measures are underway to assassinate him —it's called Operation Valkyrie and I personally know people who will kill him. The same is true for Goering and Himmler. You'll see for yourself because this event will occur shortly. I'll bring proof when this happens. We'll have a toast of cognac to their rotting bodies. I despise Hitler and what he represents. As for ODESSA, if they discover our plan or find us after the war, they'll kill us for the gold. They're not partners, only enemies."

Dale asked, "How do you intend to grab my plane without my uncle finding out and who'll fly it?"

"Together we'll tell him I saved your life in exchange for safe passage to America. We'll say that I'm Norwegian and worked for the underground. He'll be elated that you're alive and that I managed to bring you home. Not only will he be pleased to see you, he'll be compensated for assisting us. I know people better than you think. As for the plane, Andy will fly it. He's a chief engineer of a B-17 and has flown before — you simply need to talk him through the basics of a float plane and the proper route."

Dale turned to Andy. "What do you think, amigo?"

"I damn near shit myself coming into this room and I still might — I don't want to die here, Dale. What the general says makes perfect sense, this has nothing to do with America or our military and we're not harming anyone — this is about staying alive. I say we do it."

Dale looked directly at Andy. "You saved my life." He turned to Bruner. "So have you. If I say 'no,' Andy and I die — look at the position I'm in. Andy, are you convinced? You trust him not to harm us when this is over?"

"Yes, I do. I believe what he's saying. He's always been straight with me."

Dale looked toward Bruner and nodded.

"We're in. Tell us about the gold. How much are we talking about?"

The general smiled. "Excellent. I'm thrilled. You won't be disappointed with our new partnership. Your cut will be 20% of 10,000 kilos and an equal share of $250,000 in U.S. currency. That's 2,000 kilos each —approximately 2 million dollars. The balance of gold goes to our captain and crew in exchange for safe passage. There are fuel costs for the F-19 and your uncles' compensation. Those costs will be split as evenly as possible."

Andy let out low whistle. "That's a lot of dough. When will this happen?"

Bruner answered, "Patience is a virtue my friend — something Hitler never understood. Things are being arranged. It could be 45 days. Much depends on my family shipyard and whether the Allies destroy it or our U-boat. The buildings you bombed were only partially damaged. You managed to ruin windows in dummy warehouses."

"So what happens next?" Andy asked.

"Both of you'll be taken to my country home and cared for. Play convincing role as defectors, remain inside and keep a low profile. No funny stuff, because my house is heavily guarded,, and besides, we're partners. My guards will think that you're becoming spies for the Reich. I'll spend nights there and keep you abreast of developments."

Bruner leaned closer. "During our trip to Alaska, we'll refine our plan until it's foolproof. I'll tell the guards outside this room that you're defectors and being sent to Berlin. It'll spread like wildfire, adding to our ruse."

Mid-May, 1944 — The Partnership

It had been nearly four weeks since Dale and Andy had their meeting with Bruner. He visited daily to keep tabs on his new partners and informed them the Allies would soon invade France. They weren't surprised at his ability to predict the invasion and appreciated his intuition and intelligence. It was clear he had the ability to make the escape plan work. The house where they stayed was nestled into a beautiful pine forest, not far from where Dales' parachute had landed him. The home was impressive and well kept, with an immense stone fireplace in the great room. It was obvious that Bruner led a privileged life. The Americans enjoyed playing with Rudy's dog, Fritz. Andy taught him to play dead after pretending to shoot him.

Dale and Andy were in the study when a black limousine approached the front entrance. Three German officers got out —the general and two others. The trio entered the home and walked directly into the study. Bruner introduced Colonel Karl Obert and Major Günter Bruehl to Dale and Andy. Obert spoke reasonably good English, but Bruehl was a slow talker with a thick accent.

Bruner began by saying, "The protocol of this meeting will be for all parties to address each other by their rank. Aside from allowing everyone to meet, I'll update our progress and finalize our escape. Captain Olsen and Lieutenant Decker likely have little to lend to this meeting. However I want to demonstrate our sincerity as partners by keeping them informed. Besides, they may also have valuable ideas. Tell me Major, what do you think of the new U-boat XXI?"

Günter answered, "Incredible technology — if Germany had this 18 months ago, we would win the war of the Atlantic. It can slip through any harbor undetected and will serve our purpose well. I've concluded that we need to dispense with the 23 torpedoes and most of our crew because of the gold. Initial trial runs demonstrate the ability to easily operate this craft with only eight men —which means 16 rotating crew members for constant travel. This leaves us with room for the gold and extra fuel."

Bruner asked, "What about U-740 — the second boat for ODESSA?"

Günter continued. "We staged its sinking two days ago. My brother Hans is presently headed with it to Lorient and will moor next to ODESSA's other boat. I've given this much thought and I suggest that he captains our escape vessel. Allow him to hand-select his crew and give the crew members at Strasbourg to ODESSA. You know how trustworthy Hans is."

The general nodded. "I'm fine with Hans being our kommandant, so make this happen right away. Be certain Hans has a radioman who speaks fluent Russian. I have a documents expert with printing equipment who needs to be aboard, so make sure to get him settled into the XXI when Hans arrives. I have three large trunks filled with civilian clothes that need to be taken along, as well. What of XXI — when will it disappear?"

"I'd wait until we're a week from departing," Günter said. "That way we won't need to spend fuel and resources avoiding detection. I have all of the charts and arranged for a fueling U-boat to rendezvous with us in the Barents Sea at night. I'm not sure about getting a Russian-speaking radio operator on such short notice but we'll do our best. Your documents expert needs to contact me tomorrow. Then all I need is for Hans to get here and a departure date."

"Great job, Major. Let's make our U-boat disappear when Hans arrives. Hitler suspects an assassination attempt and he's quite concerned. Time is running out."

Bruner shifted his attention to Obert. "Colonel, has the gold been placed into the new containers and distributed to our families?"

Karl Obert nodded. "Yes. Our parents have received their portions yesterday and I believe they've hidden it by now. Our share remains in the bunker at Bremen and everything's in place for the transfer."

The general smiled. "Wonderful! The only two variables are departure date and Hitler's assassination. According to my sources, his astrologer advised him that the planets are poorly aligned and his death is looming on the horizon. Hitler's very cautious and won't allow anyone near him with a weapon other than his three personal bodyguards. Valkyrie plans to blow him up, but if he's not dead by mid-July, we'll leave anyway. That being said, let's choose a date gentlemen."

Andy looked at Dale, then turned to Bruner. "Are we allowed an opinion?"

Bruner nodded. "Yes, speak freely, Lieutenant Decker."

"It seems to me that if everything's in place, we should proceed immediately. Why wait for Hitler to die? The Allies will kill the bastard within a year anyway. The longer we wait, the greater the risk of discovery."

Obert looked at Andy in surprise. "I agree. He's on point. Soon this house of cards will fall, and when it does, we're finished. There are far too many risks associated with waiting. Goering contacted me this morning and wants me to transfer back to the Luftwaffe, but Himmler's resisting. If I'm transferred, things become complicated."

Bruner frowned and smiled at once. "It seems the lieutenant has a new friend and advocate in Colonel Obert; however I'm concerned about Goering. Why the transfer — do you think he suspects anything?"

"No. General Raasch was killed during an airstrike in Leipzig and Goering wants me as his replacement. He said he'd call you this afternoon to discuss his needs."

"Well, congratulations, do we call you 'general' now or wait until it's official?"

Colonel Obert shook his head. "I'm serious. This complicates matters."

The general grinned. "I'm joking, Colonel. You're correct, this is complicated. Captain Olsen, what are your thoughts about leaving sooner?"

Dale nodded. "I share their views. If Hitler finds out, it's over. Don't wait."

Bruehl cleared his throat. "What we seem to be forgetting is that the Laptev and Siberian Sea are frozen until mid-July —our U-boat isn't an icebreaker."

Dale rolled his eyes. "Please don't tell me you're thinking of taking a submarine through the Arctic Ocean. It's solid ice. If the ice doesn't sink us, the Russians will."

Bruner smiled and shook his head. "On the contrary, it's open between mid-July and mid August. The Allies sent two large convoys through last year. Our only issue is the weather. If it cooperates, we could leave by early July — if not, the end of July. That's the beauty of our plan — no sane person would expect a U-boat to pass through enemy waters in the Arctic Ocean. Major, please help me, here."

Günter answered, "The general's right. It's open but treacherous, so timing is important. As for the Russians, they won't know we're there because the XXI has a radar-absorbing skin. We travel the surface during the brief night and remain submerged during the day — completely undetected. Our boat can travel for sixty hours at silent running without recharging so our only issue is the weather."

Bruner smiled again. "Thank you, Major. Knowing these parameters, let us decide on a date."

The colonel nervously spun the SS ring on his finger. "If this new U-boat is everything we think it is, I propose we leave by mid-June. We refuel as planned, then slowly navigate through the Barents and take our time. We'll approach the Laptev Sea by mid-July, which is when the Arctic opens up. I'd rather be on the U-boat instead of waiting here. The chances of our plan being discovered grow by the minute. I can't stall Goering without raising suspicion."

Bruner leaned forward, placed his elbows onto his knees and buried his face into his hands. This was his thinking position. After a long pause, he spoke. "We've got logistical issues by moving this fast." He looked at his two subordinates. "How soon can you make this happen. No bullshit — actual time frame?"

Bruehl cleared his throat again. "Two weeks maximum. If Hans can locate a radio operator who speaks Russian, maybe sooner."

Obert turned in his chair. "I can have the gold transferred within three days."

The general nodded. "So be it, I'll arrange for our deaths. Major, you'll be lost at sea on our U-boat as soon as Hans has selected his crew." He turned toward Obert. "I'll contact Goering and stall him. If he demands your immediate transfer, we'll stage your death and you'll remain here with our American partners. As soon as Hans arrives, inform ODESSA about the two U-boats and their location — this way everything appears normal."

Bruner stood up. "Then it's June 23. Meeting is adjourned."

U-Boat Prototype XXI

Nine days later, the new XXI entered the North Sea and immediately submerged to eighteen meters. Major Bruehl was correct in his evaluation of this technological wonder. The vessel eclipsed anything the world had ever seen in submarines. Had the Germans developed the electroboot eighteen months earlier, Germany's condition would be much different. Its streamlined design enabled it to travel fully submerged at speeds faster than most convoys.

With anti-radar detection coatings and low signature profile, it was virtually undetectable. Its snorkel incorporated a device called a Tunis that identified any incoming radar beams. The XXI could remain submerged for over 60 hours while silently running at five knots. If Germany had this technology earlier, the Allied invasion would have failed.

Hans Bruehl had listened to his brother Günter bragging about the new U-boat but didn't understand the significance of his statements until now.

Hans ordered, "Up periscope. Initiate silent running. Reduce speed to five knots; course 300 degrees, west-northwest." He scanned the horizon in all directions. The only vessel within sight was a German destroyer a kilometer off their starboard side, which was totally unaware of the U-boat's presence. He continued, "Down periscope. Ahead one quarter. Maintain silent running."

Günter stood beside Hans, smiling. "What do you think of our latest achievement?"

Hans shook his head. "This is utterly fantastic — I had no idea. May I surface and see how fast it goes?"

Günter smiled. "Certainly. Be my guest."

Hans gave the order to surface while increasing the speed to one half. After climbing into the conning tower, Hans ordered full speed ahead, and the stealthy boat cut through the choppy sea like a knife. After five minutes, he asked the engineer their current speed. It was 19 knots. He wondered how fast it could travel submerged, and climbed down to the bridge and gave the order to dive to snorkel depth.

There was no vibration as the perfectly balanced twin engines propelled the vessel further into the North Sea. After reaching 21 knots, Hans gave the order to transfer power to the electric motors. There was a dramatic change in sound — the U-boat was virtually silent slicing through the dark water. They were traveling at 17 knots without a sound.

Günter was amused at the look on his brother's face. Hans was obviously impressed with the U-boat's performance. "How much further before we send our distress signal?" Hans asked.

"I suggest another hour before sending the S.O.S. Let's put some distance between us and that destroyer. When we're satisfied, we'll blow several hundred liters of oil, trash and the three bodies we brought onboard out of our number one torpedo tube. Be sure the bodies have life vests on. Then head toward our rendezvous point. We'll wait there submerged until the gold arrives."

Major Bruehl turned away and walked toward his quarters. He hoped things were going well on the other end because they couldn't return to Germany after staging so many sinkings. Upon reaching his room, he picked up his accordion and began playing a waltz. It helped him relax and took his mind off of things.

June 23, 1944 — Escape

It had rained for three days in Northern Germany, but the weather was supposed to clear by evening. Goering insisted on Obert's immediate transfer to Leipzig because the aircraft factories there required immediate attention. Allied bombers had destroyed a key facility and Obert would overlook the repairs. The Reich simply couldn't wait for General Bruner's schedule. Bruner begrudgingly congratulated Goering on his choice and told him that he'd personally escort Obert to Leipzig. He planned a small celebration and would return to Hamburg the next morning.

The late morning flight transporting the two SS officers to Leipzig taxied to the end of the runway. It was raining hard, making it impossible for the tower to clearly see the aircraft. The pilot radioed the tower and asked permission to take off. The tower's controller scanned the radar screen. The surrounding sky was void of all traffic and the converted Heinkel-111 was authorized to take off.

Moments later, the small bomber roared down the runway, lifted slightly then banked hard to its left. The wing struck the ground, forcing the bomber to skid off the runway into a grassy field. Its wheels and nose dug into the wet grass, and the tail section rose high into the air. The Heinkel immediately exploded into a fireball.

The controllers in the tower couldn't believe their eyes. They dispatched fire crews to the burning plane. The intensity of the inferno made it impossible for fire crews to approach the wreckage. Two high-ranking SS generals and their pilot had just been killed.

Who would Hitler blame?

12:00 a.m.

The Benz sped toward the country home where Dale and Andy were staying. Obert was driving. Bruner handed the Heinkel's pilot new identity papers and showed him an aluminum cylinder filled with Swiss Francs.

The general spoke. "Remember this Otto; we're on a secret mission for the good of Germany and our families. The Reich thinks the three of us died in the explosion, and let's leave it that way. I want you to remain at my home and play the role of my houseman and caretaker. My parents know about this, so when the war is over, see my father and he'll attend to your needs. Please look after Fritz — he's been a wonderful companion and I know you'll like him. I truly thank you for the many years of devoted service to my family and myself."

He reached over and hugged Otto.

Tears rolled from the older pilot's eyes. "I'll miss you Rudy, I hope you'll return someday soon — we'll play Sheepshead and drink beer."

"I'd like that very much — perhaps in time, my friend."

The Benz pulled into the driveway and the trio entered the house. Bruner provided Obert with a special Lugar with a silencer, then instructed him to take the Benz to Bremen and load the gold onto the trucks. They'd meet at 9:00 p.m. by the Am Alten dock. Obert left the house, got into the Benz and drove away. Bruner entered the study and closed the door. He wanted to call his family and say his final goodbyes.

2:00 p.m.

Dale and Andy were nervously sitting in the living room. Bruner came out of the study holding German uniforms. He instructed them to put them on and meet him in the kitchen for a quick snack. After returning to the kitchen, Andy asked, "How did it go?"

Bruner wore his usual smile, looking as if he was enjoying this. "Absolute perfection, my friends. Otto placed three bodies into the plane last night which had our dog-tags on them —he even placed a replica of Oberts' SS ring onto one of the bodies. The crash was convincing —a slow motion wreck followed by a tremendous fire ball. Otto had placed an incendiary bomb on board so it would ignite the fuel tanks. All they'll find are skeletons and dog-tags." The general laughed. "They're probably retrieving our remains as we speak. After they notify Berlin, Goering will spit lightning bolts." Bruner laughed again and left the room.

Dale chuckled while eating his ham sandwich. He threw a piece of ham to Fritz who swallowed the morsel whole, then looked for more.

Andy turned toward Dale. "Hey, pal is your heart pumping yet? This is exciting!"

Bruner re-entered the kitchen carrying a suitcase, put aside the plates and set the case onto the table. He opened it, exposing a variety of holstered handguns and ammunition. He said. "Choose whatever you please gentlemen. I promised equal footing, so here it is. I even have small caliber ankle guns and machine guns on the boat. Take whatever you like."

Before Dale or Andy could choose, Rudy grabbed a Luger with a silencer.

Dale selected a Colt .45 ACP. "Someone help me get this on. Wait. The damn holster's not going to work. Are there any left-handed holsters?"

Bruner helped out. "There are several holsters for double-action .38 Specials. Perhaps one of those will suit you — or maybe the Colt auto will fit another holster."

The Colt didn't fit any of the left handed holsters so Dale settled for a .38 Special and an ankle gun. After securing a Colt .45 to his right hip, Andy helped Dale put his weapons on. He placed an extra loaded clip into his pocket.

"Hey Rudolph," Andy said. "I've got a question. Did you intend to kill us in that room if we declined your offer?"

Bruner pulled out a chair and motioned for the two Americans to sit. "I knew almost certainly that you'd agree to my proposal and have no idea what I would have done had you refused. My plans demand your silence, but I'm not a murderer. As our friendship matures, you'll see the real me. Put past episodes behind and concentrate on the future. You'll soon appreciate my honesty and sincerity."

The general stood and walked to the door. With his handle on the doorknob, he said, "We leave in four hours. Relax, read, whatever — but don't leave the house. I suggest you stay in your rooms in case someone comes to the door. And, from now on, please call me Rudy."

He left the room.

Andy and Dale looked at each other, both dumbfounded. Dale could only shake his head. Andy grinned, pointed his index finger at Fritz and said, "Pow!"

Fritz rolled onto his side but kept an eye open to see if Andy would throw him another piece of ham. Andy smiled, threw him a sliver of meat and said, "Good boy! Damn, I'll miss you." He reached over and stroked Fritz on the side of his head.

9:00 p.m.

The black limousine approached the dock's main gate through a slight fog. Otto drove, and the other three men sat in the back seat. The gatehouse was nothing more than a small shack with windows and three guards sitting inside. The highest ranking guard noticed the general insignia on the limo, jumped from his chair and immediately ordered the gate raised, saluting as the limo passed. Otto flashed the limousine's headlights to acknowledge the salute. The dock complex stretched into two separate long-angled wings, each for different types of vessels. The floating docks had concrete tops which had several craters from Allied bombs. The hull of a sunken freighter sat against the dock's corner waiting to be removed. It had been blown in half by Allied bombs. Dale looked at the wreck and knew that the 457th had done the damage.

At the end of the south wing, the trio watched Obert supervise the unloading of two large canvas-covered trucks. The group was a kilometer from the main gate and the dock was void of any other activity. A portable crane stood adjacent to the two trucks and two low, trim vessels floated next to the dock. The trio exited the limo, and Otto turned the vehicle around and left. Bruner turned to his American partners. "These are S-26 Schnellbootes, torpedo boats. 'Schnell' means 'fast' and they're precisely that — 34 knots fully loaded. The torpedoes have been removed to accommodate our gold. We'll be loaded and underway before you know it. The two crew members on each boat are my cousins. Everything's on schedule and going exactly as planned."

The pallets being lifted by the crane had strange metal tubes with handles welded to each end. Dale asked Rudy, "Is the gold in those containers?"

Rudy nodded. "Yes. They're heavy-gauge aluminum canisters with thirty kilos of gold in each. You can drop one out of a B-17 and it won't open — the ends are machined with fine-threaded internal screw caps."

Dale shook his head. "Christ, you've got all the bases covered."

Ten minutes later, the two empty trucks drove toward the gate, and the last load was placed onto the boat. Another set of headlights approached the group from the north dock.

"Who's that?" yelled Obert.

Noticeably surprised, Bruner said tersely, "Spread apart and let me do the talking." He pulled his Luger with his right hand and placed it behind his back. Andy flanked his left side.

A small military sedan stopped next to the crane and two soldiers sprang out. Both wore Gestapo uniforms. The first was a captain and the other a sergeant. Each carried a small machine gun, which they quickly pointed at the group.

The captain barked out in German, "What's going on here? Show me your orders."

Dale and Andy couldn't understand, but knew from the tone of his voice it wasn't good.

The general yelled back, "Who do you think you're talking to? Don't ever address a general or colonel in such a tone. Lower those weapons, stand at attention and salute, or I'll have you explain yourself to Muller. He'll execute both of you. If he doesn't, I will."

They both lowered their weapons. The Gestapo captain thought for a moment, then responded, "I doubt that very much, sir. We work directly for Muller. Now what are you doing here? Show your orders . . . SIR!"

Bruner was noticeably annoyed. "This is a secret mission for Hitler. There are no orders for secret missions and Muller is my subordinate. Do you have any idea who you're speaking with?"

"Yes sir, I do. Oddly enough, you died this morning. How do you explain this? Now where are your orders? . . . SIR!"

Obert pointed towards the main gate. "There's Muller with our orders."

The Gestapo turned their heads toward the distant guard shack. The general shot the captain twice —once in the throat and once in the chest. There was little noise because of the Luger's silencer. The sergeant raised his weapon, but Andy tackled him to the pavement before he could shoot. The two men struggled, and Bruner stepped up and shot the man twice in the head.

The entire incident happened in the blink of an eye.

Bruner snapped his head toward the gate. "Do you think anyone heard the shots?"

Dale shook his head. "I doubt it. I barely heard them standing here."

Obert spoke. "I guess they should've saluted when instructed to. Quick thinking Rudy. I wasn't sure you'd shoot when I pointed."

Bruner took a deep breath, Adrenaline surged through his veins. "That insolent bastard. I was hoping for a diversion so I *could* kill him. Quickly. Load their bodies onto the boats. We'll strip them and dump them into the North Sea. Place the car in neutral and push it off the end of the dock. Andy, your performance was heroic. If you were German, I'd promote you and issue the Iron Cross for bravery. How did you know what we were arguing about and when to take down the sergeant?"

Andy said, "It wasn't hard to figure out. As soon as you showed your Luger, I figured it was now or never. Let's push the car into the drink and scram."

Dale looked at Andy. "You never cease to amaze me, amigo. I think the general just answered our question about killing us in that room. We'd be rotting in a mass grave somewhere."

10:00 p.m.

The S-26's raced toward the mouth of the Weser River and open water. After entering the confluence of the Elbe River with the North Sea, they headed 300 degrees west-northwest. Dale commented on how smooth the boat ran; that it felt like a racing boat that could turn on a dime.

After several kilometers, the boats slowed, and the bodies of the Gestapo were tossed overboard. Obert said, "Serves those Muller goons right — I couldn't believe their arrogance and insubordination. The sharks will eat well tonight."

He looked toward Rudy. "Do you think Muller or Himmler knows?"

Rudy shook his head once. "Impossible. If he did, half the Wehrmacht would've been there. They stumbled upon us by accident. What raised their suspicions was recognizing me. Remember the comment about me dying this morning? This was a freak encounter. They must work directly for Himmler, because I've never seen them before."

The torpedo boats increased speed and headed toward the rendezvous.

11:00 p.m.

The boats reduced speed and made large circles, then engines were shut off. A large spotlight was turned on and slowly rotated, scanning the open water. Out of the darkness, another spotlight appeared on the port side. It was the Bruehl brothers with the U-boat. It sat silently as the S-26s pulled alongside and tied off.

Günter yelled from the conning tower, "Greetings, I'm pleased to see that you made it. Any problems?"

Bruner yelled back, "Not really — two casualties — Muller goons. Let's get below and have the crew get to work unloading. I'll tell you about it later."

He turned to Obert. "Please see that each boat receives a canister of gold for their services."

The crew began loading canisters through the forward torpedo hatch as the partners entered the U-boat. Dale required assistance climbing down the tower's ladder and into the bowels of the submarine. So far, the partnership's plan for escape was on track.

Henry's Estate — Trinidad, California

An insistent knock on the bedroom door interrupted Frank Reid's dream and announced Henry's butler. Still in a blurry dream state, the old man managed a garbled, "Yes. One moment please."

The butler opened the door slightly. "Sorry, Mr. Reid, but it's almost 9:00 o'clock and Catherine has instructed me to check on you. Is everything alright, sir?"

Finally awake, the old man rose and stood beside the bed. "Yes James, I'm fine thank you. Please inform Catherine that I'll be joining her downstairs in a few minutes."

"Very well, sir."

Frank moved from the bedside and headed for a hot shower .

Within fifteen minutes, the study door opened and a refreshed Frank Reid walked into the room. Catherine rose from her chair and greeted him with a hug. She withdrew and placed her hands onto the old man's shoulders, looked at his face and said, "You look much better today Uncle Frank. I trust you slept well?"

"Yes, indeed I did." The old man poured himself a cup from a pot of coffee on the desk. "I'm sorry to be late, but I must have needed the sleep. Please sit down, and I'll tell Patty and you about my past — and your father's"

Frank sat across from the mother and daughter, sipped from his cup, and began.

"Henry and I met in Germany during World War II. As he explained to you many years ago, we are not brothers, but extremely close friends." He pointed to his robotic arm. "The loss of my right arm and my bunged-up left shoulder are result of war wounds — not from a mining accident in British Columbia as everyone was led to believe."

"This will be a lot to take in," he continued, "but it's important that you know. Henry's real name was Rudolph Bruner and he was born in Hamburg, Germany to a wealthy, powerful ship-building family. My real name is Dale Olsen and I'm from Pelican, Alaska. During the war he was a senior-ranking SS general in Hitler's army. I captained a B-17 bomber for the Allies.

"On March 10, 1944, my plane was shot down during a bombing run over northern Germany. I was seriously wounded, captured by the Nazis, and near death. At great personal risk, Rudy secretly took me to his family's home and nursed me back to health. He saved my life."

To say the least, Catherine and Patty were stunned by the facts their uncle was unleashing. Catherine sank deep into her chair, closed her eyes and listened as the old man continued.

"Henry — or shall I say 'Rudy'? — despised Hitler and the Nazi regime but was a victim of circumstance. He had the choice of joining ranks with Hitler and preserving his family's business or a Germany taken over by Stalin and the Communists grabbing his family's assets. His family and business associates believed Hitler was the lesser of two evils, and as long as they were allowed to manage their businesses under the watchful eye of Rudy, things would eventually work out."

Frank looked directly at Catherine.

"You need to understand that your father was the furthest thing from a typical Nazi Hitler follower. He was a loyal son who did everything possible to salvage his families' interests and heritage. Rudy was extremely bright and used his intellect to remain two steps ahead of Hitler's regime while pretending to be a devout follower. Many within the Reich were terrified of him and the power he wielded; exactly the image he strove to project."

"As the war developed and things within Germany deteriorated, he devised a plan by which the Bruner fortune would be protected while he disappeared like smoke in the wind. He convinced several lifelong friends to join him in stealing pre-war gold from the German treasury and forging a new life in America. His friends — descendants of aristocracy and industrial families — formed an alliance with the Bruners and shared in their vision.

"When your father stumbled across me, he realized that I presented him and his associates with the final element of his plan — a way to enter America undetected. After saving my life, he offered me and my flight engineer new identities and a share of the gold in exchange for our assistance. Our involvement entailed the use of my float plane — located in Pelican — to transfer gold and personnel to Washington State and finally, our help to assimilate into American society."

The old man peered over the top of his mug. "I obviously accepted. Otherwise we wouldn't be having this conversation."

Catherine asked, "How does this tie into our current situation?"

Frank looked toward the ceiling.

"It boils down to this: your father's plan was intricate and involved high-ranking individuals closely aligned with Goering. I'm not sure if ODESSA was involved in his death or if Rudy's closest associate — Karl Obert, who went berserk during our trek to Alaska — is behind this."

Catherine wiped her eyes as Frank continued.

"Let me explain. ODESSA was a group of SS officers who believed your father would flee to South America with them and further the cause of Nazism. Rudy used them as a method to gain access to the German treasury, and supplied them with two U-boats and a substantial amount of gold. Your father staged his own death in 1944, but if ODESSA found out he was still alive, they'd stop at nothing to kill him and grab his wealth."

The old man took a final swig of coffee. "The other possibility involves Karl Obert. During our submarine trip to Alaska, he had a drug-induced breakdown and insisted that the other partners kill my flight engineer and myself, take our shares of gold, and link up with ODESSA in Argentina."

"Your father was trying to clean Obert up from his drug problem when he escaped from the U-boat. I understand he was a poor swimmer, but if he managed to survive, he or his descendants could be involved in Rudy's — Henry's — death. In my mind, these are the only two scenarios that make any sense."

Catherine shook her head in disbelief. "That's one hell of a bombshell you've dropped in our laps." She glanced at her watch. "I promised we'd join the others for breakfast ten minutes ago. Perhaps we could take a short break and continue this after."

Frank answered, "A break would be good. What's important for you and Patty to understand is that dangerous people are after us, and we must exercise caution until the threat is eliminated. I promised your father that I'd protect everyone while resolving any situation like this and I intend to keep that promise."

Catherine walked to Frank and placed both hands onto his shoulders. "It's sort of beginning to make sense. I always thought Papa refused to talk about his youth because of some traumatic event, but now I know he couldn't speak about his past for fear of discovery. My sense of reality is somewhat shaken, but father will always be Papa and you will always be my Uncle Frank."

The old man smiled. "Thank you, and you will always be my fond niece."

Patty asked, "If ODESSA still exists, they'd be very old and decrepit. Why would they want a 97-year-old man or his family at that stage of their lives?"

Frank provided a terse response. "They probably have descendants who share their views."

Patty shook her head. "But the wealth is tied up in legitimate investments. They'd never be able to access it."

Frank realized Patty didn't understand the brutality and greed of these people. "I'll answer with a question; how much would you pay someone who'd just kidnapped young Henry or held Travis for ransom?"

Patty finally understood the gravity of the situation. "I see your point, Uncle Frank. They're looking for any opening to get at Grandfather's wealth, and you believe they're Nazis or their descendants?"

Frank stood and nodded. "After the war, ODESSA surfaced throughout South America and harbored people like Mengele and Eichmann. If ODESSA's not behind Henry's death, then I might assume Obert's still alive. The bottom line is this: whoever's behind this won't stop until we put an end to it, so I'm setting a trap to flush these people out. Rudy and I should've done this years ago."

Breakfast

Frank, Catherine and Patty entered the dining room and found young Henry, Travis and William the chauffeur sitting at a massive cherry-wood table. Frank asked William if he knew where the Dark Star crew was. He informed Frank they'd eaten much earlier. Rusty, Helen and several others had left the compound and would return shortly. He assured Mr. Reid everything was under control and that Rusty would speak with him upon returning to the estate.

Henry's cook and butler brought in two platters of food, one containing spinach quiche with Virginia ham and country style potatoes. The other was stacked with fresh baked breads and cinnamon rolls. Frank flashed back to Hamburg and Andy using ham to train Rudy's dog, Fritz to play dead. It seemed like yesterday

The group sat and enjoyed the fabulously-prepared meal. Young Henry watched Frank eat with his robotic arm and asked if it was bionic and had super strength.

At 9:45 a.m., the large white van pulled up to Henrys' front entrance. Whitey was stationed outside smoking a cigar. Rusty and Helen exited the vehicle. The trio stood under the entrance way, and Rusty discussed ongoing security issues. Whitey and Helen pretended to listen to his never-ending stream of senseless detail. The two had an inside joke about Rusty's annoying habit of rehashing things over and over again. Whitey called it "little man syndrome," which Helen equated to penis size. They were pleased after he concluded his talk and laughed in relief when Rusty finally entered the house. Neither respected their section chief.

Helen whispered, "I'm tired of this rubbish. Rusty's a bloody control freak. He treats us as if he's the King of England."

Whitey offered, "Don't mind Little Caesar. Besides, he's talking about retirement. With any luck, we won't have to deal with him much longer."

Rusty found the door to the dining room open, with a well-dressed security man standing by. He briskly walked past the man with no acknowledgement and entered the room unannounced. After being introduced as an "associate" by Frank, Miller asked Mr. Reid if they could speak privately. Frank excused himself and left the room with Rusty.

In the foyer, Rusty updated Mr. Reid on his progress. He informed Frank that he would keep Helen and Whitey as assistants and promised to keep them clueless about Frank's past. Frank had no qualms with the request, providing confidentiality was maintained. Rusty went on to say the Seattle and Redding airports were covered and if the mysterious Al flew a commercial jet from Juneau, he'd be followed. The tactics for the upcoming call would be discussed in detail once Helen and Frank met inside the van.

Henry's Study

Catherine entered the foyer and interrupted Frank and Rusty. Sensing the conversation was about her family's security, Catherine explained that Patty and she wished to be involved. She asked the men to come into the study so they could discuss things as a group.

In the study, another large pot of coffee and a carafe of orange juice waited on a table. After everyone was settled in, Frank asked Rusty to start by disclosing his thoughts and plans.

"From the standpoint of security," Rusty began, "I've taken the liberty of having Mr. Reid's and Henry's jets moved to Sacramento. I've altered both inbound and outgoing flight plans as diversions, which prevents our target from locating the planes and following us later. I believe the people we're after are a small, unorganized group desperately searching for information. The buffoons we captured suggests that they're amateurs and not well-funded. Nevertheless, they're extremely dangerous."

"I believe 'Al' is connected to ODESSA through bloodline or by purchasing a stake in the operation. Revenues from the operation could come from extortion, kidnapping, retrieval of lost treasure or a combination of the three. It's apparent that they're clueless as to anyone's identities other than Henry. Otherwise, they'd have already made their move."

Frank asked, "What do you suggest?"

"Remaining here presents a considerable risk for family members," Rusty said, "because this is where they expect to find you. I urge everyone to return home and allow Dark Star to provide ongoing security. After Al calls this afternoon, we'll know more, but even if things go well, I'm afraid we're several rungs short of reaching the top of their organization. With a little more time, we'll get there. That's how I see it."

Catherine asked, "Mr. Miller, what about father's house? I can't leave this behind — and what about the staff? They can't be shuttled off, and they know who we are."

Rusty smiled. "It's covered. Henry's estate is now a trap. These people will certainly make a play for the staff and we'll be ready for them. A bogus staff will be our bait. I counted seven people working here — the butler, housekeeper, a cook, two gate men, and two security guards — one of which is Henry's pilot. The cook and housekeeper are married and it's my understanding that all staff personnel live at the estate — correct?"

Frank answered, "Yes — Henry insisted upon that as a condition of employment."

Rusty proposed, "What I suggest is to temporarily replace the existing staff with our personnel while the real staff is sent somewhere secure."

Frank nodded. "It sounds like a good plan, but where to?"

Catherine offered, "Perhaps we could use the yacht and send them on a short cruise."

Rusty thought, and finally nodded. "That's a great idea. I can assign three Dark Star guards to act as captain and crew while protecting them. If the bad guys show up here they'll never leave alive."

Patty asked, "How long do you think it will take before these people are captured?"

Rusty looked at Patty and thought, *Not only is she filthy rich, she's a fine looking unit. It must be nice to be her.*

"I'm cautiously optimistic," he answered, "that we'll have this issue resolved within ten days."

Catherine asked, "Uncle Frank, what are your thoughts on all of this?"

He began, "I trust Rusty's judgment. He's an experienced professional. He and his associates neutralized three individuals yesterday who were hot on our trail. His plan to create a trap with phony staff is brilliant and I believe he'll beat these scoundrels at their own game."

Patty looked at her mother. "Uncle Frank's right. The security team has protected us without our knowledge and much of this puzzle has been solved. The plan seems prudent. Let's go home and allow these people to do their jobs."

Catherine asked, "What happens to our help if this isn't resolved within the span of the cruise?"

Rusty interjected, "We'll cross that bridge if and when we come to it. It's a detail that can be handled when the time comes. Right now, my focus is keeping everyone safe while neutralizing the individuals behind this."

Catherine asked, "Why don't we simply pay these people off?"

Rusty appeared annoyed but responded calmly. "First off, you never negotiate with thugs. They'll always come back for more. When they come back, you're right back where you started — having to protect family from extortion, kidnapping and possible death. I recommend meeting this threat head-on."

Patty placed her hand onto her mother's knee. "Currently we're in a vastly superior position because they're unaware of the information we possess. It's just a matter of time before they make a mistake. By remaining here, we'll be in the way and complicate matters. I suggest returning to Dallas as soon as possible."

112

Catherine sighed. "You're right, dear. We'll return home, perhaps even today. Uncle Frank, how long will it take to complete our conversation about Father?"

"No more than an hour. That'll give Rusty time to prepare the helicopter and jet for your departure."

Rusty kept thinking about how attractive Patty was and wondered what she saw in her dorky husband. He stood. "Excellent, I'm glad we're on the same page. I promise everyone here I'll do my absolute best to resolve this quickly. Excuse me while I call the chopper and notify Henry's staff of their upcoming vacation."

Angoon, Alaska

Jim woke to the smell of fresh brewed coffee. Ernie had been up for some time and was sitting in the living room with his coffee cup, looking out the massive front windows at Chatham Strait.

Jim poured a cup of coffee, spiked it with a double shot of Bailey's, then sat in a leather recliner near Ernie. "How long have you been up?" he asked

"An hour or so."

"I thought you were a late sleeper. You're up awfully early. I can easily move you to a different bed tonight."

"Strange bed and new surroundings, I suppose. After livin' in the same house for over sixty years, I guess I'm set in my ways. Truth is, I'm angry about Crane and couldn't sleep. If I was thirty years younger, I'd beat the tar out of him."

Jim smiled. "I believe you would. Like I told you last night, I'll handle him. We'll set a trap by giving him access to your cabin; let the village know you're staying with me until the bear's caught. He'll get wind of it and swallow the bait. After he's busted, the Clans will send him packing."

Jim finished his coffee and added, "How about some breakfast?"

The old trapper grinned. "That would be swell."

Following breakfast, Ernie sat on the couch facing the Strait and watched salmon surface while chasing a school of herring. Soon, the Kings would be heading up the rivers to spawn. While Ernie relaxed, Bennett quickly cleaned the kitchen, then went into the master bathroom, opened a false panel inside the linen closet and retrieved a plastic tub filled with surveillance equipment. The tub's contents consisted of high-end, solid-state micro-technology used by the CIA. Jim closed the panel and chuckled, knowing he'd soon have the goods on Crane and perhaps a connection to Santos and Rigby. Returning to his favorite recliner, he opened the tub and laid two miniature cubes on the glass coffee table.

Ernie peered at the devices and asked, "Are those the cameras ya talked about?"

"Affirmative." Jim held up a tiny black cylinder. "This is a wireless, motion-sensitive video camera." He produced a small black box the size of a cigarette pack. "They'll transmit images to this receiver which we'll hide outside your cabin. The receiver transmits to a subscriber satellite I'm linked to. As soon as the motion sensors are activated, an email sent to my computer will prompt me to download the images with a few keystrokes. The video runs four seconds between frames. I'll set one camera inside the cabin and one on your front porch. Then, I can access the information from my laptop in real time. After I shower, we'll install these."

Ernie picked up one of the translucent, button-sized cameras. It had a thin wire protruding from its edge. "You're telling me this is a movie camera?"

"Yep."

"What's the world comin' to? I'm a dinosaur. Did ya do this sorta thing for the Army?"

Jim leaned forward and collected his goodies. "These were some of the tools I used in Delta — its ancient technology compared to modern 'good stuff.' Imagine taking real-time, high-resolution images from outer space of targets anywhere in the world. We can direct satellites to key in on a ten-square meter area for constant surveillance. Before long, we'll be firing laser guns from space at high-value targets on the ground. Satellite surveillance and weapon technology is developing at breakneck speed. Packaging this technology into computerized systems is some of what TacSec does."

"What if this stuff got into the wrong hands and some nutcase decided to kill the president or something?"

"That's another element of what TacSec does — developing secure programs that limit accessibility, making it impossible for anyone to operate the system alone. Individuals with top-secret clearance are allowed onto the system, but never alone. The FBI constantly monitors those people as well as their families. Our government knows every time one of these guys farts. And it's such a serious issue, everything's encrypted, impossible to hack."

Ernie shook his head. "Who's watching the man who watches the man? I'm too old for this crap — let's wash up and install those cameras."

"I have to check emails and track my kids' flights."

Jim quickly accessed his hidden computer and read a short cryptic message from Lori.

"Frasier's not a happy camper — call me at four."

After verifying that his children's flight was on schedule, he turned off the computer and took a shower. While shaving, his thoughts wandered to Lori — hopefully she'd be cut loose and able to visit. If not, he would take a one-week trip to Denver after his kids returned home so he could see her. Jim closed his eyes as the shower rinsed soap from his face. He pictured her shoulder-length blonde hair blowing in the wind as she walked across the TacSec parking lot and the rectangular gold wire-rimmed glasses that accentuated her light blue eyes. Jim had wondered why such an attractive woman had only been married for a year, but later learned her ex was physically abusive and had gambling issues.

Following their divorce, she graduated with an MBA from Stanford and became immersed in her career. She was driven and fiercely independent, which enabled her to rise quickly within TacSec. Jim had long sensed that once she realized there was more to life than career and financial success, her priorities would change. He hoped that, at age 39, she was ready for something new, including a meaningful relationship.

The men arrived at Ernie's cabin as the sun reflected on Kootznahoo Inlet, providing them with a spectacular view. Several small boats trolled for salmon on the opposite shore. Soon the Kings would be returning. A vacant barrel trap next to the weathered log cabin greeted them. Walking to the cabin, Jim told Ernie they couldn't talk inside until he checked for bugs. He pulled the antenna up from his small device, opened the door and scanned the room.

"We're good to go, Ernie — no surveillance devices in here — give me a minute to determine the best camera angle, then I'll set everything up."

Ernie set Jim's laptop and a small box of components on his kitchen table. "Take your time, I ain't goin' anywhere."

Jim decided that the ideal location for the camera was on the wall opposite the kitchen because large cracks in the upper logs provided ideal concealment. After positioning the miniature camera, he walked across the room to a workbench containing several birdhouses in various stages of construction. He placed the receiving unit in a completed house, and reattached its roof. A tiny wire protruded from the entrance hole. Jim walked outside and hung the bird house in a nearby tree.

He returned and said, "That's it — we should be live and transmitting to my laptop."

Ernie frowned. "Everything's done?"

Jim opened his laptop. "Yep, as soon as I boot up, we'll see a live video of ourselves. My computer automatically accesses the signal within 300 feet of the transmitter — otherwise a government satellite picks up the signal and sends it back to earth. I can access the signal from any of the satellite dishes on my boat or at my house."

Ernie reached for the whiskey bottle standing next to the computer, removed the cork and poured two fingers worth into his glass. "Here's to catchin' Crane." Before he could take a sip, he saw himself hoisting the glass on the computer screen. He looked at the camera, back at the screen and said, "That's very impressive, Colonel Bennett."

"Thanks. Let's set up the outside camera and get to town. We'll spread rumors about you staying with me until the bear's caught — chumming the waters for Crane."

The old trapper gathered changes of clothes and looked around his cabin before closing the door, as Jim set the outer camera. Ernie was angry about being displaced. The duo met at the Humvee, and Jim checked the system one last time. Convinced it worked flawlessly, he drove up the steep hill toward town.

Seeing Pete's mini-van, Jim pulled into the store's parking lot and gave Pete the news that Ernie would stay with him until the bear was disposed of. Jim and Ernie then cruised down Chinook Street looking for Clan members who might be walking about.

As they turned onto Aanya Street, Jim saw Hilda Koostaha sweeping her porch, She was matriarch of the Raven Clan and known purveyor of Angoon gossip. When they pulled over, she smiled and walked down her steps. Jim scanned the area with his bug detector and received a positive signal, indicating a fully operational transmitter was within three hundred feet.

She kissed Ernie on the cheek, then crossed to the drivers' side.

"Good seein' ya, Mr. Bennett. Mel told me yesterday ya came back for the summer."

"Yes, ma'am. It's always a pleasure to be here with gracious people like yourself. Angoon certainly beats the heck out of urban America."

"Flattery will get ya everywhere, Mr. Bennett." She bent slightly in order to see both men. "Ernie, you're lookin' good these days."

"Other than feelin' my age and dealin' with that damn bear, I'm doing fine. If it wasn't for Jim's generosity, I'd be sleepin at Mel's till the bear's caught."

She asked, "Ya ain't stayin' at your place?"

"No. The damn thing tried to break into my cabin while I was having dinner at Jim's. I ain't returnin' till he's caught."

She nodded in agreement. "Don't blame ya a bit. I'm sure Hank will catch that renegade within a day or two."

She patted Jim on the shoulder. "Ernie, we're lucky to have a friend in Mr. Bennett. He's always helpin' folks. Did ya know he got us grant money for the new health clinic?"

Ernie nodded, and Jim changed the conversation. "If any hot dishes come looking for this old-timer, let them know he's staying at my place."

She laughed. "I'll do that. Say Mr. Bennett, Mel told me about your run-in with our new cop and showed me the report. Just wanna let ya know I been in contact with our lawyer in Juneau — he's worried about wrongful discharge. Says we can't replace 'im till we have a formal inquiry. I like the idea of havin' a town cop but I been sayin' we can do better than him. Meanwhile, ignore him. I want ya ta know that the Clans have taken a real likin' to ya, so don't confuse his actions with Angoon."

Jim smiled. "Thanks Hilda, I appreciate the support. I don't mean to change the subject but I've been wondering how your interviews are going with that writer?"

"Oh, alright, I s'pose — he's kinda strange, but who am I to judge?"

Jim asked, "What's he writing about?"

"He said it's a history of Tlingits, but he's been wanderin' off subject — more interested in stuff that happened round here since the '40s. I keep tellin' him Tlingit history goes back nearly a thousand years on this island but he's concentratin' on recent stuff — he'll never understand our people that way."

Jim countered, "It's good that someone's writing about the Tlingits. Do you have his phone number or know how I can reach him? I'd like to speak with him."

"No, I don't have his number. He just shows up every now and then. Dick at the fishin' lodge told me he went ta Hoonah to expand his research on the Tlingits."

Jim asked, "Is he friends with Mr. Santos?"

"Oh, heavens no! Mr. Santos' a very private fella He keeps ta himself."

Jim continued, "You ever seen them together?"

"Never. I seen Rigby with Crane every now and then. Why anyone would befriend Crane is beyond me."

"When you run into Rigby again, please tell him I'd like to chat with him."

Hilda nodded. "You bet. Dick made it sound like he'd be gone for a while though. Maybe ya should be talkin' with Dick cuz he knows a lot more about him than me."

"Thank you Hilda, I'll do that."

Young Otto Kankesh came tearing down the street on his red bike. "The new boat's here! The new boat's here!" he yelled. "It's at the marina." He locked up the bike's rear brake and skidded to a stop. Nearly out of breath, he managed, "It's really cool."

Hilda scolded the boy. "Dogonnit, Otto, you're gonna ruin another tire if ya keep doin' that and they don't grow on trees. Now what about the boat?"

Otto could hardly speak fast enough. "It's here. Some man just ran it down from Juneau. It's so cool. Can I go for a ride? Can I?"

Hilda sighed. "Maybe later. Are any elders down there?"

Otto answered, "Mel's there with a coupla kids — our cop drove up when I was leavin'. I think the man's gonna show Mel and the cop how it works. The man said he's gonna take the float plane back to Juneau after Mr. Bennett's kids get here."

Hilda seemed anxious about the news of the boat. "Well gentlemen, I hate to say this but I should get down there. Good seein' ya, Mr. Bennett. Ernie, I'll bring ya a batch of blueberry muffins when the berries are out — meantime, stay outta trouble."

The young, black-haired boy peddled as fast as he could toward the marina. Hilda drove off in her beat-up, oil-burning Toyota to investigate the towns' new toy. After she left, Jim exited the Hummer and walked the perimeter of Hilda's house, inspecting his scanner. On the side of the dwelling where the electrical service box hung, the signal spiked. He opened the electrical box, and found a small gray transmitter magnetically attached to the inside — someone had bugged Hilda's home. Jim returned to the truck and turned on his laptop. Ernie wondered what was happening, but kept quiet. Finally Jim spoke, "There's a wireless audio link inside her home."

"Why would someone do that?"

Jim answered, "I don't know — Crane may have planted it. Don't say a word of this to anyone, OK?"

"I ain't sayin' nothin'."

"Good. Let's get back to my place, eat lunch and decide on what to do — maybe swing by the marina to see what's shaking."

Bennett drove the olive-drab Humvee to the crest of the hill overlooking the docks. A group of two dozen onlookers watched the 18-foot Zodiac back away from the pier. On board were the delivery man, Mel and Officer Crane. As soon as Jim realized Crane would be occupied for a while, he accelerated onto Killisnoo Road toward his house. Ernie wondered why he was in such a hurry. After reaching his home, he ran inside, yelling, "Wait here, I'll be right back."

Within a minute he returned to the vehicle with a small tool box and a cordless drill. Ernie frowned. "What're ya up to now?"

"While Crane's on the boat, I'm going to wire his motor home. You'll have to be my look-out — can you do that partner? This should take less than a minute or two ."

"Of course I can. You don't miss a trick, do ya?"

The Hummer roared up Killisnoo Road to the hill overlooking the bay. The new patrol boat was out on Chatham Strait. Jim turned left onto Chinook Street to a parking area near the high school. A lone Winnebago stood on leveling jacks next to a light pole with an attached electric meter. After surveying the surroundings, Jim considered it safe to proceed.

"Give a holler if anyone approaches or if you see people watching me, OK?"

"You've got it."

Several kids were playing basketball on the opposite side of the school. Jim calmly walked past a small motorcycle parked near the main door of the Winnebago and opened his scanning device. The readings indicated Crane had no surveillance equipment in operation. He knocked on the door. Convinced nobody was inside, he walked to the far side of the camper, looked through the dinette window. He quickly slid under the camper and drilled a tiny hole through the floor. He applied

118

a dab of epoxy to the back side of a miniature microphone, pushed the tiny antenna through the hole and attached it to the undercarriage.

Jim crawled out from under the camper and looked around. No one was watching. He walked to several massive Sitka spruce standing fifty feet away. At the backside of the largest, he drilled into the tree, pushed a ring-shank nail into the newly drilled hole, attached a tiny receiver and activated it.

He returned to the Hummer and drove to the water tower facing the camper. He activated his scanner, which showed that his audio system was working. After carefully surveying the area for onlookers, he walked to the tower. He aligned and fastened a micro-camera to the side of one of the tank's metal leg with epoxy and returned to his truck. After testing both audio and visual systems on his laptop computer, he smiled.

"That's it old timer, we're off to the races."

The duo drove back to the hill overlooking the marina and watched as Angoon's new Zodiac returned to the dock.

Ernie shook his head. "Christ, you're good at this sorta stuff. It took three minutes to do all that. Is Crane bugged?"

Jim studied his laptop. "Let's link up one more time and see."

After punching in his security code and several keystrokes, he grinned. "My friend, Crane's totally wired, and he's one screwed hombre. Soon, I'll know what he's up to. If you listen carefully, you can hear the kids playing basketball."

Ernie listened but heard nothing. "I'm afraid my hearing ain't what it used to be."

"That's alright. I know we're connected. Let's get back to my place and kill some time."

After a small lunch of leftover stew and biscuits, Jim turned to his laptop and checked the hidden cameras at Ernie's house and the microphone at Cranes. The link indicated that both systems were working and all they had to do was wait. While Jim checked his email, Ernie tried to figure out how to operate his new flat-screen-DVD-player combination. It didn't take long for Jim to know he hadn't received any new information, so he assisted Ernie with his new toy. The old timer was amazed at the units' clarity and detail.

The grandfather clock near the front door chimed 12 times. Within four hours, Jim's children would arrive.

Trinidad, California —Henry's Study

After Rusty left the room, Catherine spoke about a recollection from childhood. "Now that Mr. Miller's gone," she began "something comes to mind that's important.

When I was young, Father took Mother and I for a summer vacation to Europe. We met people Papa described as old family friends in Kiel. They were shipbuilders, and father was there to purchase ships for his business. All were German, and one gentleman looked very much like father but was many years older. In retrospect, I'm convinced they were related — perhaps brothers. I had a marvelous time because everyone treated me like a princess.

"During that trip, I heard father mention ODESSA but I thought he was talking about the Ukrainian city. Names you spoke of — Bruehl and Obert — were mentioned repeatedly. I remember Papa hugging a much-older man named Johanne Bruehl. The two of them spoke for quite a while, and after the discussion, they both had tears in their eyes. It seemed that they'd been good friends from another era and shared in some common but tragic event."

"Something unsettling happened the night before returning home. A woman about father's age arrived, accompanied by a man in his mid-twenties. They appeared out of nowhere and confronted Father in the hotel lobby. The young man was very upset and began yelling at Papa in German. He was extremely combative and kept mentioning somebody named Karl. This person created such a scene that hotel security escorted him from the lobby and physically tossed him onto the street. Papa then spoke with the woman for several minutes. She was reasonable, and after they spoke, she hugged Papa goodbye."

"During the flight home, father explained why the young man had been yelling. He was Anton Keller, illegitimate son of the woman he was with. The woman was Papa's cousin and her name was Heidi Keller. It seemed that Mr. Karl Obert was her fiancée and father of Anton. I learned that Mr. Obert was a former associate of Papa's and Anton Keller felt Papa owed his father money. Papa explained to Anton that his father and family had been paid in full and for all he knew, could still be alive. Papa also told him that he owed Obert nothing more than sympathy in the afterlife for becoming such a rotten person. These are the same names you spoke of earlier."

"Indeed they are. Henry informed me of a meeting he had with family in Europe and mentioned a run-in with who he learned was Karl Obert's son, but I couldn't remember his first name until you brought it up. Henry admitted it was a terrible mistake to have gone to Europe, because it exposed him as being alive. Alfonse and Heidi Keller were Rudy's cousins. I learned of the relationship between Karl and Heidi after Henry returned home from Copenhagen. Henry said Alfonse managed the Reichsbank gold and had been tricked into handing it over to Karl. Alfonse had strong ties with ODESSA and believed it was destined for Argentina. He probably informed his sister Heidi about what had transpired during the war and had it out for both Karl and Henry. How did you remember the name, 'Anton'?"

"I use word-association games to remember difficult things — a trick Papa taught me. Anton became 'Ant,' and Keller became 'Killer,' so by thinking of 'ant killer,' I remember Anton Keller. For Obert, I used, 'Obert the river and through the woods.'"

Frank smiled. "I won't question your techniques and I trust your memory. There's a possibility that Alfonse and Anton Keller are connected to ODESSA and Henry's murder. Is there anything else you can remember about the incident?"

"Not at the moment. Perhaps by knowing more about you and Papa, other things will come to light. I'm very curious about how you managed to traverse the Siberian coast and Arctic Ocean to reach Alaska. That's an exciting and fascinating adventure worth knowing about. I know we're pressed for time, but could you tell me more about the trip? I'm dying to know how the two of you accomplished that."

Frank looked at his watch and shook his head "There's not enough time to get into full detail but I'll provide a short version.

June 23, 1944 — Alaska Bound

We escaped Germany because of Henry's — Rudy's — exceptional planning. Even though we were free from Hitler, we had to contend with Russian patrols, Arctic ice, a partner who became off-centered, and ultimately, America. We had four things going for us. First was the element of surprise; second was a U-boat with advanced technology; thirdly a Kreigsmarine kommandant and crew who were seasoned professionals; and finally, an unwavering partnership that could solve problems without argument."

"A U-boat traveling through the hostile Arctic from Norway to Alaska seemed impossible. Nobody would expect such a ridiculous maneuver, yet Henry knew it could be done. Even I doubted the outcome, but after studying the facts, every member believed in the plan."

"The U-boat Henry provided was a prototype called the XXI. Your grandparents developed and built this exceptional vessel. It was new technology capable of things that were deemed impossible up to that time. It had twin screws and two means of propulsion — diesel engines and electric motors. Surfaced, it had speeds of 18 miles per hour and a range of 18,000 miles. Submerged it ran silently at seven miles per hour with its electric motors. Besides the boat's advanced propulsion system, it had a low profile and a radar-absorbing skin. It could detect ships at a distance of 5 miles, providing further ability to avoid detection. It was designed for a crew of 56 men, but we only required sixteen to operate the boat 24/7. There were only 20 men onboard. The vessel eclipsed anything the world had ever seen before."

"The doors were difficult to get through. I shared a small cabin with partner Günter Bruehl. My flight engineer Andy did the same with Günter's brother, Hans. Henry had a private cabin, as did Obert, modified rooms added to the rear portion of the torpedo room. The balance of the torpedo room was packed with gold."

"The third element for our success was Hans Bruehl and his crew; well organized, focused, and honored to have been chosen by Kommandant Bruehl. They were quiet, professional, and always cordial toward Andy and myself."

"Numerous encounters with Russian vessels required stealth, so much of the trip before reaching the Arctic was made submerged to avoid detection. The crew performed flawlessly while silently running under entire convoys with ease. I can say that our crew was second to none."

"The final component for our success was the partnership's unwavering commitment to each other. We resolved problems by discussing solutions, then voting on how to proceed. Our partnership had the ability to make critical decisions for everyone's benefit. Henry insisted that we use democracy and vote on major issues. An example: after reaching middle Siberia, the sea was solid ice. It was too dangerous to proceed. Our radio operator spoke Russian and intercepted Soviet transmissions. We learned that a Russian supply ship was frozen in the ice and the *Krassen* ice breaker was deployed to break it loose. Open water existed sixty miles east of the supply ship. We voted to follow the *Krassen* submerged using our diesel engines and snorkel. Once we reached the rescue site, we proceeded submerged with our electric motors for 15 hours which placed us 15 miles beyond the ice sheet. It was a calculated risk made as a group."

"As we approached my home in Pelican our partnership hit a snag. Colonel Obert wanted to dissolve the partnership. He had always seemed to have a terrible attitude toward Andy Decker and myself. He insisted on killing us and taking the U-boat to Argentina. Henry locked the colonel in his cabin with an armed guard outside. He'd had enough of Obert's behavior."

"Your father said this to me after learning Obert's plan: 'My word is my honor, Dale. When we agreed to this partnership, I gave you my word not to betray you and I will always honor my word. We're standing at the doorstep of freedom and a new life. I'll never allow him to get between us.'"

"We sat down and developed a plan for meeting my family."

August, 1944 — Pelican, Alaska

The XXI entered the cove on schedule. The sun had set but it was light enough to see. Dale, Andy and Rudy were on the bridge with the Bruehl brothers. Karl remained imprisoned below. Hans raised the periscope and surveyed the waters. He noticed the small island near the right-hand shore had a sheltered notch capable of hiding the U-boat. He had Dale look through the periscope and asked, "Do fishermen ever set their nets around this island?"

Dale shook his head. "No — that's Mite Island — it's not good salmon grounds. It's also shallow — maybe 20 meters at low tide. There's no river or stream nearby, so salmon won't congregate there. I can't ever recall seeing boats in this area."

Hans nodded. "Good. Then I suggest we use this as our rendezvous point. Our boat will never be seen when surfaced. Rudy, come look." Rudy placed his hands on the knurled handles of the periscope grips and examined the small island. He agreed that it was a perfect hiding spot.

The U-boat entered the cove, and Hans came about and scanned the entire shoreline. He saw the outline of a float plane next to the main dock. It was exactly as Dale had described it. Several people could be seen walking around the dock. The cannery was operating and fishing boats were in their slips. Bright electric lights illuminated the cannery while nearby lights appeared to have a golden hue, as if from oil lamps or kerosene lanterns.

Dale turned the periscope toward his uncle's modest log home, also brightly illuminated. He pointed it out to the others.

At 10:30 p.m., the XXI passed north of the house, stopped and rapidly surfaced. A mad scramble ensued as crew members climbed to the deck and prepared a raft. Rudy, Dale and Andy made their way up the ladder and joined the crew. Rudy hoisted one of the aluminum tubes as he entered the conning tower. Günter, Hans, Rudy, Andy and Dale gathered in a small circle, shook hands and wished each other well. Rudy again cautioned the Bruehls about Karl. The three men got into the raft with Dale in the rear, from where he gave directions while Andy rowed. The U-boat slid back into the inky water as the three made their way to shore.

Within 15 minutes, the raft reached land less than 100 meters from the house. They struggled, slipped and stumbled their way up the steep, wet, rocky shoreline to the tree line. After covering the raft with pine boughs, the trio nervously approached the house. As the three walked onto the rough-cut cedar porch, each understood it all came down to this. Dale looked through a window. Carl was sleeping on the couch with a newspaper over his chest. He was a large man with gray hair. Rita stood with her back to the window drying dishes. She was short with brown hair. Gus was nowhere to be seen. Dale knocked on the door, then stood back.

Rita opened the door with a plate and dishrag in her hand. She backed away in disbelief and dropped the plate, which shattered. She screamed, "My God! Carl, it's Dale!" Rita threw her arms around her nephew and sobbed.

Carl rose from the couch mumbling, "Who the hell is coming at this hour? This better be good."

He approached the door, then stopped and turned white. "Jesus Christ —what the — this can't be."

Crying, he hugged Dale and then motioned everyone into the house. The Olsens reacted to Dale's missing arm and gimpy left side with more tears. They were jubilant, yet sad to see Dale's wounds.

Rita picked up the broken plate, and Carl led the group into the kitchen.

Dale spoke. "Please join us, Aunt Rita. I didn't mean to startle you. It's a long story, but I'm very glad to be home."

The group stood in a circle and Dale first introduced his aunt and uncle. Then he said, "I want to introduce you to my friends — these are two very special individuals. Each of them saved my life on two separate occasions. Without them, I wouldn't be here." He pointed to Andy. "This is Drew Prynne, my chief engineer — he pulled me from our crippled bomber." He nodded to Rudy. "This is Henry Weddell —he kept me from dying in Hamburg by arranging surgery and care. He also got Drew and me out of Germany."

Carl shook their hands. "Thank you for bringing our son home. We were told he died over Germany in March. I can't ever recall being this happy. Thank you both for saving him. Dale, are you OK? Your arm and all — you don't look so hot."

"I'm doing well — especially now that I'm here. I'm getting stronger every day, and I'm learning to use my left arm almost as well as my right. Soon I'll be flying my plane."

Everyone laughed as Rita kissed Dale's friends on the cheek. "You can't imagine how happy we are. We owe both of you so much. How can we ever repay you? Thank you, thank you, thank you."

Dale asked, "Where's Gus? Why isn't he here? Is he all right?"

Carl answered, "Oh he's fine — stays on his boat most of the time. He's been building a cabin near the boardwalk since the news of your death. He's been pretty busy with the fishing boat and now the cabin. The silver run' s starting so he sticks around the docks and only comes up here to sponge an occasional meal. Since your death, he's been wanting to enlist and kill Nazis — claims he'll even the score. He's the last surviving Olsen kid. We won't sign the papers till he's eighteen, which is next month. I'm going over to the boat to get him. Rita, could you brew some coffee?"

"Wait," Dale said. "First we need to talk."

Before Dale could speak, there was a knock on the door. Carl opened the door to Yanyedi, the night foreman. He was a short, middle-aged Tlingit with jet black hair nicknamed Jon. He apologized for intruding but knew that keeping the plant running was most important.

"The main generator began sputterin' so I shut it down," Jon said. "I'm runnin' off the old backup and had to shut down one of the canning lines. We gotta get the main generator goin' or we'll miss our quota."

Carl agreed. "Everyone, please. I need to take a look at the generator. We'll talk on the way down and there's always hot coffee at the cannery. Is that OK with everyone?"

The group agreed. After they left the house, Rita put her arm around Dale and bubbled happiness as they walked toward the cannery.

Carl wanted to talk, but Dale told him they needed to speak privately. Carl said they'd take a quick look at the generator, then go next door to the warehouse. After reaching the cannery, Rita went to get Gus while the men examined the ailing generator.

Andy whispered to Rudy, "Christ, it reeks of fish — makes me wonder if I could ever eat fish again."

Carl examined the massive generator and determined that it needed a new carburetor. He didn't have a replacement. The older generator would have to handle the load until he could get spare parts. Jon fetched a tool box to remove the carb, and the other four headed to the warehouse. Carl refused to put on lights because the older generator was already overloaded. He located an oil lamp and lit it. Before they could settle in, Rita returned with Gus.

Gus was a tall, muscular young man. He squinted through the orange glow of the lamp and saw Dale. "Oh my God! You're alive!" He noted Dale's missing arm and frail condition. "Are you OK — can I give you a hug?"

"Of course you can." They hugged for a long moment as the others smiled and looked on. It was obvious that the cousins were like brothers.

Carl set up crates to sit on as Dale introduced his friends to Gus. He shook their hands, then Dale began. "Everyone, please have a seat so we can talk — I've got a lot to tell."

"On my seventh mission over Germany, we were shot down near Hamburg. I was hit in my arm, scalp, and back — I was literally dead." Pointing to Andy, he continued. "My copilot was dead and Drew took control of the bomber, managed to get a parachute on me and tossed me from the plane. After my chute opened, I blacked out. I was unconscious for two weeks. When I woke, I was in Henry's parents' home. My arm was gone and I was dying from an infection. I'd been shot through the top of my left back and needed immediate care. Henry secretly arranged for a doctor to perform surgery. He saved my life and kept Drew from a German prison camp. Later, he managed to get us out of Germany — right to your front door."

Carl frowned and looked puzzled. "If the Germans captured you, how did Henry get you away from the Nazis and bring you here?"

Henry interrupted before Dale could respond. He spoke softly, in an engaging manner. "Allow me to explain the situation, Mr. Olsen. We'd planned to fib but I won't lie to you. What I'm about to say is the truth."

He waited for a moment, then continued. "I'm a former two-star general in the German SS. My real name is Rudolph. My friends call me Rudy. My role during this war was to simply protect my family from Hitler and his thugs and my rank was obtained because of my pedigree. I'm not a Nazi. I'm a German and I despise Hitler — that's why I'm here. Close friends and colleagues of mine recently attempted to assassinate Hitler but failed — I'm convinced that by now they're all dead."

Rudy turned slightly on the crate and continued to keep his audience engaged. "I come from a family which was powerful long before Hitler was born. My rank and family contacts enabled me to scrutinize Americans who could possibly assist me in leaving Germany. When Dale was captured, I immediately took measures to protect him because both he and Andrew presented me with an opportunity to flee Germany before the war's end — otherwise I would face life in prison because of my rank. I speak fluent English because I'm a Princeton graduate — applied science degree. While attending Princeton, I had the honor of studying under Albert Einstein — he's an amazing person, with brilliant intellect. Hitler would kill him because he's a Jew, which is an absurd and evil concept."

"Your son agreed to help me return to America in exchange for his escape and financial freedom. My hope is to reach Washington State — where Andrew's from — without being discovered. He is to fly me there in Dale's plane and help me get situated into American society. I'm not a spy, nor will I ever harm America. I simply want to live here, hidden from the SS and circumstances which made me leave my home, family and friends. I'm telling you the absolute truth because if the Nazis realize I'm alive, they'll track me down and kill me, as well as my family in Germany. I've disclosed this because my life, as well as my family's, depends upon your cooperation."

Dale immediately turned to Bruner. "I never expected you to say this, Rudy — I mean Henry. Ah crap, I'm a terrible liar."

He turned to Carl and Rita. "This is really my flight engineer, Andy Decker. Everything Rudy said is gospel truth. At first Rudy terrified me, and I suspected some hidden agenda. Afterwards, I found him to be incredibly honest — one of the most sincere persons I've met. His involvement with the Hitler assassination attempt is also true. He told us about it weeks before it happened. He's not a Nazi, but the man who saved my life and gave me hope."

Andy nodded. "Everything he's said is true."

Rita walked over to Rudy. "I trust Dale, so I trust you. You saved our son and I'd walk through the gates of hell for that. I don't care who you are or where you're from because you're family to me." She extended her hand. They shook hands and Rudy smiled.

Carl put his hands on top of his head. "Holy buckets, I can't believe this — he's a Kraut — and an SS General besides. I'm flabbergasted." He shook his head, hesitated, then added, "Rita's the best judge of people I've ever known and if she says he's OK, then I'm with her. This war has ruined enough lives and I'm sure Gus thinks the same way because anyone who saved our boy deserves respect. The fact that he told the truth tells me a lot about him."

He stood and shook Rudy's hand.

Gus pulled his crate next to Dale and whispered, "Is this guy for real? He's not lying? A Nazi general that wants to defect or something?"

Dale smiled. "Something like that. He's for real and he's my friend — both these gentlemen saved my life and I'm forever in their debt."

Gus shook both their hands a second time. "Whatever I can do to help, let me know."

Rudy had been waiting for an opening. He seized the moment. "I'm glad, because we need assistance. First and foremost, this must be kept secret — tell no one about our arrival or plans. Remember, the Army thinks Dale and Andy are dead and that must remain so for this to work. The three of us have new identities and after the war is over, nobody will ever know or even care. You'll be compensated for assisting us beyond your wildest dreams."

Rudy pulled the aluminum canister into his lap and unscrewed one end. He pulled out a bundle of cash, handed it to Carl, and poured out a pile of gold Swiss Francs onto the crate supporting the oil lamp.

"This is a fraction of what you'll receive — three thousand dollars and a kilo of gold, which should get us started. We need a place to stay tonight and a boat to take us somewhere very close to here late tomorrow night. Perhaps in the morning we can discuss our needs in detail."

"You can stay in the guest cabin as long as you want," Rita offered. "Dale knows where it is and I'll bring pillows, sheets and blankets. I'd really like Dale to stay with us tonight. I'll make a big breakfast in the morning so we can talk. As for compensation, bringing Dale home is more than we could ask for. The Army offered us a letter of recognition — a piece of paper, not flesh and blood."

Rudy firmly shook his head. "I insist on compensating everyone here because there's risk and expenses associated with our plan. Take it — it will help pay for cannery repairs and Gus' boat. As things progress, you'll receive more. Tomorrow we'll discuss the details of our plan."

Rudy looked at Carl. "Bring me your broken carburetor and I'll see that it's repaired within two days."

Gus offered the use of his boat when he returned from fishing. He'd come home early, unload his catch and have dinner with them.

Dale spoke to the Olsens. "Do as Rudy says — keep the money. We'll take Gus up on his offer for the boat. Let's get to bed, we've got a busy day tomorrow."

The group left the warehouse. When the door closed, a young Tlingit worker named Lena stood from behind a stack of boxes. She'd snuck into the warehouse for a drink of brandy before they entered and remained hidden, overhearing the entire conversation. Lena was excited as she snuck back into the cannery. Her mind raced. *A Nazi general in the warehouse. Money. Gold. Captain Olsen's alive. Who should I tell? Will I get fired for saying anything? Or possibly killed? What should I do?*

The Study—Trinidad, California

Frank was finishing up. "That's how we managed to reach Alaska. Your father saved my life and brought me home. During our journey we became close friends, but afterwards we became brothers. You've met Gus many times — he's not just a close friend, but my cousin from Pelican. Beyond that, Henry, Gus and I have been connected in a variety of business ventures for over sixty years."

Catherine sat back and shook her head. "Absolutely incredible. It's like finding missing chapters of a book. Do your children know about this?"

"I told them everything when Henry died."

"What about your family? Who's watching them?" asked Catherine.

"The same organization that's with us now — Dark Star."

She added, "The company you hired will find out about your past — what then?"

"They'll never find out. Only Rusty knows about my past and he just resigned from Dark Star to work directly for me. Henry and I have dealt with him before and he's trustworthy. He's handsomely compensated for his services and discretion."

Catherine asked, "Why would ODESSA or their descendants pursue us now. They must realize that our family wealth is insulated. Even if they managed to kill every last one of us, they'd never be able to steal legitimate investments."

"They're also searching for missing treasure. After arriving in Alaska, things went terribly wrong. There are nearly 20,000 kilos of gold unaccounted for — almost a billion dollars' worth today. Henry and I managed to keep what was delivered to Whatcom. However, Günter and Andy disappeared. They may have crashed and died in my plane while making the final delivery. The sub was likely lost at sea. Henry tried to connect with Hans in South America for many years but was unsuccessful. The old man you witnessed hugging Henry in Kiel was the father of Hans and Günter. Likely, neither of the brothers survived because they'd have contacted their family after the war. What happened to the gold is as big a mystery to me as it is to whoever's behind all of this."

Patty came and hugged Frank. "Thank you for being so honest and caring. I feel relieved that you're watching over us. Gramps always told me that if I ever needed help and he or Mother weren't around, to contact you. He said I could rely on you and I never doubted him."

Frank countered, "Henry would do the same for my family if the tables were turned."

Patty spoke to her mother. "Do I dare say anything to Travis about any of this?"

Catherine hesitated, then said, "Nothing about Papas' past. Tell him we've received death threats and we're being cautious. This must remain our secret for now."

Whitey knocked on the study door and stuck his head into the room. "Excuse me, Mr. Reid. Rusty asked that I inform you the helicopter was ready for departure. The phone call you're waiting for is within two hours. Rusty would like to prepare for it with you and Helen."

"Thank you Whitey. We'll wrap this up directly."

Catherine asked Frank, "Will you promise to update us daily?"

"I'll do my best, providing I'm within cell phone range. There's no telling where this journey will take me, but Mr. Miller and I will remain together on this matter until it's resolved. I promise you that."

Catherine began to cry. The past few days had finally taken their toll. She walked to Frank and hugged him. "I love you. Please be safe. Thank you for everything. You're the best."

Patty echoed her mothers' statement. She finally understood how dangerous things were and appreciated her Uncle's devotion to her family and lifelong friend. Everyone exchanged hugs and tears as the group left the study. Catherine said she would confirm the staff's willingness to leave and said she'd give each person a $25,000 bonus as spending money for their upcoming cruise. Frank's robotic arm rose to his waist and neatly tucked against his stomach while walking from the study. A natural looking artificial hand closed slightly. Young Henry sprinted across the foyer to tell his mother about the upcoming helicopter ride.

Bennet's House —Angoon, Alaska

Jim turned to Ernie and asked, "Why don't you come with me to Whitewater Bay? I've got to check on a crab pot. Besides, we've got three hours to kill. It's calm out and we could make the bay in 45 minutes. Maybe you could point out the area where you found the artifacts."

"I'd rather watch the 'Duke.' I've never seen this one — it's got Dean Martin in it."

"We can take it along and you can watch it in the cabin while we ride. You can pause the movie when we get there."

"That would be great — hope ya got cold beer on board."

Jim loaded a tool box, a small propane tank and turkey fryer and four bags of ice from his freezer into his truck, and they took off for the marina. Fifteen minutes later, they were on the *Sojourn*, heading out of Kootsnahoo Bay toward Chatham Strait. They saw Crane behind the controls of the new patrol boat as he circled the inlet. Ernie mumbled "asshole."

Ernie was content to sit on a cushioned bench seat next to a Formica table and began watching *Rio Bravo*. Jim smiled, turned his boat south and pushed the throttles forward. The *Sojourn* leapt forward and skipped over the glassy surface of Chatham toward Whitewater.

Several smaller open boats from the fishing lodge trolled the nearby shoreline for King salmon. Rounding Killisnoo Island, Jim saw a boat filled with fishermen taking pictures of a large red marker buoy crowded with four resident sea lions. The lions were less intrigued with the situation than the fishermen. This scenario was reenacted every day of the fishing season. The distant waters beyond several smaller islands southwest of Killisnoo were void of human activity. Several whales swam directly west of the boat toward Juneau.

Within thirty minutes, the boat cleared the corner of Whitewater and sped east toward the interior of the bay. Jim eyed the surrounding mountains to get a better feel for the area and its terrain. An enormous bed of kelp choked half the length of the bay's southern shore and he avoided it so it wouldn't foul his props. Ten minutes later, Jim cut engine speed to approach the crab pot he'd placed the day before. After placing the props in neutral, he took a gaff pole and snagged the buoy line connected to the pot. Slowly and methodically he pulled the rectangular steel pot from 35 feet below. By the time it reached the surface, his biceps bulged as if he'd been pumping iron.

Ernie left the confines of the cabin to watch. Jim reached over the side of the boat and struggled to get the heavy load onboard. The pot was crawling with Dungeness crabs.

Ernie whistled and said, "Holy buckets, that's a pile of crabs. I ain't seen that many crabs in probably twenty years."

"Ernie, you probably haven't been crabbing in twenty years — you can't catch them sitting in Angoon."

"That's a good point." Ernie retrieved a large cooler from the cabin and said, "I bet there's over twenty keepers in there."

The men spent fifteen minutes sorting through the pot, careful to keep only the biggest and best-looking. Jim counted eighteen keepers and used a bucket to pour seawater into the cooler with them. All the bait had been consumed, so he left the pot on the deck and retrieved the buoy line. After stowing everything, he shifted attention to the upcoming treasure hunt. He maneuvered the boat to the mouth of the inlet.

Jim pointed. "Ernie, take a look at that small stream. Have you ever searched above it or west of there?"

"Not above it — too damn steep." Ernie pointed to a flat area east of the stream. "That's where I found the metal tube." He pointed to his right. "Further east, by the end of that lake, is where I found the body."

The hillside beyond the tidal flat had been logged off and was now grown over with young trees, devil's club and ferns. Jim assessed the landscape, then turned to look at the southern shoreline of Whitewater Bay, which wasn't as steep or choked with new growth timber. He then directed his attention to the inlet, which was actually a narrow river about sixty yards across and three hundred yards long. Swift water and eddies comprised its entire length.

"I know I can get my boat through here during high slack tide," Jim said, "but I'd have to turn around in that lake to get back out. How deep is the water in there?"

"Maybe 50 feet in the middle during high tide — 30 or so at low. It's shallow along both shorelines and fed by a gravely stream on the east end. Takin' a boat this big to the other end of the lake is risky unless it's high tide. If it was me, I'd anchor in the middle and use a dingy to reach the shore. Then tide changes ain't a big deal."

Jim thought about the body Ernie had found and wondered whether anyone could swim across the inlet. He carefully studied the outgoing current to see how much flow was needed to overcome the tide. He looked toward the inlet with its swirling eddies. "I don't imagine anyone in their right mind would try swimming across this thing."

Ernie shook his head. "I'd never try it. Way too dangerous."

"The reason I asked about crossing the inlet," Jim explained, "is to rule out a few things. First off, the body would never have washed ashore. Where you found it, the current is way too strong for anything to wash upstream. He couldn't swim across the inlet from the opposite side, which means he swam to this spot maybe from a sinking boat on this side of Whitewater — or he walked down the mountain from above."

Ernie pointed into the dark water. "How could you ever find anything in this?"

"With sonar and magnetometers. I can run a search grid over the entire bay. If a boat or plane is on the bottom, I have a reasonable chance of finding it. After that, it's a matter of underwater cameras. As for the mountain, we'd need to search it on foot or cruise it with a helicopter. A foot search looks to be an ugly proposition, but I guarantee you this, if he came from above, there's a wrecked plane up there."

Ernie looked doubtful. "How will ya begin?"

"We comb the lower shoreline with metal detectors, then work our way up the mountain a few hundred yards." He pointed west. "I'm considering that steeper shoreline as a likely starting spot. If we come up empty-handed, your mystery will remain a mystery unless I can scrounge up a magnetometer and sonar."

Jim reversed the boat and backed away from the rocky point overlooking the inlet. The duo made their way back toward Angoon. Ernie settled into his movie as Jim navigated Chatham Strait. A sizable boat was headed north through the center of the strait. Since they had a few minutes to spare, Jim swung into deeper water to get a better look at the vessel. After closing the gap, he saw it was a small NOAA research vessel — Number 332. The name on the stern was *Oregon II*. A mile ahead was the Santos catamaran. The catamaran appeared to be headed toward Juneau. By the time Jim closed the gap, he'd reached the turning point for Angoon's inlet. Within minutes, they were in Jim's slip at the marina and secured the boat.

Jim retrieved the Humvee while Ernie watched the end of his movie. After setting the turkey fryer onto the dock, he filled the large kettle with fresh water and a can of "Old Bay" seasoning and lit the gas. Soon they'd be boiling crabs. While the water heated, Jim emptied the cooler of sea water, carried it onto the dock and opened the lid. A frenzy of climbing, wiggling crabs awaited the soon-to-be-boiling pot.

Ernie finished his movie, then watched Jim preparing dinner. "That was a great flick. I loved the role of 'Stumpy' Walter Brennan played. Ya ever seen *Rio Bravo*?"

"I'm sure I have — isn't that the one where Dean Martin plays the part of a town drunk and former gunslinger?"

"Yep, that's the one. Say, that spiced up water's boilin' and it sure smells good."

Jim dropped half the crabs into the pot. The water was so hot that they immediately turned bright orange. As the crabs cooked, an approaching plane could be heard in the distance. Two hundred yards to the west, several people assembled near the seaplane dock. Jim strained the cooked crabs from the metal caldron, and added the balance of his harvest into the bubbling water. He poured cold water from his boat's fresh water tank into the crab-filled cooler. After rinsing them, he threw three bags of ice onto the cooked crabs and waited for the final batch.

A blue DeHavilland Beaver with floats touched down on the glassy waters of Kootznahoo Bay. The pilot turned its massive tail rudder and accelerated the powerful engine. The plane quickly turned parallel to the dock, where a young Tlingit attentively waited to secure the plane. The pilot cut the engine and allowed the plane to coast silently to the young native. When it was tied off, Jim's children climbed down a small ladder onto the passenger-side pontoon. A quick hop from the pontoon to the dock made their arrival official.

At over six feet, Danny stood a full head taller than his sister, Audra. He was muscular and deeply tanned, with blond, shoulder-length hair. His faded orange sweatshirt with cut-off sleeves and weathered leather boots were the signature of a construction worker. Tribal and barbed-wire tattoos adorned his biceps and exposed shoulders. Audra's appearance was in stark contrast to Danny's. Her slender body, short brown hair, baseball cap and jogging outfit projected a "Seattle yuppie" look.

Jim grinned and watched them at a distance. He shut off the gas to the cooker and strained out the remaining crabs. After a short cold shower, these were added to the cooler. "Come on, old timer. We'll come back for these. Let's pick up my kids."

As Jim and Ernie approached the Hummer, Crane arrived at the seaplane dock and got out of his old black and white cruiser. He wore black slacks with a blue shirt and a sheepskin-lined leather vest with a gold police badge over the left pocket. Hustling down the ramp to the plane, he confronted the two arriving passengers. Without introducing himself or saying why, he asked for their IDs.

The pilot immediately intervened and began questioning the policeman's actions. "Officer, what's going on here? What seems to be the problem?"

"None of your damn business. Get back to your plane, mister."

The pilot shook his head. "What's this about? You haven't the right to bother my clients like this. They've not broken any laws in the short time they've been here."

Crane shoved the pilot toward the float plane. "Get out of my face or I'll arrest you for interfering with my investigation."

He turned to the two young passengers. "I asked for ID, so let's go — chop, chop."

Audra nervously fumbled with her purse but Danny defiantly placed his hands on his hips. "What's up with the IDs, dude? This isn't communist Russia. We've done nothing wrong. We're just standing here, waiting for our bags."

Crane walked directly in front of Danny and began jabbing him in the chest with the index and middle finger of his right hand. "I gave you an order, you long-haired hippie. Show me some ID, or I'll arrest you and throw your ass in jail."

A voice from behind him said, "What jail? There's no jail in Angoon. Now stop pushing my boy around."

Crane spun around to look straight into the face of Jim Bennett. The officer turned bright red as his temper soared. He pushed Jim backwards. "I'm ordering you to immediately leave this dock. You're interfering with an ongoing investigation."

Jim shook his head. "Investigation, my ass. There's no investigation going on here, only harassment. I'm telling you: leave us alone before someone gets hurt."

John Addison, the pilot, added to the fray. "You're completely out of line, officer."

Crane poked Jim in the chest, as he'd done with Danny. Jim backed off, but Crane moved forward and continued poking him in the chest.

Crane barked, "You got away with telling me to get fucked yesterday, but not today. I'm ordering you to leave this dock so I can do my job. If you don't leave right now, we'll pick up where we left off yesterday and you'll be the one who gets hurt."

"Stop pushing me, Crane, or you're gonna be very sorry."

Crane pulled his night stick and anchored it on Jim's chest. "Alright asshole, I'm placing you . . ."

Jim blocked Crane's right hand and club with his left forearm, and punched him in the nose with his right elbow. The nightstick dropped and Cranes' nose exploded with blood. With a smooth motion, Jim shifted to his left foot and swept back with his right, undercutting Crane's legs. As the officer fell backwards, Jim solidly pushed his head backwards. Crane's head bounced off of the wooden planks and the wind was knocked out of him. The takedown happened so fast, no one actually saw what happened. Crane was on his back trying to breathe, and blood poured from his nostrils.

Crane reached for his gun with his right hand, and Jim heel-stomped it, splitting it wide open. Blood gushed from the wound. Jim knelt beside the bleeding man and grabbed his larynx with a powerful right hand. Crane desperately gasped for air as Jim whispered, "Relax, fat boy, or I'll tear your fucking throat out and toss it into the ocean."

Realizing he was beaten, and soundly, Crane relaxed, but he also wondered who Jim Bennett *really* was. As a former Marine, he understood that very few men possessed the kind of moves Bennett had just performed. He wasn't some "candy-ass CEO" — he was a trained killer.

The former colonel released his grip, calmly reached over and removed Crane's Glock from its holster. He tucked it behind his belt and stood. There was no doubt in the minds of witnesses that Bennett was an experienced fighter.

Jim looked down at the frightened policeman. "Now that I've got your attention, listen carefully: screw with me again and I'll take you out. Don't ever try this sort of shit again — it's your final warning. Leave me, my family and friends alone. You're messing with the wrong person."

Jim kicked the nightstick into the water. Looked at Crane's bulging eyes, he wondered who he reminded him of. He spoke to the downed officer. "I believe you have a greater understanding of who you're dealing with. I urge you to visit the new clinic, get your nose looked at and have your hand sewn up. While you're at it, take classes on how to interact with people in a positive manner. If your cruiser has a shotgun on board, don't try anything foolish because I'm a better marksman than I am a fighter. The Clan elders will be really interested to know what just transpired here."

Crane was still trying to catch his breath on the hard wooden planks. Everyone on the dock was quiet, except Ernie, who cackled at the sight of Crane lying flat on his back. After what seemed an eternity, the officer rolled onto his left side and got onto his hands and knees. He coughed like a dog hacking up a bone as blood continued to stream from his nose. He grabbed his hat, got to his feet, wobbled slightly and looked at his bleeding hand. He walked toward his cruiser, then turned around, In a hoarse voice, he said, "This ain't over — you'll see."

Audra ran to her father and gave him a huge hug. "Daddy, what was that all about? Why was he acting like that? Are you OK? Are we in trouble?"

Ernie whispered to the pilot. "She's always askin' questions."

Danny grinned and gave his old man a hearty high-five. "Wow, Dad! You smoked that guy. You looked like you were in a tap-out match. I've never seen anything happen so fast. "

Ernie was ecstatic. "I thought I'd pissed my pants watchin' that fat bastard's head bounce off them planks — I loved it. He's gonna have one helluva a headache tonight."

John spoke. "Hey, Jim, I'll back you on this one. He had it coming. That S.O.B. was itching for a fight and shoving everyone around. I've never seen law enforcement act like that."

Jim's adrenaline began to subside. He took a deep breath. "Thanks John. Forgive my violent outburst, but I won't tolerate bad behavior directed toward me or my family."

Jim chuckled. "Does Crane remind anyone here of someone?"

The pilot commented, "Come to think of it, he looks a lot like Brad Garrett or a young Jackie Gleason."

Ernie broke into another fit of laughter, then managed, "He did look like Jackie Gleason when his eyes were all bugged out. I wish I had a picture of him layin' there."

Jim turned to the dock assistant. "Billy, I'll need you as a witness too."

The young man nodded. "I watched the whole thing. He picked the fight and got what he had comin'. Nobody here likes 'im anyway."

Jim made certain the Glock was secured under his belt, then put an arm around each of his kids. "I'm glad to see you. C'mon, let's grab your bags and get over to the boat. I've got a cooler of cooked crab waiting for us. Let's pick it up and go home."

The pilot and dock assistant emptied the plane and piled everything onto a large push cart, and the group made their way up the long ramp to the parking area. The man who delivered the new patrol boat and Mel were getting out of Mel's car. Jim stopped and told Mel about what had transpired, and handed him the Glock. Mel was more interested in the fact that Jim had a bunch of cooked crab waiting at his boat. The senior Clansman figured that he and other elders would take care of Crane after dinner.

Colonel Bennett's House — Evening

In the log home overlooking the ocean, the group sat down to a feast of crab, drawn butter, green beans and salad. Danny managed to polish off three of the red beauties before calling it quits. They talked for nearly two hours, catching up on each others' lives. Audra was excited about her new position at Boeing. As a marketing intern for the corporate giant, her future looked promising. She talked about a cooperative project between Boeing and Lockheed-Martin in which the two companies were collectively trying to convince Uncle Sam to develop a replacement for the B-2 bomber. The project appeared to be a slam-dunk, and her immediate role at Boeing was to spearhead a public relations campaign with Congress. Jim commented that his late father would be tickled to death watching Audra hob-knob with Washington insiders.

Danny said he'd filed for a patent for an idea and prototype he had developed. He managed to incorporate piezoelectric transducers into an ultra-thin solar electric membrane. He could harness solar radiation from the membrane while harvesting wind and acoustic vibrations from the piezoelectrics. Since vinyl stuck to virtually any clean, solid surface, the potential was limitless. High rise windows, vehicle tops, highway billboards, metal roofs and even road surfaces became instant candidates for electrical generation.

Everyone was taken aback by his brilliant idea. Asked what led him to the concept, he said working on hot roofs in downtown Phoenix with an electrical engineering degree had its benefits.

Jim was proud of both children, but surprised and pleased by his son's transformation. Ernie was spot-on about predicting Danny's future. Jim told his children about his recent retirement and informed them that Lori Phelps might be coming to visit while they were there. Both knew Lori and were genuinely pleased that their father had possibly found a new flame.

Ernie enjoyed being included into Jim's family circle. It was the most social interaction he'd had in quite some time.

At 6:00 p.m., Jim called Lori as promised. "What's up with Frasier?" he asked. "Did he give you time off?"

"He did, but he's unhappy about it. At times, he's such a jerk. Something else has thrown sand into the gears. I can't find anyone to watch Oscar. Both of my usual sitters have plans. I found a kennel that can take him, but he does poorly in those environments. He's an inside dog who hates staying in outdoor chain-link cages. Oscar's really old and is accustomed to his routine. It's best that I reconsider."

"Stop right there. I know where this is headed and I'm not about to give you an out. Bring Oscar along. He's well trained and I won't mind him being here."

"I couldn't expect that from anyone. He's my problem, not yours."

"Nonsense. Let's make him *our* problem."

Lori paused. Finally, she laughed and said, "All right. He's *our* problem."

"How soon can you get time off?" Jim asked

"Two days. Frasier allowed me the two weeks I have coming. I need to make reservations — now!"

"Let me make your reservations. You and Oscar are going first-class the entire way. I'll arrange for a bush flight, and you'll be here by 3:00 p.m. Thursday. I'll email you your itinerary."

"Wow. I mean, what should I bring for clothing? I've never been to Alaska and know nothing about the weather."

"Think casual and layered — bring a light jacket and a fleece vest. If it rains, I've got rain gear and rubber boots. I know you're a hiker. A light pair of hiking boots and comfortable pair of sneakers for everything else. I have a washer/dryer, so travel light. Bring a swim suit for the hot tub. Forget anything formal because you can't even order a hot dog in Angoon."

"I'm looking forward to this, Jim. But are you sure bringing Oscar is OK? I don't want to impose."

"The squirt will have a great time. He'll never want to leave."

"I hope so. Thank you very much."

"I can't wait to see you."

Lori put on her business hat. "On a different note, let me update you on Rigby and Santos. I contacted Doug at the F.B.I. and Walt Diller with the CIA. Doug said he'd call you. Diller will send an email once he's got the information. I performed a terse investigation and came up empty. It feels like Santos and Rigby changed their identities. Both names are fictitious, but I'm certain Interpol or CIA biometrics will pin them down."

"I researched Rigby's book on Hawaiian culture," she continued, "and came up empty as well. In fact, there's never been any book published by a David Rigby — he's likely using writing as a cover."

"I figured as much. Look, don't worry about any of this. Concentrate on getting up here and having a great time."

They said their farewells. Jim opened a bottle of Moet and Chandon White Star and poured everyone a glass of champagne. He raised his glass. "To my family and dear friend. May we enjoy our time together."

Later, Jim booted up his laptop and made airline reservations for Lori. The others played cribbage and talked as Jim sent Lori her itinerary. He slipped into the kitchen, logged onto his secret computer, and found an email from Doug and several security hits from both Ernie's cabin and Crane's RV. He transferred the information onto his laptop, hid the covert computer and returned to the living room. His attention focused on the video link at Ernie's cabin.

Several keystrokes later Jim exclaimed, "Bingo! Check this out. Officer Crane has officially signed his arrest warrant."

The group watched six minutes of Angoon's finest sifting through Ernie's personal effects. Crane was dressed in civilian clothing, carried a side arm and appeared calm. The affects of his fight with Jim were apparent. He made a call on his cell phone, and shifted his attention to the shelf where the cookie tin had been. Unable to locate what he was searching for, he pulled a small, dark object from his shirt pocket and placed it behind a photograph of Ernie and his late wife hanging on the wall. Crane took a final look around and left on the motorcycle that had been parked next to his Winnebago.

Audra began, "Why is he constantly doing weird things? What could he possibly want?"

"Yeah, what's this jerk doing in Angoon?" added Danny.

Looking at Ernie, Jim replied, "Perhaps Ernie can answer that."

The old man shrugged his shoulders. "Beats me. What happens now that he's swallowed the bait?"

"Before we decide, let's listen to what's going on inside the Winnebago."

Bennett switched to the audio link and listened to an earlier conversation Crane had with someone on his cell phone. They could only hear his side of the conversation and had no idea who he was talking with or what was being said by the other person.

"Hey man, it's Rich. Fuck no, things couldn't get much worse. I just got my ass kicked by the old man's friend, Bennett. He broke my nose, split my hand open and I've got a goose egg on the back of my head.

— I don't know, but he's *not* a businessman from Denver

— He fights like he's been trained for "The Octagon." This fucker's got serious moves.

— Maybe I got a little carried away, but you instructed me to get the information and control the situation in Angoon. I operate from a position of strength, that's all.

— Hey, fuck you! I can handle myself. I'm telling you, he's not what he puts on to be. Use your assets to find out who this guy is.

— Jim Bennett from Denver. The guy with the log home facing Chatham.

— Impossible. Nobody knows about us

— I tried entering his place but it was locked up. Then a fucking bear appeared from nowhere and scared the shit out of me. I had to fire a round into the air to scare him off. I got the hell out of there before someone checked out the gunshot.

— Yeah, the new boat came in today but I doubt I'll get much time on it. The Clan will probably fire my ass unless I can come up with some bullshit story. Maybe I was searching for drugs and booze coming in on the plane. If I act humble and apologize, they might keep me on.

— Serious? When do we leave?

— Fuck'n A! Civilization, restaurants and titty bars. How long will we be there?

— Man, I can't wait.

— The old coot swallowed my bear story, so he's staying at Bennett's house

— Nope, I found nothing to connect him

—When we're done talking, I'll ride down there and take another look around

— You really want to know what I think. Your information sucks! It's nothing more than rumors. There's no connection, otherwise he wouldn't be living like a fucking bum

— I'd need less than an hour with him

— Suppose you're right, then what?

— Fuck that, I won't go to prison for your shit. You do it.

— That's impossible with Bennett around. Let's try tricking him into talking.

— Yeah, I've got two more. The other one's set.

— Alright, I'm on it. I'll save the last one for Bennett. If I have problems or stumble across anything, I'll call you, otherwise we'll talk on the plane."

That concluded the call. They could hear Crane rummaging around his RV, followed by the door closing. Moments later a motorcycle could be heard starting up and going away, down the hill.

Jim looked at Ernie. "Alright partner. There's something going on here that you're not telling me. What are these guys after?"

"Christ, Jim, I don't know. If I did, I'd tell ya."

"People don't break into someone's house and plant bugs without reason. They're after something you have. What is it? Information about your past? Maybe something in that cookie tin?"

Audra interrupted. "Hold on a minute, Dad. Stop interrogating him; you're not in the Army anymore. If Ernie says he doesn't know, then let it be."

Ernie followed. "My past is the same as it is today. Takin' each day as it comes. As for the tin, it's filled with sentimental items I've had for over sixty years. Crane doesn't want my old trinkets. I'll show ya everything that's in it after you search Whitewater."

Jim knew Ernie was lying, and that Crane wanted that cookie tin. Avoiding a confrontation, he offered, "Sorry Ernie. Audra's right, I can get abrasive."

"It's OK Jim. Sounds as if Crane's plannin' a trip. Where ya s'pose he's going?"

"I haven't the foggiest, but I bet he's going with Rigby. Soon we'll know what he wants, then use his audio bug against him."

Danny walked over to where his dad was sitting on the couch, stood behind him and began massaging Jim's shoulders. "Good idea Pop, now you're talking. Feed him false information through his own bug. This'll be a fun vacation."

Jim closed his eyes and tilted his head forward as Danny moved to the thick of his neck. The massage felt wonderful.

Jim murmured, "We need to be careful. Crane's dangerous and has an accomplice. Ernie, you need to remain here until we're certain it's safe for you to go home — agreed?"

"I ain't gonna argue. Maybe we can all go treasure huntin' tomorrow. I don't feel safe bein' here alone."

Jim nodded. "Meantime, I want you to think about what they're after. No matter how obscure the idea may be, you need to share it with me — I'm trying to protect us."

Ernie said, "I'll do my best."

Danny stopped the massage and lightened the conversation by opening a second bottle of champagne. "Let's have another glass of bubbly. Here's to a great day of fishing tomorrow and the answers to all of life's riddles. Soon, I need to hit the sack. I was up late last night and need some Z's."

After the group retired for the evening, Jim's cell phone rang. Caller ID indicated Hilda Koostaha was calling. Jim considered the bug located on Hilda's phone box, then answered, "Good evening Hilda. How are things?"

There was a long pause. "Uh — fine. How'd ya know it was me callin'?"

"Caller ID."

"I need to get that for my phone. Say Mr. Bennett, I'm in a meetin' with Mel and a couple other elders. I understand ya had another run-in with the village idiot. We called the pilot and he told us his version. Mel spoke to Billy Thompson too. They both said Crane picked a fight with ya, so ya taught him some manners. First off, are ya OK?"

"I'm quite well, thanks."

"I'm glad to hear that. Secondly, will you be pressin' charges against him?"

"I've yet to decide. It depends on his future behavior."

"Do you plan on holdin' the Clan responsible for his actions?"

"Absolutely not! He's the one that got hurt, not me."

"You're a tolerant man, Mr. Bennett — more tolerant than us elders. We agreed he ain't worth keepin' on. We're gonna fire him and send him packin'."

Jim's mind raced —he needed Crane to remain in Angoon long enough to flush out his partner. "Could you wait another day or two? Suspend him while you perform a formal investigation and document things. That way you avoid wrongful discharge claims."

"That makes sense. I'll give the idea to the elders."

"Excellent. It's in everyone's best interest to have a formal investigation, where everything's open and in writing. It also enables him to explain his side of things."

"Very well. I didn't expect ya to stick up for him. I'll keep ya informed of our final decision —thank ya for your understanding. Good night Mr. Bennett."

The house was silent. Jim stared out his vaulted glass windows toward Chatham. He was disappointed by Ernie's stonewalling. He sensed something Ernie knew or possessed was behind Crane and his accomplice's actions. They were deadly serious about something. He wanted the biometric reports he'd requested. With any luck, he'd soon know who Rigby was and possibly what he wanted. Jim's mind was tightly wound and racing as he tried to understand recent events, in particular, Crane's telephone call.

Everyone but Jim slept and darkness finally overtook the protracted daylight. Convinced it was dark enough to proceed, Jim entered his bedroom and retrieved a metal suitcase from behind the false panel in his bedroom closet. He quickly changed into camouflaged clothing. He applied a thin coat of lamp black to his face and hands, strapped the Desert Eagle to his hip and walked outside. The former operative quickly worked his way up the rocky coast toward Angoon. In 20 minutes, he reached the water tower overlooking Angoon. Several dogs barked in the distance as he scaled the tower's ladder. Only a few yard lights illuminated the sleepy village, as Jim looked toward Crane's Winnebago. After ten minutes of calibrating a control panel inside of his briefcase, he closed the lid and murmured, "OK asshole, let's dance."

The former colonel silently maneuvered through Angoon back to the rocky coastline. Within sight of home, he sat on a boulder overlooking the water to think things out. He breathed deeply and several owls hooted in the distant timber. After several minutes it came to him. Convinced he knew what was going on, Jim smiled and returned home. He immediately went to bed, and slept better than he had in days.

Trinidad, California - Evening

Frank Reid and Rusty Miller stepped into the van. Helen was busy at the control panel. It was thirty minutes until the upcoming call, and she connected a small receiver to the cell phone in order to record the conversation. The three went over their plan one final time. Rusty — posing as Gary Wiser — would tell Al to go to the Bayshore Mall in Eureka. Outside of the mall pet store was a bank of public telephones. The phone closest to the store would ring, and Al would be given final instructions. This afforded the crew opportunity to see if Al was alone and what he looked like. The final drop point would be outside of Weddell's warehouse.

The old man informed Rusty of Catherine's recollection about Anton Keller, the illegitimate son of Karl Obert. Rusty's intuition told him that Al was more than likely Keller. "Helen, run an INTERPOL and FBI profile for Anton Keller from northern Germany. I need photos if available."

Helen contacted the D.C. office to fast-track Keller's file. She was directly linked with two agents at the Seattle airport. No passengers from the early Juneau flight connected to Redding or Sacramento. Two passengers were headed to San Francisco but both were female. The afternoon flight was due to arrive within an hour. The Redding agents were instructed to watch for private jets as well as incoming commercial flights. So far, nothing was coming together.

At 4:00 p.m., the phone rang. Helen immediately began tracing the caller's location. Rusty was calm as he answered. "I'm all ears."

"Mr. Wiser?"

"Yep."

"I've had a slight snag on my end. My partner won't authorize me to pay anything without proof of goods. As a show of good faith we need something — anything that demonstrates the information you possess is of value to us. It's imperative that we clearly understand your value."

"Where are you now?"

"I can't divulge my location but I assure you I'm close."

Helen looked at Rusty and shook her head. She scribbled "Sitka" on a note pad.

"You lying shit bag — you never left and don't have my money."

"That's not true. I've got a quarter million with me but can't release anything without an adequate demonstration of value."

"Fuck your value crap — fuck you, and fuck your partner. How does the name Keller strike you? I know more than you can possibly imagine. I'm getting my own crew to shake down the Olsens and find the gold myself."

There was dead silence on the phone. Rusty wondered if he overplayed his hand. He looked at Helen, asking with his eyes, "Are we still connected?" She nodded.

After what seemed an eternity, Al responded, "Did Weddell give you that name?"

"Fuck you. I'm done talking — hasta la vista."

"Wait, wait! Please wait. Don't hang up. I believe you have what we need, but my partner's skeptical. He'll kill me if I pay for worthless information. What if I raise my own capital and we throw in together — fifty-fifty partners. I'll pay you $200,000 up front, bankroll the operation and we'll share any gold we find. All you need to do is supply me with the information and a two man crew."

"What about your partner?"

"Like you said before, fuck my partner. I'm not married to him. If he's not prepared to take a risk, then he's out."

"When will I get the bread?"

"I can have the cash within twenty-four hours. We'll meet in two days. I'll return my partner's money and tell him the sample you provided was worthless."

"Who pays my crew?"

"We offer them ten percent of anything we get plus a meager salary — maybe
a hundred thousand."

"Now you're talking. I'll assemble my guys. I expect a call in a day to confirm
that we're on. We'll meet in two days. That's your drop dead date. Otherwise I'm
proceeding without you."

"Perfect. I won't let you down Mr. Wiser. I'll call tomorrow at 2:00 p.m. We'll
meet in two days at a place of your choosing."

"I'm warning you, don't fuck with me. You already owe me a boatload of money
and you've stood me up. If you piss me off, my gang will fuck you bad."

"I'm being sincere. When this is over, we'll both be extremely wealthy."

"Call me tomorrow or else. Got it?"

"Yes."

"Goodbye."

Helen was ecstatic. "He's a big fat liar with his pants on fire. He's not in
Sacramento and he's not in Juneau. Juneau is simply the strongest translator in his
area. I triangulated his position between three translators in the Sitka area. He's
somewhere between the three, definitely on the water. I've narrowed it down to a
twenty-square-mile area east of Sitka; really remote."

"Can you ping his location right now?"

Before she could answer came the "thump —thump —thump" of Henry's helicopter returning from Sacramento. Once the chopper landed, she responded. "I
tried after the previous call. He doesn't have a 911 default on his phone, so the
only time I can track him is when he's calling or has his phone turned on. I'll contact Seattle and have them keep a 24/7 scan for his phone. If he turns it on and
uses it, we'll triangulate the location."

"What about hacking his SIM card or IMSI code?"

Helen shook her head. "I tried. He's got a TMSI module on his phone."

"What the hell's that?"

"Temporary Mobile Subscriber Identity module — it randomly changes
his IMSI code so we can't hack his SIM card. With a TDMA signal interceptor within four hundred meters of his phone, I could hack the module so a cell

phone of our choice would ring whenever he made a call. We could also turn on his phone whenever we want — it's the same technology used by the FBI and Homeland Security to monitor suspected terrorists."

"Christ," Rusty said. "If I were within four hundred meters of him, I'd shoot the son-of-a-bitch. Isn't there another way to hack into his phone?"

"Not with the TMSI module he has."

Rusty said, "So this guy's either a techno-geek or someone set the module up for him."

"Roger that, Red."

Rusty shook his head in disgust. He told Helen to contact the airport agents and have them stand down. He also asked her to locate all cruise lines operating around the triangulated area in case Al was a passenger. It was time for him and Frank to have another private discussion.

The two men stepped outside the van and walked toward the helipad. "Things didn't go as planned," Rusty admitted, "but we have an opportunity here. We'll go over maps and satellite images of the triangulated area. I'm convinced these guys are already searching for the gold, but like a needle in a haystack. We can assess the area by sending two agents as tourist fishermen. If he uses his phone while they're there, they can charter a chopper to recon any boat he's on. If he doesn't use his phone, at least we'll have a heads up of the area. He sounded sincere and I bet he shows up as promised, so let's use this time to develop a foolproof plan to capture him. If we're successful, that leaves his partner and crew. There may be light at the end of the tunnel."

Frank smiled. "Excellent. I know that area like the back of my only hand. We can go over the maps and send a few agents on a fishing trip. Do we have any other assets at our disposal that might help locate Keller and his partner?"

"What's needed is real-time military satellite imagery for when he calls or uses his phone. We could immediately GPS the transmission source, then take satellite pictures."

"How do we accomplish that?"

"You don't unless you know someone in the Pentagon or CIA."

Reid asked, "Do you or anyone at Dark Star have those connections?"

"No, but there's a person I know of who can access satellites. I haven't talked to him in years. He's a private sector contractor with incredible connections. His security clearance with the CIA is higher than 99 percent of top military brass and field agents. He can zoom in on any coordinate we provide and constantly track any target."

"What are our chances of having him work for us?"

Rusty shook his head. "Slim. He sells top-secret military computer programing to the Pentagon, CIA and FBI. There's no reason for him to want to work for us.

Knowing him, he'll balk unless we specify why we need his resources. Once he knows, he'll tell us to take a hike."

"Who is this man?"

"Colonel James Bennett, a retired hybrid of Army Delta and CIA. He commanded my Delta Troop — a West Point grad. Airborne Ranger. Special Forces operative and so on. I worked under him as an assault member and we trained Contra death squads in Central America. He was recruited into the CIA's Special Operations Group and became their top agent. This guy orchestrated the take down of the Sandinistas, Noriega and Escobar. Our team was about to poison Castro, but Clinton squashed the mission. He's the 'real deal' and has more contacts than anyone I can think of."

"After leaving the CIA, he formed a company that provides the government with software systems for high tech weapons and secure communication links. He's way beyond the capabilities of Dark Star."

The old man asked, "When can you contact him?"

"That's the tough part, because he's insulated. The last time I tried reaching him, it took him over two weeks to return my call. Besides, if I were able to reach him, he'd never discuss details over a cell unless I had an encrypted phone identical to his. He'll insist on a face-to-face meeting. But let me see what I can do."

Frank shook his head. "This is a bad idea. If he's as connected as you say, he'll use his assets to discover things about Henry and myself — I can't involve any more people unless it's unavoidable."

"OK. Let's send Whitey and Helen to Sitka tomorrow morning. She has the tools and resources to intercept the call and Whitey has the expertise to track him down. We're betting on the fact that he'll be calling from the same area so it's a calculated risk, but if he does call from there, the payoff would be enormous."

"How can you pull this off with only two people?"

"We'll have your pilot Jeff Elliott fly them there and tag along. He'll fly the surveillance chopper. I'll arrange for a rental van when they arrive in Sitka. Helen will run surveillance while Whitey and Jeff provide transport and muscle. When Helen identifies the phone's location, they take off to the source."

The old man shook his head. "It sounds unreasonable to think that two operatives and my pilot can handle such a huge undertaking."

"They'll handle the situation."

Reid asked, "Will Helen and Whitey agree to leave on such short notice?"

"They'll enjoy the change of scenery. Besides, they're getting paid beaucoup bucks."

"I don't agree with the amount of personnel, but go ahead and put the wheels in motion. I also insist that Helen be in charge of the operation. She's a quick thinker."

Rusty nodded. "She's my first choice as mission leader too.

The old man reluctantly acquiesced. "Alright. Make it happen. I'll button up loose ends here and head home to Port Angeles. William can drive the limo while you, Helen, Whitey and I take my jet. How much time do you need to finish here?"

Rusty paused for a moment. "I can have things completed within three or four hours. Dan Cranston will be in charge of operations at the estate including the removal of Henry's staff. The yacht will be ready within an hour and your captain should arrive from Seattle by 6:00 p.m."

"Splendid, I'd like the yacht taken to Port Angeles before going on the cruise. It's only a thirty-hour trip to my home by ship and provides me with time to think about what we're doing with Henry's staff. I'm not convinced that a protracted sojourn on such a small vessel is in their best interest. When the staff arrives at Port Angeles, they can stay at my estate until I've decided on a proper course of action."

"Whatever you say, Mr. Reid. If you're more comfortable that way, by all means do it."

"Good. As for returning, I'd like to swing by Henry's grave before we depart. I never had the opportunity to pay my respects or say goodbye."

"I'll have Whitey and a blocker car follow your limo. When you're done at the cemetery, we'll take the chopper to Sacramento to pick up your jet."

A strong gust of wind tore across the grounds overlooking the ocean. The men turned their backs to it and walked back to Henry's home without saying a word.

CHAPTER FOUR

June 11 — Angoon — Morning of a Big Day

Jim Bennett awoke to the smell of bacon frying. It was 8:00, and he'd overslept. The skies were overcast and rainy. The barometer had fallen considerably, forecasting bad weather. He poured a cup of coffee and sat at the kitchen table.

Danny and Audra were cooking breakfast while Ernie showered. Jim listened as his children updated each other on their lives. He appreciated that they got along so well. Even as children, they never really fought, just jostled and joke with each other. Jim knew this trait came from their mother, not him.

Ernie entered the room, poured some coffee and sat across from Jim. He placed his cookie tin and Luger onto the table.

Danny announced, "It's farmer's omelet and bacon. Toast is coming right up. Hey Ernie, what's up with that pistol? Are you expecting Bin Laden or maybe Crane for breakfast?"

"When we're done eatin', I wanna show you kids something. It's about the treasure hunt we talked about last night."

"Cool. If we find an extra hundred grand or two lying around, I'll be able to pay off my patent attorney."

Ernie smiled. "One never knows, you might find a fortune."

After breakfast, Jim cleared the table while Ernie showed off his Luger to Audra and Danny. He explained the circumstances behind its discovery, and produced the Nazi medals. Audra held little interest in the artifacts, but Danny was totally immersed in Ernie's story. Ernie promised to divulge another tidbit, once the hunt in Whitewater Bay had concluded. Jim used the opportunity to convince Ernie into returning the Luger and the tin to his cabin before heading out. That way, if Crane returned, they would know if he was after those items. Ernie agreed, providing the tin was emptied of its contents.

Everyone was anxious to get their day underway. Jim retrieved a small inflatable raft, two metal detectors, a shovel, rubber boots and rain gear from his shed.

He made a point of taking the Desert Eagle and a short-barreled, tactical shotgun along. From his experience, brown bear encounters in remote tidal flats were common, especially during salmon runs.

Jim engaged his home surveillance system and led the group to the Humvee. He carried an aluminum attaché case in his left hand and a small cooler in his right. After returning the Luger and cookie tin to Ernie's cabin, they took off for the marina. Audra captained the boat as her father sat back and operated a small control panel located inside of the attaché case. He attached a cell phone to the panel, then walked to the boat's deck, leaving the case inside the cabin. Jim produced a second phone from his pocket and dialed. Somewhere, another phone rang.

"Hello."

"Is this Officer Crane?"

"Yes it is, My caller ID says 'private.' Who is this?"

"Jim Bennett."

There was a prolonged silence, then, "Yeah, what do you want?"

"I'd like to apologize for injuring you yesterday. I should have used greater restraint. I'm calling to see if you're OK. Perhaps we can get together and try to reach some sort of an understanding that's mutually beneficial."

"I'm fine and I don't think it's in anyone's best interest to try to strike up a relationship until things blow over."

"The Clan contacted me last night and informed me that they were prepared to terminate you; however, I recommended that they reconsider and try to work things out."

"So what's your point?"

"My point is that this is a small community and we need to get along. If Angoon elects to continue your employment, I'm prepared to bury the hatchet and move on. I'm hoping that we can coexist without further problems."

"Yeah, whatever. Look, I've got shit to do. Goodbye."

Jim smiled as he reentered the boat's cabin. After checking the briefcase, he removed the attached cell phone and placed it into a top pocket. Danny looked quizzical.

Jim grinned and said, "It was a nothing call. Let's get out of here."

The weather in Chatham Strait was unusually rough, with three-foot seas coming from the south. Jim asked Audra to take the passage between Killisnoo and Admiralty Islands in order to avoid as much rough water as possible. As the boat approached the fishing lodge on Killisnoo, he noticed the owner standing on the main dock. Jim asked Audra to stop by the dock so he could speak with him. Danny tied off the boat while Jim approached the short, heavy-set man cleaning trash from a large catamaran.

The two men shook hands. "Hey Dick," Jim began, "how's life treating you these days?"

"Good —how about you?"

"Quite well, thanks. How's the fishing been?"

"Not good. Kings aren't in yet. We've got eight people staying here and they've only boated one King all week — can't seem to locate them. Big halibut are too damn deep for most people and unless you're in five hundred feet of water, you'll catch nothing but small chickens. I'm guessing the water temperature is still too cold."

"Give it another week or ten days and you'll be cleaning more fish than you can handle."

Dick nodded. "That's how it usually works. Looks like you and the kids are going fishing. Plan on trying for Kings?"

"Yes, but it's rough out there today. We'll stick to the southern shorelines so we won't get blown off the water. Say, is Mr. Rigby around? I'd like to ask him something."

The heavy-set man shook his head. "He took a float plane to Hoonah three days ago. Said he'd be back in a couple days."

"Can I leave a message for him? It's important that I talk with him when he returns."

Dick pointed to a red cabin behind the dining hall. "He's renting the red unit over there. You want me to get a message to him?"

"I don't want to interfere with your work. If it's alright with you, I'll slide a note under his door."

"Knock yourself out — saves me the walk."

The two men said their farewells, and Jim returned to his boat and opened his attaché case. Danny took a look inside and knew his father was up to something. Jim sat at the table and wrote a short note in a spiral notebook:

Dear Mr. Rigby:
I'd like to talk with you regarding your current project. I'd also like to purchase a copy of your prior book. Please call me at 907-788-3121.
Yours,
Jim Bennett

Tearing the page from the notebook, he folded it and proceeded to the red cabin. The wind was blowing hard as he walked onto the porch of Rigby's rental unit. Bennett produced the bug detector from his shirt pocket and scanned the porch. Rigby had no surveillance equipment in operation, so he tried the door.

To his surprise, it opened. He stuck his head into the small cabin and took a quick, careful look around. The inside was unusually neat and orderly. Jim noticed that the front door's interior trim was warped and pulled away from the jam. He squeezed a dab of epoxy onto the backside of a miniature audio receiver and stuck it behind the top of the door's trim. Satisfied, he placed the folded note between the door and its jam, then closed it shut.

Three pine trees to the side of the dining hall swayed in the wind as he walked toward the dock. Jim stopped and fastened the receiving unit to the trunk of the largest tree. After initiating the unit, he calmly returned to the boat. When Ernie asked what he was doing, he shrugged his shoulders and said, "Taking care of loose ends."

Jim turned on his laptop. Within a minute, he nodded, turned it off and asked Audra to take the boat into Hood Bay. She obliged her father by opening the throttle as soon as the boat cleared the lodge's dock. Ten minutes later, the boat approached the summer home of Vicente Santos. A large yellow catamaran was secured to the dock. Several Tlingit workers were fastening thick planks to the new dock. Jim asked Audra to turn the boat southeast and away from the compound.

Jim checked his scanner for any incoming signals. Faint signatures told him that Santos had some type of surveillance system in operation. Jim asked Audra to swing the boat wide to the south in order to place a long peninsula between them and Santos' house. The peninsula blocked the workers and any cameras from viewing his boat. A narrow cove provided shelter from the wind and access to the tip of the peninsula. Jim took over the controls from Audra and piloted the boat into the cove, then beached it on the rocky shoreline.

Ernie was watching his movie, not to be disturbed. Jim said to his children, "I'll be back in ten. Sit tight and have some coffee."

Jim attached a rope ladder to the side of his boat and climbed down into knee deep water with a gym bag over his shoulder. After securing the boat to shore, he ran up the bank and into the timber toward the north. Danny looked at Audra, shrugged his shoulders, and jumped into the shallow water and followed his father.

Several minutes later, Danny low crawled into an opening that had an unobstructed view of the house and dock. He had snuck up on his dad.

"What are you up to?" he asked

Though surprised to see Danny, Jim explained. "I'm setting up a video link to my computer. I'm also deploying a cell phone interceptor. As soon as Santos receives a call, I'll infect his phone. Afterwards, every time he receives a call, it'll ring through to my phone. I'll also be able to monitor outgoing calls."

"You can do that?"

"I can."

"Is it legal?"

Jim smiled. "As long as you don't get caught. This is the same system used by the government to track terror cells. I installed the identical set-up on top of Angoon's water tower last night and I hacked Crane's phone when I called him this morning."

Danny asked, "Is that what you were doing when we were leaving the marina?"

"You bet."

Less than a thousand feet separated the dock from Jim and Danny on the peninsula. Jim zipped open the bag and produced the metal attaché case. He removed a black plastic globe and a three pronged antenna. Jim explained to Danny that the black globe was a multi-function video camera with night time infrared capabilities. It operated from a battery pack with hard wiring to a satellite transmitter. After carefully mounting the system with epoxy to a large boulder, Jim took the antenna and low crawled to an adjacent tree. He fastened it to the trunk, then returned to Danny. The metal case contained a built-in computer with an array of electronic meters and a keyboard. Danny watched in awe as his father plugged a cell phone into the array and began typing on the keyboard. Seconds later, Jim dialed the Santos cell phone number given to him by Mel Franks.

"Hello."

"Is this Mr. Santos?"

"Yes, who is this?"

"My name is James Bennett. I have a summer home in Angoon."

"Oh yes — I've heard of you. You're the gentleman with the large log home facing the Strait. What can I do for you?"

"I'm calling to inform you that I had a run in with Officer Crane and that the Clans are considering his termination. I understand that he was hired at your request and that you've purchased a patrol boat for the village. I'm hoping that if the Clans ultimately decide to fire him, perhaps you'd consider allowing them to keep the boat with the understanding that they'd find a suitable replacement within a reasonable time frame."

"Do you represent the Clans of Angoon, Mr. Bennett?"

"No sir — but I am very close with village elders and advise them on occasion."

"As a matter of protocol, I should be having these discussions with Clan members however; I assure you that if they elect to terminate Mr. Crane, I'd support any suitable replacement. My offer for a patrol boat and salary participation will remain intact."

"That's a generous position and I appreciate your support for the natives of Angoon."

"Very well Mr. Bennett — perhaps someday we'll have the opportunity to meet face-to-face. I don't wish to be rude, but I need to cut this conversation short as I have a prior commitment. I'll contact Hilda Koostaha and Mel Franks regarding our conversation."

"Thank you for your time, sir, and have a good day."

Jim closed the case and placed the phone into his top pocket. He told Danny, "Let's go."

"Were you blowing smoke up his ass in order to hack his phone?"

"You bet I was. Now every loose end is wrapped up. Soon, we'll be having fun."

The father and son team hustled back to the boat. They'd been gone for fifteen minutes by the time they returned to the boat. Ernie was still watching his movie when Danny climbed back onboard. Jim pushed the boat into deeper water, climbed on and asked Audra to start the engines. He turned on his laptop and performed a few tests. Danny smiled while looking at the Santos complex on the computer monitor. After explaining to his sister what they'd just done, she smiled, as well. She headed the boat for Whitewater.

Sitka, Alaska - Morning

At 10:00 a.m. the private jet carrying Whitey and Helen began final descent into Sitka. Both mercenaries sat in plush leather recliners as the pilot notified them over the intercom that they'd be landing in twenty minutes. The albino neatly folded an outstretched topo map of Baranof Island that he'd been studying for the past hour while Helen laid back in the comfortable recliner with her eyes closed and an MP-3 player plugged into her ears. Her right foot, fitted with a calf-length black leather boot, kept rhythm to music only she could hear. Tight fitting faded jeans and a tailored black leather jacket rounded out her Euro-rocker look. Whitey reached over and tapped her on the leg, signaling their arrival. She reluctantly opened one eye, and flipped him the bird while he lit a cigarette.

She adjusted the chair into a sitting position and removed her headphones. "Hey, dude. Fire one up for me,"

He handed her a lit Marlboro. "Thought you were trying to quit. I've been studying the maps. Our best option is to position ourselves on the east side of Baranof. There's a large island where we can set up an observation post. We'll have an unobstructed view of Chatham Strait."

"What if our mark decides to call from somewhere else this time?"

"Unless he's within range of our chopper, we're screwed."

She studied the map. "Let's have Jeff sneak onto this ridge system from the south, then we'll set up my equipment overlooking the Strait to the north. If I determine that our target's location is beyond my equipment, we'll fire up the chopper and pinpoint him.

What's our arsenal?"

Whitey said, "One fully automatic M4, two Uzis, three 9-mm autos, six frags and plenty of extra ammo clips."

"That's airy-fairy."

Whitey frowned. "What the hell does that mean?"

She smiled and winked. "Lacking strength — like you."

She looked out the window at the dark clouds and rain streaking across the glass. After shaking her head she asked, "Did you pack rain gear? Otherwise I'm staying in the motel room and watching the telly or perhaps in a pub with a nice warm fireplace. I'm far too old and way too cute for this rainy shit."

"We've got camouflaged slickers and rubber boots. I agree with the cute statement but you're certainly not too old."

"Shit, dude. I'll be thirty in two weeks. I'd planned on being retired by now."

"You're a young pup, so quit bitching. You can start a 401K when this is over. Rusty said he'll give the three of us a hundred grand bonus if we can find Mr. Al. You'd never earn that kind of dough working for Blackwater or Aegis. Besides, you'd be reassigned to Pakistan or Iraq hunting down camel jockeys. That's what happens with PMC's like us."

She shook her head. "Never again. I hate the fucking Mid-east."

Whitey nodded. "Rusty told me he quit Dark Star yesterday and he's working directly for Reid. I'd like to work for him when I return."

Helen shook her head. "There's no job security with that scenario. So Rusty quit Dark Star and is working directly for the old man?"

"That's what he told me yesterday."

Helen stared at the glowing end of her cigarette. "I could freelance and be better off than working for Rusty. Last month, Alpha 5 asked me to work for them in any capacity, but I was noncommittal." She chuckled and said, "Maybe I should start my own gig and hire people like you and Rusty."

Whitey gave her a smirk. "Good luck. It would take a small fortune to get started. If it was so easy, we'd all be doing it. When we arrive in. . . " He stopped talking as several violent bumps rocked the jet.

Jeff Elliott immediately voiced into the intercom, "It's probably a good idea to put on your seat belts. The weather ahead looks rough."

Helen murmured, "I hate this shit."

"As I was trying to say — when we land, a van will be waiting for us inside a private hangar. We'll drive into town, go to our hotel and change clothes. I'm told the hotel has a good restaurant — we'll get a late breakfast. Afterwards, we'll recon the town and act like tourists."

"Good, I'm starving."

As the Gulf Stream approached Japonski Island, rain and strong winds greeted the sleek bird. After landing, the jet taxied to an obscure hangar and parked inside. A yellow and white Bell 212 helicopter sat outside the hangar. Two ground crew closed the large overhead door and assisted the passengers with their baggage.

"Welcome to Alaska," one of the men said. "Your chopper is fueled and ready to go whenever you please. The van has the keys in the ignition and is topped off with fuel. The only road leading from the airport will take you over the bridge onto Baranof Island. Don't blink or you'll miss Sitka. You're staying at the Westmark Lodge, across from the marina. Any questions?"

Helen couldn't resist, "Any pubs near the lodge?"

"Yup. There's a bar inside the lodge and at least four more within walking distance."

"How about clubs. Where are they located?"

The young man frowned. "I don't understand — you mean like Kiwanis or Rotary?"

Helen giggled as Whitey shook his head. "C'mon let's go. We've got work to do."

After checking into the hotel and showering, the trio met in the restaurant. Helen sipped a mug of black coffee and stared out a plate glass window. The wind subsided but it continued raining. She laughed at seeing "reindeer sausage" on the menu and commented that Rudolph must've pissed off Santa Claus.

Whitey unfolded his regional topo map and pointed out the area where he wanted to set-up, then asked Jeff if he could sneak them onto a flat bench directly below the island's summit to avoid detection from the surrounding area.

The former combat pilot responded, "No problem. We'll fly low, just above the trees while crossing Baranof, then drop down to the Strait — maybe 50 feet above the water. I'll turn north and hug the coastline at high speed. The sun will be at our backs so anyone to the north won't see us. When we reach Kelp Bay, here, I'll swing hard to the west and gain enough altitude to clear the trees. We'll be out of sight from anyone to the north. After a mile, I'll turn northeast and climb to your LZ. It'll be fun — just like the old days."

The rain stopped before they finished eating breakfast and blue skies slowly replaced the dark cloud cover. The trio was about to leave when Helen's phone rang.

She answered, "Hey, Red — what's up?"

"Checking to see if everything's a go for our two o'clock call."

"Everything's on schedule. We were about to head to the chopper. We're setting up on top of a mountain overlooking the last GPS coordinates."

"Good choice. Call me at 1:45 to confirm final mission details. I expect to remain connected throughout the call so make certain your phone's fully charged."

Helen shook her head. "Knock the crap off, Red. I'm prepared and you don't need to micromanage me."

"Stop being testy, Ms. Moorcroft, and don't fuck up. Bye."

Helen grabbed the pack of smokes from Whitey's shirt pocket, lit a cigarette and said, "Little Caesar's freaking out again — he's a bloody twit."

Whitey tried to calm her down. "C'mon, let's get to the marina and snoop around. If Al's on a boat, he'll eventually come through this harbor."

A long ramp connected the upper parking area to the docks below. The marina was choked with boats of all sizes, but there was virtually no human activity. The bad weather recently passed kept a majority of people indoors. A lone dock worker emptied chained-up garbage cans into a large-wheeled cart. Helen pointed him out as a possible contact and walked toward him. Jeff asked why not go to the marina office and ask a manager for a manifest.

She smiled. "Never ask a general when you can talk with a corporal. Top brass are never in touch with what's going on in the trenches. They'll end up asking him anyway. Watch. You might learn something."

Helen introduced herself to the man pushing the gondola. She shook hands with him. "Good morning. Do you work these docks every day?"

Talking with the most beautiful woman he'd ever seen made him nervous. "Ye-Yes, ma'am. Ca-can I help you?"

"My name's Helen, what's yours?"

"A-Art W-Welling."

"Relax, Art. If I give you a description of a boat or small ship, will you be able to tell me who the owner is and how to get in touch with him?"

The man settled down and removed his baseball cap. "If he uses this marina, chances are good. Why?"

"Just asking. I might require your services later. I pay handsomely if you're able to help." She gave Art a hundred dollar bill. "Like I said — handsomely."

The man grinned. "I'm here at seven every day and work till late sometimes. If I'm not on the docks, I'm in that building." He pointed to a gray block structure on shore. "I know all the regulars and can get you copies of the manifest and transient registry if you like." He pointed to a different building. "That's where the manifests are kept."

"Can you arrange for rental of a quality fishing boat with gear and sleeping accommodations? No captain. Just the boat. Price is no object. A complete set-up with radar, GPS, and auto-pilot."

"Sure. You want me to contact the owner?"

"Not yet, Art. Perhaps later. Do you have a cell phone so I can reach you after hours?"

Art provided her with his number and they shook hands again. The trio then walked up the ramp to the van. As the pilot drove them to the hangar, Whitey laughed. "Christ, aren't you the crafty one. You had him eating out of your hand."

Dark Fortunes

Jeff pulled the van next to the helicopter and opened the rear doors. Helen and Whitey loaded the chopper while the pilot began his pre-flight check. Clear skies enabled Helen to see the snow-covered volcano, Mount Edgecombe. She stood in amazement, soaking in the landscape, and thought, *This must be the place Mum described.*

She lit another of Whitey's cigarettes and leaned against the hangar. Peering at the distant volcano, Helen resisted hearing her late mother's words. The thought of her dear Mum in bed dying from brain cancer was almost too much to deal with. Her words poked at Helen as she gazed up at Edgecombe, then looked at her feet on the wet tarmac. Finally she allowed the past to flow into her head.

Helen was in tears, sitting beside the thin, bald woman with dark sunken eyes. Her devoted mother spoke softly. "Don't despair, child — soon, I'll be at peace. One benefit of my illness is that I've had many visions lately, a good thing. I believe that this cancer serves a greater purpose — survival of you and your brother, Wayne. Listen carefully Helen, because your life depends on what I'm about to say."

Helen stroked her mothers forehead and whispered, "Shhh — try to sleep."

"You're not listening. This is important."

Helen smiled. "OK Mum, I'm listening."

"Soon you'll encounter difficulties in the Mid-East. Two friends will face death at the hands of men with swords. If you're concealed and act with courage, you'll save them. Be brave and no harm will come to you or your friends. That's my first vision."

Helen now listened intently because she'd just gotten word from her employer that she may be sent to Baghdad. She hadn't told her mother and wondered if, in fact, she *could* see the future.

She asked, "Did Wayne tell you that I might be going to Iraq?"

"No. I told you. I saw it in a dream. Let me continue." She sipped water through a straw. "Years later you'll visit a land where snow-covered volcanoes loom to the heavens from icy seas. This is a mystical land where thundering waterfalls merge with deep waters. It's beautiful and captivating, but it's also filled with danger and death. You will be surrounded by evil people consumed by greed; a confusing time when friends become enemies and perceived enemies are your friends. Survival depends upon clear thinking and swift action. When danger surrounds you, ask Wayne to be there and together you'll triumph. While . . ."

Whitey interrupted Helen's reverie. "Hey Ms. Moorcroft, can you hear me? Wake up, we've got work to do."

Helen snapped back to the present. She wiped her eyes with tissue. "I'm fine — just thinking about my Mum, that's all. I had no idea Alaska was this beautiful — I'm impressed. Is all of Alaska like this?"

Seeing Helen's tears, Whitey patted her shoulder. "It is —you OK?"

Helen nodded. Changing the subject, he asked, "Care to go clubbing tonight or sight-seeing?"

Helen considered her mother's words. "Screw clubbing and that worthless life-style, let's roll."

The pilot motioned the duo into the chopper while warming up the turbo. Warm oil began flowing throughout the motor and moments later he started the engine, then engaged the blades. A rhythmic "thump-thump -thump" beat deeply into their chests. After achieving suitable oil pressure and tower clearance, the white-and-yellow chopper rose vertically, then banked left over Sitka Sound. Helen remained glued to the window as the mercenaries headed southeast toward the bright sun.

Jeff flew treetop level over Baranof Island as promised. After cresting the midpoint, he hovered to assess potential boat traffic on Chatham Strait. Five miles south, a cruise ship headed toward Petersburg and Wrangle. Another small boat was ten miles to the east, leaving Whitewater Bay. No other vessels were visible. Convinced that he could proceed undetected, Jeff dropped the helicopter's nose and sped toward the Strait. The pilot performed the sequence he'd discussed during breakfast, and within minutes the chopper had landed on the bench, two hundred yards below the summit of Catherine Island. Jeff quickly cut the engine to avoid unnecessary noise and possible detection.

The trio unloaded two suitcases filled with gear and armed themselves. The summit was near, but the climb proved to be wet and exhausting. As they approached the top, the group low-crawled to an unobstructed view of the Peril- Chatham intersection. To the north, three boats were visible, clearly within the GPS zone from the last call. Whitey set up a high powered spotting scope while Helen and Jeff unloaded the cases. Helen set up two small satellite dishes on tripods and a peculiar looking antenna system, then attached them with coaxial cables to the first suitcase. With a headset on, she began working at a laptop computer.

Five minutes later Helen said, "I'm golden — what's up with these targets?"

Whitey whispered, "The large white one's a NOAA research vessel, *Oregon II*. Another's a commercial fishing boat —registration number 64839, the *Catchum*. The third is a catamaran — I can't make out its number but the name is *Salsa*. A white sport fishing boat is moving into view from behind the ship — number 72132 — but I can't see its name but it looks like a Bertram. The *Oregon II* seems to be anchored."

"Jeff, keep an eye on the four targets," she ordered. "Whitey, contact Red."

The two men changed positions while Helen focused on her duties. Al would be calling within thirty minutes.

Port Angeles, Washington — Frank's House — Morning

Frank Reid entered his corner library and pulled back the flower-patterned drapes, exposing a spectacular view of Sequim Bay and the Strait of Juan de Fuca. Modest in comparison to Henry's estate, the six bedroom mansion on eighty prime waterfront acres provided Frank with a casual and elegant lifestyle. Proximity to the Sequim marina and Port Angeles airstrip afforded the former pilot immediate access to the outside world. His nearest neighbor was Gus Olsen, who owned an equally impressive abode. Though his children lived far away and his wife had died years earlier, Frank never felt alone because of Gus and his wife Lena.

He became consumed with thoughts of his former partner and best friend while pacing the library. Distant events bothered him, but he finally sank into a soft, comfortable couch. He stared blankly at his robotic arm as concern for his family and friends nearly overwhelmed him. The distraught old man desperately wanted to put an end to this.

A light knock on the library door announced the arrival of Gus. They hugged, then sat next to each other.

Tears welled into Frank's eyes as he spoke. "It's a terrible mess I've gotten us into Gus. Why didn't we fight this battle in our youth?"

Gus shook his head. "The threat was non-existent when we were young. Besides, you didn't cause this to happen — relax before you have a stroke, for God's sake. Dark Star caught the men responsible for Henry's death, and we remain anonymous. We couldn't ask for more."

"I want the bastards behind the men we've captured. It won't end until they're dead."

"It'll be resolved shortly. The wheels are in motion. Let Dark Star do their job."

Frank was about to respond when there was a loud knock on the door. Rusty entered to update the two cousins.

"We're rolling, gentlemen. Whitey, Helen and Jeff are in Sitka. They'll be in position within an hour and Mr. Al will be calling in slightly over two hours. We'll either capture him today or lure him to Eureka tomorrow. Either way, greed will be his downfall."

Frank looked at the ceiling. "It's not him I'm worried about. How many others are looming on the horizon?"

"As I suggested before, not many — maybe two or three. After interrogating Al, we'll know what we're up against. Until then, don't get upset over things you can't control."

Gus added, "By the end of the day, you'll be relieved. I've a gut feeling we're going to experience something like destiny —we can't help but win."

Rusty continued, "The yacht is making excellent progress. They'll be here very late tonight, which presents us with a minor problem, Unless our Sitka team captures Al today, we need to be in Eureka tomorrow. How do we handle Henry's staff?"

Reid answered, "I'll remain here and take care of the staff with Dark Star. You can take care of business in California. I want every shred of information possible, then eliminate that son-of-a-bitch. No prisoners — understood?"

Rusty nodded. "Yes. Helen's replacement is outside. Will you join us for the two o'clock call?"

"Absolutely, I wouldn't miss this for anything. Are you satisfied with the security situation both here and with our families?"

"Please relax, Mr. Reid — everything's going as planned."

"I'm not sharing your optimism. Come get me before the call."

Rusty left the library to the two cousins. Gus offered to play a game of two-hand Sheepshead which Frank eagerly accepted. It reminded him of playing with Rudy, Andy and Günter on the XXI. Soon both men sat laughing and carrying on as if they were teenagers once again. Time passed, and the two men were interrupted by a knock on the door. Rusty peeked inside to say they were approaching the expected call.

Angoon —Mid Morning

Ten minutes of hard running positioned the *Sojourn* at the confluence of Hood Bay and Chatham Strait. Jim and Danny changed into dry clothes as Audra sat in the cushioned captain's chair piloting the cruiser. Large breaking waves pounded the boat, demanding Audra's undivided attention. She was an experienced operator and enjoyed the challenge of heavy seas. The dry, heated cabin provided the group with more-than-adequate protection from another incoming squall. After turning the corner into Whitewater Bay, the water settled considerably. The bay's southern mountains and shore offered a much-appreciated windbreak. Audra reduced speed while approaching the inner reaches of the bay.

It was 11:00 a.m., two hours before slack tide. Several Kings were observed chasing herring near the inlet. Rather than risk taking his boat into the inlet during the end of the incoming tide, Jim decided to set up two mooching rods and fish for the salmon. He was banking on better weather and slack tide conditions before entering the inlet.

As soon as the first mooching rig was set, a vicious strike peeled out the heavy line. The reel hissed, spitting vapor into the air as Danny jumped to the rod and began fighting the huge fish. Audra placed the boat into neutral and Danny yelled, "Wooo-hooo!"

The King made three deep runs before finally breaking the surface. It danced on its tail, then spit the hook. Danny yelled, "Damn it!"

Jim soothed his son's frustration. "Chill out. Look in the water. There must be dozens of salmon surrounding the boat. Dick at Killisnoo Lodge thinks it's too early for Kings — that's a crock. Get the other pole into the water." He turned to Audra. "Make large, slow circles."

Within minutes, another King was peeling line, but Danny remained silent while fighting the fish. Audra placed the boat in neutral and watched the battle. Though smaller than the first, it was definitely a nice fish. Five minutes later, the King was on its side next to the boat and Jim landed the twelve pounder and threw it into an ice filled cooler. Danny took over the controls of the boat, and Audra tried her hand at fishing.

The commotion had spooked the schooling fish into deeper water, so the rods were returned their holders, and Danny maneuvered the boat away from the inlet. Ten minutes later, one of the rods bent into the dark abyss as the line peeled furiously toward the shoreline. Audra panicked and jerked the pole back to set the hook, pulling it out of the salmon's mouth. Before she could even complain, the other pole bent, and line peeled from the reel. Jim encouraged her to play the fish without setting the hook. Eight minutes later, she pulled a 20-pounder to the boat.

Jim netted the King and Audra exclaimed, "Now that's what I call fishing!"

Ernie smiled. "Somethin' tells me they're havin' a good time. That one's a lot bigger than Danny's. They like to needle each other but they get along really well. You should be proud."

They stowed the poles in the overhead racks and Jim turned his attention to the inlet. The wind had slowed considerably. The sun was breaking through the clouds to the southeast, but it afforded little comfort since the weather above them was dark and dismal. Though it was an hour before slack tide, Jim felt confident that he could safely navigate the narrow inlet. The twelve-foot-wide boat wound through the channel and into the small interior lake. The depth finder indicated a fifty-foot-deep flat bottom. Jim slowly approached the northeast shore, where Ernie had found the body. The bottom came up rapidly, so he anchored off. Minutes later, the raft was loaded and being rowed to shore by Danny. Ernie remained aboard, watching an old western in the comfort of the well heated cabin.

Reaching the shallow flats, Jim jumped in and pulled the raft onto the muddy shore. He slung the short shotgun over his shoulder and made his way up a hillside thick with grass. Danny wore the Desert Eagle on his right hip and carried a metal detector, as did Audra. After discussing their search pattern, the trio proceeded with their hunt. Jim kept them parallel to the shore, swinging the detectors in overlapping straight lines so as not to miss anything. Mosquitoes swarmed them, but the rain gear and rubber boots kept them at bay. Danny's detector screeched and garnered everyone's attention, but it turned out to be a section of frayed steel cable.

A half-hour later, two rusty oil cans and several links of broken chain rounded out their first search grid. The trio focused their efforts to the west since the steep area above them had been logged off. They agreed that if anything had been there, it would have been destroyed during the logging operation. Besides, the logged area was choked with devil's club with its poison barbs. A tedious half hour passed without a single hit. Jim pointed out a sow and cub brown bear at the far end of the opposite shoreline. The mother was awaiting the upcoming salmon spawn, and the Bennetts silently watched the two bears saunter off to the east. Jim would watch their movements to keep safe.

The trio moved west into sparse timber where a brook with ice cold water rushed from the higher elevations and merged into the tidal flat. They were about to call it quits when Audra's detector gave a flurry of faint screeches. Jim carefully dug into the wet mossy dirt and recovered a dark metallic button-shaped object. Scouring the wet dirt yielded three additional buttons. Danny took one to the stream, cleaned off the mud, opened his raincoat and furiously rubbed it on his shirt. The polishing brought out the dull luster of oxidized silver.

He ran back to the others. "Check this out — a miniature skull made of silver. I think they're coat buttons."

After that, the trio had renewed interest and a sense of accomplishment. The buttons were all imprinted with the shape of a human skull. Jim figured the buttons were from the shirt or uniform of the torso that Ernie had found. The buttons were fifty yards west of where Ernie discovered the canister.

Jim commented, "These aren't trinkets from an American G.I. These came from the body of a Nazi soldier; most likely an officer. Let's see what else is here."

Both children scanned the area near the previous find, and Danny's detector went off. The screech was faint but audible. Audra continued searching while Jim and Danny uncovered their prize; a green-stained lower human jaw bone, including teeth. Three silver fillings had triggered the detector.

The trio swept the surrounding area. Audra's detector sounded off as faintly as Danny's previous hit. After several minutes of digging and sifting, a small, corroded metal tag made of aluminum or zinc was added to their treasure list. Careful examination led Jim to conclude it was a military dog tag. It was badly pitted and would require careful cleaning in order to read anything legible.

DARK FORTUNES

They searched another thirty minutes before beginning back to the water. Audra unleashed myriad question as they made their way to the shoreline. Though they'd searched this area, Danny swept his detector in large arcs as they walked toward the raft. A tremendous screech interrupted Audra's endless stream of questions; the loudest hit they'd gotten so far. It was near where Ernie had found the metal cylinder in 1945. Danny stopped dead, bent over and swept the moss away to find a half-buried, corroded metal pipe with a handle on its end. The handle broke off when he tried pulling it from the mud. Jim shoveled around the object, completely exposing it, and Danny picked it up. He wiped off the mud and gave it a hard shake. It rattled slightly, forecasting unknown contents. The handle connected to the opposite end of the pipe hung by a thread. Jim explained that the Nazi medals Ernie had found were located inside of an identical cylinder. Both children were ecstatic at the find. Once in the raft, Danny paddled against the wind to the boat. They couldn't wait to get home and open the container.

The foul weather had stopped and blue skies overtook the ominous clouds which had engulfed the area earlier. The Bennetts were glad to take off the wet gear and get inside the heated cabin. This woke Ernie, who had fallen asleep watching his movie. The three shared their treasure-hunting escapade with the old man, while Jim distributed sandwiches and mugs of hot coffee.

Ernie looked as if he'd seen a ghost when Danny brought the cylinder into the cabin. "When we get back and you've opened the tube, I'll tell ya the story I promised this mornin'. You'll wanta come back after I tell ya what went on here in 1944."

At that, the group decided they'd come back and refine the search area. Jim elected to leave the raft attached to a spare anchor. He wouldn't have to deflate it or tow it back to Angoon. The tide was almost high slack as they left the lake and approached the bay.

Again, salmon were congregated at the mouth of the inlet. Several trophy-size Kings circled the stacked up school as if ushering the others toward the inlet. Jim cut the engine and drifted into the bay while Audra set out a mooching rod with a herring. Almost instantly, the line went taught as a hungry King grabbed the bait. Ten minutes later, Danny netted a monster for Audra. The four took bets on the weight. Ernie guessed within a pound — a 41-pound, chrome-colored fish made its way into the ice box.

Audra piloted the boat west to the confluence of Chatham Strait. The ocean was much calmer than earlier. After carefully cleaning the four buttons, Jim and Danny struggled to remove the corroded cap from the aluminum tube. They soon realized cutting around the tube's outer wall with a hacksaw was the only method of retrieving its contents. The rattle indicated it was filled with something light-

162

weight and metallic. Danny's excitement level rose with every shake of the canister, convinced he'd found the Holy Grail of Admiralty Island.

Jim returned to the deck and filleted the three salmon while the boat made its long return trip to Angoon. He carefully sliced, rinsed and packaged the enormous filets into zip-lock bags. He would vacuum pack the catch later. The scraps were kept in a pail for catching crabs when Lori arrived. His duties turned to hosing the deck of the fish cleaning mess.

Inside the warmth of the cabin, Ernie inspected one of the buttons. The skull was cocked slightly to one side with deep set eye sockets and a mouth that seemed to grin. Each side of the skull had tilted leg bone ends that protrude outward as if they were an artistic version of the classic skull-and-cross-bones used by seventeenth century pirates.

He told the young Bennetts, "Sure looks like something a Nazi would wear — must be a shirt button."

"We'll know after searching the internet," responded Danny.

"You're like your pop — always getting' answers from computers."

Danny smiled. "I'm helpless without my computer — modern society would suffer a protracted collapse without them."

"You're likely right — your dad showed me stuff the other night that was amazing."

Jim finished cleaning the cruiser's deck and glanced eastward. A fast, low-flying helicopter approached Peril Strait from the south. The chopper banked hard left toward Baranof Island, then disappeared into a narrow bay. Within seconds, it reappeared from the west, climbing the back of Catherine Island. He recalled this anti-detection maneuver, used by savvy combat pilots from his Army days. The chopper hovered for a moment, then landed.

Jim entered the cabin and tapped Audra on the shoulder and pointed toward the ship near Peril Straight. "Slow down, sweetie, and head toward that white dot."

Audra slowed the boat to quarter throttle and aimed for the white dot.

Jim's view of the chopper was now blocked, so he turned his binoculars north. The *Oregon II* was at the entrance of Peril and three smaller boats were within a half mile of the ship. A white commercial fishing boat with tall masts trolled near the point of the island. Another sportfishing boat approached the ship's stern. A third vessel drifted east of Peril. It looked to be the Santos catamaran. Jim concluded that the helicopter had been avoiding detection from those vessels. Back in the cabin, said, "Let's cross the Strait and explore the entrance of Peril."

Audra wondered what had piqued Jim's interest, but relished the opportunity to run wide open. She pushed both throttles forward, aimed the boat toward the mouth of Peril and said, "We'll be there within fifteen minutes."

Catherine Island Ridgetop —Afternoon

The Dark Star duo kept a vigilant eye on events surrounding Chatham Strait. Whitey contacted Rusty while Helen studied her computer monitor. Jeff pointed out a boat approaching from the east. Things had become complicated — they now had five targets to contend with. Helen spun the antenna toward the oncoming boat and began typing. Al would be calling within minutes, and they had no idea which boat to target.

Whitey spoke with Rusty. "We have another boat approaching from the east. That makes five targets. The place looks like a Walmart parking lot. Keep Al on the line for as long as possible, because we've got our work cut out for us."

Frank heard the comments over the van's intercom and said, "We need more resources up there. We'll never pull this off."

Rusty responded, "Don't panic. If Al calls from any of those boats, Helen will determine which one it is."

Helen heard the comment over her headset but ignored the compliment. She opened a small metal case and connected a coax cable from the inside to a miniature hand held dish. A second cable connected the case to her computer. Finally, she pulled a cell phone from her pocket and plugged it into the laptop. Sensing an enormous accomplishment, she spoke. "Relax people. Remember that I infected his phone? If he calls from any of these boats, I'll configure his phone to mine. I've got my interceptor set. When he calls, it'll ring through to me as well. From now on I'll know who he's talking with and what's being said."

Rusty said, "You're stellar, If you can manage that, you'll make my day."

Whitey spoke. "The catamaran is motoring across the channel They're leaving."

The ridge overlooking the water was dead silent as the trio lay on their stomachs and watched the other four boats. The control van located in Frank Reid's driveway remained silent as well. Everyone understood the importance of the moment.

Rusty rehearsed his lines while holding the Wiser phone.

Jim's Boat

Audra, Danny and Ernie were unaware of events taking place outside. Jim, however, slid open a side window and glassed the ridge top. Two satellite dishes on tripods were barely visible, but he knew someone had pointed an antenna at his boat. He asked Audra to stop and told Danny to take a halibut rod out of the rack, bait it with the smallest salmon head and get it into the water. Confused, Danny reluctantly got on deck and set up a pole. Jim opened his laptop and turned the boat's antenna toward the ridge top. He opened the case of his cell phone interceptor and connected it to his computer and a new disposable cell phone. Convinced he was set, Jim walked on deck and put his hand onto Danny's shoulder.

"Try fishing here for a few minutes. I need time to check on the things we did at Santos' place. We need to look like innocent fishermen."

Danny tipped the heavy rod over the side and allowed the huge lead weight to send the bait to the bottom. "Have you ever fished this area before?" He asked.

"No, but it doesn't matter —we won't be here long."

Jim sat at the cabin table and typed away at his laptop. The computer verified a cell phone signal coming from the ridge, even though there was no conversation. His computer was programmed to constantly scroll through cell phone channels and radio frequencies, then capture conversations. Jim wondered if the people on the ridge were game wardens checking on the commercial fishing boat or perhaps the Coast Guard. As the boat drifted north, Danny yelled and asked Audra what the depth was. She told him 160 feet and deepening. Realizing that they were drifting over an underwater shelf, Jim dropped his windlass anchor in a rapid free fall, adding to their ruse. He continued to glass the ridge but saw nothing other than the two satellite dishes.

Minutes seemed like hours as Jim split his attention between glassing the ridge and watching the computer. Audra and Ernie stood on deck and watched Danny rhythmically jigging his line up and down so the bait would bounce off of the bottom. An icon in the shape of an eyeball popped up onto Jim's monitor. Either his home or Ernie's cabin was transmitting a signal from one of his hidden cameras. He minimized the radio scanning program and transferred to the visual monitoring system. There was Crane snooping around inside of Ernie's cabin. The officer took the Luger from the post and inspected it, then took several photos of it with his cell phone. He wrote what was likely the Luger's serial number into a small spiral notebook, then returned it to the post. Jim called for Ernie as Crane removed a cookie tin from the upper shelf and set it onto the table. Ernie arrived in time to see Crane reach into the tin, then yank his hand back with a rag and something else attached to his fingers. The old man broke into a fit of laughter while Crane struggled to remove a rat trap from his hand.

Jim laughed. "Ouch! You put a trap inside that tin, didn't you?"

"Ya bet your ass I did —placed it under a rag. I hope that hurts like hell."

They watched Crane toss the trap across the room, look at his fingers, then grab the tin and throw it to the floor. After several hearty foot stomps, he must have realized the consequences of his tantrum. He picked up the trap and damaged tin and left.

Jim looked Ernie in the eye. "Well partner, we've come full circle. There was something in the tin that he wanted. Any ideas what it might be?"

"At first, I didn't think he was after the tin," Ernie said, "but I was wrong. I'll show ya what was inside when we get back."

Audra yelled, "Danny's got a fish on. Hurry up, we need help."

They watched Danny try to crank the reel of the thick pole. The severely-bent pole shook violently as he tried placing it into a rod holder. His arms were no match for whatever was on the other end of the line. Jim ran and helped him secure the pole into a rod holder. Sensing the fish was too big to bring aboard, Jim grabbed a harpoon-looking device, a heavy wooden club, and a small .410 shotgun from a sidewall compartment. After looping the harpoon cable around a side cleat, Jim opened a cooler, removed three beers and handed one each to Ernie and Audra.

Jim took a swig of his beer. "Wish you could join us for a cold one, Son, but you seem preoccupied. I need to go into the cabin so give a holler when you can see the fish."

Danny yelled back, "It could be awhile. It's a big one. Maybe two hundred pounds. Anyone feel like taking over?"

Audra couldn't resist. "Nah, I'm enjoying my Heineken and dad's busy, so don't be a girly man. Finish what you started." Danny grimaced and kept cranking.

Jim sat back at the computer and minimized visual monitoring. After reentering the radio and phone transmission programs, the computer froze. Too many programs were running concurrently. Jim thought, *Quick, shut it off and reboot.*

Before he could, Danny yelled, "I see the fish! It's huge!"

Jim restarted the computer and anxiously waited what seemed forever. Finally, he was able to enter the phone surveillance program. The computer froze again. Jim shook his head and shut it off, wondering why the program kept freezing. He disconnected the phone intercept module and turned the computer on once more. The laptop rebooted and he pressed the radio scan icon and the program responded with ease. Jim reattached the phone hacking module and the system worked. As he calibrated the frequency ranges, Danny yelled for help.

"C'mon! The fish is tired and coming up. Someone help me get this jacket off. I'm sweating to death."

Jim abandoned the computer to help Danny land the fish. A glance over the side verified Danny's statement — the fish was big, bigger than any Jim had seen in years. He held the pole while Danny stripped down to his tattered orange construction sweat-shirt, exposing pumped up biceps. After returning the fishing pole to Danny, Jim grabbed the harpoon and leaned over the side to assess the situation.

All eyes were on Jim as he spoke. "Danny, a fish this big is dangerous so here's the drill — gently coax her head near the side of the boat but don't break the surface or she'll run. Keep tension on the line and I'll harpoon her through the gill plate — she'll try to run but I've got the harpoon line tied to the rail. When she tires, we'll loosen the rope and pull her up. While I'm doing that, place the rod into the holder, loosen the drag and grab the 4-10 shotgun. As soon as she reaches the top, shoot her behind the eyes. Open the transom door, then take the other gaff and stick her in the head. When you do, we'll both pull her onto the deck. If she thrashes around, stand back. If not, I'll knock her in the head a few times to make sure she's done."

He turned to Audra. "Could you please press the "enter" key on my laptop. There's an important program I need to run."

Audra ran into the cabin while Danny moaned, "Oh, please. My arms are near dead. Let's hurry up and do this."

Control Van —Port Angeles

Eerie silence permeated the van as the anticipated phone call drew near. The phone rang at two o'clock sharp, shattering the quiet. Rusty allowed it to ring five times before answering, "Yeah, I'm listening."

"Hello again my friend, how are things?"

"You tell me — ya got my money?"

"I certainly do. Have you made arrangements for a crew?"

"I've got three good hands lined out — they're tough and they're smart."

"Excellent. I trust they have enough hardware to complete the job."

"They're fully tooled."

"Wonderful. Let's arrange for a face-to-face meeting tomorrow — just the two of us."

Ed Prible, Helen's replacement, scribbled a note for Rusty, showing the coordinates of the cell transmission. It was coming from the same tower as the previous call. He nodded to Prible and continued, "Are you familiar with the Eureka mall off of Highway 1?"

Al answered, "I know where it is. Is that where you'd like to meet?"

"Yep. There's a pet store near the rear of the mall. Next to the store is a bank of public pay phones and some rest rooms — I'll call you on one of the phones for your final instructions. I'll be watching you, so you'd better be alone. If everything's cool, we'll meet."

Al asked, "You seem paranoid. Is there a problem?"

"Look pal, my cousin met you and he's dead. I'm not ending up like him, so we're gonna meet in a public place. I'm taking precautions, that's all."

"I had nothing to do with his death; however if you're comfortable meeting at a mall, then so be it. My agenda is to become very wealthy when this is over. When you're satisfied with my sincerity, I'd like you to meet one of my men. You may have met him already, through the Hell's Angels. He's the gentleman who introduced me to your cousin."

"Greg talked about a dirty cop. Is that the dude?"

"Indeed it is."

"You don't need him. I've got all the muscle we need."

"I want him for my personal protection. Besides, he's connected to several of your gang members and his services will be at my expense."

"That's fine with me. What about your other partner? Is he going to create problems later on?"

"He's no longer my partner, so he won't interfere. Besides, he won't live long enough to bother anyone. My police associate will handle that end of it."

"I like the way you do business. We think the same way."

Al pressed on. "So let's set a time — I can be at the mall by 1:00 p.m."

"That works for me. Wear a red baseball cap so I can ID you. Once I'm satisfied everything's cool, you'll know me because of my colors."

"What do you mean?"

Rusty wondered if Helen had pulled a joke on him while interrogating Wiser. He hesitated, then said, "My club jacket."

"Well, what color is it?"

Rusty continued, "Colors means a club jacket — it's faded denim with many patches — you can't miss me."

"Oh. Now I understand. OK, my friend, 1:00 p.m. at Eureka Mall. You'll have your money and we can set the wheels in motion."

"Later, dude."

"Goodbye."

The Ridgetop —Catherine Island

Rusty quickly spoke to Helen atop Catherine Island. "Do you have him?"

She motioned to Whitey for a cigarette. "Somewhat — narrowed down between the research ship and a small boat. The ship is unlikely but still in the mix. They were too close to each other for me to pin down. The Angoon tower screwed everything up by forwarding the signal to Juneau. By the time I filtered out the towers, the call was over."

Rusty pressed. "Can you follow both vessels?"

She took a deep drag on her newly-lit cigarette. "Not if they go in opposite directions. I'm betting the small boat is the source. The ship can be tracked by contacting NOAA."

Rusty continued. "I'll have our sources check out the ship. Again, can you follow the boat without detection?"

Whitey interrupted. "Al's coming to Eureka tomorrow so why risk scaring him off? If he thinks we're onto him, he won't show — end of story. A chopper flying around this area is out of character."

Reid overheard the conversation and added, "I know this area really well. Why doesn't Jeff fly everyone back to Sitka, then charter a boat and head north through Peril Strait. It should take under three hours to accomplish. If the boat is still there, pretend to be fishing. That way you can keep tracking the target without raising suspicion."

Whitey added, "That works because Helen already lined out a boat this morning."

Helen raised her hand while Whitey was talking with Rusty.

"Hold on, Helen needs to say something."

She exhaled another drag and said, "First off, I'll find out why the NOAA ship is here. Second, nobody asked me about hacking Al's phone."

Rusty asked, "Well, what? Did you get in?"

"I'm in. I've got it. Whenever he uses his phone, it'll ring through to me and when it's turned on, I can ping his location."

Rusty sounded annoyed. "That doesn't help me unless I've got the phone."

Helen was perturbed. "You're not getting me, Red. I can record every call he makes and immediately forward it to you. If you'd like, when we reach Sitka, Jeff can take the phone and fly it back to Port Angeles. That way you'll have it within a few hours, Whitey and I can secure a boat then follow our mark all night, need be. Mr. Al's probably flying commercially from Sitka or Juneau tonight. If we can track him, we'll book seats on the same flight. If he's got his own wings, there's nothing we can do other than fly back anyway."

"I don't appreciate loose ends," Rusty said. "Besides, both of you have been going non-stop for days. Are you up for this?"

Helen bantered back, "Dude, take a chill pill, we can handle ourselves including the phone. I've got two disposable cells with me. I'll configure another phone to match the one I used to hack his. That way two phones are linked to his, giving us zero gaps. If he receives a call before Jeff returns, I'll simply forward the recording."

Rusty was appeased. "Great, let's . . . "

Helen yelled, "Stop! Hang up! I repeat! Hang up! This call is being monitored!" She turned off her phone and aimed the handheld antenna toward the ship and trailing boat for several seconds, then at the boat directly east of the island. The scan was coming from the boat to the east. She pointed to the boat while Whitey placed the spotting scope onto the target.

Jim's Boat

Danny positioned the fish with his rod as Jim sank the harpoon completely through its gill plate. Jim struggled to hold the fish because the "slip-knot" pulled loose from the cleat. Seeing the problem, Danny swung the other gaff deep into the fish's mouth. The enormous fish splashed and flailed as the two men wrestled to keep it against the side of the boat. Jim yelled, "Audra, open the transom door! We've got to get her aboard now or we'll tire out before she does."

Audra sprang to the door, locked it in open position, and scrambled back toward the cabin yelling, "Clear!"

Danny turned to his tired father. "On three —here we go. One — two — *three!*"

Jim and Danny groaned as they dragged the huge fish onboard. Both men ran as it thrashed up and down on the deck. Jim ordered everyone inside the cabin until the fish settled down. Inside, he glanced at the computer. It had intercepted a transmission several minutes earlier. He turned toward the fish and said, "Danny, she's calming down — finish the job."

With several massive blows to the head with a club, Danny subdued the fish. A stream of blood poured from its mouth as Jim slit its gills with a knife. It was too large to fit into the live well. They would have to leave the fish on the deck until they returned to Angoon.

Jim asked Danny to raise the anchor so he could check his computer. After typing "retrieve" onto his keyboard, he listened to a woman's voice with an English accent saying, "That way two phones are linked to his, giving us zero gaps. If he receives a call before Jeff returns, I'll simply forward the recording."

A man answered. "Great, let's . . . "

The woman yelled "Stop! Hang up! I repeat! Hang up! This call is being monitored!" That was the end of the recorded transmission. Jim glassed the ridge top and noticed that the satellite dishes were gone and it appeared several lumps were on top of the ridge that hadn't been there before. A glint of reflective light betrayed the lens of a spotting scope. Bennett knew his boat was being watched from the ridge top by people with sophisticated equipment and they understood he'd monitored part of their call. Had it not been for the fish, he'd have gotten much more. Jim continued to glass the ridge. He asked Audra to start the motors as soon as the anchor was stowed.

The Ridgetop

Whitey asked, "Are you sure about the location? Those guys are fishing. They just landed something the size of a Buick."

Helen answered, "I'm positive because their scanner's still on. It's a scrolling module just like ours and they have an IMSI catcher masquerading as a land based station. These guys are good, almost too good." Helen slid next to Whitey. "Let me have a peek."

Helen put an eye to the scope, and another part of her mothers' vision immediately flooded her mind. "While lying in the clouds, you'll see your future husband for the first time. He will be far below you on a boat. His blonde locks, muscular body and brightly-colored shirt will be unmistakable. You will meet this handsome man and you will fall in love. But beware. This is the beginning of life-threatening events."

Whitey asked, "What do you think?"

She looked through the scope in utter silence as Danny stowed the anchor, then wondered, *How could Mum predict this? It's scary.*

"Earth to Helen —do you copy? Are you sure about the location?"

Helen continued looking through the scope. *Whoa, maybe I will check out the young dishy hunk in the orange teeshirt — that's one hot slab of beef. Perhaps Mum was right after all.*

Finally Whitey slapped the back of her head. "Are you daydreaming or what? I asked if you were sure about the transmission source."

Helen turned toward Whitey. "Absolutely. And stop hitting me."

Whitey snapped back, "C'mon. Did they hack our phone?"

She shook her head. "Not enough time. But they heard the end of our call."

"Could Al be on that boat?"

"Negative. His call came from the north — either the ship or that small boat."

"They must be spotters for Al. Why else would they be scanning us?"

Helen pitched her cigarette. "Maybe, maybe not, They could be Homeland Security. They didn't have enough time to pinpoint our location or figure out what the conversation was about."

Whitey adjusted the scope and said, "I can't read the boat's number but it has a satellite dish, directional antenna and two marine antennas on top of the wheelhouse. Their engines are running and they've pulled anchor. Wait. I see a wake.

They're moving — probably toward Angoon. I can see the boat's name on the transom — *Sojourn*. Let's get back to Sitka and charter a boat. You'll need to update Rusty. He's having a coronary by now.``

The trio scrambled down the hill to the chopper and within ten minutes they were in the air heading to Sitka.

The Sojourn — *Chatham Strait.*

Audra piloted the boat at half throttle toward Angoon. Jim remained at the computer while Danny took another look at the enormous halibut. He opened his own Heineken, sat next to his dad and asked, "What went on back there?"

Jim explained the helicopter situation, then played both the video link at Ernie's cabin and the cell phone intercept. Danny put it together. "You used halibut fishing as a ploy for surveillance?"

"Yep, but I never expected you to hook Moby Dick. Had I been able to stick with the computer, I'd..." The cell phone he'd set up for intercepting Crane rang in his pocket. He asked Audra to stop the cruiser and shut engines off. When Crane answered, Jim listened while cupping the mouthpiece.

"Yeah, this is Rich."

A voice on the other line said, "Everything's set for tomorrow. We need to be in Eureka by 1 p.m."

"Good, I can't wait to leave this shit hole. That old fucker McKinnon pisses me off. He hid a rat trap inside of an old cookie tin I figured had info. Mangled two fingers. Now he'll knows someone's been snooping around his place."

"Did you find anything?"

Crane answered, "No, just the serial number from the gun. But get this: Mel Franks saw me leaving McKinnon's cabin and confronted me. I told him I was looking for Ernie, but he didn't buy my story and gave me my walking papers."

The other voice commented, "It doesn't matter anymore; we're taking a completely new approach. A float plane will pick you up in 30 minutes so hurry and pack. We'll meet at our usual spot. Bye."

Jim asked for everyone's attention as he placed the phone back in his pocket. "Crane is leaving Angoon in thirty minutes. He was fired by Mel after being seen in Ernie's cabin. The voice of the caller had a European accent. It was undoubtedly Rigby. They're going to Eureka —probably California."

Ernie asked, "Do they plan on comin' back?"

"I don't know. That was the end of their conversation. Crane did say that he's got two mangled fingers."

Ernie cackled. "Serves that fat bastard right for diggin' through my stuff."

As Ernie completed his sentence, Jim's personal phone rang. Caller ID said it was Rigby. Jim asked everyone to remain silent and answered, "Good afternoon, this is Jim."

"Good afternoon sir, my name is David Rigby. I was told you tried reaching me earlier today. How may I help you?"

Jim asked, "Did you get my note?"

"No sir. I called Dick today, and he said you wanted to speak with me."

Jim began, "Yes I did. Thank you for calling back. I understand you're researching Tlingit culture. I'd like to offer my services as an expert on Tlingit lineage. Prior to moving here, I spent three years tracing the various Clans and their origins. The information I've gathered could be of great benefit for your project."

"I appreciate the offer, but I'm preoccupied for the next few weeks. Perhaps we can discuss this when my schedule is less demanding."

"I totally understand. Mel Franks told me that you're a published author and wrote a book about Hawaiian culture. I've always been intrigued with Pacific islanders and would enjoy reading your book. Would you happen to have a copy that I could either purchase or borrow?"

"Not with me. I believe that it's no longer in print."

Jim asked, "Perhaps I can locate one on E-bay. What's the title and who's the publisher?"

There was a pause followed by, "You're breaking up —hello —hello — Oh, I've lost you." The phone went dead.

Danny asked, "Was that Crane's friend Rigby?"

"Affirmative. He's a sham. I asked for details on his previous book. He pretended to have phone problems and hung up. He's the same person who called Crane."

Ernie offered, "That means he and Crane are in cahoots."

"That's another affirmative. Things seem to be adding up. Let's get back to the marina."

Audra restarted the engines and headed for Angoon. Twenty minutes later, a float plane landed as the *Sojourn* entered Kootznahoo Bay. Jim passed beers around. Cool, overcast weather greeted them as Audra approached the marina and placed the boat into neutral. Audra asked her father to park the boat. Jim sat down and drank his beer. Audra shrugged and the *Sojourn* simply drifted as they watched several locals fish for salmon. Jim watched through his binoculars as Crane climbed into the float plane and the plane took off toward Sitka. After finishing his beer, he parked the boat in his slip.

Jim shoveled a pile of ice from his live well onto the halibut and stowed the gear. The four walked to the Humvee with their new-found treasure and a cooler full with salmon filets. Danny and Jim would come back to clean the halibut after Audra and Ernie got settled into the house. Audra eagerly offered to cook one of the larger salmon filets.

As the group exited the Humvee, Jim suddenly asked everyone to stop. The surveillance system had been triggered. He asked Danny for the Desert Eagle and walked the perimeter of the house, looking for signs of a break-in. The large double doors overlooking Chatham were closed, but Jim knew a bear had tried forcing it open. Wide, deep claw marks had taken the anodized finish off of the door frame but the LED light next to his stereo indicated no interior breach.

"The Clan needs to catch this bear before I'm forced to kill it," Jim said. "I'll call Hank Stites and have him move the barrel trap over here. We'll bait it with the halibut carcass."

Sitka

The chopper arrived in Sitka, and Whitey called Rusty to inform him about the intercepted call. After discussion, they decided to continue with the original plan. Jeff would return to Port Angeles while Helen and Whitey sniffed around Angoon.

Helen contacted marina worker Art and told him that she wanted to charter a boat immediately and it needed to be stocked with food. Whitey went to the hotel and grabbed their bags while Helen met with Art at the marina. She asked about the NOAA ship and described the catamaran.

"NOAA spent last season here taking deep water temps and salinity tests; something to do with global warming, but I didn't know they were here again. There's a rich fella living on Admiralty who owns that big catamaran."

"Where on Admiralty does he live and what's his name?"

"I can't remember, but I think he's Mexican. His home is somewhere near Angoon."

Helen handed Art two crisp Franklin's and thanked him for his help. She looked skyward as a corporate jet took off from Jablonski Island, announcing Jeff's departure. Whitey arrived and honked the van's horn, signaling that he required help bringing the equipment to the waiting boat. Within fifteen minutes, a 34-foot Bayliner Cruiser motored from the marina and into Sitka Sound. Helen lit a cigarette, and punched the GPS coordinates into the boat's navionic system.

Whitey accelerated to full throttle, and Helen asked, "Dude, you ever run a boat this big?"

"I grew up on Cape Cod — spent plenty of hours on my old man's boat fishing for tuna. Sit back and relax, we'll see the mouth of Peril Strait within ninety minutes."

Helen said, "This landscape is out of control, dude. I'm taking a real shine to Alaska."

Whitey commented, "I never pictured you to be into this sort of stuff. Figured you for a hip city chick."

"London and New York are cool, but so is this. It's completely opposite and strangely magnetic. I'd relish spending summers up here and winters in a big city."

"Stop dreaming and get your equipment ready for the next phase."

The Bayliner skipped across the inland passageway of Neva Strait toward Salisbury Sound. A red Boston Whaler with two men aboard came racing from the opposite direction. Whitey slowed the cruiser to quarter throttle. As a courtesy, he didn't want his wake to endanger the smaller craft, but the Whaler maintained full speed, going airborne as it jumped over Whitey's wake.

Helen said, "They're in a bloody awful hurry. Haven't we seen that boat before?"

"We've seen hundreds of boats today. Maybe you saw it in the harbor this morning."

"It'll come to me sooner or later. How about some food? I'm starving." Helen made several sandwiches as they continued the trek to Chatham.

Angoon

The phone's answering machine was beeping as the foursome entered the house. Mel and Hilda had left messages explaining Crane's termination. Jim asked the group to get comfortable while he called Lori and returned the two other calls. Ernie poured himself some whiskey and Audra began dinner. Anxious to open the metal container, Danny went to the tool shed and got to work.

Lori answered, "Well Mr. Bennett, how are things?

"Stop that crap. Call me anything but Mr. Bennett."

"How about Colonel?"

"You're testing the waters aren't you? Is this a prelude of things to come?"

"Absolutely."

Jim shook his head and smiled. "Are you packed and ready for tomorrow?"

"Actually I'm still at work. I've got a mountain of paperwork to complete before taking off. Frasier wants an outline for the magnetic pulse project by tomorrow, and I've got three more memos to get out — I'll be working for another two hours."

"Call me tomorrow from the airport so I know everything's on track."

Lori said, "You'll still be sleeping when my plane takes off. I'll text you instead."

"I'll be awake."

"Jim?"

"What?"

"I can't wait to see you."

He smiled. "Thank you. I can't wait either. Have a safe trip, but contact me in the morning."

Jim hung up and called Hilda, interrupting an elder meeting. Hilda, Mel, Hank and several others were discussing the Crane dilemma. Hilda put Jim on speaker. They were concerned about the possibility of losing the patrol boat and potential litigation from Crane, but Jim explained he'd talked with Santos earlier in the day, which soothed part of their concerns. The status of Crane still plagued the group.

"Crane is no longer a problem," Jim offered. "I can't go into detail because these phone lines are not secure but believe me when I tell you that if he creates any further trouble, I'll have him prosecuted for numerous felonies. I've got enough on him to put him away for quite a while. He'd be an idiot to try and build a case at this late stage."

Mel asked, "What about phone lines?"

"Under the circumstances, it's best to assume that they're bugged. In fact, for the time being, I suggest holding future meetings outdoors or in my house."

Hilda asked, "You can't be serious?"

"I am. Let's meet by my boat at 9:30 a.m. Make sure Hank's there. I'll show you some things and we'll be able to talk in private. In the meantime, don't worry about any of this. Crane's no longer a problem and Mr. Santos will support any replacement the Clan decides to hire."

Hilda was relieved. "Thank you Mr. Bennett. You're a gentleman."

"You're welcome and good afternoon."

Audra was busy preparing a marinade for the freshly caught salmon and the smell of freshly chopped herbs with shallots seeped from the kitchen into the living room. Like her mother, Audra was an outstanding cook who enjoyed preparing gourmet meals. After her father completed his calls, she placed several CD's into the stereo system for music while cooking. Because the old man was a sucker for old movies, Jim mixed Ernie a drink and sat him in front of the large plasma flat screen with another old western called "True Grit."

Jim entered the tool shed and was greeted by the smell of burning marijuana. "What the hell are you doing?" he barked. "You'll get us both busted. Do you have any idea how Tlingit's feel about drugs?"

"Don't worry. I only brought a tiny bag along. No one could ever find such a small amount."

"I did without even trying. Damn it Danny, you're jeopardizing what I've got going on up here. I don't care about you smoking pot or what you do back home, but please don't do that shit around this house. Take a walk on the beach or something."

Danny looked down at the rough-cut floorboards and apologized. "Sorry. I won't toke up around here anymore."

"Good, I appreciate that. So what's with that canister?"

Danny pointed to the corroded container. "It's almost open."

The metallic cylinder sat firmly anchored in the jaws of a large vice and metal filings littered the floor as Danny made his final cut. He carefully finished the job. The end cap dropped to the floor, exposing a dark hole. Jim laid a large rag onto the bench and Danny tipped the contents out. A handful of small metal rectangles and ovals and over a dozen small booklets tumbled onto the bench.

Danny looked at the contents. "That's it?" He expected something more exciting.

Jim briefly inspected three of the metal pieces, two of which were WW II American dog tags, then set them down. He picked up one of the booklets. "I think this is a German Soldbuch. It's remarkably preserved and definitely Nazi."

"What's Soldbuch?"

"An ID for the German Army — the SS on the cover means this belonged to an SS soldier."

He opened the booklet, careful not to tear the fragile pages. A faded photograph of a stern looking soldier in dress uniform stared at the duo. Pages of the soldier's information nearly filled the inside the small booklet as Jim read out loud. "This soldier's name is Karl Johann Obert, a Standartenfuhrer in the Wehrmacht. He was born on March 6, 1917. I've seen this face before— a photo of a John Doe found in 1944."

"What does Standarten and Wermak mean?"

The Wehrmacht is the name for the German army, and Standartenfuhrer means a full colonel. He was an SS officer." He picked up one of the American dog tags. It read:

ANDREW F. DECKER — USAAF 16273566
Lt.2 — DOB 01-20-23 — CATH O+

"This belonged to Second Lieutenant Andrew Decker, born January 20, 1923. He had O+ blood type and was a Catholic. He was in the Army Air Force and may have been a pilot."

Danny picked up one of the ovals. "This one's completely different. It looks like the piece of metal we found in Whitewater. I think it's German."

Jim nodded. "Nazi dog tags. This other one is another Allied dog tag."

As he silently read the name, Jim felt a rush of blood flush into his temples. He put the tag in his pocket. "Come on, let's get these inside."

"So we found a bunch of worthless crap?"

"I wouldn't say that. Maybe Ernie will shed some light on the subject."

When they entered the house, Ernie was engrossed in his movie as Audra prepared dinner. The salmon needed to marinade and that dinner was a ways off, so Danny decided to return to the boat and filet the halibut. Jim offered to help, but his son insisted on handling the job. After he left, Jim took the dog tag to his study and turned on the computer. While booting, up he re-read the tag:

DALE C. OLSEN — USAAF 16473595
CPT. — DOB 09-18-22 — ND O+

Captain Dale Olsen had died in his B-17 during March of 1944. Somehow his dog tag ended up on Admiralty Island. Jim pondered the situation, then began typing. After several minutes, the name "Andrew Decker" came up as a crew member of the B-17 Olsen piloted. Both men were listed as KIA. Dale Olsen's plane was the one reported missing from the Pelican cannery.

After placing the tag in his shirt pocket and buttoning it shut, he thought, *Coincidence? No fucking way.*

Chatham Strait

The Bayliner slowed as it passed NOAA Ship 332. Helen took a series of digital photographs of the cabin. *Oregon II* was painted on its stern. It was anchored with its rear boom gantry extended over the water. A peculiar feeling struck Helen as she observed the ship, but she couldn't understand why — something was out of place. The catamaran and commercial fishing boat were gone. The duo in the cabin discussed the situation.

"Whitey, do you notice anything strange with this ship?"

"Other than a lack of crew, no. Why?"

"I can't put my arms around it, but something's wrong. It'll come to me. Where do you imagine the small white boat went?"

Whitey scanned the horizon to the north with his spotting scope and saw nothing but water. He repeated his survey to the south with the same results. "I don't see it anywhere."

Helen looked through a pair of binoculars at the ship. She tapped Whitey on the shoulder and pointed. "There's the white boat — it's tied to the ship."

"I'll be damned, you're right."

"That's not all, dude. Remember the red open boat we encountered coming toward Sitka that wouldn't slow down?"

178

"Yeah, what about it?"

"It was on the rear deck of the NOAA ship earlier today. That's why its crane is still deployed. Al's with this ship — he passed us while we were coming here."

"Holy shit, I think you're right. He's in Sitka right now and about to fly out."

Whitey immediately called Rusty while Helen set up the scan detector. The two men made small talk until Helen nodded that the call was clear. Excited about the revelation, Whitey began. "Here's what we uncovered, Al was on the NOAA ship earlier — its number is 332 and the name is *Oregon II*. Al's in Sitka right now and about to fly out."

Rusty asked, "How do you know that?"

"The ship's harbor boat's gone. It passed us about 90 minutes ago. We didn't realize it until now. There were two people aboard and they were in one hell of a hurry."

"Did you get a good look at them?"

"I did," responded Whitey.

"Good. We'll post folks at SeaTac. We'll check out the NOAA ship as well — it's probably bogus. What about the catamaran and the boat that intercepted our call?"

"We're going into Angoon for the night, so we'll investigate that."

"No. That's a game changer. I'll send a float plane to Angoon to pick you up ASAP. Take the earliest flight to Seattle in case Al's on the plane. I need you with me in Eureka tomorrow. "

"What about Helen snooping around Angoon?"

"She can stay with the boat for a day or two and perform recon. You'll return to Sitka in two days and help her wrap up the investigation."

Whitey looked at Helen and shrugged his shoulders. "Are you up for this?"

"Only if you teach me how to run this bloody boat."

Whitey spoke to Rusty. "OK, let's do it — send a float plane to Angoon."

The Bayliner accelerated toward Angoon with Helen at the controls. The weather warmed considerably and the skies were bright blue as Whitey gave Helen boating lessons. She was a quick study.

Angoon

Danny drove the Humvee to the base of the marina's dock system. There was a large "No Parking" sign, but he didn't feel like lugging a heavy cooler up the hill, so he ignored it. After looking in all directions, he placed a small pipe to his lips and took another hit of pot. Danny left the Hummer, and a large cabin cruiser approached the dock just as he jumped onto his father's boat. A pale man with white hair hailed from the cruiser. "Hey, big fella. Where can a person dock a boat for a few nights?"

Danny answered, "I'm not sure what the village requirement is but I'm sure if you tie off next to me and go up the hill to the store, someone can help you out. Things are pretty laid back around here."

"Thank you. Is the store far away?"

Danny pulled off his windbreaker exposing his faded orange construction shirt. His muscles bulged as he dragged the fish toward the center of the deck.

"It's about a five minute walk. If the store's closed, keep walking to the third house on your right. It's owned by a Clan elder named Mel. He'll be able to help you out."

"Thanks again. I appreciate your help."

Danny replied, "Hey man, my pleasure."

The albino tied off the Bayliner. A beautiful woman wearing large black-framed sunglasses with short cropped raven hair came out of the cabin. A tight-fitting black t-shirt exposed several tattoos on her upper arms. Danny was utterly stunned at her appearance and happily surprised when she smiled at him. He helped tie off the Bayliner, watching her from the corner of his eye. He thought she was looking at him too, but couldn't see her eyes because of the sunglasses.

She turned to the albino. "Hey Whitey, see if they have a restaurant or pub. I'll hang by the boat while you take care of business."

He nodded. "Sure thing, I won't be long."

Whitey trotted up the dock and proceeded up the hill. Helen secretly closed a handheld scanner. She glanced toward the *Sojourn*, where Danny was back at the enormous fish,

"Whoa, dude, that's a hell of a fish — you must be a local."

Danny answered, "No, but I come up for a few weeks every year. I wish I could afford to live here during the summers."

Helen assessed Danny's features as he sharpened a long-bladed knife. She wondered if this was the man her mother had predicted she'd meet. An out-of-character sense of nervousness overtook her, and she wondered what to say next. A barrage of thoughts flew through her mind, *Is this really the guy? Was Mum in a drug induced state of confusion while having her so-called "visions?" How could Mum see the future? Christ he's a dishy hunk; look at that rock-hard body and his shoulder-length hair. He looks exactly how Mum described him, including the shirt. I saw him from afar while lying in the clouds. It must be him. How do I proceed without acting overt or eager?*

Danny maneuvered the halibut to begin filleting. Kneeling next to the fish, he glanced toward Helen to see if she was watching him. She was. *She's gorgeous*, he thought. *Too bad she's with that pale dude. She's definitely English. I wonder if I should talk to her? Nah, put-downs suck. Just clean the damn fish and get back home.*

Helen finally said "Permission to come aboard your mighty vessel, Captain?"

Surprised and pleased, Danny stood, wiped his hands and replied, "Permission granted, fair lady. Be careful not to slip. The deck's wet." Danny reached out to help her onto the boat. Both of her hands wrapped around his right bicep as she stepped onboard. Once on deck, the top of her head came to the height of Danny's eyes. He took a good look at the woman and once again was struck by her beauty and perfectly proportioned body.

"What's your name?"

"Helen Moorcroft. How about you, Captain?"

"Danny Bennett."

She held out her right hand. "Pleased to meet you Captain Danny. Those are some mighty big pipes that helped me aboard. You must work out."

Danny wiped his right hand with a clean deck rag and shook her hand.

"The pleasure is all mine Helen. As for working out, I've been known to pump a little iron every now and then. You're from the UK."

"Jolly good observation. I'm from Liverpool."

"I'll be damned — a Scouser."

She frowned. "How do you know the term Scouser?"

"I just finished a book about the Beatles — they were from Liverpool. It's my understanding that people from Liverpool are called Scousers."

Danny began fileting the halibut. "What brings you here?"

"I'm on holiday and my cousin from Seattle offered to take me fishing in Alaska."

Relieved to hear "cousin" Danny asked, "That guy's not your old man or boyfriend?"

She answered, "Heavens no. I'm not hooked up."

Helen thought, *Keep it going — ask about his status.*

After a pause she asked, "What about you, committed dude or maybe married?"

Danny shook his head. "Not even close. Excuse me for being forward, but you're incredibly attractive. How do you manage to keep the hounds at bay?"

She finally relaxed and settled down. "Practice."

Again he shook his head. "Excuse me. I don't get it. You're too attractive to be single — unless you swing both ways. Maybe a lesbo or something?"

She ripped off her sunglasses. "EXCUSE YOU INDEED! THAT WAS BLOODY RUDE! You weren't joking about being forward. I'm not a carpet muncher. I happen to dig men. If I was lesbo, I'd slap you silly. I'm not hooked up because my work doesn't allow relationships. Besides, I've never met a man who's worth a shit —including today."

Danny felt like a fraternity idiot at a mixer. "Sorry. Really I am. Sorry I offended you." He stood up and looked into her hazel-colored eyes. "Please forgive me. That wasn't the brightest thing to say."

In a modulated voice, Helen responded. "Apology somewhat accepted, but not completely."

There was awkward silence as the two of them wondered what to say next. Finally Helen broke the ice. She pointed at his biceps. "I see you're a tat freak. Yours look to be a combination of tribal patterns and barbed wire — very biker-esque. You got more of those under that shirt?"

Danny noted that her tight t-shirt telegraphed her well-shaped breasts and perky nipples. He knelt on the deck with his left knee to reposition the halibut. "I've got a few more and I happen to ride a bike — a Harley Fat Boy. I'm not a hardcore biker, though — no gangs or crap like that. You've got a few tats of your own. Not many chicks dig that much ink."

"It was a phase when I was younger. Maybe later you can show me more of yours."

Danny hesitated, then shook his head and grinned.

Helen immediately asked, "What?"

Danny couldn't resist. "Only if I can see more of yours."

She smiled. "One never knows what the future holds. That was a clever retort; not rude like before, but still somewhat brash."

Silence followed as Helen perused Danny's physique as he deftly sliced huge slabs of snow-white flesh from the enormous fish.

"I envy you for being able to come here as often as you do. Is this your boat?"

"It's my dad's. He built a summer home here about five years ago. I simply leave my work behind and enjoy the fruits of his labor. He's very generous and pays my way to be with him and my sister."

Helen knew she had a job to do, but felt guilty asking, "Your pop must be coined up. What's his vocation?"

"He recently retired as a CEO of a defense contracting firm. Mostly computer software for weapons."

"How about you, You're obviously well educated. What's your vocation, Captain Danny?"

"I have an electrical engineering degree, but I work construction in Phoenix. How about you; where do you live and what do you do?"

Helen knew she couldn't tell the whole truth but offered, "I worked for the Yard but recently moved to the States. I stay at my cousin's place in Belleview. I've been offered a job there, but I haven't decided if I'll take it."

He asked, "What's the Yard. What do you do?"

She thought, *That's a harmless question —go ahead and answer.* "Scotland Yard. I've got a degree in computer science. After seeing Alaska, I wish there were employment opportunities here."

"Were you a cop?"

"Indeed, Captain. I was a Bobby, working in surveillance. Too bad Alaska doesn't need my services. I'd move here in a heartbeat."

"Winters can be brutal and there's little summer work that pays for shit," Danny said. "My old man has the idea: accumulate enough bread so you can migrate like the birds."

Danny finished filleting the fish, took the boat's freshwater hose and carefully rinsed the massive filets.

"How long do you plan on staying in Angoon?"

As Danny spoke, Helen leaned with her left hand on the cabin's roof and stuck a tiny GPS tracking module inside the roof's drip gutter.

"That depends on my cousin," she said. "I'd love to remain here long enough to get to know the area and its people — including you."

Danny looked up, "Are you yanking my chain?"

"Assuredly not. I noticed you as soon as I arrived and thought you were a person worth checking out. Aside from the lesbian comment, the more we talk the more intrigued I am with you. At the risk of rejection, I find you dishy and would like to know you better. That's if you don't mind hanging out with a Euro punk."

Danny didn't hesitate. "I dig your look — sort of a young Joan Jett but much prettier. Any guy would be crazy to reject eye candy like you. Frankly, the way you dress adds to your look."

Helen sported a huge grin. "Thank you for the magnanimous compliment. What do you think? Perhaps we could spend a few hours and get to know each other over a drink or something?"

Danny had to think. Finally he said, "Um, I'm not sure how family commitments are shaping up, but I'm sure we could go boating or hiking for a few hours tomorrow."

Helen now knew her Mum had seen the future. This had to be "him."

"I'd truly like that, Captain Danny. You could be my personal tour guide."

Whitey ran down the pathway toward the boat as a Cessna 180 float plane approached the bay, landed, then taxied toward the large dock several hundred yards to the west. The albino motioned for Helen to meet inside the adjoining cruiser. Danny watched in confusion as Helen sprang from the boat onto the dock.

Inside of the cruiser, Whitey said, "That's my ride. I called Rusty and my flight leaves Sitka in ninety minutes. How you doing with young Tarzan over there? Any information?"

"Not yet, but I'm working on it."

"You're on your own for two days, so find out everything you can about Tarzan's boat, the catamaran and the NOAA ship. I can't take any ordnance with me because

I'm on a commercial flight, so keep it hidden. I paid for seven days' moorage and you're set until I return. There's a bit of bad news though. Angoon has no bars or restaurants. There's a small store at the top of the hill but it doesn't sell alcohol — that's about it."

Her voice raised several notches. "Fuck all! No pubs, ale or restaurants? I'll die here!"

"There's a sixer of Bud in the fridge. That's two beers a day. Look, I've got to scoot or I'll miss the last flight from Sitka."

Whitey grabbed a small gym bag, jumped onto the dock and sprinted down the shoreline toward the waiting Cessna. Danny watched the events unfold while stacking the massive filets into the ice chest.

Helen exited the cabin, clearly upset. "My cousin's been called away for an emergency meeting in Seattle. I don't mind staying on the boat while he's gone but he said there are no pubs or restaurants in Angoon. What's up with that?"

Danny answered, "Angoon's a dry village. Look, let me get the fish packaged and into the freezer while you settle in. I'll return later with a half rack of beer from my old man's stash. We'll party down with a few cold ones and continue our talk. I can make it back in an hour or so."

"That would be terrific, Danny." With his help, she crossed onto Jim's boat. She grabbed his head and pulled him to her lips. Her breasts pressed firmly against his muscular chest as they kissed. Her fingers ran through his sandy blonde mane while Danny's felt her braless back and sides.

After separating Danny said, "Wow, you don't mess around."

"You're the one who asked if I was lesbo. I'm merely setting the record straight."

He smiled. "I certainly asked and I'm glad I did. Hang loose. I'll be back within an hour or so."

Helen returned to the Bayliner while Danny transferred the cooler onto the dock, set the boat's security system and hauled the halibut to the Hummer. He reached the house overlooking Chatham and carried the cooler onto the front deck. Inside, the others were seated at the dining room table going through the contents of the metal tube. Jim's laptop was on, with a photo of a Nazi officer on its monitor.

Danny sat down next to Audra, sporting a huge grin.

She took a look at him, laughed, and sang, "Danny's got a girlfriend; Danny's got a girlfriend."

Jim frowned with confusion. "What're you talking about?"

Audra explained. "Every time he wears that silly grin, he's dialing in on a chick. Believe me, I know my brother."

Danny elbowed his sisters' side. She blurted, "Ouch. Stop that."

Jim asked, "How could you hustle up a girlfriend in an hour of cleaning fish?"

Danny answered, "There's a hot tourist down at the marina. We started talking. Before you know it, I've got a date with her."

Ernie laughed. "I'll be damned — a modern day Casanova. Is she good lookin'?"

Danny nodded. "Totally hot."

Jim shook his head, and redirected the conversation. "I showed the treasure trove to Ernie and Audra, and cleaned the corroded tag we found in the dirt. Here's the interesting part. It belonged to a man named Hans Bruehl, a U-boat commander reported killed in the English Channel on D-Day. Also, one of the German ID photos matches a John Doe recovered in Rodman Bay in 1944. He had three gunshot wounds and he was naked. *He* was reported killed near Hamburg in June of that year.

"I've researched the other names and found that they're all listed WWII KIAs."

Jim handed Danny the German ID booklet and a photograph of the "John Doe" — Colonel Karl Obert.

"Ernie was about to share a story when you came prancing in. He claims he has some juicy tidbits. So, Mr. McKinnon, give us the juice."

The old man had already set a faded old shoebox onto the table. He opened the lid and removed a handful of papers, a small booklet and another German dog tag. Passing the objects to Danny on his left, he began, "The name on this tag is Günter Bruehl — it matches the name in the booklet. Besides these things, there were six of these that I pressed onto parchment paper. That's the real treasure I found inside the pipe."

Danny examined a small rectangular pattern imprinted onto the paper, then passed it on. Audra did the same. Ernie had five more of the stenciled reliefs. Jim studied the imprint. It measured two by four inches, emblazoned with a Nazi Imperial Eagle standing on a circle with a Swastika in its center. Six distinct lines of print started at the center of the rectangle and ended at its bottom:

DEUTSCHE
REICHSBANK
1 Kilo
FIENGOLD
999.9
DR076441

Jim blurted, "Holy buckets Ernie — gold bars. You found these inside the canister?"

"Yep — there were six of 'em. The tube was chained to the dead man's belt."

Audra asked, "What did you do with them?"

"First, I tried to sell one at a pawn shop in Juneau but the owner said it was fake. I ended up filing them down and sellin' them as placer gold. Asked where I found the gold, I said in a creek on Green Island. Before ya know it, there was a small gold rush in the area. Funny thing happened, though — people started finding gold in nearly every creek on Green Island."

"So that's what this is about," Jim said, "gold with a capital 'G.' Who else knows about the bars?"

"Just Jenna and she's dead."

Danny said, "That's what Crane and Rigby are up to. They're after gold. How do you imagine they found out?"

Ernie continued. "I became the talk of Angoon — a legendary prospector because of all the gold I kept bringin' into Juneau. I s'pose when Rigby interviewed the Clans, the word of me findin' gold after the war came up. When Rigby saw my Luger, he probably put it all together."

Jim seemed relieved but annoyed at the same time. "You should have told me sooner. We could have avoided a lot of guesswork and danger."

"I wasn't sure 'til the night ya got a call from your friend about Gus Olsen. I wanted to wait so it wouldn't spoil your treasure hunt."

Jim frowned in confusion. "What's the deal with Gus Olsen? He's dead."

Audra interrupted. "Do you think there's more? I bet there's more. Can we go back and look again?"

Ernie smiled over Audra's stream of questions. "Gus ain't dead. He was at Jenna's funeral. He married Jenna's cousin Lena back in '46. She sent me a card for my last birthday. My wife and Lena were like sisters cuz both were raised by their grandma. Lena and Gus visited Angoon many times through the years and I'm good friends with both of 'em. After the funeral, Gus said they moved from Seattle and gave me his private phone number. If I ever needed anything, I was s'posed ta call."

"Jenna died three years ago," Jim said. "Do you still have their number?"

Ernie poked around in the shoe box and handed Jim a piece of paper with a telephone number on it. He entered it into the memory of his personal phone and returned the paper. Audra left the table to check on dinner. Danny studied one of the etchings.

Jim looked at Ernie. "This may sound paranoid, but I suspect serious trouble is brewing. Rigby, Crane and possibly Santos think there's more gold to be found. From the comments Crane made during the intercepted call, they want to interrogate you. When Crane said he wouldn't spend his life in prison for Rigby, I'm convinced he was referring to murder. What else do you know that's so important to them?"

Ernie answered, "I'm thinkin' they're after Gus and Lena."

Jim asked, "Why?"

"My wife told me a story about Lena just before she died. Lena said she witnessed a meetin' between the Olsens and a Nazi general at the Pelican cannery in 1944. There was an exchange of gold for passage to the lower 48. This was a time in Lena's life when she drank a lot, so things she said were taken with a grain of salt. The day after talkin' with my wife, Lena went missin' and was presumed drowned. Her coat was found on the end of a dock with a half-empty bottle of booze. She reappeared days later and told everyone she was on a bender and had tried walking back to her home in Hoonah. When Jenna asked her about the cannery story, she played dumb and said she couldn't remember the conversation."

Jim wasted no time. "You must contact Gus and Lena to explain the present situation. They staged their deaths to avoid detection from the likes of Rigby — their well-being is in jeopardy. After I receive information about Rigby and Santos from my contacts at Langley, you must — and I repeat *must* — contact them."

Ernie asked, "When will that be?"

Jim said, "Very soon. It's important for everyone here to be on guard and above all, keep your mouths shut. We're dealing with bad people. I suspect there's more gold to be found and we'll consider looking for it, but in a safe manner. Are we in agreement about what I've just said?"

Everyone nodded.

The aroma of dinner permeated the dining area. Danny said that he would vacuum pack the halibut filets while Audra finished cooking. Jim collected the articles on the table, put them away, and turned on the stereo. Soft tranquil music flowed through the house as Ernie sat in the living room, looking out the massive windows.

Jim went to the front deck to help Danny package his fish and asked, "So you sport a silly grin every time you have a new girlfriend?"

Danny shrugged. "I never noticed. Audra's such a butthead."

"Do you think your new friend would care to join us for dinner?"

Danny frowned. "I don't know. We hardly know each other."

"Would you like to invite her? There's more than enough food. I'll package Moby Dick while you run into town and ask her."

Danny smiled. "That's terrific. You wouldn't mind a stranger coming for dinner?"

"Not at all. We'd be more than happy to accommodate your new friend. Have her bring her bathing suit so you guys can soak in the hot tub after dinner."

"You're awesome. I'll run into town right now. I hope she doesn't turn me down."

"She'll accept your invitation. But remember what I said about keeping our secret — no conversations about treasure, Nazi's or Whitewater Bay."

Danny assured him, "Believe me, I won't say a word."

Jim finished vacuum packing the fish and informed Audra about a possible dinner guest. He made certain that any evidence of their Whitewater trip was hidden from prying eyes and that Ernie would remember to remain silent.

Port Angeles, Washington — Frank's Library — Late Night

The Reids and Rusty sat in the library recapping the long day's events. Whitey had boarded the Alaskan flight and called from the plane. No one on board fit the profile and description of their target. Frank's Bell picked Whitey up at SeaTac and brought him to the estate for debriefing. Upset with the day's failures, Frank needed to clear the air.

The old man looked at Rusty and began, "I'm not pleased, and I don't expect to hear any more bad news or excuses as to why Al isn't apprehended. If he's a 'no show' tomorrow, I want the cavalry sent to Sitka. If he does show up, I expect to have him captured. No excuses."

Rusty nodded. "Understood sir. I took a calculated risk which failed. I fully intend to capture him tomorrow and extract every shred of information."

Frank kept on. "Very well. I'll arrange to meet with Henry's staff on the yacht in the morning and decide how to proceed with protecting their well-being. They may wish to fly somewhere exotic rather than take a protracted cruise. Maybe Tahiti."

"Excellent plan, sir. Keep me informed about your final decision so I can arrange security."

The old man asked, "Are you fully prepared to handle the situation in Eureka?"

"Yes, sir. I'd like Whitey to assist with the interrogation process because he's trustworthy and knows what I'm after."

Frank agreed. "I like him. He's very business-like. However, I'm deeply concerned about Helen working alone. How will you extract her if things go haywire? I'm concerned for her safety. She reminds me of my granddaughter and I wouldn't want anything to happen to her."

"I'm not concerned. She's capable of taking care of herself. Not only is she the best techno-geek I've ever worked with, she's an accomplished soldier. I heard a story about her killing four Al Qaeda combatants in Iraq without blinking an eye."

"Tell me about Helen in Iraq."

There was a knock on the door. Jeff and Whitey peaked in. Jeff smiled and waved the cell phone Helen had used to infect Al's phone.

"I hope we're not interrupting," he said, "but I know you're looking for this."

"Please come in," Frank said. "We were just finishing up. Rusty was about to tell me about Helen's escapades in Iraq."

Rusty said, "Perfect timing, Whitey. Tell Mr. Reid the story about how Helen saved you and Bachman from Al Qaeda."

Whitey said, "You really don't want to hear that, do you?"

Rusty nodded, and pointed to an upholstered chair.

Whitey sat and began. "The three of us were transferred from Islamabad to Baghdad with orders to locate and rescue two Blackwater operatives captured near Eufrat. Bachman and I traced them to an Al Qaeda safehouse deep inside the city. Helen ran the techno part of the operation while Bachman and I were the team's muscle. Bachman and I were jumped in a market near the safehouse. We were stripped naked, bound and interrogated in another building. Six hours later, we were tied up and forced to kneel on the floor. These guys pulled out a camcorder and began taping us. They instructed us to read a manifesto. One of the guys had a huge sword and I'm certain he was going to lop off our heads as soon as we were done reading. All we could do was stall and hope someone would intervene. Helen had configured our phones to act as locators and microphones. She also had placed GPS transmitters inside the cuffs of our pants. She realized how desperate the situation was and took matters into her own hands."

Reid seemed shocked. "What did she do?"

Whitey continued, "After locating us, she changed into an abaya and hijab, then . . ."

The old man interrupted. "A what?"

"An abaya is a loose-fitting robe — sort of a dress — and a hijab is a head scarf that covers a woman's face and hair. Only the eyes are left uncovered."

Frank nodded. "Oh yes. I've seen that. Sorry I interrupted; please continue."

"Anyway, there was a solitary guard sitting outside by the front door. Helen carried a Tech-9 machine gun with a silencer under her abaya and approached the guard with a tray full of fruit. What she told us later was that she balanced the tray with her left hand and bowed to the guard while offering him some fruit. When he looked at the tray, she dusted him in the throat with the Tech-9. She entered the house and sprayed the other three insurgents. Helen stood guard and we got dressed. When we left the building, a small crowd had converged by the fallen guard. She pointed the gun at the onlookers, and they scrambled like rats. We made it to a minivan and split. Helen saved Bachman and me from certain death."

Reid looked dumbfounded. "Mercy. She's a hardened soldier and a hero besides. I'd have never guessed her tough-ass demeanor is for real."

Whitey nodded. "She's a seasoned veteran. If not for her, we'd be dead. Bachman and I have tremendous respect for that gal. She's like a younger sister to me and I owe her my life."

Frank looked at Whitey and Jeff. "Maybe she'll handle herself after all."

Whitey nodded. "You can count on it. You'd never want to get on her bad side."

The old man looked at Whitey. "Give me an assessment of the situation in Angoon."

Jeff tossed the phone to Rusty, and Whitey began. "We really could have used another team in a boat so we could pin down the source of the transmission, but hindsight is always crystal clear. The really troubling issue was the attempted monitoring of our final call. A boat to our east was the source."

Frank asked, "Do you think they pinpointed you or gained information from our call?"

"I'd say negative to both of those questions, sir. We snuck into position with little chance of detection and Helen immediately cut the communication off when we were scanned."

Jeff nodded in affirmation. "Immediately."

"Good. She's on top of things," Reid said. "I'm relieved. Whitey, do you have any theories regarding the person who monitored our call?"

"They either work for our target or it may have been a Homeland Security boat checking cell phone traffic in the area. You'd be surprised at how many agents are working our coastlines."

"Gentlemen, we can analyze this thing to death," Rusty said, "but we'll never arrive at a definitive answer. Our only hope lies in the events of tomorrow. Whitey, Jeff and I should pack our gear and get rolling."

He looked at Mr. Reid. "Unless you have anything else, I'll contact you when we're in position. Keep me posted on your decision about Henry's staff."

After the three mercenaries left the room, Gus spoke. "I know you're overwhelmed, but you need to relax. Remember what I said about destiny? We can't lose. I've got a good feeling about this."

"I hope you're right. Let's find Lena and get a bite to eat at a nice restaurant."

The two cousins left the library and closed the door behind them.

Angoon

Danny parked the Humvee at the end of the pier and walked toward the Bayliner. Helen had heard the truck's arrival and walked onto the boat's deck. She'd changed into a tight pair of black jeans and a long-sleeved white blouse. Seeing Danny without beer, she threw her arms to the sky and yelled, "Where's the half-rack of ale?"

He reached the boat. "There's a new twist. Perhaps you'd care to join us for dinner instead. We're a very casual group and we'd love to have you over."

Helen hesitated. "I'd feel out of place. Not many people dig the way I dress or my persona."

"What are you talking about? The way you look and dress is totally rad — and you're incredibly hot. Besides, after telling Dad about meeting you, it was his idea

190

to invite you. He's a hip dude and knows the score, and you'll get a kick out of my sister. My dad even recommended that you bring a swim suit for a dip in the hot tub after dinner. We'd really enjoy having you over for dinner."

Helen smiled. "That's very gracious, but I really don't know about this."

"C'mon Ms. Moorcroft. Please say 'yes' and grab your suit."

Helen was apprehensive but really wanted to be with Danny. She finally caved. "I didn't bring a suit. Would it be inappropriate to wear workout shorts and an oversized t-shirt?"

"Not at all. C'mon. Grab your shit and let's ride."

Helen went to the cabin and placed a cell phone, hand-held scanner, trunks and t-shirt into a small, black leather bag. She fumbled for a pack of smokes Whitey had left, then looked at herself in the mirror. She unbuttoned her blouse, removed her nipple rings, straightened her hair and wiped off her lipstick. After taking another look in the mirror, she twisted her nipples so they would perk up, buttoned her blouse and left.

When she reached the deck, Danny whistled. "Hot mama — you look terrific."

She smiled and winked. "I'm trying to impress you, Danny Boy."

Fifteen minutes later, Danny and Helen walked up the steps of the luxurious seaside home. She looked at the small scanner in the palm of her left hand, closed it shut and placed it into her bag.

Helen was taken aback by the massive beams and vaulted ceilings. She was ushered into the dining area, and Danny introduced her to his family and Ernie, then asked if anyone would care for a drink.

Audra commented, "Danny wasn't kidding when he said you were a hottie. I love the way you dress and what you've done with your hair. You belong on a runway or in Hollywood. He's always had good taste, if not good sense."

Helen grinned. "Thank you. Danny didn't exaggerate when he said you were wonderful people."

Ernie added, "If Danny doesn't treat ya good, date me. I know how to treat the ladies."

Helen laughed. "I bet you do Mr. McKinnon, you must have slayed the birdies when you were younger."

Danny showered and changed into a tight tank top that showed off his chiseled frame. His father taught him the advantages of being fit and muscular at an early age. Helen winked at him when he returned. She knew he was trying to impress her. Jim set the table and asked everyone to sit. Audra brought two large platters; one cradling the marinated grilled salmon and the other contained au gratin potatoes. Tequila lime butter with tarragon and dill complimented the pecan-crusted salmon. A tureen of lump crab bisque and an oblong bowl containing French-style green beans with almonds rounded out the elegant meal. Jim passed out wine glasses and opened two bottles of Blanc Bordeaux.

The sun slid behind the coastal mountains west of Angoon, producing a beautiful red sunset. The waters of Chatham were glassy calm as evening overtook a stormy day. Everyone complimented Audra on the outstanding meal. Jim offered to clean up so the others could retire to the living room with their wine and enjoy the sunset. It took little persuasion, and the group sat and enjoyed the panorama. The four of them talked for an hour about their lives, experiences and future plans. The group interacted effortlessly. Helen came to feel at ease in the Bennett household.

Jim had already recognized Helen's voice from the intercepted call coming from the ridge. He joined the group and sat across from her. "I understand you're here on a fishing trip. The waters around Angoon provide excellent sport fishing opportunities. How have you done so far?"

Helen responded, "Actually I've yet to soak a line. As soon as we arrived at the marina, my cousin was called back to Seattle. Some sort of business crisis. He'll return in two days and I'll try my luck then."

Jim asked, "How will you spend your time? There's not much happening in Angoon."

She hesitated, noting the scar on Jim's cheek. "I'll experiment with operating the boat and explore the area. The sightseeing here is awesome."

She changed the subject. "I do say your house is magnificent and the views from the windows are stunning. Whatever prompted you to build in such a remote location?"

"A friend told me about the area and I'd been looking for a place to spend my summers. I fell in love with this area and, in particular, its people. The rest is history. I overheard you say you're involved with computer software and worked for Scotland Yard. What type of work did you do?"

"I worked in the crime lab. Other than that, the nature of my work was classified, and I'm not at liberty to discuss specifics. I hope you'll understand."

Jim nodded. "Sorry I asked. I thoroughly understand the need for confidentiality. Perhaps you and Danny would care to sit in the spa and chat. I've got emails to check, Ernie would love to watch a *Lonesome Dove* DVD, and Audra can find something to occupy her time."

Helen smiled. "That would be top drawer, but anyone wishing to join us is welcome."

Audra asked, "Would you mind if I joined the two of you for a short while? I've a few questions I'd like to ask Helen — things about London and Europe. I promise I won't interfere for very long."

Danny grinned. "Of course you can, provided you volunteer to be designated bartender."

Jim set Ernie up with the first episode of *Lonesome Dove* while Helen, Danny and Audra prepared for the hot tub. Jim went to his computer room and got to work. He'd taped the hour-long conversation of the other four while cleaning the kitchen. His voice analysis program came up with a 97 percent match between the voice of the woman on the ridge and Helen. He saved the comparison, then deleted the taped conversation. After pondering the situation, Jim emailed General Hobson with the British Secret Intelligence Service and asked him to run a terse profile for Helen Moorcroft of Liverpool. He returned to the kitchen and quietly booted-up his hidden computer. It had received documents during dinner, which he downloaded to a flash drive. The trio in the spa could be heard laughing. He turned off his secret system and returning to his computer room. Jim plugged the drive into his other computer and read the Rigby file.

INTERPOL had yet to report, but he was pleased to see the FBI and CIA reports had been consolidated by Walt Diller. Walt and Doug had combined efforts to determine the identity of David Rigby — also known as Roger Albert Krantz. The reports were welcome. A facial recognition program verified the identity of Krantz. He was born in Rostock, Germany in 1942; the second son of Albert Krantz; a German officer listed as MIA by the Waffen in 1944. Albert was classified as a war criminal due to involvement with the Dachau concentration camp. Roger's mother Emma moved the family to Buenos Aires in January of 1945. How she managed to leave Germany was a mystery. Speculation about Albert's disappearance during the war led most investigators to believe that he'd transferred his family assets to Argentina through Persia. Albert never surfaced, but he was known to be involved with ODESSA and thought to be living in Argentina. The Krantzs had lived a privileged existence as guests of the Peron government.

Roger moved to Puerto Alegre, Brazil, in 1964 and married Maria Sanchez in 1966. Maria came from a family of wealthy oil distributors. She divorced Krantz in 1973. In the settlement, Krantz was given 1.5 million dollars by the Sanchez family to simply go away.

Maria disappeared shortly after the divorce, never to be seen again. Fearing blame and reprisal from the Sanchez family, Krantz changed his name to David Rigby and fled to Chile. He resided at the notorious Colonia Dignidad compound near Parral as a guest of his friend, Paul Schafer. Schafer had strong connections to President Pinochet and basked under his umbrella of protection. Rigby's spending habits never matched his known assets. He continually spent more than was reported in bank accounts.

The FBI concluded he was funded by his family in Argentina. Rigby also owned a small apartment in Hamburg and a respectable villa in Chile but both were sold in 1998. His whereabouts were unknown — until today. Diller recommended that the FBI apprehend him for questioning since he was on the Homeland Security watch list. Pawning himself off as an accomplished author provided ammunition for further scrutiny. Jim immediately connected Krantz, AKA Rigby, to the search for Nazi gold.

Jim moved onto the Vicente Santos report. He was a man who surfaced in Brazil from out of nowhere. There were no known records of his birth although he claimed to have been born in the slums of Rio in 1944. It was assumed he grew up on the streets of Rio. He became a field worker near Santos, Brazil, and took the name Santos while living there. He mysteriously raised enough money by age 30 to purchase a small pineapple farm outside of Rio. A year later, he sold it to a gas and oil refinery, which accounted for much of his wealth.

His citizenship was listed as Brazilian, but he had a peculiar accent and appears to be well educated. Street urchins from the slums of Rio seldom read or write and never rise to the level of wealth that Santos accumulated. He owns an apartment complex in Hamburg, a coastal villa in Rio and a summer home in Angoon, Alaska.

Because of many similarities between Vicente Santos and Roger Krantz (Hamburg, oil and gas and Brazil), the CIA recommended an in-depth analysis of the Santos' Hamburg connections as well as his personal income stream. The combination of unanswered questions about his past seemed odd, but Santos was considered legitimate and non-threatening to American interests.

Bennett leaned back in his chair and thought. He knew that Crane and Rigby were connected to the Nazi gold, but the disposition of Santos was unclear. The hiring of Crane by Santos seemed more than coincidence.

He shifted attention to Helen; she appeared sincere, but that's how coverts operate — infiltrate without suspicion. Maybe she was with Homeland Security — he'd wait for a report, but hoped that Danny wouldn't get burned in the process.

Jim took his encrypted phone from a desk drawer and called Walt Diller. After six rings, the voice mail kicked in. "This is Walt, you know the drill. I'll return your call ASAP."

Jim began to leave a message. "Hey Walt, this is Jim. Just checking . . ."

The agent answered the call. "Hey friend, you got my email. Is this line secure?"

Jim responded, "Yes — good to hear your voice, Walt. How's the family?"

"Fantastic! I'm finally a grandfather! Samantha had a baby girl last week. This is a special time for the Diller household."

"Congratulations are in order. How's Rachel?"

Walt knew that whenever Jim asked "How's Rachel?," it really meant to communicate via a special computer Jim had furnished him.

Walt answered, "She has a cold — otherwise she's a proud grandma. Say Jim, can I call you later? Rachel needs my help with something."

"No problem Walt — I'll call you another time. Congratulations on the new baby."

"Thanks Jim — bye."

Jim went to the kitchen and booted up his covert computer again. After activating the live video program, he contacted Walt on a secret system Jim had formatted at TacSec. He opened a live link to Walt sitting at a desk, smiling at the screen. A graying Black man blinked at the monitor and said, "This must be important Jim — what's up?"

"First off, I'm thrilled that you're a grandfather — what's the babies' name?"

Walt rolled his eyes. "Tarysha."

"A unique name. I'm really glad for you — it's a marvelous addition to your life."

Walt smiled. "Thanks partner. I appreciate your comment, but it's an awful name. I bet you called this meeting because of the report I sent."

"Yes. I need another favor related to the report."

"I'm at your beck and call," Walt said. "What can I do for you?"

"I need the latest high-resolution satellite images downloaded to Elmendorf for southern Admiralty Island from NORAD sats that pan southward. If I find what I'm looking for, I'd want a link so I can pinpoint my target and zoom accordingly. I also need the SAR deep-water radar imagery for Whitewater Bay."

Walt squinted, exposing deep lines at the corner of his eyes. "That's sensitive material Jim, is your system 100 percent secure and encrypted?"

"Affirmative — TacSec wrote the program."

Walt asked, "Is this about Krantz?"

"That's a big affirmative."

Walt nodded. "Can I provide you with a real time link?"

"That would be outstanding. I also need a baseline matrix of the area for comparisons. Ideally clear midsummer pics from '06 and '07 for the following coordinates: Latitude 57° 14' to 29', Longitude 134° 33' to 36'. Two klicks in all directions of those coordinates would be helpful."

Walt wrote the numbers onto a note pad. "I can arrange that. How long will you require real-time images?"

Jim paused. "Four days. I need mid a.m. and p.m. swings — fifteen minutes per pass."

Walt nodded. "Okay, I'll contact the Pentagon and General Runkle at Elmendorf. If I'm asked, you're my direct agent working to pin down Krantz."

The former colonel and CIA operative was pleased. "Thanks, my friend. Keep me posted on the Santos-Hamburg investigation. I need to know why these guys are here."

Walt rummaged through a small booklet and said, "Write this down — your access code is Alpha Tango 616 for the NORAD satellite and Echo Charlie 210 for the SAR imager. You'll be able to link up by 7:00 a.m. tomorrow. I'll have General Runkle forward the baseline matrix tonight."

Jim saluted his friend. "Thanks Walt. We'll talk again soon. Congratulations on becoming a grandfather. Give your darling wife a hug for me. By the way, are you still planning on coming up for the silver run in August?"

"I wouldn't miss that in a million years. If it's anything like last year, I'll fill my freezer with scrumptious filets. Would you mind if I brought my son-in-law George along? He's a good kid and loves fishing."

"That would be great. I met him at the wedding. He's a terrific kid."

"Thanks partner. I'd better be going. Say hello to your family for me — bye."

Audra left the hot tub and dried off with an enormous beach towel. She chuckled at Ernie — snoring while his western played.

Jim shut down his system and went to hug his daughter. "I'm glad you came to visit. You're always welcome here, and if you care to bring a friend, they're welcome too. Now that I'm retired, I'd like to visit you in Seattle from time to time if that's OK."

She smiled. "I'd love that — I could show you around town. It's a really nice place."

Jim added, "I'd like that. Remember, if there's anything you need or require help in any way — financially or emotionally — don't hesitate to call me."

"I appreciate the offer. Things are going fine. If I do need help, you'll be the first to know."

Jim was pleased. He changed the subject. "How are the two love birds doing out there?"

"Wonderfully — they're a perfect fit. I know Danny's falling head over heels for her and she's just what he needs. We talked about her life and family in Liverpool, which was rather sad. She grew up in poverty in a two-bedroom flat above a small pub. Her father was a heroin addict who died of an overdose when she was nine. She and her brother were raised by her mother, who died of brain cancer three years ago. I'm of the opinion that she's had a rough go of things when she was young."

Jim asked, "Is she close with her brother?"

"Yes. He's two years younger and in the Royal Navy. I must admit, I like her a lot — she's very engaging and promised to visit me in Seattle."

"Do you think she likes Danny?"

"Oh boy — the way she keeps looking into his eyes, I'd say she's swept off her feet. If you haven't noticed, Danny's quite handsome and she knows it. And, she's incredibly attractive, don't you think?"

"She's a cutie. I hope things work out so neither of them gets hurt — that's the important thing." He looked at the snoozing prospector. "I'd better wake Ernie and send him to bed. I'll turn down the lights, start the fireplace and play some Moody Blues for our two love birds."

"You've turned into a romantic. Remember to do the same for Lori when she gets here."

He hugged Audra, kissed her on the forehead and said good night.

Helen had repositioned herself next to Danny as soon as Audra left. They sat silently watching the waters of Chatham. The lights dimmed inside the house and soft music flowed from the outside speakers. Turning to Helen, Danny focused on a beautifully-drawn butterfly on her upper right arm and asked, "Do you mind if I take a better look?"

She smiled and pulled the short sleeve to her shoulder, exposing several other well-crafted designs. Close examination revealed an unusual butterfly sitting with outstretched wings on top of clustered, round, neon-pink flowers. An electric blue followed the wing's shape to the outer wing, transforming into shimmering purples and ending in black. The unique coloration gave the appearance of one butterfly sitting on top of another, yet it was clearly a solitary being. Long, thin, purple antennas draped over the flowers as if guarding their nectar.

Danny commented, "I've never seen anything like this before. It's incredible."

Helen smiled. "That's a female Ulysses Blue Swallowtail from the Australian rainforest. She's feeding on Doughwood tree flowers. It's a rare insect indeed."

His eyes wandered to another unique tattoo which was actually connected to the neon pink flowers. The Doughwood tree's thin branches and waxy green, spear-shaped leaves contained a slender brightly-colored snake, crimson with black and yellow diamonds on its back. It was wrapped around a branch and looked toward the feeding swallowtail.

Danny asked, "Any symbolism going on between the snake and the butterfly?"

"Indeed — I am the butterfly and my vocation is the snake. The Ulysses Swallowtail appears to be two separate creatures but they're one. Like the butterfly, my persona is different from who I am — someday I'll explain. As for the snake, you would think that it has the upper hand and is about to have lunch but the distance between the Doughwoods' flowers and its branches gives the advantage to Ulysses. By draping her antennae over the flower, she can feel the vibrations of the snake as he tries closing the gap. The tree's characteristics prevent the snake from coiling up and striking, forcing it to slowly extend itself toward the flower, giving itself away. Like the butterfly, I'll never allow my profession to consume me."

"Wow — that's deep. Do all of your tats have hidden meanings?"

She nodded. "Every one tells a story and someday I hope to have the opportunity to explain them."

"I can honestly say that I've never seen this level of quality or detail before. Knowing that they all have meaning simply blows my mind."

Helen caught movement inside the house. She turned and watched Jim enter his bedroom, then laid back in the spa and said, "Tell me about your father."

"There's nothing to say other than he's a terrific person who cares about his family and friends."

"How did he get the scar on his face? It's not what you'd expect of a CEO."

"Remember when you said your former job was classified and you couldn't talk about things?"

"Of course. Is that the case with your father?"

"Yes, and to be honest with you, I don't know the exact specifics. He never talks about it and avoids questions related to work. However, this is a matter of public record: my late grandfather Bennett was a Senator and Yale graduate who belonged to the Skull & Bones Society. He chaired the armed services committee and was aligned with the Department of Defense and CIA. He and my father were extremely close."

"I've heard of the Skull & Bones Society. Aren't they a campus organization of students whose goals are to become high-level politicians and business leaders within America?"

"That's the rumor. Grandfather wanted me to attend Yale and follow in his footsteps, but I disappointed him by declining. Imagine anyone passing up a free education at Yale."

She ran her fingers through his long hair. "I can say this much about your father. He's a gracious host, raised wonderful children and has excellent taste in music. I love the Moody Blues. So, Danny, I want to know about you and what you expect from life."

Danny shrugged. "OK. Let me collect my thoughts."

After a brief pause, he said, "First and foremost, I want to understand existence — why we're here and what it's all about. Since tripping on psychedelics in college, I've been obsessed with those questions, but answers to life are elusive — always beyond our grasp and constantly changing. Since graduation, I've had an overwhelming feeling that I'm destined for something extraordinary, but I can't put my finger on it. It's frustrating. My mother pushed religion on me as a teenager, but I couldn't dig it. In college, self-indulgence became all-consuming. I partied like a rock star. That became a trap, but I buckled down and graduated a year behind schedule. Now I'm compelled to do something worthwhile with my education — something that contributes to the grand scheme of things. I'm evolving as a person, I hope in the right direction."

Danny repositioned himself in the spa.

"Recently, I developed and filed for patents on an extremely simple and effective piezoelectric harvesting system which harnesses energy from vibrations, motion and strain. Marketing it is my immediate goal, so I'm busting my ass in construction to save enough money to see this through.."

"Imagine grabbing energy from the sound of a city or the movement of traffic over congested highways. I've done it with prototypes and I know I can do it on a grand scale. My attorneys are so high on the idea that they're absorbing a portion of the patent costs in exchange for one percent of my net. My dad offered to help me out financially last night, but I want to do this on my own."

Helen smiled. "That's fantastic. Intellect, independence and looks!"

"Haha. Thanks." He continued. "The story of trying to figure shit out now brings me to relationships. Several college buddies say really connecting with a woman is an awesome thing, but I've never experienced it. I thought my parents had it figured out, but they got divorced. That made me skeptical. If they couldn't make it work, what makes me think that I can — and I've never met the right person. Maybe someday I'll find that connection. Right now, It feels like I'm on a treadmill, searching for life's mysteries and trying to make a difference."

Helen clapped. "Bravo! That's an incredibly honest assessment of yourself."

Danny turned to the beautiful woman sitting next to him. "You know my story — or much of it. Tell me what Helen expects from life."

Helen smiled and turned away. "Helen expects you to rub her shoulders," she teased. Soon Danny's muscular hands were at work.

"Similarly," she said as she pushed back against the massage, "I'm hung up on human consciousness and why we're here. It's a constant process with no end in sight. My grandmother — like your mum — pushed religion on me when I was young. As I matured it became a useless stream of ritual and dogma based on the fear of death. I wanted — needed — to climb from poverty, so I excelled in school, which led me to my current career. I'm grateful for the money, but I despise my work and find myself lacking direction. I envy you having a meaningful goal with your energy harnessing thing. Like you, I find myself stuck on a treadmill — consumed by work. There's little time to consider anything else. That's pretty much it."

Danny asked, "What about relationships?"

He ran his thumbs down both sides of her spine.

199

"Mmmmm," she said. "As noted on your fathers' boat, my employment makes it impossible, but like you, I'm looking for someone I can connect with. At the risk of immediate rejection — why wait, right? — I am drawn to you. You're fascinating, handsome and smart."

He smiled and kissed her cheek. "Thank you. There'll be no rejection from me. You're beautiful and captivating. And, you must've heard that countless times before."

Helen moved to straddle Danny's lap. She smiled. "Maybe, but I'm glad you said it." She looked into his eyes and kissed him with a slightly open mouth. Danny slid his hands under her shirt, planted his hands firmly on her back, and pulled her to his chest. Her breasts pressed against him as they explored each other's mouths. Danny's right hand gently massaged the side of her left breast, perking its nipple. Helen retreated slightly and giggled.

Danny pulled his hand back and whispered, "Sorry. Too fast?"

Helen pulled his hand firmly back to her breast. "That doesn't bother me. I laughed because I felt your stiffy while we were snogging. Sorry I laughed — it's delightful that I arouse you."

Danny frowned. "I can guess what a stiffy is, but what's snogging?"

"French kissing. I'm not making fun; I'm flattered that you find me attractive." She kissed him again. "Do you like me Danny?"

He answered, "I do. You're fantastic."

"That's uppermost, because I feel the same about you. Perhaps you should take me back to my boat so we can check out each other's tattoos?"

Shocked and pleased by her boldness, Danny smiled. "I'm all over that. Let's saddle up and hit the trail."

Thirty minutes later, they were in the Bayliner's master birth. Helen pulled back the blanket of the queen sized bed and turned to Danny. He held out a small pipe and asked, "Care for a toke?"

She grinned. "We're getting blazed before booty call — jolly good plan."

After several tokes each, Danny unbuttoned her blouse, exposing firm breasts with hard pink nipples. She grabbed his hair with her left hand, kissed him and gently placed her right thigh into his groin. They tumbled onto the bed.

For the next few hours, they explored each other's bodies, during which both were taken to heights they'd never experienced.

Early morning sun interrupted the couple's seemingly endless embrace.

Helen was confused. "It can't be morning. What time is it?"

Danny reached onto the floor for his watch and looked at it. "It's 4:35 — days are awfully long this far north."

"Bloody hell indeed!" She wrapped her arms around him and kissed him again.

She became pensive. "Danny, I'm afraid of what's happening here. I'm falling for you, but I can't allow this to happen — at least not now."

He was confused. "Why not?"

She considered the risk, but she felt she had to be upfront with this man. "Because part of my work may involve you."

Danny flashed on what his father warned him about. "I thought you were between jobs."

"I am, but I'm not. I'm on a temporary assignment — it's a complicated situation."

Danny pressed her. "How am I involved with your work?"

Helen hesitated, then offered, "I'm on a fact-finding mission. Every person in and around Angoon should be off limits to me."

"Then why did you sleep with me?"

She wiped a tear away and said, "I've said too much —far too much."

She thought about her mother's visions. "I'm very confused right now, but if I knew you felt about me as I do about you, I'd quit this bloody job and hang onto you like a new tattoo."

Danny turned toward her. "That's heavy. Look, my feelings for you are strong as well —so where does that leave us?"

"I'm not sure. Let's spend the day together and see what happens. You can teach me more about how to operate this boat while we explore the area and each other. If things continue to click, I'll contact my employer and tender my resignation."

He asked, "You'd quit your job for me? Just like that."

"I'd have to — I'd want to. Besides, my position would be compromised. There are so many things I want to tell you, but I can't right now."

Danny added, "I'm curious how this relates to me and the people of Angoon, but I won't dig into into your job. I agree. Let's spend the day together and see what happens."

She touched his cheek and kissed him. "Thank you. You're tops."

"Since it's light enough to see, roll over and let me get a good look at your tattoos."

Helen smiled, kissed him again and rolled onto her stomach. A tastefully-done work of art ran the length of her back. A combination bird and fairy-like creature stood on the cheeks of her buttocks and ran up the center of her back to her shoulder blades. The figure was looking over its shoulder. It's face was almost identical to hers but had long, flowing black hair. The creature's outstretched wings wrapped around Helen's sides and the feathered tips ended at the sides of her breasts.

The tattoo was beautifully colored with expertly shaded blues, greens, yellows and reds. Its outstretched wing tips and feathers seemed to change color from different angles — almost like a chameleon changing with its environment. Danny had never seen such a unique tattoo.

He touched the face. "It's absolutely stunning. Where did you have this done?"

"London. The face is that of my mother. I had it done when she was diagnosed with cancer. She loved it. My Mum was the finest person I've ever known. I believe she'd love you too."

Danny commented, "She looks — or I should say, 'looked' — exactly like you."

Helen nodded. "My worthless Pop always said so."

Within an hour, the couple had fallen asleep with Helen's breasts pressed against Danny's back with her right arm wrapped around his torso.

CHAPTER FIVE

June 12 — Angoon, Alaska

Helen snuck out of bed, quietly dressed, and stood at the end of the bed watching Danny sleep. She smiled. Amazed at Angoon's silence, she stepped onto the dock. The sun illuminated the snow covered peaks to the east. Rain clouds loomed on the northern horizon, but weather over the sleepy village was clear and calm. She called Rusty but got voice mail, so she tried reaching Whitey only to encounter his voicemail. Helen avoided leaving messages. She called Mr. Reid's private number.

Frank was speaking with Henry's staff aboard the yacht. He excused himself and answered.

"This is Blue Marlin."

"Top of the morning to you, sir," Helen said. "I'm calling to furnish an update. Rusty and Whitey didn't answer. They must be busy. Am I interrupting anything?"

"Not at all. It's very good to hear your voice, young lady; I've been worried sick about you — are you alright?"

Helen walked in small circles, looking down at the wooden planks. "Yes, sir, I'm very well indeed. I'm embedded in Angoon with the family who owns the boat that scanned us yesterday. I believe they're legitimate and unconnected to our targets."

He asked, "Is this conversation secure?"

She scanned in all directions. "Yes, sir. I've scanned the area and we're clear. Besides, my phone has a built-in alarm if I'm being monitored."

Frank said, "Very good. Tell me, how do you explain the phone interception and attempted monitoring yesterday?"

Helen offered her only logical explanation. "I can't say with certainty, but I believe the owner of the boat is a government employee — perhaps Homeland Security. He's merely monitoring cell phone chatter along the coastline — nothing more."

Reid asked, "Why do you think he's with the government?"

"By the way he presents himself. I've been trained to look for certain characteristics and mannerisms — he fits the mold.

"Why would he monitor our call?"

"Uncle Sam has intercept stations and personnel everywhere. He's not our adversary, sir."

"Who is this person?"

"Jim Bennett. He's from Denver with a summer home in Angoon. He's also the son of the late Senator William Bennett, chair of the Armed Services Committee."

"That name sounds familiar but I can't quite place it. You believe he's not a threat?"

"Correct. He's top-shelf. I had dinner with his family last night and they're totally genuine. I'll run his name through our database and see what comes up. Today, I plan on tracking down the *Oregon II* and catamaran. I also placed a GPS tracker on Bennett's boat so I can monitor his movements.``

"Very well. I trust your judgment, but be careful. These are dangerous times. If anything goes haywire, lay low and contact me directly. I'll have you extracted."

Helen stared into the water as a school of minnows swam by. "I understand, sir."

"Now that you're working for me, I want you to know that a sizable bonus has been set aside for you personally — this is above and beyond what I've allocated to Rusty' crew. Please don't disclose this information to other team members, as it would create friction. You're doing a magnificent job and I appreciate your attention to detail."

Helen was confused. "I didn't know I was working directly for you, sir. Rusty simply alluded that I might have an employment opportunity with you in the near future. It's troublesome. I never notified Dark Star about leaving."

"That's odd. Has Whitey mentioned working for me as well?"

"No, sir. I'm sure he's under the same impression as me. We work for Dark Star."

Frank was concerned at Rusty's lack of attention to detail, but defended him. "Rusty must be overtaxed and forgot. I'll handle things from here. I need to start from the beginning — will you entertain working directly for me? I'll double what you're making at Dark Star. Regardless of your decision, you'll receive a $250,000 bonus when you return to Port Angeles."

"That's a sizable offer, sir. And difficult to resist." She paused, thinking hard. After a moment, she said, "I accept the offer. I'll contact Dark Star and tender my resignation. Your generosity is only surpassed by your charm. We'll enjoy working together, but I need to be up front. I don't plan on this line of work for much longer. I'm burning out and I'd like to settle down."

Frank was pleased. "I appreciate your candor and hope you'll see my mission through to its conclusion. As for your decision to quit the profession, I'm thrilled for you. I think you deserve the best in life, and you're making an excellent choice.

If there's anything I can do for you afterwards, don't hesitate to ask. You're a wonderful young lady."

Helen smiled. "Thank you very much, sir. Since Rusty's tied up with the California project, shall I report directly to you?"

Frank said, "That would be best."

Helen ended the conversation. "I must go now. Thank you for the bonus — it's greatly appreciated."

Helen said, "Bloody hell! What a way to start the day." She looked at her phone — it was 7:15. She turned toward shore. Jim Bennett was walking down the hill toward the marina. The Hummer was still parked next to the boat ramp from the night before. She murmured to herself, "It's a terrible predicament you've gotten yourself into Ms. Moorcroft." Helen walked up the dock to greet Jim.

In a business-like tone, Jim said, "Good morning. Is Danny on my boat or yours?"

"My boat, sir — he's sleeping."

Jim commented, "It must have been a long night."

Helen blushed. "Not long enough I'm afraid."

Jim placed a hand on her shoulder and pointed her toward shore. "Let's take a short walk and discuss a few things."

Her heart dropped. She felt cornered and intimidated. They walked up the path toward town. When the marina was out of view, Jim stopped and took out a folded paper from his top pocket. He looked her square in the eyes.

"Friends in the British Secret Service sent me a report. You currently work as an operative for Dark Star — a startup PMC. You worked undercover in Pakistan and Iraq for a short time, and recently reassigned to the U.S. Prior to that, you worked for Scotland Yard, which only lasted two months. Before that, you worked for the British MI-6 in their intelligence division. I know who you are. What transpired on top of Catherine Island yesterday afternoon?"

She shook her head. "I'm sorry Mr. Bennett, but that's classified."

He asked, "Why are you here? It's not for fishing."

"I'm not at liberty to say. You, of all people, should understand."

The former colonel was noticeably annoyed. "You know little, if anything, about me. Besides I'm asking the questions."

Helen shook her head. "That's rather one sided, wouldn't you say? I could be asking similar questions of you, sir. Why were you eavesdropping on a private telephone call and why did you try to infect my phone? Why do you have VME, TDMA and IMSI antennas on your boat — not to mention the military SATCOM-5 satellite dish? That's uncharacteristic equipment for a fishing boat. Are you a private military contractor or a CIA operative? Shall I go on?"

Jim smirked. "Please do. This is entertaining."

"Very well, sir. Who are you working for, and how did you get the beef jerky scar on your face? It wasn't in the corporate world. CEOs fight with attorneys."

Jim winced and instinctively nodded. "Touché. You have quite an acid tongue, young lady. Dark Star has plenty of resources. You'll know about me soon enough. The problem with your organization is their reputation for working both ends against the middle."

"PMC's don't care what the mission is or who's paying the bill as long as there's enough money involved. We're both professionals who know the score. We may be adversaries. Then again, we could be allies. It's too early in the game to know, because it's the nature of what we do, but there's a huge difference between us. You do it for money. I do it for the freedoms we enjoy."

Helen wanted to provide a nasty retort, but Jim's comments were on point. That's why she hated her profession. She managed a civil response. "Don't be hypocritical, sir. We share the same line of work. What we do is never black or white. It's always littered with gray. That's why I despise my job — allies today may be enemies tomorrow."

"Are you playing my son to get at me or McKinnon?" Jim asked

"No, sir. I'm not playing your son."

"It sure seems that way."

She turned to him and looked into his eyes. "I say this on my mother's grave: I'm not playing Danny. I'm very fond of your son; honestly drawn to him. I hope he feels the same about me. I admit to being a PMC but my specialty is surveillance, not combat. I'd never harm Danny."

Jim softened. "I'm being a hard-ass, but if you're telling the truth, we share something special — we both have feelings for my son. If we're on opposite sides of the fence, understand this: I'll kill for my children. After reading my dossier, you'll understand how efficient I can be. If you or your employer threatens my family, you'll witness a shit storm of biblical proportions. Understood?"

Helen nodded. "Yes, sir. I believe you and don't doubt your abilities. We're both bats on a sticky wicket, but I promise you this: I'll remove myself from this project before jeopardizing your family."

They heard the Humvee coming toward them from below. Jim wondered what "bats on a sticky wicket" meant, but he was out of time.

"I appreciate your candor. It's best we keep this conversation between the two of us. The last thing I want in life is to alienate myself from my son. Why don't you grab a change of clothes and take a shower at my place. We'll have breakfast and try to put this conversation in perspective. At least for the time being. Are you agreeable to that?"

Helen was angry but polite. "Yes, sir, and thank you. I don't say this lightly — I may be in love with Danny and would never do anything to harm him or your family."

The Humvee pulled alongside Jim and Helen, and Danny powered down his window. "Hey Dad, sorry about not returning your rig — I overslept."

Jim smiled at his son. "That's perfectly alright. Helen and I were just talking; she agreed to come home for breakfast and a hot shower. She needs a few things from her boat. Why don't you grab her things while I jog back — I need the exercise."

Returning to the boat, Helen remained silent. Danny felt her tension and asked what was wrong. Tears welled into her eyes, and she threw her arms around him.

"You're wonderful, Danny Boy. No matter what the future brings, you've got to know that spending last night with you was splendid."

"Say lover girl, the feeling's mutual." He let her go, and she went to gather her things.

When she returned to the Humvee, he said, "I had the weirdest dream just before waking up. We were together on a beautiful white yacht. Standing on deck, I pulled on a thick rope, expecting a crab pot, but somehow I managed to get tangled with a submarine propeller. My subconscious is telling me something."

Helen smiled. "Later I'll tell you about my mum's dreams. You'll think she was either totally wacko or fall madly in love with me. Come on, let's go."

Early morning — Trinidad, California

Eleven Dark Star personnel assembled in Henry's study before Rusty and Whitey entered. Absolute silence filled the room as Rusty sat behind a desk facing the group. Whitey stood to the side of the desk.

Rusty began, "I'm only going over this once, so pay attention. Our target will be at the Eureka Mall by 1 p.m. He has an accomplice. They must not escape. Apprehending them inside the mall is out of the question, so every exit must be covered."

He turned to one of the men. "John, you will get a cell phone video of our main target when he's outside the pet store — he'll be wearing a red baseball cap. Live stream the video to our van for everyone to see."

Rusty continued, "Here's the plan — I'm calling him on the corner phone by the pet store. I'll arrange a meeting in the rear parking lot. The lot faces Humboldt Bay, so he'll be boxed in. Once he's outside, cover the two rear exits to prevent him from reentering the mall. I want each end of the parking lot sealed so he can't escape. You can bet his accomplice will be tailing him from a distance and that they'll have a method of communicating. This is where it gets sticky."

"I'll be sitting on a motorcycle near the bay wearing a Hell's Angels vest. I plan on talking with Al while sitting on the bike, then encourage him to have his accomplice join us for an introduction. When he shows, we apprehend both marks. I need these guys alive. No gunfire unless they start shooting or if escape is imminent. If that happens, make sure they're dead, then disappear. Afterwards, we'll meet at the warehouse. Any questions?"

One of the operatives asked, "What if the second mark doesn't show?"

Rusty answered, "He'll be there. It's just a matter of identifying him. If I can't convince Al into having him join us, we grab Al and watch the parking lot to see who splits in an awful hurry. Follow that vehicle and run him off the road. If he dies, then so be it."

The room remained silent. These were professional killers who knew what was expected. As the meeting was about to adjourn, the phone Helen had infected rang. Rusty placed his fingers to his lips and walked to the corner of the room.

Angoon — Morning

On the table were platters with French toast, fresh baked muffins and bacon and a carafe of coffee. Danny sat between Helen and Audra with an arm around each of their shoulders and commented about how lucky he was to sit between two beautiful women. Ernie said he envied Danny

A cell phone rang in Helen's tote bag near the front door. Helen asked to be excused, then hurried to answer her phone. Jim got up and walked into his bedroom. He looked at his IMSI monitor and placed a headphone to his ear.

Audra asked, "What are the chances of both of them leaving the room at the same time?"

Ernie shook his head. "Always askin' questions."

"Put a sock in it Ernie. Why do you mock me?" Audra retorted.

Ernie couldn't resist. "There ya go again — always askin' questions."

Audra laughed and threw a piece of bacon at Ernie. He picked it up and began eating it.

Helen walked onto the front porch. Jim remained in his bedroom. In Trinidad, Rusty stood in the corner of Henry's study and listened in as well. "Al" was making a call.

"Buenos dias. I'm checking in as promised."

"You've arrived?"

"We got here late last night. We're at a restaurant having breakfast."

"What we recovered yesterday turned out to be a sunken barge so your meeting today is crucial. Don't screw it up."

"I won't."

"Call me after the meeting."

"I will. Goodbye."

That ended the call. Helen returned to the table, kissed Danny on the cheek and continued eating breakfast. Audra taunted Danny by humming her song from yesterday. "Danny's got a girlfriend — Danny's got a girlfriend." Danny elbowed her and the table erupted with laughter.

Jim went from his bedroom to his computer room and scrolled through several programs on his laptop. The call had originated from an outside source connected to a 907 area code. His surveillance video of the Santos compound showed the catamaran still parked at his dock. Jim noted that the caller's number didn't match one used by Rigby. However, the voices sounded exactly like Rigby's and Santos'. Bennett concluded that Rigby had simply used a different phone. He returned to the table and sat down.

"Sorry for the interruption," he said. He looked at Helen. "Enjoying breakfast?"

She winked at Jim. "Yes, sir, it's wonderful. I appreciate your hospitality."

Jim said, "Don't thank me. Audra's been the chef lately."

Trinidad

In Henry's study, Rusty spoke into his shirt cuff microphone. "Did you pin down the location of his call?"

His earpiece said, "It's coming from a Eureka cell tower. That's as close as I got."

Rusty addressed his team. "He's here and so is his accomplice. They're at a restaurant having breakfast somewhere in Eureka. It's early. Break into teams and scour all the local breakfast joints around town. Look for two men. One's in his sixties, the other's in his late thirties or early forties."

"If the man I saw yesterday is Al," Whitey said, "he's around five-foot-ten, 180 pounds and going bald. We've heard him speak — he's got a European accent."

Rusty nodded. "Alright gentlemen, let's do this."

Angoon

Danny finished eating and announced, "If you guys don't mind, I'd like to take Helen sightseeing today. We'll take her boat. I promise to be back before Lori gets here."

Audra loved ribbing her brother. "I plan on quizzing Helen about the sights when she returns. It better not be the color of your eyes."

Danny tried elbowing her again but she was prepared and intercepted the blow. Jim told him that he didn't mind. He had calls to make and needed to meet with the Clans at the marina. Ernie offered to be Helen's tour guide if she'd leave Danny behind, which made her laugh. She stood and began clearing the table. Jim said he'd handle the cleanup, but she insisted on helping.

While Jim and Helen were alone in the kitchen loading the dishwasher Jim asked, "Tell me something. The call you listened to. Good guys or bad guys?"

"Not the sort of men I'd bring home to meet my Mum."

Jim smiled and asked, "What's a 'bat on a sticky wicket?'"

Helen replied, "A difficult and awkward position."

Jim nodded, then patted Helen on top of her head. "Both responses are encouraging."

Danny entered the room with a handful of coffee cups. "Hey, leave my lady friend alone. Keep that up and I'll tell Lori you're hitting on a woman half your age."

Jim laughed. "Whoa there, big fella, I wouldn't want that. You love birds get your things together so I can take you to the marina. I need to meet the Clans soon and there's no sense in making two trips."

Audra and Ernie stayed behind while Jim drove the others to the marina. After disarming his surveillance system, Jim moved the fifty-gallon garbage bag of halibut remains from *Sojourn's* deck to the pier.

Helen started her boat and Danny continued the lesson that Whitey had begun. He explained the procedure for backing away from the dock. She placed the cruiser into reverse and allowed the idling engines to slowly back the boat away from its birth. After it cleared Jim's boat, she placed the control levers into neutral, turned the steering wheel toward open water and engaged the engines without accelerating. She smiled with a sense of accomplishment as the large boat chugged into the bay. Once the cruiser reached a safe distance from the dock, Helen cracked the throttles slightly open.

Danny stood behind her and coached her through the rocky inlet toward Chatham Strait. When the boat cleared the rocks, they accelerated into the channel. Helen smiled the entire time.

She turned to Danny. "You're a wonderful teacher."

Jim wasn't satisfied with the job Danny had done rinsing his deck. He hosed it down and began scrubbing with a long, wooden-handled brush. As he finished the final rinse, five Clan members walked toward his boat. Jim climbed onto the dock and greeted them. Hilda hugged her friend as the others looked on.

"Thank you for showin' up, Mr. Bennett. We got a call from Mr. Santos. He said we could hire a replacement of our choice, but he'd like it done soon. Ya got any ideas?"

"Run ads in the Juneau and Sitka papers and post a help-wanted message on the State website — you'll get someone to respond. The quickest solution is to hire a security guard from a temp agency in Juneau. That way, replacement is immediate but you'll be paying a middle man — the agency."

"I like that idea," Hank said. "It's quick and painless. I'll call an agency today."

Hilda asked, "Is your offer for background checks still good?"

Jim nodded. "I'm more than happy to help. That way you have a known commodity."

Mel said, "I heard ya talkin about phone taps. What's that about?"

Jim explained the situation with Crane and Ernie's cabin. He jumped into his boat and retrieved three color photos of Crane taken inside Ernie's cabin. While handing them out he said, "Anyone who enters another person's house, plants a bug and rummages through their belongings can't be trusted. He tried entering my place, and he's been into Ernie's cabin several times. As a former Sacramento policeman, he has access to wiretaps and surveillance equipment. It doesn't surprise me that he's using those resources in Angoon. He's smarter than we give him credit for."

Mel asked, "What good would any of that do him now. He's been canned."

"At the very least, he's got to return and get his motorhome. He might hang around for a while. For all we know, he could be a new neighbor."

Hilda barked, "Over my dead body. I'll drown that damned rat."

Mel offered, "Why not feed him to the bear? We oughta take Jim's advice and hold meetin's at the school till he's out of our hair."

A large group of ravens flew over the dock and circled, cawing to each other. Over thirty birds juked and jived in different directions.

Hilda said, "There's a battle comin' — ravens never do this unless a big fight's on the horizon."

Mel nodded. "Yup. Judgin' from the number of birds, it's gonna be a doozy."

Jim asked, "Tlingit prophecy?"

The group nodded in agreement.

Jim shifted gears, noting that the nuisance bear was hanging around his house and that he'd appreciate it if Hank moved the trap to the tree line next to his shed. He offered the halibut carcass as fresh bait, and Hank eagerly accepted. They said their farewells, and Jim reset the security system on his boat, walked to the Humvee and returned home.

Chatham Strait

Danny leaned in and said to Helen, "Stop the boat for a moment."

She obliged him and asked, "What's up?"

"Let me show you how to use the navigation system to plot a course. That way you'll never get lost."

Helen looked serious. "I did that with Whitey yesterday. Watch this."

Within moments, the navionic system was set for the mouth of Peril Straight. The boat's current position was highlighted as a tiny red triangle and their route was a dashed line ending at a circle surrounding an "x." Danny wondered how she learned how to set a navigational system so quickly and why she chose Peril Strait. Helen advanced throttle to full speed, and the Bayliner skipped across Chatham. After ten minutes, a pod of whales came into view. She cut the engines and started taking pictures. She confessed she'd never seen a whale before.

Helen whispered, "They're totally lit. I can't believe how big they are. Is it dangerous to be this close?"

"No, and there's no need to whisper. They can't hear you. Climb to the pilot-house to get a better view."

She climbed to the upper bridge and watched in amazement as the whales passed within a hundred feet of their boat. Enormous tails effortlessly propelled them through the crystal clear water. Twenty-foot water spouts blew toward the sky as their curved backs crested the calm surface. Helen took several close up photos of the passing herd, then scrambled down to the main captain's chair.

"Danny, how do I run the boat from up above?"

"It's no different from the cabin. It's all connected. There's another nav system on top, so the only difference is you're exposed to the elements."

Helen replied, "Let's go above. It's a better view."

After thirty minutes of open running, the Bayliner reached the mouth of Peril Strait. Helen was disappointed to see the *Oregon II* was gone. She cut the throttles and entered the narrow passage and asked, "Would you mind operating the boat from below while I get to the internet and check for messages. Let me run down and get my bag. I need to be alone for just a bit."

"That's fine, but where do you want me to go?"

"Continue into the entrance, but very slowly."

As Danny went below, he commented, "Whatever the lady wants, the lady shall have."

Helen returned to the flying bridge and pointed a small satellite dish toward the southern sky. She turned on her laptop and entered a secure government site through Dark Star. Several minutes of searching provided her the dossier of Colonel James D. Bennett. Specific information about his background was classified "top secret" and blacked out, but she clearly understood he wasn't bluffing about his efficiency. His experience as a Delta commander with interconnecting ties to the CIA and Oval Office meant his experience level was light years beyond hers — he was definitely a "big time" player. She wondered if TacSec was a legitimate defense contractor or another CIA front. Perhaps it was a combination of the two.

Helen closed the program and looked up NOAA ship Number 332. To her surprise, its location was listed as Catalina Island, California. It was recently refitted and was performing fish surveys on the Catalina Shelf, where it was scheduled to remain for the summer. Afterwards, it would move north to the Coos Bay fishery off the Oregon coast. The ship she'd seen yesterday was a fraud.

She immediately contacted Mr. Reid. He answered on the second ring.

"Greetings Helen. Is everything alright?"

"Yes, sir. I've got important news. The operative I spoke of is not our target. He's a former Army commander with ties to the CIA. I'm sure he was monitoring cell phone chatter for the government when he stumbled into our call. Bennett's good at what he does. He approached me after we spoke this morning and encouraged me to investigate his record. He's not sure about us, but he's been watching our targets."

Frank thought a moment. "At least he's not our adversary, which is a plus. Now that you've identified him, I recall where I heard his name. Rusty worked with Bennett years ago and spoke highly of the man. Whatever you do, don't tell him why you're in Angoon."

"Yes, sir. I have more. The ship that we saw yesterday is a fraud. The real *Oregon II* is currently stationed near Catalina Island. Whitey and I felt strongly that the small craft passing us yesterday came from that vessel. I'm at the mouth of Peril Strait searching for it now."

"Be cautious. The waters in Peril can be tricky. If you find the ship, remain at a safe distance but try intercepting any transmissions."

"Affirmative, sir. I'll report this afternoon — unless I have breaking news."

"Thank you. Be careful and goodbye."

She climbed down to the cabin and placed her arms around Danny from behind. He remained focused on navigating the passage but enjoyed the attention. After passing the northern tip of Catherine Island, they had an unobstructed view of Peril. The *Oregon II* was visible at a distance of six miles. Helen got the spotting scope from Whitey's bag and adjusted the focus while leaning against Danny's chair.

The ship had left the mouth of Rodman Bay and was turning into the Strait. Its large, U-shaped crane extended over the rear deck just above water line and a thick steel cable attached to a drum was dragging something behind the ship.

When the ship completed its east turn, a small white boat came into view. The boat followed several hundred yards directly behind the ship. Helen watched the ship for ten minutes while deciding what to do. Finally, she asked Danny to stop the boat.

"Can we set up some poles and slowly fish our way toward that ship?"

"You want to put the sneak on them?"

Helen smiled and winked. "C'mon sport, don't ask about my work."

Danny looked for tackle. To his surprise, the owner had a wide array of fishing gear. He set up an electric downrigger on each side of the boat and rigged two salmon rods with flashers and lures. One had a cream-colored "hoochie" squid for bait while the other had a green and blue plug. After setting one downrigger at sixty feet and the other at forty, they crept toward the oncoming vessels.

Helen asked, "Have you seen that ship before?"

Danny looked through the scope and replied, "Yep."

"How long has it been here?"

Danny couldn't resist. "That's classified."

"Oh, you shit. C'mon, how long?"

"It'll cost you a kiss."

Helen leaned forward. "You're a fast learner."

After kissing him, she retreated. "OK, time to pay up — how long?"

"They were here for the entire season last year and spent most of their time near Tenakee Inlet. Dad said they returned a week ago."

"There was a catamaran near it yesterday. Have you seen them together before?"

Danny chuckled. "That'll be a new rate. This time a snog."

Helen giggled and planted her partially opened mouth on his. After a brief kiss she said, "Pay up, lover boy."

"Yesterday's the first time I noticed them together, but I've only been here a few days."

"Who owns the yellow catamaran?"

"Standard rate please."

Helen lifted her shirt, flashing her breasts. She quickly pulled down her shirt, limiting him to a brief glimpse. "That's got to be worth ten answers. Now get busy, lover boy."

"That's what I call sightseeing," Danny said. "It belongs to a man named Santos who lives in Hood Bay. He's 'coined up' and comes from Brazil. But, he's got a North European accent."

"How long has he lived here?"

"Maybe three years."

"What does he do for a living?"

"I think he's in oil. If you want the real juice on this character, talk with my dad. Why don't you try asking him?"

Helen smiled. "Does he charge the same rates?"

Danny cocked his head. "I sure hope not. There'd be nothing left for me."

Helen carried a small briefcase to the upper bridge while Danny trolled toward the oncoming vessels. She engaged the scanning radio and cell phone interceptor, placed her headphones on and listened. After 15 minutes, she intercepted a radio transmission between the white boat and the ship. They were transmitting on a low-band radio frequency ideal for short distances. Helen listened carefully.

"I've got a solid hit on the magnetometer. It's directly below us at 300 feet. Over."

"Copy that. Mark it with your GPS and give me the coordinates. We'll follow in your wake for a sonar signature. Over."

"Copy. There's a sport fisherman approaching from starboard. Should we retract our cable or continue?."

"Continue on course as planned. When you reach the outer grid, return and widen the search by twenty meters."

"Copy that. Over and out."

Helen mumbled, "I've got your arses." She immediately called Mr. Reid.

The old man answered, "Good morning again. Problems?"

"No problems, but some good news. I've located the bogus NOAA ship and they're definitely searching for something. The ship's using a magnetometer while a smaller boat is following with sonar. They're the same boats we saw yesterday. I intercepted a radio transmission verifying what they're up to."

"Wonderful news, young lady. Can you determine how many people are involved?"

"I see one crewman operating the cable drum, and there are two people in the boat. There's no visible human activity on deck, which tells me the crew is minimal."

"Where are they searching?"

"Eight miles inside Peril Straight, near Rodman Bay."

"Any other traffic in the area?"

"No, sir."

"Leave the area immediately. They're dangerous and you don't want to draw attention to yourself. I'm not concerned about losing track of the ship. It's too large to hide."

"Yes, sir. I have one more lead to track down and my recon's complete."

Reid replied, "Excellent job. Update me later."

Helen turned off the roving scanner and closed the case. Upon reaching the cabin, she planted a big kiss on Danny's cheek.

"I'm almost done working, Danny Boy. Life is good. Take me somewhere exotic."

"We'd never reach Tahiti in this boat. You'll have to settle on Warm Springs Bay."

Danny performed a wide, slow 180-degree turn and headed east. Helen stowed her gear and produced two Budweisers from the fridge. She pecked Danny on the cheek again and handed him a beer. A school of porpoises swam next to the boat, but before Helen could retrieve her digital camera, they were out of range. Danny assured her that they'd see many more before the day was over.

The *Oregon II* and smaller craft were gaining on their slow-trolling boat. Helen used the opportunity to take a series of pictures of the oncoming vessels.

Jim's House

Jim, Ernie and Audra sat on the couch and talked about the upcoming call to Gus Olsen. Ernie felt it was best for them to talk in private so anything of a personal and sensitive nature would remain that way. Jim produced one of his private cell phones and handed it to the old man.

Jim and Audra went outside and found the enormous brown bear looking at them from beyond the Humvee. Father and daughter watched in anticipation as the bruin approached the barrel trap. It sniffed and then bolted backwards. It looked at the duo and shook its head and clacked its teeth as if to say, "Not this time — I'm not that hungry."

The bear stood its ground and snorted several times, watching the people on the porch. It then sat in the gravel, content with the situation. Jim whispered that the old fellow probably had a difficult time competing with younger bears and had adopted Angoon as his new feeding ground. Moments later the bruin turned and walked toward Killisnoo road.

Audra commented, "I feel bad for him. He looks really old."

Jim grabbed the Desert Eagle from the house and they walked to the beach. Audra skipped stones on the surface of Chatham.

Ernie stood near the window with the phone at his ear.

"Good morning, Lena. This is Ernie. How are you these days?"

Lena answered, "Ernie, I can't complain — wouldn't do any good if I did. How are you?"

"Pretty good but I really miss Jenna. Soon we'll all be joinin' her in Tlingit heaven."

Lena knew he was right. "That's a fact. Not a day goes by that I don't think about her. I always considered her my sister instead of a cousin."

"Undertsood," Ernie said. "Where's Gus?"

"Out and about. I expect him home anytime now."

"There's something I need to ask both of ya when ya have time."

There was a momentary pause. Lena asked, "Is anything wrong Ernie?"

"Actually, there is. Some folks are after me 'cause of things I found when I was young. Things about Germany and the Olsen family. It has to do with the story ya told Jenna when ya was workin' at the cannery in Pelican. It's gotten so bad round here that I'm stayin' with my best friend. He's been protectin' me from the scallywags."

Lena asked, "Are you safe where you're at?"

"Yep but there's more. I think they're after you and Gus, too. We need to have a heart-to-heart talk."

After another pause, Lena asked, "The fella that's helping you — can he be trusted?"

"Besides you and Gus, he's the only friend I got. I trust him with my life."

She asked, "What's his name?"

"Jim Bennett."

"Is that where you're staying?"

"Yep.

"Stay where you are and don't go anywhere. Gus and I will call you back within a few hours. Don't tell anyone you talked with me, OK?"

"Gotcha."

Jim and Audra returned from their walk, and Ernie informed them he'd be getting a call within a few hours. Audra challenged Ernie to cribbage. Jim said he had to make a personal call and went into the kitchen. After the others were settled in, he booted up his covert computer, typed in the AT-616 access code and began downloading several hours' worth of recent satellite imagery. Scanning Chatham in real time, he quickly located the boat Danny and Helen were on. The NOAA ship and a smaller craft moved slowly west of the Bayliner's position. Jim zoomed into the ship's deck and noted its crane overhanging the water with an attached cable. The other boat had a small jib crane attached to a cable running into the ocean. Jim figured they were searching for the missing plane from 1944. After transferring the information to the computer in his study, Jim restored the covert system to its hiding spot. He informed Audra that he was done with his call and that he'd be in the study.

Inside the study, Jim carefully compared baseline imagery to the recent satellite photos. He zoomed in and out of each nook and cranny above Whitewater Bay, hoping to find traces of an old crash. It was a tedious task that might take hours to complete.

Eureka Mall

Rusty sat on the customized red Harley and listened to the constant surveillance chatter flooding the low frequency channel. The morning attempt to locate

Dark Fortunes

Al proved fruitless, and he understood that it was now or never. The control van with two occupants flanked the south end of the parking lot as two men in a white sedan covered the north end. An agent dressed as an elderly woman sat on a bench in perfect view of the pet store while additional agents posing as shoppers covered the entrances. At 1:20 p.m., a man carrying a small satchel walked to the pet store window and looked at a large cage filled with puppies. He glanced at his watch, opened his shirt and pulled out a red baseball cap. After putting it on, he stepped away from the window and nervously stood near a bank of phones. The elderly woman pretended to cough and spoke into her palm.

"Target acquired. Subject's alone."

Rusty immediately dialed the public phone number. A charcoal-colored late-model Honda drove past him. The driver glanced at the biker, then turned away. The car circled the back lot and pulled into a vacant spot with its engine running. Rusty whispered into his sleeve. "Dark Honda may be our second target."

The man answered the phone by the pet store.

"Who is this?" Rusty asked.

"Your new partner, Al."

"Are you alone?"

"Yes, how do we meet?"

Rusty asked, "Got my money?"

"Yes."

Rusty continued. "Follow the corridor to the rear exit. Come into the parking lot. Head west to the water's edge. I'm sitting on my bike."

Rusty hung up the phone and placed it in his vest pocket. Seconds seemed like hours as he fidgeted on the bike's seat. Finally, he saw a bald man in his sixties exit the mall and look around.

After seeing the biker, the man looked in all directions and slowly proceeded. He walked within fifteen feet of the dirty-looking biker and asked, "Are you Gary?"

"Yeah — and you're Al."

Al smiled. "It's nice to finally meet you." He reached out with the satchel and said, "I know you've been waiting for this, but, like the saying goes, 'shit happens.'"

Rusty took the case with his left hand, then shook hands with his right. He sat back on the seat of the Harley and examined the case's contents. Rusty grinned and said, "Alright dude, we're square. Where's your backup? I know he's here somewhere."

"I didn't think you'd want him here so he's been instructed to keep his distance."

"We should get together and discuss our plan. Is he close so we can talk?"

"One moment." Al produced a cell phone and called. He spoke for several seconds and hung up. The dark Honda drove up next to the men and stopped. A

218

large man in his early forties got out and approached the biker. His right hand was tucked inside his coat, as if he had a gun.

The man spoke. "You don't look anything like your cousin Greg. Who's the leader of the Hell Bents?"

"Moose Titoni, why?"

"Just checking. How's Moose doing these days?"

"Not well. He's got advanced prostate cancer."

The man nodded at Al, affirming that Gary was legitimate, then said, "I heard that too — nothing worse than losing one's virility."

Rusty responded, "I don't know what that means, but let's get down to business."

He pointed to the white van parked next to a light pole. "That's my old lady's ride. Let's go inside and talk."

Al asked, "Does she have a phone with her?"

"Yeah."

"Call her and have her leave the vehicle. We can't have her involved in any of this."

"That's cool, but this is the last time you'll order me around. I planned on making her split with my bike and I don't like being told what to do. Do you understand me?"

Al apologized. "I didn't mean to ruffle your feathers. I'm merely being careful."

Rusty called the van. "Hey bitch, time to split. Leave the keys in the ignition."

Moments later, a greasy-haired woman wearing chaps and a leather vest exited the driver's side door. The vest was partially buttoned and enormous, braless breasts spilled out its sides. She walked past the approaching men and said, "Fuck off asshole. Call me bitch one more time and I'll cut your balls off when you're sleeping."

Crane nudged Al with his elbow. "Don't you just love these people. They're so colorful."

Rusty stood to the side and opened the sliding door. Greeted with tasers, both targets dropped to the ground convulsing as more agents rushed the van and maneuvered them inside. In the van, they were hogtied and duct tape sealed their mouths. Rusty barked into his microphone, "Targets secure, everyone converge on the rear lot. Form a convoy, two rigs in front and four behind. Let's get out of here."

Rusty immediately called Mr. Reid. "Good news, sir — we've secured both targets."

"Splendid work — absolutely splendid. You know what to do. Make it happen."

Rusty closed by saying, "I'll call you when we're done."

Whitey drove the van to the warehouse and parked beside the huge structure. Six agents escorted the prisoners into separate rooms and strapped them to gurneys. Rusty sent the crew back to Henry's estate with the exception of two guards posted outside. Both captives were terrified and struggled to free themselves. Rusty instructed Whitey to remain with the "fat man" while he interrogated Al. After closing the door, Rusty walked over to Al and ripped off the duct tape that covered his mouth. Rusty smiled. "We're about to have some fun Mr. Al. What do you think? Are you ready to party and have a good time?"

Peril Strait

The *Oregon II* had almost overtaken the Bayliner, but made a large sweeping turn back to the west. Helen took several closeup photos of the ship and the trailing boat. As she returned to the cabin, one of the rods bent and line peeled from the reel. A fine mist rose into the air.

She yelled to Danny, "I think there's a fish on this pole."

"Reel up the slack and keep tension on the pole."

Danny put the boat in neutral and went on deck.

Helen's tough, independent attitude evaporated. "Danny, I don't know what to do. Please, you take the rod."

"No way gal, it's all yours."

He brought up the downriggers and reeled in the other pole.

"I've never fished before. I'm afraid I'll lose it."

"That won't be the end of the world." Danny got behind her, gently massaged her shoulders and coached her as she fought the fish. He told her to keep the rod tip up and allow the fish to run when needed. The salmon went airborne and peeled out additional line. Helen begged Danny to take over, but he refused and after ten grueling minutes, the fish was pulled to the boat. Danny scooped the tired fish into the landing net and hauled it on deck. Helen jumped back, afraid of being bitten. He clubbed the fish and placed it into a livewell.

Helen was running on adrenaline. "That's the first fish I've ever caught!" she burst out. It was totally kickin'! Is that a big salmon?"

"Big enough — probably twenty pounds. Do you have any ice on board?"

Helen shrugged. "I haven't the foggiest but we do have a few cold beers and several hours to kill." She grabbed Danny and kissed him. "Thank you for today. I'm having the time of my life. Days like this should last forever!"

"The day's still young. Let's get to Warm Springs and buy some ice. It's a ten minute hike from the dock to some spectacular thermal pools. If no one's around we'll skinny dip. You captain the boat while I filet your fish."

Helen located the bay on the screen and locked in its bearing. She pushed both throttles forward, and the cruiser skimmed over the crystal water. Storm clouds loomed far out on the horizon, but the weather above them remained sunny and calm. Mesmerized by the spectacular surroundings, Helen engaged the autopilot in order to enjoy the views. She was thinking, *This is my last mission.*

Jim's House

The former colonel examined satellite images from the past two summers and compared them to the most recent. Overlaying older images on recent photos, he searched for anomalies. He filtered out snow fields on the steep terrain surrounding Whitewater without finding anything unusual, then sat back and considered other possibilities. If a plane had crashed on the mountain above the area where the artifacts were found, it could be buried under years of accumulated snow. Another possibility would be that the plane went down in the water and sank. It would be impossible for anyone to survive a crash, then swim to shore with a canister of gold and a pistol on his hip.

After several minutes of deep thought, it struck him. The body of Colonel Obert couldn't have ended up in Rodman Bay unless the body was dumped there by the plane prior to its crash. Forty miles separated the two bays, making it impossible for Obert's body and Bruehl's body to be part of the same crash. The plane and crew may have landed in Peril Strait, dumped Obert's body, and took off again. The plane may have then crashed near Whitewater. Jim pulled out his USGS map and determined a probable take off sequence from Rodman Bay toward Chatham. According to the Navy reports, the weather that day was socked in with a fog layer between 200 and 3,000 feet. A pilot taking off for the southeast from Rodman would head due east into the open expanse of Chatham, then turn south toward Ketchikan.

Jim placed the map on his desk and pulled out a ruler. He penciled in the probable course, then had an epiphany. His map noted a strong magnetic disturbance at the juncture of Chatham and Peril. A seven-degree north variation exists there which creates severe problems for a pilot relying on compass readings. Executing a safe turn under those circumstances would be difficult. The colonel penciled a seven-degree deflection onto the map and replotted the flight path. He drew a southerly course. If the plane executed a perfect 90-degree turn, it would strike the mountains above Whitewater.

Jim leaned back in his chair and said, "BINGO!" His attention focused on his computer and the satellite images. Using older images, he estimated the location of the likely flight path and began enhancing the area with his mouse. Most of the mountains above Whitewater Bay were more than 3,000 feet tall and a Stinson F-19 couldn't have gained that elevation within such a short distance. A likely crash site was west of those peaks. Jim identified a likely strike zone and debris field, then plotted a path down the mountain to an upthrust of rock. The stone wall contained a narrow canyon on its uphill side and was covered in snow. Above the wall, Jim made out an unusual and out-of-place rounded object. He thought it could be man-made.

Jim re-entered the real-time satellite link and located the rock wall. He magnified the image, and spoke aloud. "I'll be damned."

An airplane tail protruded above the snow. Nothing else was visible. A person would have to be literally hovering above the tail to notice it. Without satellite imagery, he'd never have located it. The rugged terrain and the snow field had prevented its discovery for decades.

He panned back for a broader view and nodded. *That rock wall and canyon is less than a mile above the area where we found the artifacts*, he thought. Jim printed the image, turned off his computer and got a beer.

Audra was bored with playing cards, so he offered her a reprieve by turning on the DVD with the *Lonesome Dove* series for Ernie. She winked at her dad as Ernie became entranced in the movie. Jim sported a huge smile and asked if she'd like to go on a real treasure hunt tomorrow. Her eyes beamed with excitement, knowing quite well that her father had uncovered something interesting.

Warm Springs Bay

After entering the bay, Helen executed a right turn and motored toward a modest dock system. A long elevated boardwalk led to several brightly-painted cabins with metal roofs. Only one other boat was in the bay when Danny tied off the Bayliner. They stepped onto the dock. The white commercial fishing boat *Catchum* Helen had observed a day earlier lay at anchor several hundred feet away. Two fishermen were repairing a net strung up on a tall vertical mast. Danny waved at the duo working on the net. Several hundred yards beyond the cabins, a steep river rushed into the bay. When they reached the cabins, the thundering roar of water was heard in the distance. Misty clouds rose above the treetops from a hidden waterfall. Beyond a bathhouse, a small store with a green metal roof awaited their arrival.

Helen said, "This is amazing. What is this place?"

"This is Warm Springs. It's full of geothermal pools and hot springs. I wasn't sure the store would be open but the door's wide open. This place has changed hands so often that you never know what to expect. Sometimes it's packed, and other times, it's just like this."

"I love it. It's totally mystical, almost as if I've been here before."

"Having a touch of déjà vu? C'mon, let's get your fish on ice, then walk to the hot springs."

They bought ice at the store and Danny packed it onto the fish. He grabbed the towels he'd packed, and they walked up the hill on an old wooden walkway. The boardwalk turned into a gravel path next to the waterfall. Helen looked in awe at the cascading torrent as it fell toward the sea. The sheer power of the scene was overwhelming, and she remembered her Mum's words: "It is a mystical place where a thundering waterfall joins serene water."

Danny pointed to a ledge above them and said, "There are several natural hot-tubs up there carved into the rocks. This is perfect. Nobody's here."

At an upper pool, Helen looked around, then stripped off her clothes. Danny followed suit and admired her perfect body as they entered the pool. They sat next to each other in the warm water on smoothly polished rocks. The pool overlooking the spectacular river created a perfectly romantic setting. They snuggled and talked for nearly an hour about their lives. Helen finally said, "You really know how to swoon the birdies, Danny Boy. I've never experienced anything this romantic. I could remain here forever."

"I'm glad you like it. Tell me something. Earlier today you commented about quitting your job. What are your thoughts about that now?"

"As soon as we left Peril Strait, I decided this is my last project. Regardless of what happens between you and me, my present occupation is over."

Danny nodded. "Now that we've gotten that out of the way, I'm going to be very blunt. I know you were on top of the ridge yesterday talking on a cell phone — I recognize your voice from my dad's laptop. The reason he was talking with you this morning is because you're a spy."

Helen shook her head. "We had an understanding that asking about my work was out of bounds."

"Look, I really dig you — more than any other woman I've ever met. But I'm concerned for my family and how your work fits into all of this. My feelings for you are real, but I'm afraid you're working me to get at my father."

Again, she shook her head. "You're a clever observer but wrong. I've been an agent for Britain. Now I freelance. As I told your father this morning, I'm not playing you — in fact, I'm likely falling in love with you. Details about my mission can't be discussed, but it has nothing to do with you or your family."

"When will your current project be completed?"

"I suspect rather soon. Why?"

"Because you're not the only one with deep feelings. I want to spend as much time with you as possible but not at the expense of my family."

Helen turned around in the pool and straddled his lap. Her nipples were adorned with silver scorpion rings that matched her earrings. She gently pressed her warm open mouth against his and they kissed embracing each other's bodies.

Helen retreated. "Do you believe in the metaphysical and seeing into the future?"

Danny frowned. "Somewhat. Why?"

"After you mentioned your dream this morning, I wanted to tell you about mine. I've had a recurring dream for several weeks now and it involves you. As soon as we met, I knew you were the person from my dream."

"Tell me about it."

"We are on the deck of a white ship. Suddenly, flames leap out of the water. Both of us are panic stricken while the flames surround the ship, but they immediately subside and disappear. Then we depart for an around-the-world voyage — a wonderful feeling of adventure — sort of like astronauts might feel going to space for the first time. The dream changes and we close and lock enormous steel doors behind us as the skies become filled with brilliant orange clouds."

"That's it?" Danny asked. "We close steel doors and the sky turns orange. What makes you think it's me in your dream?"

"I'm certain of it. There's more. Before dying, my mother had visions and told me about my future. At first I dismissed it as her cancer, but later I realized she somehow managed to live in the unconscious future. So far, everything she predicted about me has come true. She described this place and meeting you. She spoke of danger and a white ship, the skies and the steel doors. Mum also said we would meet under stressful circumstances and fall madly in love. This is destiny, Danny, I'm convinced of it. It sounds silly, but I know we'll be together when this project ends."

He kissed her. "So you're a witchy woman who can foresee the future. You probably put a spell on me so I'd fall for you too."

She smiled, then winked. "Would that be such a terrible thing?"

He smiled. "Not at all. I'm actually digging it, especially the part about falling in love.

He paused. "It's interesting that both our dreams involve a ship."

Helen continued. "When you mentioned your piezoelectric patent, I considered offering to finance the endeavor, but I didn't know how you'd react or how you felt about me."

He ran his fingers through her hair, and cupped her head in his hands.

"You'd do that for me?" he asked

"As long as we're partners in love and life, it would be a dream come true."

They began kissing again. Their hands ran up and down each other's bodies. Finally Helen reached into the warm water and gently massaged his penis until it became throbbing hard. She maneuvered herself over him and placed him inside of her.

When they had finished, they remained in place until distant voices from the path below announced the arrival of other bathers. They broke their embrace, and Helen asked if they should get dressed, but Danny said "No." They'd sit still and allow other bathers to claim their own pool further up river.

"I lied about my dad's past and his scar," Danny confessed. "His profession was the primary reason my mother divorced him.

"I know about your father and he knows about me," Helen said. "Not only was he a Delta commander, he was a covert operative within the CIA's Special Operations Group. He worked in Granada, Nicaragua, El Salvador, Panama, Columbia, and the Mid-East."

"How could you possibly know all that?"

Helen shrugged. "It's my job to know these things. I've got a file on him at the boat, but the majority of his past is redacted. How I see it? This world needs more Colonel Bennetts. So tell me lover, how did he get that nasty scar?"

"Which? He's got a body full of them, but I assume you're referring to the one on his face."

"I am."

"He broke into a Panamanian prison and extracted a fellow agent who was facing execution. A guard shot him, but Dad smoked him along with several others."

Danny pulled her to him and they kissed. He asked, "Exactly what do you do?"

She giggled. "You're a smooth operator Danny. I trust you enough to give you some basics but nothing about this operation. My specialty is surveillance and I was trained by the British Secret Service and worked for MI-6. After one tour of duty, I left to take a job at Scotland Yard but it was too autocratic. That's why I became a PMC."

Danny nodded. "Private military contractor."

"Yes, and that's where this conversation ends."

Danny let that soak in. "Have you ever had to kill anyone?"

She nodded. "Yes."

"Tell me about it?"

She hesitated. After a moment, she said, "My mum predicted the incident as she was dying. There was a situation in Eufrat. I killed four Al Qaeda. I don't regret it — they were evil people. This line of work exposes you to the scum of the earth — another reason I need a change."

"What happened in Eufrat?"

"I don't like talking about it. Let's leave it at that.

"I get it. You and my old man have a lot in common."

"Not really. Like your father said earlier, he does it for freedom. I do it for money."

Danny's head snapped back. "He said that?"

Upset about breaking her word, Helen grabbed Danny's locks with both hands and looked him in the eyes. "Yes he did. But please don't tell, because I promised him I wouldn't tell you. He's correct about me. I respect your father, so please, please, please, don't tell him I told you about our conversation. He asked me not to share it, because he didn't want to jeopardize his relationship with you."

Danny was silent for a moment. "OK. I promise."

"Because of your dad's contacts, he knows everything about me. He knows that I've been a free-lance mercenary for over four years. He has little respect for people in my profession because they'll sell out to the highest bidder. He's right. He accused me of using you to get at him, but I told him that I have deep feelings for you. Your father trusted me enough to reinvite me home so *we* could be together — it shows his love for you."

"Sounds like my old man. I've never doubted his love for Audra and me, but the poor guy's been on a guilt trip for years. Mom rubbed his nose in the fact that he wasn't around when we were growing up, but she never understood how resilient kids are. We grew up on an Army base and considered it normal to have our dad gone for long stretches. So did the other kids on base."

"I sympathize with your father's guilt. That's why I've avoided relationships for years."

Bad for you, but fortunate for me," Danny said. "Otherwise you'd have been snagged a long time ago."

"Danny, I'm happy we're connecting with each other. I could sit here forever, but I need to call my employer. I also need to cruise by the home of Mr. Santos — take a few photographs and get his GPS coordinates. The sooner I put this project behind me, the sooner we can be together."

He gave her a kiss on the cheek, and reached for the towels. "Let's boogie."

Port Angeles

Frank Reid was alone in his library when his private phone rang at 3:30 p.m. Caller ID was blank, but he realized it had to be Rusty calling about the questioning. He nervously answered, "This is Blue Marlin."

"This is Rusty. I've got good news and bad news. What do you want to hear first?"

"I don't want bad news but you'd better get on with it."

"Whitey was shot and killed while watching the cop from Sacramento."

Dark Fortunes

Frank remained silent, but he slumped toward the desktop. He didn't know how to respond. Whitey had been a consummate professional with several years of service as a bodyguard. Even though he was not a direct employee, Reid considered him a friend.

Rusty broke the silence. "You alright Mr. Reid?"

There was a long gap as the old man tried to regain his composure. He finally responded in a choked voice. "No I'm not. How could you let this happen?"

"I'm not sure. While questioning Al in the other room, someone ran past my door. I checked the other room. Whitey was on the floor with a head wound. His pistol and silencer were missing. I ran into the warehouse. The cop was running toward the bayside door. He turned and I shot him in the chest, but he managed to dive into the water and swim under the dock. He dropped the gun on the pavement and there's a blood trail to where he dove in. I called the two outside guards. We watched the water around the warehouse, but he never surfaced. I'm convinced he died and sank to the bottom. He must have a torso full of water."

Frank was upset. "Now I have two pieces of terrible news: Whitey's dead and our second captive escaped. I'm questioning my choice of hiring you for this operation. We missed an opportunity to finish this in Alaska because of inadequate planning and now this. Your good news had better be earth-shattering."

"I won't apologize for Whitey. It was his own carelessness. I'm quite certain that our second guest is dead. The blood on the pavement was pink and foamy, indicating a solid lung shot. I'll accept responsibility for not having enough resources in Alaska, but my decision was based on keeping your past from as many people as possible. Shit happens in this business and death is one of the risks we take."

Reid barked, "You've made your argument, but I'm not convinced that things were handled correctly. You claim to have good news. Let's hear it."

"We're rapidly approaching a suitable resolution to our problem. The man I interviewed is an ODESSA member whose father set up the Dachau concentration camp. His family escaped from Germany to Buenos Aires. His cover name is David Rigby but his real name is Roger Albert Krantz. He lived in Brazil for a while, then moved to Chile and joined Colonia Dignidad. It's a Nazi camp created by former SS members with close ties to the Krantz family. He learned about you and Henry from his father, who happened to be friends with a man named Karl Obert. Obert talked about an escape plan developed by SS General Rudolph Bruner and two Americans. I assume that you're one of the Americans and that Henry Weddell was Bruner. He mentioned the name Olsen as being a key player, which is probably you. Several ODESSA members tried locating Bruner and Obert after the war, but were unsuccessful until Rudolph was seen in Europe during the '70s. That spawned attempts to locate Bruner, but without success. Are you with me?"

227

Frank finally said, "Go on, I'm listening."

"The original members of ODESSA are all dead, but their descendants are alive and well. Two of them teamed up and are searching for a submarine filled with gold and a transport plane used to carry treasure to America. They narrowed the search to a cannery in Pelican, Alaska, but were unable to locate the Olsen family or Bruner. As bad luck would have it, a photo of Bruner, AKA Henry Weddell, surfaced in Fortune Magazine. It was seen by Albert Krantz, who died in 1999. His son Roger has been trying to locate Bruner for the past nine years."

"What about the escaped man who killed Whitey?"

"He was a hired gun, like the Wiser cousins. The NOAA ship has six employees who work directly for Krantz. The second partner is located at the Colonia Dignidad compound. His name is Anton Keller, the illegitimate son of Karl Obert. Any of these names ring a bell?"

"Yes. Do the people on the NOAA ship know what they're looking for?"

"Negative. They're salaried and Roger Krantz planned on killing them if and when the gold was recovered."

"What's the status of Krantz?"

"He's been injected with a double dose of our psychotropic cocktail — his mind is mush. I plan on planting Whitey's gun on him and sending him to Sacramento. I'll leave him in his rental car and tip off the police about a suspicious character parked in a vehicle near the airport. We'll dump Whitey's body on the shoulder of the road near the car. I found the shell casing from Whitey's gun and I'll plant it near the scene. I've already placed Roger's fingerprints on the weapon and fired the gun with his hand around its handle. The cops will have gunshot residue on Krantz, a weapon, a shell casing, and a victim. That ought to seal the deal for Krantz."

The old man asked, "What about the body of the escaped cop?"

"We'll scour the bay for a floater but I'm sure the crabs will make short work of his remains. The bay is cold, so he won't float."

Reid said, "That leaves Anton Keller in Chile and the ship in Alaska. How do we deal with those two situations?"

"According to Krantz, the ship's crew is responsible for marking all anomalies on a GPS map, then taking high resolution sonar scans of each anomaly. Krantz said he'd return and decide what data is worth pursuing. They've got weeks' worth of work to do, so I recommend letting sleeping dogs lie. As for Keller, I want your permission to immediately leave for Chile, track him down and kill him. That should wrap it up."

The old man remained silent as he weighed his options in conjunction with their recent failures. He finally asked, "What about the families of Keller and Krantz?"

"That's the beauty of it, sir, they have no heirs. Both were married and divorced without having children. Krantz had an older brother who died last year and Keller had no siblings. Once I've neutralized Keller, it's over with."

"Alright. Track him down and kill him. I'm extracting Helen immediately. We'll deal with the ship when you return. Now comes the unpleasant part. I need to know about Whitey's family so I can do something for them."

"His real name is Mike Stoddard. His father's dead and his mother's in a nursing home suffering from Alzheimer's. He's been married and divorced twice. He has a son named Mike Jr. from his first marriage who's a senior at Old Dominion University. I'll get the information from Dark Star and forward it to you before I leave."

"Very well. Send the info on Whitey. Call me from Chile unless problems arise before your departure."

Frank walked from behind his desk and sat in his leather chair. His mind raced, trying to grasp the events of the past week. He needed to extract Helen immediately, but before he could call her, the library door opened. Lena and Gus entered, bad news written all over their faces.

"We have problems in Angoon," Lena began." Ernie McKinnon called and said he's in trouble — people are after him. He wants to talk with Gus and me about Nazis and the Olsen family. Says he found some items including a dog tag with the name Decker."

Frank blurted, "Shit! This is absolutely splendid. When it rains, it pours. Is he safe?" Lena answered, "I think so."

Frank wasted no time. "Grab several days' worth of clothes while I arrange for the limo to drive us to my jet. I've got to bring one of my people back from Angoon anyway, so we'll talk during the flight and decide how to handle this. We want to be in Sitka before dark."

Gus and Lena left and Frank called his pilot and chauffeur. After arranging transportation, he contacted the captain of the yacht and asked him to evacuate Henry's staff. He instructed him to transport them to Hawaii on one of Henry's cruise ships without notifying Dark Star of the change in plans. He then instructed the captain to start a small ship owned by P.C.I. from Seattle to Sitka and wait for his instructions. The captain was also instructed to take the yacht directly to Ketchikan without delay. After arrangements were complete, the old man looked at a photograph of Henry and himself taken when they were much younger. He spoke out loud. "Rudy, I sure could use your help right now. Things are out of control and people are dying. You were the brightest man I've ever known. If you can hear me, give me the wisdom to get this right."

He left the room to pick up Gus and Lena.

Warm Springs Bay

Danny and Helen made their way back to the Bayliner. They held hands the entire time and talked about how they'd make the transition after Helen resigned her employment. In the boat, Helen backed the Bayliner from the dock and plotted a course to Hood Bay. The wind increased slightly, creating small choppy waves. Whale spouts rose into the air to the south of them but this time Helen ignored them. She needed to get coordinates and photos of the Santos residence.

Forty minutes later, the cruiser slowed as it approached the newly constructed dock. The catamaran was gone, suggesting that Santos was on the water. A solitary man walked the perimeter of the house with a rifle in his hand. He stopped and glassed the Bayliner with a small set of binoculars.

Helen gathered GPS information and took photographs of the facility. She turned the boat around and headed back toward Angoon, and her phone rang.

She answered, "This is Helen."

"Good afternoon, young lady. This is Frank. Where are you?"

"I'm on my way back to Angoon. I've concluded my reconnaissance."

"Good. When you arrive in Angoon, I need you to locate a Mr. Ernie McKinnon and bring him to your boat. I'll have both of you extracted within two or three hours. It's important that you have him on the boat when our float plane arrives."

Confused, Helen asked, "Is there a problem, sir?"

"Yes. I'll tell you about it when I meet you in Sitka."

"You're coming to Sitka?"

"Yes. I'm in the air now and should arrive within ninety minutes."

"This is highly unusual, sir. Can you tell me the nature of the problem?"

"I can't provide specifics, but we experienced problems in Eureka. I have reason to believe that you and Mr. McKinnon may be at risk."

Helen understood. "You wouldn't be coming here unless we had casualties. Please tell me who."

"We'll talk after we meet."

Helen shook her head. "I hate this crap. What about the boat? Return it to Sitka?"

"Whitey rented it for a week. Leave it in Angoon. Gather your things and make sure McKinnon's there when the float plane arrives at the main dock. I suggest that you arm yourself in case there's interference."

Helen stared at Danny. "Yes, sir. I've met Mr. McKinnon, but I'll have problems getting him to the dock."

"How so?"

"He's friends with the Bennetts; staying at their home. I'm convinced they won't allow McKinnon to leave with me unless he agrees."

The old man said, "Don't worry about that. An old friend of his will call him and explain the situation. He'll understand and Bennett won't interfere."

Helen asked, "If things are this dire, should the Bennetts be warned?"

"No! Absolutely not! We can't involve anyone else. Besides, I'm certain the colonel can take care of himself. From what you've said and the Dark Star report, he's more than capable. Concentrate on your own safety, as well as McKinnon's."

"Very well, sir. I'll wait for the float plane." She ended the conversation.

Reid's Private Jet

Sitting in a soft leather recliner aboard the jet, Lena dialed the number Ernie had called from. Gus sat adjacent to her as the phone rang. Jim Bennett answered, and Lena asked to speak with Ernie. Jim handed the phone to Ernie and went to his computer room where another phone was, configured to the SIM card on the phone Ernie was using. Jim listened as Lena spoke.

"Gus and I are flying into Sitka and should be there shortly. We're sending a chartered bush flight to pick you up, so we can talk about the situation you discussed."

Ernie asked, "Why don't ya just come to Angoon?"

"Hold on a moment, I'm putting you on speaker phone so Gus can hear this too." Seconds later, Gus spoke. "Hey Ernie, how are you?"

"'Getting' older by the minute. How 'bout you?"

"That depends. I understand things are getting rather chaotic in Angoon. Lena and I are worried about you, so we'd like to send a plane to pick you up. We'll meet in Sitka. We've got an employee in Angoon who'll escort you."

Ernie answered, "As I was tellin' Lena, why not come here and talk?"

"I'm afraid that's too dangerous for everyone involved. After you hear our story, you'll understand."

"Who's gonna escort me?"

"A woman named Helen Moorcroft. She said she's met you and she's worked for us in the past."

"Oh yeah, I met her — a real looker."

Lena spoke. "Ernie, please listen to her and follow her instructions. It's important for us to talk with you and explain a few things."

"I don't wanna leave my friend and his family behind. He's been a big help and knows a lot about what's goin' on around here. He should hear what ya got to say."

231

Gus interjected. "Your friend doesn't need to know. It could jeopardize Lena and me."

Ernie asked, "This is about the Nazis, isn't it?"

Gus hesitated. "Yes. Yes it is. We need to explain the situation in private."

Ernie asked, "Can I at least tell him about our meetin'?"

Again Gus spoke. "I don't think it would be wise. Just tell him you've got an opportunity to see old family and friends for the evening. Please keep Bennett uninvolved."

Ernie reluctantly answered. "I s'pose — but I don't plan on spendin' much time away from here. When will I be back home?"

Lena spoke. "I swear on Jenna's spirit, you'll return as soon as I'm sure things are safe. Soon you'll understand what's happened in the past. Please trust me Ernie, we're family."

Ernie finally agreed. "Alright, we're family. Should I bring some of the things I've found so ya know what I'm talking about?"

Gus replied, "It's not necessary."

Ernie asked, "When's this gonna happen?"

"Helen will meet with you within an hour or so," Gus said, "She'll call us when things are secure. OK?"

"Alright. I s'pose.

"See you soon," Gus said. "Bye."

Ernie pressed the "end" button on the phone as Jim entered the room. He handed the phone to Jim. "I gotta go to Sitka and meet with Jenna's cousin and her husband."

"I was listening in and understand. Call me when you arrive Sitka so I know you're OK."

Ernie nodded. "I'll do that."

"We need to get down to the dock and pick up Lori," Jim said. "Her plane arrives in fifteen minutes."

Chatham Strait

The Bayliner cleared Killisnoo Island when Reid's call was completed. Danny looked expectantly at Helen after she hung up. She asked to be excused and walked into the sleeping birth. She retrieved a holstered pistol, then put on a fleece jacket to conceal the weapon. When she returned to the bridge, Danny said, "I couldn't help but overhear your conversation. What's happening?"

Helen shook her head "I'm not sure. My employer is sending a plane for Ernie and me within a few hours. He said there's a problem with the mission and that we're being picked up. Ernie's been contacted and knows all about it."

Danny asked, "What kind of problem?"

"I haven't the foggiest, but I'm sure it isn't good."

Danny said, "You said 'Should the Bennetts be warned?' Warned about what?"

Helen was upset. "Listen carefully Danny. I don't know exactly why I'm here other than to collect information, but I can tell you this much: a very wealthy man was murdered several days ago who was my employer's best friend. His murder has something to do with Angoon and Ernie McKinnon. Ernie may know my employer and possibly the murder victim. Several shady characters were involved in the murder, including the Hell's Angels in Sacramento. Something terrible happened earlier today, so I'm being extracted. My employer won't elaborate until he meets with me in Sitka. Ernie's been told I'm escorting him out of Angoon."

Helen looked deep into Danny's eyes. "I'm quitting when I return, and I'll call you within a day or two. I'm telling you this because I love you. Promise me you'll be careful while I'm gone."

Danny hugged her. "Don't worry about me or my family. We'll take care of ourselves. When this blows over, we'll look back and laugh."

She looked down. "I hope you're right. I'll need to leave the boat here for a few days. Can you keep the keys?"

"Of course. Don't panic. Things will work out."

Helen turned the cruiser into Kootznahoo Bay. She piloted the boat into the marina and helped Danny tie it off. At that moment, the Humvee containing Jim, Audra and Ernie pulled up to the seaplane dock. Danny whistled and waved to get his father's attention. The bush plane containing Lori glided toward the bay from the west.

Recognizing the opportunity to secure this flight instead of waiting for the pre-arranged plane from Sitka, Helen said, "Danny, I'm going to try to talk the pilot into taking Ernie and me to Sitka."

"Relax. You're stressed out, lover. Dad knows the pilot well. He'll arrange it. Let's pack your things before the plane docks."

She asked Danny to move the duffle bag containing her arsenal onto the pier. Two other large suitcases containing her surveillance equipment waited on the cruiser's deck. As soon as Danny lifted the bag, he knew what it contained and realized he couldn't carry it to the plane in time. Danny whistled at the group and motioned for them to come and pick him up. Audra obliged his request and drove to the marina as the float plane touched down several hundred yards away. Danny threw the salmon filets into a small cooler for Helen to take with her.

They loaded her gear in the waiting Humvee and drove back to the seaplane dock as a dock attendant tied off the plane. Within minutes, Danny, Helen and Audra had emptied the truck.

A striking blonde in her early forties, dressed in blue jeans, a light blue windbreaker and white running shoes climbed out of the cockpit onto the pontoon. Her shoulder-length hair was tied back with a barrette, forming a preppie-looking ponytail. A small Jack Russell terrier with a short red leather leash was under her arm. Upon safely reaching the dock, she put the dog on the deck.

She smiled at Jim and said, "Well?"

Jim squinted in confusion. "Well what?"

She shook her head. "Are you going to kiss me?"

Jim blushed, turned to see if anyone was looking, which they were, then walked forward. Lori pulled him toward her, demonstrating how a first kiss should be. She slightly lifted her right foot as her dog obediently sat at her left side and watched. After several seconds, they separated while the Bennett group converged on the plane.

Lori said, "I wanted you to remember our first kiss. You never know. It could be our last."

Jim grinned. "It won't be the last if I have anything to say about it. But, I'm a little embarrassed. My kids are watching."

Lori laughed. "Big deal. They're both adults and know the score."

Audra asked Danny in a whisper if he thought her dad and Lori made a cute couple. Danny told her to hush and let nature take its course. After the obligatory greetings, Helen and Ernie were introduced to their new arrival.

Lori looked at Helen and commented, "I love what you've done with your hair. It really adds to your good looks."

She turned to Danny. "Listen, young man. Don't let this one get away — she's a knockout."

Helen smiled at the compliment. Danny placed his arm around Helen's shoulder. "I'm trying my best to keep her around but she's leaving me for a much older man."

"Temporarily!" Helen said.

He turned to his dad. "Can you talk the pilot into taking her and Ernie to Sitka. I guess something's come up you may not be aware of."

Jim nodded, and thought, *You have no idea, kid.* But, he said, "I understand completely." He went to speak with the pilot.

Audra petted Oscar, who didn't budge from his spot next to Lori. The pilot agreed to take Helen and Ernie to Sitka, and Jim asked to speak with Helen alone at the end of the dock. Danny loaded her gear into the plane while Helen and his father spoke privately.

Jim handed her a tiny button-sized object. "Here's the GPS tracker you placed on my boat. I listened to your calls today. We're *not* adversaries."

Helen stared at her feet. "Sorry about the tracker, I'm only doing my job. As for the phones, jolly good job. My monitor never detected an interceptor. You impress me Mr. Bennett."

Jim added, "Tell Gus Olsen that Ernie's always safe with me and I won't interfere with his decision to visit dead relatives. As for your employer, I wouldn't mind talking with ghosts from the past."

Helen frowned. "I'm afraid I don't understand."

"That's alright. Gus, Lena and your employer will get it. Meanwhile, please see that Ernie's looked after and accept my apology for this morning's confrontation."

Helen shook her head. "There's no need for that . Your comments were spot on. Mr. McKinnon's in good hands. Watch your back side. They'd never extract me unless shit's hit the fan somewhere."

Jim said, "I've got eyes in the back of my head, girl. Besides, when Ernie returns, he'll tell me about the trouble in California."

Helen nodded. "I'm sure he will. By then, both of us will know the score."

Jim shook his head. "I'll have it figured out long before then."

She smiled. "That wouldn't surprise me at all. Thank you again for your hospitality and I hope to see everyone shortly. I'm tendering my resignation when I return and hope to be welcome in your home again."

He offered a handshake. "Leaving this profession is a wise move — one you won't regret. Aside from that, you're welcome in my home any time, young lady. I know Danny's been swept away by you and I trust his judgment."

She smiled. "Thank you for opening your home for a complete stranger. As for Danny, he's not the only one swept away. I'm in love with him. Please keep him safe."

Jim nodded. "I'm on it, but he can handle himself. Let's get back to the others."

Helen called Frank and canceled the inbound bush flight. He sounded confused but she assured him everything was under control. While she spoke with Frank, Jim informed Ernie about the change of plans and helped him into the plane. Danny and Helen said their farewells and kissed each other. The plane started up and taxied into the bay. Everyone waved as the plane roared skyward. They took Lori's bags and headed for the house.

Sitka

The Gulfstream 550 touched down and taxied across the tarmac of the Sitka airport. At a top speed of over 650 mph, the flight had taken less than two hours. Parked at the outermost hanger, Jeff shut down both engines. Frank and Jeff left the cockpit for the main cabin. The pilot opened the cabin door, stepped onto the asphalt and inspected the outside of Reid's multi-million dollar aircraft. Gus, Lena and Frank sat together in the cabin and considered whether Ernie should be introduced to Frank. Everyone agreed it would be best to keep him clueless regarding the former B-17 pilot and only tell him selected bits about former events. Frank would remain in the cockpit while the group flew to Ketchikan for the evening and remain onboard until Ernie was escorted to his motel room. Later, he'd meet with Helen and inform her of Whitey's death.

Lena looked out of her window as a white van pulled alongside the jet. Helen helped Ernie from the sliding side door onto the tarmac. The bush pilot unloaded gear as the duo approached the Gulfstream's stairway. Frank retreated to the cockpit and closed the door. Gus and Lena stood to greet the duo as they entered the cabin. Helen was relieved to be in the Gulfstream, but she wondered where Frank Reid was. Gus informed them they would spend the evening in Ketchikan for security reasons. Helen looked at Gus and opened her hands with her palms skyward, silently asking where Frank was. He looked toward the cockpit, then nodded his head slightly. She understood. Minutes later, the jet was in the air, heading toward Ketchikan.

Angoon

Lori asked about the barrel trap adjacent to Jim's shed. Jim told her about the bear, and the four entered the massive log home. Jim gave her the grand tour. She was awestruck by the beauty and quality of the home. Jim had characterized his summer home as a cabin instead of a miniature mansion.

Oscar followed Lori and obediently sat next to her whenever she stopped to talk. Jim bent down, grabbed the dog and tucked him under his arm before climbing a metal spiral staircase to an upstairs loft containing a work-out room, two small bedrooms and a spacious bathroom. The views of Chatham Straight from the upper loft eclipsed those from the main floor. Lori asked if she could sleep upstairs so she wouldn't impose on anyone. Jim said she could stay wherever she liked. Audra and Danny were busy in the kitchen, and he placed his hands onto Lori's shoulders, leaned forward and kissed her. He retreated and smiled.

He said, "Thanks for everything you've done for me through the years. Without your help I'd never have been able to grow the company to its current level and afford retirement at such a young age. I'm thrilled you're here. It's good you managed to convince Frasier into letting you off on such short notice."

Lori's rectangular gold wire rimmed glasses accentuated her blue eyes

"Well?" she said.

Jim pulled her forward and kissed her. "Well, what?"

She smiled. "You're catching on. I've often wondered if I'd ever get to know you on an intimate level. I think you've answered that."

Jim kissed her again, wondering why he waited for all these years. After separating, he said, "I've asked myself many times why I haven't made a play for you, but military conditioning prevented that. I avoided a relationship with you because I was your supervisor. Now — thanks to you — I'm free to do as I please and it would please me very much if we connect with each other."

She smiled. "That would please me more than you can imagine."

Jim placed his arm around her. "C'mon downstairs. Let's have a drink and plan dinner."

Audra was rummaging through the refrigerator when Jim and Lori entered the kitchen. Danny was speaking with Helen on his cell. Lori walked up to him and kissed him on his cheek. "Say hello to your girlfriend for me." He grinned.

Jim pulled a container of homemade spaghetti sauce from the freezer and put it in the microwave. Audra was relieved Jim found something quick for dinner. That gave her time to check her email and contact friends at Duke University.

Lori boiled a pot of penne, and Jim prepared morel mushrooms with caramelized onions and red bell peppers. She was impressed with his ability to cook. She remembered that Special Ops soldiers could make shoe leather taste like steak. The four sat at the dining room table and ate heartily. They remained at the table and talked for over an hour. Before he cleared the table, Jim commented on how fortunate he was to be surrounded by the most important people in his life. He invited everyone to sit in the hot tub and continue their conversation. The sun was setting soon. It would be the end of a nearly perfect day — for nearly everyone.

Ketchikan

A misting rain greeted the short flight from Sitka to Ketchikan. Helen walked down the staircase from the parked Gulfstream, and looked in all directions. Satisfied that the situation was secure, she saluted the pilot, indicating the all-clear. A white stretch limo Frank had reserved prior to landing approached from a service road to transport Ernie, Gus, Lena and Helen to the Cape Fox Lodge. Ernie had no idea another person was inside the jet's cockpit as the four entered the limo. He called Jim as promised, to let him know where he was and that everything was OK.

Jim wasn't surprised Ernie and Helen were removed from Sitka for security reasons. He asked Ernie who met him at the airport, and Ernie said Helen, Gus, Lena and the pilot were with him. Jim wondered if it was Gus Olsen who had changed his name to Frank Reid and was, in fact, Helen's employer. He'd run a voice analysis comparison from his archived calls to determine if Gus and Frank were one and the same.

The limo pulled up to the entrance of the Cape Fox Lodge and parked. Helen was given a note from Jeff to check in for five rooms and to arrange for a conference room so Gus, Lena and Ernie could have their talk. After clearing each room and searching for surveillance systems, Helen returned to the limo and escorted Ernie and the Olsens to their respective rooms. She set up her monitoring equipment and anxiously awaited Mr. Reid's arrival. Twenty minutes later, there was a knock on her door. Jeff asked her to gather up the Olsens and Ernie and take them to the meeting room for dinner. Frank would remain in his room and speak with her afterwards.

Awkward silence permeated the small meeting room while the group picked away at their meals. A darkening sky outside was a prelude to heavier rain. Frank Reid paced in his room and pulled open the drapes, exposing the clouds. He nodded his head and mumbled to himself, "Surprise, surprise, surprise — always raining in Ketchikan. No wonder I hated flying into here when I was young."

His telephone rang, breaking his constant pacing. The old man looked at his phone and knew it was Rusty. Frank answered, "This is Blue Marlin.."

"Rusty here. I leased a jet and it's being refueled in Mexico City. I won't make Santiago until late this evening. By this time tomorrow I'll be outside of the Colonia Compound, figuring out a way to get inside."

The old man tilted his head and paused. Finally he responded. "I've extracted Helen from Alaska. Who's in charge of the California situation, and what's his number?"

Rusty answered, "Dan Cranston's still in charge. I'll text his number when we're done."

Frank asked, "Did the cop's body surface?"

Rusty hesitated. "Not that I'm aware of. I'll ask Tristan when we're through talking."

Frank asked, "Did the police capture Mr. Al and fall for the ruse?"

"Yes, sir. It worked as planned. He's in custody and should be charged by now."

"Is Mr. Cranston still at Henry's estate?"

Rusty wondered why Reid was asking so many questions but decided to avoid a confrontation. "Yes, sir. He's managing the entire operation from there. If things go as planned, we should be in a stand-down mode within 72 hours. Our loose end should be neutralized, which only leaves the *Oregon II* to contend with."

"Who witnessed the police apprehending Mr. Al? Or should I say Rigby?"

Rusty was annoyed. "I did, damn it. Don't you trust me?"

The old man barked back. "Listen here, young man, you work for me. You're responsible for numerous miscalculations which are unacceptable. I intend to verify that Rigby is completely incapacitated and the escapee is dead. If the Rigby situation is not to my liking, I'll find a way to have him neutralized. Do your job by eliminating the target in Chile without further problems."

Rusty responded in an annoyed manner. "I understand your frustrations and I'll eliminate the target. Goodbye."

Frank tossed the phone onto his bed in disgust. He was a perfectionist and demanded flawless performance from his subordinates. That's how he flew his B-17 and that's how he would manage this from now on.

A slight knock on his door announced Helen Moorcroft. Now he had to inform her of the disastrous events in Eureka. He opened the door, hugged her and said, "So good to see you again. Let's go for a short walk outside."

Frank wrapped a sweater around her and put a light windbreaker on himself. The duo walked silently through the hallway to an outside door. A misty drizzle filled the air as they walked on a pathway overlooking the lights of the small city. Helen finally broke the silence. "It must be extremely bad news because you haven't said a word since we left the room. Get on with it."

He stopped walking, looked directly at her and gave out a big sigh. "Whitey was killed this afternoon."

Helen stood motionless, then turned and stared at the lights of Ketchikan. Frank felt awkward and didn't know what else to say. She remained silent and began throwing stones off the embankment. She finally said, "Give me the details. I want everything."

The old man answered, "I'm sorry for your loss. I know the two of you were close. Last night he confided in me about the events in Eufrat and described you as heroic. He had tremendous respect for you."

She continued to stare at the city, showing no emotion. "Details. I want details."

"All the information I have is second hand. The crew apprehended both targets and had them secured at the warehouse. While Rusty was interrogating one of them, the other broke loose and somehow managed to shoot Whitey with his own gun. Rusty shot the target as he was fleeing. He fell into the bay and sank."

Helen shook her head. "Total rubbish. Whitey was on top of his game and would never allow that to happen."

Frank placed his left hand onto her shoulder as she lowered her head and looked at the gravel walkway. "I find this incredibly hard to accept as well," he said, "but I have to rely on the facts. I believe he fell asleep, which provided his captive opportunity to escape."

She asked, "Where's Rusty?"

"On his way to Santiago, Chile. Our final target is there and he's been sent to eliminate him."

Helen looked at Frank and wiped tears onto her sleeve. "I can't do this anymore. I've entertained leaving this profession ever since Eufrat, but today's the proverbial straw that broke the camel's back. I loved Whitey like family, and now he's dead. I've compromised your trust by falling in love with Bennett's son. My effectiveness to you as an operative is worthless. I have no choice but to resign."

Frank hugged her. "Nonsense. You're not worthless. To the contrary, you're invaluable. You're the only operative I can trust and I've considered you as extended family for quite some time. I need you as my personal advisor until this mission is concluded. Your relationship with Bennett's son doesn't bother me at all. In fact, it's imperative that you remain involved because you have a vested interest in the outcome — vis-a-vis the young Bennett. His proximity to the problem and his fathers' relationship with Ernie McKinnon demands your involvement."

Helen paused while considering Frank's comments. She nodded. "If I'm to remain with you until this project's concluded, you'll have to tell me everything about your past and what's behind the events in Alaska, Eureka and Chile. Otherwise I'm off for Angoon to help the Bennetts."

Frank smiled. "Come on trooper. Let's go inside, and I'll tell you everything, providing you promise to take my secrets to your grave."

She shook her head. "I can't promise that unless I'm the only person who knows the truth, but that's not the case, is it? I'm convinced Ernie, Lena and Gus know. Jim Bennett instructed me to tell my employer that he'd enjoy talking with ghosts from Ernie's past. He also suggested that he'd soon have everything figured out. Besides, I bet Rusty knows everything so what's the point? The cows have left the barn."

Frank was shocked by her retort, but also impressed. He cleared his throat. "You're absolutely correct. Kudos to Mr. Bennett. I *am* a ghost, as are Gus and Lena. If too many people knew the truth, it would destroy our families. Some very bad people have found this out and you've seen the results. So I ask for your indulgence by promising to keep the secret within the group of people you've just mentioned."

Helen nodded. "I'll make that promise providing you'll tell me everything. Otherwise I'm out of here."

The old man answered, "You have my word. I'll tell you everything."

They walked back into the lodge as a lightning bolt flashed across the sky. Frank held her hand as they walked to his room. Inside, he opened the small refrigerator and removed two bottles of water and handed one to Helen. They both sat in large cushioned chairs facing each other. Helen folded one leg under the other. Finally she would know the truth.

CHAPTER SIX

June, Friday the 13th — Angoon — Early Morning

A partly sunny day greeted Jim as he rolled out of bed to the smell of brewing coffee. He threw on a pair of sweatpants and walked into the kitchen. Lori sat at the table with Oscar in her lap. She smiled at her former boss as he poured himself a cup of coffee and sat down next to her. Oscar growled slightly as if unhappy with his new surroundings. Jim frowned at him and asked, "What's up, little guy, don't you like it here?"

Lori calmly replied, "No, he loves it here. But, he's not thrilled with the bear you caught this morning."

"I'll be damned!"

Jim bolted to the rear porch and approached the barrel trap. The bear was calmly laying down watching him. Heavy steel bars on each end of the device allowed Jim an unobstructed view of the bruin. He spoke softly. "Hey old fella, sorry for the inconvenience, but we're going to move you somewhere else. Maybe a place where the fish are always spawning and the lady bears will be falling all over you."

A soft laugh caused Jim to turn around. Lori stood on the porch with Oscar at her side. She couldn't resist. "So lady bears will be falling all over him, huh? You're a softly after all."

The enormous bear remained quiet and watched Jim return to the porch. He placed his arm around Lori. "How long have you been awake?"

"Since the bear woke me up — probably two hours now."

"Let's make some breakfast and contact the Clans. They'll pack our hairy guest away. After the kids get up, we'll plan our day."

The smell of frying bacon piqued the interest of the younger Bennetts, convincing them to get up. After everyone had eaten and showered, Jim called a meeting about the upcoming day. Lori realized he managed his household just like he did TacSec — always holding short meetings to brief personnel on upcoming projects and issues. She wondered if he developed this management style while in the Army.

The kids and Lori sat on the couch as Jim knelt next to the large glass coffee table and presented a pile of paper and photographs. The former colonel began to explain. "I've got a proposal for everyone here. We talked about events surrounding Angoon in the hot tub last night, but I failed to disclose several key facts. After I tell you my theory and what I've found, we need to vote on whether we'll risk our lives for something historically significant and potentially valuable. Unless there is consensus, we'll let it go and allow the vultures to fight it out."

As usual, Audra began questions. "Do you know where more gold is? Did you find a hidden Nazi camp, when can . . ."

Danny stopped her before she got rolling. "Hold your horses, sis. Let Dad talk, then ask your questions."

Lori looked amused and Jim began. "Here's what I know: Captain Dale Olsen and Lieutenant Andrew Decker were in a B-17 shot down over Germany in March of 1944. They were listed as MIA and later confirmed as KIA. Dale lived in Pelican, Alaska, prior to the war and owned a bush plane and flight service. He also had an aunt, uncle and younger cousin Gus who lived in Pelican during the war. Dale's bush plane was reported missing in the fall of '44 and its pilot and one-man crew were considered lost at sea. Ernie found the container of gold and Nazi relics in 1945. Gus and Lena Olsen staged their deaths years ago in order to hide their identities. Ernie is related to them through his late wife Jenna. Those are the facts."

Jim passed out the photographs, dog tags and ID's for the others to examine and continued, "Here's my theory: Captain Olsen and Lieutenant Decker didn't die in their B-17, but cut a deal with Nazis to transfer gold to America. They managed to escape Germany somehow and made their way to Pelican in the fall of '44. While bringing gold to the Lower 48, the plane crashed and has never been found. The current problems surrounding Angoon are based on a mad dash by shady characters trying to recover the gold lost with the plane."

Lori wasted no time. "So that's the hornet's nest you've managed to stir up. How do Crane, Rigby and Santos fit into all of this?"

"I can only speculate. They could be descendants of the Nazis who were involved in the original heist. Crane and Rigby are certainly after the gold, but the jury's still out on Santos. He could be an innocent bystander; then again he could be the ringleader. Until I get the INTERPOL report on him or Walt Diller uncovers something, we have to consider him as a suspect."

Lori added, "I have little faith in INTERPOL, but if Walt's involved, he'll get the skinny on Santos. I personally think he's up to his eyeballs in this thing and is probably the ringleader."

Danny asked, "How does Helen fit into this?"

"She's a hired gun for the Olsens."

Danny took a bit to swallow that. "So are the Olsens good guys or bad guys?"

Jim hesitated. "They're somewhere in between. Gus and Lena probably had a hand in helping cousin Dale when he returned to Alaska, but from their history and what Ernie says, they're good people. We can't judge them without knowing all of the facts. I'll tell you this much, though — Crane and Rigby are absolute slime balls."

Audra raised her hand as if she were still in school. Lori laughed and placed her hand over her mouth.

Jim said, "Just because Danny jumped your ass, doesn't mean you need to raise your hand, honey."

She asked, "So what's the life threatening vote we need to take?"

Jim nodded. "Good question. Keep thinking like that and you'll be a millionaire someday. Here's my discovery. I know where the plane is, and it's probably loaded with gold."

Lori blurted, "Bullshit!"

"Oh, ye of little faith." Jim handed her the satellite photo of the tail section. Danny and Audra leaned over and crowded Lori, trying to distinguish details of the photograph.

Lori looked up and said, "I see trees, rocks and snow, nothing else."

Danny grinned. "It's right there." He pointed to a shadowy object sticking out of the snow near a rock wall. He examined another larger view of the area and said, "Look, it's directly above where we found the canister."

Lori grabbed the original photo, looked at it and then exclaimed, "I'll be dipped in shit! Sure as hell! That's the tail of an airplane."

Jim spoke, "If you're superstitious, this is Friday the 13th. Is it worth the risk of life and limb to climb to the wreck? The vultures involved in this affair are ruthless bastards that wouldn't hesitate killing us if we get in their way."

Danny asked, "How much gold are we talking about and what would we do with it? Can we legally keep it?"

"I've researched the plane," Jim answered. "It's a Stinson F-19. It could easily have carried tens of millions of dollars in gold at today's price. I'm not sure what the laws are for finding treasure that originated from Nazi Germany, but frankly, I have no need for it. However, I don't speak for everyone in this room."

Audra asked, "What's the point of risking our lives if we don't intend to keep it?"

Silence filled the room as they considered their options. Finally Lori broke ranks and offered, "I'm with Jim. I don't need the money, but a couple million buys a lot of happiness. I haven't a clue about treasure laws — especially when it comes to Nazi reparation — but you know the old adage, 'finders keepers.' What do you kids think?"

Danny commented, "The IRS will be all over us if we suddenly start spending money like rock stars. That's another risk. It's called income tax evasion. If we turn it in, it'll be confiscated. If we keep it, we could go to prison."

Lori shook her head "Not if you set up off-shore accounts in Belize or Costa Rica. Those countries refuse to share any personal financial information of depositors with any other country."

Audra looked at her dad. "Is that true?"

Jim nodded. "She's got an MBA from Stanford. What more do you want? Look, let's focus on the real issue. Do we or do we not risk going for the plane today?"

Danny was first. "I'm up for it."

"Me too," exclaimed Audra.

Lori looked at Jim. "It occurs to me these photos are real-time satellite images. Walt hooked you up with NORAD, didn't he?"

Jim nodded. "That's a big affirmative, Ms. Phelps."

She grinned. "Stop the 'Ms. Phelps' crap, Mr. Bennett — do you have real-time access?"

Jim answered, "Yes and I know where you're going with this. If we go up the mountain after the wreckage, we can keep an eye on the entire area by bringing my encrypted laptop, external battery pack and the MS-5 dish from the boat. We can monitor everything from Angoon to Kake, and Wrangell to Sitka."

Lori nodded, as if satisfied. "What do you have for armaments?"

Jim laughed. "Enough to wage a small war — from shoulder-held M72 rockets to fully-automatic M4A's, and everything in between."

Danny's eyebrows went up. "What are we waiting for?"

Jim said. "The vote must be unanimous. We've not heard from Lo . . ."

Before Jim could finish, Lori snapped back. "I'm in and so are you. Otherwise you'd never have mentioned any of this."

The "William Tell Overture" began playing from a cell phone inside Jim's pocket. It was the phone he'd configured to intercept calls from Santos. Jim asked everyone to be quiet as he pressed the phone's green button and listened.

"Why are you calling me on this line?" Santos asked. "I gave you specific instructions to always use the radio."

"Relax. This line is more secure than the damn radio. Besides I've got three boats within sight that could be scanning the radio channels."

"Alright. What have you found?"

"We used the underwater ROV on both anomalies. They're total junk — one is a fishing boat that must've sunk fifty years ago and the other's an old rusted out channel buoy."

Santos asked, "Have you located any other anomalies within Peril Strait or Hoonah Sound?"

"Nope. It's void of wreckage. I suggest working a grid pattern in Chatham between here and Whitewater Bay."

"Commence the new search grid and keep me abreast of any developments."

"What about the additional crewmen you promised? I need at least another set of hands if I'm gonna get good data."

"I have a few of your Hell Bent friends lined out."

"Well that totally sucks. I gotta train Hell Bent greenhorns. Who are they?"

"I'm not sure, but that's beside the point. Quit your whining and get back to work. You'll have extra hands by tomorrow."

"Fine. I'll contact you by radio providing there are no other boats around. Otherwise I'll use the cell. Hasta la vista, baby."

The line went dead. Jim motioned for everyone to take a seat. He started, "Does anyone know what 'Hell Bent' refers to?"

The group shrugged their shoulders. Jim continued, "I've not heard of them either, but the jury just came in on Santos. He's definitely part of this — maybe the ring leader.

Danny countered, "So what? We're all in, so let's go."

Jim stood. "OK. Audra if you make us a sack lunch, I'll pack up my laptop and some weapons."

Audra jumped to her feet. "Hot damn. Let's find a pile of gold."

Lori offered, "Wait up girl, I'll give you a hand."

Ketchikan - Early Morning

At 8:00 a.m., Helen gently knocked on Ernie's door. He answered and found her holding a tray filled with food. She flashed back to the incident with the fruit tray in Eufrat.

"I'll be go ta hell," Ernie said. "This is the first time I've ever had room service. Whose idea was this?"

Helen looked tired, but managed a smile. "Compliments of Lena and Gus. How did your meeting go last night?"

The old man sat at a small desk and bit into a piece of bacon. "We musta talked till midnight. I finally understand what's been goin' on around Angoon lately. It makes perfect sense now that I think about it. Everyone thinks I might know where the gold is."

Helen nodded and patted him on the shoulder. "Can you promise me you'll remain in your room until I return? I've got something to do. I'll be back in less than two hours."

Ernie was taken aback. "Shit girl, I ain't needin' no nursemaid. Why do I need ta hang around in my room?"

Helen attempted to diffuse his attitude. "Jim said I'm responsible for your safety. Besides, it's raining cats and dogs outside."

Ernie nodded. "OK — Jim's usually right — especially with what I learned last night. Is that why you're wearing that gun under your jacket?"

"Yes, sir. Remain here until my return. I'll put the 'do-not-disturb' sign on your door and I already notified housekeeping to skip your room. When I return, I'll have figured out how to proceed with our day. Lock the door behind me."

She left the room and took the elevator down to the first floor. She lightly knocked on the conference room door.

Frank opened the door holding his cell phone. "I've been expecting you. I see that you're still packing heat. How did your four hours of sleep go?"

"Under the circumstances, as well as can be expected. I only slept an hour or so. I keep thinking about Whitey."

The old man looked down the hallway and shuffled her inside. "Excuse me for a moment. I need to finish this call."

Helen sat in a chair at the table and stared out the window as Frank continued with his call. She knew it was Rusty on the line from the tone of the conversation.

If they've got an electrified fence and surveillance cameras around the entire compound, how do you plan on neutralizing the target?"

Rusty calmly answered, "I've located numerous soft spots where large tree branches overhang the fence. After dark, I can easily penetrate the fence. Once inside, I'll find a sniper position. Corn fields and fruit trees surround the main complex so I can set up without detection."

"How will you identify Keller?"

"I've done my homework. I downloaded numerous photos from INTERPOL. When I see him, he's dead."

"What about escaping the compound after neutralizing him?"

"I've got a C4 satchel charge. I'll blow my way out if need be."

"Excellent — make it happen. I want our next conversation to be a cause for celebration."

"I'm on it Mr. Reid. I'll contact you when it's done."

The old man placed his phone on an end table and sat next to Helen. "That was Rusty. He's about to kill the ringleader."

"I gathered that. I'm going on record as not trusting Rusty. Whitey was a consummate professional and too smart to be overtaken by a captive. Rusty's not telling us everything."

"I share your feelings. However we have little choice but to let things take their course. Are you ready to pick up where we left off? This shouldn't take long."

Helen nodded and leaned back. "Yes. I'm intrigued by the fact that you escaped from Germany with the help of the SS. Your exploits are incredible and I'm anxious to hear how you managed to get the gold to Seattle without being caught. More importantly, I'd like to know how your past fits into our current situation."

The duo settled into the room, and the former captain continued his story:

***

After being confined to a U-boat for nearly six weeks, it was a blessing to walk in the open spaces of Alaska. Andy was unable to sleep on the second night in Pelican, so he took a stroll to the canary warehouse. We'd taken my portion of gold, canned it . . ."

"Canned it?" Helen asked. She was incredulous and impressed at once.

"Yes," Frank said. "Canned it and concealed it on a pallet inside the warehouse. Andy knew the warehouse was locked, but someone with a lantern was inside rifling through our secret stash. He managed to catch the perpetrator; a young female Tlingit worker. A fight ensued and Andy ended up knocking her out and breaking her nose."

"It turned out she had been in the warehouse the previous night and overheard the meeting between my family and partners. She knew everything about our plan. We hid her until we could decide what to do. My cousin Gus knew her well and they were fond of each other. We decided to fake her death by drowning and keep her in the U-boat. This was a really big deal. We couldn't kill her because my family insisted on not harming her. We stood a good chance of the entire operation going south because of this situation.

"To make matters worse, we had already discovered Obert was addicted to drugs and absinthe. Henry — General Bruner — hoped to clean him up, which became a fool's errand. While pretending to recover, he was caught trying to reach ODESSA on the sub's radio. After our fifth successful trip to Whatcom, he escaped through the forward torpedo hatch and tried swimming to shore. He was presumed dead.

"The woman Andy caught at the warehouse is Lena — the wife of Gus. She promised to never divulge what she knew in exchange for her life. Obviously, she has kept her promise."

"Our partnership had developed a plan for transferring the gold to Whatcom. My uncle Carl provided us with registered flight plans to Bellingham, Washington, under the guise of bringing another canning line from Seattle to Pelican. He'd often expressed desire for three production lines, so the flights back and forth were inconspicuous."

Helens left leg had fallen asleep. She groaned as she stood and began massaging her calf. The old man offered her a glass of water while she walked around in small circles.

"No, but thanks," she said. "Now I understand the connection between Lena, Gus and yourself. So your cousin Gus ultimately married Lena, Ernie's late wife's cousin. Lena and Jenna were both raised by their grandmother and were like sisters. You're almost related to Ernie McKinnon by virtue of Gus. In the end, Rudy — AKA Henry — and you transferred the gold to Washington. Our dilemma is linked to you and the partnership's wealth."

The old man shook his head. "Not quite. The partnership dissolved because of events beyond Henry's and my control. Shall I continue?"

Helen replied, "Absolutely, but a few quick questions. I need to get a handle on our current situation. Besides your family, who else knows the truth about your past?"

Frank considered the question. "Until Henry's death, I've managed to remain in the background. Besides my family and Henry, only Rusty, Lena and Gus knew who I am. However, the people we apprehended in Trinidad and their bosses were in hot pursuit. Rusty insists that there's a connection with descendants of ODESSA and the illegitimate son of Karl Obert. After neutralizing the people apprehended in California, Rusty claims that only one individual remains — Obert's son — Anton Keller, who resides in Chile."

She asked, "So Rusty's been mobilized to Chile?"

The old man nodded. "He should be in position to eliminate Keller later today or early tomorrow."

"Is he acting alone?"

Again, Frank nodded. "Yes."

Helen paced the room thinking, then asked, "What about the ship I confirmed as hostile in Peril Strait? Who's running that operation?"

"At first I considered Bennett as our likely candidate, but Rusty said that the men apprehended in Eureka were behind the Alaskan operation as well as the problems in California. Both worked for Anton Keller of Chile."

Helen sat back down. "If Rusty's assessment is correct, then our only loose end is the bogus NOAA ship and its crew. What's that ship searching for?"

Frank was anxious to continue. "That's what I'd planned to divulge when your leg fell asleep — I'll continue with the details of our gold runs.

Mid August, 1944 — The First Trip

Intermittent fog surrounded Lisianski Strait and Pelican Cove as the fishing fleet left the docks for the fishing grounds of Icy Strait. Exhausted from too many late nights, Gus sat in a cushioned chair as his first mate operated the boat. He figured the fog would force Dale to stay another day, but he didn't know his cousin as well as he thought. Being a B-17 pilot had transformed Dale into a fearless man with incredible focus and stamina.

Aunt Rita prepared breakfast with the help of Rudy and Andy, and uncle Carl went to the cannery and radioed Juneau, Sitka, Ketchikan, Powell River, Bellingham and Seattle. He confirmed the flight timetable, refueling stop, weather reports and radio frequencies. Everything was on track, including the components he needed for another production line. The weather would clear by noon and steadily improve the further south the plane traveled. The Navy supply ship would be at his docks by late morning, so he quickly pulled a fuel cart over to the F-19 and topped off its tanks. He checked the engine oil, then threw a small canvas tarp over the gold laden cylinders.

After breakfast, Dale spread two maps on the kitchen table and Andy pulled up a chair to study the proposed route. Dale was a perfectionist when it came to flying, and the maps were pre-marked with pencil lines, compass headings, radio frequencies and notes. Rudy knew that Dale and Andy were professionals, yet he was impressed with their preparation. By the time the duo refolded their maps, Rudy knew they could reach Whatcom blindfolded. He left the house and entered the guest cabin to retrieve his sea bag and jacket. The bag contained three pistols, an aluminum cylinder and a change of clothes for the trio. Upon return, he sat next to Carl, opened the canister and handed him another three thousand dollars.

"I'm sorry for all the problems we've encountered, but I think things are finally on track. Each trip you'll receive three thousand dollars and upon completion, another two kilos of gold. That's a total value of fifty thousand dollars. I hope this takes the sting out of our intrusions."

"Rita and I appreciate your generosity and we're glad to help Dale and his friends. It's a blessing to have him back and when the war's over, please come back to visit. You're always welcome in our home."

"Thank you. I'd like that. Perhaps we could go fishing with Gus or hunting." He pointed toward the far wall. "I noticed the moose antlers above your desk and the other set above your door. I'd enjoy doing that sort of thing when the war's over. Dale tells me you're an avid hunter. There's nothing to hunt in Germany except deer that pale in comparison to moose."

"That would be fun. We could fly into the interior and call in a big old bull. After you've shot it, the real work begins. Dealing with a 2,000 pound animal is a tough project.

Carl stood. "Time to get down to the cannery and load the supply ship. You guys need to filter down to the plane separately and get into the plane a minute or two apart. No one will pay attention unless you're in a group. I'll keep the cannery busy while you guys take off, then I'll radio ahead to Rupert. Good luck and Godspeed."

Carl put the money in his bedroom, and left for the cannery.

Rudy emptied the canister, and handed out documents to Dale and Andy. The trio already possessed new passports, military ID's and dog tags. Now, Andy was given a Canadian birth certificate and Dale received military discharge documents. Rudy also handed over social security cards and drivers' licenses. On paper, the group appeared completely legitimate. Rudy opened the sea bag and distributed the pistols and jackets, then suggested that Andy leave for the plane. He'd follow. Dale would go last.

Ten minutes later, Dale said goodbye to Rita, and headed to the plane. Walking toward the dock, Dale knew they'd be at Lake Whatcom before evening. At the dock, he hugged his uncle goodbye and entered the cockpit. Carl pushed the F-19 away from the dock with a long oar and moments later the engine was humming and the plane was headed toward the inlet. It was foggy and drizzling, but blue sky was breaking through in spots. Andy sat in the left seat with Dale in the right. Behind them, Rudy sat on a large upholstered bench-style seat. They all wore light jackets to conceal their sidearms. There was a slight southerly wind, so Andy taxied north, set the altimeter to zero, and turned the plane south. He adjusted the trim bar for takeoff, pushed the throttle forward and the F-19 immediately sped forward. Within thirty seconds, it stepped up onto its pontoons and the plane easily skipped along the top of the water.

Dale began coaching Andy. "Keep a neutral position on your wheel. Let the engine pull you up. Perfect — keep it steady while gaining speed." The green and yellow plane raced down the inlet at over 110 mph. "Great job, amigo — now gently pull back on the wheel."

Andy eased back the wheel as the F-19 pulled clear of the water. Dale said, "Excellent job Andy. Now, slowly advance the trim bar to the flight position."

The plane rose steadily as Andy reset his trim.

Dale continued with his coaching. "Pay attention to the end of this inlet and the mountain valley directly ahead. It leads into Hoonah Sound and Peril Straight. You'll see it as you gain altitude."

Andy said, "I see it." He looked over his shoulder at the scenery below, and the F-19 banked slightly to the left. "This is gorgeous country."

Dale responded, "Stay focused. Set your bearings according to our compass numbers on the map." Andy looked at the map and brought the F-19 onto a course of 135 degrees southeast. He flawlessly executed a slight left turn as the plane continued to gain altitude.

Dale said, "This heading places you to a straight line between Lisianski and the right-hand corner of Peril Strait. You'll see the Strait in a minute. Ahead and to your right is Sitka — just over those mountains. Behind your left shoulder is Hoonah, then Juneau."

The plane continued to gain altitude and speed, traveling at 155 mph. Dale said, "The idea is to have enough altitude to clear Catherine Island without changing course. If you're able to do that, you can remain on this bearing all the way to Rupert. If you can't, follow Peril into Chatham Strait and turn south until you have enough altitude to clear the tip of Admiralty Island. Then re-establish the 135 southeast heading."

Andy smiled. "This ain't bad at all. I see Catherine directly ahead of us. We're at 2,800 feet and climbing. According to the map, we'll have plenty of clearance by the time we get there."

Dale patted Andy on the shoulder. "Fantastic job, amigo, you're on track for Rupert." He radioed the cannery to inform Carl that they were on course and everything was normal.

The weather began to clear as they approached Chatham Strait. The F-19 operated flawlessly and Rudy occupied himself with the views. Scenery in every direction was breathtaking. Enormous snow-covered mountains rose from the sea. Heavily-timbered shorelines and steep mountainsides were littered with cascading waterfalls. Shaded high-mountain valleys were choked with snow and numerous glaciers were visible to the east. He completely understood why Dale loved Alaska, especially from this vantage point.

Dale looked at the speedometer, then glanced at the flight clock. They'd be flying over Ketchikan in 85 minutes and Rupert was only 40 beyond that. Since Rupert was in the Pacific Time Zone, they'd lose an hour and be refueling by 3:30.

He put his left hand to the wheel to see if he could control the plane. It was easier than he imagined.

"Let me try to hold her, Andy." He quickly felt that the trim wasn't properly set and said, "Push the trim bar slightly forward. The nose should drop. That way you won't need to constantly push on the yoke."

As soon as Andy adjusted the trim, the engine quieted and the plane increased speed. Dale discovered that he could easily manage the plane once airborne. Rudy looked forward and said, "Like a duck in water — throw him in and he swims. Someday, you'll fly again."

After reaching the southern tip of Admiralty Island, Dale said, "At this juncture, you need to be at least 4,000 feet. The inland waterway to Seattle is dotted with small villages, so you're never very far from civilization. On your left is a Tlingit village called Kake. The map points out every refuge imaginable. By maintaining this altitude, you'll be able to glide to a nearby village if you're in trouble."

Andy looked to his left and saw Kake about twelve miles away. He looked ahead and noticed solid white clouds engulfing the islands and waterway. Low-level clouds stretched to the horizon.

"What's going on here? I'd never be able to land in this soup."

"It looks worse than it really is. I avoid Ketchikan because these clouds typically stretch to there. They get so damn much moisture there people catch giant slugs for fun — they even hold slug races. I've seen eight-inch slugs. If you have to get into Ketchikan, head toward the ocean and approach from the south. Once you clear Ketchikan, the clouds disappear. It has something to do with mountains on Prince of Wales Island trapping moisture in Clarence Sound."

Andy responded, "You're bullshitting about the slugs, right."

"Not at all."

Rudy busted out laughing. "Slug races?"

"I'm not joking. They bet on the goofy bastards. It's a big deal."

The cloud cover below them made it difficult to see landmarks, so Andy contacted Ketchikan airfield and verified his course. Broken clouds and Prince Rupert lay directly in front of the F-19 as they passed Ketchikan. Andy calculated they'd be landing in 35 minutes.

Rudy used the time to ask Andy about Lake Whatcom's southern end, where his grandparents had homesteaded. The Decker family owned several large tracts below Blue Canyon that were eventually given to Andy and his sister. The original homestead was four miles east of the lake near an area called Doran. His maternal grandparents were Dorans and the main farm road was called Doran Road. His father grew up just north of Doran in a town called Acme. His parents met attending school in Acme.

As Andy explained the situation at Whatcom, Prince Rupert became visible ahead. He maneuvered the F-19 into a landing path, cut the throttle back and adjusted the trim tabs. Dale radioed the docks at Rupert to identify the incoming flight and request fuel. Three minutes later, the plane taxied toward the fuel depot. Two men stood on the dock to greet the flight. One was in an Army uniform.

Rudy asked Dale, "Is it customary for military personnel to be involved with a routine fuel stop?"

"Remember, we're at war. If they suspected anything unusual, we'd have dozens of armed men waiting for us. Relax. Andy and I will do the talking."

The plane pulled adjacent to one of four fuel tanks and the corporal motioned for Andy to open his door. Andy did and asked, "How's the weather south of here?"

"Great, from what I'm told." The corporal handed a large, green, cloth-covered booklet and pencil to Andy. "Regulations require that you log in. Enter the plane's registration number, time, origin, destination, pilot's name and how many passengers on board. Just follow the top column to the line where I've signed my name."

Andy nodded. "Roger that. Who do I pay for the fuel?"

The soldier pointed to the man in civilian clothing. "He'll take the money. My job is to track air traffic."

Andy carefully executed the manifest and handed the pencil and book back to the corporal. The young man thanked him and walked toward buildings at the end of the dock complex. After the fuel attendant was paid, the plane was pushed back into the harbor. It started and taxied south. Moments later, Dale admired Andy's flawless take-off.

Airborne, Rudy commented, "The re-fueling was easier than I'd imagined — not a single question or raised eye-brow. What will refueling in Bellingham be like?"

Dale answered, "We'll make a point of buying fuel at a private facility near the Canal Street docks. It'll be just as easy as here, providing I show them my uncle's letter."

"Excellent — a pleasant surprise."

Dale explained the remainder of the flight to Andy as the plane roared south. Steep coastal mountains to the east and open ocean to the west provided a clear pathway to Bellingham. He pointed out the small town of Powell River as an additional fuel stop if headwinds were to prevent them from making Lake Whatcom. Clear weather and slight cross winds enabled the plane to reach Vancouver, B.C., within three hours but air traffic increased dramatically as they approached the U.S. border. Scores of newly-manufactured PBY's flew in formation toward Seattle — destined for deployment overseas. Rudy thought to himself that Germany and Japan had been fools for taking on America's industrial might.

Dale kept in radio contact with a variety of military towers, identifying themselves as a registered Alaskan cannery flight. Their presence went unchallenged.

It was near evening by the time Andy circled their destination. No activity was observed on the lake as they flew over Andy's barn. The trio was tired of flying and anxious to land. Andy executed a tight, spiraling turn into the wind and set the plane on the lake. He turned it toward the barn and taxied to a small adjoining dock. They arrived as the sun transformed into a disappearing orange ball on the horizon.

Rudy tied the plane to the pier, and the three men walked 50 yards up a gravel road to the barn. Its front doors were chained and locked. Andy lifted a flat rock near the corner of the barn and retrieved a brass key. After opening the two large doors, he went to a central vertical post and grabbed a large kerosene lantern. He shook it to see if it had fuel and pulled a farmer's match from his top pocket. The barn's interior was lit by the lamp's yellow light. A dusty 1936 Ford coupe stood under a hay loft storing tons of old, decaying hay. Andy went to a large work bench against the left wall and produced another lantern.

Dale asked, "Does the car run?"

"It ran like a champ before I headed overseas. Her nickname's 'Jewel.' It's been two years since I drove it. Dad must've put it here. I left it at the house."

Andy opened the driver's side door. He was surprised when the dome light came on. There were no keys in the ignition. On the dashboard was a photograph of himself in a football uniform and a dried bunch of flowers. He figured his family parked it in the barn because it reminded them of their loss. A rush of guilt came as he sat behind the wheel. His parents were suffering grief while he was alive and well. A fifteen-minute ride separated his parents from the truth and their much deserved relief. After gathering his thoughts, he left the car and reached under the rear bumper to retrieve a hidden key. He sat behind the wheel again, placed the Ford in neutral and turned the key. The engine coughed and sputtered several times before starting. The trio now had an unexpected and much-needed means of ground transportation. They also had an easy method of bringing their cargo from the plane to the barn.

"Let's empty the plane and get some sleep," Andy offered. "You guys can use 'Jewel' tomorrow for reconnaissance while I fuel up the plane and get Carl's parts. If we get an early start, we could return to Pelican by tomorrow night."

Rudy was confused. "What happened to your plans for hiding the gold?"

"I totally trust you guys. I'm comfortable stashing it in the barn. You guys can do what you want with yours."

"I'm good with that," Rudy said. "I'll keep mine here as well. Günter will agree that this place is as secure as any. We can be done transporting within a week."

He paused. "We can't tell Karl about any of this."

The trio agreed and began the laborious task of bringing the canisters from the plane to the Ford. Life had suddenly become easier.

Mr. Reid was near the end of his story. "Rudy, Andy and I successfully made five trips to Whatcom. Rudy — now Henry — and I remained in Whatcom while Andy returned to Pelican on the sixth and final run. Karl's mental state had improved so dramatically that he was allowed to move about the U-boat with only slight supervision.

He was banned from the radio room and the weapons room. To our relief, everything about him appeared on track and normal, but, like I said earlier, he deceived us."

"During our fifth trip to Whatcom, Hans surfaced the U-Boat during the dead of night so his crew could get a breath of fresh air. Karl used the opportunity to knock out our navigator, steal his pistol and escape through the forward torpedo hatch. Men on deck watched in disbelief as he dove into the ice-cold water and disappeared. Obert couldn't swim well and everyone assumed he died from hypothermia or drowned.

"Afterwards, Hans searched his room and found a near-empty bottle of Eukodal he'd managed to squirrel away from prying eyes. The crafty bastard regained our trust in order to escape. His survival is doubtful, and to my knowledge he was never seen again. The partnership was somewhat relieved he was gone."

Frank paused and sighed. "On the final trip, the Stinson went missing with Günter and Andy aboard. It was never found. I'm convinced the NOAA ship and the people we've encountered are searching for my plane."

" Now I get it," Helen said. "Not only are they intent on extorting money from you, they know there's a plane full of gold somewhere near Pelican."

"That's only part of it. The sub crew never established contact with Rudy or their families after the war. Henry believed Karl somehow sabotaged the U-boat prior to escaping because Gus witnessed an enormous oil slick near Lisianski Inlet on the morning of the final flight. It's where the U-boat had been hiding which suggests its demise."

"Bloody hell! An airplane *and* a U-boat filled with gold. No wonder you've got worms crawling out of the woodwork. Anyone else know about your past you may have overlooked?"

"No."

Helen frowned. "I'm convinced Bennett has figured it out. Remember? He told me to tell ghosts from Ernie's past that he'd like to have a conversation with them. What about Rusty? Does he know about the gold?

Frank sighed. "Yes. I felt it important that he knew the specifics of my problem."

"Do you trust him?"

Before Frank could respond, there was a knock on the door. Helen peeked through the peep-hole. She turned and whispered "Gus" and opened her palms skyward as if saying, "Should I open?"

The old man nodded. Helen ushered Gus into the room and glanced up and down the hallway before closing the door. Gus said to Frank, "I have information from my meeting with Ernie you need to be aware of. It's unsettling — perhaps we should talk in private."

Frank shook his head. "Go ahead. Helen's my gal Friday."

Gus tipped his head to one side and grimaced. "You sure about this?"

Frank nodded. "Anything you need to say to me can be shared with Helen."

Gus rolled his eyes in doubt. "Alright. Here goes. Ernie found a canister of gold and Günter's pistol in 1945. His friend Bennett found several dog tags two days ago. Your and Andy's tags were among them. He's got mountains of incriminating artifacts and knows about me. Ernie said he's got FBI and CIA files on all of us — including Helen."

Helen smiled at that.

"He knows Lena and I are alive. It gets worse. He learned Obert's body was found in Peril Straight days after the plane disappeared. For Christ sake, Dale, we didn't even know that."

"Obert's body was processed through the Sitka police department as a homicide because the body had bullet holes in it. Here's a complete stranger who knows more about this affair than we do. There's a chance he's part of what happened to Henry and Whitey. Ernie insists he's not. I don't understand how he knows all of these things unless he's part of it. Nobody has access to this much information without being involved."

Frank sat back in his chair speechless, trying to digest what Gus had said. Helen asked Gus to sit and watched her boss deal with the news. Concerned about the amount of stress confronting the old man, she got behind him and began massaging his shoulders.

"Bennett had nothing to do with Henry or Whitey," she said. "I seriously doubt he'll narc on either of you. Not his style. He's legitimately concerned for Ernie's welfare."

Helen asked Gus, "Did Ernie show Bennett the items he found in 1945?"

Gus replied, "Yes — several days ago."

She swiped her left hand into the air. "There you have it. Ernie initiated the situation. Bennett simply used his resources in order to connect the dots. He couldn't have been involved with Henry's murder because he hadn't seen Ernie's treasures until after Henry's death."

Frank realized she was correct. "You're right. The question is what he intends to do with the information he has?"

Helen thought for a moment. "Why don't I call him and ask?"

Frank frowned. "You can't be serious?"

"I'm dead serious, sir. He's asked to speak with ghosts from Ernie's past. Let's lay it all out and see why he wants to talk."

Silence permeated the room as Frank and Gus pondered her suggestion. Gus offered, "He certainly knows about me but maybe not you. He probably believes you died in your B-17, and that I was the person involved with the Krauts."

Helen shook her head. "He's smarter than that. Let's bring Ernie in here and have him call Bennett. When they're done, I'll take over and broach the subject of speaking with ghosts. If you are comfortable with his remarks, I'll prod him for more information. As long as we don't divulge anything he doesn't already know, perhaps he'll enlighten us about who's behind the problems in Alaska and California. In my opinion, he could prove to be our greatest asset."

The cousins looked dumbfounded, but Gus admitted, "She's right. Ernie is key to an introduction. I said in Port Angeles I had a gut feeling about everything working out. This is it — our golden opportunity. Dark Star's good, but they're hamstrung by our need for secrecy, whereas Bennett already knows more than we do — and he's friends with Ernie. Ernie needs to say that he expects our identities to remain anonymous because we're family. If he's truly Ernie's friend, he'll cooperate."

Frank shook his head. "I'd be placing my family's well-being in the hands of a complete stranger. I'm uncomfortable with that."

Helen sat at her employers' side and placed a hand to his knee. "You've already done that with Rusty and look where it's gotten you. Answer me this — do you trust me?"

The old man nodded. "I do."

Helen said, "Then contact Bennett and see what he has to say. I've met him and I know he's sincere. If Ernie asks him to remain silent, he'll do so."

The old pilot leaned deeper into his chair. "For Christ's sake, I hope you're right. Get McKinnon and Lena in here. Let's get on with this before I have a Goddamn stroke."

A few minutes later, Lena and Ernie were escorted into the conference room. Ernie was nervous and confused by the presence of the one-armed man at the head of the table. Helen placed an aluminum briefcase on the table, opened it, and sat next to Ernie.

Lena introduced Frank as Dale Olsen, cousin of Gus. Ernie awkwardly offered his own left hand. Dale smiled and assured him that new acquaintances often had the same problem. Gus provided a brief recap of last night's conversation, and explained the capture of Officer Crane and Rigby. Gus also divulged Dale's past. After completing Gus' terse summary, Ernie managed one of his cackled laughs.

He looked at Gus. "I figured ya got rich from inheritin' your parents' dough. The gold I found was a drop in a bucket compared to what ya guys musta raked in. That's why ya got private jets and all. I heard war stories about Captain Olsen and how he got killed durin' the war. I gotta hand it to ya boys, ya sure fooled everyone, includin' me."

He turned his attention toward Dale. "Did ya lose your arm durin' the war?"

The former B-17 pilot nodded. "I did. Now that you know the truth about us, can we have your promise you'll keep this information confidential? The well-being of our families depend upon your silence."

Ernie was annoyed. "I'd never snitch ya guys out. Lena and Gus are family."

"Being sure," Frank said. "You told Gus and Lena your friend Mr. Bennett has volumes of material related to us and our past. He also has insight into the situation surrounding Angoon. We've managed to defuse the immediate threat, but Mr. Bennett has sensitive information which could assist in determining if anyone else may be involved. What bothers me is whether he'll expose us if we spoke with him?"

Ernie was near anger. "Jim's no snitch either. He's the best friend I've got and he's a patriot. He cares about me and treats me like I'm part of his family. Ask the young missy sittin' next to me — she's seen what kinda fella he is. The reason he got involved in this mess was because of me. Crane kept fuckin' with me, so Jim handled him — beat the tar outa him. Not only did he kick Crane's ass, he kept me safe while figurin' this shit out."

Lena reached across the table and grabbed Ernie's hand. "Relax Ernie. We don't doubt Mr. Bennett's friendship or sincerity toward you, but we need to determine if we can talk to him without him turning us in."

Helen placed her hand on Ernie's shoulder. "Mr. McKinnon's correct about the colonel. I'm convinced that if Ernie asks him to remain silent, he will as a matter of friendship and respect for Ernie."

Ernie added, "You're damn right he'd keep quiet."

He turned to Helen. "Hey Missy, how'd ya find out he was a colonel?"

Helen smiled. "It's my job to know these things."

Ernie asked, "Just what do ya think ya know about Jim?"

Helen smiled. "He's a former C.E.O. who's joined at the hip with the Pentagon and CIA. He received the Silver Star for extracting an agent from a prison in Panama. He has two Purple Hearts and was a full colonel in Delta Force. Later, he transferred to the Special Activities Division and took down Escobar. Years of government service led to his divorce and he recently retired from TacSec, which is possibly a government front. I characterize him as extremely honest and trustworthy. If you ask for his silence in exchange for a candid dialog, he'll honor that commitment."

Ernie smiled. "I told ya guys. Miss Moorcroft met him three days ago and already knows what kinda fella he is. I'll ask him to promise silence before ya talk."

Frank Reid finally agreed. "OK. Ernie, call him now and we'll put the phone on speaker so everyone can join in. Do you approve, Ernie?"

Ernie nodded and Helen placed the call. The gadgetry inside her metal case was ready to record and track the colonel's location. She set the phone at the center of the table when it rang.

Jim answered, "Good morning Miss Moorcroft, how are you today? Is Ernie with you?"

"This ain't Miss Moorcroft. It's Ernie."

"Then let me rephrase. Good morning Ernie, how are you today?"

"Couldn't be better except it's rainin' like cats and dogs over here."

"The weather's quite nice in Angoon. I sense you need something. What can I do for you?"

"Actually I do — a big favor ta ask before we go on."

"Go ahead, buddy. Maybe I can accommodate you."

"If I let ya talk with some ghosts from my past, would ya promise to keep everything private and never rat them out — no matter what they told ya? Would ya promise?"

Jim set the phone down and motioned for Lori, Audra and Danny to sit close. "My system indicates a phantom intercept. Is Helen monitoring this call? If not, we need to stop talking."

Helen interrupted. "Top of the morning to you, Colonel. It's my system you're detecting. I'm simply doing my job. No other line breaks, so it's safe to continue."

Jim placed his index finger to his lips for the group surrounding the coffee table. "Very well then, let's move forward. Ernie, you asked me to promise silence. I agree with your request, providing what I hear won't jeopardize national security. Beyond that, I won't cast judgment on people and events from 60 years ago. I'll keep an open mind regarding your family members, but it's important to understand that until my termination contract arrives from TacSec, I'm subject to random lie detector tests and interrogation from our government. The prospect of that occurring is slim, but I did pull strings with the CIA to arrive at the point of understanding what's currently happening in Angoon. I'll eventually need to justify my recent requests but it's nothing that I can't handle. Knowing this, your family may reconsider conversing with me."

Helen looked at the others, who nodded approval. She added, "On behalf of everyone here, we accept those risks and are prepared to proceed. However, I suggest we speak in hypothetical terms, which is a handy way to beat lie detector tests."

"I understand your approach."

Helen looked at Frank who again nodded in approval.

"I believe we're all on the same page, sir, so let me enlighten you regarding my role. My involvement is no longer through Dark Star. I'm working directly for individuals within this room. Recently a dear friend of my employers was murdered. He was shaken down by unscrupulous individuals for money and information. We captured and interrogated several of those individuals and realized that more are involved. They managed to kill one of our operatives yesterday and we have reason to believe that part of their organization is in Southern Alaska. These people want to interrogate Ernie, which is why he was spirited away yesterday. That being said, who would care to begin?"

Ernie jumped in. "Jim, I'm in a room with four other people — three of 'em are dead and I'd like it to stay that way, if ya know what I mean."

Jim understood. "If they're dead, we'll let their souls rest in peace. Allow me to run a theory by those resting souls: Suppose that the current situation surrounding Angoon and the problems facing the deceased has its roots in Nazi gold. Imagine an American B-17 pilot and his crew being shot down over Germany and then coerced into assisting the Nazis to transfer gold to America. Perhaps they exchanged their assistance for freedom and wealth. Let's assume that the B-17 pilot was from Pelican, Alaska, with the name of — give me a moment to dream up some names. I've got it — Captain Olsen, and maybe a Lieutenant Decker, as well as several top SS officers, perhaps named Obert and Bruehl, among others managed to pull off the heist of all heists. They faked their deaths, stole a U-boat from Hitler and loaded it to the gills with Reichsbank gold. Maybe Olsen's role was to provide a tricked-out bush plane for making runs to the Lower 48 — somewhere like Washington State. But things went terribly wrong. A shipment of gold disappeared with the plane, the U-boat sank and one of the key Nazis was murdered in Hoonah Sound. What if someone stumbled onto these events? I'd bet it would ignite a flurry of interest in finding the gold as well as locating individuals involved in the original caper. Are you with me so far?"

Frank shook his head and smiled. "Please continue, Mr. Bennett."

Jim wondered about the new voice, but moved on. "Suppose a dirty cop from Sacramento and a so-called author with family ties to the SS appeared in Angoon. The likelihood of them being interested in helping the Tlingits or documenting their history would be slim to none. The reason for their presence in Angoon is driven by greed. They're after a dark fortune. A cop and a bogus writer could never recover treasure in a remote area of Alaska without a financial backer, which means someone with sophistication and resources would be pulling their strings. Therefore, the individual or group behind the search would also be looking for persons directly involved in the original exodus from Germany for the purpose of extortion. Any survivors from the original heist are at risk."

Jim concluded, "My theory has gaps which I trust can be elaborated upon."

Frank answered. "Your power of deductive reasoning is incredible, sir. What if the policeman and author suddenly disappeared and the person pulling the strings was identified as a former ODESSA heir residing in Chile. What if he were to be neutralized as well? Would we see light at the end of the tunnel?"

A long pause was followed by, "No, things would just be heating up."

The group in Ketchikan looked at each other in disbelief. Frank stared down at the table while shaking his head. He asked. "Please explain, sir."

"You mentioned a man in Chile — he's likely located at the Colonia Dignidad Compound. It's reputation is that of a former Nazi lair. However, the CIA and Amnesty International years ago convinced the Chilean government to apprehend the compound's leadership and allow interrogations. They were tipped off by Chilean officials, and the Nazi big shots fled the compound before the sting operation was concluded. Subsequently, only a handful of low level Nazis were apprehended. Afterwards, several were convicted of child molestation, not war crimes. Our government knows that after World War II, ODESSA scattered throughout Argentina and Brazil and integrated into legitimate enterprises. ODESSA wouldn't subject themselves to the high profile lifestyle practiced at Colonia Dignidad and it's unlikely that current residents of the compound could orchestrate a meaningful search in Alaska. Is the person of interest residing at the Colonia compound?"

Frank hesitated and looked at Helen. She nodded. Frank answered, "Um, yes — again, sir, your grasp of the situation is uncanny."

Jim continued. "Helen, pay attention here. Is his name Vicente Santos?"

"No, sir, it's Anton Keller."

Jim wrote down the name. "I doubt you've located the source — just a subordinate player. Don't talk yourself into believing there's light at the end of the tunnel. The light you see may be an oncoming train. Unless the real facilitator and his organization are eliminated, things will only escalate. If ODESSA is involved, there's a litany of individuals throughout the globe who'd want to recover this 'dark fortune.' I also recently learned a group called the 'Hell Bents' is involved in this, as well. Do you know anything about them?"

Helen quickly offered, "They're a motorcycle gang from Northern California who've been retained by the organization behind our problems. They're a splinter group of the Hell's Angels who managed to murder one of our men — they're dangerous and must be taken seriously. Why are you mentioning them? Are they connected with Santos?"

"Yes, they are. I intercepted a conversation today indicating that Hell Bents are here and more are headed this way."

A long silence followed. Frank rubbed his eyes. Finally he continued. "Let's shift gears for a moment. Much of the information we've gained came from an independent contractor who uses identical interrogation techniques employed by the CIA. Would you be inclined to rely on that information?"

"Absolutely. Captured subordinates typically tell the truth when pressured correctly. However, they're often given misinformation by superiors in case of capture. Its standard counter-intelligent protocol, so separating fact from fiction is tricky."

Helen nodded at Frank before he responded. "Well put, sir. If you were one of the original hypothetical participants, how would you go about solving the situation?"

"Eliminate the root cause, then dilute the facts with conjecture and misinformation."

Frank spoke. "Please explain."

"The root of this hypothetical problem isn't ODESSA, former SS members, their heirs or even the Hell's Angels. It's this hypothetical 'dark fortune.' As long as anyone thinks it's still out there, greed will continue to fuel the oncoming train. Here's a likely solution; imagine a missing plane from 1944 is accidentally discovered by the Tlingits of Angoon. With the wreckage is several hundred ounces of gold without any Nazi connection. The Tlingits have sovereign rights on Admiralty Island, so the wreckage and gold technically belongs to them. Only Uncle Sam can challenge those rights but that's politically incorrect. Are you with me so far?"

Frank nodded. "I think so. Please continue."

"Assuming identities of the pilot and his assistant are verified as those who disappeared from Pelican in 1944 — new IDs and all — and that no evidence of Nazi involvement was found in the wreck, the cannery owners are absolved from complicity. The presence of gold is simply a mystery. The pilot and crewmember and the gold's true origin could never be ascertained. The Tlingits who stumble on the gold, immediately spend it on a commercial salmon enterprise and because it's spent, further involvement from outside sources including ODESSA goes away."

Frank managed to smile. "Brilliant scenario, sir. Let us imagine that the survivors have no connection to ODESSA and no desire for this 'dark fortune.' Let us also assume they have established new identities. Do you feel that their situation would improve?"

"Absolutely. However, I would encourage them to take every step necessary to eliminate their enemies, including the Chilean fellow — hypothetically speaking of course."

Frank nodded. "There are several hurdles which require further thought. First the wreckage must be located. Next, the wreckage requires preparation because the amount of gold far exceeds 200 ounces. Finally, the gold could be in a variety of forms. Swiss Francs, Austrian Coronas, and Reichsbank bullion. Coronas and Francs are explicable but anything connected to Nazi Germany is problematic. Do you follow me?"

"I do. How much gold are we hypothetically speaking of?"

"Fifteen hundred kilos, perhaps more."

The other three sitting around Jim's coffee table looked at each other in disbelief. Jim had no reaction other than to say, "That's a significant amount. No wonder there's so much interest."

Frank asked, "I don't imagine you know the location of the hypothetical wreckage?"

"I can't speak to that at this time, but if personnel from the hypothetical original group were alive today, I'd encourage them to rest easy and concentrate on matters regarding anonymity and the person in Chile. Meanwhile, the Tlingit community might accidentally stumble on a wrecked plane without Nazi ties which contains two hundred ounces of Swiss Francs."

Frank felt relieved for the first time in over a week. "You're a gentleman I'd like to meet someday. Both Ernie and Helen were correct in their assessment of your abilities and character. Thanks for your insight and assistance. We're forever indebted to you, sir. Meanwhile, we'll attend to loose ends."

"My pleasure — just see Ernie's cared for. On another note, I'm convinced my son Danny would like to speak with Helen in private if that's alright?"

"Most certainly. Here she is."

Helen picked up the phone, turned off the speaker and walked into the hallway. By then, Danny had walked onto the deck with Jim's phone.

Helen began, "Hey, lover boy, how are things?"

"Splendid, how about you?"

"Hanging in there. It's only been a day and I already miss you. Hopefully it won't be long before I'm done here. I know things are moving unusually fast between us but you rock my world. Is the offer still good for hooking up when this is over?"

"You bet it is. This is awesome — we're talking as if we're a couple."

"I know — it's tickety-boo, isn't it?"

"Say what?"

"Tickety-boo. Look it up."

"Oh, more of your witchy woman stuff."

"No. My Mum's predictions are merely coming true."

Danny's tone turned serious. "Promise you'll be careful."

"Don't worry about me. I'm trained and get paid to do this crap. Say, I understood your dad's comment regarding Santos. He's the ring leader, not Keller — unless they're one and the same."

"Stay clear of Santos and the NOAA ship we saw yesterday. Hell's Angels are aboard and they're dangerous. After we hang up, I'll suggest to my employer that we immediately return to Angoon to defuse the situation. You asked me to be careful but that cuts both ways. You too."

"I'll tell my dad about our conversation, but listen up: my old man is a crafty dude and he's on top of things, so you might reconsider sending the cavalry. Don't expose your employer to unnecessary risks. We can handle the situation here."

Helen winced. "I'll take that under advisement."

"I'd better get going," Danny said. "We've got a day trip planned. I'll see you in a few."

"Alright, Danny. Bye."

Angoon — Mid-morning

Danny informed the group about his conversation with Helen. Jim was happy to understand the connection between Santos, the fake *Oregon II* and the Hell's Angels. They'd heed Helen's warning about steering clear of them until the plane wreck was located and cleansed of anything incriminating.

Jim thought to himself, *When this is over, I'll take care of these dirt bags on my terms.*

Lori and Audra gathered warm clothing and sack lunches while Jim ushered Danny into the master bathroom and showed him a secret door in the linen closet. He pressed a button behind the interior door trim, and the back wall and shelves rotated 90 degrees, exposing a dark void. Jim flipped a switch behind the panel, illuminating the chamber below. They walked down twelve steps into a concrete bunker Jim designed prior to building the house. Danny was impressed with the neatly arranged shelves filled with canned food, clothing, and blankets. A small sink and toilet sat behind a retractable curtain. On the far side of the room stood an imbedded steel vault with a large combination lock and stainless steel wheel.

Jim said, "It's a simple word combination — 'ACES.' Can you figure it out?"

Danny hesitated then counted on his fingers. "1-3-5-19?"

Jim smiled. "Right on. All those puzzles and anagrams as a kid paid off. Open it."

Danny's intuition told him that the first turn was to the left. Within seconds, he managed to open the vault. Inside were crates filled with military ordnance, including M4 assault rifles, grenades, rockets, claymores, mortars and ammunition galore. Two shoulder-held Stinger missiles hung from overhead brackets while several M-240 machine guns with external box magazines stood in the corner. A modern version of a .50 caliber sniper rifle rounded out the contents of the vault.

Danny shook his head and exclaimed, "Holly buckets. These look like fun, but they can't be legal."

Jim laughed. "They are if you don't get caught."

He reached into the corner and gently picked up an M72 LAW rocket. He asked Danny to grab two M4 rifles and a Tech-9 from a wall rack. Jim took a cell phone from a shelf, six grenades for the M4s and said, "We need four sets of Kevlar vests and four of those camouflage jumpsuits. Two extra-large and two small."

They stuffed material into two large green canvas duffle bags.

Before closing the vault, Jim assessed the Tech-9 that Danny had secured. Content that it was loaded, Jim grabbed four full Tech-9 clips and four M4 clips, and spun the vault's tumbler as they left. They climbed out of the chamber and returned the upper closet to its original condition.

"You're the only person besides me that knows about this," Jim said, "If anything happens to me, you're welcome to take whatever you need providing it's used for the right reasons. Audra's also welcome to share if things go south."

Danny said, "You sound as if you're expecting a confrontation."

"You were a boy scout — remember the motto?"

Danny smiled and nodded. "Yeah. I understand where you're going with this."

"There it is. If you're going to a knife fight, bring a gun. If you're going to a shootout, carry grenades. Considering the people we're dealing with, it's the only way to roll."

Danny loaded the ordnance into the canvas bags and placed them near the foyer. Jim was gathering his computer and surveillance equipment when a knock on the front door announced the arrival of Hank Stytes, who had promised to remove the bear before 10:00 a.m.

Jim glanced at his watch. It was 9:30. He accompanied Hank to the culvert trap. As they approached, he noticed an ulcerated wound on the bear's rear paw. He pointed it out to Hank, who was unconcerned. Several minutes of talking and a hundred dollar bill later, Stytes understood that the reason the old fellow became a town bear was because of his injury and treating the bruin with a massive dose of antibiotics prior to relocation was in the Clans' best interest. Jim spoke calmly to the bear as Hank injected the animal with medicine in its wounded hind quarter. The bear was so large and confined it couldn't turn around to confront the sting of the syringe. Hank promised to administer another dose later in the afternoon just before releasing him. When asked where he planned to relocate the bruin, Hank simply said, "South."

Upon return to the house, Jim found the group gathered around the kitchen counter, talking about their trip. He sat at the coffee table, booted up his laptop and connected it to the NORAD satellite link. The group intently watched him. Upon gaining secure access, Jim typed commands to the satellite, which immediately sent live images of Chatham Strait. He set the resolution at two miles and scrolled from southern Angoon to the tip of Admiralty Island. The area beyond Hoods Bay was void of activity to the junction of Chatham and Frederick Sound. The NOAA ship was visible inside off Peril Strait. Jim panned inner Whitewater Bay and was pleased. There was no activity. He zeroed in on the aircraft tail section.

Lori leaned and placed her chin on Jim's shoulder as he enhanced the image. She pinched his side and said, "You're a crafty devil. This is a 'Keyhole,' satellite isn't it?"

Jim nodded. "Affirmative. It's infrared sensitive with resolution down to a meter. I can look inside buildings during total darkness and detect a human sitting in a chair."

"Jim, see if you can locate Santos."

He scrolled north into Hoods Bay and identified the Santos catamaran tied to its new pier. Someone was kneeling over its engine compartment, servicing the twin Penta diesels. He zoomed in on the residence and noticed nothing unusual. After careful observation he said, "He's inside the house . . ."

Jim's private encrypted phone rang. The caller had blocked his ID.

Jim answered. "I'm all ears."

"This is Walt. I've got the goods on Vicente Santos."

"Hey buddy. Good to hear your voice again. Let me guess, his real name isn't Santos and he's from Germany."

"Damn, Jim. You hit the nail on the head. His real name is Anton Obert Keller, born out of wedlock in Hamburg, Germany, October 16, 1944. His father, Karl Johann Obert was an SS colonel killed in a plane crash earlier that year. Karl had close ties to Goering and helped orchestrate the ODESSA movement prior to the allied invasion. The Obert family was 'old wealth' — Luftwaffe manufacturers from Dessau, Germany. As an infant, Anton moved to Argentina with family in 1945, and returned to Germany with his mother in 1963. He has close ties with a cousin — Roger Albert Krantz, aka David Rigby. Santos has broken the law by using a false passport; he's in the U.S. illegally. If you want, I'll arrange for his immediate arrest."

"Give me a couple of days without raising any red flags. I'd like to see how things play out."

"No problem. I can justify delaying his arrest based on you acting as my agent. You're simply casting a wider net for bigger fish. Get my drift?"

"Roger that, boss. That's exactly what I'm doing. The way I see it, Santos isn't going anywhere soon. I'll contact you when my investigation's complete."

"Excellent. If things get dicey and you require assistance, call on this line. I can immediately deploy resources from Anchorage via chopper. Meanwhile, keep your head down."

"Can do Walt. Thanks for the update."

"My pleasure friend. I'll wait for your call."

Jim ended the call and looked at Lori and his children. "Good news. That was Walt. Vicente Santos is the son of John Doe, AKA Colonel Karl Obert; found murdered in Peril Strait in 1944. Santos' real name is Anton Obert Keller."

Lori asked, "What's good about that?"

"It verifies Santos is the ringleader. I doubt anyone in Chile is involved. We're dealing with a rag-tag group of bikers and a few bungling idiots. Santos is the only person with the least bit of intelligence, but he's not trained to handle this sort of operation. We'll easily outmaneuver him with our resources and fill him with misinformation. Afterwards, he'll be apprehended by the CIA for a litany of felonies. He'll spend the rest of his life behind bars."

Danny asked, "What type of misinformation are you talking about?"

"You'll see soon enough."

"Should we alert Helen and her boss? They think Keller is in Chile."

"No. No offense to Helen, but maybe that'll keep them out of our hair for a while. We have a treasure hunt to attend to."

Ketchikan — Late Morning

Helen returned to the conference room and asked for a private conversation with Frank. Frank and Helen went to his room. Lena, Gus and Ernie continued their talks at the table. Helen set her aluminum suitcase filled with equipment on the desk in Frank's room. After booting up her computer and accessing the Dark Star database, she explained to Frank, "I'm digging up everything I can on Vicente Santos. Bennett likely mentioned Santos because he wants us to know he's the ringleader in Angoon. Have you ever heard of this guy?"

Frank shook his head. "Never."

"Well, we have now. A report from Dark Star indicates he comes from Brazil." She showed Frank a copy of his passport on her monitor. "Does he resemble anyone from your past?"

Frank studied the monitor and said, "Not particularly — he's got to be in his sixties. That's too young to be a former SS or ODESSA member. You're considering him as a descendant of a Nazi expat, aren't you?"

"That's a big affirmative, Mr. Reid. I'll run biometric comparisons on every missing SS member from the Jewish Documentation Center and the Sam Wiesenthal archives. I need the last name of every SS member on board the submarine so I can narrow the search."

"What good does any of this do?"

"If we match him as a descendant of someone aboard the sub, chance of ODESSA's involvement is non-existent. If he matches someone believed to be an ODESSA expatriate, then, as Colonel Bennett said, the light at the end of the tunnel is an oncoming train."

"I understand. Start your scan on Karl Obert now. I've recently learned that he had an illegitimate son named Anton Keller."

Helen began searching through the Jewish Documentation Center. There was no military ID or photograph of Obert. The comment field stated that he died in a plane crash on June 23, 1944. His skeletal remains, SS ring and dog tags were recovered from the wreckage. He was unmarried with no known descendants. She shifted gears by using the Wiesenthal Center's database. Within seconds, a copy of Obert's military ID photo appeared on screen. Helen ran the biometric program between pictures of Santos and Keller. Less than a minute later, the program confirmed an 88.5 percent match between Obert and Santos. She turned to Frank and exclaimed, "Santos matches as Obert's offspring. Santos is likely Anton Keller."

"Fantastic job young lady. Then who is Rusty after in Chile?"

"You'll have to ask Rusty. I wasn't privy to the interrogation of David Rigby."

"This complicates things. Rusty's in Chile, trying to kill Keller. How can Keller be in two places at the same time?"

Helen said, "He can't, but two scenarios come to mind. Santos could have an accomplice in Chile who Rigby believes is Keller, which means Rigby was unaware that Santos' real name is Keller. Otherwise, Rusty would have learned about Santos during Rigby's interrogation. Santos may have created a decoy in Chile to insulate his true identity."

Frank asked, "That's only one scenario, what's the other?"

"Rusty's lying."

Frank nodded. "Yes. But how can we determine that?"

"When he calls, I'll track his phone location. If he's in Chile, he's telling the truth. If he's not, he's gone rogue. When are you expecting his next call?"

"As soon as he kills Keller — or whoever — which should be today."

Helen thought for a moment. "We can remain together so I can track his location when he calls, or I can infect your phone so it rings into mine."

"I prefer the latter. Tell me about the Santos home in Angoon."

Helen uploaded her digital camera to her computer. She pointed at a photo on the monitor.

"Danny showed me this place yesterday in Hoods Bay. It's extremely isolated, on the waterfront and surrounded by mountainous forests — virtually impossible to defend. A savvy sniper could lay in wait for him without detection. There's no better place to run a hit operation." Helen hesitated, then continued. "You said you trust me, so here I go. It's important that we make our way to Angoon now. We have a fantastic opportunity to eliminate most, if not all of our problems."

"I'm ahead of you. When Rusty gave me the bad news of Whitey's death, I dispatched a small ship my company owns from Seattle. The ship and Henry's yacht are both headed to Sitka. Each vessel has a skeleton crew and should arrive in Sitka tonight. We'll fly to Sitka this evening and spend the night on the yacht, which will serve as our base of operation."

"Brilliant maneuver, sir. You've doubted Rusty's information, too?"

"I'll defer judgment until this mess is over. We'll find out soon enough. What you and I need to do is develop a plan to eliminate Santos and his crew."

Angoon – Late Morning

Audra operated the boat in choppy seas. Jim, Lori and Danny operated the NORAD satellite program. They observed the *Oregon II* moving north parallel to the junction of Chatham Strait and Peril Strait. A person stood at the controls of the large horseshoe crane and cable drum at the rear of the ship. No one else was observed, so Jim panned to the Santos residence. His catamaran remained parked at the dock.

In order to clear Russian Reef, Audra turned wide left toward Whitewater Bay. The boat cruised effortlessly into the wind as she entered the long bay. Convinced that the NOAA ship and Santos were preoccupied, Jim turned off the computer and disconnected the MS-5 dish from the cabin roof. He returned to the cabin and studied the tide table. He realized the incoming tide surge against brisk easterly winds would create tide rips at the head of the bay. Short walls of turbulent water awaited them in the narrow inlet. Audra was relieved when Jim took over navigation through the inlet.

Jim slowly circled in the inlet mouth. Layer upon layer of tide rips awaited them. After reviewing the situation, he told everyone to hang on, advanced the throttle and entered the inlet. The boat plowed directly into the turbulent waves, causing it to climb every crest and dig into each trough. Lori watched in agitated awe as Jim kept the boat perfectly on course. The rocky shorelines on each side of the inlet gave way to the small choppy lake. Directly ahead of them Jim's yellow raft lay tethered to an anchor line. The colonel cautiously set anchor upwind of the raft, and slowly let out line until the boat swung next to the raft. The raft and boat were anchored seventy five yards from the tidal flat where Danny unearthed the aluminum canister.

Jim gathered everyone for a short meeting, opened one of the duffle bags and handed out several items. "Listen up. Everyone needs to wear flak jackets, camouflage and carry weapons."

He demonstrated how to use the safety and selector switch on each machine gun. "Point the gun and squeeze the trigger in short bursts. Tracer rounds will show you where the bullets are going. Put the tracer lines on your target — it's that simple. Danny will take everyone ashore with the raft. As soon as you reach the mud flats, Lori and Audra advance into the trees. Danny will return to the boat for me. When we're together again, we'll slowly maneuver up the mountain. It's important we remain concealed."

The trio nodded their heads. The excitement of being armed and ready glowed in their faces.

Danny rowed the small craft with Audra, Lori and Oscar aboard. After unloading his passengers and cargo, he returned for Jim. The father and son loaded the surveillance equipment, a spade shovel, two pack frames and a metal detector into the raft and made their way to shore. The weather was clear, but windy. Jim concluded that it was safer to climb the steep terrain under the cover of timber to the west than be skylined in open sawgrass and devil's club. Lori released Oscar's leash while Jim checked the safeties on each weapon. He kept the balance of the arsenal inside of the second duffel bag and hid it under a large deadfall tree with all watching.

After securing the Desert Eagle on his right hip, Jim pulled the large pack frame onto his back. As they embarked up the hill, Oscar began to dig furiously at the base of an enormous cedar tree. Lori demanded that he return, which resulted in the first find of the day. Oscar obediently returned — with a green-stained human arm bone in his mouth.

Jim set the pack frame down and walked to the cedar. The forest floor was covered in moss-covered rocks, ferns, brush and devil's club. Upon reaching the cedar, Jim found a three-foot-wide triangular cavity at its base which merged into the tree's trunk at head level. He bent over and peeked in with a flashlight. Inside the hollow tree was a partial human skeleton; a rib cage, arm- and hand-bones. The top of a human skull lay in the far end of the dark abyss.

Remnants of a rotted leather jacket and another aluminum canister also came to light. Jim retreated and called, "Here's the rest of the corpse Ernie found in '45. Good Job, Oscar!"

Oscar ran and danced in circles, barking, knowing he was a hero for the moment. Lori knelt and petted her old-time companion. "Good boy, good boy."

Jim pulled on the container. Much to his surprise, he was unable to pull it out on first attempt. He said, "This SOB weighs a lot more than I thought."

Another try failed to extract the tube from its grave. Finally he managed to pull it out of the cavity into the light.

Danny removed a hatchet from his pack and said, "Let's break it open and have a look." Jim backed away as Danny knelt in front of the tube and began swinging. Five massive blows produced desired results. The cylinder top was torn apart enough to expose a pile of dull yellow Austrian Coronas.

"Hot damn!" Danny said. "Check it out." He handed one to his dad. "What's this worth?"

Jim laughed. "At least $1,000 per coin. Probably three-quarters of a million in that canister — maybe more."

Danny said, "Holy shit! We're rich."

Lori stared in disbelief at the coins. Audra asked, "There's a body in there? Whose is it?"

"Either the pilot or co-pilot from the wrecked plane," Jim said. "The body must've been decomposed to the point that it came apart when a bear pulled on its legs. Sixty years ago, this tree would've been smaller. He couldn't get at the torso because it's too tight of squeeze to get inside."

Audra had more questions. "What about the jaw bone? Did it walk over to where we found it?"

Jim shook his head and smiled. "How the hell do I know? Maybe a marten or weasel carried it off. Let's put the gold in the duffel bag and leave it here."

With renewed vigor and growing excitement, the group hiked up the steep mountainside. To limit the ability of anyone to follow them, Jim had the group walk single file up a narrow stream, walking in its gravel bed. They trudged up the mountain for almost an hour before resting. They remained concealed in the timber while Jim looked at his GPS. A hundred yards above, the tree line gave way to a large grassy meadow. Above the meadow to the east, a snow field stretched along a craggy ridge. The base of the snow field was open and exposed. He carefully set up a satellite system to evaluate the situation in and around Chatham Strait.

The *Oregon II* continued its grid search for the wreck. Santos remained at home. A Tlingit barge carrying the captured bear was in a short, narrow cove directly south of Whitewater Bay. Four men were visible aboard the barge as it approached the rocky shoreline, four miles south of Whitewater.

Jim determined things were under control. It was time to finish the arduous trek. They'd be skylined for the final stretch, and Jim realized this should have been a night operation. There was danger in exposing themselves in the opening, but they were less than a quarter mile from the upthrust that held the plane. The wind ceased and the temperature dropped. The group was anxious to start moving to keep warm. Leaving the security of the timber, Jim instructed them to move through the opening quickly and hunch down when they hit the snow field. Once there, he had lightweight white Tyvek jumpsuits to wear over their clothes so they'd blend into the snow.

After reaching the snow line and putting on their suits, Lori pointed. "I see the tail on the right."

"Good eyes," Jim said. "I thought it was higher up."

The rusted, weathered tail sat upright at a slight angle. A faint white "A" was barely visible on it. Danny and Audra moved sidehill to the site. The snow was hard-packed ice pellets. Even though they only sank an inch or so, hurrying was difficult. Jim looked down at his boat as Lori grabbed his belt and asked for help traversing the icy slope.

By the time Jim and Lori reached the site, Danny and Audra were digging into the snow. Jim and Lori assessed the surrounding area and came to the conclusion that the fuselage was below them nearly a hundred yards. Jim whistled to his kids and pointed down the mountain to a vertical wall of rock. A small section of the upper fuselage was visible near the wall. Apparently the plane's tail section had broken off while sliding down the mountainside.

The foursome approached the cliff. "Let's not randomly start digging," Jim suggested. "Let's study this for a moment. Remember, the Tlingit's are supposed to find this thing undisturbed. Let's determine door locations without making a mess of things."

The rock upthrust ran parallel to the upper ridge and tapered to where it met the meadow below. The rock wall holding the wreck was nearly ten feet above the fuselage. Looking up the mountain at the tail section, Jim deduced that the plane stalled trying to clear the summit. It likely hit with its pontoons, then slid to the rocky wall, tearing off the tail section. Both wings were attached and distinguishable under a layer of icy snow. The rear fuselage rose several feet above the wings, exposing it slightly. Jim leaned against the rock wall and saw the crumpled propeller sticking two inches above the snow. He returned to the left side of the plane and stood behind the wing.

He said, "The pilot's door is directly below me."

Audra asked, "How in the heck would you know that?"

Danny began digging. Jim immediately told him to stop.

Jim climbed to the rear of the plane where the tail section would have been. A three-foot-diameter hole at the end of the fuselage presented them with a perfect access point. The bottom of the hole was even with the hard-packed snow. Jim pulled a mini mag flashlight from his pack, stuck his head in the hole and illuminated the inside of the plane. He backed out, stood up and smiled.

"We're in business. We can access the interior right here. I'm going inside. No digging needed, but if this damn thing collapses, dig me out where the door is."

Danny, Lori and Audra peered into the hole and saw nothing but a dark void. All three shook their heads as Jim carefully climbed into the chilly hole. Once inside, the fuselage opened into a large dark tunnel. Jim shined the light toward the cockpit. Twenty five feet away he could make out the instrument panel. Between the cockpit and where he knelt lay a jumbled mess of aluminum tubes. The tight quarters opened into an expansive tunnel right where the mound of tubes began. Almost able to stand up, he grabbed a tube by one handle and maneuvered it toward the entrance. As he approached the opening, he yelled for Danny to grab the heavy object.

Danny pulled the tube out, and Jim shimmied out of the plane.

He gathered the group. "There are dozens of these laying in a pile amidship. We need to figure a way to get most of them out without disturbing the inside of the wreck. We also need to ensure nobody *thinks* it's been discovered. The surrounding area needs attention to detail. Any ideas?"

They backed away from the fuselage and silently considered the problem. Time stood still as they considered how to pull this off without detection.

Cradling Oscar in her arms, Lori broke the silence. "Audra and I certainly can't handle the extraction of the canisters from the inside. They're too heavy. However, once you get them to the entrance we can each grab a handle and stack them away from the plane. We're limited to stacking and watching for prying eyes via the satellite. Danny's the strongest person here so he picks them up inside and shuttles them toward the entrance. Jim takes over and hands them to me and Audra."

Jim nodded. "I was thinking along the same lines. There's got to be at least 45 canisters inside — 70 to 75 pounds each. It will take Danny and I three minutes per load, maybe less. That's a full two hours of ball-busting work. Afterwards we've got to clean up the site and strip the cockpit of any incriminating evidence. That's another hour at least. We need to get busy."

Lori set Oscar down and asked, "How in hell are we going to get the gold down to the boat?"

Jim smiled. "Not sure. But I'll figure out something."

Forty-eight canisters and two hours later Jim and Danny sat next to each other outside of the fuselage and breathed a sigh of relief, drinking water and eating sandwiches. They were weary from their workout. Danny complained about the musty smell of rotted leather he endured while shuttling canisters. He also reported skeletal remains crumpled against the yoke in the left front seat.

Audra said, "There's a body in there — a skeleton? Whoa!"

Lori looked at Jim. "Now what — where do we go from here?

274

Jim stood and pointed toward a grassy area. "The three of you take two canisters and the hatchet to that clearing and carefully open them. We need to gather two hundred ounces of coins and place them back in the wreck. Beyond the clearing, there's a small group of trees. Select a bushy one away from us and chop it down at ground level. We don't want anyone to see one's been cut down. Drag it back and use it to level out our footprints and other signs of our presence. While you guys are doing that, I'll start working on the plane's interior."

Once inside the wreck, Jim made his way to the cockpit. He carefully examined the area with his flashlight and soon realized that the only piece of evidence that might link the crash to Dale Olsen was an aluminum clipboard with words scratched into it. The pilot had left a message prior to dying. A switchblade knife lay nearby on the floor with a holstered, heavily-rusted Colt .45 service pistol. He placed the clipboard on the rotted bench seat behind him and focused on the front passenger seat, finding it empty and devoid of anything incriminating. He closely examined the skeleton. Small remnants of khaki trousers remained on the exposed leg bones. The left leg was broken below the knee and both feet were still inside a pair of heavy leather shoes. A rotted leather jacket covered some of the rib cage and the intact skull lay on the floor against the left door.

The windshield and door windows were intact. The pilot's door was partially open and the hinges were bent. The door had probably jammed on impact. Apparently, the pilot was trapped with a broken leg. This had to be Andy Decker. He must have suffered for hours — maybe days.

He focused his attention on the back seat and saw nothing of significance. Most of the seat's leather cover was gone, exposing rusty metal springs. There were a few wrenches on the floor.

Satisfied that the surrounding area was clear of anything incriminating, he examined the side cargo door. Its built-in pocket contained a rotted flare.

Finally, he gently brushed the cargo area with his hands to erase any boot prints that he or Danny may have created while removing the canisters. Convinced that the plane was clean, he returned through the dark cavern to the fuselage opening.

At the entrance, Danny handed him a small backpack. "There's 70 one-ounce coins in here. Dump them and bring back the pack. I'll reload it twice."

Jim took the backpack to the cargo area, and randomly scattering the coins. He returned with two more loads. Knowing he had spread nearly $200,000 worth of gold on the floor, he smiled and left the plane with the clipboard Andy Decker had left behind.

Jim surveyed the area surrounding the plane. "Great job everyone. This ought to do it. If we get a skiff of snow up here this place will look totally untouched."

Lori suggested, "Perhaps you should boot up the satellite and check out Chatham."

"Good idea. Maybe the new Santos crew members have arrived."

While checking his surveillance equipment, the cell phone used to intercept the Santos line rang. Jim motioned for everyone to remain silent and listened to the conversation.

"I instructed you to never use this line unless it's an emergency. This better be good."

"It's an emergency. I was at my camper and our new associate just uncovered an audio bug. He left it intact so we can use it to our advantage."

"Where are you now?"

"We're at the marina. What should we do?"

"Who saw your flight arrive?"

"Nobody. The dock was empty when we got here. It was an unscheduled flight so we sorta slipped in. I doubt anyone noticed us walking to my camper."

"Good, remain near the marina but out of view. I'll send John to pick you up with the Lund — he'll be there in 30 minutes. Who do you think placed the bug?"

"Our partner says its high-end equipment used by the military. He says Bennett's a former Special Ops colonel. He must've planted it. That also explains how he was able to beat the crap out of me. I told you he wasn't what he appeared to be."

"Did you talk near the camper before locating the bug?"

"No. Our associate used a tricked-out sensor when we got here. He'll take us to new levels of sophistication. He's got hardware we should've had months ago."

"I hope he's as good as you say. Remain out of view and we'll talk when you get here."

Jim switched to the video link located on the water tower. Crane and a man wearing sunglasses and a baseball cap were visible. The man carried an oversized sea bag over his shoulder and wore a black windbreaker. Jim switched programs to the NORAD satellite and watched as Crane and the mystery man disappeared under a rain shelter at the end of the pier. The mystery man reemerged from the enclosure and mounted a small device onto the shelter's outer support column which faced Jim's slip at the marina.

Jim explained, "Our beloved town cop has returned with a someone new. They discovered my audio bug under his camper but not the video camera I planted on the water tower. Their replacement knows about my past so he's obviously a professional — maybe former Special Forces who joined the Hell's Angels. He just planted a camera onto the rain shelter by the sea-plane dock and it's aimed toward my slip."

Lori said, "This complicates things. Should we quick get the heck out of here?"

"Not at all. It's troubling that they know about me but this is our only chance to work on the wreck. I need you guys to monitor their movements while I go further up the mountain to plant a radio relay."

Jim demonstrated how to manipulate the satellite image, then walked up the hill with a small backpack. He carefully stuck to the grass and rocky areas to prevent footprints in the snow.

The other three watch the screen. Audra pointed. "There's an open boat heading to Angoon. It must have come from Hoods Bay. The *Oregon II* is still in front of Peril Strait."

While Jim trekked up the mountain and the women watched the computer screen, Danny walked to the stack of canisters and tried opening one. Danny groaned while trying to unscrew the canister's cap. The women watched in amazement as his powerful hands finally unscrewed one of the end caps. The inside was packed with small gold coins and Danny handed out several for the group to inspect. Oscar curiously watched as Lori held one up to the sky and turned it in the light.

"How many coins do you think are inside that tube," asked Audra.

Danny squinted into the tube. "Hundreds. No, thousands. They're tiny."

"These are 20-franc Swiss gold pieces." Lori said. "The inscription around the woman's head on the front of the coin is *Confoederatio Helvetica*. The Swiss cross is on the obverse within a shield surrounded by a wreath. The number 20, letters FR and the date 1893 tell me they're 3/16 of an ounce of pure Swiss gold. They're magnificent specimens in perfect condition. These are rare collector coins worth more than the gold content. I'd bet this coin is worth at least $300."

Danny frowned. "How do you know all that?"

"I've been collecting coins since I was twelve. My grandfather gave me one just like this for my sixteenth birthday. What do you think the tube weighs?"

Danny said, "I bet each weighs between sixty five and seventy pounds. What's the total number of tubes remaining?"

Audra smiled. "There's are 46 beside the two we emptied in the plane. We also have one down below."

Lori petted Oscar and looked into the sky, thinking. Finally she said, "With the tube we found below, that makes 47. At $1000 per ounce, that's over 56 million dollars. If you take into account that some of these are rare collector pieces, the final tally could easily reach 70 million. Not bad for a day's work."

Jim had snuck up on the trio. He said, "Let's not count our chickens quite yet. Even if we pull this off, we've still got to sell them without raising suspicion."

Lori smiled. "I can help. I've got two excellent contacts — one in Paris and the other in Dubai. They're discrete and completely reliable. Either one can afford to purchase the entire lot with cash — no questions asked. Afterward, I'll show you how to put cash into Costa Rican banks without raising any red flags."

Jim looked into her blue eyes. "I knew you were good with money, but I never took you for a money launderer. Here I am, a West Pointer and defense contractor getting schooled on how to beat our government out of taxes. There's a term for conversations like this. It's called conspiracy. What's become of me?"

Lori shook her head. "The civilized world is sliding into socialism, including America. Politicians will extract every pound of flesh possible from people like us. Insulate your success from redistribution of wealth by hiding your assets in off-shore accounts."

Danny clapped. "Right on Lori — I dig your style. The shit's gonna hit the fan so go with the flow — you won't regret it, Dad."

Jim smiled. "I'll consider it. Costa Rica, Belize, Huh?"

Lori shrugged her shoulders. "Do what suits you, but both are safe havens for cash and prosperity. Remember what Mark Twain said: 'Patriotism is supporting your country all the time, and your government when it deserves it.'"

She looked at the computer monitor. "Crane and Mr. X are leaving the marina in an open boat and NOAA's setting anchor in Chatham."

Jim looked at his watch. It was 5:00 p.m., though the bright sky said noon. "We need to get out of here. We'll cover the gold with our white suits and leave it behind."

Danny jumped to his feet. "I'd like to take another canister back to the boat."

Jim stood. "Take one, Danny. I'll cover the rest."

Danny tied a full container of gold to the bottom of his aluminum pack frame. Jim shut off the surveillance equipment. He firmly strapped the metal surveillance case to his pack frame. He quickly covered the stockpiled containers with Tyvek suits and snow and said, "Let's get off this damn mountain; I'm cold and hungry, and I could use a stiff drink."

Lori added, "That's the best idea I've heard all day. Some hot spiked cocoa sounds really good. Look at Oscar, he's shivering."

Jim reminded everyone to remain in single file and watch their footing while traversing the hill to the tree line. When they reached the small stream, Jim had everyone walk in the gravely bottom to avoid footprints. The fours clambered silently down through the timber. The only sounds were the stream and an occasional scolding from a red squirrel as they passed. Within thirty minutes, they reached the deadfall tree which hid the duffel bag and first canister of gold.

Audra looked up the mountain and commented, "That's one heck of a hike — I don't care if I . . . . OUCH!" Looking back uphill, she had stepped into a small hole between two moss covered boulders. She fell to the ground and rolled in pain, holding her right ankle.

Jim dropped his pack and ran back. "Audra, are you OK?"

She grimaced in pain and assumed a fetal position. "I wasn't paying attention and twisted my ankle. That was my fault and stupid of me. It hurts *really* bad." Holding her ankle, she thought, *It is Friday the 13th.*

Jim examined the ankle and realized it could be broken. "Alright, I'll carry Audra and an M4 to the raft while the two of you keep a sharp eye on us from the tree line. Once Audra is situated in the boat, she'll keep the M4 and I'll meet you here and take over lookout position while you guys go to the raft. When you're situated on the boat, call me and I'll run to the mouth of the inlet to guard your exit." He turned to his son. "Tie the raft to the transom and pilot the boat through the inlet and pick me up on the right hand shore. This is our most vulnerable time, so remain alert and don't dawdle."

Minutes later, Danny maneuvered the boat to the steep rocky shoreline where Jim stood. He climbed onto the bow and walked to the stern. Lori had wrapped a towel filled with ice around Audra's ankle. Jim glassed the western horizon as Danny backed the boat into deeper water. He got a Vicodin from his first aid kit and gave it to Audra with bottled water.

He reluctantly left the warmth of the cabin, vented the raft's air chambers so it could be stored and helped Danny stow the raft in a large transom compartment.

"The salmon are stacked up near the inlet," Danny said, "just like yesterday. I'm thinking that if we brought a few back to Angoon and made a point of cleaning them there, it would look as if we were fishing all day."

"Fire up a mooching rod while I position the boat. We'll only give it a few minutes. I'm afraid Audra has a broken ankle."

Jim returned to the cabin and explained the plan. Fortunately, Audra's pain was subsiding from the combination of Vicodin and a spiked hot cocoa Lori made. On deck, Danny cut the head off a herring and secured the body to a double hook harness. He pulled the harness line tight so the herring would slowly spin as if it were injured, then tossed the bait toward the inlet, allowing the herring to sink. After counting to ten, he slowly retrieved the bait, giving the rod tip an occasional twitch to further entice a King. He saw the bait approach the boat when a silver flash announced the arrival of an enormous salmon. The reel hissed as the King peeled out line and Danny yelled toward the cabin that he had a fish on. Jim placed the engines in neutral and once again left the warmth of the cabin.

The drugged, semi-drunk Audra blurted, "Danny's a butt licker. If that fish is bigger than mine, I'll castrate him."

Lori patted Audra's head, attempting to make her feel better. On deck, Jim stood ready with the net as the King began to tire. Danny positioned the fish next to the boat and Jim scooped him into the net. Jim kept the net against the hull and Danny quickly stuck the halibut gaff through the King's massive the lower jaw, then hoisted it to the deck. The monster King thrashed on deck until Jim dispatched it with a wooden club.

Jim was excited. "That is the biggest King I've seen caught on hook and line. It's a hog — must be a female. Bait up and I'll position the boat again."

Audra pouted in the cabin. "He's a jerk — had to show me up. I hate men."

Jim smiled. "That's the pill talking darlin'. Danny's helping us with misinformation, that's all. When he catches another one, we'll get you to a doctor and have your foot examined."

Danny yelled, "Fish on."

The two men repeated the process, netting a much smaller, but decent, salmon. Jim asked Danny to gut and gill both fish, then pack them on ice. If either had roe, the eggs would be good for steelhead fishing in the fall. Jim returned to the cabin, turned the boat toward Chatham and accelerated to full throttle. When Danny finally entered the warm cabin, Audra was laying on the seat with her foot elevated on top of the table. Audra began singing a "James Brown" tune while bouncing her head to an imaginary rhythm. "Whoa-oa! I feel good . . I knew that I would . . I feel good . . I knew that I would . . . So good, so good, I got you — bomp, bomp, bomp, Whoa-oa! I feel nice . . like sugar and spice . . . yeah, I feel nice . . . like sugar and spice. So nice . . . so nice, I got you — bomp, bomp, bomp."

Jim, Lori and Danny laughed as Audra demonstrated her Vicodin-enabled vocal abilities. Danny piloted the boat as Jim and Lori watched Audra perform her singing audition..

Jim dialed Mel. Two cell phone rings later, Mel answered, "Hello."

"Hey buddy, this is Jim. I need a quick favor."

"Sure Jim. Whatcha need?"

"My daughter slipped on deck and rolled her ankle. Can you call Hilda, have her contact someone who knows how to operate the x-ray machine and meet me at the health trailer in about thirty minutes? She may have a broken ankle."

"That's awful. I'll call Rhonda instead and have her there lickety-split — she's the Clans' nurse and knows how ta run the darn thing. She's been known to roll casts too."

"Thanks a bunch Mel! I owe you one. By the way, would you care for a King? Under the circumstances, I don't have time to deal with cleaning fish."

"You guys have the hot hand when it comes ta fishin'. Nobody else has been catchin' 'em. I don't mind cleaning fish. I'd love a King."

"Meet us at the marina and I'll hook you up buddy. Rhonda can have one as well."

"I'm sure she'd love that. See ya there Jim."

Jim focused his attention to Peril Strait and the NOAA ship as his boat passed Russian Reef. He booted up the Keyhole satellite and saw the vessel's radar dish turning. "If the bad guys are paying attention to their radar," he said, "they've seen us coming out of Whitewater."

His boat's radio scanner locked onto a transmission on channel 60. He asked Danny to slow the boat to half speed in order to hear the conversation.

"This is Softail to Fortuna. Come in Fortuna." There was a ten second pause, then the transmission repeated. "Softail to Fortuna; come in Fortuna."

"This is Fortuna. Go ahead."

Jim recognized Santos' voice returning the transmission to Softail. The Softail continued, "Package is passing Russian Reef heading north. Over."

"Is McKinnon on board?"

"Negative."

"Where did the package originate?."

"I'm not sure. I just noticed it on my screen.."

"That's unacceptable. From this point forward, I expect to know the exact location of our package at all times."

"Go fuck yourself. I've only got five men besides myself. I can't track shit while running this ship. I told you I was short-handed yesterday, and I'm frankly sick of your constant bitching."

"Listen to me, asshole. Keep this up and I'll send you packing with your worthless buddies. I told you yesterday you'd have two additional men tonight. No more excuses. OVER AND OUT!"

Danny accelerated the boat as Lori spoke. "Sounds like there's dissension within the ranks. Santos has temper issues and lacks people skills. At least, now we know we're being watched and they haven't a clue where we were today."

Jim nodded. "We'll shift gears tomorrow and keep them guessing."

Audra changed songs. "Cisco Kid was a friend of mine . . . Cisco Kid was a friend of mine . . . He drink whiskey, Poncho drink the wine." She pointed at the galley. "Hey, got any wine or beer in the fridge? I'd love another drink, right about now."

Jim shook his head. "You're already buzzed. How's your foot feeling?"

"What foot?" She touched her lips and added, "Come to think of it, I can't feel my lips. Those pills are kickin' good."

"Good. Let's keep it that way. Danny, do you have the keys to Helen's Bayliner?"

"Yep. Why?"

"Providing Audra's foot isn't too bad, tomorrow we'll clean up the crash site while having fun with Santos. Here's my plan: You sneak onto Helen's Bayliner tonight and take it to Warm Springs. Spend the night on board and we'll meet you there early tomorrow morning. We'll leave the *Sojourn* and take the Bayliner into Whitewater Bay and troll the shoreline as if it's just another fishing charter. By leaving my boat there, they'll think we're spending the day soaking in the hot springs."

"They don't have resources to follow a charter boat, so we'll slip right by them. If by chance anyone follows the Bayliner, we'll abort the plan, but if things go as planned, the girls can drop us off on the point by the inlet. You and I will make a quick trip up to the crash site and perform a final clean up. While we're doing that, Lori and Audra can pretend to fish for a couple of hours, and pick us up when we're done. We'll go back to Warm Springs and Lori and I will pick up the *Sojourn*."

Danny liked his father's plan.

They rounded the corner of Kootznahoo Inlet and made their way to the marina. Mel and a short, dark-haired woman waited at Jim's slip. Mel tied off the front of the boat and the woman climbed aboard and into the cabin to see the first patient of the new clinic. Danny made a point of lifting the two salmon for everyone to see, then handed the Kings one at a time to Mel. If Santos had planted cameras as suspected, the ruse of fishing all day would convince any disbeliever.

Mel dragged the larger fish up the dock. "I ain't seen a King this big in nearly twenty years. So much for Friday the 13th and bad luck. I'll clean 'em, and give half ta Rhonda. Damn Jim, you guys have the hot setup for catchin' fish."

Inside the cabin, the nurse unwrapped the towel and ice on Audra's ankle and said, "Ya did a great job of keeping the swelling down with this homemade ice bag. So young lady, you've got a bad wheel do ya? Let's take a better look — oh yeah it's a doozy. My name's Rhonda, what's yours?"

In an extremely deep voice, Audra said, "Bond. James Bond."

"Oh, we have a comedian on our hands. Let's get ya to the trailer and take some pictures. It doesn't look broken but we'd better take a closer look. Got any more jokes for me, 007?"

Jim laughed. "Excuse my daughter. I gave her a pain pill earlier and she's been on a tear ever since."

"Ah, that explains our comedian. Enjoy the ride, young lady. When it wears off, you'll wish it hadn't. C'mon 007, let's take a few pictures."

Danny retrieved the Humvee during Audra's comedy debut and parked it next to the dock. Jim and Danny helped happy Audra into the Humvee and drove to the clinic. During the examination at the trailer, Danny and Jim stood outside. Danny said he would return to the boat, unload the gold into a large wheeled cooler and deposit it in the vault at the house.

Jim nodded. "Take it to the house. Return here after it's transferred. Don't act nervous and for God's sake, be quick.."

Jim went inside and spoke with Rhonda as she examined the x-rays. "I've never seen you here before. Are you a native of Angoon?"

"I'm originally from Kake, but I moved here when I was ten. I'm with the Dog Salmon Clan. Ya probably never saw me before because I just got outta the Army. Twelve years as a triage nurse — two tours in Iraq."

Jim shook her hand. "Good for you, I admire your commitment."

"I learned a lot over there. More than I could by bein' a civilian nurse. Ya know — hands-on kinda stuff."

"That's fantastic. Are you here to stay?"

"Yep. My time was up and I figured I'd do the Clans a service by runnin' the clinic."

Rhonda focused her attention on 007. After studying the films, she nodded as if she'd found something, then walked over to a shelf full of casting material.

Ketchikan — Late Afternoon

Helen asked the inn's chef to cook the salmon she'd caught with Danny, telling him to prepare half of the fish and keep the rest for himself. While the Olsens and Ernie indulged themselves with the wonderfully-prepared meal, Helen sat in her room and stared at the town below. She shook her head at the current situation. She couldn't believe her friend and mentor was dead. Helen loved Whitey like a brother. His comment about betrayal and emptiness going hand-in-hand with this profession haunted her. He was right — it was time to hang it up.

She leaned back in her chair, looked toward the ceiling and closed her eyes. Soon, Frank's yacht and service ship would arrive in Ketchikan, and she needed to develop a plan for taking out the NOAA crew and Santos. Thoughts of armaments, personnel, surveillance and communication equipment flooded her mind. After nearly an hour of thinking, the phone she'd configured with Frank's rang. Helen began tracking the call.

Frank answered, "This is Blue Marlin."

"It's Rusty — I got him. No time for details. I'm on the run. Sleep well. Your problem's neutralized. He dropped like . . ." Gunshots echoed through the phone's earpiece and it sounded as if the phone was dropped.

"Rusty! Do you require assistance or extraction?" Frank asked

"Not now — can't talk. I'll call when it's safe." The line went dead.

Helen tossed the phone onto the bed and shook her head. Before she had time to digest what had happened, a knock on the door announced Frank.

She let him in, and he asked, "Did you pinpoint his location?"

"Not even close. The conversation was too short."

"He sounded sincere. Did you hear the gunfire?"

"I heard everything." *Why would Rusty call under such perilous circumstances?* Helen thought to herself. *Wouldn't a person call when the heat was off?*

Frank said, "We'll have to wait for his next call. I hope he's alright."

Helen shook her head. "Rusty can handle himself. He's been at this for 25 years." She changed gears. "Can we talk about the mission?"

Frank nodded and Helen began, "Before I get rolling, we need to have an understanding about chain of command. You're my employer. I admire you and I answer to you, but what we're about to undertake requires a manager with experience in covert operations. That person must direct a crew that follows orders and is willing to kill if ordered to do so. I'm that person and I fully intend to orchestrate this operation the way I see fit. Furthermore, I won't be involved in pissing matches with subordinates when it comes to who's in charge. If you have problems with that, we can say our goodbyes now. I'll head to Angoon to assist the Bennett's. Otherwise, I've got a litany of questions for you that require honest answers. It's the only way I can develop a strategy that guarantees success."

Frank remained silent while considering her statement. Helen was quite capable, but he wondered how other operatives would handle a woman giving orders.

"Please give me a minute to think this through."

Helen was careful not to show her annoyance. She still had time to hire a bush flight for Angoon if Frank balked at her demands. Finally, she said, "Take your time."

"OK. I'd intended for Dan Cranston to run this operation, but you're more qualified than him. Your candidness is sometimes overbearing but your knowledge and loyalty is exemplary. I will completely support you and stand behind you 100 percent."

Helen smiled. "Good. You won't regret your decision and I guarantee success."

"Where do we begin?" Frank asked.

"First, describe your incoming ship, its armaments, captain and crew."

"It's a newly-refitted, 210-foot medium-endurance cutter with sparse accommodations. It's virtually identical to a second-class Coast Guard patrol boat with a vacant front turret that will accept a variety of heavy cannons. The cutter is equipped with radar, deep water sonar, GPS, satellite links, autopilot and a computerized wheel house. The rear deck is elevated and carries an orange Sikorsky HH-52A Seaguard helicopter. Also aboard is an orange 24-foor Zodiac with Coast Guard markings powered by twin 115-horse Mercury outboards for shallow draft combat and possible ship boarding. The ship's white. I plan to disguise it as a Coast Guard cutter with magnetic Coast Guard markings when we arrive in Chatham."

"Cranston was in charge of armaments and he assures me what he's bringing will do the job. The fake NOAA vessel won't enter into a fight with a well-armed government ship. After whatever transpires, we remove the Coast Guard markings, fly the chopper to Seattle, toss the armaments into the sea. *Voila!* It instantly becomes one of many research vessels in coastal Alaska."

"Brilliant. Does Rusty know about this?"

"No."

"What about a crew?"

"I'm moving Cranston and his men from Henry's estate to Sitka. Dark Star and Cranston don't know all the specifics. They arrive late tomorrow. I plan on changing the cutter's crew to Dark Star operatives the following morning."

Helen asked, "What are the bare-bone manpower for operating this style cutter?"

"Two — a captain and his mechanic. The balance of the crew is armed muscle."

"Who selected the weapons and crew?"

"Cranston."

"Is Dark Star the weapons supplier?"

"Yes."

Helen winced. "How many operatives will Cranston bring with him?"

"Five."

"Alright, we'll get back to the cutter and crew in a moment. Tell me about the yacht — same questions; brief description, any armaments, captain and crew."

"You saw it in Eureka. It's white, 200 feet long, steel construction, fitted for trans-oceanic voyages. State of the art electronics, radar, sonar, auto pilot, GPS, two satellite communication links including internet, luxury accommodations. It's the real deal. I intend on using it as our control center. Two people can operate the vessel — captain and his mechanic"

"I'll send Lena and Ernie to Port Angeles from here. My cousin Gus will captain the yacht after it arrives in Ketchikan. He's been piloting boats and ships since he was sixteen and is well versed with this stretch of water. As for on-board weapons, the yacht always carries small arms. I've yet to decide on how to handle the mechanic issue."

Helen said, "OK. Thanks. Now, let's analyze real needs. I believe that less is best. The more people involved, the more potential of uncovering the true reason for our mission. Afterwards, you and your family may be exposed to the same set of problems you're currently facing."

"I'm not following you."

"Hired guns and soldiers of fortune work in a dirty business. Many operatives are honest and hard-working, but some are opportunists who'll do anything for a buck. Cranston is a middle-of-the-roader who I don't trust. The same is true of Rusty. I want you to call Dark Star manager, Brandon Phillips and tell him we're nearing conclusion of the mission and their services are suspended for the time being."

"I see your point, but how do we fill the void?"

"I have several associates who are reliable and trustworthy. I'll contact two when we're done talking. I'll try to get them here by 10:00 a.m. tomorrow."

Helen paused, then said, "Here's what I propose: Leave the yacht here. It only complicates matters. We need to consolidate and control our resources. Gus can captain the cutter with you as his assistant. Jeff Elliott's been your pilot and confidant for over a decade. He's a former combat pilot and he can run the chopper. During slack time, he can also assist with ship duties. My friend Dave Bachman lives in Phoenix and owes me big time. Whitey and I worked with him in both Pakistan and Iraq. He's an exceptional person and trustworthy. My brother Wayne is on leave from the Royal Navy, partying with friends in Cabo San Lucas. He's a military diver and underwater munitions expert. He's also a skilled diesel mechanic who can stumble his way through any potential engine problems. Most important, Wayne's completely honest and would never screw me over. I'll manage the crew and perform all surveillance and communication duties. I'm an excellent shot who can handle any combat duties.

She looked at Frank. "That's my plan to minimize your exposure to future risk."

Frank frowned. "I like your ideas, but we'll be outnumbered."

"Numbers won't matter because our enemies are not professionals. Between Bachman, Elliott, my brother and myself, we'll tear these guys apart — quickly and forever."

"Is Bachman one of the men you saved in Eufrat?"

"He is."

Frank nodded. "The idea of eliminating Dark Star from this project is outstanding. I trust your judgment. If you know your crew can handle the job, then make it happen."

Helen fought down the urge to high-five Frank.

"Alright. Let's do this right. I need resources. For armaments, I want an 81 mm mortar cannon for the cutter's front turret. Additionally, each side of the wheelhouse requires armaments. Starboard side, an M134 Gatling gun. Port side, a .50 caliber machine gun. Fit the Zodiac with an M240 machine gun. Defensive gear for everyone — Kevlar vests and helmets, night vision goggles and an integrated radio system for everyone. I want infrared surveillance cameras and a GTX radar jammer mounted on the cutter's tower. I'll integrate a 40-inch monitor into the wheel house with infrared night vision capabilities for both surveillance and night time navigation. That way, we can maneuver the cutter at night without detection. Finally, everyone requires authentic Coast Guard work uniforms."

"That's a hell of a wish list. How can we obtain these things on such short notice?"

"Bachman can handle it. He'll have everything by the time we meet in Sitka. We'll change crews at that time. When everyone's on board, I'll explain the details of my plan. Rather than wait until tomorrow, Jeff should fly Ernie and Lena to Port Angeles right now. When the cutter arrives tonight, have it re-fueled so we can take off for Sitka as soon as Jeff returns with the jet."

"Can you accomplish all of this by this evening?"

"It's a mad dash, but doable. Please contact Brandon Phillips with Dark Star and have him abort the mission while I make the arrangements."

Angoon — Late Evening

Convinced that his home's security hadn't been breached, Jim stood behind Audra as she navigated the porch with her new crutches. She was diagnosed with a bad sprain and a minor fracture at the end of her fibula that Rhonda described as a crack rather than a break. As a precaution, Rhonda rolled a short walking cast, which needed to be worn for three weeks. The pain pill had worn off and Audra was exhausted.

Danny followed Jim, lugging the cooler up the steps and into the house. After taking another pain pill, Audra went to bed. Jim and Danny stowed the gold in the munitions vault. Inside the vault, Jim pointed out another door hidden behind a roll-around shelf. What appeared to be a concrete wall was actually a stucco-covered metal door with two large stainless steel handles.

Jim said, "Behind this door is an exit tunnel that leads into the forest north of the shed. There's a vertical metal culvert with a built-in ladder and rotating lid similar to a sewer entrance on the other end. Santos may have surveillance cameras watching the house, so you're going to sneak out this way tonight. Once outside, walk north until you hit the beach, then follow it into Angoon and make your way to Helen's boat. It's about a mile and a half trek."

Jim walked to the corner of his vault, then reached onto the top shelf and retrieved a black metal box. The device had a four-foot coax cable with a split tee on the cable end. He smiled. "Attach the tee end of this cable to Helen's radar cable. A pair of pliers and an adjustable wrench, will tighten the connections. This is a radar jammer with a thirty-mile range. It'll enable you to pass the NOAA ship in the dark without detection."

Danny asked, "They taught you this stuff in Delta?"

"Nope. Most of my counter-intelligence knowledge came from CIA field agents — people like your grandfather and Walt Diller."

Danny frowned. "Granddad was an agent?"

"Yep. He was recruited by Director Helms after winning his second election. As chairman of the Armed Services Committee, he monitored other senators and congressmen and reported his findings to a litany of CIA directors including Turner, Casey, Webster and so on. With diplomatic immunity, he traveled the world collecting information from field agents like Walt. He also advised Reagan's National Security Council."

"His plan for me when I entered Delta was to have me rise to general so he could have me appointed to the Joint Chiefs of Staff, but I had other plans — I became a special activities agent."

"Holy shit, you and granddad were both CIA operatives! That's awesome."

"That's what I thought, but your mom had serious issues with it. Deservedly so."

Danny shook his head. "What other surprises do you plan to unload on me?"

"I'm just getting started. You guys wanted the gold so the wheels are in motion. Tonight you'll be disguised as a seventy-year old charter boat captain. Your mother wouldn't recognize you if you were sitting at the same table. Tomorrow, you're our escape mechanism from Warm Springs."

Returning from the vault, Danny wondered how many people his father had killed and whether his former CEO position at TacSec was a CIA cover. He also wondered if he could ever kill another human. Somehow he knew these questions might be answered in the near future.

The duo reached the kitchen to find Lori rummaging through the pantry for a quick fix dinner. Though he had elk stew with Ernie three days earlier, Jim offered to open another jar, which everyone embraced.

After dinner, Jim retrieved a large suitcase from his bedroom closet. The inside was crammed with disguise materials including authentic looking latex masks, beards, hairpieces and more. Lori watched in awe as Jim painstakingly transformed his son into a salty, old sea captain. White hair and a short scruffy beard coupled with a deep-pocked whiskey nose, weathered skin and round wire-rimmed glasses made him look completely authentic.

"Hollywood makeup artists have nothing on you," Lori said. "Is this how you actually look or have you been wearing some elaborate disguise for the past ten years? Maybe you're an ugly old cuss who looks exactly like Danny right now."

Jim smiled. "I guess you'll have to see me while I'm taking a shower. That's the only way to know for sure."

Lori blushed. "C'mon Jim, your son's sitting here."

Danny laughed. "It's dark enough for me to hit the trail. I'd better leave the two of you alone so you can check out each other's disguises. How long do I keep up this masquerade?"

"Until we leave Warm Springs in the morning — maybe longer. There's a dead spot with no cell service near Killisnoo Island. I'll keep the house VHF radio tuned to channel 10. Call me via cell when you arrive at Warm Springs. If you encounter anything strange or have trouble, contact me immediately."

Danny's heart pumped with excitement as he and his father entered the vault for the second time. Jim handed him a loaded Tech-9 with two additional 30 round clips. He commented that they had netted several million dollars today, but tomorrow could easily surpass that amount. At the end of the tunnel, Jim hugged his son and told him that he loved him and was proud of him. Danny smiled and returned his fathers' feelings.

Danny felt a strong sense of arrival. He knew that a family baton had been passed on. He scrambled up the ladder with his sea bag and disappeared into the timber. Fifteen minutes later, he reached a clearing and he could see Helen's boat. Soon he'd be headed to Warm Springs.

Jim returned to the living room to find Lori standing next to the bar with her back to him wearing a fluffy white robe. She turned, and the robe was open, exposing a sexy red negligee. Two whiskey drinks sat on a serving tray. He reached out, and pulled her toward him and kissed her. She kissed back, her tongue teasing his.

Lori was flushed when they broke apart. She asked, "What say you, Colonel? You've been talking the talk, can you walk the walk?"

He placed an arm around her shoulders. They picked up the drinks and walked toward the bedroom. "That's a big affirmative, Miss Phelps."

She jabbed him with her elbow. "Please. No more of this Miss Phelps crap."

CHAPTER SEVEN

June 14 — Ketchikan — Morning

The early sun dimly illuminated the dense fog, creating the illusion of fluorescent lighting. A cell phone in Helen's room rang several times before she could gather her senses. It was 4:45 a.m. She answered while fumbling to engage her tracker. "Blue Marlin. Rusty, are you okay?"

"I'm fine and you're not Blue Marlin. Where's the old man."

Still half asleep, she struggled to watch the scanner. "Um, you woke me up. It's not even five o'clock here. The old man's sleeping. He thought you might call too early for him, so he gave me his phone and instructed me to handle the situation."

"What situation?"

"Your extraction, of course. He said you were being chased and in danger. Where are you so I can arrange things?"

"I'm in the jungle on foot. I'll make Parral by first light. Where are you and Mr. Reid?"

The scanner began its job of backtracking and identifying base stations. In a few seconds, she'd have a fix on his location. She stalled. "We're at his residence in bloody Port Angeles. I arrived here two days ago, and it's been raining the entire time. Look, the old man has instructed me to send his jet to pick you up. He's worried sick about your safety. Let's arrange a rendezvous."

"It's not necessary. I'll charter a private flight to Santiago. From there, I'll toss my weapons, then take a commercial flight to Bogota. I should be in L.A. by noon tomorrow. Tell Frank that everything's wrapped up and I'll call him when I'm in L.A. I've got to get out of this mosquito-infested mess and into Parral."

"Rusty, I've been instr . . ." The phone was dead. The tracking device indicated the Ketchikan and Juneau base stations had forwarded the call to her. Helen sat on her bed confused as the cutter slid gently through the waves. She could only backtrack and determine the closest translator responsible for sending the incoming call. Her tracking only went to Sitka.

Her attention was focused on a hot shower and a warm cup of tea. As the only woman aboard the ship, she was assigned a stateroom with its own bathroom. After showering, she stood in front of the mirror and inserted tiny skull nipple rings. She dressed in black leather pants with a silver studded belt and a black tank top with an electric chair silk-screened on its front. Ghosted lettering above the chair said, "Too Fast for Most." Underneath was, "Too Young to Die." She assessed her image, put a black leather motorcycle jacket over the tank top and left her room for the deck, confident that she portrayed an attitude of dark competence. She took a deep drag off a cigarette, retrieved a cell phone from a jacket pocket and strolled onto the cutter's deck. She walked past the orange chopper and dialed Dave Bachman's number.

Several rings later the phone responded. "Leave a short message and I'll get back with you."

"This is Helen. I'm checking . . ."

Dave interrupted. "Hey, doll — I'm here. Wassup?"

"Were you able to get the ordnance and other items I requested?"

"Affirmative. Everything's being delivered this morning to a friend's warehouse. I've chartered a jet and I'll be in Sitka by 5:00 p.m. Are you going to meet me on the tarmac?"

"That's the plan. We'll arrive by ship early this afternoon. Our cruiser's faster than I imagined. We're making fabulous time. If brother Wayne diverts to Phoenix, could you give him a lift to Sitka? He's on shore leave and will work with us on this project."

"No problem at all. Have him call me when he arrives at Sky Harbor and I'll meet him in the baggage terminal. Once he's got his luggage, I'll escort him to a private portion of the field."

"Wonderful, Dave. I appreciate your help." She paused and cleared her throat. "Look, there's something you need to know. Whitey was killed two days ago. He and I had been working on a project for over a week. He was called away to work an interrogation with Miller. He was shot to death in California during a detainee escape. Sorry to break this news, but it's better coming from me rather than someone else, I guess."

Silence followed. Finally Dave managed a response. "This is totally fucked up. Whitey was unquestionably the finest person I ever worked with. Maybe except for you. How are you holding up girl?"

"Not well, I'm afraid. He was tops, and I loved him like a brother. This is an extremely bitter pill to take, but I've got a job to do."

"Is our project connected to Whitey's murder?"

"Indeed."

"Then I'm pulling out all the stops. I'll kill every last one of the mother fuckers." There was a brief pause. "I need a bit to gather myself. I'll call you after picking up your brother. Have him call me as soon as he lands. Give him my number. I'll see you soon."

After Dave hung up, Helen broke into tears. She stared at the white foam following the cutter's propellers and sobbed. The situation was bittersweet. On one hand, she had met Danny Bennett, who could very well be the love of her life. On the other, she lost her best friend and colleague, and she understood killing Whitey's murderers would never fill the vacuum of his death. It was as if she'd lost her mother again. While she looked toward the red southern sky, a gentle hand touched her shoulder. She turned to find Mr. Reid.

"You're crying about Whitey?"

"I was. I'm sorry you saw me this way, but I'm utterly mournful. He was my best friend."

"You're not alone young lady. We've all shed too many tears within the past week. Come inside and warm up. It's freezing out here."

"I need to call my brother and arrange his transportation to Sitka. I'll come inside in a few minutes and update our developments."

Frank nodded. "Understood. I'll be in the galley waiting for you." He walked away.

Helen called her brother, who was in a taxi heading to the airport. She explained the change of plans and gave him Dave's phone number.

He could tell his sister was upset. "You OK, sis? You don't sound so chipper."

"Dave will fill you in during the flight to Sitka. You'll understand why I'm distraught. Call me as soon as you hook up with Dave, OK?"

"Very well. I look forward to seeing you, sis. It's been far too long."

Helen walked to the galley and found Frank and Gus drinking coffee. She poured hot water into a large mug, dropped in a tea bag, then took a seat at the table.

Gus reached across the table and held her hand. "I haven't had the time or opportunity to tell you how much I appreciate your allegiance to the Olsen family. I'm honestly sorry for your loss. I wish I could bring Whitey back, but I can't. I can offer words of support and encouragement, but they're mere words. I hope your anguish diminishes with time and that, as a team, we don't experience any more senseless loss of life. Please accept my condolences."

Helen nodded. "Thanks to both of you. I've enjoyed working with your family. However, we'll likely experience additional killing before this is over. Considering the nature of our adversaries, it's a given. Any future casualties need to be on their side, not ours."

Frank agreed and added, "On deck, you mentioned recent developments. What's the latest update?"

She sipped tea and began, "Rusty called, apparently from Parral, at 4:45 a.m. He said he's hiring a private charter to Santiago, then continuing to Bogota on commercial airlines. He'll call us when he arrives at LAX. I couldn't get a fix on his location. The call was too brief, but I doubt he called from Parral. I backtracked through the Sitka translator before he hung up."

"He asked where we were. I told him Port Angeles. He'll be in Seattle tomorrow evening."

"Did he sound sincere?"

"That's irrelevant. He's trained to sound sincere even when he's lying. He's managed to keep his calls short and untraceable, which demonstrates his professionalism. He's a cunning Dark Star operative. The good news is that Bachman and my brother will arrive in Sitka by private jet at around 5:00 p.m. Bachman secured all of the items on my list. We'll be rolling later tonight."

Frank smiled. "Excellent job. Gus and I spent considerable time on the bridge last night. Our cutter is quite user-friendly so we shouldn't have any operational difficulties. As soon as we're done with our coffee, the two of us plan to take control of the vessel while the skipper scrutinizes our performance."

"What's our ETA for Sitka?"

"No later than 3:00 p.m.," Gus said. "How long will it take you to retro-fit the night vision monitor and radar jammer?"

"Perhaps two or three hours. Why?"

"Gus and I considered avoiding Sitka by sending the on-deck chopper with our current crew to the airport. That way, we remain incognito and eliminate real Coast Guard or police scrutiny. We're hoping you can mount both systems while on the water."

"I can handle the installations while we're underway," Helen said, "but will we have enough fuel to safely accomplish the mission?"

Gus answered. "There's enough fuel to perform our mission and return to Ketchikan without even trying."

Helen took another sip of tea. "You're ahead of the curve. I suggest anchoring at the tip of Baranof Island where it meets Chatham Strait. We can slip into position under the cover of darkness."

Frank stood. "The three of us make a great team. Come on cousin, let's inform the Captain about our changes and learn more about this fine cutter."

Helen remained at the table with her tea. She wondered if Mr. Reid's management style was taught to him by the Army or from his long association with Henry Weddell. She realized it was likely both.

Angoon — Early Morning

At 6:00 a.m. Lori entered the kitchen and hugged Jim from behind as he stood at the stove making breakfast. He turned to her and smiled. "Hey there, sleepy head. I trust you slept well. I figured the smell of coffee and ham frying would pique your interest."

"You're what piques my interest, James Daniel Bennett, not the smell of food."

Oscar stood at Lori's side and tipped his brown and white head to one side. "What do you think Oscar? Want a sliver of ham? Ask your mom."

He danced in a small circle, then pawed at Lori's foot.

"Go ahead and give him some. You're spoiling him."

Jim sliced off a small portion of ham and knelt on one knee. "Well buddy, she thinks I'm spoiling you instead of her. As I see it, if I get on your good side, she'll like me even more." Oscar gladly accepted Jim's morsel and a few pats on his side.

Audra entered the kitchen on her crutches. "I'm starving. Man, that smells delicious. Is breakfast ready? What's on tap for today? Where's Danny?"

Lori laughed. "Ernie's got you pegged young lady. You're always asking questions."

Audra responded, "The only dumb question is the one not asked."

Jim answered, "It's ready in five minutes. How's your foot feeling, 007?"

"Oh crap. I remember that. I was trying to be funny . . ."

"And it worked," Jim said.

Audra laughed. "My ankle feels much better than yesterday. It's been throbbing, but the nurse said to expect that. It'll be fine. Man, those pain pills kicked my butt yesterday. I hope I didn't offend anyone."

Jim couldn't resist. "Come to think of it, your singing was pretty offensive."

Audra poked her dad with the tip of her left crutch and Oscar growled. "I'm a great singer. You didn't like my choice of songs, that's all. Where's Danny? His room was empty when I walked by."

"He's waiting for us at Warm Springs. He spent the night there on Helen's boat. I spoke with him at 5:00 and he wants us to bring plenty of food because he's starving — just like his sister. We should hustle and get the day underway. If things go well, we'll haul down another three million today and have the crash site totally prepped."

Audra looked at Lori. "Hot damn! Let's boogie. I'll be ready ten minutes after eating."

An hour later, Jim walked onto the float plane dock with a plastic baggie in his left hand. He snuck around the corner of the rain shelter and located the button-sized camera. After carefully applying a thick coating of Vaseline to its tiny lens, he waved to the Humvee. Within minutes, the *Sojourn* motored past Killisnoo Island. The fishing lodge was buzzing with activity. Several small craft were headed north toward Chichagof Island. Apparently, the lodge owner Dick and his guides didn't have a clue about locating early stages of the King run. Jim swung wide into Chatham and made certain the *Oregon II* spotted him. Within seconds he intercepted a radio transmission from his scanner and turned up the volume while cutting his throttle.

"Softail to Fortuna — come in Fortuna."

"This is Fortuna, go ahead."

"Our package is entering the channel and heading in our direction. Over."

"Good. We've lost our live video link at the marina. Is McKinnon aboard? Over."

"I've got a spotting scope on them but they're moving too fast to tell."

"Copy that. I want to know the exact destination of our package."

"Understood. If the package goes out of sight, should we follow with the Whaler?"

"Negative. If our package travels beyond radar range, its destination is of no use to us. Over."

"Roger that Fortuna. We'll keep posted on the package's status. Fortuna out."

Two miles past the *Oregon II*, Jim throttled to full speed. Lori took over the controls while he inspected the ship's deck with a powerful spotting scope. Two men stood near the horseshoe crane. Jim got a good look at the ship's bridge. One person was visible inside the wheelhouse navigating the ship. It turned slowly south directly in front of Peril Straight. Soon the ship would be facing Jim's course and Warm Springs Bay.

Within twenty minutes, the *Sojourn* was nearly 12 miles from the ship. It slowed and executed a large sweeping right turn. Once again the radio sounded off.

"Softail to Fortuna, Softail to Fortuna. Over."

"This is Fortuna. Over."

"Our package is headed south and turning into Warm Springs Bay"

"Copy that. Maybe our package plans on taking a dip today."

"Affirmative. They've entered the bay. Shall we investigate?"

"Negative. Continue working but monitor the mouth of Warm Springs with your radar. Contact me when they leave."

"Copy that. Softail out."

Audra busted out laughing. "These morons don't have a clue do they? They don't even know Ernie's gone."

The harbor was almost empty, so Jim coached Lori on how to dock his craft. A white-bearded old man on the dock offered to assist them by tying off the boat. He tied them off next to Helen's Bayliner and climbed aboard the *Sojourn* as if he owned it.

Audra was shocked. "Do you know this guy?"

"Yep, and so do you," Jim said. Audra frowned.

"Come on," Jim said. "Let's transfer to the Bayliner before someone notices us. Don't forget your crutches."

Lori smiled as the old man silently helped Audra change boats. She thanked the old-timer, who remained still. Within minutes, the gear was loaded into the Bayliner. Audra finally asked Lori, "Where the heck is Danny, and what's Dad doing with that old-timer on our boat?"

Lori smiled. "Always asking questions. They're probably setting the alarm and surveillance systems. Danny will be here shortly. Why don't you sit in the captain's chair and get ready to operate this beast? It's too big and complicated for a rookie like me."

Audra settled into the seat and assessed the controls. Confident that the Bayliner wasn't a challenge, she started it. Jim entered the cabin and closed the door while the old man untied the boat, then jumped onto the rear deck. He motioned for Audra to back away from the dock.

Confused, she barked, "What the heck is going on here? Where's Danny? Who's the geezer?"

The "geezer" entered the cabin and asked in Danny's voice, "Where is my breakfast? I'm starving."

Astonished, she looked at the "old" man. He placed a hand on her head and said in a scratchy voice, "Aar — what's the matter missy? Ain't ya ever seen a salty old dog before?"

Audra punched him on the arm. "You guys are cruel. Where in the world did you get that goofy disguise? Let me get a closer look."

Lori and Jim both roared. Finally, Audra laughed along.

Audra lightly pinched Danny's cheek and found it was covered with a thin latex film. After pulling on his bushy white eyebrows, she said, "It's so real, you could fool Jesus Christ himself. Dad did this to you?"

"Last night while you were sleeping."

Danny looked at his father, "When can I remove this itchy thing?"

"When we reach the tip of Admiralty."

Jim handed Danny two large vinyl banners with black lettering: AK61532. "Stick one on each side of the bridge before we leave the harbor. We'll look exactly like a chartered fishing boat. When you're done with that, go to the upper bridge and pretend you're operating the boat. Take the small cooler. It has two breakfast burritos in it. I need to set up my scanning equipment."

The Bayliner smoothly skipped forward and soon reached its cruising step. Its powerful engines effortlessly pushed the boat at 18 knots while Jim set two sea bags vertically on the bench seat and draped jackets over the bags. He plumped the bags tops and placed baseball caps on top of the puffed-up areas. As soon as the boat cleared the harbor, the NOAA ship sent another radio transmission.

"Softail to Fortuna — come in Fortuna"

"This is Fortuna. Over."

"We've picked up a radar signature and have a visual on a large charter boat leaving Warm Springs. They're heading across the strait toward Admiralty."

"Can you see anyone on board?"

"An old fella with a white beard at the controls. Several people are inside the cabin."

"A fishing charter?"

"Affirmative. It has Alaska charter boat numbers on the bridge."

"They're fishing. Don't waste time tracking them. I'm sending someone to Angoon to repair our video link and possibly locate McKinnon, so focus on our package. If the package leaves the bay, contact me immediately. Over."

"Roger that. Softail out."

"Your ruse is ticking like a fine Swiss clock," Lori said.

Jim nodded. "Hook, line and sinker. Audra, when you reach the other side, turn north for about a mile, then cut the engines to trolling speed. Danny will set up the downriggers and rods without lures or bait so we *appear* to be fishing. When you reach Whitewater, turn and troll into the bay. As soon as they lose sight of us, we'll blast off to the drop point."

Forty-five minutes later, the NOAA ship was out of sight. Audra pushed the Bayliner's throttles wide open. The boat would reach the bay's headwaters and rocky point in ten minutes. Jim set his surveillance equipment on the cabin table and instructed Lori in its various operations and settings. She easily learned the system, which operated satellite observations, audio and video links located at the house. Jim's boat, Ernie's cabin, Crane's camper, Santos' house and the water tower in Angoon were all connected. The radio scanner would alert her in case Santos decided to switch bands or change to walkie-talkies. Jim decided they would communicate by cell phone, and carried a compact military walkie-talkie as well.

Danny asked to have his disguise removed, and Jim carefully obliged. The mask was needed for their return to Warm Springs.

After reaching the rocky point, Jim took over the boat's controls and showed Audra how to maneuver the Bayliner's bow onto a small, sandy spit adjoining the point. He returned control to Audra and had her duplicate the maneuver.

Lori was impressed with Audra's ability to operate the Bayliner. She deduced that Jim must have spent hours teaching her the subtleties of handling a boat. When the boat was nestled onto the sand, the men changed into camouflage, donned their packs, took up weapons and jumped off the bow into the wet sand. Jim pushed the boat off the spit as Audra throttled backwards.

Jim yelled, "You know where the weapons are. Don't hesitate using them if you're confronted by Santos or his men. I'll call when we reach the wreck. I'm leaving our walkie-talkies on as well as my cell phone." Lori waved as Jim and Danny slipped into the dark, thick timber.

The duo force-marched up the mountain until they reached the first opening. Jim timed their ascent. They would reach the snowfield in five minutes. After reaching the wreck in record time, Jim looked toward the bay but couldn't see the Bayliner. He immediately called the boat on the two way radio.

Danny unfolded a telescoping rake and groomed the snow around the wreck while Jim spoke to Lori. "We're at the site. How are things below?"

Lori answered, "There's no way you guys could be there this soon unless you flew. You left only thirty minutes ago." Lori changed the satellite image and saw Jim sitting near the snowfield edge as Danny groomed the site. "Hey! I see both of you. You weren't bullshitting."

"We're indeed here. What's going on down there?"

"We trolled about two miles, then made a big turn. We're on the south shore, directly across from the drop-off zone."

Jim saluted. "Any unusual activity I should know about?"

"A small boat just left the Santos dock with one person aboard, headed toward Angoon. I bet he's going to check on the camera you disabled. Without it, there's no way for them to track your boat unless they see you on the water."

"You're right about the camera. I'll call when we reach the bottom."

"Be careful. I'll contact you if there's anything to be concerned about."

Jim looked at the job Danny had done. "Excellent. With any precipitation, a person would never know we were here." Jim pointed. "Let's move this pile of canisters away from the plane to that small grassy area."

After relocating the canisters Jim asked, "Can you safely carry a canister on your pack frame down this mountain?"

Danny boldly said, "I can handle two."

Jim smiled. "I'm too old for that. I'd never handle two. Let's go for one each."

"OK. Let's roll, Pops."

They covered the stash of gold with camo canvas and loaded their packs. The duo carefully made their way to the small stream. The pack weight was more than either of them had expected, but neither man would cry "uncle" for fear of being outdone. Fifty minutes later, nearly exhausted, the father-and-son team reached the rendezvous point. They removed the packs, dropped to the soft, mossy ground and lay on their backs.

Several minutes passed before Danny spoke. "I'm in pretty good shape, but that was ridiculous."

"I agree. After that, I've got an idea. Our bush pilot, John Addison, was a Warrant Officer chopper pilot during Desert Storm. If we pay him handsomely, we can retrieve everything during the dark. I've got night vision equipment in the vault. The entire operation would take only twenty minutes."

Danny stood and shook out the cobwebs. "That's makes sense. Could we do it tonight?"

"I'll call him from the boat to see if he can get hold of a logging chopper. Even so, we need to develop a fool proof plan before committing ourselves. Let's get this gold loaded, then get back to Warm Springs."

Jim called the boat for pick-up.

The Bayliner slowly pulled onto the narrow sandy spit and the men exited the timber line. Danny cupped his hands, providing his dad a step for climbing onto the bow. After taking the canisters and backpacks aboard, the former colonel pulled his son onto the boat. Audra gently backed away from the spit and turned the boat around. They cruised the northern shoreline and stopped as they approached the Strait. Jim reapplied Danny's disguise and sent him to the upper bridge. Within minutes, the Bayliner rounded the corner and headed north toward Russian Reef as if fishing the shoreline.

After 15 minutes of trolling, Audra placed the boat in neutral while the "old man" retrieved the downriggers and poles. He made a point of affording the *Oregon II* a good view of himself.

Jim used the time to call John as the boat headed back to Warm Springs.

"Hey, John. This is Jim Bennett. How are things?"

"Busier than a cat trying to bury shit on a marble floor. Saturdays are always this way for me. What can I do for you?"

"Are you free tonight?"

"I've a 4:00 p.m. flight to pick up a group of fishermen at Pelican. Why?"

"Can you get your hands on a logging helicopter by tonight?"

"There's one in Petersburg gathering dust. It belongs to Northern Lights Logging and I know the owner."

"Are you interested in doing a small job late tonight?"

"What's it pay?"

"How does a hundred thousand sound?"

After a short pause, John said, "I could pay off my plane. Is it legal?"

"Borderline. No drugs or weapons, but the job is strictly on the QT. Payment in cash upon completion. Probably 30 to 45 minutes of fly time."

"Outta sight, Jim. Look, I've got a charter in a few minutes and need to contact a friend about getting the chopper."

Jim added. "I need a cable winch and cargo net too. Is that a problem?"

"The grasshopper I have in mind is fully equipped. I'll call at 5:30 for details."

"There's no need for that. Secure the chopper and call me when you're ready to leave Petersburg. I'll give you details then."

John responded, "I'll call tonight."

Jim hung up the phone, walked behind Lori while she was watching the computer monitor and kissed the top of her head. She turned in surprise. "Hey, handsome."

"Up for an all-nighter in order to get the balance of the gold out in one swoop?"

She stood. "I couldn't walk up that mountain again to save my soul. Especially in the dark."

"All you have to do is stay at the house and run the surveillance equipment."

"What about me," Audra asked. "Am I included?"

"Affirmative. You'll communicate with us by radio. I'll fill in the blanks over dinner."

As they began turning into Warm Springs, the *Oregon II* was headed directly toward the center of Chatham Strait with a long wake trailing the ship, leaving the waters of Catherine Island. They'd be searching the opening of Whitewater Bay and beyond on Sunday unless Jim managed to divert their attention.

The Bayliner approached the Warm Springs slip where it had been earlier and slowly parked. Danny returned to the deck and helped tie off the craft. He looked at Jim. "What's the plan for tonight? Are we good to go?"

"It looks that way. You can remove the disguise while I transfer things to my boat. Be careful not to destroy your mask. We may need it again."

By two o'clock, the four had switched boats, locked up the Bayliner and headed into open water. Lori was still watching the monitor. "Someone is repairing the Angoon video camera," she said. "I watched him park his boat at the marina and wander around town. He stopped at the store, then walked to the float plane pier."

Jim studied the monitor and added, "He looks like an albino."

Danny took a look. "That's Helen's cousin. I mean, he works with Helen. I met him the night they arrived in Angoon."

Jim asked, "Are you certain?"

"Yep. I helped him tie off the Bayliner."

Jim watched as the albino cleaned the camera lens and walked away.

He said, "That's an interesting turn of events. You're absolutely sure?"

"Yep."

The radio scanner sounded off. "Softail to Fortuna — come in Fortuna."

"This is Fortuna. Over."

"Package is headed toward Angoon from Warm Springs. Over."

"What's their exact position — I've got a man at the marina who needs cover if they're close."

"Ah, Christ, they're at least ten clicks south of us. We're centered between Peril and Whitewater. They're another hour from Angoon."

"Great. Let me know if anything changes"

"Roger that. Out."

Jim enhanced the satellite resolution to one meter, zoomed in on the albino and asked, "Is this the guy?"

Danny studied the grainy image. "That's him alright. Helen called him 'Whitey.'"

"That means Helen and the Olsens are playing us for fools or this guy changed sides and is now working for Santos. If it's the former, Ernie's life's in danger."

Danny shook his head. "I can't believe she's playing us. You overlooked the possibility of Helen's people infiltrating Santos."

"I doubt that, but it's a possibility."

Lori pulled on Jim's arm as a cell phone inside his metal case rang. It was Santos making a call. Jim cut the throttles and placed it onto speaker mode.

Someone answered on the fourth ring. "Yeah, I'm all ears."

"The package is on its way to Angoon. It'll be there within an hour."

"Thanks for the heads up. I need to check out McKinnon's place before leaving. By the time they return, I'll be long gone. Hopefully he won't take the inside passage by Killisnoo."

"Hurry up and don't get caught."

"Chill out. It's under control. Later."

Jim instructed Audra to head for the inside passage. She pushed both throttles forward and re-set the boat's trim. Moments passed and the boat's speed climbed to 28 knots. Lori changed links to Ernie's cabin and watched as the albino removed a portable scanner from his pocket and perused the cabin's perimeter. The man immediately stepped back and jogged toward his boat.

"He knows the place is bugged." Jim replayed and freeze-framed the man.

Danny looked at the monitor and nodded. "That's him."

Jim called the phone he'd given Ernie. After many rings, the old man finally answered. "Ya — I mean, hello."

"Ernie, this is Jim."

"Hey there friend. I thought ya'd be callin."

"Where are you?"

"At a house haunted with ghosts — somewhere near Seattle I think."

"Are you OK?"

"Of course. Why?"

"We've had a few developments over here. Listen carefully. Where are Helen and your ghost friends right now?"

"Ain't sure — maybe Ketchikan. She sent me here last night with Lena — said it was safer for everyone."

"Since you left Angoon, have you seen an albino man or heard anyone mention the name 'Whitey?'"

"Never saw anyone like that, but I overheard Gus and Lena mention that name. They said Helen was upset that someone by that name got killed."

"I need you to do something for me. It's important."

Ernie said, "Sure, whatcha need?"

"Tell Lena that Helen's cousin Whitey tried to break into your cabin about ten minutes ago, and I've got video to prove it. Carefully observe her reaction — she should be upset and immediately call Gus. If she doesn't, take the phone and get the hell out of there. Find the nearest police station and have the cops call me by using the re-dial function on the phone I gave you. Can you do that?"

"Ya, but what if she calls Gus — what do I do then?"

"Nothing. They'll figure out how to contact me."

"Ya sure know how ta scare an old coot."

"Sorry Ernie, but you may be in danger. If she immediately calls Gus, everything's good and you're safe."

"OK. I'll do it now. Bye."

Sitka Tarmac — 4:30 p.m.

Helen stood next to the Sikorsky helicopter as Jeff walked to the co-pilot's side and opened the large sliding bay door. She waved to a small white one-ton delivery truck approaching the hangar. The truck pulled next to the chopper and the driver got out.

He asked, "You the people who ordered the plywood?"

"Yes. Did you cut the sheets into the sizes we need?"

"Yes mam. My boss said I was only to accept cash. It's gonna be $74.25. You got the money?"

She handed him a hundred dollar bill and said, "You can keep the change if you load it into the chopper."

The delivery man smiled and began packing the plywood into the helicopter. Helen noticed a medium-sized jet approaching from the north and figured it was Dave Bachman's plane. Her phone rang as the plane touched down. She expected her brother to call but it was Frank Reid.

She answered, "Yes, sir."

"Bennett just called Ernie. He claims to have video of Whitey trying to enter McKinnon's cabin about twenty minutes ago. This is very confusing."

Her phone indicated a "call waiting" and said, "I'll handle this. I've got another call coming in. Give me a few minutes to get back with you."

She switched over to the incoming call. "Yes."

"Hey sis, how do we find you?"

"Turn northeast and you'll see an enormous orange chopper standing next to a blue hanger. Taxi over here and park the jet inside the hanger. Sorry bro, but I can't talk right now — I'll see you when you get here."

She immediately contacted Bennett. His phone rang several times and she was surprised to hear Danny answer, "This is Danny."

"Hey lover, what's this rubbish about Whitey?"

"I'll upload his photo to your email as soon as we reach the house. We've got a video of him snooping around Angoon and Ernie's cabin. What the fuck's going on?"

"I honestly don't know, and I don't appreciate that tone of voice. Whitey was killed two days ago while interrogating a prisoner. That's why Ernie and I were extracted."

As the jet approached the hanger, Helen cupped her ear and walked away from the noise. "Listen carefully Danny, I swear to you that I'm not part of whatever's going on over there. Neither is my employer. I need a straight on close-up photo so I can run a biometric comparison."

"I already said I'd forward it to you when we get in. Where are you?"

"I'm sorry, but I can't tell you. Please understand. It's my job."

"I don't understand, and quite frankly, I'm tired of all this cloak-and-dagger bullshit. It occurs to me that you and your 'cousin' may be after the gold and I'm being played for a fool. Are you the woman who touched my soul or something dark and vile? Will the real Helen Moorcroft please stand up? Look, I've had enough of this shit for one day." Danny hung up in anger.

Helen panicked and walked further away from the hanger as her tall, gangly brother yelled for her return. She motioned for him to remain there as she re-dialed the number. After several rings, Jim answered.

"Good afternoon, Helen."

"Likewise, Mr. Bennett, but not real good. May I please speak with Danny?"

"I'm sorry but he's on the rear deck. He's rather upset and asked me not to bother him if you called back."

"I'm sorry he feels that way. I swear that I know nothing about the event that just unfolded. I was convinced Whitey was dead. And now . . . ." She took a deep breath, . . . "I have a favor to ask."

"What do you want?"

"I want you to remain off the water for the next few days."

"Why."

"I don't want your family to be confused as combatants or suffer collateral damage. If you can't oblige my request and find yourself in a dire situation, will you immediately contact me at this number?"

"I can't make promises I know I won't keep. If you're being honest with me, I suggest you delay whatever plans you have until you've determined the extent of defection within your ranks. I recall telling you PMCs often change sides for more money and that's why I dislike them. You called me a hypocrite the other day, but maybe now you'll appreciate my point of view. If we find ourselves like 'bats on a sticky wicket,' I'll consider contacting you. Otherwise, I urge you to keep a sharp eye over your shoulder."

"Splendid that you remembered my phrase, sir. I'll heed your advice. Please send my regards to your family."

"I will. Goodbye."

Helen ran to her waiting brother and hugged him and he lifted her into the air. They walked hand and hand toward Dave and the waiting chopper. She threw her arms around the older man and kissed him.

Dave said, "You're looking hotter than ever darlin'. I see you're still sporting the rock star image."

"Got to keep the men at Dark Star wondering. You know how it works."

"I understand completely and I don't blame you a bit. Most of the guys over there are worthless saps anyway. I'm glad I've left them."

Helen formally introduced Jeff to Wayne and Dave. They climbed aboard the Sikorsky and Jeff handed out earphones to the passengers. The chopper warmed up while Jeff explained safety procedures over the radio and told Helen to extinguish her cigarette. The massive chopper made a deafening roar as it ascended to five hundred feet, then banked toward the open ocean. Helen stared out the window, trying to parse out what had just transpired in Angoon. She kept checking her phone for the video from Danny.

Knowing what close friends Dave and Whitey had been, she wondered if Dave could be involved as well. Nothing added up or made sense. Helen questioned the status of Rusty. Could he be involved? Her thoughts shifted to Danny and how suspect he was of her. He had every right to be. She turned toward the window and wiped her tears with a Kleenex. Ten minutes later she spoke into her mic and asked Jeff to inform Frank they were inbound and would arrive shortly. Bumpy air greeted the chopper as it banked east over Whale Bay. They'd be landing on the cutter in ten minutes.

Helen turned to Wayne sitting next to her and kissed him on his unshaven cheek. He smiled and gave her a one-armed hug, and kept his arm around her shoulders. Helen knew that no matter how bad things are, she'll always have her brother.

The orange chopper tore across Whale Bay and the tip of Baranof Island at over 90 mph. After clearing Baranof, the helicopter entered Chatham Strait and turned into Rowan Bay on the west shore of Kupreanof Island. The cutter sat anchored deep inside the bay, hidden from view. In spite of swirling winds, Jeff safely set the chopper on the cutter's deck. Helen went to the wheelhouse as the other three strapped the chopper solidly onto the rear deck.

Frank greeted her, and she said, "We've got to meet privately. Now. I'll fill you in when we get to the galley."

Angoon — 5:30 p.m.

As the *Sojourn* approached the buoy near the tip of Killisnoo, an open boat sped through the narrows between Admiralty and Killisnoo. The albino's shoulder length white hair was clearly visible as he rounded the corner and headed into Hood Bay. Jim had anticipated this encounter. He took several photos with his digital camera from 50 meters away. Whitey never looked toward Jim's craft.

After entering Kootznahoo, Jim asked Audra to place the boat's bow against the western edge of the float plane dock and keep it there. The colonel exited the boat and pulled the portable scanner from his top pocket. He walked to the camera's transmitter, found it high on the opposite side of the rain shelter and pulled it from the wooden post. He tossed it into the bay and returned to the boat.

"Their camera's toast without a transmitter. Let's unload the boat and get back to the house for a meeting."

Danny drove the Humvee home as Jim called John to finalize the details of the night's project. At the house, he checked the perimeter security system and entered the beautiful structure. Danny moved the gold to the secret vault while Jim examined all of his perimeter videos. Both beach cameras had captured Whitey running his Lund onto the gravel shore and scanning Jim's house. The albino quickly retreated to the boat. He had detected surveillance equipment. Jim transferred all videos of Whitey to his laptop, then forwarded them to Helen's email.

Lori began cooking a beef roast she'd left out to thaw earlier in the day. Audra elevated her leg, complaining that it was throbbing as a result of sitting in the pilot's chair all day. Jim gave her some aspirin and a quarter of a pain pill. After Danny returned from the vault, Jim called for a meeting. They sat at the glass coffee table as Jim unfolded a map.

"There's been a shake up within the Olsen camp. One or more of their operatives are working in concert with Santos. Helen insists she's not involved and I think she's telling the truth. The Olsens are rich and have nothing to gain by going for the gold. They simply want this thing to go away. However one or more of their hired guns want the gold. These are professional, real-time mercenaries with the same assets at their disposal as me. They'll likely kill Santos and his lackeys once they've got the gold and they'll kill anyone else who gets in their way. It appears that someone at the top is involved. At this point, we have two options. Either we go for the gold tonight, or I can contact Diller and let the CIA sort this out. The safest scenario is to allow Walt to do his thing and we settle for the couple million we currently have."

"Diller's involvement can be a dangerous proposition for everyone involved," Lori said. "What happens to Helen and the Olsens?"

"The Olsens will likely lose everything they have and go to prison for the rest of their lives. As for Helen she might get off with conspiracy and obstruction of justice charges. Worst-case scenario: 10 years of prison, possibly a suspended sentence. Ernie gets to go home."

Audra bristled. "That's not an option."

Lori nodded. "If we defer to Walt, we also run the risk of prosecution. We'd be individually questioned by people other than Walt, so we'd need to get our stories straight."

Jim cocked his head to one side and rubbed his scar. "Walt will sweep our involvement under the rug if I deny keeping any of the gold. He owes me that."

Danny asked, "Do you have any clue where Helen and the Olsens are right now?"

Jim nodded. "They're close. I tracked Helen's last call from a Sitka tower."

Danny looked at Lori and Audra. "I say grab the gold. What about you guys?"

Audra wasted no time. "I'm with Danny. Let's do it."

Lori added, "Providing Diller never gets involved, I'm in too."

Jim spoke. "Okay. We need to act. Here are the parameters. First off, the Dark Star defectors are pros and must be taken seriously. They don't have any idea where the plane is but they think Ernie or we do. They'll track our movements for a while, but if that doesn't lead them to the gold, they'll grab one of us and hold them for ransom. Second, the Olsen crew is inbound, which exacerbates the situation. We're being drawn into a confrontation and we're not prepared. Finally, we're out of time. Events have taken a turn for the worse. I think our salvation is to remove the gold. Taking another water trip into Whitewater is suicide. We'd be boxed in. However, if we remove the gold tonight and the Tlingits found the wreck tomorrow, we'd be in control."

Lori said, "I'm in agreement with you, except I don't see how we'd be in control."

"After the Clans 'find' the wreck, we'll set a trap for Santos and Dark Star — they'll think that the gold is hidden somewhere near the wreck and wait for us to recover it. When they follow me into Whitewater — deep into the inner lake, I choke them off so they're the ones boxed in — then I'll smoke 'em."

"When they follow you, you'll smoke ' em?" Lori barked. "You're crazy and you've already made up your mind about 'smoking 'em?' I've got a terrible feeling about this, Jim. Dark Star defectors add a whole new dimension to the Santos crew. You've forgotten a great alternative. Do nothing. Let these bastards fight it out between themselves."

Jim nodded. "Yes. I wish. I considered that but there's a likelihood the Olsen crew will be unsuccessful. There's a defector in their ranks. That leaves Santos and the defector or defectors — and possibly Dark Star against us. They're convinced that Ernie, Olsen or ourselves know where the gold is. I'm not going to be at the mercy of these guys. We get the gold out, then set a trap and eliminate them."

Lori reluctantly agreed. "OK. So how, without getting any of us killed?"

"Are we all on board?"

Everyone nodded, and Jim continued, "First, I planned a slight diversion — just in case we agreed."

"Way to go, Dad," Audra said.

"John's got access to a chopper and should be in Petersburg to get it by now. I'll have him hover over the southern tip of Chichagof near Peril and send out a bogus message that he's verified the location of a plane wreck that was found earlier in the day by a ground-based timber crew. He'll spend ten minutes or so making passes over a steep ravine across from Rodman Bay. Santos should swallow the bait, which buys us time to retrieve the gold tonight."

Lori walked to the bar and poured herself a small whiskey.

"Hold on," she said. "Anyone care for a drink? As a group, it could be our last."

Hood Bay – 5:30 PM

Whitey opened a bottle of Heineken and looked at the medium-built bald-shaved man. "We need to talk outside. Away from your body guards and caretaker."

The man answered with a distinct European accent. "No need for that. We'll talk in my study."

"Walls have ears my friend. Let's go out back into the timber. The front of your house and pier are under surveillance by Bennett."

"Nonsense, that's impossible. My cameras are operational 24/7 with infrared capabilities. I would have noticed him planting bugs."

"His equipment's on the point directly across from your home. I detected it when I got here. He's probably bugged your phones, too. The camera at the marina has stopped working again. He disabled it."

Vicente pulled back a white curtain and peered out over the open water toward the island. "He's clever. I'll take pleasure in killing him. Let's go out back."

The two men walked 50 meters into the dense timber, then the albino spoke, "Your organization is strictly minor league, Vicente — or should I call you Anton? I've assessed the situation and I demand a new deal. Without me, you'll spin your wheels until hell freezes over. Old man Olsen told me there's fifty million on board that plane and I'll find it. I want half."

"That's unacceptable; I have partners that expect their cut when this is over. They're not the kind of people you'd want to betray."

"Fuck your partners. They're a bunch of dirtbag hoodlums. They're expendable and so are Olsen's people. For my half, I'll deliver the gold and both Olsens, plus one giant tidbit."

"What's the tidbit?"

"The Olsens know where the U-boat was before your father sank it. That means there's over a half billion worth of gold in shallow water waiting for you to grab."

"You talk as if the Olsens are coming here."

"They're supposed to meet with my Dark Star co-workers in Sitka tonight and they're coming here to kill you and your thugs."

Santos asked, "They know about me?"

The albino smirked. "Of course they do. I told them."

Santos paused. "OK. You've got my attention. Keep talking."

"Excuse me for a minute." The albino tipped his head and began to methodically pull off sections of a full-facial latex mask, including hair. Seconds later, he was undisguised. Rusty Miller dropped the mask to the ground.

"Sorry," he said. "I couldn't stand that thing any more."

Santos backed away and drew his Glock. "What the hell? Who the fuck are you?"

"Relax. I'm the guy who's going to make you filthy rich. The disguise was to confuse Bennett, the Olsens and Dark Star. By now, they're wondering how a dead operative and myself figure into all this. They think I'm currently returning from Colonia Dignidad after killing you. Did Whitey and I infiltrate your organization on their behalf, or are we working in concert against them? They don't know who to trust or where to turn. While they're regrouping, Bennett will have the gold. Then, we kill Bennett."

"Again," Santos said. "Who the fuck are you?" The Glock was still pointed at Rusty's chest.

"My name is Russel Miller — call me 'Rusty'. I'm in charge of the Olsen crew, trained under Bennett and run Dark Star's security team. Ask Crane. I kept him alive so you and I could join forces."

"I've got the resources to track Bennett. I've known him for a long time and he's the best operative around. He'll lead us to the wreck. Instinct tells me he's already found it. All we need to do is have your goons intercept him when I give the word. When the time comes, I expect your crew to be under my command."

"How will you eliminate my crew and deliver the Olsens?"

"I'll let Bennett eliminate your crew. Then I'll kill him and his family."

"What about your people?"

"I've got an insider who'll eliminate everyone except the Olsens by the time I reach Henry's yacht. Once aboard, I'll kill my insider. That leaves the Olsen cousins and me on the yacht."

"Where am I during all of this?"

"You'll remain in the background as an observer with your bodyguard. I might need you as backup transportation if any of our craft takes a hit. Your guys will use the Bertrum, Boston Whaler and Lund while Crane and I use the Zodiac from Angoon. Your location depends on where Bennett leads me."

"How can I trust you?"

"You can't. And I can't trust you. Those are risks we take in a risky business. Personally, I'm quite content with twenty-five million and a tricked-out yacht. I'll sail south and disappear. You take your share and do whatever, but if I were you, I'd hire a new captain and two deck hands from Juneau. Pay them handsomely to run the NOAA ship and locate the sub."

Santos lowered the pistol.

"I like your style, Mr. Miller. How do we proceed?"

"I'm taking the Lund and my equipment across the bay." He pointed. "I'll set up on top of that ridge. When I've got the goods on our colonel, I'll contact you and your crew and we'll spring the trap. Be prepared to leave on a moment's notice — possibly as soon as tonight."

"You believe he's close to finding the gold?"

"As sure as your name is Anton Keller. When we're done talking, send your bodyguard and a caretaker to pick up the Zodiac. If the natives freak out, tell them that you'll return it when they hire a new cop. I want Softail anchored tonight on the east side of the strait. I expect them to man the radar 24/7. No more sonar or magnetometer bullshit. I need Crane transferred to your place tonight. He can take the Boston Whaler from Softail or you can pick him up with your catamaran. Later on, he'll be in charge of running the Zodiac."

"How do you plan on staying up all night on that frozen ridge?"

"That's my problem."

The two men shook hands before walking back to the house.

Rowan Bay — 5:30 p.m.

Frank and Helen met privately in the galley. Before she could talk, her phone chimed, announcing an incoming email. She studied the downloads, threw the Blackberry across the small table and placed both hands on top of her head while leaning back into her chair. Frank took a look at the Blackberry and realized why she was distraught.

The old man frowned. "Rusty, Whitey and Cranston are taking us for a ride. God knows how many other Dark Star personnel are involved. They're after the gold. Your pal Bachman could be involved as well."

Helen thought about her mother's prophecies, then said, "That's exactly what went through my mind on the return flight, but I know Whitey wouldn't do this to me. We were very close friends — things aren't as they appear."

Frank reached over and touched her hand. "I'm sorry I've gotten you into this situation. The Bennetts and ourselves are in grave danger. I have no idea how to proceed."

Helen looked at her Blackberry again and said, "I'm at a loss for words if Whitey and Bachman were involved. Before I finalize my plan, let me enhance these images on my laptop and compare them with the biometrics of Whitey. I also need to see the coroner's report for the corpse in Sacramento."

She opened her laptop, turned it on and waited for it to boot up.

Frank picked up his phone and dialed. Helen watched and listened. "Hello John. John Benton, this is Frank Reid. How are you today? Are you enjoying your cruise?"

There was a pause "So, it's your first time to Hawaii. Marvelous. Enjoy tonight's luau. Say, the reason I'm calling is that I remember you have a daughter working in the Sacramento police department forensics department."

After another pause, Frank said, "Yes, yes that's her — Laura. Could you do me an immense favor and have her call me at this number ASAP. It's rather important."

After a bit, he said, "I understand. Anything you can do is greatly appreciated."

The conversation was ending. "Thanks, John. Please have a fantastic time in the islands. I look forward to her call. Goodbye."

Helen asked, "Was that Henry's gatekeeper?"

"Yes it was. You have a keen memory. I'm certain his daughter has access to the coroner's report."

Helen turned her laptop around and pointed to the screen. "His face looks identical to Whitey, but he appears shorter and heavier."

"It's difficult for me to tell," Frank said. "The face and hair looks identical, but I can't make out his eyes. This photo was obviously taken at a great distance. His eyes had such a unique color."

Helen manipulated the image. "This is the clearest photo we have. I can't do better than this."

"I still can't make out his eyes, but it definitely looks like Whitey."

"We'll run another biometric as soon . . ."

Frank's phone rang. He placed it in speaker mode and put it on the table. "This is Frank."

"Hello Mr. Reid, my name is Laura Kimball and I'm calling on behalf of my father. How can I be of assistance?"

"I believe a murder victim — an albino male — was processed through your department three days ago. Do you recall?"

"I processed the gunshot residue sample in my lab. Why are you asking? Do you have information about this crime?"

"No. A friend told me the victim could be someone I know. Do you have a name and maybe a photograph that could be emailed to me? If it's the person I know, I'd like to send condolences and flowers to his family."

"The vics' name was Michael Stoddard, nickname 'Whitey.'"

"Who told you his nickname?"

"His son Michael, Jr. He'll be here tomorrow to identify the body. The vic carried ID and will be released to his son for internment. Standard protocol prevents me from sending out coroner reports and autopsy photos, but since you're friends with my father, I'll go back to the lab and cut a few corners. I must warn you: the bullet entered the back of the skull and exited through the face. It's not a pretty picture. What's your email?"

"I appreciate your assistance. My email is marlin@yahoo.com. Thank you very much."

Helen looked at Frank. "What do you think? It sounds like the dead man is Whitey. I'm not sure how I feel about that. But, look at the scan I completed from the Bennett video. The center of the eyes in relation to the nose and mouth are different. So is the width of the eyes. The match likelihood is only 40%. I'm reluctant to say it's not a match because enhancement creates a 20% margin of error, but I have doubts about this being Whitey."

"Let's wait for the email from Sacramento. How well do you know Mr. Bachman?"

"Very well. I consider him a close friend who's always treated me with respect and dignity. Most women in my profession are treated poorly by male counterparts, but he's never been that way with me. One of the reasons I dress and act like this is because it intimidates fellow workers and gives me room to navigate. It provides me with an advantage. Dave recognizes my ploy and kids me about it whenever we're alone. I find it incomprehensible that he'd blindside me."

Frank stared at the floor. "The only other wild card on this vessel is Jeff. He's been in my employ for over ten years; a conscientious and loyal worker. I suppose he could have been coerced into working with the bad guys at some point, but he's never said or done anything peculiar to indicate that. He had a failed marriage and no children. I pay him extremely well — more than any commercial pilot — and he's very meticulous when it comes to safety. I find it hard to believe that he'd cut a deal with anyone."

"Considering what we've uncovered, we have no choice but to wait for the coroner's report before pointing fingers. We're short on time and I need to have Wayne and Dave build the floor panel for mounting the machine gun on the Zodiac. While they're doing that, I'll retro-fit the radar jammer and night vision equipment. By the time that's completed, we should have the report from Laura."

"Can Gus or I be of any assistance?"

"Perhaps when it comes to installing the monitor in the wheelhouse. Please inform me as soon as Laura's email arrives. Forward it to my email so I can run a biometric scan. Let's introduce you to my brother and Dave Bachman."

The duo left the galley and headed to the deck.

Hood Bay — 6:00 p.m.

Wearing a hoodie, Rusty climbed into the Lund, started the outboard and motored to the backside of the point overlooking the Santos property. He found a small gravelly cove near the southern tip of the island and beached the boat. After walking the shoreline with his scanner, he located the audio and video equipment Jim had planted. A watertight transmitter and adjustable video camera were connected to a small satellite dish pointing information skyward. This was high-end equipment worth tens of thousands of dollars. He quickly cut the positive lead to the power source, removed everything from the battery, and placed them into a duffle bag.

Rusty's cell rang as he climbed into his boat. Caller ID said private but he recognized the number. He answered, "Hey Mr. Cranston, what's happening."

"You wanted updates so here's the latest. Dark Star informed me old man Reid canceled the mission last night. We're not coming to Sitka tonight as planned. So,

Dark Star's out of the picture. I won't be able to participate in the special deal you alluded to. Now what?'"

"Where's Reid?"

"No idea. He pulled the plug."

"Where's Helen?"

"No clue. She doesn't report to me. What about the deal?"

"Shit, I don't know. I need to speak with Reid. I'll get back to you." Rusty hung up.

Rusty sped across the bay, returned to the pier and brought the dismantled system into the house. Keller looked at it and said, "You were correct about Bennett's surveillance equipment. He's clever."

Pointing across the bay, Rusty said, "I've got to climb that mountain before dark. Help carry my gear to the Lund and we'll talk on the way. I won't be able to communicate with you for about two hours, so this is our last chance."

The duo spoke while walking to the dock, then loaded the boat. Rusty handed Santos six identical-looking cell phones. "These are for Softail, Crane, the Boston Whaler, and you. The other two are spares if the crew needs to split up. Once they're distributed, this will be our only method of communication. No more radio, landline or personal cell phones. Bennett's infected all modes of communication. These phones are totally clean from infection and linked together. When one rings, they all ring — they act like their own tower."

Santos asked, "Can they be intercepted?"

"Only if someone has an IMSI catcher and infects our SIM cards. In order to avoid infection, keep the conversations short and to the point — always under a minute."

"I don't understand any of this 'catcher' and 'infection' jargon."

"It really doesn't matter because I do. Follow my instructions and we'll remain impenetrable."

Angoon — 6:30 p.m.

Jim sat on the couch with Danny and Audra as Lori finalized dinner. He held an M4A2 assault rifle with a detachable XM-320 grenade launcher. Both kids carefully observed Jim demonstrate how to load and fire the weapon.

"The launcher lobs 40-mm grenades and its adjustable sight makes it easy to send shells accurately providing you know the target distance."

He handed a cigarette pack sized device with an attached neck lanyard to Danny and said, "This is a laser-operated range-finder. It will provide you with the exact distance to your target. All you do is set the launcher site to that distance and squeeze the trigger.

313

It lobs grenades up to 300 meters. The grenade creates a three-meter kill-zone. It will kill anyone within that circle and severely wound anyone within a zone twice that size."

Jim's focused on the weapon's optics. "The variable-power scope provides you with ass-kick accuracy for firefights. Place the scope to your target and squeeze off one-second bursts. The M4A2 can cut a man in half at 100 meters."

Jim then demonstrated how to adjust and use the PVS-764 night-vision goggles. He carefully fit the standard version to Danny's Kevlar helmet. After tightening the harness, Jim explained its operation and focal adjustment.

Jim's children watched in awe as their father explained the various military hardware. Confident that his children were prepared for the mission, he mixed himself a drink. The phone rang before he could take his first sip.

Jim answered, "This is Jim."

"It's John. I'm entering Chatham from the Hoonah Sound side. I've made a big circle around Baranof Island. I'm currently making a huge spectacle of myself by circling the mouth of Peril. Turn your VHF radio to multicom channel 122.85. We'll have some fun."

"You've got it. Lori will do all of the talking on this end."

The enormous green chopper looked like a praying mantis as it flew up and down the gullies of Chichagof Island. Several minutes later John spoke into his radio. "This is flight 606 to base. Come in base."

Lori responded, "We copy you 606. Over."

"The timber cruiser is correct. I'm hovering over an old plane wreck in a steep ravine."

"Copy that 606. What's your current location?"

"Directly across from Hannus Bay in Peril Strait."

"Copy that. We logged the lower portions of that area ten years ago. I'm surprised our timber crew didn't find it then."

"The wreck's in a very steep drainage not worth logging The craft is vertical. It appears to have crashed nose first; looks like it's growing right out of the ground. It's surrounded by four large pines. You'd never find it unless you're right above it. Did our crew investigate the crash site?"

"Negative. They said it was too dangerous to climb into the ravine without ropes. That's why Marty called the office."

"Copy that. They'd need to descend from above with ropes and harnesses. That wouldn't appeal to anyone."

"What's the wreck's elevation?"

"I'm at 1900 feet. The wreck is probably 500 feet below me."

"How long do you think the planes been there?"

"Fifty years, maybe more."

"Copy that. Have you marked the location?"

"I've saved the coordinates to my GPS. Should we contact the authorities about the wreck?."

"Negative. I'd better discuss this with management."

"I'm low on fuel and the wind is squirrely. I need to head out. Over."

"Copy that 606. Return to Sitka. Out."

The Bennett group laughed at Jim's ruse. Audra commented on how authentic the conversation sounded. Before Jim could comment, his scanner picked up another transmission on channel 66.

"Softail to Fortuna. Come in Fortuna."

"This is Fortuna — over."

"We've been watching a Northern Lights logging helicopter and intercepted a conversation with their office in Sitka. They've located an old plane wreck in a steep ravine across from Hannus Bay."

"Copy that. My scanner picked up the transmission. We scoured that area last fall and came up empty handed, but it could be our target. Check the area while there's adequate light. Over."

"Copy that. Softail out."

Santos wondered about his new partner, Mr. Miller. He seemed convinced that Bennett knew where the wreck was and we was spinning our wheels, but a helicopter may have just located it. Miller was right about one thing They couldn't trust each other. Santos mumbled, "If I find the wreck without you, I'll let you kill my crew, deliver the Olsens, and then I'll kill *you*."

Jim noticed that his link at Santos' property was down. At first he thought it was as a result of battery failure, but then considered the possibility of Whitey disabling it. *We'll rock-n-roll soon enough, pal*, Jim thought. *Tell mama to sell the shit-house because your ass is mine.* He switched to the satellite program and saw the cutter heading toward Peril straight.

He called the Clans biologist, Hank Stytes. Hank answered and Jim began another ruse. "I saw our bear friend near the Whitewater tidal flats. You must've released him somewhere close by."

"Yep. Me, Mel and my boy released him in Wilson Cove. What time did ya see 'im?"

"Around 11:00 o'clock this morning."

"Wow. He's a real gypsy, isn't he? We released him late mornin' two days ago. That means he covered over ten miles a day. Exactly where did ya spot 'im?"

"We were at the end of the bay setting a crab pot — near the inlet. My daughter spotted him in a high meadow on the north side of that small lake."

"How do ya know it was him?"

"I carry a spotting scope. We beached my boat and watched him for over 20 minutes. I could make out the white markings on his head."

"I hope he ain't headin' back to the village."

"He looked content. He hunkered down next to a snow field. When I pulled the pot, he was in the same spot."

"He could be havin' a bad reaction to the antibiotics I gave him. Maybe ya can point it out on a map. I'll investigate tomorrow mornin'."

"I can show you, but I'll do you one better. When tomorrow's charter flight arrives for Dick's fishing camp, I'll pay them to do a quick fly over with you."

"That's mighty nice of ya Jim. What if I come right over so ya can show me the spot?"

"No problem Hank. I'll see you in a few."

Lori had listened Jim's end of the conversation. She nodded. "I wondered how you'd manage to have the clans find the wreck."

Jim smiled. "Let's assemble and I'll explain how tonight and tomorrow should shake out."

The Cutter — 7:00 p.m.

Frank, Helen and Gus met privately in the galley prior to a scheduled crew meeting. She hadn't received the coroner's report, but Helen felt that time was of the essence and that they must proceed as planned. Concerned about a mole in their ranks, Frank reluctantly agreed, providing David and Jeff surrender their personal phones and remain in the dark about detailed plans until the coroner's report arrived.

"I'll speak in general terms," Helen promised, "and stall regarding final plans, but once we mobilize equipment, I'll need to furnish specifics. The phone idea will upset them and it's best to avoid a confrontation — remember, I can't afford to lose anyone."

Frank nodded. "Do your best."

A knock announced the arrival of Jeff, David and Wayne. They got situated, and Helen offered coffee. Then, she unfolded a map. "I brought everyone here to begin mission preparation. For security reasons, I need everyone to surrender their cell phones"

Dave frowned. "Bullshit. What's that about?"

"I can't afford any breaches at this stage. We're about to embark on a sensitive and dangerous mission. There'll be no more slip-ups like what happened to Whitey. Not on my watch."

Wayne and Jeff eagerly surrendered their phones but Dave challenged her. "I didn't come out of retirement and fly halfway around the world to relinquish my only link with civilization. We've been friends for a long time, darlin'. Give me the real reason. I'll accommodate your request when you tell me the truth."

Frank intervened. "She's following my orders."

"Then I ask you, sir: why all the drama?"

Frank handed the Blackberry with the photos of Whitey to Dave and said, "We have reason to believe people from Dark Star are operating against us. They may have infiltrated this group. Until we can verify Whitey's death with the coroner's report, we have no choice but to take preventative measures. The success of this mission and our lives depend upon it."

Dave took a hard look at the pictures. He shook his head. "I appreciate your point, but this isn't Whitey. This guy's too short and stocky."

"Helen said the same, but I have decided to play it safe."

Dave slid his phone across the table toward Helen. "I'm insulted, but I guess I'm the prime candidate until the report arrives. Look, if you guys don't trust me, I'll bail now, no questions asked, but understand this: Whitey was my best friend. I intend to track down his killer and send him to hell. I did my own investigation this morning, and trust me, he's dead."

Frank smiled. "Helen, you may return everyone's phone. They surrendered their connection to the outside world. I'd say they're trustworthy. I'm sorry if I offended you Mr. Bachman. I had to be certain. Don't blame Helen. I ordered her to ask for your phones. I accept full responsibility. Can we put this behind us and discuss the mission?"

Dave was still angry. "Get this operation moving forward or I'll change my mind and leave."

Helen said "Dave, please chill. Just doing my job.

"Our objective," she continued, "is to capture a phony NOAA ship with its crew and a man known as Vicente Santos." She nodded her head toward Mr. Reid. "They're currently trying to locate the wreck of a plane once owned by Frank. They won't stop until they've retrieved it. They've already murdered Whitey, it seems. We'll set up surveillance stations and watch their movements until opportunity presents itself. We're now disguised as a Coast Guard cutter performing routine checks. We'll board the *Oregon II* on that pretense. After capturing the crew and disabling their communications, Dave, Frank and I will interrogate the crew. I also need to extract information from Santos. We must apprehend him alive so we can ascertain who the Dark Star mole is. That said, this is a kill-as-needed operation. Don't be a hero by trying to capture someone who appears threatening. We have several important tasks to complete before planning our initial strike."

Dark Fortunes

Helen pointed at the map. "First, Jeff and I need to take the chopper to the top of this island and set up my equipment."

She circled a spot on Catherine Island and another on Admiralty Island with a pencil. "I need two relay stations: one here and the other, here. Dave, you're in charge of setting up MS-5 dishes on each of these positions above the high tide line. You'll utilize the Zodiac for this after Gus positions the cutter into Echo Cove." She circled a long narrow bay on the southern tip of Catherine Island.

Helen continued. "I need the cutter anchored here with her bow facing Chatham Strait. When it's positioned and Dave returns, keep the Zodiac tethered to the cutter. I want Dave and Wayne to mount the front cannon and port side Gatling gun and cover them with canvas. Secure the medium machine gun to the Zodiac's new plywood floor, then attach the magnetic Coast Guard graphics to our ship. We have vinyl Coast Guard graphics to attach to the Zodiac. All must be completed by 2100 hours."

Gus asked, "Explain the armaments please. I'm unfamiliar with the cannon and Gatling gun. If Dave and Wayne get sidetracked in the Zodiac, Jeff or I may be forced to operate them."

Helen turned to Dave. "You have the honors — it's your ordnance."

Dave began, "Besides M16 assault rifles, we have an 80-mm breech-loaded single-shot cannon, an electrically-operated M134 Gatling gun, an M240 machine gun and a .50-caliber machine gun. I'll demonstrate the M16 to anyone not familiar with its operation. They're simple to use. The cannon shoots a small artillery round. Using a rangefinder, anyone can easily place a round onto a ship's bridge. The destruction factor is so substantial that I don't suggest using it other than to scare these guys. Our primary weapon is the Gatling gun. It's remarkably easy to operate and vicious. It fires depleted-uranium, armor-piercing rounds at 4,000 per minute. The gun will hit a 40-foot-diameter target at 4,000 yards with 85 percent accuracy and the projectiles will penetrate one-inch steel plate at that distance. A five-second burst will virtually destroy a small ship. We'll use it only if we plan to quickly sink our opponent. I'll instruct everyone on its use but use it sparingly because I've only got a minute's worth — 4,000 rounds. The .50 caliber machine gun is simple to operate. When we're done here, I'll train anyone who wishes to learn. I'll mount one next to the bridge, and one inside the chopper, overhanging the passenger side bay door. With the aid of tracers, you merely place the red lines onto the target while the gun is firing. The M240 for the Zodiac is a medium-rated machine gun."

Wayne spoke. "I'm proficient with all of these armaments, including the Gatling gun."

Dave nodded. "Excellent."

Gus asked, "Does the Gatling gun kick?"

"No, sir. It's electric. It has no kick, but it does chatter."

Silence followed and Helen stood. "Excellent, gentlemen. Every one upstairs for weapons training."

Mountain Top – Hood Bay — 10:00 p.m.

Brilliant red clouds scattered across the skies north of the snow-covered peak as Rusty dropped his pack to the ground. He had little interest in the beautiful surroundings. After catching his breath and a hearty drink from a canteen, he felt relieved. The cold penetrated his insulated pants as he sat and unlaced his boots. He quickly realized he'd need a small fire if he was going to spend the night on top of this inhospitable peak. After rubbing his sore calves, he chose an area to set up an infrared scanner, radar system and radio interceptor. Confident he'd accomplish his tasks before dark, he unzipped his coat pocket and retrieved two cell phones. He dialed Crane.

Crane knew where Rusty was. "Hey man, what's it like up there?"

"Damned, awful cold."

"Get this," Crane said. "Both he and my men on Fortuna intercepted a radio transmission from a logging helicopter. The chopper pilot located an old plane wreck near the mouth of Peril. Fortuna headed over there and sent a ground crew ashore."

"Hold while I check this out with my spotting scope."

Rusty dialed in the high-powered scope. The *Oregon II* was anchored on the north shore of Peril. With cold and shaking hands, he unfolded a map to pinpoint the area and its topography.

"This could be the real deal, partner. That sucks if it's legitimate."

"Why?"

"I won't be able to control the recovery process. We're in an awkward position with me up here. If it *is* the wreck, that means Bennett's not involved and I've been barking up the wrong tree. I'd planned on Bennett to eliminate our crew but we may be forced to do it ourselves. If we're lucky, Santos will take the initiative and eliminate the Fortuna crew with his two goons. If he does that, he'll try taking us out too."

"I see your point. What should I do?" Crane asked.

"Remain awake and keep me posted on Fortuna's progress. Buddy up to Santos and watch his movements. I'll also monitor movements and communications from here, but if Fortuna finds the plane, call me immediately. By then I'll have developed a killer plan."

"I like your choice of words. Is that it for now?"

"Affirmative — later."

Miller wasted little time setting up the surveillance equipment with its attached bank of batteries. Afterwards, he cleared an area and pitched a small survival tent. Satisfied that he was set for a cold night, he walked to the edge of the snow field and into the thick timber. Six short trips later, the traitor had managed to stockpile enough firewood for the night. He was prepared for whatever events unfolded.

CHAPTER EIGHT

June 15 — Angoon — Midnight

Carrying a Kevlar vest and weapons, Jim opened the secret closet entrance to the vault below. Danny lugged a fully-loaded pack through the narrow passageway. Audra and Lori looked on in amazement as Jim explained using the word "ACES" as a code for opening the vault.

Audra stared at her father. "Crap, oh dear, what have we here? I never knew you were a survivalist. This is crazy."

Danny grinned. "But wait, there's more." He rolled the wheeled shelf back and opened the passageway to the outside. "This puppy leads to a vertical shaft and ladder about 50 yards from here. All you need to do is close and lock everything behind you and boogie. You can slip in or out of the house in less than a minute without detection."

Lori shook her head, then shook her finger at Jim. "You're far too sneaky for this city girl. What kind of person dreams this sort of thing up?"

Jim shrugged his shoulders. "People like me, I guess. Look. This is how you'll exit the house tomorrow morning. There's an internal lock mechanism on this door that works from either direction. It's encased in one-inch, case-hardened steel — impenetrable. The combination is also ACES. Set the surveillance system before you leave and we're golden. Got it?"

Lori hugged Jim and kissed him on the lips. "Be careful, James D. Bennett —I want you back in one piece when we meet this afternoon."

Danny looked at Audra and grinned. "Don't even think of doing that to me."

She kicked him with her casted leg. "You're such a butt-sucker."

The two men ducked low and walked into the tunnel. The girls retreated back into the house, closing everything behind them.

Jim pushed the hinged lid open slightly. Convinced they were safe, he opened the hatch and offered Danny a hand into the outside world. They cautiously maneuvered through the timber toward Angoon. By 12:20, they reached the far southern end of the marina where many of the natives kept open aluminum boats.

Jim climbed into a 16-foot boat with a 40-horse motor and helped Danny aboard. It was overcast and dark. Both men donned night-vision goggles, and they navigated toward the inlet of Kootznahoo.

It was low tide, and the rocky outcrop near the inlet was clearly visible via their night technology. Jim motored at quarter throttle to remain undetected to anyone still awake in Angoon. Before reaching Chatham, Jim made a right turn into a shallow channel leading to Mitchell Bay.

Well away from Angoon, Jim opened the throttle and sped through the narrows into Mitchell Bay. He turned 90 degrees to the right and carefully passed several small islands, then followed the bay's southern shore for another quarter mile. He beached the boat on a tidal flat, and Danny strung out 200 feet of rope to the nearest tree. The boat would be afloat when the tide returned.

Danny looked at his watch and said, "Almost 0100 hours."

Jim answered, "Listen for our ride. When we hear it coming, I'll pop a flair."

A few minutes later, the thump-thump-thump of a big chopper was heard. Jim popped a short red flair and set it into the sandy flat.

"This'll be our LZ. Stand back until he's landed."

The logging 'copter approached low and quickly from the east. The pilot wasted no time setting down on the hard-packed sand. Jim tossed the flare into the water and the duo ran to their ride.

John flipped up his night-vision goggles and took a hard look at the pair. "This brings back memories, Jim. Were you in Special Forces?"

"Roger that John. I've been known to do this once or twice."

"That's how you decked that fat-ass Crane so easily. Hoo-rah, Jim Bennett. I'm liking you more as time goes on. Goggles and headphones on. Let's fly the friendly skies of Praying Mantis Airlines."

Jim said, "Keep as low as possible John. Go out the exact same way you came in. Instrument lights only."

The chopper rose fifty feet above the tide, then tore across the bay and through a narrow valley leading to Gambier Bay on the opposite side of Admiralty Island.

Mountain Top - Hood Bay —1:00 a.m.

Yellow and orange flames crackled and red sparks flew skyward as Rusty kept a sleepy eye on his monitors. Hours of climbing and constant review of the screens were taking their toll. In his trance-like state, the distant sound of a helicopter made him believe he was back in Central America. Years of Special Forces operations flashed him back to jungles and small villages of El Salvador. Then, the infrared monitor beeped, tearing him from his trance. In seconds, he realized a chopper was entering the area north of Angoon from the east. He jumped to his feet and pulled fourth-generation night-vision goggles over his eyes. Stepping away from the fire, he barely saw a helicopter clear a ridge and descend out of view. A red hue illuminated the sky but he couldn't pinpoint the origin. In less than a minute, the illumination ceased, leaving him with nothing to see but the lights of Angoon. The rhythmic thump of helicopter blades echoed in the distance, and he anxiously awaited another sighting, The sound began to move east, and he was afforded a brief glimpse of the chopper before it disappeared into the black.

He returned to the fire, warmed his hands, unfolded a map and oriented it with the area where the red light had appeared, Rusty contacted his partner by phone.

"Yeah, what time is it?"

"Just after one, asshole. You were sleeping after I told you to stay awake. I just saw a funny-looking chopper pick up something — very likely Bennett —in Mitchell Bay. Wake your fat ass up and get over to the marina. When I see the chopper returning, I'll call you. Wait for Bennett to return — see what he's carrying. If he's picking up the gold, we've got to pin down his location and movements."

"What about Softail? They've been searching across the strait."

"It's a decoy — get over to the marina. Hide where Bennett won't see you, and call me when you're in position."

Rusty cupped his hands behind his ears and listened for far off helicopter blades. Silence filled his anxious ears.

He thought, *Bennett's doing it right now —but where?*

Echo Bay —1:00 a.m.

Helen stood alone in the wheelhouse watching her monitors. For 90 minutes, she had watched a small campfire on a mountain in Hood Bay. Infrared sensors on Catherine Island forwarded images of someone with surveillance equipment while other monitors detected radar and infrared waves coming from the mountain top.

She frowned."Whoever's on that ridge has scanners too — they're sophisticated."

Loud, oscillating beeps interrupted her thoughts as the infrared scanner, night-vision sensor and radar picked up a bogey to the northeast. All three green monitors caught a chopper clearing a ridge and then dropping into cover of an apparent valley. A red glow suddenly filled the upper quadrant of the infrared screen. Moments later, it disappeared and the screen turned solid green.

That was a flare, Helen thought. Shortly, her screens lit up again and oscillating beeps filled the wheelhouse. The bogey reappeared, crested the ridge again, and dropped out of sight where it had originated from. By measuring the distance on her IR screen to the bogey, she identified the area where the flare had been and the ridge the bogey had crossed. She whispered to herself, "I bet that's Bennett."

Helen spoke into her headphone. "Wayne, I need you in here ASAP."

"On my way."

Her tall, slender, unshaven brother entered the dark wheelhouse wearing a coast guard suit with a Kevlar helmet and vest. Night-vision goggles and an M16 rounded out his attire. He flipped up his goggles. "What's happening, sis?"

Helen pointed to a map. "I just got a positive hit on a chopper over here and a flare over there. Did you hear anything on deck?"

"Absolutely. But it must have been twenty miles north of our position."

She pointed to the mountain near Hood Bay. "Check out the dipstick with the campfire. He's monitoring the Straits, just like us."

"Do you think it's Dark Star or Santos or both?"

"Most likely one of those combos. Watch these screens for me and call if anything changes. I'll be on top of the bridge with my 'Big Ear.' Maybe I'll be able to ascertain the chopper's flight path."

Helen ran to her stateroom and retrieved the audio enhancer. She scrambled up the ladder to the roof of the bridge. With her headset held to her right ear, she slowly began sweeping the dish from left to right. A chopper's sound was audible to the north. An ever-increasing rhythmic thumping clearly defined the chopper's course as north-to-south. Helen spoke into her radio. "Wayne, it's east of our position and getting closer. Can you see anything on the monitors?"

"Nothing — just our neighbor with the campfire."

Helen dropped the headset and pulled her goggles down. She looked toward the oncoming sound. Almost magically, the enormous bird cleared a ridge east of Whitewater Bay, then dove back into the darkness. Wayne confirmed the bogey and marked its location. The chopper reappeared, climbed the north slope of the bay and then hovered. Helen and Wayne observed the event without saying a word.

Mountain Top — Hood Bay —1:15 a.m.

Rusty strained to see the chopper southeast of his position. Several peaks blocked his view as he desperately searched for the helicopter. He adjusted the night goggles and cupped his ears in order to enhance the thumping sound. He struggled in vain to locate the craft, which seemed to be hovering several miles south of him. He yelled "GOD DAMN IT!" and kicked the snow in anger.

He called Crane. "Where are you?"

"Getting into the Zodiac."

"I think Bennett's picking up the gold just south of here. Get over to the marina before he returns. Call me when he gets there."

"I'm on it."

The turncoat stomped the snow in frustration, listening to the thumping blades.

Whitewater Bay —1:15 a.m.

The chopper sped over the steep, narrow mountain pass separating Whitewater from Eliza Harbor and ducked into a valley. Relying strictly on his night-vision goggles, John deftly maneuvered the helicopter through the rugged terrain to the innermost tidal flat. Choosing a suitable spot, he gracefully set the chopper onto the flat and spoke into his helmet radio. "This is as good a spot as any. This is our jump-off point. Danny, communicate with us at all times. We can't see what you can. Let's get busy."

Danny had pulled a snowmobile suit over his clothing during the short flight from Mitchell Bay and secured a five point harness to his body. He wore night goggles, heavy gloves, a Kevlar vest and a helmet with an internal radio connected to the chopper's frequency. An M16A2 was slung over his shoulder. Jim unstrapped, tossed out the cargo net and quickly unwound one hundred feet of steel cable from the winch. Danny stepped out of the side bay door and looked at his father.

Jim spoke into his helmet microphone. "We rehearsed this at home. Make certain each side of your safety harness is attached to the cable, and fasten the chest clip as well. Place your feet on top of the steel ball — not the net. Can you do this?"

"Piece of cake. I'll contact you when I'm set." Moments later, he said, "Let's do it."

The chopper rose until the cable slack disappeared, and John hovered while Danny secured his harness. Danny spoke over his radio. "I'm secure."

Standing next to the winch, Jim tapped John's shoulder and gave thumbs up. John nodded and slowly ascended to 1,000 feet, then turned the bird uphill.

Danny's heart pounded with excitement as he stood on the large steel ball. The timber below him shrank, and he laughed out loud. He thought, *This is the coolest thing I've ever done.*

John slowly angled up the steep slope. Jim pointed to the upper meadow. "John, there's a snowfield to the right of that meadow. Position us over the bottom right hand edge of the snow near the rock upthrust. Danny? We're almost there. Get ready to bail."

Danny responded, "I hear you and I can see the snow field. I'll let you know when the headache ball touches the turf."

John positioned the giant "mantis" with surgical precision and slowly descended. Jim watched the cable's heavy steel ball touch ground.

Danny yelled, "I'm down."

Within seconds, he released his harness from the cable, unhooked the cargo net and motioned to his father to back the chopper away.

John moved the chopper laterally to the downhill side and maintained his altitude. Jim watched his son drag the heavy cargo net ten meters to the stockpile and unfold it.

Danny was running on pure adrenalin and carried two canisters at a time to the net, but after three trips, his body said, "No more double loads."

Time stood still for the trio as the net slowly filled with gold-laden canisters. Jim surveyed the surrounding landscape for intruders and kept track of Danny's progress. Soon all the canisters would be positioned on the net.

Winded, Danny finally pulled the net's four corner straps together and spoke into his radio. "Ready for the cable."

John put the chopper and cable over Danny's position while Jim kept a sharp eye on the heavy steel ball. The rigging was stable but ten feet higher than before. John was prepared to lower the chopper, but Jim insisted on lowering the cable with the winch for greater control. The last thing he wanted was Danny hurt. The cable and ball were in place, but Danny struggled with connecting the last corner strap to the large hook. The weight of the net prevented him from pulling the strap any closer. He fought to make the awkward connection.

Finally, Danny said, "I need a foot of slack. I can't attach the last corner."

Jim obliged by lowering the winch another foot. Danny continued struggling with the final strap. Looking below, Jim realized the gold was not centered within the net and that additional slack was not helping. He instructed Danny to unhook the other three straps and attach the problem strap first. He would utilize the winch to pull the strap even with the other three. Danny was reluctant, but soon realized it was an easy fix. In less than a minute, all four straps were connected and Danny's harness was secured to the cable.

Jim spoke into his radio "Are you ready? It's going to be a long, cold ride."

Danny was tired and achy, but he said, "I'll manage — let's boogie."

Jim lifted the cable 20 feet above the ground, enabling the cargo net to hang freely. "Alright John, let's go."

John said, "I don't know what's in that net, but it's heavy. This beast is maxed out. How are you doing down there, young fella?"

Danny answered, "Freezing my ass off."

Jim spoke. "That's enough chatter. Concentrate on what we're doing."

Rather than descend into the valley, John headed directly into the pass linking Whitewater to Eliza Harbor. Jim retracted the cable another 20 feet, ensuring adequate ground clearance when making the Eliza crossing.

Danny shivered as he hung onto the thick cable, but he felt a sense of accomplishment like he'd never experienced before. The fear, excitement, adventure and an unparalleled adrenalin rush was addicting. He understood how his father must have felt during Delta missions. Danny's thoughts shifted to Helen and her insistence of leaving this profession. *She must be playing me —how could anyone our age not enjoy this.*

Finally, he considered that killing other humans would throw another twist into things. Would it add to the excitement or leave an unwanted psychological scar? Helen had brushed off his question earlier. He'd have his father enlighten him about this at a later date.

The chopper cleared the pass and began a descent into a valley leading to Eliza Bay. John followed a small river which ended in a small bay on Eliza's west shore. Jim saw the old salmon cannery on the east shore of the long narrow bay. Mother Nature had decided to reclaim the cannery decades ago. Trees had grown through and now towered above the fallen structure. The colonel pointed to the tidal flats at the mouth of the river and said, "This is our landing zone. Twenty meters upstream will be the drop point."

John nodded and positioned the chopper over the landing zone while Jim lowered the cable. Jim spoke to Danny. "This is where you get off. We'll stow the net 25 meters west of here. I'm throwing the camouflaged tarp out the bay door. Get to the drop point and unhook the net. I'll retract the cable while you cover our cargo. We'll set down at the landing zone to pick you up."

"I'm on it."

Five minutes later, Danny entered the heated cab of the helicopter, shivering from the cold ride. John handed him a thermos of hot coffee which he gladly accepted. Jim slapped his son on the top of his helmet and said, "Great job son! We'll be in Petersburg in 15 minutes."

Echo Cove —1:30 a.m.

Helen flipped up her night goggles, picked up the "Big Ear" and returned to the wheelhouse. Helen opened the door and found her brother hunched over with a ruler and compass in hand, studying a USGS map of Admiralty Island. He looked up at Helen, down at his map, then back at the night-vision monitor. By comparing the infrared and radar screens with the night-vision monitor, he located the precise area where the bogie was observed. He penciled in its entry and exit routes as well as the hover zone.

"Well, bro, what do you know?"

He pointed to the map. "Here's their route and this is where they hovered. Did you manage to see anything?"

"I watched the entire event. I'm convinced it was Bennett. The chopper carried a sling when they left. They may have found the wreck and cleaned the site. What's our friend across the way doing?"

"He just restoked the fire. That's about it."

"Any traffic on Chatham or Hood Bay."

"Negative. The NOAA ship is still anchored inside of Peril. Aside from the chopper and our neighbor across the strait, it's been quiet."

"Go downstairs and wake Jeff. It's your turn to get some sleep."

The tall, gangly man left the wheelhouse while Helen studied the map. She murmured to herself, "Be careful Danny."

Mountain Top — Hood Bay — 1:30 a.m.

As the chopper sound subsided, Rusty focused back toward Mitchell Bay. If his theory was correct, the helicopter would return within a half hour. He used the opportunity to call his partner. "Hey, where are you?"

"I'm entering Angoon harbor. I'll be at the marina in less than 5 minutes."

"Good. Hide somewhere with a view of the opening to Mitchell Bay. The chopper should be arriving shortly. I want to know how Bennett's dealing with the cargo. Call me when you know something."

Shivering profusely, he returned to the warmth of the fire and his tent. He'd hunker down for another twenty minutes before watching Mitchell Bay.

Warm Springs Bay — 6:15 a.m.

The blue De Havilland Beaver descended and gently landed on the glassy-slick waters of Warm Springs Bay. Jim immediately texted Lori. "All systems go. Get to the seaplane dock ASAP." He then assessed the bay for activity.

As they taxied toward the small marina, John turned to the white-haired old sea captain. "How long do you plan on staying in Warm Springs, Mr. Smith?"

Danny laughed, and a stocky, gray-haired Tlingit sitting in the rear seat answered. "Just long enough for an espresso. Listen up, John. What we did last night is confidential and strictly between us. Don't ask any questions and we'll tell you no lies."

"For a 100 grand, I'll take this little adventure to my grave. I finally own this bird free and clear. I won't jeopardize that."

The De Havilland reached the dock next to the Bayliner and both passengers stepped out onto the plane's pontoon. Jim handed John a satchel filled with hundred-dollar bills and said, "There are seventy bank packs containing two grand each. I figure a bonus is in order for a job well done."

John beamed. "Now I can even afford fuel!" he joked.

Jim said, "Tell Audra and Lori that we'll meet them later today. Thanks again and have a safe trip."

Jim pushed the plane away from the dock while Danny lugged a heavy pack to the Bayliner. Moments later, the powerful plane turned into the wind for take-off. Danny warmed up the cruiser as Jim untied mooring ropes and pulled the inflated fenders onto the deck. The Bayliner backed out of its slip, in time to watch the blue plane roar toward Angoon. Jim entered the cabin and said, "We'd better top off with fuel. It's a long haul to Juneau."

Angoon — 6:30 a.m.

Both women giggled as they looked at themselves in the master bathroom mirror.

Audra said, "You're lookin' mighty decrepit these days, Candice. Ya better take your Centrum Silver along with a hearty dose of Boniva. Wouldn't want ya ta break a hip."

Lori turned sideways to get a better view. "Well, let me tell ya something gal. Ya ain't no spring chicken yourself. Ya musta gained fifty pounds since I last saw ya."

They broke into laughter at the disguises Jim had concocted the night before. Lori asked, "Did Jim ever do this to you kids for Halloween?"

"No. Come to think of it, I can't remember him being home for Halloween."

"Oh dear, I'm sorry I asked. I should have known. Come on, we've got to set the security system, get down to the vault and into the trees before your dad calls. Are you going to be able to walk without your crutches?"

"If we walk slowly."

After setting the alarms and negotiating the vault, Lori opened the outside escape hatch and looked around. Convinced that they were safe, she placed two small duffel bags, and two Tech-9s onto the mossy ground and climbed out. She reached into the cavity and helped Audra onto the forest floor. Oscar whined from the confines of his soft, black traveling bag. After closing the steel lid, Lori assured him that he wouldn't need to be in the bag much longer.

The women stowed their guns under heavy old coats and began the trek to Angoon. Lori's Blackberry chimed. She'd received a text message. A quick look verified everything was a go. They were to proceed to the main dock. Upon reaching the school, they changed course to the marina. The timber was sparse and littered with trash the bear had spread around on one of his many nightly raids.

Before long, they passed several houses with barking dogs. Oscar growled from his prison as the duo maneuvered around homes, walking between trees. After passing the buildings, the main dock came into view and they were greeted by the asphalt road that paralleled the bay. The roar of an incoming seaplane announced John's arrival. The women carefully looked up and down the road before exiting the timber. Convinced it was safe, they walked onto the pavement and quickly toward the dock.

A large man hidden in the trees above the marina observed the incoming plane. He immediately contacted someone by phone as the flight touched down.

"I hope you're calling to say Bennett arrived."

Crane said, "I haven't seen anything other than the plane that just arrived. You must have seen it coming in."

"I did. It came from somewhere south of here. Maybe Bennett's on the plane."

"Hold on. Two people are walking down the gangplank. Nah, it's Candice Engels and a native woman. It's the same plane Bennett always uses —a blue De Havilland from Juneau."

"What's the pilots' name?"

"I don't know. Hold on. He's docked. I'm glassing him. No one besides him on board. He's simply picking up the two old hags."

"This sucks. Did you see anyone come out of Mitchell Bay last night?"

"Nope."

"Anything unusual happen at the marina?"

"Yeah. I stood in the cold and got chewed by mosquitoes. How much longer do I need to hang around this dump?"

"Give it until 10:00. I'll call you then."

The plane accelerated toward the mouth of Chatham and soon became airborne. Lori released Oscar onto her lap and asked John, "Have you ever seen such good looking babes as the two of us?"

"Can't say that I have. Jim sent his regards and said he'll meet up with both of you later today."

Audra said, "I hope everything went OK last night. Any broken bones, cuts or bruises?"

"Other than Danny freezing his ass off, I'd say it was quick and painless."

John banked the airplane north and gained altitude. Lori pointed out several whale spouts to Audra as John concentrated on his duties. Distant rain awaited as the dark blue plane headed toward Juneau. Lori looked east into the endless landscape of snow-covered mountains, rivers and waterfalls. She understood why Jim came here to clear his head.

Helen stood in the wheelhouse and sipped hot tea, still observing the monitors. The radar indicated an easterly flight originating from the Frederick Sound area. She set down her cup, and located the plane with her powerful binoculars. The plane banked north and began to descend on a path to Warm Springs. Groggy from lack of sleep, she flashed back to the wonderful time she had with Danny at that mystical spot. She wondered if and when she'd ever speak with him again.

The wheelhouse door opened, tearing her from her thoughts. Frank and Gus entered. She relocated the inbound flight with the binoculars and recognized it as the plane she flew on with Ernie.

Frank asked, "Why don't you get some sleep? You look exhausted."

"Not yet. I had a busy night and I believe Bennett was at the center of it. It could be him in that plane."

"What happened last night?"

"Not yet. I'm watching."

Moments later she said, "Kudos to you Mr. Bennett. I bet you pulled it off."

Frank was puzzled. "Pulled what off?"

"Located your wreck and cleaned the plane out for you, that's all. I'll fill you in as soon as the plane lands."

Moments later, she briefed the cousins on the events that had taken place. She pointed out the helicopter's flight path and hovering location. She also pointed out the person camped out on top of Hood Bay. The De Havilland left Warm Springs. She stopped her dissertation and studied the plane with her binoculars. This time, only a pilot was visible as it passed by. The radar atop Catherine Island tracked the flight toward Angoon. She felt it would be a while before it took off again, and continued her report. As she finished, the ship's radar picked up a boat leaving Warm Springs.

Looking through her binoculars, she giggled. "Bennett's a crafty bugger alright. He's got *my* boat altered to look like a fishing charter. They're heading to where I lost sight of the chopper last night. I'll bet you a biscuit that he's picking up the gold."

Frank looked at Gus and shrugged his shoulders. He asked Gus, "Are you getting any of this?"

"Not at all."

Helen turned and said, "That's all right gentlemen. All you need to know is that I'm damned sure Bennett managed to get the gold out last night."

Gus asked, "What now?"

"Sit and wait. I'll send our chopper out in about an hour to see that Bennett's not interfered with. Other than that, we look for an offensive strike opportunity."

Eliza Harbor —7:30 a.m.

The Bayliner stopped at the mouth of the long narrow bay on the southern end of Admiralty and Jim scanned the surrounding water and sky for other boats or planes. Certain they were alone, he instructed Danny to hurry toward the cove so they could retrieve the gold. Within a few minutes, Jim pointed to the small river where they'd dumped their cargo. The tide was in and the tidal flat was flooded with six feet of water.

Danny said, "This doesn't look like the spot. Is this it?"

"It is. Drop the front anchor and back toward shore. When it gets too shallow, I'll have you cut the engine and I'll jump in."

Standing on the swim ladder, Jim motioned for Danny to stop and jumped into the cold, waist-deep water pulling a rope he'd attached to a transom cleat. On shore, he pulled the slack out of the rope and walked to the waiting pile of gold. After tying the rope tight to one of the canisters, he began the arduous task of bringing the gold to the rear swim step. Danny stowed the canisters in the bowels of the craft while Jim acted as transport mule. It took over two minutes per trip and Jim tired from the weight and cold water. Ninety minutes later, though, he made a final trip to the waiting Bayliner. After climbing aboard, he happily changed into dry clothing.

Danny lifted anchor and accelerated out of the cove. A Coast Guard helicopter passed overhead as the boat cleared the bay. Danny pointed to it with a puzzled look.

Jim assessed the situation. "Don't worry about it. They're heading away from us."

Jim frowned. "The boat's sitting weird. It's front-heavy. We're plowing through the water. We need to redistribute weight to the stern so we can get on step. Ten containers should do the trick. I'm beat up. You've been drafted. I'll navigate while you balance the boat. We'll take Stephens Passage, which is new to me, but we won't be seen by anyone from the Chatham side. I'm thinking we're four, maybe five hours from Juneau."

After completing his assignment, Danny stood next to his father. "Is it balanced?"

"Much better. We're only making twenty knots, so sit back and enjoy the ride."

Danny asked, "Are you hungry or thirsty?"

Jim responded, "No thanks, I'm fine. Tell me, though. What did you think about our little adventure last night?"

"Ass-kickin' cool — I enjoyed the hell out of it. How about you?"

"It brought back memories — some good, some not so good."

"While I was riding that cable last night I wondered what it felt like to kill someone."

"Whatever made you think of that?"

"Here we are, armed to the teeth, pulling off a dangerous mission with all sorts of bad people looking for us. The thought of using lethal force crossed my mind. I wondered what it felt like."

Jim sighed. "I never thought about it while it was happening. When people are trading lead, shit just happens."

"So do you think about it afterwards?"

"Of course. Not a day goes by without thinking about what I've done — not one. When you kill someone, you've taken away everything they have. I rationalized my actions by telling myself it's part of my job. Being a soldier, it's either them or me, and the desire for self-preservation is pretty damn strong. If not, *you* end up in the body bag."

"Any regrets?"

"About what? Killing someone or life in general?"

"Both."

"I have no regrets about the people I've killed. They made the same choice as me. During combat, you do a better job than your enemy or you die. However, I regret what I did to our family. I chose my country over all else, which ultimately led to endangering the family. Your mother was right when she said that my ideology jeopardized you kids."

"I don't get it. We had a great childhood and were never in any danger."

Jim hesitated, then said, "That's not true. A hit was ordered on me and the family by the Medellin Cartel. That's when you moved to Grandad's ranch in Wyoming."

"I thought we moved to Casper because mom got tired of living at Ft. Bragg."

"After the Contra affair, I transferred to the CIA's drug unit and orchestrated the take-down of Pablo Escobar. I quickly identified his network as a major cocaine distributor in Miami. Simultaneously, Walt Diller infiltrated Escobar's Panamanian connections, which gave us access to the Cartel. Once inside, we identified the big players and made plans to destroy them. Walt was exposed in Panama, and Escobar realized who I was. He ordered the hit."

"Holy crap."

Jim kept his eyes on the water and continued. "Grandfather whisked the family away to Wyoming. I went to Columbia to organize 'Los Pepes,' the group that achieved the death of Escobar. I coached Los Pepes death squads and commanded Delta operatives who assassinated people involved with the Cartel. Satisfied with the results — after Escobar was dead — I went to Miami, personally hunted down his U.S. network and destroyed them. The DEA and Miami police thought a turf war had broken out between competing distributors. In actuality, we simply killed every distributor we found. After the dust settled, Escobar's distribution network was destroyed."

"Jesus Christ! That's what got between you and Ma?"

Jim looked down and nodded. "The Escobar contract on us was the last straw. I'd dug such a deep hole by jeopardizing the family, I couldn't crawl out. Every day I regret what I put her through."

Danny said, "Wow, I had no idea. The other day, Helen said your military record was virtually blacked out, which meant you were involved in top-secret shit. What if you hadn't transferred into the CIA? What then?"

"I'd probably be a two-star general on the Joint Chiefs of Staff. Truth is, I'd rather be here with you. Family and friends are what's important in life. I should've understood that before burning bridges with your mother, but I got swept up in myself."

Danny nodded. "The rush of what we did last night and what we're doing now makes me feel very alive. That's it, isn't it?"

Jim nodded. "It's addicting — and like all addictions, it's also a trap."

"What about Helen and PMCs like Dark Star?"

"Fuck 'em. Most are adrenalin junkies and money grubbing whores."

"Do you think that way about Helen?"

"Not quite."

Danny frowned, "Why not?"

"I've researched her. She was British Special Ops and damn good at it. She has stellar reviews, which speak to her character. After her time with MI-6, she joined Scotland Yard, but couldn't handle the monotony. I think she joined Dark Star out of boredom with promises of adventure and money — the same adrenalin you're experiencing. She seems fed up with Dark Star and wants out. She may be in love with you. I don't know. Only you can answer that. I will say this: she's got a face and body that will let her get away with anything when it comes to men and she knows that. You know what I'm saying."

Danny nodded. "She's told me the same thing about Dark Star. As for looks, she certainly has a face and body that lets her get away with stuff. I've fallen for her, but I question if I'm being played."

"Follow your instincts son."

"What do your instincts tell you about her?"

"She was taken over by the rush of being a PMC but realizes it's a dead-end street. Like me, she's trying to dig out of a self-created hole."

Danny patted his dad's shoulder. "Thanks for telling me the truth about the past and giving me your insight. You're awesome."

Jim smiled. "I couldn't ask for a better son."

The Bayliner sped along the inland waterway and approached an elegant white cruise ship. Scores of people stood on deck, soaking in the magnificent panorama. They would probably conclude their cruise in Skagway and headed straight back to Seattle or Vancouver. Danny used the opportunity to text message Helen and apologized for being so confrontational.

Juneau —9:00 a.m.

The two old hags finished breakfast in a small diner, giggling like teenagers at a slumber party. It was exciting to play the role of someone else without anyone suspecting. Oscar laid obediently in Lori's lap as she sipped her coffee. Occasionally, she'd slip him a tidbit from her plate. Light drizzle fell outside, and a group of tourists walked the sidewalks, umbrellas in hand.

Most cruise lines promoted Juneau as a must-see destination. Scores of souvenir shops —dependent on tourism — lined Main Street. Most of the shops were owned by the cruise lines and operated by locals, and tourists were compelled to buy things they didn't need. Most items ended up in thrift shops or garage sales after the buyer discovered they were made in China.

Audra scoured the Sunday paper for a one-ton pick-up truck with a canopy. Two vehicles matched their needs but both were older than Jim wanted.

She pointed them out to Lori. "They're old, but might be worth looking at. The more expensive one is only $4,500."

Lori said, "Who cares if it's old. All it needs to do is run from the dock to a storage unit. Jim will sell it when we're done anyway."

"You're right. Call for addresses while I hail a cab."

A few minutes later, a beat-up, dirty-yellow taxi picked up the two women from the shelter of the restaurant's awning. Rather than get out and open the trunk for their bags, the driver popped the lid from inside and waited for his passengers to get in. Audra didn't mind, but Lori didn't appreciate his lack of manners. Inside, a dirty, unshaven man in his early forties asked, "Where to."

Audra answered, "Twenty-one-twelve Dogwood Lane."

The driver placed the car into gear. The cab reeked of stale beer and cigarettes, which annoyed Lori. The smell was so bad, Oscar buried his head in Lori's coat during the short ride. After seeing the first truck from inside the cab, Lori asked to be taken to the second address. The cab driver shrugged and drove on.

The second truck was a one-ton Dodge Ram with a canopy and looked much better than the first. Audra remained in the taxi while Lori knocked on the door.

A heavyset woman answered the door and walked to the truck with Lori. The woman had a difficult time climbing into the truck due to her weight. After she started it, Lori asked, "Why are you selling?"

"My husband got a job on the North Slope and told me to sell it. Says he's buyin' a new one when he returns. I got my Honda and never use this diesel-smellin' heap."

Convinced that the truck was adequate, Lori said, "If you have a clear title, I can do the deal today."

"Yep."

When the woman returned with the paperwork, Lori said, "I'll give you what you want for it but I need the plates too."

"My husband would kill me."

"I don't want to hassle with registering this thing right away, so I'll throw in an additional $500. Once it's registered, I'll return the plates prior to their expiration date."

The heavy-set woman thought for a moment. "They expire in August — that OK with you?"

Lori reached into her purse and counted out fifty 100-dollar bills. "That works. Sign the title and the cash is yours. I'll return the plates before the end of August."

After retrieving their bags from the taxi's trunk, Lori went to the drivers' window to pay the bill. The man rolled down the window and said, "That's sixteen bucks."

Lori dug into her purse and found a ten, a five and four quarters. She handed it to him.

He barked, "Hey, what about a tip, lady?"

"Yes indeed, here's a tip: shower and shave every day, learn some manners, clean the stench out of this piece-of-shit cab, handle your customers luggage. And, smoking will kill you. Six tips. Priceless."

The driver mumbled something obscene and sped off. Audra laughed at the cab driver's reaction to Lori's remarks. She high-fived Lori.

After getting into their new ride, Audra said, "This is perfect for the job. We need to find a place called Glacier Storage Center on Shuane Drive. Dad said he wants a private indoor unit that's lockable."

With a false Alaska driver's license — provided by Jim — Lori filled out paperwork for a rental unit. The manager barely looked at the license. He was more concerned about the first month's payment. After satisfying the manager's request, the old hags headed to the hardware store for a case hardened padlock and a hand truck. The plan was to meet Jim and Danny at the marina and transfer the gold.

Angoon —9:30 a.m.

Hank and Mel handed an Alaska Seaplane Charter pilot three hundred-dollar bills — also provided by Jim — and entered the De Havilland. Several Tlingit women at the seaplane dock were irritated at the change in regular service, but Hank explained that the flight would return in twenty minutes to pick them up and that the flight was in the best interest of the Clans. Grudgingly, the unhappy group looked on as the commandeered flight took off without them.

Hank sat in the co-pilot's seat with an open map in his lap as the powerful plane became airborne. The pilot executed a large circle over Chatham to gain altitude before flying over Whitewater. Mel kept his nose glued to the window and watched the world below. The weather was deteriorating on mountaintops surrounding Angoon as another weather front near Juneau made itself known. Content that he had enough altitude to safely negotiate the rugged peaks, the pilot flew over mountains above Whitewater Bay. Hank pointed out the meadows where the Bennetts said they had observed the bear while the pilot made large banking circles. After five minutes of circling the area, Hank pointed out something peculiar to Mel.

"Hey Mel, is that the tail of an airplane on that snowfield or are my eyes playin' tricks on me?"

One circle later Mel answered. "I'll be dam'. It's the tail of an old airplane alright. Look against that rock wall. I can see wings just under the snow."

"I see what you're talking about. Judgin' from the rust on that tail, it musta been here for a God-awful long time," added Hank.

"Yeah. It's really weathered. I don't see no sign of the bear, so he must be OK. Let's head back and rassle up a party to go look at that plane."

"Garfield and Sam ain't doin' nothin' special today. They can be our shovel brigade."

The pilot asked, "Are we done here gentlemen? I've got a schedule to keep."

"Yep," said Mel.

The De Havilland banked to the south and five minutes later it taxied to the seaplane dock. Hank and Mel thanked the pilot and apologized to the anxious passengers standing near the rain shelter. The Tlingit elders hurried up the ramp to gather a search party.

Echo Bay — 9:30 a.m.

Helen watched her monitors and chugged an ice cold Coke. Another aircraft landed in Angoon, then took off toward Whitewater Bay. The plane circled the area where the helicopter had been the night before. It was a different plane than the previous one and the pilot was much more tentative. The circles were large and deliberate when he banked the De Havilland; not crisp and quick like the chopper.

She marked the plane on her radar and compared its circular pattern to the hovering helicopter's. They were obviously after the same target. The plane's flight was short-lived and returned to Angoon. Helen called her outbound chopper on a multicom channel and asked, "CG 27 to CG 31. Do you copy?"

"Roger CG 27 —we copy. Over."

"What's your location."

"Stevens Passage."

"Have you made visual contact with the target vessel?"

"Yes."

"Return to base."

"Roger that. Out."

The Sikorsky banked left over Admiralty, intercepted Chatham Strait 20 miles north of Angoon and pitched slightly forward, speeding across Chichagof Island toward Sitka. After crossing Peril Straight, it ran toward Sitka until the *Oregon II* and the observer above Hood Bay were beyond visual range; then crossed Baranof Island into Kelp Bay. Fifty feet above the ocean, it rounded the corner of Catherine Island and snuck into Echo Bay. It landed on the deck of the cutter and quickly shut down. Wayne ran to the wheelhouse while Jeff secured the chopper.

"Well, bro," Helen asked, "where's Bennett going with my boat?"

"He's headed to Juneau through Stevens Passage."

"Did he see our chopper?"

"Perhaps while leaving Eliza Bay, but after initial contact, Jeff flew seven thousand feet above and two miles behind him. I'm convinced they didn't notice us."

"What about the NOAA ship. Still anchored off the tip of Baranof?"

"Yes. They've got a small boat tied to shore, which tells me there's personnel on the ground."

"Is Santos' catamaran tied at his dock?"

"Yes."

"That's it. Did you see the observer above Hood?"

"Yes. He's got a small tent and several satellite dishes aimed toward the Strait."

"Could you make him out?"

"When he heard the chopper, he scrambled into the tent. You want me to hike up there and grab him? I could have him before dinner."

"Not yet. Let's see what he does. If things don't develop by tonight, we'll take him out."

338

Helen changed the subject. "A bush plane just flew circles around the same area we observed the chopper in last night. Then it returned to Angoon. Ten minutes later, it took off and headed toward Tenakee. Did you notice anything unusual in that area or on the ridge top overlooking Whitewater?"

"I inspected the area with my binocs flying over Admiralty, but I didn't see anything but snow, rocks and trees."

"I think it's the wreck site," Helen said.

"Maybe, maybe not." Wayne paused. "At the risk of upsetting you, you're spaced out and look like crap — you need sleep. I can keep an eye on the monitors. Get out of here."

"Not now, bro. Maybe later."

Frank and Gus entered the wheelhouse. Frank looked at Helen and asked, "Have you had any sleep yet?"

"No, but I will soon enough."

Frank gave her an enormous hug with his left arm. "I appreciate all you're doing, but I insist that you at least take a nap. There are enough of us on board to handle things and we're at a standstill anyway. After you update me, I expect you to get a few hours of sleep. That's an order, young lady."

Helen knew Frank and Wayne were right. If she was to be of value to the team, she needed to rest. After briefing Wayne about what might happen in Whitewater, she provided the Olsens with an update. Minutes later, she was lying in bed thinking about Danny. Helen wondered how to reconcile with him when a text message came through her Blackberry. It was from Danny, who apologized for being rude. He added that he missed her and that he'd make up for his cheeky remarks when they hooked up. Relieved, Helen's mind slowed. She relaxed and her eyes grew heavy. Moments later, she slept.

Mountain Top – Hood Bay —9:45 a.m.

A cold and wet Rusty watched with powerful binoculars as a float plane circle Whitewater. Earlier, a Coast Guard helicopter had passed overhead, and he wondered if there was a connection between it and the plane. He was plagued with unanswered questions and his mind raced: Why didn't Bennett return to Mitchell Bay last night? Where might he take the gold? Where was Frank Reid and why did he cancel the operation? Why was the Coast Guard cruising the Straits? And what was behind the logging chopper reporting a wreck late yesterday? He sat in cold isolation as the float plane returned to Angoon.

Suddenly, he understood Bennett's ruse.

"Goddammit!" He immediately called Santos.

Santos answered, "This is Fortuna. How are things on top of the mountain?"

Rusty answered, "Cold and wet. Let's see if everyone's connected to this phone system. Rich are you there?

"Affirmative, I'm listening from metropolitan Angoon."

He then asked, "Softail are you there?"

A raspy voice answered. "I read you loud and clear."

Rusty continued, "What's the status of your men on Chichagof?"

"They've just finished clearing one ravine. I swear it was the one that the chopper was hovering over but apparently not. They're about to cross over into the next ravine and work their way down the mountain."

"They won't find anything because it's a decoy used by Bennett. He's been busy all night recovering the gold."

Santos barked, "Nonsense. How can you make such a preposterous assertion?"

"Because I watched him being picked up by a chopper in the Angoon backwaters at 1 a.m. last night. I'm convinced he removed the gold from a mountain south of my position. Rich has been watching the marina since 1:30 to see if he returns."

Santos asked, "Rich, is Bennett's boat at the marina?"

"Yes, sir."

"How can you explain that Mr. Miller? His boat's at the marina and his Humvee is in the driveway?"

"He's using a different boat and he's got a secret way of leaving his home. I want everyone to listen to what I'm saying because I'll only say this once. I'm good at what I do, but he's the best there is. He trains people like me. Misdirection and confusion coupled with real-time information is how he operates. Right now he's at least two steps ahead of us. The chopper we saw yesterday afternoon is the same one Bennett used to recover the gold. He's removed us from the equation with misdirection. Our assets were in Peril Strait when they should have been at the entrance of Whitewater. Now he's engaged in another ruse to divert our attention by having a float plane circle the area he was in last night. I also believe he's orchestrating the Coast Guard chopper that's been flying around us all morning."

Rich added, "Hey, a Coast Guard chopper cut across Admiralty ten minutes ago."

Softail chimed in. "Yeah. It headed across Peril toward Sitka just as you called. I also saw a float plane circling a ridge above Whitewater."

"I intercepted a Coast Guard communication about ten minutes ago," Santos said. "It seemed quite routine. Mr. Miller, what do you propose we do?"

"I need to track Bennett's movements in real time. Get our men off of Chichagof now and position the ship at the confluence of Peril and Chatham. Keep the engines running so you can leave on a moment's notice. Vicente, there's a sea bag full of cameras and transmitters in the bedroom I slept in. Each unit has an instruction manual explaining their setup. Someone place a camera and transmitter on both sides of Bennett's house and another on Killisnoo Island across the narrows facing his house. The camera at the seaplane dock is down. I need another one placed. Vicente, on some pretense, call the natives and find out who was circling the ridge at Whitewater."

"Here's the tough one, have someone bring two fully-charged car batteries up here. That'll free me up to operate my equipment remotely. Finally I need all of our boats in the water, topped with fuel and ready for action."

Santos was upset. "If Bennett has the gold, what good will any of this do?"

"He's moved the gold down the mountain but couldn't have moved it out of Whitewater. It weighs too much. He should make a play for it shortly. If not we storm his house and extract the information the old fashioned way."

Santos sounded pleased. "I can only imagine how thrilling that would be. Mr. Miller, what's the status of the two cousins?"

"They should be here shortly. As soon as they arrive, I'll contact you."

Santos confirmed the orders. "Alright gentlemen, you've heard Mr. Miller. Let's get moving. Keep two men aboard the ship, and send everyone else to my dock with the Boston Whaler, Lund and Bertrum."

Juneau — 11:45 a.m.

The rented Bayliner cleared Gastineau Channel and turned into Juneau's marina. Danny piloted the boat as Jim texted Lori on his Blackberry. His message simply said, "Arrived, meet @ transient dock."

Jim observed the two "old hags" walking down the ramp while tying off the boat and smiled at how authentic their disguises were. Lori pushed a heavy-duty rubber-tired hand truck with Audra and Oscar in tow.

The foursome exchanged greetings, then Audra asked, "Did you get it all out? Are we rich yet? Tell me what happened."

Jim looked around and assessed the area. "Did you get the truck and storage space?"

Audra continued, "Yes — we're set. You never answered my questions, Dad. At least tell me what happened."

Jim smiled, reached down and petted Oscar. "Just like Ernie says, always asking questions. My answers are 'yes,' 'yes,' and 'no comment' other than 'mission accomplished.' Where's the truck parked?"

Lori pointed to a tan Dodge pickup next to the ramp in a loading zone. "It's perfect for what we're doing. Let's get moving."

The four sprang into action. After eleven back-breaking trips, the Bayliner was empty. Thirty-nine canisters weighing 70 pounds each made their way into the waiting truck. The Dodge sank deep onto its suspension, and Jim and Lori slowly drove to the storage compound. Danny and Audra remained at the boat and talked while waiting for their father's return. After parking the Dodge in the unit, Jim re-stowed six of the canisters onto the front seat floor to take weight off the back axle. Satisfied with the results, he locked the storage unit,

Jim slipped the middle-aged storage manager Aluit a fifty-dollar bill for a ride, and ten minutes later, they were back at the marina.

After refueling, they pointed the Bayliner toward Angoon.

Whitewater Bay —1:00 p.m.

Stinging sleet pelted Mel and Hank as they watched four strong, young Tlingit's expose the plane's fuselage and passenger door with their shovels. The wreck was easy to locate, but the trek up the mountain was brutal for the two older men. Hank stood guard with a bolt-action .378 Weatherby in case the bear showed up. Mel instructed the digging crew to expose the fuselage so he could determine if the plane had a registration number. The four teenagers were anxious to open the door, but the Clan elder told them to wait. A couple of tons of dense snow lay in a pile near the right wing tip when the four youngsters walked away from the wreck. The registration number wasn't a number at all; it was a series of letters: OB-BBN.

"This is a mighty old wreck," Mel said, "before registrations had numbers. I bet it was built in the thirties."

Hank said, "You're ranking elder. Ya gonna sit and BS all day or open the door ta see what's inside?"

Mel clambered to the plane with a flashlight and pulled on the heavy door. It screeched as if in agony, resisting Mel's efforts. Finally, it gave and Mel stuck his head inside. "Mother of mercy," he yelled, "there's a skeleton behind the wheel. And, holy buckets, there's coins scattered all over the floor. I think they're gold."

Hank got to the wreck and looked inside. "I'll be damned, it's gold alright. I'll crawl inside and start handing 'em out. Mel, count every coin and put 'em into a rucksack. This is our lucky Sunday."

One of the young Tlingit's pointed down the mountain at the small lake. "We got company. It don't look like a Clan boat."

Mel looked at the boat with his binoculars. "I seen that boat before — it's with the research ship. Whatcha s'pose they're doin' in here? Boys, keep an eye on 'em. Let me know if they start up the mountain."

Mountain Top — Hood Bay

Miller asked, "Can you see anyone?"

"Yep, they're about a mile above us — there's five that I can see — above the tree line in a snow field."

"Can you make out a plane?"

"Not from this angle, but there's a pile of new-looking snow next to the five guys and one has a shovel. Wait, there's one more. That makes six. Should we get up there?"

"Negative. Take pictures and return to the compound. I'm leaving the ridge. I'll meet you in an hour."

Echo Bay —1:00 p.m.

Wayne glassed Whitewater for signs of the Boston Whaler he'd seen earlier. He asked Frank, "Should I wake Helen? These guys are part of the Santos group. They followed a Tlingit boat into the end of the bay and haven't come out."

Gus intervened. "Let her sleep. The Clans can take care of themselves, and the Santos boat is probably on a scouting mission."

Jeff added, "I could check things out with the chopper."

Gus shook his head. "Wait to see what happens."

Frank's phone rang, interrupting his train of thought. He saw it was Rusty. He looked at David Bachman and pointed to his phone. "We need to determine where this is coming from.

Bachman watched Helen's tracker as Frank answered. "This is Blue Marlin."

"Hey, it's Red. Where are you?"

"At home. Where the heck are you?"

"Stuck in LAX at customs. They've detained me because security dogs smelled gunshot residue on me. Homeland Security is coming to ask me why I've got gunshot residue on my right hand, arm and face."

"Are you carrying any weapons?"

"I dumped them in Parral. This delay isn't a big deal. I should make my 2:30 flight to Seattle. I'm thinking that I should go to Angoon and deal with the phony ship and its crew. Do you feel like taking a quick trip with me tonight?"

"Actually I have plans. Helen has resigned and I promised to fly her and Whitey's son to Cape Cod for a small service. Would you care to join us?"

"I'd like to, but better not. This is the final loose end and I plan on taking care of it."

"So we're completely done with Obert's relatives and anyone else in Chile?"

"Yes, sir. A brilliant head shot at fifty meters. Hey, my company has arrived and I'm sure they're anxious to interview me. I'll call you from Angoon."

Frank looked at Dave. "What did you find?"

He shook his head. "Sorry. I needed more time. I only got as far as the Angoon translator, which is odd. I should have at least seen a connection to Seattle."

"That's alright. I didn't expect him to talk as long as he did."

"Since the NOAA ship is just around the corner," Dave said, "I suggest striking them when the tender boat returns from Whitewater. I can jam their radar and we can board the vessel within minutes."

Frank said, "I know everyone here is anxious for results, but that's Helens decision. She's in control of this operation and it's her call. We'll give her another two or three hours of rest before even thinking of waking her."

North Chatham Strait — 1:00 p.m.

Rough water greeted Audra as she piloted the Bayliner around the northern tip of Admiralty and entered the junction of Icy Strait and Chatham. Jim and Lori watched the Tlingit's digging out the plane from their satellite link as Danny slept in the lower berth. After panning out for a broader view, they saw the Boston Whaler circling the inlet at the inner part of Whitewater. Lori ventured that they were afraid to enter the turbulent narrows in such a small boat, but before Jim could respond, they negotiated the inlet.

Lori asked, "What's Santos going to do when he finds out the Clans found the gold?"

"Once he realizes only a fraction was recovered, he'll come looking for us."

"You think so?"

Oscar left the comfort of Lori's lap and sat next to Jim, laying his head on Jim's thigh. "I guarantee it. And here's how we deal with Santos and Dark Star when we return."

Jim opened a map and explained his plan to Lori and Audra.

Angoon —4:30 p.m.

The high school gym was packed as Mel and Hank prepared to address 16 Tlingit elders sitting at three large tables. Middle-aged and younger Tlingits on folding chairs waited for the two men to speak. Several teenagers played basketball on the other end of the gym.

Mel stood and began talking. "OK boys. Please stop playing. I've got important news that affects all the Clans of Angoon." Silence overtook the gymnasium.

344

Mel continued. "By now some of ya prob'ly heard rumors about Hank and me finding a plane wreck on Chaik Ridge this mornin. We did find an old plane — with a skeleton inside."

Immediate chatter began between the elders. The matriarch Hilda responded, "Quiet everyone." Silence returned. She asked, "How old is the wreck?"

Mel continued. "At least fifty or sixty years. What's really important is that the plane was carryin' gold."

The gymnasium erupted in noise. Again, Hilda raised her arms to restore order. "Quiet down everyone!"

She asked, "Whatcha plan on doin' with the gold Mel?"

Mel and Hank handed out several small coins to the elders. "It's on native ground. I say it belongs to all of us — as a group."

Hilda smiled. "I kinda thought you'd feel that way. Do ya have any idea what the gold is worth?"

"Hank should answer this one — he looked 'em up on his computer." Mel turned to Hank and nodded.

Hank stood and held up a coin. "I Googled the coins. Most are Swiss francs from the 1800s. Others are Austrian Coronas. Several of the Swiss coins are for sale on eBay at $285 each and the Coronas are selling for $1,000 each. We found eighteen hundred and seventy seven coins. We have in our possession over a half million dollars' worth of Swiss and Austrian gold coins.

Gasps, applause and laughter erupted throughout the gymnasium. Hilda stood and put her arms out to silence the exuberant crowd. "Before we get too happy, there are questions. Can we legally claim this or do we face a big fight with the government?"

Mel answered, "We don't give the government a chance to challenge anything. We been talkin' for over two years about convertin' the old processin' plant into a smoked salmon factory run by the Clans, but we never had the money. Jim Bennett sent samples of our product to a couple grocery chains in the lower 48. He said they'll buy everything we can produce as long as it's packaged as a gourmet Tlingit product and USDA approved. One grocer offered to help design a vacuum package with a Tlingit totem pole on it. Jim gave me the paperwork for USDA approval and estimated a start-up cost of $250,000. If we spend it right away on projects like this — ones that benefit of our people — the government won't interfere."

The gymnasium exploded with a roar of applause and whistles. The Tlingit's would finally have native-controlled employment opportunities for their tiny village. Mel and Hank were instantly elevated to the status of Tlingit "rock stars."

At the marina, the Bayliner pulled into the furthest stall from Jim's boat and tied off. A perfectly disguised elderly Tlingit walked toward the parking area, followed by an old charter captain and his "date." The Tinglit that was Jim held his scanner against his chest and realized there was a transmitter located in the trees to his right. He suspected it was aimed toward his boat and the seaplane dock. After walking behind the trees, he verified his suspicions. The four walked past the parking area, crossed the pavement and slipped into the timber. The old captain pointed out over 20 cars parked near the gymnasium as they passed the school's running track.

Jim whispered, "I bet the Clans are having a meeting regarding the wrecked plane — probably wondering what to do with the gold."

Ten minutes later, they reached the hidden entrance behind the shed. Jim surveyed the area with his scanner and identified three different transmitters. He whispered to the group, "Santos has been a busy beaver — he's got three cameras aimed at the house."

Lori looked around. "Can he see us now?"

"No." Jim pointed to the edge of the driveway, then south of the house, and finally at Killisnoo Island. "He's got one on a tree over here, another across the parking area, and one on the island. The shed is blocking his view of our entrance."

Convinced it was safe, the four entered the tunnel and closed the camouflaged lid behind them. At the vault, Audra asked, "What are we going to do with the four canisters of gold sitting here?"

"Save it for a rainy day," answered Jim.

Lori laughed. "Jim, it's been raining all day. Why don't you take us all out to dinner at Chez Paul tonight."

Jim shook his head. "Sorry, that's in Denver, and I've got work to do."

They entered the main floor and removed their disguise in silence. Everyone knew that tomorrow morning would define their future.

Santos Compound — 6:00 p.m.

Two armed guards walked the perimeter of the main house in the rain with AK-47s at the ready. They were both large. One wore a dirty denim jacket with a Hell's Angels insignia on the back. The other wore a hooded fleece coat and gloves.

Icy sleet covered the dock and walkway leading to the main house as the two men passed each other. Inside the massive dwelling, Santos, Miller and Crane sat at an enormous oak table overlooking Hood Bay. Rusty watched his three monitors for activity as Crane drank a beer and Vicente played a game of solitaire.

Miller said, "They're back, I see movement inside of Bennett's house. Our cameras never picked them up. His secret entrance must be beyond camera line of sight. Vicente, why don't you contact one of the Clan elders. I want to know what they found today."

Hilda answered her phone and Santos said, "Top of the evening to you Hilda, this is Vicente Santos. I wanted you to know that I have no intention of keeping the Zodiac. As soon as the village hires a replacement officer, I'll immediately return it."

"That's what Mel told me. We ain't hired no one yet, but we're workin' on it."

"Very good. Say, I noticed a lot of activity around the peaks just south of Chaik. Did someone get hurt hiking in the snow?"

"Oh heavens no. The Clans found an old plane up there earlier today and we was investigatin' it."

"Ah, that makes sense. How old of a plane was it?"

"I'm told it was really old. It didn't have any numbers on it — just a coupla letters. Hank says that means it's been up there for over sixty years."

"That's exciting to say the least."

"Yeah —there was a skeleton inside. They said it was the pilot."

Santos asked, "Only one person on board?"

"That's what I was told."

"Did they find anything else?"

Hilda hesitated. "Can ya keep a secret?"

"Of course."

"The plane had some gold coins in it — old Swiss something-or-other — and I been told they's worth a few bucks. Now we can fix up the old cold storage plant near Killisnoo and turn it into a salmon processin' factory."

"That's wonderful, Hilda. I'm happy for the people of Angoon."

"Thanks — the whole village is on cloud nine."

"That answers the mystery of what I saw from my house today. Remember about the Zodiac — when Angoon hires a police officer, I'll return it immediately. So long."

Vicente hung up and turned to Rusty. "They found the plane with some gold coins on board. The amount of gold recovered doesn't match our information."

"Old news. I told you I watched Bennett get it out last night."

"Richard told me you were good, but I needed to find out for myself. I'm convinced that you're on the right path. Soon we'll have my father's gold."

Echo Bay —6:00 PM

The solid rumble of diesel engines vibrated through the cutter and Helen opened one eye. Lost in the recurring dream of her and Danny leaving on a cruise, Helen wondered where she was. Finally the constant tone of the engines reminded her she was on a mission in Alaska. A quick glance at her wristwatch told her she'd gotten six hours of sleep. She sprang to her feet and ran to the shower. Fifteen minutes and a fresh change of clothes later, she was being briefed in the wheelhouse by the entire crew. Convinced that things had developed satisfactorily, she understood it was time to explain her strike plan.

"Here come details for tonight. I'll give you the facts, define the parameters, then tell you what I want. Santos likely knows about Bennett finding the gold because of his surveillance set-up above Hood Bay. They watched him last night but don't know that he moved the gold with my Bayliner. They probably think the gold is down the mountain but not in Bennett's possession. *Oregon II* is anchored at the north edge of Peril with engines running —though the radio chatter told me last night that they were getting low on fuel. An oiler is supposed to come meet them tomorrow. The current position tells us they're prepared to intercept Bennett as soon as he makes a move for the gold. We observed the Bennetts — in disguise — return to Angoon with my boat, which suggests the gold is already hidden. Santos doesn't know that."

"The Bennetts are planning an elaborate trap for Santos. Bennett won't do anything wild or crazy without the cover of darkness. Tonight's the night. We've not intercepted any recent radio transmissions from Santos because he's using cell phones with identical SIM cards that are configured to a master phone. The master serves as a translator and can't be hacked. There's only one Dark Star operative who knows how to do that besides me — Rusty Miller."

Frank interrupted. "Whoa, Helen. How can you make such an incriminating claim?"

"Because I taught him how to do it. Think about it. All incoming calls from him are tracked to Sitka — no further. Coincidence? I think not. He's our defector, he's here and he killed Whitey."

Frank closed his eyes and Bachman interjected, "I never liked that arrogant prick. I'm on record for claiming rights to dispatch him — medieval style."

Helen smiled and nodded. "That brings us to our neighbor on the mountain across from Hood. He's using a satellite dish to forward the dedicated cell phone signal. That same dish has radar with infrared transmitting capabilities. Step one is to knock out their surveillance and communication capabilities. When it gets dark, Jeff and Wayne will take the chopper and destroy their equipment. I'll deploy our jammer on Catherine Island so the chopper isn't detected. If anyone is still manning the ridge top, kill them."

She continued, pointing at the map. "Step two is to pull anchor at dark and reposition the cutter outside Echo Bay with lights out — after Jeff and Wayne return. If the *Oregon II* is still at its current position, Dave and Wayne will take the Zodiac and board NOAA while Jeff mans the Gatling gun. If NOAA tries to move, we overtake them."

Helen drew a circle around Russian Reef. "Step three is to pump what's left of *Oregon II's* diesel into our tanks, if it's significant, and then sink her here. Wayne will place C4 charges under the hull while Dave opens all doors and bulkheads. The water surrounding the reef is 500 feet deep so if we remove their fuel, or it's already nearly gone, an oil slick will be undetectable."

She circled the Santos compound. "Step four is to get Santos and his men. He'll only have one or two bodyguards with him and may be on the water with his boat, which makes him easy pickings for the Gatling gun. If he remains at his compound, we land our chopper on his dock and tell his people it's a Coast Guard emergency. When he comes out, kill him and his men and clear the house. Finally, if we fail to apprehend Rusty, the Olsens will take off for Seattle with the cutter. Dave, Wayne and I take the Zodiac to Angoon, secure my boat and scour Angoon for him."

Dave asked, "So if Bennett's on the water tonight, how can we avoid collateral damage? Won't Santos go after him? He's at risk from both ends."

"I'm *counting* on Santos going after him. Bennett will take care of himself. He'll draw them either into Whitewater Bay or Eliza Harbor, which means their ship and Santos will be trapped with no way out. It simplifies our operation."

Dave asked, "What happens to Bennett afterward?"

Frank interjected, "Nothing. We leave him alone. He's been our greatest benefactor."

Wayne frowned. "He could get in the way — then what?"

Helen kissed her brother on his forehead. "He's too good for that. He works in the shadows. Any other comments?"

The group was silent. "OK team," Helen said. "Prepare to get underway."

Chapter Nine

June 16—Angoon —12:00 AM

After shaving, Colonel Bennett ran a finger over the deep facial scar he saw in the bathroom mirror. He wondered if it was luck or skill that prevented him from dying that night in Panama. He decided it was a little of both. He opened the linen closet door which led to the vault, then walked into the dining room area.

"Who's escorting me to the vault?" he asked. "I'm arming up and on my way."

Lori set Oscar on the floor and everyone followed Jim into the tunnel. Oscar managed to beat Jim to the vault.

Once inside the vault Lori said, "I've got a bad feeling about this. You shouldn't be taking these guys on by yourself."

Jim simply smiled. "I've got this handled and we've already discussed this to death. C'mon, help me get my gear together."

After loading a lightweight pack frame with a variety of weapons, he turned and smiled.

Danny said, "Wait."

"What?"

"I should come with you."

Jim hugged Danny, then held his shoulders. He looked directly into Danny's eyes and said, "I need you here to guard the others, Don't hesitate using force — shoot first and ask questions later. You belong here."

"You're totally outnumbered."

"Not really. Vegas has it 100-to-1 in my favor. I'll be back in time for breakfast — eggs over medium, bacon well done."

He bent down and removed a holster and his beloved .357 Derringer from his right boot. He handed them to Danny he said, "Here's something I want you to have — it saved my life in El Salvador. It chambers two rounds — simply pull back the hammer and shoot. Repeat for a second shot. Wear loose-leg pants so it's hidden. It comes in handy if you're hit or captured. By the way, it kicks like a mule. Hold on tight."

350

Danny inspected the pistol, knowing it was another rite of passage. He hugged his father and thanked him.

Jim and Danny walked to the end of the concrete tunnel, climbed the ladder and rotated the metal lid into the open position. Jim peeked out and assessed the area. Convinced it was clear, he asked Danny for the pack stuffed with ordnance and his surveillance equipment. Danny handed up the weapons and closed the lid. Jim donned his night-vision goggles and slipped through the trees toward Angoon. After passing the school and hustling across the pavement, he entered the safety of thick undergrowth surrounded the parking area. Confident that the marina was clear of activity, he ran to his boat and started it. Rather than wait for the twin diesels to warm up, he cast off the dock lines and forced the throttles forward. He was underway.

Hoods Bay —1:00 a.m.

Rusty tore through the Santos house yelling, "GET UP! GET UP! GET UP! HE'S ON THE MOVE! COME ON, GET UP! THIS IS IT! HE'S ON THE MOVE! C'MON EVERYONE! LET'S GO!"

He pulled a phone from his top pocket and called Softail.

"Rise and shine, gentlemen. Our package is leaving Angoon. Position the ship in the center of the Strait. After he passes, block the Whitewater entrance and anchor. Follow him with the Whaler and Lund. Leave one man aboard to man the bridge. I want every available asset to track our package."

"Who do you want to stay on board Softail?"

"Whoever's the best shot with the .50 cal. We'll block the lake's inlet with Vicente's boat and the Bertram. He'll never get out of there alive."

"OK. I'm leaving John with the ship. We'll be under way in less than ten minutes."

Crane gulped a mug of coffee. "Where is he now?"

Miller looked at his monitor. "He's in the narrows between Angoon and Killisnoo."

Santos and his two body guards stood near the kitchen counter and poured themselves hot coffee. Vicente asked, "How soon before we can follow?"

"As soon as he clears the southern point of Hood — no more than 15 minutes."

Vicente turned toward one if his bodyguards, a large man with a clean-shaven head. "Mr. Poole, would you be so kind as to warm up my boat. Take two fully loaded AK-47s for us and place them inside the cabin. They'll come in handy if Mr. Bennett decides to make a run for it. If things go well tonight, we shall recover my father's long-lost legacy." The enormous man nodded and walked away.

Rusty sat at the long oak table, studying his monitor while sipping a mug of coffee. He grinned, knowing he finally had the infamous Colonel Bennett.

351

Echo Bay —1:05 a.m.

Helen, Frank, Gus and Dave huddled around their monitors and watched the *Oregon II* with their IR scanner.

Dave pointed at the screen. "They've pulled anchor."

Helen spoke over the radio. "CG -27 to CG -31 —come in CG- 31."

Jeff answered, "This is CG-31 —over."

"All jammer's are on, proceed to target."

"Roger that —over and out."

The Sikorsky, with no running lights on, raced over the jagged, snowy peaks between Chaik Bay and Eliza Harbor, then dropped into a dark, timbered valley. It banked hard and fast toward the icy ridge that held communication and surveillance links for the Santos operation. Jeff set the bird down lightly on the ridge and Wayne jumped into the snow. He sprinted to the equipment and opened fire with his M16. Chunks of plastic and metal flew helter-skelter as Wayne unloaded a full thirty-round clip into the electronic array. The lanky man kicked and stomped equipment, tearing apart wiring connections as he went. He perused the area one final time, then ran back and climbed into the helicopter.

Helen watched her monitors as events unfolded at breakneck speed. Bennett's boat passed by the rocky outcrop beyond Killisnoo Island, while the NOAA ship headed toward Whitewater. Then she intercepted a radio transmission.

"Softail to Fortuna, Softail to Fortuna —come in."

Vicente responded, "Go ahead Softail."

"I've lost my radar and my phone doesn't work. Besides, I can't see shit."

Helen heard a familiar voice respond. "Turn off your damn bridge lights and wear the night goggles I gave you. They've got a three power central lens —simply adjust it like you would a binocular. My surveillance link is also down and won't respond, so we'll make do with night-vision gear until I can rectify the problem — over."

"One moment — much better. I can see what's going on. What about my phone?."

The same familiar voice responded, "I'm working on it — use the radio for now."

"Ah, copy that —When are you guys leaving?"

"We're underway. Repeat my instructions."

"Do you think we're dumb or what? We follow the package, making sure we're not seen, take control of his boat and apprehend him when he returns."

"Excellent. Whatever happens, don't kill him unless he's got the gold. We'll meet up in thirty minutes — over and out."

Helen looked at Dave. "That bloody red-headed turncoat. I knew it was him."

"He's a dead man. Too bad I can only kill him once," responded Dave.

Frank turned to Gus. "I wouldn't want to be in Miller's shoes."

Gus nodded. "Me neither." Looking at Helen, he asked, "Should I get underway?"

Helen sported a huge smile. "Relax Gus —we'll wait for the chopper to return and allow these pillocks to get into position. Then we'll piss all over them."

Chatham Strait —1:15 a.m.

Jim's radar quit working and he engaged his auto pilot in order to safely continue. He'd intercepted the radio transmission from Santos' crew and knew they'd swallowed his bait. He stepped away from the controls, opened the metal surveillance case. After booting up his computer, the KH-12 satellite ELINT program indicated that someone was jamming his radar system. The program traced it to a ship in Echo Bay. There was nothing he could do about the jammer other than see where the signal was originating so he switched the KH-12 satellite over to its SBIRS mode, giving him a complete infrared picture for all of Chatham. Jim watched a helicopter round the corner of Admiralty Island and head directly toward the ship sitting at the mouth of Echo Bay. Moments later, the helicopter landed on its deck. He could just make out Coast Guard markings. He shook his head and mumbled, "The Coast Guard never jams other vessels' radar unless it's under attack. It's the Olsen crew."

Jim saw the *Oregon II* heading directly toward Whitewater with two smaller boats in tow. Within Hood Bay, Santos was visible leaving the compound with his catamaran and two other boats. The open Zodiac had two men on board but he couldn't see how many men occupied the other boats. He set his case on top of the boat's dashboard, then pushed both throttles wide open.

Convinced that everything was going according to plan, he used the opportunity to contact his house with his encrypted radio.

Audra answered, "Are you in trouble? Where are you? What's happening?"

"Whoa. Slow down — I'm just checking in. Is everything OK on your end?"

"Yep. Everything's fine here. Where are you?"

"I'm approaching Chaik Bay. Tell Danny I believe Helen's watching events from a Coast Guard ship. According to my IR satellite, I've got the entire Santos crew following me. They're keeping their distance which gives me ample time to set up inside the lake."

Danny interrupted, "I overheard your comment about Helen. Is she working with the Coast Guard against us?"

"Negative. She's pretending to be the Coast Guard, which is beneficial. Her radar jammer is slowing down Santos but it doesn't affect me. I figure she'll seal off Whitewater once Santos is inside."

"Should I contact her?"

"Negative. Just keep the radio on so we can communicate. Look, I'm passing Chaik Bay so I need to concentrate. I'll contact you when I'm in position."

Echo Bay—1:15 a.m.

Wayne and Jeff entered the wheelhouse to find the group huddled around Frank's laptop. Frank had finally received the coroner's report. Helen turned away from the gruesome photograph of Mike Stoddard, AKA Whitey. A nickel-sized exit wound was directly above the bridge of his nose, forcing both eyeballs to nearly bulge out of their sockets. As a result, the eyelids didn't cover his bulging, bloodshot eyes, making for an ugly and gruesome sight.

David Bachman gritted his teeth and said, "Fuckin' Miller did this — rest in peace Whitey, because I'll make that fucker pay. Medieval torture's got nothing on me. I can't wait to get my hands on him."

Helen asked, "Could you please turn that off? I don't want to remember him like that. Besides, we've got work to do. Bennett's heading toward Whitewater and he's alone. My IR camera on top of Catherine Island indicates there's only one person aboard the *Oregon II*. Hope she doesn't run out of fuel. We'd have to tow her."

She looked at her brother. "When Softail anchors, you and Jeff sneak to the ship in the Zodiac, take it over and destroy its radio. Don't hesitate to kill anyone who gets in the way. As soon as it's secure, try to intercept the Santos catamaran with the Zodiac while Gus maneuvers our ship into Whitewater. Keep Santos alive for questioning. Gus will set the cutter up broadside to the back inlet and Jeff can eliminate anyone who tries to escape with the Gatling gun."

Dave said, "What about Miller? I want the satisfaction of taking him out. If he tries escaping through the inlet, you guys will smoke him with the Gatling gun."

Jeff said, "I'll do my best to avoid killing him."

Helen looked at Jeff. "It's important to keep him alive — we need to interrogate him and determine who else is involved."

Dave said, "When he's captured, I want to spearhead the interrogation!"

Helen smiled. "Be my guest. I bet you'll make him sob like a little girl."

She pointed to her monitor. "Bennett's at full throttle entering Whitewater. Santos and the other two boats haven't even entered Chatham." She pointed to her radar. "NOAA is halfway across the Strait. When Santos reaches the inlet, we'll take off."

Russian Reef —1:30 a.m.

Jim kept a keen eye on his quarry while cutting to the inside of Russian Reef. After turning into Whitewater, he reset his auto pilot and studied the satellite image of the inlet. Satisfied that it was safe to proceed, he turned off his computer and pulled the night-vision goggles down from atop his helmet. The total darkness transformed into an eerie green fluorescent landscape. The twin-engine boat cut effortlessly through the inky-black water. Jim sat back and poured a second cup of coffee from his thermos.

Ten minutes later, he disengaged the auto-pilot and cut both throttles to one-third. Even at low tide, Jim had grown accustomed to the entrance, so he confidently entered the narrow passage. Once through, he turned east into the small lake and headed toward its headwaters. Knowing it was low tide and that the lake would rise another four feet within the next two hours, Jim backed the boat toward a soft sandy point and disengaged the props. The *Sojourn* drifted into the soft sand and stopped. After deploying the front windlass anchor from inside the cabin and allowing enough slack for the incoming tide, he walked to the rear swim step, tossed a long rope to shore and tied it to the boat. He locked the cabin door, then placed a small walkie-talkie into a bucket next to the transom. After lifting the bulky backpack to his muscular shoulders, he grabbed the metal case with his right hand and his assault rifle with his left. Jumping into the thigh deep water, he waded to shore, tied the boat's rear rope to a clump of alder and disappeared into the darkness.

The colonel trotted east along the shoreline to the wide, shallow stream that fed the lake. He crossed the frigid knee-deep water to the south shore. After climbing a small embankment, he took off his pack and untied two carbon fiber tubes. Each tube was three feet tall, three inches in diameter, with a folding aluminum stake at their base for securing them to the ground. He positioned the tubes so their open tops faced skyward, then forced the stakes deep into the ground. Satisfied with their location, he pulled a small retractable metal antenna from each tube's bottom and secured it to their tops. The antennas would act as a receiver and an arming mechanism. Jim grabbed his gear and headed west along the shoreline.

Thick sawgrass and brush covered the bank above the lake. Jim pressed onward and reached a well-traveled game trail paralleling the shore. Enormous bear tracks were visible in the trail's mud as he jogged toward the lake's inlet. After stopping to catch his breath, he opened his surveillance case, knelt in the wet grass directly across the lake from his boat and stared at the monitor. Santos' crew had entered Whitewater with five vessels — two from the anchored *Oregon II* and three from Hood Bay. Within

20 minutes, they'd be at the lake's entrance. He also noticed the Coast Guard cutter and another Zodiac leaving Echo Bay, heading towards Whitewater. Jim turned off his computer, closed its case and trotted toward the lake's entrance.

He carefully studied the surrounding terrain in order to determine his best offensive position. A narrow, tree-filled point protruded into the lake two hundred meters ahead of him. It was the perfect location to view the inlet, his boat, and both shorelines of the lake Even though he was winded, Jim ran on toward the timbered point. Once there, he dropped to his knees, threw off his heavy pack and pulled in deep breaths of ice-cold air. Ignoring the burning pain in his chest and side, he unloaded his pack and secured five sixty round clips of ammo, two 80 mm grenade shells, and a modified claymore mine. He fortified his position with boulders, logs and brush, and hunkered down. He was nearly out of time.

A cold southerly wind brought rain into the bay. Jim turned on his helmet radio and made contact with his house in Angoon. "Hey guys, do you copy?"

Danny quickly answered, "We copy you loud and clear. The relay on top of the ridge works well. We've been waiting for your call."

"I'm in position waiting for their arrival. Just testing radio contact."

Understanding that his eye in the sky was about to be negated, Jim opened the metal case, unfolded a twelve inch satellite dish and turned on his computer. He'd have to turn it off before the Santos crew entered the inlet, so he carefully studied the screen one last time. The Lund, carrying three men, landed on the same side of the inlet he was on. They pulled the boat onto the rocky shore. They were wearing night-vision equipment and carrying AK-47s. The Boston Whaler and Bertram proceeded into the inlet. Both boats contained a two-man crew equipped with night-vision goggles and AK-47s. The Santos catamaran beached itself onto a sandy spit outside the north side of the inlet. Jim's infrared system showed two men in the cabin of the catamaran. The slow-moving Zodiac circled the inlet, then pulled next to Santos' cat. It carried two men fitted with night-vision hardware. Surprisingly, the Zodiac then sped off in the direction from which it came, traveling at full throttle. Jim shut off his computer and contacted the house.

Audra answered, "Are you OK?"

"Yes. Listen up. The Zodiac is heading out of Whitewater. They know I'm occupied, so they're probably coming to the house. The party's about to begin and I won't be able to monitor their movements until it's over. The Zodiac is problematic, so I insist that everyone gets into the vault now. Leave all the house doors unlocked. Once inside the vault, turn off the large breaker panel but leave the vaults panel on —got it?"

"What about . . ."

Jim interrupted. "Not now Audra. Just get into the vault and do what I say before it's too late. Over and out."

The Whaler and Bertram entered the lake, made one short circle, and pulled onto the north shore, the side Jim's boat was on, but nearer the outlet. Both boats beached in a tiny pocket a third of a mile from the *Sojourn*. The four men scrambled into the timber, then walked slowly in and out of the trees along the shoreline toward Jim's boat. He heard voices 50 meters behind him. The Lund's crew was on the game trail he'd just left. Jim knew they were executing a classic pincer assault on his boat.

You fools are already out-maneuvered with no place to go but through me, he thought. *So there's nine men here, including Santos and the two in the Zodiac. There's at least one more on the NOAA ship for a total of twelve.* Jim wondered if Santos had additional personnel at his dwelling and if he was in his catamaran.

As the trio behind him approached the headwaters, Jim picked up the claymore mine and low crawled to the trail. He followed the trail toward the stream for fifty meters, then set the modified claymore's wire legs deep into the soft, moist ground. The unit was altered to deploy five seconds after being activated by a tripwire. That way, Jim didn't need to activate the mine with a hand-held trigger. He pulled the trip wire taught and secured it to the base of a small jack pine. He returned to his makeshift fortress and watched as both teams slowly negotiated the dense undergrowth choking both shorelines. Soon they'd be in position.

Chatham — 2:00 a.m.

Gus navigated the cutter toward Whitewater while Helen pointed out *Oregon II's* anchored position on the IR monitor. Jeff stood on the starboard deck, manning the Gatling gun as Dave and Wayne approached *Oregon II's* stern at full speed with the Zodiac. Bachman piloted the craft and Wayne knelt behind the machine gun.

Helen spoke over their encrypted radio system. "So far so good, Dave. There's one person inside the wheelhouse and he's focused on Whitewater Bay. The deck is empty. You're cleared for boarding."

Dave cut his throttle as the Zodiac came within 50 meters of the vessel. "Affirmative. We're almost there. I'll inform you when Wayne's on board."

The Zodiac softly touched *Oregon II's* stern. Wayne moved to the bow with a shoulder-held grapple launcher. He whispered for Dave to back the Zodiac away from the ship and placed the launcher against his shoulder. Wayne squeezed the trigger, which was followed by a loud pneumatic "POP." A four pronged grappling hook pulled rope over the ship's railing and landed onto its metal deck with a "CLANK."

Dave said to Helen, "We just sent our hook onto the deck. Did our target move?"

"Negative. He looks preoccupied. It's OK to proceed."

Wayne pulled the grapple tight and attached a portable battery-powered winch to the rope. He connected his harness to the winch, pushed the hand-held trigger and was lifted to the deck's upper railing. After clearing the rail, Wayne pointed his M16 toward the wheelhouse. A long-haired man stood on the starboard side of the enclosure peering toward Whitewater with night-vision binoculars.

Wayne whispered into his radio, "He's alone. I'm taking him now."

Helen answered, "Clear to go. Be careful, brother."

Wayne dashed across the deck and placed his back against the side of the metal bridge. His heart pounded as he took his M16 off safety and peeked around the corner. He looked left and right for any others. It was clear. He counted twelve steel steps separating him from the wheelhouse. On one knee, he turned and looked up the steps, then whispered into his helmet speaker, "Tell me if he moves."

"Affirmative. He's static."

Crouching, Wayne pointed his M16 forward, then slowly and methodically took one step at a time until he reached the upper landing. A man with a short beard was inside, focused on whatever events were transpiring in the darkness of Whitewater Bay. A steel door with a small window separated the two men. Wayne stood, placed his left hand on the door's rusted handle, and lifted it. He pushed the heavy door open and the man turned toward the noise and lowered his binoculars.

Wayne yelled, "Coast Guard! Don't move!"

The man instinctively reached forward and tried to knock the barrel of Wayne's gun to the side, but before his hand touched the barrel, Wayne pulled the trigger. The impact of several rounds knocked the burly man against the control panel and he crumpled to the floor. Wayne stood over him and pointed the M16 at his head.

Blood poured from his wounds as Wayne asked, "How many more are on board?"

The wounded man said, "Fuck you," flipped Wayne the middle finger, took a ragged breath and died.

Wayne spoke into his helmet microphone, "One dead. Tried grabbing my rifle. What an arse."

Helen said. "I saw the flash and heard the noise over the radio. You alright?"

"My heart's pumping out of my chest, but I'm much better than him. I asked if anyone else was on board. He looked right at me and said 'Fuck you.' Then he flipped me the bird."

"I heard that too. Disable the radio, toss his body overboard with something heavy, and return to the Zodiac."

Helen looked at the Olsens. "We're clear to proceed into Whitewater."

She pointed at the monitor. "Whoa, hold on. A vessel's rounding the bay and heading north toward Angoon. It's too small to be Santos or Bennett. Let's watch where it goes."

Helen ran to the bridge and saw through her night-vision binoculars two men in a Zodiac. She waited until it passed Russian Reef, then returned to the wheelhouse.

"It's clear sailing, Gus." She pointed at her monitor. "Position us in this zone so we're within range of our Gatling gun."

Gus pushed the ship's throttles forward and asked, "Who was in that Zodiac?"

"Two of Santos' crew. They're probably heading to Bennett's house."

Frank asked, "Rusty and someone else?"

Helen nodded. "I believe so, but there's nothing we can do about it other than contacting Danny."

Frank nodded. "Call him."

The phone rang several times before Danny answered, "Hello."

Helen said, "Danny, there's no time to explain, but a boat is headed toward your position with two men after you and the family. Get the hell out of there."

"Don't worry. Dad already told me. I'm expecting them." Danny hung up.

Helen shook her head. "Stubborn Irishmen."

She turned to Gus. "Let's get into position. We'll deal with Rusty later."

She hurried to the bridge and called the Bennett land line. The phone rang until the answering machine picked up. "Danny, this is Helen. If you're there, please answer. Danny I need to . . ."

Danny answered, "Hey, good lookin', I told you. It's handled."

"Listen carefully, Danny. Professional killers are headed your way and they're not paying you a social visit. Shelter somewhere safe until your father or I can get there."

"I appreciate your concern, but I've got this. How far away are they?"

"Thirty minutes. Maybe less. Danny, please don't engage them."

"Thanks for the heads up." The phone went dead.

Helen snapped her phone shut and mumbled, "Damn him."

Chaik Bay —2:15 a.m.

Richard Crane operated the boat while Rusty Miller sat next to him and laughed. He yelled over the sound of the outboard. "Santos and his crew are finished. Bennett will eliminate all of them. He'll be busy long enough for us to grab his family. They're our bargaining chips. He's a family man and will pay anything to keep them alive."

Crane shook his head. "You know we've got to kill all of them when this is over, otherwise he'll track us down."

Rusty simply nodded.

After passing the mouth of Chaik at full speed, Crane asked, "Do you think his kid will put up a fight?"

"Of course. When he does, try to keep him alive. If Bennett knows his family's alive, he'll trade."

"You're certain he's got the gold?"

"I'll bet you my share against yours."

"No thanks. I never gamble unless the game's rigged in my favor."

"Spoken like a true cop on the take. Look, run this puppy onto the beach in front of his house. Like Normandy, we'll storm the place."

Crane nodded as he followed the shoreline leading toward Hood Bay.

Bennett's House — 2:15 a.m.

The Bennett clan disconnected the upstairs radio, grabbed Jim's computer, and went to the master bathroom closet. Audra opened the secret passage and turned on the lights below. Danny closed the closet door behind him and neatly arranged the towels before entering the cavity below. After securing the false wall to its original position, he turned out the lights and entered the vault. He closed the heavy steel door and spun the internal tumbler. He walked over to a large electric panel and threw off all the breakers except the one controlling the vault. The electrical service was underground, so it was be impossible to disconnect the vault from the power grid. If the grid went out, Jim's generator would immediately kick in. Twenty fully-charged twelve-volt batteries and an inverter were neatly stacked in the vault's corner for additional power needs. Two large PVC pipes ran vertically from the vaults ceiling, through the house's framing, then penetrated near the top of the home's steep roof. The pipes were concealed in the interior walls and virtually tamper proof. Both pipes contained blowers which provided a constant flow of fresh air to the vault.

Danny pulled back canvas tarps, exposing Jim's large arsenal and shelves of military MRE's. In the corner were four neatly stacked polypropylene 55-gallon drums of distilled water. Rain gutters also diverted water through pipes that entered the vault. A diverter valve enabled unused water to exit the building. This provided the vault's occupants with a vast supply of water.

Audra assessed the vault. "I didn't know dad had all of these guns and stuff"

She unknowingly picked up a LAWS Rocket Launcher. What are these goofy looking things? He's got dozens of them. He's a friggin' survivalist."

Danny said, "I suggest you put it down. It's a rocket launcher. You say 'survivalist' as if it's a bad thing. I'll ask you, where would you want to be if the shit ever hit the fan? In downtown Seattle or here? He's simply prepared for every contingency."

Audra continued, "But what does dad plan to do with all these weapons?"

Danny shook his head and turned his attention to the shelves. He began assembling combat gear.

Lori defended Jim. "It's his insurance policy. Your father managed to piss off a lot of people through his years of service and I wouldn't be surprised if there's a price on his head with the KGB and China. I've read your father's personnel file. He's hard core and hates Communism. Even at TacSec, he carried a gun under his suit coat. I bet you didn't know his Audi in Denver is armor plated, compliments of our government. There's justification for this room because of his past."

Audra smiled and said, "You really like my father, don't you?"

"Yes and I have for years. Beyond that, I respect his convictions. Younger people may think he's a dinosaur, but it's people like Jim who provide freedoms we take for granted. He's a man with deep convictions."

Audra looked at Lori. "I'm glad you said that because I've always looked at him that way. The two of you would make a great couple."

Danny donned a Kevlar vest and put a helmet equipped with night vision. She asked, "What the hell are you doing?"

"I'm going outside to kill these bastards."

"You're doing no such thing. We're instructed to remain here until he returns, and that's exactly what we're going to do. It's not the time for ego driven bravado."

"Look, I'm an adult and I make my own decisions. Besides, I don't answer to you. I know exactly what I'm doing. I'm not sitting on my ass while these jerks tear through Dad's shit, then ambush him when he returns. There's no time to argue, so get over it."

Audra shouted, "DANNY, DON'T! YOU KNOW WHAT DAD SAID!"

Danny shrugged his shoulders, opened the outer vault door to the secret tunnel and tossed a canister of gold into the dark void. He slung an M4A2 over his shoulder and placed two extra clips into his ammo pouch.

"No matter what, don't open this door, not even for me. I'm going to trap these fuckers inside the tunnel so don't open this door under any circumstances." He closed the vault and disappeared into the darkness.

In a broken voice Audra asked, "Should we call dad?"

"No darling — it wouldn't change anything and we can't interfere with him at the moment. We'll tell him when he calls."

The younger Bennett reached the ladder of the tunnel and opened the canister filled with gold. He intentionally dropped its contents onto the cement floor as bait. Knowing his unwanted guests were still some time away, he swung the pivoted lid to one side and climbed out. After looking around, he decided to set up 20 meters to the east. The thick foliage and higher terrain was an ideal ambush point. Rather than closing the lid, he left it partially open so it would be found. He walked in a large half circle and entered his ambush area from the east. He carefully attached a sniper's ghillie poncho over his back and helmet, then hunkered down.

The Lake —2:30 a.m.

Jim lay on his stomach and watched his adversaries' movements. The four across the lake had positioned themselves near his boat while those on his side split apart.

On Jim's side of the lake, one man crouched in a thicket of brush within 100 meters of him while the other two lay in the grass near the mouth of the stream.

Dark clouds towered above as a slight breeze came from the south. The tide was coming in and Jim's boat started bobbing with the wind and rain. He wondered if his adversaries were waiting for daylight, but one of the combatants across the lake suddenly sprinted toward his boat and disappeared. Jim opened a Snickers bar and took a hearty bite. Even with a big dose of insect repellent, mosquitoes swarmed his body. He smiled as the Santos crew swatted and fidgeted from swarms of insects. Experience in jungle warfare allowed him to remain calm as his targets kept telegraphing their positions.

The man nearest his boat came into view, maneuvered to the side and tried to pull himself aboard. He was obviously out of shape and too heavy to pull himself onto the deck. On his third attempt, he fell into the knee deep water. In desperation, he whistled for someone to help him onto the boat. Jim shook his head in disbelief and considered their ordeal comical. He thought, *These clowns wouldn't last an hour in Delta.*

Once aboard, the man found the bulkhead door leading to the cabin was locked. Before allowing the man to break into the cabin, Jim pressed the transmit button on his walkie-talkie. Its companion unit sounded off in the bucket on the deck to the sound of the General Lee horn from the *Dukes of Hazzard*. The overweight man grabbed it out of the bucket.

Jim started, "Hey mister. What are you doing on my boat? Don't you realize that breaking and entering is a felony?"

"Who is this?"

"The owner of the boat you're trespassing on."

The man looked toward shore. "Where the fuck are you?"

"Very close. Say, why don't you and your friends leave before someone gets hurt?"

The burly man looked around, then toward the person who helped him onto the boat. He spoke into a different walkie-talkie to the rest of his crew. "This stupid fucker just called me. He says we should leave before we get hurt. He's a damn comedian."

362

Laughter erupted from the dense grass. The hidden man yelled back, "Tell him we'll leave after we have the gold."

"Did you hear that Bennett? Actually it's a simple concept. Give us what we want and we'll leave. That way you and your family won't get hurt."

Jim increased the magnification on his goggles and saw the man peering into his cabin. "What exactly do you want?"

The man talked into his radio. "He's playing dumb. Can any of you see where he is or hear him talking?"

The man closest to Jim answered. "I can't hear a thing. I sure as hell can't see him."

One of the men near the mouth of the river said, "He's probably above you. That's where the plane is. If we wait for daylight, I'll follow his tracks to locate him."

"Fuck, Marty, you ain't Tonto. Besides, I want him now." Annoyed by the situation, the man spoke into Jim's walkie-talkie. "Stop playing games, asshole. Where's the gold."

"If I show you where it is, what guarantee do I have that you'll leave Angoon without hurting me or my family?"

"Look asshole, we want the gold. Nobody cares about family bullshit."

"Alright then. The gold's in the water, directly under my boat. Look over either side or better yet walk onto the swim step and look down. You're wearing night goggles, so you'll see what I'm talking about."

Again the man spoke into his radio. "He's on the opposite shore because I'm standing against the bulkhead door. He knows I'm equipped with night-vision. Someone above the boat wouldn't see me. He says the gold's under the boat. I think it's a trap."

The man closest to Jim said, "Keep him talking while I walk the shoreline."

"So the gold's under your boat. Now why would you dump it in the drink?"

Jim held a small transmitter in his left hand. It had a short antenna with three separate red buttons on its front surface. He answered, "I stacked it in the mud flats yesterday during low tide. I'd have gotten it out tonight if you guys wouldn't have shown up."

The man looked over the boat's side while holding the walkie-talkie at his hip. He straightened up, walked to the other side and looked over, then said, "Hey, fuck you man. I don't see shit."

"Maybe the wind and tide pushed my boat closer to shore. Try looking off the back swim step."

Jim laughed as the man opened the transom door and stepped onto the heavy swim platform. He looked into the water with the walkie-talkie at his side, then raised it and said, "There ain't shit over here."

Jim could barely contain himself. "You're breaking up. Can you hear me?"

"Yeah, I hear you fine."

"Good —now listen real careful so you understand what I'm saying."

Jim had pressed the transmitters' first button.

"I'm lis . . ." BOOM.

A bright white flash of light followed, and a loud explosion echoed across the lake. The man's right hand and part of his head disappeared. He dropped dead into the frigid water. The booby-trapped walkie-talkie had served its purpose.

Jim spun to his right and pressed the second button. Something exploded out of one of the tubes Jim had planted near the stream with a loud "POP." A yellow and red line of sparks ascended 200 meters skyward. A white phosphorus flare ignited and a parachute deployed to keep it from falling fast. The entire bay lit up.

Jim aimed a laser-operated rangefinder at the two men near the mouth of the stream and raised his M4A2. After adjusting his elevation site, he squeezed the upper trigger of the grenade launcher. A hollow "CACHUNK" sound followed and a line of sparks defined the grenade's trajectory. Jim counted, "one thousand one, one thousand two, one thousand three, one thou . . ." —an intense white flash was followed by a deafening "KABOOM," which roared through the bay.

Jim was certain that he saw a boot tumbling through the air and land in the lake. Jim located the second man ten meters beyond the blast zone, wounded and stumbling toward the stream. Bennett moved the M16's selector switch to fully automatic mode and located the man in his scope. He heard men yelling something from across the lake but focused his attention on the target in the scope's crosshairs. He squeezed off a short burst. The man crumpled into the shallow water.

Gunfire exploded from all directions. Jim ducked into his makeshift fortress as bullets ricocheted from shoreline rocks 30 feet to his left. The men on the other side of the lake had mistaken his position and were blindly firing into the shoreline opposite them. Before he could return fire, another volley came from his front. Several rounds hissed over his head while others ripped across the top of his Kevlar vest. He rolled to the left side of his fortress, placing it between him and the incoming rounds. Bullets whizzed over his position or were absorbed by the wall of rock and logs. Muzzle blasts lit up a thicket 100 meters away. Jim smiled. Chinese versions of the AK-47 seldom have flash suppressors, making them easy targets during night combat. He raised his weapon and unloaded his gun into the muzzle flashes. The firing from the brush stopped, but the men across the lake opened up again.

Needing to reload and knowing his position was compromised, Jim sprinted into the trees, dove to the ground and snapped another 60-round clip into the rifle. He heard a man moaning before three separate groups of muzzle flashes came from the opposite shoreline, striking his previous location. The flare had extinguished and drifted with the parachute into the lake.

Unsatisfied with his position, Jim crawled to his left and slipped into the lake. Ignoring the frigid water, he maneuvered behind a floating tree still attached by its roots to the shoreline. Awaiting another volley, he scanned the opposite shore to no avail.

A loud "BOOM" from behind him announced the tripping of his Claymore mine. The combatant he'd shot in the thicket had made it to the trail. Gunfire erupted from the far shore and sprayed Jim's previous fortress. He placed his night-vision scope onto the nearest muzzle flash and fired several two second bursts. A man stumbled away from the shore and into an alder thicket while holding his left thigh.

"Bill. Charlie. I'm hit! C'mon, help me get to the boat."

The other two combatants sprinted toward their wounded friend as Bennett unloaded his weapon. They ran in and out of alder thickets, and disappeared into the darkness. Jim immediately pressed the third button on his transmitter, setting off his final mortar flare. Two seconds, later the flare exploded, flooding the bay with light. Knowing the wounded man and his friends were making a dash for their boats, Jim climbed out of the water and ran back to his fortress as he reloaded. He placed his rifle across a downed log and waited for the combatants to cross a 50-meter clearing as they ran toward their boats.

Two men sprinted into the opening. He placed the crosshairs of his scope in front of them and squeezed the trigger as they came into view. One stumbled toward the lake. The second man managed to reach another alder thicket as the wounded man fell into tall grass near the shore.

The flare was nearly out when Jim caught movement in the alder thicket to the right of the clearing. It was the combatant he'd wounded prior to engaging the men in the clearing. He thought, *Sure, leave your buddy behind while you get away. Some friends.* The flare went out, and he lost sight of the wounded man.

Jim grabbed his gear and headed for the inlet. He'd seal it off, then deal with Santos. After reaching the trail, Jim sprinted for the inlet. They'd never escape the inlet without going through him.

It was nearly 2:40 a.m. and he'd eliminated three men and wounded another three. Since his immediate surroundings were secure, Jim opened his computer and assessed the area near his house. He saw the Zodiac nearing the fishing lodge. He immediately turned on his helmet radio and called home.

Lori answered, "Are you okay?"

"Everything's going well. But, the Clan's Zodiac with two men in it are five minutes away from you. Stay tight. I'll be back within an hour."

"Bad news, Danny took it upon himself to engage these guys. We couldn't stop him. He's armed and somewhere outside."

"SHIT!" Several seconds passed before he said, "Stay put and don't open the vault. No matter what. Stay where you are —I'll try to hurry."

"We will. Be safe."

He closed his computer, grabbed his pack, positioned his night goggles, picked up the rifle and headed down the trail. A well-defined line of blood led toward the inlet. His Claymore victim was still alive. He slowed his pace to avoid an ambush.

In a few minutes, he approached the last bit of cover before the open inlet. Jim set down his pack and surveillance case and low crawled through wet grass for the final 20 meters. A slim man knelt in the mud with his arms hung over the sidewall of the Lund, as if he was too weak to get inside. Jim was close enough to see that the back of his shirt and thighs were covered in blood as the man desperately tried to stand. The Santos catamaran was neatly tucked into the cove on the north shore of Whitewater. Bennett was reluctant to close the gap.

Jim assessed his situation. After flipping his night goggles up, he heard the sound of a boat on the east end of the bay. A Coast Guard Zodiac paralleled the shoreline, then stopped. Bennett scanned the entire bay with his binoculars and saw the same Coast Guard cutter that had jammed his radar. It was 2,500 meters away and moving towards his position. Well beyond the cutter, the *Oregon II* lay at anchor.

Olsen's "Cutter"

Helen saw the bright flash in the east while inside the wheelhouse and dashed onto the bridge. Another flash was followed by a loud explosion rumbling in the distance. Sounds of small arms fire echoed through Whitewater Bay. She immediately contacted her brother. "Wayne, can you see what's going on from your position?"

Before he could answer, another white flash was followed by an explosion and more gunfire echoed from deep inside the hidden lake.

Wayne responded, "There's a firefight going on about a half click from here," Wayne reported. "Hold on, I just spotted the Santos catamaran. It's beached near the mouth of an inlet and there's a small aluminum boat beached across the inlet from the catamaran. Over."

"That leaves the Bennett boat and two others —can you see any of them?"

"Negative. They must have gone through the inlet. That's where the firefight is."

"Do you see any movement?"

"Negative."

"Very well. Proceed along the south shore and position yourself to block the exit but don't interfere with Bennett if he tries to leave. If you have the opportunity to take Santos, do so."

"Copy that. Over and out."

The Zodiac accelerated along the shoreline and closed the gap. Dave tapped Wayne on the shoulder and yelled, "There's movement on the catamaran. A man just ran into the cabin. The other's crouched down on the bow."

The Inlet

Jim was surprised when the Zodiac announced its presence over a loudspeaker.

"Ahoy, yellow catamaran. This is the United States Coast Guard. All hands on deck and prepare to be boarded. I repeat, this is the United States Coast Guard. All hands on deck and prepare to be boarded. Failure to respond will result in immediate action."

Someone aboard the catamaran began pulling its windlass anchor from inside the cabin. The catamaran began to back out of the cove.

The wounded man kneeling next to the Lund raised his head, looked at the Zodiac, then struggled to his feet. He lifted his AK-47 to his waist and fired at the Coast Guard vessel. Bennett raised his weapon, aimed and shot the man in the head, dropping him into the Lund. Jim mumbled, "You needed help getting into the boat."

Wayne responded by firing a pedestal-mounted M-240 machine gun at the Lund. Chunks of metal flew in all directions as the gun tore the small boat apart. Jim retreated into thicker grass and said to himself, "For Christ sake, he's dead already."

The catamaran re-beached and Santos and an enormous man walked onto the deck. Both men held assault rifles at their right sides while waving with their left arms, as if surrendering. The Zodiac accelerated toward the catamaran. From the hidden lake, the Boston Whaler approached the mouth of the inlet.

Bennett was familiar enough with the bay to know that unless it was high tide, the Zodiac would run aground on a shallow sandbar. It struck the sandbar on its port side, throwing Wayne against the machine gun and tearing it loose from the floor. Dave was thrown overboard and the Zodiac was helplessly grounded. Dave had a kill switch cable connected to his belt which stopped both outboard motors as he stood in the frigid water.

Jim ran to an enormous pile of driftwood in order to provide cover for the Zodiac and intercept the possible exit of the catamaran.

Santos ran across the bow and jumped to shore, leaving his bodyguard behind. As Santos escaped into the timber, his body guard opened fire on the grounded Zodiac. At over 1,000 meters away, his shots were short, wild and ineffective. Jim aimed his M4A2 at the man's head and squeezed the trigger. The bodyguard dropped to the deck.

The sound of the oncoming Boston Whaler announced its exit from the lake. Jim spun and opened fire, tearing through the vessel and killing its single occupant. The pilot was dead, but the boat continued moving until it struck the rocky shoreline and flipped onto its side. Its outboard motor screamed wildly for several seconds, sputtered and died.

Jim maintained his position while changing clips, and focused his attention on the Bertram. A wounded man was setting up a heavy machine gun with a bi-pod on the boat's bow while another entered the cabin and started its engines. Santos desperately waved at them from shore as they backed away. They didn't return. Jim reached into a pocket and grabbed a grenade for his assault rifle. He sat down, loaded the shell and raised his weapon. With no time to use the rangefinder, he judged the distance and squeezed the trigger. The grenade hissed in flight and struck the starboard stern of the fast-moving boat. The ensuing explosion rocked the turning boat and took off the port side transom. Jim sprinted toward the underbrush and a torrent of M60 rounds closely followed his escape. Out of grenades and not eager to engage the heavy machine gun, he dove behind a clump of driftwood.

Jim focused on the narrow part of the inlet, hoping to unload his clip into the Bertram's cabin as it passed. Knowing that the machine gunner on the bow couldn't turn fast enough to fire at him, Jim stood and raised his weapon. Before the Bertram came into Jim's view, its gunner began firing the M60 at the distant beached Zodiac.

Wayne yelled into his helmet. "They're coming out HOT and shooting at us with a heavy machine gun. We're sitting ducks."

Helen heard Wayne's transmission while standing near the cutter's Gatling gun. She nudged Jeff to the side and manned the gun.

Knowing the gunner was focused on the Zodiac, Jim stood and prepared for a final take down. When the Bertram came into view, he trained his weapon on the pilot and unloaded a sixty-round clip. Bullets tore through the fiberglass sides and windows, and the pilot slumped against the control panel. Blood splatter covered the cabin's interior.

The boat passed and its engines coughed. Jim had hit the pilot and managed to disable both engines. The boat slowed, but a following wake pushed it forward into Whitewater Bay. The Bertram's machine gunner changed his ammo belt as Jim frantically dug for another clip. Raising his weapon, he saw the Coast Guard cutter had come about. The Bertram was in a direct line of fire between them. On instinct, Jim dove to the ground The ship opened fire with its Gatling gun.

The surrounding landscape became engulfed with bright red, orange and yellow bullet fragments. Red metal tracers tore through the Bertram. An enormous yellow fireball followed by flying chunks of fiberglass signaled the boat's destruction. The boat was completely destroyed, but Jim also found himself on the receiving end of the Gatling's projectiles. He held onto his helmet as the cutter finished its assault. Searing pain from his back, leg and foot let him know he'd been hit. The colonel's Kevlar vest was no match for depleted uranium shells.

What seemed like an eternity had lasted just four seconds, but the damage was done. Jim lay wounded as pieces of the exploded boat rained from the sky. He remained motionless, face down in the gravel and covered in mud and debris. Burning pain shot through the right half of his torso. Knocked breathless and semi-conscious, he knew he was wounded, but he was unable to react. The hit in his torso was the most intensely painful wound he'd ever garnered. Eerie silence followed and an odd-smelling thick fog engulfed the entire area.

A much-needed adrenaline surge enabled him to rise to his hands and knees. He began choking on fumes and smoke. Survival instinct told him to hold his breath and move — move fast. Sheer will pushed him away from the shoreline. Thirty meters and many agonizing breaths later, he wobbled and fell to his knees. Surrounded by a yellowish cloud, he continued to breathe in acrid air. He rolled onto his side and watched a long cloud of smoke rise over the ocean and shoreline.

The pain subsided, and his mind began to clear. He assessed his wounds. His left boot had two buckshot-sized burn holes. Shrapnel had traveled completely through his foot. He cut open the side of his left trouser and found a cauterized hole in his upper leg. Shrapnel rested deep within the muscle or against his femur. It hurt terribly, but there was little blood. Hot metal had literally cooked the wound shut. Jim pulled off his Kevlar vest and jacket and stretched his left hand around the small of his back. Though he couldn't see the wound, he could feel it deep inside his thorax. He managed to touch the wound. It was much larger than his leg wound. The cauterized hole refused to bleed.

Jim thought, *Get the fuck out of here.*

He gathered himself and stood. He slowly limped to his backpack. Feeling woozy, he sat on the bow of the bullet-riddled Lund. Jim looked at the dead man and whispered, "Sorry mister. It's better you than me. For a moment, I thought you were the Energizer Bunny — you just kept banging that drum."

Shaking his head clear, Jim stood and walked toward the lake's headwaters, and into the dense vegetation. Ten minutes later, he came upon the man who'd been concealed near the river. He was missing a leg and was split apart from the grenade.

Direct hit, Jim thought. *You never felt a thing.*

Jim tied a long piece of orange flagging ribbon to the closest alder branch, and commenced to cross the stream, now over waist-deep from the incoming tide. A bullet-ridden body floated in the water near the opposite shore. Jim grabbed the corpse's shirt and dragged it to shore. Again, he tied a piece of flagging to the nearest tree, and proceeded toward his boat.

Near the *Sojourn*, the man he'd killed with the walkie-talkie bomb bobbed up and down against the shoreline. The corpse was too large to move, so Jim cut some rope from his bow line and tied it around the man's belt. The dead man was wearing a faded denim jacket with a "Hell Bent" motorcycle gang emblem embroidered on it. He tied the other end of the rope to a stand of saplings, then flagged the spot.

A voice from the alder thicket to his left said, "Put your hands in the air and don't move." Santos stood 30 feet away with AK-47 pointed at him.

"No nonsense," Santos said. "I won't hesitate shooting. Now, where's the gold?"

As Jim raised his hands, the bear with a white patch on its face appeared out of the brush behind Santos. Jim almost laughed out loud. In a soft, raspy voice, he said, "The bear behind you will see that you won't kill me."

"I'm done talking. This is your last chance. Tell me now or I'll shoot."

The bear moved and growled, and Santos swung around. The AK-47 went off and the bear charged. It knocked Santo to the ground with one swipe of a front paw. The AK-47 flew away and the bear jumped on him. Santos screamed as the bear began pounding him into the ground..

Jim backed into the water and tossed his gear over the transom. He struggled to get onto the swim step, but the thought of the danger at home enabled him to ignore his pain and climb aboard. He locked himself in the cabin and started both engines. On shore, the bear was tearing Santos to shreds. Both propellers churned up sand and silt, but with the push of a button, the windlass anchor pulled the boat into deeper water. Jim turned the *Sojourn* toward the inlet and accelerated.

Bennett's House —3:30 a.m.

Crane circled the Zodiac in front of the log house and assessed the situation. The house lights were off and the setting was quiet and peaceful. The eastern sky had begun to lighten with pink and red clouds, but the timber surrounding the house provided an inky, black setting. Both men continued to wear their night goggles. Crane placed the boat in neutral and asked, "What the hell's going on here? The place looks deserted."

"They're sleeping. Or maybe it's a trap. Before my cameras went berserk, I could see the entire group from across the narrows. They're here somewhere. Motor into shore and we'll recon the place."

Crane beached the boat on the rocky shore and cut the engine. They scrambled from the Zodiac, split apart and ran to the front corners of the house. The dwelling appeared empty as they circled its perimeter. Jim's Humvee sat in the driveway near a wooden tool shed. Rusty felt its hood for heat and met up with Crane on the rear porch. He whispered, "Their rig's been parked here for days, but they've been using his boat. He's got a 'gopher hole' somewhere."

"Do you think anyone's here?"

"Let's find out." Rusty walked onto the porch and tried the door handle which turned freely. He placed his back against the wall, turned the handle again and nudged the door open with his foot. Pointing an M16 into the doorway, he peeked inside, then snapped his head back outside. He motioned for Crane to join him and whispered, "Go inside while I cover you."

Crane shook his head and didn't bother whispering. "Bullshit, this is the sorta crap *you* do. *You* go inside and I'll cover you."

Miller peeked one more time, pointed his rifle inside, and moved into the dark house. As he snuck from room to room on the main floor, it appeared empty. He felt the coffee pot and oven for heat, but they were cold. Careful to examine every room and closet, Rusty concluded the main floor was unoccupied. After sneaking up the steps, he searched upstairs. The rooms were also empty and all the beds were made. Looking over the upper banister into the vaulted living room, he thought, *So this is how a Senator's son lives. Not too shabby, Colonel —not too shabby at all.*

After trying several light switches on the main floor, Rusty realized someone had tripped the main breaker. A doorway under the stairs led to the basement. He turned on his head lamp, walked down the stairs and examined the basement walls for a hidden exit. He noticed that the main floor footprint didn't match the basement footprint. The basement was shorter than the main floor.

He turned to Crane, who had followed him like a puppy. "He's crafty alright. There's a hidden chamber under the east end of this house. When we find it, we'll find the gold."

It was light enough to operate without goggles but too dark to see details without a flashlight. Rusty estimated where a concrete partition might separate the basement from a hidden chamber, and the duo began tearing away throw rugs and moving beds, appliances and furniture. Convinced a chamber existed, Rusty examined each closet for signs of a doorway. Tearing apart the linen closet, he found the back wall had uncharacteristic perimeter molding. Careful examination revealed a slight gap at each side of the wall. Realizing that the wall pivoted on its center, Miller pushed on its edges but it wouldn't budge. He kicked the wall in frustration. It moved slightly but not enough to gain access into the chamber. Crane pushed him aside, laid on his back with his shoulders against a wall and pushed with his legs. Snapping studs and tearing sheetrock provided Rusty with enough room to crawl into the dark void.

Inside the vault, Oscar growled at the massive steel door. Audra placed her ear against the door and listened carefully. She jumped back and whispered, "Someone's out there —they're trying to turn the wheel."

"Don't worry, they'll never get in — not before Jim returns. Besides, we were expecting company. We'd better radio Jim and give him a heads up."

Whitewater Bay —3:30 AM

Wondering if the cutter might mistake his intentions and cut him apart with their Gatling gun, Jim cut the throttle, removed a white pillow case from the state-room bed and tied it to his radio antenna.

Suddenly he heard Lori's voice on his helmet's radio.

"Jim, do you copy?"

In a weak and scratchy voice, he answered, "I hear you."

Lori asked, "Are you alright? You sound like crap."

"Just a few nicks — that's all. What's up?"

"Someone's trying to get into the vault."

"Whatever you do, don't open it. Arm yourself and remain calm. I'll be there shortly."

Jim pushed both throttles wide open passing through the inlet. The Coast Guard Zodiac remained beached on the sandy spit as Jim entered the bay. He made a point of broadsiding his boat to the cutter so they could see his white flag. Jim's cell phone rang as he passed Santos's catamaran. It was Helen.

"Top of the morning to you, Colonel," she said. "I tried calling earlier but you must have been preoccupied."

"I've been very busy. I assume you're on the Coast Guard vessel. Tell your gunner not to confuse me as a combatant."

"Jolly good observation. Our gunner's aware. Would you be so kind as to pull our Zodiac into deeper water? It's run aground."

Jim coughed several times and brown coagulated blood spewed from his mouth. "I'm really strapped for time." He coughed again as more of the foul stuff left his lungs. "I've got unwanted visitors at my house."

"It should only take a minute. Afterwards, pick me up. I'll be your back-up. From the sound of your cough and voice, you probably need it."

Jim swung his boat toward the beached craft. "I'll pull the boat free, but your men need to clean up a mess inside the inlet. I ribboned two casualties that need to disappear on the south shore. There's another inside the Lund and one in the tipped Whaler and a body on the catamaran deck. The exploded Bertrum has two casualties.

"Interesting fact: Santos escaped the catamaran, only to be killed by a bear. Don't tell. I'm eternally grateful. What's left of him is near an orange-flagged body halfway down the lake on the north shore. That's nine bodies."

Helen responded, "Once the Zodiac's free, I'll send a crew to clean up. We'll handle that. Pick me up. I really want to join you."

Jim hesitated, assessing the extent of his injuries. "OK, but don't dawdle. Danny's alone outside dealing with unwanted visitors."

"God, no! I'll be on the starboard side rope ladder waiting."

Jim arrived at the Zodiac and threw them a rope. The older of the two men saluted and said, "It's an honor to finally meet you, sir. I've heard much about you."

Coughing, Jim managed, "I'd like to chat, but I've got shit going on. Tie off to your rear cleat and I'll pull you loose."

Moments later, the Zodiac was free and Jim raced toward the cutter.

Helen told Frank, Gus and Jeff, "It's almost 4:00 a.m. and we're running short on time. I'm going after Rusty with Bennett. The three of you are responsible for wrapping things up here."

She looked at Gus. "Pull the captured ship's anchor and tow it to the outer edge of Russian Reef. It's likely out of fuel, or very close, so Wayne can go ahead and sink it. At 500 feet, the currents will disperse any residual fuel."

"Make certain the Straits and sky are void of any traffic. Radar will tell you if things are clear. Stay out of Wayne's way unless he asks for help. He's a demolitions expert and knows what to do. While it's being towed, Jeff needs to remove all life rings and open all hatches and bulkheads so when it blows, it sinks immediately. Chain the Santos catamaran to the ship and sink them together. I want everything deep-sixed by the time I return. Afterwards, remove all of our Coast Guard markings and return to Echo Bay."

"Why did Dave and Wayne go to the lake?"

"They're cleaning up casualties and any other evidence. Santos is dead along with his entire crew. And get this. A bear killed Santos. A freaking bear! Mr. Bennett's got friends, I'd say. All the bodies have to be aboard the *Oregon II* when it's scuttled. I've gotta go."

Helen ran to the rope ladder hanging from the starboard side as Jim's boat approached the cutter. She wore a flak jacket, helmet and pistol, and an M16 was slung over her shoulder. Moments later she was inside the cabin of Jim's boat. He was ashen, and she saw the coagulated blood on the floor and his shirt. She touched a clump of brown material on his shirt and realized it was semi -cooked blood.

"Christ, this blood's yours! Where are you hit?"

"Pretty much all over, I took a pile of hot shrapnel." Jim accelerated to full throttle towards Angoon. "Listen up, we've got a job to do and time is running out, so let's focus on the mission. We'll deal with this ancillary crap after we're done."

"Nonsense. You're wounded and you look like shit." She lifted the back of his shirt, and saw hole as large as a dime. Whatever made it didn't exit the front of his chest. "This isn't good — not good at all."

"I can handle it."

Helen immediately called the ship. "Jeff, when the ship's positioned at the reef, bring the chopper. The colonel's got a chest wound — I'll be done there by the time you reach Angoon."

"Can do — I'll call when we take off."

The boat sped toward Angoon as Bennett coughed up more chunks of dark blood. Helen removed his helmet and kissed him on top of his head. "Hang in there, Colonel. You can't die on my watch — Danny would hate me."

"Relax. I'm not ready to cash in quite yet, and Danny needs our help." Jim pointed to a small red box. "Kindly open that first-aid kit and find the yellow prescription bottle that says "Vicodin." Give me a tablet with some water please."

Helen fumbled with the bottle as Jim continued on course. With trembling hands, she gave him a pill. He swallowed it with a swig of water. He coughed and bright red blood trickled from his nostrils onto his shirt. Helen winced while watching him wipe his nose onto his forearm.

"Thanks," he said.

"Colonel, you need some serious care.

"All in good time. We have some other shit to take care of first. Here's the plan: I drop you off 100 meters south of my place. When you're on the beach, push me back into the narrows. I'll run aground on the beach in front of my house. That'll get their attention and keep them occupied while you slip into the timber and flank them. There are two combatants — a big galoot named Crane and your albino friend who ain't an albino. Shoot to kill. The girls are in a downstairs vault but Danny's outside, so be careful who you're shooting."

The boat passed Hood Bay and Helen said, "I should stay with you. You're in no shape to be point man."

"They don't know that. I'll draw their fire while you blindside them. No sense in both of us taking the heat. Can you adjust your helmet radio to my frequency?"

"Certainly, what is it?"

"Sixty-six."

Helen changed the frequency on her helmet, then stood behind the colonel.

Bennett's House - 4:05 a.m.

Rusty quickly realized that breaking into the vault was hopeless. Placing his ear against its heavy steel door, he thought he heard voices. Examination of the chamber led him to believe there was another entrance. He crawled back from the dark void and explained the situation to Crane. The duo retreated outdoors and considered their options.

A steady rain greeted them. "I'm convinced the gold's in that vault," Miller began, "and so is Bennett's family. There has to be a fresh air supply, otherwise they'd suffocate. If we can locate it, we'll force them out by pouring gasoline down the pipe. When they realize what we're up to, they'll exit like rats."

Crane argued, "Bennett might show any minute. Wasting time looking for it's senseless. We'll grab him when he returns, then force him to open it."

Rusty thought to himself, *You dumb ass, nobody forces Bennett to do anything and the odds of capturing him are slim to none. You'll be my sacrificial lamb.*

He appeased his partner by saying, "We'll do both. Conceal yourself and be my lookout. He's got to pass by in order to get home and when he does, call me. If there's no time and he storms the house, shoot for his legs."

Crane smiled, "Good plan. I'll post myself at the northwest corner of his deck. Stay in radio contact."

Crane positioned himself against a large support column out of the rain while Rusty stood at the east end of the house and studied the roof above the vault. He stood back and saw that a white PVC pipe with a 180-degree return fitting exited the roof near its ridgeline. Bathroom vents were visible lower down the roof and lacked the return fitting. The uppermost PVC pipe had to be the air vent, but it was impossible to reach without an enormous extension ladder.

Considering the placement of his cameras and the fact that Jim hadn't been seen coming or going, the secret exit had to be beyond the view of both cameras. Rusty noticed a wooden shed sitting north of the house. He went to it, opened the door and searched for a trapdoor. Finding nothing, he focused on locating a ladder tall enough to gain access to the roof vent but came up empty. But there was a battery-powered saw stored on a workbench and a gallon container of gasoline on the floor. The saw would easily cut through walls and plastic pipe.

Rusty walked outside and looked at the pipe again. Confident that he could tear apart the walls on the upper floor and find it, his attention turned toward locating the hidden entrance. Logic dictated that a trench would have been dug and a large pipe or culvert installed, then covered with soil. Excess rock and dirt would have been stockpiled and re-spread after the ground settled. He searched for surface depressions and any unusual mound. Rusty smiled knowing that the entrance had to be somewhere beyond the shed. He crisscrossed the area and quickly located Jim's "gopher hole." Its lid was partially open, and Rusty looked in all directions for signs of other people.

Danny remained perfectly still as Miller peered at the overgrown mound. Danny's scope was trained on Rusty's chest and his right index finger touched lightly on the M16's trigger. His heart pounded so that he thought the world would hear it.

Satisfied he was alone, Miller pivoted the lid to one side, knelt and pointed his head lamp into the dark. A dull aluminum object lay on the floor of the cement, and dozens of gold coins. After turning in all directions, he pulled his pistol and clamored down the eight-foot ladder.

Danny sprung to his feet and sprinted toward the lid with a grenade. He pulled the pin, let the handle fly, dropped it into the culvert and pulled the lid over the hole. A dull explosion rattled through the ground, pushing the lid into a vertical position. Stunned and knocked down by the blast, Danny rolled to his knees, got up and ran toward his hiding spot.

Crane cleared the corner of the shed as Danny ran toward the mound. He raised his Glock and fired off an entire clip. Danny crumpled. Crane re-loaded and ran to the vault entrance

Smoke billowed from the dark hole. He knelt and yelled, "Rusty, are you in there?"

Silence followed. He talked over his radio. "Rusty, where are you?"

Again, no answer. Crane pulled a small mag light from his pocket and shined it into the hole. There was the gold. He looked at Danny's body, then climbed into the culvert. Seventy feet inside the concrete tunnel, a bright head lamp lay on the floor illuminating Rusty. He lay face down with tattered, smoking clothing. Crane stood over his partner and gave him a nudge with his foot. Convinced Rusty was dead, Crane walked to the end of the tunnel and shined the light on a stainless steel bank vault door. After trying to turn the immense wheel, he kicked at it and yelled, "You fucking rats!"

Walking back to the entrance, Crane talked to himself. "There's only one way I'm gonna get this gold. I've gotta catch Bennett when he returns."

Crane climbed from the tunnel and walked to Danny and realized the young Bennett was wearing body armor. His Kevlar helmet was torn apart on the upper left side. The helmet had deflected a bullet. Another bullet had torn into his Kevlar jacket directly below his shoulder blade. Crane drew his pistol and rolled Danny onto his back. Blood covered the side of Danny's face and he faintly moaned. Crane kicked him in the side. With his gun pointed at Danny's head, he yelled, "Wake up, Come on, wake up you miserable fuck."

Blinking profusely, Danny looked up and saw three blurred figures standing over him. Knowing the three were actually one Crane, he tried to gather himself. He needed to buy some time — enough to formulate a plan. He pretended to pass out.

"C'mon kid, wake up."

Danny's eyes fluttered, then he rolled onto his right side, assuming a fetal position. His right foot rested on top of his right hand. Crane walked to his other side, rolled him onto his back with his foot, demanding again that he wake up. Again his eyes fluttered, then opened slightly

"That's right kid, open your damn eyes. Wake the fuck up."

The three images merged. Crane pointed his Glock at Danny's head and asked, "What's the combination kid?"

Danny closed his eyes again and Crane kicked his foot. "C'mon kid, give me the damn combination."

Danny pointed with his left arm toward the shed. Crane turned and Danny lifted his right hand and pulled the trigger of the Derringer. The .357 hollow point struck Crane in his left side, knocking him backwards. Dropping his Glock and holding his lower rib cage with both hands, Crane stumbled toward the beach.

Danny took a deep breath and murmured, "Combination is THREE-FIFTY-SEVEN, asshole!" He closed his eyes.

Five minutes later, a tattered and bloody figure emerged from the colonel's "gopher hole." Clear of the tunnel, Rusty fell to the wet ground. Lying there, he saw Danny's body near the overgrown mound. He looked at his watch, stood, then wobbled toward the beach. He found Crane in the Zodiac with a massive wound.

He returned to Danny.

Rocky Point —4:20 a.m.

Hearing a loud explosion, Lori called Jim but had no response. His radio helmet was on the rear deck. He and Helen rounded the fishing lodge, then headed straight down the narrows toward Jim's house. Jim cut the throttles and nudged the bow onto the shoreline just south of his house. Helen helped him stand and secured his bullet-ridden Kevlar vest to his shrapnel-riddled body.

Helen kissed him on the cheek, and placed his helmet on. "Stay alert, Colonel. I'll have you on a chopper in a few more minutes."

She ran to the front of the boat and jumped off. After pushing the boat back into the narrows, Helen sprinted into the timber with her assault rifle in hand.

Wanting to draw attention, Jim tore past the beach at full throttle and made two large circles while assessing the situation. After his second turn, he saw Crane crouching behind the Zodiac's steering pedestal with an AK-47 in hand. The blood-soaked cop stood and raised his weapon and Jim pushed both throttles forward. Aiming directly for the Zodiac, Bennett accelerated at full speed, then cut both engines a split second before ramming the rear of the boat. Jim's huge boat completely swallowed the small Zodiac as Crane awkwardly dove sideways. Bennett ran from the cabin and jumped off of the rear transom plate into the frigid water. Pain shot through his lung and bright red blood spewed from his mouth as he bent over and peeked around the port side of the boat. Not seeing Crane, Jim crept along the starboard hull until he spotted him beside it.

He walked to Crane and shot him twice in the head. He spoke out loud. "How do you like being dead, asshole?"

Helen whispered into her headset. "What's happening? Talk to me."

Jim managed, "Crane's dead."

Helen responded, "Where are you?"

"Next to my boat by the Zodiac."

Lori's voice came through the radios. "Jim, I just tried calling you. There was a big explosion inside the tunnel ten minutes ago. Later, someone tried opening the vault."

Jim whispered, "Stay put. Have you heard from Danny?"

Lori answered, "No. Is Helen with you?"

"Yeah. Look, we're both busy. Don't call us, we'll call you. Helen, where are you?"

She whispered back, "Twenty meters south of the house. I can see you now and I have a good view of the rear and side door."

Jim said, "I'm making a run for the deck, cover me."

What Jim called a run turned into a pathetic hurried limp. Reaching the deck, he bent down and coughed. More blood ran from his opened mouth while he gasped for air. He saw one of the waterfront doors was wide open.

Hearing him cough, Helen asked, "Are you alright?"

Jim struggled to answer. "Short of breath, that's all. You can't cover me from where you're at so watch the other doors. I'm going in."

Jim's adrenal gland somehow kicked in. He ran up the front steps and ducked behind the hot tub. Though it was raining, he saw blood drops on the patio and wondered if it was coming or going. He also wondered if it might be Crane's — or Danny's. After looking behind him, he pulled a small pocket mirror from his vest, held it beyond the corner of the spa and looked into the house. It appeared empty.

Only ten feet separated him from the log wall separating the two large glass doors. He bolted to the wall and placed his back against it. Again, he held the mirror out and examined the living room but several small blind spots prevented him from getting the complete picture.

He whispered, "I'm at the door. Fresh bloods on the patio and inside carpet — can't tell if it's coming or going. Anything back there?"

Helen answered, "Negative. No movement, no blood. Since you're at the door, I'll swing around to your end of the house and cover you."

Again whispering, "Negative — cover your end of the house. If shit goes south, you'll hear it over the radio. Be ready to come in from your side."

Jim entered the house. His eyes scanned the room as he swung his M4 from side to side. From his vantage point, noticeable blood drops were visible on the kitchen floor. He crept past the bar, then stood near the dining room table. He peeked into the kitchen, and saw Danny tied to a chair with a gag in his mouth. He took a step forward and the distinct sound of a cocking pistol announced someone behind him. A voice ordered, "DROP IT!"

Jim set his rifle to the floor and turned. Standing behind the bar with a .45 ACP pointed at Jim's head was a red-headed man in a shirt covered in blood.

"Long time no see, Colonel." He waved his pistol toward the couch, "Have a seat. We need to talk. Remove the helmet and flak jacket. No funny stuff or you're dead."

Outside, Helen overheard the order being given to Jim. So did Lori and Audra in the vault.

Jim sat down. "I'll be goddamn — Staff Sergeant Russel J. Miller. So you're the Dark Star mole. You ought to take better care of yourself, you look like roadkill."

Miller walked around the bar with a whiskey bottle in one hand and his pistol in the other. He spun a black leather recliner around so it faced Jim and sat. "You're not looking so hot yourself." He took a swig from the bottle. "Tell me Jim, do you miss Delta?"

"Not at all."

"Neither do I. Come to think of it, I hated working for you and your nigger friend."

"Who are you talking about?"

"That fucking CIA spook, Diller. I'm the one who dropped a dime on his black ass to the Columbians. I got 50 grand out of the deal. That's when I realized I could make more money on the outside."

Jim wanted to rip Rusty apart. "So you're the fucker who blew our cover. I never took you for a turncoat or a racist. Because of you, Escobar put a hit out on me and my family. All these years, I figured General Clark got shit faced and shot off his mouth about our operation. You've stretched the boundaries of bad behavior."

"You're right about Clark. That's how I found out Diller was CIA instead of a drug distributor from Miami."

Rusty put the bottle on the floor. "Enough chit-chat, Jim. You know why I'm here."

Jim looked beyond Rusty. Danny had blood oozing down the side of his head and face. Trying to buy time, he asked, "What did you do to my son?"

"That prick fragged me when I was in the tunnel searching for your vault. Crane shot him after he fragged me. Your kid shot Crane, somehow. So here we are. You're shot up. Your kid's shot up. Crane's shot up. I'm shot up. It's a mess for sure."

Rusty pointed his pistol at Danny. "He's dead if you don't give me the gold."

Jim coughed up blood but managed, "If I give you the gold, then what?"

"I want you and whoever's downstairs to load the gold into the Hummer. Then, I tie everyone up, and disappear. It's easy. Give me what I want and I'll go away. That way nobody else gets hurt."

"If I do that, you'll kill us."

"I have no interest in killing anyone. I simply want the gold. Listen up, Colonel, there is a plan "B." I can shoot you and the kid now, tear through your walls and expose the air pipe leading into the vault. After I pour gasoline into the vent, I bet the gals in the basement flee before I get a chance to toss a road flare down the pipe. Get my drift?"

Jim coughed repeatedly and bright red blood spewed from his mouth. A steady thin stream trickled from his nostrils. Jim held out his right arm and tried to speak. Struggling to remain conscious, he leaned back in the couch, closed his eyes and tried to catch his breath.

Miller shook his head. "What a shame. I don't think you're going to survive this time around, Colonel. Unlike the uncanny luck you had in Panama, the reaper's got your number today. I told Noriega's goons about Diller's rescue plan. I even delayed your extraction chopper. You were so frickin' lucky that night. Both you and that jig-a-boo got out alive, but I'm afraid you've run out of luck. I guess it'll be 'Plan B,' as in 'barbequed bunker.'"

Jim opened his eyes. He smiled, pulled himself erect, wiped blood on his sleeve and managed, "You fucking racist. Now, you have pissed me off. Here's my proposal, asshole, put down your weapon and you won't get hurt."

Miller smiled. "That's the dumbest thing I've heard in years. Now why in the fuck would I do that? You're in no shape to suck any more lead."

"Because an old friend of yours has an M16 aimed at your head."

"I get it. This is when I turn around so you can make a play for my Colt. Go ahead, Colonel. Make your play."

The distinct "click" of an M16 selector switch sounded behind him and a cold steel barrel pressed against the back of Rusty's head.

"No! This where I resist blowing your bloody brains out," said Helen.

Rusty sank into the recliner. Jim limped over, grabbed his gun and pistol-whipped him. He moved to Danny, removed his gag, untied him and examined his wound. Then, he returned to the couch and collapsed.

Helen butted Rusty's head with the stock of her M16, knocking him to the floor. "That's for Whitey, you miserable fuck. There's a lot more of that coming." She zip tied his hands and feet together, then went to Danny, who was removing his father's burnt and bloody shirt.

The colonel looked at Danny's blood soaked head and saw a short section of missing scalp. White skull was visible under the dried, crusty blood.

Jim pointed to the sofa. "Sit down, son. You're hurt."

Danny sat. He was dizzy. "Christ, you're hurt a lot worse than me. Your back looks terrible. We've got to get you to a hospital."

"No hospitals, they ask questions. We'll all end up in prison. Helen, please call the girls on your radio. Tell them it's over. If they balk, I'll talk with them."

Before Helen could speak, the lights came on. Shortly after, Audra and Lori arrived. They had been listening, but they were stunned at what they saw. Audra knelt next to her father and cried while Lori grabbed several wet towels and two blankets. Lori carefully wiped Jim's back clean. Blood slowly oozed from the hole and he labored to breathe. She rolled him onto his right side and elevated his legs. She covered him with a blanket, then looked at Danny's wound.

"Danny likely has a concussion," she said. "Jim's going into shock. He's bleeding internally. His right lung could be fried — he needs immediate care."

"NO!" barked Jim. "I've treated worse."

Struggling to breathe, he gathered himself and managed to say, "My lung isn't sucking air. The holes are cauterized. Blood's pooling in my chest. Lung's collapsing, I need a drain tube."

Lori shook her head. "You need a doctor."

His head slumped forward. "Drain blood now. I'm dying."

Helen and a woozy Danny dragged Miller onto the patio and Helen called the ship. Audra Googled lung wounds as Jim mumbled to Lori about Rhonda Kadake.

Helen told Frank, "We captured Rusty, but Bennett's dying. He's drowning in his own blood and refuses to go to a hospital. He claims hospital staff ask too many questions. We need someone to administer a chest drain to keep him alive, and deal with his wounds. Can you please help? We can't let him die!"

"How long can he hold on?"

Tears rolled from Helen's eyes. "Not much longer."

"Keep me informed. I'll arrange something."

Audra ran out to Danny and Helen. "Dad's right. Chest wounds require immediate draining. Dad just reminded me that the nurse who casted me was a triage nurse in Iraq. She must know how to perform this procedure. Help us get Dad into the Hummer and down to the clinic."

Lori leaned over Jim. "C'mon lover, time to get that drain tube going. We're going to help you into the truck. Can you stand?"

With blue hands and lips, he managed to sit up on the edge of the couch, and hold out his arms. "I need help."

She kissed him on top of his head, placed her arms under his and whispered, "On the count of three. Here we go, one . . . two . . . three."

Jim wobbled, but stood. Lori, Danny and Audra helped him to the Hummer while Helen stood over the unconscious Rusty. Lori raced the Humvee down Killisnoo Road to the health clinic. Knowing Rhonda lived in the new doublewide directly behind the clinic, Lori laid on the horn, then ran to her front door. She beat on the door yelling, "Rhonda! Get up! It's an emergency."

Lori pounded on the door and the short, dark-haired woman answered in her robe. "Darlin, do ya know what time it is? It's barely 4:30. This better be good."

"Jim Bennett's in the truck dying. He needs a chest drain right away. Have you ever done that before?"

Rhonda immediately woke up. "Too many times. Get him into the clinic. It ain't locked. I'll be right over."

Back at the house, Rusty awoke to find himself hogtied and laying in the rain. He struggled briefly, then realized escape was impossible. Helen stood in the doorway looking down at her captive. "Bachman said he'll go medieval on you and I agree."

She shook her head in disgust and radioed the ship.

Gus answered. "Frank's been on the phone with an intern in Sitka. From the sounds of it, he's got him lined out to work on Bennett in exchange for something. He and Jeff left with the chopper five minutes ago. How's the Colonel holding up?"

"Not well. It's dire. His family took him to Angoon. There's a small clinic and a nurse who may be able to install a chest tube. If not, I'm afraid . . . hold on, my phone is ringing. It's Bennett's daughter."

Helen told Audra, "Please tell me the nurse can help him."

Audra answered with panic in her voice. "The nurse says his wound is really bad. He's unconscious and she's trying to revive him. Lori and Danny are inside helping her. I'm so afraid he's going to die."

"My employer is lining up a physician as we speak. If the . . . hold on, he's calling."

Frank spoke via radio. "I've got an off-duty intern in Sitka ready to go. I also have a pulmonary surgeon from Harbor View in Seattle who's inbound on a chartered jet. I'm counting on the intern to keep Bennett alive and stable until the surgeon arrives. I'm in the air now and will have the intern there within 30 minutes. Can he hold on until we get there?"

"I don't know. That may be too late. I'm not at the clinic, but his daughter says a nurse is trying to revive him. Please hurry, we're running out of time."

"All evidence is deep-sixed, and Dave and Wayne are headed your way with the Zodiac to pick up Miller. Where do we land the chopper?"

Helen had to think. "There's a running track near the school. We'll pick you up there. What's the name of the intern?"

"John — John Spaulding. Look, call me if anything changes."

Helen spoke to Audra. "Did you catch that Audra? We've got a doctor coming shortly. When you hear the helicopter, drive to the school and pick him up."

Helen immediately contacted a friend at Dark Star.

"Bill, this is Helen Moorcroft. No chatting. I need an enormous favor. Run complete profiles on Doctor John Spaulding of Sitka, Alaska, and Nurse Rhonda Kadake from Angoon, Alaska. Send the results to my Blackberry. This is a category-ten situation, so get it to me immediately."

The man replied, "Shit, Helen. You don't work here anymore. Old man Reid pulled the plug on the entire operation."

"Bill, this is a *category-ten situation*! You're the only person I can turn to. *Please* help!"

"Alright, gal. Buy me a few drinks the next time you're in Seattle."

___

The Clinic — 5:00 a.m.

Audra winced and turned to the wall as she talked to Helen on the phone. "Oh, sick. She just poked a huge needle between dads' ribs. She's sucking out blood through the syringe — I gotta go."

Rhonda withdrew the syringe. "That's the problem. The pleural cavity's filled with blood. A lung is collapsed. Lori, keep giving him mouth to mouth. Dan, I want ya to slowly push on his chest when I tell ya to. We need to time this thing and mimic a natural breathing rhythm. After Lori fills his lungs with air, you push down to evacuate the blood. It's our only hope."

She compared the needle's depth with the catheter's probe, inserted the probe between his ribs, then told Lori to force air into his mouth. Blood immediately trickled into a vented glass bottle connected to the clear plastic hose. She looked at Danny and nodded. "Gently push down son."

Blood slowly moved through the tube as Danny pushed down. Not satisfied with the results, Rhonda repositioned the tip of the catheter and told Lori to give him another lung-full of air. Acting like a pump, the expanding lung forced blood from the pleural cavity into the jar. Rhonda calmly whispered, "Good. Dan, push down gently, as if your dad's exhaling." Blood now flowed faster into the jar. Rhonda nodded while listening to Jim's heart through a stethoscope. She smiled. "OK guys, keep doin' what your doin — nice easy rhythms. His heart rate is better and he might start breathin' on his own. I've gotta set up a plasma I.V."

Rhonda secured her only bag of plasma and began setting up the drip stand when Lori said, "It seems as if he's trying to breathe. Yes. I'm sure of it. Maybe we should stop."

The collection jar was almost two-thirds filled. Plugging the I.V. into Jim's muscular arm, Rhonda looked at his face. "No. Keep pumpin' that blood out. If he opens his eyes, let me know."

Audra felt sick watching the gruesome scene and went outside for fresh air. When she reached the porch, she dropped to her knees, threw up and began sobbing uncontrollably. She was trying to regain her composure and stand when her phone rang. She looked at caller ID and answered in a shaky voice. "Hey, Helen."

Helen wondered if it was too late. "How's your father?"

"I don't know. Everything's a blur. They're trying to revive him. I'm outside. I got sick and threw up. Where's the helicopter?"

Helen grabbed the two background reports from Jim's printer as she answered. "They're five minutes out. I've been informed to contact you."

Audra managed a considered response. "I think the chopper should land by the town landfill. That way we won't wake up half of Angoon. It's secluded and flat and I can leave now if you can contact them."

"Brilliant idea. I'll contact them immediately. My guys are here picking up our prisoner. I'll meet you there in three or four minutes."

Audra couldn't face the idea of going back into the clinic and watching her father die. Still crying, she said, "OK, I'm on my way."

Danny watched out the front window as the Humvee sped off. "Audra's leaving. I guess the doctor's about to land."

Jim opened his eyes. He tried talking but only managed an incoherent gurgle. Rhonda smiled. "Looks like our patient's comin' round. Whatcha tryin' to say Mr. Bennett?"

Lori leaned over and wiped his forehead. "For Christ's sake Jim. We thought you were gone. Rhonda here just saved your life."

Jim looked at the I.V. and catheter. He looked toward Rhonda and finally realized where he was. Unable to speak, he slightly raised his left hand and gave a thumbs-up.

Danny leaned in and placed his hand onto his father's forehead and smiled.

Confident that Jim had stabilized, Rhonda asked for help adjusting the gurney so Jim could sit up. She wanted to drain the bottom of his lung cavity from any remaining blood.

After the adjustment, she said, "Ya ain't outta the woods, Mr. Bennett. Your excellent physical condition and quick thinkin' by your family is what kept ya alive. Most men wouldn't of made it this far. Now I need ya ta take a series of deep breaths. Can ya do that?"

Jim nodded and took a short breath, then repeated the process. With each laborious cycle, he slowly increased his ability to breathe. Within five minutes, a second jar was one quarter full and his skin color had turned from blue to gray as more and more oxygen entered his blood stream. Still extremely weak, he finally spoke.

In a shaky voice he managed, "Much better. Thanks."

Rhonda said, "We gotta keep ya sittin' up till nothin' else comes out.

She looked at Jim directly. "I seen these kinda wounds before. They come from hot shrapnel. What happened to ya, Mr. Bennett?"

Jim thought about it and offered, "Hot water tank explosion."

The dark-haired Tlingit shook her head. "Baloney. These are combat wounds. I treated this sorta thing in Iraq. The holes are cauterized shut cuz they're from hot metal. Probably depleted uranium rounds. Ya need to tell the truth."

Still groggy, Jim responded. "No — tank exploded."

"I ain't stupid. There ain't any burns from hot water. Look, I ain't gonna tell anyone about this cuz the Clans respect ya and you've done a lot of things for my people. I need to know if these wounds are what I think they are cuz if they're uranium shrapnel, ya can die from uranyl poisoning. That means these fragments hafta be removed right away."

Lori moved to diffuse the situation. "There's a surgeon coming within a few minutes. He'll remove whatever needs to be taken out."

Jim looked at Rhonda. "You saved me. I won't lie. You're right. Keep this quiet or my water tank story stands."

"My loyalty's with you and your family. Since you got a surgeon comin', let's take a slew of x-rays and determine the exact location of the fragments. Afterwards, I'll treat your son."

Two War Horses —*5:15 a.m.*

As Audra approached the dump she was surprised to see Helen at the entrance. She screeched to a stop, turned off the engine and left the vehicle. She was crying as she ran to Helen and hugged her. The roar of an incoming chopper announced the arrival of Frank and the intern.

Helen stepped back. "Is he alive?"

"I don't know. He seemed to be dying when I got sick. I'm sorry, but I couldn't stand seeing him like that. He's always been my pillar of strength, but he's completely helpless. It's more than I can handle. I can't believe how fragile he is."

Helen waved her arms as the helicopter from the south. Satisfied with the landing zone, the pilot gently set the bird onto a sandy flat. A torrent of white plastic bags, milk cartons and other debris flew in all directions. Frank and the doctor jumped out and began grabbing equipment.

Moments later, the Humvee sped toward Angoon. Frank stretched his neck to watch the helicopter take off to the east while the doctor ogled the striking dark haired woman sitting next to him. He wondered who was so important as to require private treatment with such a large entourage. Perhaps a wealthy politician awaited him.

He broke the silence. "So who's waiting for my services — Governor Palin?"

Frank was about to respond, but Helen barked, "Listen up John Paul Spaulding: I'm special agent Andrews, assistant deputy director of the C.I.A. You're involved in a matter of national security. You'll be debriefed on a need-to-know-basis. No more questions. Do I make myself clear?"

The young physician stared at Helen. There was dried blood on her hands and shirt sleeves. He wondered how she knew his middle name. *He* never used it. She scowled at him. Shaken by her aggressiveness, he managed a nod.

"Loud and clear, ma'am. I promise. No more questions."

Frank silently chuckled.

Helen continued, "Good. I understand you've spoken with the older gentleman in the front seat, but get something straight: he works for me and I'm calling the shots. He's a reasonable person but I'm not, so you'd better remain focused and do your job. If my operative dies under your care, you'll experience one hell of a shit storm. Understood?"

The intern wondered if this beautiful woman was bluffing or capable of following through with her threats. She intentionally shifted her body so he could see her holstered Colt .45.

He swallowed, nodded and said, "Sorry, Agent Andrews, I didn't mean anything by my Palin comment. You have my full cooperation."

The Hummer skidded into the parking lot at the clinic. Helen escorted the doctor into the clinic, but Audra remained frozen behind the steering wheel. Tears rolled down her cheeks. She fully expected someone to return with bad news about her father.

Frank introduced himself and said, "I sense your fear young lady. You're afraid your father may have died while you were gone. I'm truly sorry about the way things have turned out. Remain here. I'll go inside to see how things are going."

She managed a scant smile. "Thank you Mr. Reid."

Frank walked into the clinic to find the doctor looking at several x-rays mounted on a wall screen. Rhonda was suturing Danny's scalp as Helen scanned the room with her transmission detector. The colonel was awake on the gurney and turned, expecting to see Audra. His eyes locked on Frank's as the one-armed gentleman walked to the end of the gurney. Frank placed his left hand on the colonel's shin. Neither man said a word; they simply looked into each other's eyes. Jim knew the man at the foot of the gurney was Captain Dale Olsen — the ghost.

Doctor Spaulding looked at the x-rays again and announced that Danny didn't have a fractured skull. Then, he focused on Jim's vital signs for a second time. He asked Jim to breathe as deep as possible while he listened with a stethoscope. Then he focused on Jim's heartbeat and took his pulse. He asked, "When was the last time you urinated?"

Jim pulled his mask back and answered, "Maybe four hours ago."

The doctor asked, "Do you have the urge to urinate?"

"No, but my kidneys are throbbing and burn like hell."

The doctor nodded. "Hypoxia. The lack of oxygen and loss of blood is causing your organs to shut down. What's your blood type."

Jim took another breath, "O-positive"

"You're certain?"

"Yes."

The doctor said, "He needs blood immediately. Is anyone here O-positive?"

Frank Reid wasted no time. "I am."

The doctor asked, "You're certain about that?"

Frank answered, "Absolutely."

Jim looked at the one armed man at the foot of his gurney. He removed his oxygen mask and managed, "Good morning, Captain Olsen. It's a pleasure to finally meet you."

"To the contrary, sir, the pleasure's mine. It seems we have many things in common — including blood types."

He turned to the doctor. "Well young man, let's get on with it. Before I forget, there's a beautiful young lady outside who's thinking the worst of her father's condition. Perhaps someone can fetch her before our vampire friend begins."

Lori hurried to the door. "I'll get Audra."

There was only one gurney in the clinic, so the doctor sat Frank in a chair and began the blood donating procedure. The old man looked away as the large needle penetrated the vein in his left arm. Blood soon flowed into a pint-sized plastic bag. Moments later the outside door opened.

Audra cautiously approached the gurney and peeked over Jim's shoulder. He was awake with an oxygen mask covering his nose and mouth. His skin color appeared better and father and daughter smiled at each other. She wanted to hug him, but the I.V. and chest tube made it impossible.

She cried and said, "I'm sorry for leaving. I couldn't bear the thought of watching you die. I ran away like a coward."

He moved the mask aside. "Don't be silly, I was unconscious. Besides, who in their right mind would want to watch their old man croak. Thanks to Rhonda, I should be fine."

Jim turned to the doctor and said, "Tell her, doc. I'll be dancing in no time."

The nervous young man turned away from his microscope and said, "You'll be out of the woods providing we get some fresh blood into you and remove the fragments."

Rhonda finished suturing Danny's scalp and instructed Lori that because of his possible concussion, he couldn't sleep for more than an hour at a time for a while. The risk of him slipping into a coma was her only lingering concern.

Helen placed her hand on Danny's shoulder and said, "OK, all non-essential personnel out of here. Doctor Spaulding and Rhonda have their work cut out for them and there's no room for bystanders. Danny, Lori and Audra: into the Hummer. I'll brief the three of you outside in a minute or two."

Jim pulled off his mask and pulled Audra over to him and kissed her on the cheek. "Don't worry, I'll be out of here shortly. Listen to our fearless leader over there — she'll handle things here. I love you and we'll be having breakfast in no time."

Helen followed Lori out. "This is going to be tough and risky," Helen said.

In the rain, Helen handed Lori a phone. "I'm working on convincing the doctor and Rhonda that this is part of a government affair demanding secrecy. The trailer's too cramped for all of us and the house needs purging of any signs of a struggle. You, Audra and Danny need to go home and take Mr. Reid. He'll join you in a few minutes. Clean up as much incriminating evidence as possible. My crew has cleared the outside, including the crashed Zodiac. I'll handle the situation here. When we're done, I'll call you."

Helen walked to Danny as he was about to enter the Hummer. She smiled. "I'll see you shortly, lover boy."

Audra sniffed, but she smiled a little and hummed, "Danny's got a girlfriend."

Frank appeared at the door. When he got to the Hummer, Helen hugged her employer, thanking him for what he'd done for the colonel. After settling him into his seat, she returned inside.

"He's got adequate blood," the doctor told Rhonda, "but he's still lacking oxygen — he's hypoxic. I can't risk opening his chest, he'd crash. We need to wait at least a few hours."

Rhonda shook her head. "We don't have hours. He'll die. Those fragments are toxic."

Spaulding looked puzzled. "What are you talking about?"

"They're radioactive."

Helens heart fell to her feet. Jim had been hit by the cruiser's Gatling gun and she was the one who opened fire. She'd inadvertently shot the colonel.

Too much information had already been breached and time was running out for Jim. Instinctively she interrupted and produced several sheets of folded paper from her pocket. "Listen up. I'm about to disclose extremely sensitive information about a top-secret mission which needs to remain in this room forever. In my hand is a complete dossier on each of you. I know everything about you, so locating you later is child's play."

She continued. "Rhonda Kadake, you're originally from Kake, but your father was born and raised in Angoon and currently lives here. You were recently discharged as a First Lieutenant Nurse from the U.S. Army and spent time in Iraq. Because of your past military service, you certainly understand the need for silence. As for you, Doctor Spaulding, you were born and raised in Portland. Your parents divorced when you were ten. You were a high school track star. Graduated from University of Wisconsin Medical School in 2006. You enjoy rock climbing, fine wines and old movies. Shall I continue?"

The doctor shook his head. "There's no need."

Helen then produced a badge and an ID which had her photograph under a large circular emblem containing a shield with an eagle's head inside. The perimeter of the emblem contained the words, Central Intelligence Agency.

"My name is Helen Andrews and I'm assistant deputy director of the CIA's counter-terrorism unit. I want complete cooperation from you. The person on the gurney is a retired Special Ops colonel who was asked to monitor this section of Alaska. The older gentleman who donated his blood works for me and recently uncovered a joint North Korea - Al Qaeda plot to disrupt the Alaska missile defense system. That threat was thwarted last night due to the bravery of Colonel Bennett. He was struck by depleted uranium shrapnel and will die if they're not removed soon. His service to our nation is beyond heroic, therefore death is not an option. I want to know how you intend to proceed."

The colonel listened intently to the discourse and laughed inwardly at how convincing Helen's ruse was. He thought to himself, *She'd make an excellent agent.*

Spaulding spoke. "Ms. Andrews, my lips are sealed." He pointed at the x-ray. "There's actually four fragments here. Three smaller pieces are lying against the pleura which are easily removed but there's one large irregular piece that went through the lung and is resting against his rib. That's a serious wound and requires immediate attention. That requires general anesthesia which he'll never survive due to hypoxia."

Rhonda held up a hand to stop the conversation. She asked, "Did you happen to inhale foul smelling smoke or mist after you were hit?"

Jim remembered the acrid cloud that surrounded him and the need to run for fresh air he said, "Yes —it was awful. I had to get out of there."

Rhonda turned to the doctor. "Besides, his wounds, he's got uranyl ion poisoning in his lungs. He breathed in radioactive by-products from the exploded shells. It's nephrotoxic and collects in the kidneys, which is why he can't urinate. Unless we give him an I.V. of 1.4 percent sodium bicarbonate ASAP, his kidneys will be destroyed, the uranyl won't be excreted and he'll die from radiation poisoning."

The doctor opened his medical bag and retrieved a small bottle. "This is an aqueous solution of pure sodium bicarbonate which I use during CPR. I'll set up an I.V. of Ringer's solution. Do you have any baking soda for an oral dose?"

Rhonda opened a small refrigerator and retrieved a box, walked to the sink and poured a glass of water. After mixing a hearty spoonful into the glass, she handed it to Jim. "Drink this. When you're done, we'll do it again."

Helen looked on as the doctor administered the I.V. Rhonda filled another glass of her nasty looking concoction. She finally spoke. "What about the fragments?"

The doctor said, "It doesn't do any good to remove shrapnel if he dies from radiation poisoning in two or three days. Rhonda's right. I've read reports that emphasize the need to flush the kidneys immediately for uranyl poisoning. We've got to purge his system before he reaches the point of no return."

Jim listened, knowing he could die from what he'd inhaled. He closed his eyes and wondered how his kids and Lori would handle the situation. How would they avoid prosecution for what he'd done? Minutes seemed like hours as his mind hashed through one scenario after another. The room was silent, but suddenly an urge to urinate overtook Jim.

He opened his eyes. "Sorry to interrupt, but I've got to take a leak."

The doctor looked at Rhonda, "Is this possible?"

Rhonda answered, "Yep, I've seen it before but we gotta keep the Ringer's goin'. By continuing to do this, the bicarbonate will bind with the uranyl and be discharged through his urine. We need to keep him drinking the solution no matter what."

After relieving himself into a bed pan, Jim said, "My kidneys aren't pounding nearly as bad. You guys are onto something."

Doctor Spaulding said, "I think we have the uranyl situation figured out, so let's determine how to proceed with removing the shrapnel. I can administer a large dose of lidocaine in and around the wound and remove the others without anything else. I'd make a small incision under his armpit and try locating the larger fragment with curved forceps —it will be painful, but we'd avoid him crashing from general anesthesia."

Jim urinated a second time. "This stuff is working. My kidneys feel much better. By the way, I've got a few holes in my foot and another in my left leg. See what you can do for those while you're at it."

Helen looked at his boot and closed her eyes in disbelief. Three sizable holes were visible on top of his boot and a burn hole in the back of his camouflaged pants announced another wound. She leaned in and whispered, "I'm so sorry Colonel. I'm responsible for the wounds. I was the gunner."

"Shit happens, Ms. Andrews. All in a day's work."

"Can you handle the surgery without thrashing around?"

"I'll handle the pain providing you get me whiskey from my bar and two Vicodin from my medicine cabinet. Make it good whiskey."

She called Danny and instructed him to bring what Jim asked for. Minutes later Audra sprinted into the clinic. She set the bottle down and handed the pills to her father. Before Dr. Spaulding could speak, Jim swallowed the vicodin and took several hearty swigs from a bottle of Crown Royal.

Spaulding said, "I don't like this at all. Now I get to deal with an inebriated patient. Bad idea."

Bennett shook his head and took several more swigs. "This should knock me out long enough for you to get the piece out of my lung. Everything else is a snap." He took two more slugs of whiskey, and his voice slurred. "Get the Lidocaine started and get to work before this wears off." After a few more hits from the bottle, he passed out.

Rhonda quickly inserted a urinary catheter while Spaulding administered Lidocaine under Jim's armpit. Several minutes later the doctor began his surgery.

Rain pounded the roof of the small clinic as the doctor and Rhonda assembled their instruments.

Helen stood up. "What can I do to help?"

The doctor said, "Remove his boots and his trousers so I can inspect those wounds."

Jim's House —6:00 a.m.

After entering the expansive living room, Frank thanked the Bennett kids and Lori for their courageous actions over the past days. Silence followed. There didn't seem to be anything to say. A blood trail on the floor was a stark reminder of recent events. Lori tossed two oriental rugs from the upstairs loft over the rail. Danny concealed carpet stains with the rugs while Audra wiped the kitchen floor clean. The trio continued to tidy up the mess, which helped to divert their concerns for Jim. Lori found time to brew a pot of coffee and Frank used the opportunity to contact Gus.

Gus asked, "How's Bennett?"

"He's stable and I predict he'll survive. The nurse in Angoon undoubtedly bought him precious time and we'll need to do something special for her when things are concluded. Give me an update. How's our prisoner?"

Gus answered, "Bound and gagged. I'd bet he's shitting his pants right about now. Dave wanted to tear into him, but I told him he'd have to wait for your return so he's keeping a sharp eye on him. After sinking *Oregon II*, we repositioned the cutter inside of Echo Bay where we initially set up. I really like this spot because it's so isolated. Jeff returned with the chopper and can pick you up as soon as you give the word. Wayne's got the Zodiac and is picking up more debris inside of Whitewater."

Frank asked, "How bad was the oil slick after you sank the *Oregon II*?"

"Virtually nonexistent. Wayne wore a wetsuit and placed several pounds of C4 along one side of the hull below the water line, then detonated it from the cutter. Before he sank her, we transferred an ROV from NOAA's deck to our cutter with our crane. It's got robotic claws, cameras and much more. It could be useful."

Frank asked, "For what?"

"Maybe to locate the U-boat at Pelican."

Frank smiled. "It never occurred to me. That's an excellent idea."

Gus added, "Lena called from the yacht. They left Ketchikan last night with our initial cutter crew. They should be approaching Rowan within an hour. I'm sure Bennett will enjoy the company of his friend Ernie and vice versa."

Again Frank smiled. "Wonderful news. Have them anchor in Chatham. We'll exchange vessels after the interrogations are complete. I should be going. The Bennetts need help cleaning up. Keep me posted on further developments."

Back in the house, Frank found Audra wiping blood from the leather couch. Danny rested in the large recliner as Lori paced back and forth with a cup of coffee. The house appeared clean, so he sat in a chair near the bar. Lori pointed to her cup as if to ask if he wanted coffee. He smiled. "With a dash of cream please."

"Would you care for a shot of Bailey's, instead?"

The old man beamed. "That would be excellent. Thank you."

After Audra finished cleaning the couch, Lori sat down opposite the white-haired gentleman. Oscar immediately found a spot on her lap. She was nervous about Jim's condition and made small talk. "Are you the gentleman related to Ernie?"

At the question, Audra sat to listen in. Danny opened his eyes. Sipping his coffee, the old man considered how he should answer. After an awkward silence, he decided they probably already knew more than he expected. Helen had suggested they posed no risk.

"Helen insisted I can trust the Bennetts — you — to keep this confidential, so the answer to your question is 'no.' My cousin Gus Olsen's wife Lena was Ernie's late wife's cousin. My real name is Dale Olsen, and I'm from Pelican, Alaska. I was a B-17 pilot during World War II. My plane was shot down, and my flight engineer and I were spared and brought home by an SS officer, which, all these years later, precipitated this entire mess. You found my bush plane. The bones of Andy Decker — my flight engineer — and another man named Günter may well have still been in the craft. In any case, I assume you've located the gold, as well."

Lori grinned. "In fact we did. Jim was right all along. He guessed your name and assumed you fled Germany in a U-boat. Did you lose your arm during the war?"

Dale nodded. "Indeed. Mr. Bennett possesses extraordinary powers of deduction. Andy dragged me from the plane, and I parachuted into a tree and was captured. SS General Rudolph Bruner had his private family doctor perform surgery on me several times. Rudy saved my life. Together with Andy and several associates of the general, we fled Germany in a U-boat and made our way to Alaska."

Audra asked, "Were you a Nazi?"

The old man laughed. "Heavens no. We were escaping from them."

Audra said, "It sounds like a fantastic adventure. Please continue."

"Upon reaching Alaska, my aunt, uncle and cousin Gus, who had been told I was killed near Hamburg, helped us reach Washington State with a fortune in gold. During the final run to Washington, Andy evidently crashed. He and the gold were never found — until now. In the process of all this, General Bruner became my best friend, mentor, and business partner. He was an incredible individual."

Frank paused. "Rudy — who became known as Henry Weddel — was murdered last week at the behest of Santos. Santos' real name is — was — Anton Keller. He was the illegitimate son of one of the men who fled from Germany with us in 1944. His father's name was Karl Obert. Karl had ties to ODESSA. Karl had become addicted to pain medication due to combat injuries and he went berserk during our exodus. His son Anton has been trying to locate General Bruner and me for decades. Anton had strong connections with Nazis in both Germany and South America."

Frank asked, "Have you heard of ODESSA?"

"From what I understand," Lori said, "they're the genesis of the Fourth Reich."

She stood and Oscar jumped to her side." Excuse me. I want to retrieve some items that Jim has been saving for the ghost of Captain Olsen."

She left the room with Oscar trotting behind.

During Lori's absence, Frank turned to Danny. "You're a fortunate young man. Helen has confided in me that she's fallen in love with you. Because of that, she has tendered her resignation. I've known her for several years and she's a brave, honest, and hard-working young woman — a wonderful person. I consider her part of my extended family. A good friend of hers was recently murdered by Rusty Miller, the unsavory character you managed to capture this morning. After realizing the value of my plane's contents, he joined forces with Santos. Greed is a powerful force which brings out the darkness in people. I think very highly of Helen, so I'm compelled to ask you a personal question. Do you share the same feelings for her?"

Danny relished hearing that Helen confided in someone else about her feelings for him. He smiled. "I do, sir."

Once again, Audra couldn't resist humming, "Danny's got a girlfriend."

The old man frowned at her antics, but offered, "Love with the right person is an incredible thing. Unlike greed which brings out the darkness in people, love brings out the light in people. If things develop and the two of you ever decide to 'tie the knot,' I'd appreciate an invitation to the wedding. Furthermore, my yacht and its crew can be at your disposal for the honeymoon."

Audra chimed in. "Wow! A yacht. Hey Danny, you'd better take the plunge and buy her a ring. I'll be Helen's bridesmaid."

Lori returned with an old aluminum clipboard, a switchblade knife, dog tags, a pencil and several pieces of paper. She presented the items to Mr. Reid.

"Jim recovered the clipboard and knife from inside the cockpit. Your pilot friend scratched a message on the clipboard with the knife. If you lay a piece of paper over the scratches and run a pencil over them, you'll be able to retrieve his message. The dog tags were found inside of a corroded tube in Whitewater Bay. I believe one set is yours. We found another tube next to a partial skeleton in Whitewater. The tube contained gold coins."

Frank shook his head in disbelief. Anxious to read Andy's message, the old man tried to hold the paper on the clipboard. His robotic arm proved worthless for the task, and Audra assisted him by holding the paper steady. The former pilot began running the pencil lead back and forth across the scratches.

He asked, "Has anyone here read this?"

Lori shook her head. "No, sir. Jim insisted the note was meant for your eyes only."

Olsen considered the comment. "I admire his intentions, but to hell with it. There'll be no more secrets between us. I expect that you're keeping the gold so we're all joined at the hip. It's only fitting that we read this together."

He handed the finished stencil to Lori and said, "You have the honors, Ms. Phelps."

With Oscar sitting on her lap, Lori read aloud. "Hey, Pal, about to die, left Pelican, oil slick at Soapstone, Karl under tarp, tried to overtake plane, laughed about destroying us, Gunny killed Karl, landed, dumped Karl, took off, no visual, altimeter shot in fight, relied on compass, broke from clouds into peaks, climbed but stalled, crashed here, pinned against yoke, broken leg, Gunny hurt, went for help, desperate, won't last night, been a good ride Pal, your friend, Amigo."

Andy's message cut through him just like the Messerschmitts cutting through their B-17. The old pilot looked at the switchblade Andy used to cut a cargo strap from the B-17, the strap that became the tourniquet that stopped him from bleeding to death. Though it had been over 60 years, thinking of Andy's final moments caused tears to fill Frank's eyes. He shook his head as Lori handed him the paper.

Sensing his loss, Lori offered, "He must have been a dear friend. I'm sorry."

Dale looked at the note, and pointed to his robotic arm. "Andy pulled me from a crippled B-17. I wouldn't be here without him. He'll always be my friend."

Before Lori could ask another question, the phone Helen had given her rang. A tidal wave of fear overcame her. Walking toward the kitchen, she answered. "They can't be done this soon. What happened?"

Standing outside the clinic in the rain, Helen smiled. "I regret to inform you that you'll have to put up with his antics for quite some time. The doctor just finished removing the large fragment from his chest — without anesthesia. It was immense. The colonel's a tough customer, and the whiskey did its job. He never flinched. They're removing the smaller pieces now and we should be done in an hour. How's Danny?"

Lori let out a sigh of huge relief. "He's resting on the recliner. Would you care to speak with him?"

"Not now. Let him rest. I'll call you when we're ready to be picked up."

All eyes focused on Lori as she strolled to the bar and poured herself a two fingered shot of whiskey. Entering the living room, she raised her drink in the air, then slammed it down without so much as a shudder.

"That's for Jim Bennett," she said, "the toughest person I know. They're almost done and he'll survive."

After the wonderful news, the four engaged in open and honest conversations about their lives. Dale told of the tragic death of his parents when he was ten and how his aunt and uncle raised him in Alaska. He described how he and his German partner managed to integrate into American society and amass their fortunes without raising suspicion.

Lori discussed childhood in Arizona, education at Stanford and a failed marriage to an abusive gambling addict. She admitted she had strong feelings for Jim from the moment she was hired at TacSec but always kept those feelings to herself. She hoped that one day Jim would feel the same way about her, which always seemed unattainable.

Audra shared childhood memories of Fort Bragg, spending summers on the Bennett ranch in Wyoming, and her bitter reaction to her parents' divorce. She never understood what drove them apart, but couldn't blame either one for what happened. Audra said she loved both her parents dearly and she chose business as her career at the encouragement of Grandfather Bennett. Because of her new-found wealth, she was wondering about her future with Boeing.

Danny added that he had a normal childhood, but admitted to experimenting with peyote and magic mushrooms during college, which served to awaken him. Though he tripped relatively few times, he claimed it gave him a heightened sense of awareness. He credited his father for prompting him to buckle down and finish college. Asked about Helen, he admitted he'd never felt so connected to another woman as he did with her.

Before concluding their talk, Frank's phone rang. The caller ID showed "private," but he knew it was Gus. He answered without leaving his chair. "I'm all ears."

"Major development, Dale. Dave needs to speak with you. Here he is."

Dave came on line. "Mr. Reid, we've got a crisis on our hands. Miller's bleeding from his nostrils and mouth. Blood's weeping from the corners of his eyes and he's pissing blood. The colonel's son threw a grenade at him. There's minimal shrapnel damage, but the concussion must've torn up his insides. He's rapidly deteriorating and about to lose consciousness. I either interrogate him now, or we get him immediate medical attention. I prefer the interrogation route. What should I do?"

"Let me think." Knowing Dave despised Rusty, and could get over-enthusiastic, Reid considered waiting until he returned. But if Rusty died before interrogation, precious information regarding links to other Dark Star personnel would vanish. Gus verified the gravity of Rusty's condition, and Frank spoke with Dave again.

"Mr. Bachman, question him. I want to know who else was involved; in particular, his connections with Dark Star operatives and ODESSA. I'm not interested in motives. I already know. Don't waste time on nasty physical stuff. Inject him with the KGB truth serum. Are you familiar with injecting someone?"

Bachman answered, "Yes, sir. I've used it before."

Frank paused to consider what to do after the interrogation. He said, "I need to speak with Gus please."

Gus answered, "What's the plan, cousin?"

"Oversee the questioning and take notes, Let Jeff manage the cutter's bridge. Direct the questioning so we can ascertain the depth of this fiasco."

"What should we do with him afterwards?"

"Have Mr. Bachman dispose of him. No residual evidence. Look, Helen's calling so they must be done with the colonel. Please arrange for a float plane to pick up our doctor friend from the Angoon docks."

The Clinic — 6:45 a.m.

Helen stood outside of the health clinic and spoke with Lori. Rain soaked into the gravel parking area as she asked Lori to drive over with Frank. Audra and Danny needed to remain at the house. Several minutes later, the Humvee pulled up and Helen got inside. Lori wanted to run into the clinic, but Helen insisted that she remain with the vehicle.

Helen looked at Lori. "Mr. Bennett's fine, so relax."

She turned toward Frank. "I convinced the doctor and nurse that you and I are the CIA and that the colonel assisted in thwarting a North Korean terror attack against the Alaska missile defense system. They bought it. They pledged their silence, so play along. My story leaves the colonel in the clear and provides a logical explanation for his wounds. Lori needs to remain here while the two of us debrief them."

The former pilot patted Lori's knee. "We'll only be a minute."

He turned to Helen. "Is the colonel ambulatory?"

"No. He needs assistance. He's also ablaze on booze and pills. He's going to have a doozy of a hang-over"

"I bet," Frank offered, "Let's bring him out in a wheelchair, then debrief the doctor and nurse. That way Ms. Phelps and Mr. Bennett can be alone."

Lori looked at Helen for approval. "That would be terrific. Can you do that for me?"

Helen nodded. "Of course. I'll bring him out immediately."

Jim's head leaned forward as he was rolled down the ramp to the parking area. Rhonda lifted his left arm over her right shoulder, and Helen steadied him into the Humvee back seat. They sat him down in the Hummer, and closed the door. For once in his life, Jim was at the mercy of others, too weak to resist. Lori kissed his ashen cheek as Rhonda and Helen returned to the trailer. Once inside, Helen continued her ruse.

"Jolly good job — to both of you. Remember what I said about silence. No matter who may question you about what happened here today, play ignorant. You know nothing about their questions. It's crucial. Two of the covert infiltrators miraculously 'escaped' and will return to North Korea with bogus information about our defense system. This will provide inside moles and future intelligence about China, North Korea and their ties with Iran."

Frank added, "For your service and silence, our government is in your debt. I've been authorized to return the favor as follows: Doctor, you'll receive a letter from your college loan program notifying you that all financial obligations are satisfied. You'll receive another letter furnishing particulars about an untraceable off-shore account in your name. It will arrive within two weeks. Consider it seed money if you should decide on opening your own practice. A float plane will arrive at the dock shortly and return you to Sitka.

As for you Ms. Kadake, you'll receive a substantial sum of money in an off-shore account as well. Do what you please with it. Additionally, the Clans of Angoon and Kake will be gifted with permanent health clinics and adequate funds for full time nurses at each facility. The funds will arrive as an anonymous donation from a blind trust listing you as the administrator. It's to be utilized for the benefit of Tlingit health care. Of course, we expect everyone's absolute cooperation and silence about the events which occurred here today. Do both of you understand?"

The short, stocky Tlingit threw her arms around the old man. She said, "My people are blessed. Thank you. Both of ya. I love my people and America."

The doctor smiled. "This is fantastic." He turned to Helen. "I swear on my soul — what happened here this morning remains here."

In the Humvee, Oscar sat in Jim's lap. Seated next to him in the back seat, Lori gathered her courage. She finally spoke. "I damn near had a meltdown seeing you at death's door. If your kids hadn't been there, I'd have bawled like a baby. I should've said this years ago. I love you, Jim. I have for a long time. At the risk of rejection, I'd like to know where I stand with you?"

Jim winced in pain and leaned over to pull Lori toward him and kissed her cheek. "I'm still a bit lit, but you're standing on solid ground, lady. I'm not very articulate at expressing feelings, but I'm really drawn to you. More than you can imagine. So where do we go from here?"

Lori kissed Jim. "Nowhere in particular. It just needed to be said. Let's take things slow and see where it leads us. In the meantime, stop getting shot."

Jim laughed which caused him to cough up blood. He wiped it on his sleeve. Petting Oscar, he said, "Next time I'll duck. How's my boy doing?"

"Other than a headache, he's fine. Teach him how to duck, too."

Jim grinned, and then groaned. "Smiling even hurts. What's your assessment of Captain Olsen?"

Lori talked about the conversations between the old pilot, Danny, Audra and herself. Jim immediately understood Lori liked the old man and considered him to be sincere. Lori explained that Olsen was legitimately concerned for Jim's health and also appreciated his assistance in the matters of the day.

Jim had unraveled the ongoing threat against the Olsen and Bruner families, and Lori was sure that Dale felt obligated to disclose the truth about his past in hopes of gaining the Bennetts' trust and by some small measure demonstrate his gratitude. Jim had trusted Lori's intuition and judgment since meeting her. He agreed. Olsen was OK.

His wounds were painful, but Jim leaned over and kissed Lori again. Shortly after, Helen and Mr. Olsen entered the vehicle.

Lori asked, "Are you done in there?"

Helen smiled. "We're good. Take me to see Danny please."

Bennett's House — 7:00 a.m.

Audra sat near her brother and watched him sleeping in the recliner. She realized how similar to her father he'd become. Danny had grown into a brave, focused individual since last year. She knew Danny cared for Helen. Because of their parents' failures, she also wondered if he'd actually pursue a relationship with her. She knew that Helen was like her father and brother — intelligent, fiercely independent and strong-willed. Together, Danny and Helen could accomplish anything they set their minds to.

Audra had liked Helen from the moment Danny introduced her to the family. She hoped the two of them would get together when this was over. While considering that, she heard the Hummer pull into the driveway. Moments later, Oscar ran to his water bowl in the kitchen and Lori and Helen helped Jim to the couch.

Audra had placed several pillows and an afghan on the couch, expecting her father's return. After Jim settled in, Audra sat on the floor next to him with Oscar by her side.

She looked at his ashen face and asked, "How are you feeling?"

Jim placed a hand on her shoulder. "Much better than I did several hours ago. Everyone did an outstanding job this morning."

Danny woke from a brief nap to find Helen sitting on the floor next to his recliner. The two of them simply looked at each other and smiled. Lori began preparing breakfast, and Mr. Olsen sat in a leather chair near Jim. The brief silence was interrupted by the old man's cell phone. After looking at its screen, he walked onto the deck and closed the door behind him.

He answered, "I'm listening."

"Where are you?" Gus asked.

"At the colonel's house — he's a little worse for wear, but he'll live."

"That's great news on top of great news. We've completed the questioning and things couldn't have turned out better. It's over. It ends here."

Frank said, "Give me the details."

"Rusty was working entirely alone. With opportunity to make a fortune, he formed an alliance with Crane, killed Whitey, and planned on grabbing everything for himself. He would've eliminated Keller, Crane, the colonel and his family, and vanished before we knew what happened. The greedy bastard thought we were at home and in no position to intercept him. According to him, Keller had no living family or other ties with ODESSA. His only link was with Roger Krantz, who's now a raging lunatic facing murder charges in California. Krantz received a double dose of some psychotropic drug and will never recover. It's over."

Relieved to hear the verdict, Dale took a deep breath. "Marvelous. I'll be able to sleep without having nightmares or flashbacks. What's the status of the inbound doctor and the yacht?"

"Jeff took the chopper to pick up the doctor from Seattle in Sitka. He lands in thirty minutes. The yacht is maybe twenty minutes from my position. Would you like to be picked up now?"

Dale hesitated, then said, "Not yet. Instruct the inbound doctor to return to Seattle. Arrange to pay him for his trouble. Whatever he wants. His services aren't needed, but Spaulding told me Mr. Bennett requires two more units of O-positive blood, two week's worth of 1000-mg. Cipro antibiotics, and a few days worth of sedatives for sleep. I'm sure the incoming surgeon has these things with him, vis a vis our original instructions. If not, get whatever is missing from Spaulding when you return him to Sitka. I'll contact you when I'm ready to leave here."

The old man re-entered the house to the smells of frying bacon and fresh brewed coffee. Lori pointed toward the pot. He nodded, and sat next to Jim. "Mr. Bennett, I owe you an enormous debt of gratitude. How can I ever repay you?"

Jim looked at Mr. Reid. "Start by calling me Jim — then tell me where Ernie is."

Frank answered, "That's not enough, Jim. Ernie's doing well and is on my yacht with Lena. They're nearing Rowan Bay and I could have him here within an hour if you'd like. However, I'd prefer if your family were to join us for an early dinner tomorrow aboard the yacht. If you're feeling up to it, that is. That way, you'd be able to get some much needed rest, and later meet my cousin Gus, his wife Lena, Helen's brother Wayne, and several other extraordinary people. After dinner, I'll disclose a pleasant surprise for you and your family."

Jim considered the risk of exposing his family to someone he really didn't know. "Why not anchor out front and come here for dinner. We can pick everyone up in my boat."

The old man understood the real reason for Jim's counter proposal and wondered how to convince him that he wasn't a threat. Before he could respond, Lori interrupted.

"We'd love to meet your family on the yacht." Looking at Audra and Danny, she asked, "Wouldn't we?"

In concert, both said "Yes!"

Lori sat next to Jim, leaned over and whispered in his ear, "Let it go, Jim. He'd never hurt us."

Jim looked around the room and saw the anticipation on everyone's face. Sensing their desire to accept the old man's offer, he said, "Very well Mr. Reid. Or Captain Olsen. What time, and what can we bring?"

The old man smiled. "Jim, it's only fair that you call me Frank — and thank you for accepting my invitation. Just bring yourselves. The yacht will be anchored beyond the inlet within a few hours. We'll pick you up with the helicopter. How does 4:30 sound?"

Again Lori intervened. "That would be wonderful Frank."

Mr. Reid sported a huge grin and stood. "Helen and I should really be going. There are several loose ends that need tidying up and the four of you need plenty of rest. Rhonda will be here in an hour to administer more blood and medication."

Surprised, Lori asked, "What about breakfast? Can't this wait?"

Standing next to Danny's chair, Helen said, "I'm sorry, but my employer's right. We need to go now. I hope you'll understand."

She leaned over and kissed Danny. "Audra, could you please drive us to the landfill so the chopper can pick us up?"

Within minutes Jim fell fast asleep. Oscar carefully snuck onto the foot of the couch as if he was consoling his new-found friend. The Bennett clan smiled, knowing that he'd recover.

Two hours later, Rhonda made her promised house call with the much needed blood and medications. Jim slipped in and out consciousness until the sedatives kicked in. Afterwards he slept the night while Lori sat in a recliner next to him.

June 16 — The Yacht — 5:00 p.m.

Jim gazed at the flames of the immense see-through fireplace which was a focal point in the yacht's grand salon. His eyes wandered above the travertine mantlepiece to an authentic, brightly-painted African shield with two crossed spears. The entire salon was decorated with artwork and memorabilia from around the world. Beautiful hand-woven Persian rugs on top of polished marble floors defined the lives of both Henry Weddel and Frank Reid. A remarkable ebony bar with under-lit glass shelves accented one side of the salon while a massive horseshoe couch with a central glass coffee table occupied the other. Beyond the fireplace and toward the bow stood a dark walnut dining room table with hand-carved legs and matching chairs. Jim was legitimately humbled to be in the presence of such wealth.

Above the grand salon, sun rays shot through the large, tinted, oval window of Helen's quarters. Standing away from the mirror, she looked at herself and finished applying a coat of slightly crimson lipstick. She wanted to impress Danny without other guests thinking she looked cheap. Turning away from the mirror, she peered over her right shoulder at her perfectly proportioned torso and hips and readjusted the outfit Wayne had brought from Mexico. The combination of white blouse, flowing white skirt, black belt and matching black high heels accentuated her beauty. A barely-visible black lace bra wouldn't go unnoticed by Danny if they sat together. Satisfied with her appearance, she smiled and thought, "You're mine, Danny boy — you're mine, and I'm yours." She left her stateroom and walked down the spiral staircase to the grand salon.

The Bennetts were gathered near the bar, talking with Ernie and Lena. Dale and Gus tended bar while John, Dave and Wayne sat on the horseshoe couch and discussed sports. As soon as Audra caught a glimpse of Helen near the top of the staircase, she whistled and said, "Holy hot stuff! That's the finest looking unit in all of Alaska."

The three men on the couch clapped as a smiling Helen made her entrance. Sitting in a soft leather recliner with his feet elevated, Jim silently agreed with the accolades. A wheelchair stood nearby. Oscar happily laid in Jim's lap, enjoying the company and an occasional scratch behind his ears.

Audra asked, "What do you think of your girlfriend, Danny?"

Sitting on a barstool, Danny grinned and held out his hand. "She's gorgeous. I'd be honored if she'd come over here and sit with me."

Ernie butted in. "No, no. Over here darlin' — that young buck don't know squat about the ladies."

Lena laughed. "Watch out. Danny. Ernie's trying to steal her from you."

The group laughed and Helen pecked Danny on his cheek and sat beside him. She tipped his head toward her and inspected the sutures on his scalp and winced, then whispered in his ear, "How are you feeling, lover boy?"

Noting her lacy bra, Danny placed his arm around her waist. "I'm fine, birdie."

Dave Bachman added, "I've known Helen since Iraq. I'm warning you Danny — she's a shark. Cross her and she'll tear you to shreds. Just ask the four Al Qaeda men with Allah and their forty virgins."

Helen shook her fist at him and countered. "Rubbish! That'll be enough out of you David. Wayne, if he so much as utters another word, cork him one."

Wayne laughed. "You can handle Dave without me. Besides, you always kicked my arse when we were kids."

After another round of laughter, Frank raised his glass and offered, "Before we eat I'd like to propose a toast to good friends and family. Recent events have proved challenging for everyone here. Some have lost friends while others have sustained serious injuries. Fortunately, we've managed to prevail against darkness and I'm grateful for everyone's courage, sacrifice and commitment. Thank you all."

Frank nodded to Gus, who then walked around the room and handed out envelopes to Helen, Wayne, Jeff and Dave. While the four recipients inspected the contents of their envelopes, Frank turned to Jim and whispered, "After dinner, I'd like to meet with you and your family on deck. There's something important I'd like to discuss."

Helen opened her envelope and stared at a bank draft from Belize for two million dollars. She walked to her boss and handed the envelope back.

"Sir, I'm afraid I can't accept this. It's far more than we agreed upon."

Frank kissed her forehead. "Please call me 'Frank' — or perhaps 'Gramps' — if you'd please, but not 'sir' any more. You're part of my extended family now, not an employee. Remember? You have quit. Keep the draft or you'll hurt my feelings."

He turned to the group. "Those of you who just received an envelope: as for the amounts on these bank drafts, you've exceeded my expectations. Therefore, I've paid all of you more than what was agreed upon. Consider it a bonus. The funds are from an off-shore account and are untraceable. There will be no tax consequence. Because of my friends Henry Weddel and Andrew Decker, I'm alive and wealthier than I ever imagined. Beyond that, I have many friends and a family who've filled my life with untold happiness — the true measure of wealth. Accept this as a token of my appreciation."

The three men sitting on the couch had received half a million each. They looked at each other in disbelief. Jim sat in his soft recliner, fascinated by Mr. Reid's generosity. Lori was correct in her assessment of the old pilot.

An awkward silence permeating the room was broken as the chef and the yacht's housekeeper brought in platters filled with savory food. During dinner, the group engaged in conversations ranging from politics to music. Classical tunes played over the salon's stereo system including Henry Weddel's favorite composer, Johann Strauss. The "Blue Danube" reminded Frank of the endless days aboard the U-boat.

Jim remained unusually quiet during the meal and picked at his food. Lori sensed he was in pain and needed rest. His lips began to turn blue and he was tiring rapidly. Lori asked if he'd prefer sitting in a recliner near the bar. He accepted her offer as the concerned group looked on.

The room turned silent as everyone watched Lori maneuver the wheel chair away from the table toward the recliner. Doctor Spaulding had advised that Jim required pure oxygen from time to time. Helen asked Audra where the oxygen bottle Rhonda had provided was. It was aboard the chopper. Helen excused herself and sprinted to retrieve the bottle.

Frank got up and went to sit beside Jim. The two made small talk while the others continued eating. After several minutes of pure oxygen, Jim recovered from a downhill spiral. He said to Lori and Frank, "Please finish your meal. I'll rejoin everyone later."

His words were meant to comfort the old man, but Frank understood the gravity of Jim's situation. In reality, he should be hospitalized. Frank and Lori elected to remain with Jim while the group continued eating and talking. By the time dessert rolled around, the colonel's color had returned and he was alert once again.

Looking at Lori and Frank, he insisted, "Go on you guys. Eat your dinner. Otherwise I'll be forced to get up and join you."

Knowing Jim's stubbornness, Lori retreated to the table. Frank simply sat and smiled at Jim as if to call his bluff. He placed his hand onto Jim's leg and said, "You outrank me, Colonel, but you really should respect your elders. I've lost my appetite and I want to speak with you. I doubt you'll return to the table, so let's use this opportunity to get to know each other. I understand you were a West Point graduate and a Delta Commander. What did you think of combat? Were you ever afraid?"

Jim smiled and shook his head. "In combat, things happen too fast; you simply react so you can accomplish the mission. As for fear, I've always held a somewhat casual and fatalistic view of it. If your time's up, it's up." He took several drafts of oxygen, and asked, "What was it like piloting a B-17?"

The old man sported an enormous grin. "Thrilling beyond description. Like you, my only thought was to accomplish the mission. Everything else became secondary and inconsequential." He went on to describe the joys of flight in general, including his short career as a bush pilot.

Then, Frank asked, "What's the most important thing in your life?"

Without hesitation Jim answered, "Family and friends."

The old man nodded. "The same."

Frank grinned. "What are your thoughts about Helen and your son?"

Jim lifted the mask to his mouth and took several breaths. "I think it's wonderful for both of them. I've seen an enormous change in Danny and believe he's deeply attracted to her. Hopefully things work out for them. I like her."

"Does her former — and recent — vocation bother you?"

Jim shook his head. "Not at all. If it did, I'd be a hypocrite, which she made a point of telling me a few days ago." He took several deep breaths from his mask. "What became of Sergeant Miller?"

The old man looked down. "After questioning, he was eliminated. I hope that doesn't bother you."

Jim nodded. He didn't ask for details.

A moment later, Jim said, "Here's an unrelated question: how did you manage to get your hands on a U-boat and make it to Alaska?"

The old man placed his index finger over his lips. "The general who saved my life — Rudy — stole it from under Hitler's nose," he whispered. "We navigated it through the Arctic during summer. It was quite a daring adventure."

It was apparent Mr. Reid wished to keep this quiet. Jim nodded and whispered back, "Ah, the Arctic. That makes perfect sense."

Frank leaned closer and murmured, "How did you discover we had a U-boat?"

Careful to speak quietly, Jim answered, "A Naval intelligence report investigated an oil slick near the cannery. A native claimed he saw an iron whale near the cannery before the slick. It had to be a submarine."

The old man murmured, "This is what I alluded to when I said I wanted to speak with you and your family. I have something important to offer you. Would you like me to continue, or shall I wait?"

Jim was itching to know, but he placed the oxygen mask on his face and held out a hand as if saying, "Wait." The old man looked toward the dinner table. The group had finished their meal, He patted Jim on the knee, stood and returned to the table and offered everyone drinks.

Lori sat with Jim and chatted while Audra talked with Wayne. Helen and Danny seized the moment and walked onto the deck to be alone. The others at the table laughed and had a great time listening to Ernie. He managed to keep his audience in stitches by spinning yarns about his exploits building the Alaskan highway. If people were to believe him, he single-handedly fed the construction crew by hunting moose and trapping bears along the way. He even cooked what he shot to keep the project moving on schedule. Jim enjoyed watching the old trapper having such a good time, knowing quite well that soon Ernie would spend another winter in isolation.

On deck, Danny looked into the choppy waters of Chatham with his hands on the rail and said, "This is déjà vu. I dreamed about this yacht the night we met. Do you remember me telling you about that?"

Helen nodded. "I do. You said you were pulling on a rope connected to a submarine propeller. Do you recall me telling about my mum at Warm Springs, her 'second sight?' She predicted we would meet under troubling circumstances."

Danny laughed. "She was right about that!"

"I promised you I'd disclose more of her predictions. Get a load of this: she told me the two of us would marry after I left Dark Star and that we'd find an enormous amount of gold on the ocean floor. Afterwards, we'd have a wonderful baby girl and…"

"Hold the phone, birdie. Her visions are totally mixed up. We found a fortune in gold on top of a mountain, not in the ocean." Danny grinned. "Besides, if I ask you to marry me, I'd want two kids."

Helen placed her hands on Danny's shoulders and looked into his eyes. "Let me finish lover boy. This is serious, so don't interrupt until I'm finished. In the hot tub, you said you always had a feeling that you were destined for something important but didn't know what. Well here it is: Mum prophesied that the world will experience an apocalyptic event that will alter society as we know it. Much of mankind will perish, but the two of us will become part of a group who create a new society. Our destiny is to usher in a new era. During this period, we'll have two children; a girl, then a boy."

Danny frowned, then stepped back. "Your mother told you all of these things?"

"Yes — while she was dying. And everything she's told me so far has come true. It's our destiny, Danny. I told you before, you're my future."

Danny wondered if she was yanking his chain or absolutely crackers. But he also wondered why — or how — she would fabricate such absurdity.

The sound of people approaching caused them to turn. Mr. Reid, Jim, Audra, and Lori approached. Lori pushed Jim's wheelchair while Oscar sat in his lap. Helen knelt to pet Oscar, and Mr. Reid asked the group to gather around.

The old man began, "I have a very important topic to discuss — a proposition of sorts. I'm offering the Bennett clan — I assume it will include Helen — the opportunity of a lifetime."

He had their attention.

"In 1944, several partners and I escaped Germany in a U-boat carrying 25,000 kilos of pre-war gold. One partner and I pooled our shares and settled in America. The U-boat, still containing over 15,000 kilos of gold, was sunk by Karl Obert, father of Vicente Santos. By weight alone, the gold is worth a half billion dollars. By collectible gold coin value, that may double."

He paused and smile. "Gus, Lena and I offer this information as a gesture of appreciation and we expect nothing in return. We're already wealthy, at the end of our lives, and our families are well provided for."

The group was silently attentive, each wondering where this was going. Frank knew his next words would raise eyebrows and blood pressures.

"I know the precise location of the U-Boat."

The others on deck simultaneously sucked in a breath.

Frank smiled and continued. "Recovering the treasure should prove incredibly simple. It's in only 80 feet of water. You're welcome to utilize this yacht and the ROV recovered from the NOAA ship if you decide to go after it. Gus is an experienced captain and can navigate the yacht if you so desire."

Frank stepped back. "I don't expect an answer right away. You folks can discuss this matter in private." Frank turned and walked into the warmth of the salon as the group stood in utter disbelief.

Danny's mind raced. *My dream about this yacht and a submarine — always feeling I was meant for something important — meeting under troubling circumstances — a fortune in gold on the ocean floor — two children — apocalypse — shared destiny — mankind's survival."*

He had unintentionally tuned out a conversation taking place among his father, Lori and Audra. He came back from his thoughts, pulled Helen to him and kissed her on the lips. "I guess that seals the deal. Anything else I need to know?"

"There's more and it's all good. I don't have time to explain but what really counts is that we love each other. I certainly love you."

He smiled. "I knew that. So what's your thought about getting married, birdie?"

"Are you asking me to marry you?"

He nodded. "Yes, but I've yet to buy a ring."

Helen jumped up on Danny and wrapped her legs around his waist. She kissed him and said, "Yes! Of course I will."

"Did I just hear something about marriage?" Lori said. "Danny, did you just propose?"

Holding Helen, he turned and said, "I just asked and she just accepted."

Lori and Audra went to hug the love birds.

Jim leaned back in his wheelchair and clapped. "Outstanding! Congratulations! I'd hug you guys, too, but I'm not keen on hopping across a wet deck on one foot."

Helen went to Jim, knelt and carefully placed her arms around his neck. She kissed his cheek. "Thank you for everything. You'll never regret having me as your daughter in-law. I love Danny very much and I'm very happy. It's uppermost."

The group formed a small circle around Jim. Danny asked, "So what about Mr. Reid's offer? Do we accept?"

Jim laughed. "While you were busy proposing, three of us decided we'd be crazy not to. As you know, we don't need the money, but holy crap — half a billion is too much to ignore. I'm sure you guys will put it to good use. Hopefully we won't die trying."

Helen smiled. "Trust me. We won't. It's our destiny. My Mum told me so."

Jim wondered what she meant by that. Before he could ask, movement on the Strait caught his eye. A pod of whales swam near the yacht.

"I believe you're right, Helen," Jim said. "Our humpback friends over there have confirmed it. Come on, let's get inside and talk with Captain Olsen. We've got a lot of planning to do."

THE BEGINNING OF THE END

Made in the USA
Middletown, DE
05 February 2025

70196946R00248